TREASON AT LISSON GROVE

This Large Print Book carries the Seal of Approval of N.A.V.H.

A CHARLOTTE AND THOMAS PITT
NOVEL

TREASON AT LISSON GROVE

ANNE PERRY

THORNDIKE PRESS
A part of Gale, Cengage Learning

GALE
CENGAGE Learning

Detroit • New York • San Francisco • New Haven, Conn • Waterville, Maine • London

GALE
CENGAGE Learning·

LIBRARY OF CONGRESS CATALOGING-IN-PUBLICATION DATA

Perry, Anne.
    Treason at Lisson Grove : a Charlotte and Thomas Pitt novel / by Anne Perry.
        p. cm. — (Thorndike Press large print basic)
    ISBN-13: 978-1-4104-3522-4 (hardcover)
    ISBN-10: 1-4104-3522-9 (hardcover)
        1. Pitt, Charlotte (Fictitious character)—Fiction. 2. Pitt, Thomas (Fictitious character)—Fiction. 3. Women detectives—England— London—Fiction. 4. Police spouses—Fiction. 5. Police—England— London—Fiction. 6. Large type books. I. Title.
    PR6066.E693T74 2011b
    823'.914—dc22   2011000806

Published in 2011 by arrangement with The Ballantine Publishing Group, a division of Random House, Inc.

Printed in the United States of America
1 2 3 4 5 6 7 15 14 13 12 11

TO KEN SHERMAN
for years of friendship

CHAPTER 1

"That's him!" Gower yelled above the sound of the traffic. Pitt turned on his heel just in time to see a figure dart between the rear end of a hansom and the oncoming horses of a brewer's dray. Gower disappeared after him, missing a trampling by no more than inches.

Pitt plunged into the street, swerving to avoid a brougham and stopping abruptly to let another hansom pass. By the time he reached the far pavement Gower was twenty yards ahead and Pitt could make out only his flying hair. The man he was pursuing was out of sight. Weaving between clerks in pinstripes, leisurely strollers, and the occasional early woman shopper with her long skirts getting in the way, Pitt closed the gap until he was less than a dozen yards behind Gower. He caught a glimpse of the man ahead: bright ginger hair and a green jacket. Then he was gone, and Gower turned, his

7

right hand raised for a moment in signal, before disappearing into an alley.

Pitt followed after him into the shadows, his eyes taking a moment or two to adjust. The alley was long and narrow, bending in a dogleg a hundred yards beyond. The gloom was caused by the overhanging eaves and the water-soaked darkness of the brick, long streams of grime running down from the broken guttering. People were huddled in doorways; others made their way slowly, limping, or staggering beneath heavy bolts of cloth, barrels, and bulging sacks.

Gower was still ahead, seeming to find his way with ease. Pitt veered around a fat woman with a tray of matches to sell, and tried to catch up. Gower was at least ten years younger, even if his legs were not quite so long, and he was more used to this kind of thing. But it was Pitt's experience in the Metropolitan Police before he joined Special Branch that had led them to finding West, the man they were now chasing.

Pitt bumped into an old woman and apologized before regaining his stride. They were around the dogleg now, and he could see West's ginger head making for the opening into the wide thoroughfare forty yards away. Pitt knew that they must catch him before he was swallowed up in the crowds.

Gower was almost there. He reached out an arm to grab at West, but just then West ducked sideways and Gower tripped, hurtling into the wall and momentarily winding himself. He bent over double, gasping to catch his breath.

Pitt lengthened his stride and reached West just as he dived out into the High Street, barged his way through a knot of people, and disappeared.

Pitt went after him and a moment later saw the light on his bright hair almost at the next crossroads. He increased his pace, bumping and banging people. He had to catch him. West had information that could be vital. After all, the tide of unrest was rising fast all over Europe, and becoming more violent. Many people, in the name of reform, were actually trying to overthrow government altogether and create an anarchy in which they imagined there would be some kind of equality of justice. Some were content with blood-soaked oratory; others preferred dynamite, or even bullets.

Special Branch knew of a current plot, but not yet the leaders behind it, or — more urgently — the target of their violence. West was to provide that, at risk of his own life — if his betrayal were known.

Where the devil was Gower? Pitt swiveled

around once to see if he could spot him. He was nowhere visible in the sea of bobbing heads, bowler hats, caps, and bonnets. There was no time to look longer. Surely he wasn't still in the alley? What was wrong with the man? He was not much more than thirty. Had he been more than just knocked off balance? Was he injured?

West was up ahead, seizing a break in the traffic to cross back to the other side again. Three hansoms came past almost nose-to-tail. A cart and four clattered in the opposite direction. Pitt fumed on the edge of the curb. To go out into the roadway now would only get him killed.

A horse-drawn omnibus passed, then two heavily loaded wagons. More carts and a dray went in the other direction. Pitt had lost sight of West, and Gower had vanished into the air.

There was a brief holdup in traffic and Pitt raced across the road. Weaving in and out of the way of frustrated drivers, he only just missed being caught by a long, curling carriage whip. Someone yelled at him and he took no notice. He reached the opposite side and caught sight of West for an instant as he swung around a corner and made for another alley.

Pitt raced after him, but when he got there

West had disappeared.

"Did you see a man with ginger hair?" Pitt demanded of a peddler with a tray of sandwiches. "Where did he go?"

"Want a sandwich?" the man asked with eyes wide. "Very good. Made this morning. Only tuppence."

Pitt fished frantically in his pocket; found string, sealing wax, a pocketknife, a handkerchief, and several coins. He gave the man a threepenny bit and took a sandwich. It felt soft and fresh, although right now he didn't care. "Which way?" he said harshly.

"That way." The man pointed into the deeper shadows of the alley.

Pitt began to run again, weaving a path through the piles of rubbish. A rat skittered from under his feet, and he all but fell over a drunken figure lying half out of a doorway. Somebody swung a punch at him; he lurched to one side, losing his balance for a moment, glimpsing West still ahead of him.

Now West disappeared again and Pitt had no idea which way he had gone. He tried one blind courtyard and alley after another. It seemed like endless, wasted moments before Gower joined him from one of the side alleyways.

"Pitt!" Gower clutched at his arm. "This way! Quickly." His fingers dug deep into

11

Pitt's flesh, making him gasp with the sudden pain.

Together they ran forward, Pitt along the broken pavement beside the dark walls, Gower in the gutter, his boots sending up a spray of filthy water. Pace for pace, they went around the corner into the open entrance to a brickyard and saw a man crouching over something on the ground.

Gower let out a cry of fury and darted forward, half crossing in front of Pitt and tripping him up in his eagerness. They both fell heavily. Pitt was on his feet in time to see the crouched figure swing around for an instant, then scramble up and run as if for his life.

"Oh God!" Gower said, aghast, now also on his feet. "After him! I know who it is!"

Pitt stared at the heap on the ground: West's green jacket and bright hair. Blood streamed from his throat, staining his chest and already pooling dark on the stones underneath him. There was no way he could possibly be alive.

Gower was already pursuing the assassin. Pitt raced after him and this time his long strides caught up before they reached the road. "Who is it?" he demanded, almost choking on his own breath.

"Wrexham!" Gower hissed back. "We've

been watching him for weeks."

Pitt knew the man, but only by name. There was a momentary break in the stream of vehicles. They darted across the road to go after Wrexham, who thank heaven was an easy figure to see. He was taller than average, and — despite the good weather — he was wearing a long, pale-colored scarf that swung in the air as he twisted and turned. It flashed through Pitt's mind that it might be a weapon; it would not be hard to strangle a man with it.

They were on a crowded footpath now, and Wrexham dropped his pace. He almost sauntered, walking easily, swiftly, with loping strides, but perfectly casual. Could he be arrogant enough to imagine he had lost them so quickly? He certainly knew they had seen him, because he had swiveled around at Gower's cry, and then run as if for his life.

They were now walking at a steady pace, eastward toward Stepney and Limehouse. Soon the crowds would thin as they left the broader streets behind.

"If he goes into an alley, be careful," Pitt warned, now beside Gower, as if they were two tradesmen bound on a common errand. "He has a knife. He's too comfortable. He must know we're behind him."

Gower glanced at him sideways, his eyes wide for an instant. "You think he'll try and pick us off?"

"We practically saw him cut West's throat," Pitt replied, matching Gower stride for stride. "If we get him he'll hang. He must know that."

"I reckon he'll duck and hide suddenly, when he thinks we're taking it easy," Gower answered. "We'd better stay fairly close to him. Lose sight of him for a moment and he'll be gone for good."

Pitt agreed with a nod, and they closed the distance to Wrexham, who was still strolling ahead of them. Never once did he turn or look back.

Pitt found it chilling that a man could slit another's throat and see him bleed to death, then a few moments after walk through a crowd with outward unconcern, as if he were just one more pedestrian about some trivial daily business. What passion or inhumanity drove him? In the way he moved, the fluidity — almost grace — of his stride, Pitt could not detect even fear, let alone the conscience of a brutal murderer.

Wrexham wove in and out of the thinning crowd. Twice they lost sight of him.

"That way!" Gower gasped, waving his

right hand. "I'll go left." He swerved around a window cleaner with a bucket of water, almost knocking the man over.

Pitt went the other way, into the north end of an alley. The sudden shadows momentarily made him blink, half blind. He saw movement and charged forward, but it was only a beggar shuffling out of a doorway. He swore under his breath and sprinted back to the street just in time to see Gower swiveling around frantically, searching for him.

"That way!" Gower called urgently and set off, leaving Pitt behind.

The second time it was Pitt who saw him first, and Gower who had to catch up. Wrexham had crossed the road just in front of a brewer's dray and was out of sight by the time Pitt and Gower were able to follow. It took them more than ten minutes to close on him without drawing attention. There were fewer people about, and two men running would have been highly noticeable. With fifty yards' distance between them, Wrexham could have outrun them too easily.

They were in Commercial Road East, now, in Stepney. If Wrexham did not turn they would be in Limehouse, perhaps the West India Dock Road. If they went that far they could lose him among the tangle of wharves with cranes, bales of goods, warehouses, and dock laborers. If he went down to one of the ferries he could be out of sight between the ships at anchor before they could find another ferry to follow him.

Ahead of them, as if he had seen them, Wrexham increased his pace, his long legs striding out, his jacket scarf flying.

Pitt felt a flicker of nervousness. His muscles were aching, his feet sore despite his excellent boots — his one concession to sartorial taste. Even well-cut jackets never looked right on him because he weighted the pockets with too many pieces of rubbish he thought he might need. His ties never managed to stay straight; perhaps he knotted them too tightly, or too loosely. But his boots were beautiful and immaculately cared for. Even though most of his work was of the mind, out-thinking, out-guessing, remembering, and seeing significance where others didn't, he still knew the importance of a policeman's feet. Some habits do not die. Before he had been forced out of the Metropolitan Police and Victor Narraway had taken him into Special Branch, he had walked enough miles to know the price of inattention to physical stamina, and to boots.

16

Suddenly Wrexham ran across the narrow road and disappeared down Gun Lane.

"He's going for the Limehouse Station!" Gower shouted, leaping out of the way of a cart full of timber as he dashed after him.

Pitt was on his heels. The Limehouse Station was on the Blackwall Railway, less than a hundred yards away. Wrexham could go in at least three possible directions from there and end up anywhere in the city.

But Wrexham kept moving, rapidly, right, past the way back up to the station. Instead, he turned left onto Three Colts Street, then swerved right onto Ropemaker's Field, still loping in an easy run.

Pitt was too breathless to shout, and anyway Wrexham was no more than fifteen yards ahead. The few men and one old washerwoman on the path scattered as the three running men passed them. Wrexham was going to the river, as Pitt had feared.

At the end of Ropemaker's Field they turned right again into Narrow Street, still running. They were only yards from the river's edge. The breeze was stiff off the water, smelling of salt and mud where the tide was low. Half a dozen gulls soared lazily in circles above a string of barges.

Wrexham was still ahead of them, moving less easily now, tiring. He passed the entrance to Limehouse Cut. Pitt figured that he must be making for Kidney Stairs, the stone steps down to the river, where, if they were lucky, he would find a ferry waiting. There were two more sets of stairs before the road curved twenty yards inland to Broad Street. At the Shadwell Docks there were more stairs again. He could lose his pursuers on any of them.

Gower gestured toward the river. "Steps!" he shouted, bending a moment and gasping to catch his breath. He gestured with a wild swing of his arm. Then he straightened up and began running again, a couple of strides ahead of Pitt.

Pitt could see a ferry coming toward the shore, the boatman pulling easily at the oars. He would get to the steps a moment or two after Wrexham — in fact Pitt and Gower would corner him nicely. Perhaps they could get the ferry to take them up to the Pool of London. He ached to sit down even for that short while.

Wrexham reached the steps and ran down them, disappearing as if he had slipped into a hole. Pitt felt an upsurge of victory. The ferry was still twenty yards from the spot where the steps would meet the water.

Gower let out a yell of triumph, waving his hand high.

They reached the top of the steps just as the ferry pulled away, Wrexham sitting in the stern. They were close enough to see the smile on his face as he half swiveled on the seat to gaze at them. Then he faced forward, speaking to the ferryman and pointing to the farther shore.

Pitt raced down the steps. His feet slithered on the wet stones. He waved his arms at the other ferry, the one they had seen. "Here! Hurry!" he shouted.

Gower shouted also, his voice high and desperate.

The ferryman increased his speed, throwing his full weight behind his oars, and in a matter of seconds had swung around next to the pier.

"Get in, gents," he said cheerfully. "Where to?"

"After that boat there," Gower gasped, choking on his own breath and pointing to the other ferry. "An extra half crown in it for you if you catch up with him before he gets up Horseferry Stairs."

Pitt landed in the boat behind him and immediately sat down so they could get under way. "He's not going to Horseferry," he pointed out. "He's going straight across. Look!"

"Lavender Dock?" Gower scowled, sitting

in the seat beside Pitt. "What the hell for?"

"Shortest way across," Pitt replied. "Get up to Rotherhithe Street and away."

"Where to?"

"Nearest train station, probably. Or he might double back. Best place to get lost is among other people."

They were pulling well away from the dock now and slowly catching up with the other ferry.

There were fewer ships moored here, and they could make their way almost straight across. A string of barges was still fifty yards downstream, moving slowly against the tide. The wind off the water was colder. Without thinking what he was doing, Pitt hunched up and pulled his collar higher around his neck. It seemed like hours since he and Gower had burst into the brickyard and seen Wrexham crouched over West's blood-soaked body, but it was probably little more than ninety minutes. Their source of information about whatever plot West had known of was gone with his death.

He thought back to his last interview with Narraway, sitting in the office with the hot sunlight streaming through the window onto the piles of books and papers on the desk. Narraway's face had been intensely serious under its graying mane of hair, his eyes almost black. He had spoken of the gravity of the situation, the rise of the passion to reform Europe's old imperialism, violently if necessary. It was no longer a matter of a few sticks of dynamite, an assassination here and there. Rather, there were whispers of full governments overthrown by force.

"Some things need changing," Narraway had said with a wry bitterness. "No one but a fool would deny that there is injustice. But this would result in anarchy. God alone knows how wide this spreads, at least as far as France, Germany, and Italy, and by the sounds of it here in England as well."

Pitt had stared at him, seeing a sadness in the man he had never before imagined.

"This is a different breed, Pitt, and the tide of victory is with them now. But the violence . . ." Narraway had shaken his head, as if awakening himself. "We don't change that way in Britain, we evolve slowly. We'll get there, but not with murder, and not by force."

The wind was fading, the water smoother.

They were nearly at the south bank of the river. It was time to make a decision. Gower was looking at him, waiting.

Wrexham's ferry was almost at the Lavender Dock.

"He's going somewhere," Gower said urgently. "Do we want to get him now, sir — or see where he leads us? If we take him we won't know who's behind this. He won't talk, he's no reason to. We practically saw him kill West. He'll hang for sure." He waited, frowning.

"Do you think we can keep him in sight?" Pitt asked.

"Yes, sir." Gower did not hesitate.

"Right." The decision was clear in Pitt's mind. "Stay back then. We'll split up if we have to."

The ferry hung back until Wrexham had climbed up the narrow steps and all but disappeared. Then, scrambling to keep up, Pitt and Gower went after him.

They were careful to follow from more of a distance, sometimes together but more often with a sufficient space between them.

Yet Wrexham now seemed to be so absorbed in his own concerns that he never looked behind. He must have assumed he had lost them when he crossed the river. Indeed, they were very lucky that he had not. With the amount of waterborne traffic, he must have failed to realize that one ferry was dogging his path.

At the railway station there were at least a couple of dozen other people at the ticket counter.

"Better get tickets all the way, sir," Gower urged. "We don't want to draw attention to ourselves from not paying the fare."

Pitt gave him a sharp look, but stopped himself from making the remark on the edge of his tongue.

"Sorry," Gower murmured with a slight smile.

Once on the platform they remained close to a knot of other people waiting. Neither of them spoke, as if they were strangers to each other. The precaution seemed unnecessary. Wrexham barely glanced at either of them, nor at anyone else.

The first train was going north. It drew in and stopped. Most of the waiting passengers got on. Pitt wished he had a newspaper to hide his face and appear to take his attention. He should have thought of it before.

"I think I can hear the train . . . ," Gower said almost under his breath. "It should be to Southampton — eventually. We might have to change . . ." The rest of what he said was cut off by the noise of the engine as the train pulled in, belching steam. The doors flew open and passengers poured out.

Pitt struggled to keep Wrexham in sight. He waited until the last moment in case he should get out again and lose them, and, when he didn't, he and Gower boarded a carriage behind him.

"He could be going anywhere," Gower said grimly. His fair face was set in hard lines, his hair poking up where he had run his fingers through it. "One of us better get out at every station to see that he doesn't get off at the last moment."

"Of course," Pitt agreed.

"Do you think West really had something for us?" Gower went on. "He could have been killed for some other reason. A quarrel? Those revolutionaries are pretty volatile. Could have been a betrayal within the group? Even a rivalry for leadership?" He was watching Pitt intently, as if trying to read his mind.

"I know that," Pitt said quietly. He was by far the senior, and it was his decision to make. Gower would never question him on that. It was little comfort now, in fact rather a lonely thought. He remembered Narraway's certainty that there was something planned that would make the recent random bombings seem trivial. In February of last year, 1894, a French anarchist had tried to destroy the Royal Observatory at Greenwich with a bomb. Thank heaven he had failed. In June, President Carnot of France had been assassinated. In August, a man named

24

Caserio had been executed for the crime. Everywhere there was anger and uncertainty in the air.

It was a risk to follow Wrexham, but to seize on an empty certainty was a kind of surrender. "We'll follow him," Pitt replied. "Do you have enough money for another fare, if we have to separate?"

Gower fished in his pocket, counted what he had. "As long as it isn't all the way to Scotland, yes, sir. Please God it isn't Scotland." He smiled with a twisted kind of misery. "You know in February they had the coldest temperature ever recorded in Britain? Nearly fifty degrees of frost! If the poor bastard let off a bomb to start a fire you could hardly blame him!"

"That was February, this is April already," Pitt reminded him. "Here, we're pulling into a station. I'll watch for Wrexham this time. You take the next."

"Yes, sir."

Pitt opened the door and was only just on the ground when he saw Wrexham getting out and hurrying across the platform to change trains for Southampton. Pitt turned to signal Gower and found him already out and at his elbow. Together they followed, trying not to be conspicuous by hurrying. They found seats, but separately for a while, to make sure Wrexham didn't double back and elude them, disappearing into London again.

But Wrexham seemed to be oblivious, as if he no longer even considered the possibility of being followed. He appeared completely carefree, and Pitt had to remind himself that Wrexham had followed a man in the East End only hours ago, then quite deliberately cut his throat and watched him bleed to death on the stones of a deserted brickyard.

"God, he's a cold-blooded bastard!" he said with sudden fury.

A man in pin-striped trousers on the seat opposite put down his newspaper and stared at Pitt with distaste, then rattled his paper loudly and resumed reading.

Gower smiled. "Quite," he said quietly. "We had best be extremely careful."

One or the other of them got out briefly at every stop, just to make certain Wrexham did not leave this train, but he stayed until they finally pulled in at Southampton.

Gower looked at Pitt, puzzled. "What can he do in Southampton?" he said. They hurried along the platform to keep pace with Wrexham, then past the ticket collector and out into the street.

The answer was not long in coming.

Wrexham took an omnibus directly toward the docks, and Pitt and Gower had to race to jump onto the step just as it pulled away. Pitt almost bumped into Wrexham, who was still standing. Deliberately he looked away from Gower. They must be more careful. Neither of them was particularly noticeable alone. Gower was fairly tall, lean, his hair long and fair, but his features were a trifle bony, stronger than average. An observant person would remember him. Pitt was taller, perhaps less than graceful, and yet he moved easily, comfortable with himself. His hair was dark and permanently untidy. One front tooth was a little chipped, but visible only when he smiled. It was his steady, very clear gray eyes that people did not forget.

Wrexham would have to be extraordinarily preoccupied not to be aware of seeing them in London, and now again here in Southampton, especially if they were together. Accordingly, Pitt moved on down the inside of the bus to stand well away from Gower, and pretended to be watching the streets as they passed, as if he were taking careful note of his surroundings.

As he had at least half expected, Wrexham went all the way to the dockside. Without speaking to Gower, Pitt followed well behind their quarry. He trusted that Gower was off to the side, as far out of view as possible.

Wrexham bought a ticket on a ferry to St. Malo, across the channel on the coast of France. Pitt bought one as well. He hoped fervently that Gower had sufficient money to get one too, but the only thing worse than ending up alone in France, trying to follow Wrexham without help, would be to lose the man altogether.

He boarded the ferry, a smallish steamship called the *Laura,* and remained within sight of the gangplank. He needed to see if Gower came aboard, but more important to make sure that Wrexham did not get off again. If Wrexham were aware of Pitt and Gower it would be a simple thing to go ashore and hop the next train back to London.

Pitt was leaning on the railing with the sharp salt wind in his face when he heard footsteps behind him. He swung around, then was annoyed with himself for betraying such obvious alarm.

Gower was a yard away, smiling. "Did you think I was going to push you over?" he said amusedly.

Pitt swallowed back his temper. "Not this close to the shore," he replied. "I'll watch you more closely out in mid-channel!"

Gower laughed. "Looks like a good decision, sir. Following him this far could get us a real idea of who his contacts are in Europe. We might even find a clue as to what they're planning."

Pitt doubted it, but it was all they had left now. "Perhaps. But we mustn't be seen together. We're lucky he hasn't recognized us so far. He would have if he weren't so abominably arrogant."

Gower was suddenly very serious, his fair face grim. "I think whatever he has planned is so important his mind is completely absorbed in it. He thought he lost us in Ropemaker's Field. Don't forget we were in a totally separate carriage on the train."

"I know. But he must have seen us when we were chasing him. He ran," Pitt pointed out. "I wish at least one of us had a jacket to change. But in April, at sea, without them we'd be even more conspicuous." He looked at Gower's coat. They were not markedly different in size. Even if they did no more than exchange coats, it would alter both their appearances slightly.

As if reading this thought, Gower began to slip off his coat. He passed it over, and took Pitt's from his outstretched hand.

Pitt put on Gower's jacket. It was a little tight across the chest.

With a rueful smile Gower emptied the pockets of Pitt's jacket, which now sat a little loosely on his shoulders. He passed over the notebook, handkerchief, pencil, loose change, half a dozen other bits and pieces, then the wallet with Pitt's papers of identity and money.

Pitt similarly passed over all Gower's belongings.

Gower gave a little salute. "See you in St. Malo," he said, turning on his heel and walking away without looking back, a slight swagger in his step. Then he stopped and turned half toward Pitt, smiling. "I'd keep away from the railing if I were you, sir."

Pitt raised his hand in a salute, and resumed watching the gangway.

It was just past the equinox, and darkness still came quite early. They set out to sea as the sun was setting over the headland, and the wind off the water was distinctly chill. There was no point in even wondering where Wrexham was, let alone trying to watch him. If he met with anyone they would not know unless they were so close as to be obvious, and it might look like no more than a mere casual civility between strangers anyway. It would be better to find a chair and get a little sleep. It had been a

30

long day, full of exertion, horror, hectic running through the streets, and then sitting perfectly still in a railway carriage.

As he sat drifting toward sleep, Pitt thought with regret that he had not had even a chance to tell Charlotte that he would not be home that night, or perhaps even the next. He had no idea where his decision would take him. He had only a little money with him — sufficient for one or two nights' lodging now that he had bought a train ticket and a ferry ticket. He had no toothbrush, no razor, certainly no clean clothes. He had imagined he would meet West, learn his information, and then take it straight back to Narraway at his office in Lisson Grove.

Now they would have to send a telegram from St. Malo requesting funds, and saying at least enough for Narraway to understand what had happened. Poor West's body would no doubt be found, but the police might not know of any reason to inform Special Branch of it. No doubt Narraway would find out in time. He seemed to have sources of information everywhere. Would he think to tell Charlotte?

Pitt wished now that he had made some kind of a provision to see she was informed, or even made a telephone call from

Southampton. But to do that, he would have had to leave the ship, and perhaps lose Wrexham. He thought with surprise that he did not even know if Gower was married, or living with his parents. Who would be waiting for him to get home? This thought in his mind, Pitt drifted off to sleep.

He awoke with a jolt, sitting upright, his mind filled with the image of West's body, head lolling at an angle, blood streaming onto the stones of the brickyard, the air filled with the smell of it.

"Sorry, sir," the steward said automatically, passing a glass of beer to the man in the seat next to Pitt. "Can I get you something? How about a sandwich?"

Pitt realized with surprise that he had not eaten in twelve hours and was ravenous. No wonder he could not sleep. "Yes," he said eagerly. "Yes, please. In fact, may I have two, and a glass of cider?"

"Yes, sir. How about roast beef, sir. That do you?"

"Please. What time do we get into St. Malo?"

"About five o'clock, sir. But you don't need to go ashore until seven, unless o' course you'd like to."

"Thank you." Inwardly Pitt groaned. They would have to be up and watching from

32

then on, in case Wrexham chose to leave early. That meant they would have to be half awake all night.

"Better bring me two glasses of cider," he said with a wry smile.

Pitt slept on and off, and he was awake and on edge when he saw Gower coming toward him on the deck as the ferry nosed its way slowly toward the harbor of St. Malo. It was not yet dawn but there was a clear sky, and he could see the outline of medieval ramparts against the stars. Fifty or sixty feet high at the least, they looked to be interspersed with great towers such as in the past would have been manned by archers. Perhaps on some of them there would have been men in armor, with cauldrons of boiling oil to tip on those brave enough, or foolish enough, to scale the defenses. It was like a journey backward in time.

He was jerked back to reality by Gower's voice behind him.

"I see you are awake. At least I assume you are?" It was a question.

"Not sure," Pitt replied. "That looks distinctly like a dream to me."

"Did you sleep?" Gower asked.

"A little. You?"

Gower shrugged. "Not much. Too afraid

of missing him. Do you suppose he's going to make for the first train to Paris?"

It was a very reasonable question. Paris was a cosmopolitan city, a hotbed of ideas, philosophies, dreams both practical and absurd. It was the ideal meeting place for those who sought to change the world. The two great revolutions of the last hundred years had been born there.

"Probably," Pitt answered. "But he could get off anywhere." He was thinking how hard it would be to follow Wrexham in Paris. Should they arrest him while they still had the chance? In the heat of the chase yesterday it had seemed like a good idea to see where he went and, more important, whom he met. Now, when they were cold, tired, hungry, and stiff, it felt a lot less sensible. In fact it was probably absurd. "We'd better arrest him and take him back," he said aloud.

"Then we'll have to do it before we get off," Gower pointed out. "Once we're on French soil we'll have no authority. Even the captain here is going to wonder why we didn't do it in Southampton." His voice took on a note of urgency, his face grave. "Look, sir, I speak pretty good French. I've still got a reasonable amount of money. We could send a telegram to Narraway to have someone meet us in Paris. Then we wouldn't be just the two of us. Maybe the French police would be pleased for the chance to follow him?"

Pitt turned toward him, but he could barely make out his features in the faint light of the sky and the dim reflection of the ship's lights. "If he goes straight for the town, we'll have no time to send a telegram," he pointed out. "It'll take both of us to follow him. I don't know why he hasn't noticed us already.

"We should arrest him," he continued with regret. He should have done this yesterday. "Faced with the certainty of the rope, he might feel like talking."

"Faced with the certainty of the rope, he'd have nothing to gain," Gower pointed out.

Pitt smiled grimly. "Narraway'll think of something, if what he says is worth enough."

"He might not go for the train," Gower said quickly, moving his weight to lean forward a little. "We were assuming he'll go to Paris. Perhaps he won't? Maybe whoever he's going to meet is here. Why come to St. Malo otherwise? He could have gone to Dover, and taken the train from Calais to Paris, if that was where he wanted to be. He still doesn't know we're on to him. He thinks he lost us in Ropemaker's Field. Let's at least give it a chance!"

The argument was persuasive, and Pitt could see the sense in it. It might be worth waiting a little longer. "Right," he conceded. "But if he goes to the railway station, we'll take him." He made a slight grimace. "If we can. He might shout for help that he's being kidnapped. We couldn't prove he wasn't."

"Do you want to give up?" Gower asked. His voice was tight with disappointment, and Pitt thought he heard a trace of contempt in it.

"No." There was no uncertainty in the decision. Special Branch was not primarily about justice for crimes; it was about preventing civil violence and the betrayal, subversion, or overthrow of the government. They were too late to save West's life. "No, I don't," he repeated.

When they disembarked in the broadening daylight it was not difficult to pick Wrexham out from the crowd and follow him. He didn't go, as Pitt had feared, to the train station, but into the magnificently walled old city. They could not risk losing sight of him, or Pitt would have taken time to look with far more interest at the massive ramparts as they went in through an entrance

36

gate vast enough to let several carriages pass abreast. Once inside, narrow streets criss-crossed one another, the doors of the buildings flush with footpaths. Dark walls towered four or five stories high in uniform gray-black stone. The place had a stern beauty Pitt would have liked to explore. Knights on horseback would have ridden these streets, or swaggering corsairs straight from plunder at sea.

But they had to keep close to Wrexham. He was walking quickly as if he knew precisely where he was going, and not once did he look behind him.

It was perhaps fifteen minutes later, when they were farther to the south, that Wrexham stopped. He knocked briefly on a door, and was let into a large house just off a stone-paved square.

Pitt and Gower waited for nearly an hour, moving around, trying not to look conspicuous, but Wrexham did not come out again. Pitt imagined him having a hot breakfast, a wash and shave, clean clothes. He said as much to Gower.

Gower rolled his eyes. "Sometimes it's easier being the villain," he said ruefully. "I could do very well by bacon, eggs, sausages, fried potatoes, then fresh toast and marmalade and a good pot of tea." He grinned.

"Sorry. I hate to suffer alone."

"You're not!" Pitt responded with feeling. "We'll do something like that before we go and send a telegram to Narraway, then find out who lives in number seven." He glanced up at the wall. "Rue St. Martin."

"It'll be hot coffee and fresh bread," Gower told him. "Apricot jam if you're lucky. Nobody understands marmalade except the British."

"Don't they understand bacon and eggs?" Pitt asked incredulously.

"Omelet, maybe?"

"It isn't the same!" Pitt said with disappointment.

"Nothing is," Gower agreed. "I think they do it on purpose."

After another ten minutes of waiting, during which Wrexham still did not emerge, they walked back along the way they had come. They found an excellent café from which drifted the tantalizing aroma of fresh coffee and warm bread.

Gower gave him a questioning look.

"Definitely," Pitt agreed.

There was, as Gower had suggested, thick, homemade apricot jam, and unsalted butter. There was also a dish of cold ham and other meats, and hard-boiled eggs. Pitt was more than satisfied by the time they rose to

38

leave. Gower asked the *patron* for directions to the post office. He also inquired, as casually as possible, where they might find lodgings, and if number 7 rue St. Martin was a house of that description, adding that someone had mentioned it.

Pitt waited. He could see from the satisfaction in Gower's face as they left and strode along the pavement that the answer had pleased him.

"Belongs to an Englishman called Frobisher," he said with a smile. "Bit of an odd fellow, according to the *patron.* Lot of money, but eccentric. Fits the locals' idea of what an English upper-class gentleman should be. Lived here for several years and swears he'll never go home. Give him half a chance, and he'll tell anyone what's wrong with Europe in general and England in particular." He gave a slight shrug and his voice was disparaging. "Number seven is definitely not a public lodging house, but he has guests more often than not, and the *patron* does not like the look of them. Subversives, he says. But then I gathered he was pretty conservative in his opinions. He suggested we would find Madame Germaine's establishment far more to our liking, and gave me the address."

In honesty, Pitt could only agree. "We'll

send a telegram to Narraway, then see if Madame Germaine can accommodate us. You've done very well."

"Thank you, sir." He increased very slightly the spring in his step and even started to whistle a little tune, rather well.

At the post office Pitt sent a telegram to Narraway.

Staying St. Malo. Friends here we would like to know better. Need funds. Please send to local post office, soonest. Will write again.

Until they received a reply, they would be wise to conserve what money they had left. However, they would find Madame Germaine, trusting that she had vacancies and would take them in.

"Could be awhile," Gower said thoughtfully. "I hope Narraway doesn't expect us to sleep under a hedge. Wouldn't mind in August, but April's a bit sharp."

Pitt did not bother to reply. It was going to be a long, and probably boring, duty. He was thinking of Charlotte at home, and his children Jemima and Daniel. He missed them, but especially Charlotte, the sound of her voice, her laughter, the way she looked at him. They had been married for fourteen

years, but every so often he was still overtaken by surprise that she had apparently
never regretted it.

It had cost her her comfortable position
in Society and the financial security she had
been accustomed to, as well as the dinner
parties, the servants, the carriages, the
privileges of rank.

She had not said so — it would be heavy-
handed — but in return she had gained a
life of interest and purpose. Frequently she
had been informally involved in his cases, in
which she had shown considerable skill. She
had married not for convenience but for
love, and in dozens of small ways she had
left him in no doubt of that.

Dare he send her a telegram as well? In
this strange French street with its different
sounds and smells, a language he understood little of, he ached for the familiar. But
the telegram to Narraway was to a special
address. If Wrexham were to ask the post
office for it, it would reveal nothing. If Pitt
allowed his loneliness for home to dictate
his actions, he would have to give his home
address, which could put his family in real
danger. He should not let this peaceful
street in the April sun, and a good breakfast,
erase from his mind the memory of West lying in the brickyard with his throat slashed

open and his blood oozing out onto the stones.

"Yes, we'll do that," he said aloud to Gower. "Then we will do what we can, discreetly, to learn as much as possible about Mr. Frobisher."

It was not difficult to observe number 7 rue St. Martin. It was near the towering wall of the city, on the seaward side. Only fifty yards away a flight of steps climbed to the walkway around the top. It was a perfect place from which to stand and gaze at the ever-changing horizon out to sea, or watch the boats tacking across the harbor in the wind, their sails billowing, careful to avoid the rocks, which were picturesque and highly dangerous. In turning to talk to each other, it was natural for them to lean for a few minutes on one elbow and gaze down at the street and the square. One could observe anybody coming or going without seeming to.

In the afternoon of the first day, Pitt checked at the post office. There was a telegram from Narraway, and arrangements for sufficient money to last them at least a couple of weeks. There was no reference to West, or the information he might have given, but Pitt did not expect there to have been. He walked back to the square, passing a girl in a pink dress and two women with shopping baskets. Ascending the steps on the wall again, he found Gower leaning against the buttress at the top. His face was raised to the westering sun, which was gold in the late afternoon. He looked like any young Englishman on holiday.

Pitt stared out over the sea, watching the light on the water. "Narraway replied," he said quietly, not looking at Gower. "We'll get the money. The amount he's sending, he expects us to learn all we can."

"Thought he would."

Gower did not turn either, and barely moved his lips. He could have been drifting into sleep, his weight relaxed against the warm stone. "There's been some movement while you were gone. One man left, dark hair, very French clothes. Two went in." His voice became a little higher, more tightly pitched. "I recognized one of them — Pieter Linsky. I'm quite sure. He has a very distinctive face, and a limp from having been shot escaping from an incident in Lille. The man with him was Jacob Meister."

Pitt stiffened. He knew the names. They were both men active in socialist movements in Europe, traveling from one country to another fomenting as much trouble as they could, organizing demonstrations, strikes, even riots in the cause of various reforms. But underneath all the demands was the underlying wish for violent revolution. Linsky in particular was unashamedly a revolutionary. Interesting, though, was that the two men did not hold the same viewpoints, but instead represented opposing sides of the socialist movement.

Pitt let out his breath in a sigh. "I suppose you're sure about Meister as well?"

Gower was motionless, still smiling in the sun, his chest barely rising and falling as he breathed. "Yes, sir, absolutely. I'll bet that has something to do with what West was going to tell us. Those two together has to mean something pretty big."

Pitt did not argue. The more he thought of it the more certain he was that it was indeed the storm Narraway had seen coming, and which was about to break over Europe if they did not prevent it.

"We'll watch them," Pitt said quietly, also trying to appear as if he were relaxed in the sun, enjoying a brief holiday. "See who else they contact."

Gower smiled. "We'll have to be careful. What do you think they're planning?"

Pitt considered in silence, his eyes almost

closed as he stared down at the painted wooden door of number 7. All kinds of ideas teemed through his head. A single assassination seemed less likely than a general strike, or even a series of bombings; otherwise they would not need so many men. In the past assassinations had been accomplished by a lone gunman, willing to sacrifice his own life. But now . . . who was vulnerable? Whose death would really change anything permanently?

"Strikes?" Gower suggested, interrupting his thought. "Europe-wide, it could bring an industry to its knees."

"Possibly," Pitt agreed. His mind veered to the big industrial and shipbuilding cities of the north. Or the coal miners of Durham, Yorkshire, or Wales. There had been strikes before, but they were always broken and the men and their families suffered.

"Demonstrations?" Gower went on. "Thousands of people all out at once, in the right places, could block transport or stop some major event, like the Derby?"

Pitt imagined it, the anger, the frustration of the horse-racing and fashionable crowd at such an impertinence. He found himself smiling, but it was with a sour amusement. He had never been part of the Society that watched the Sport of Kings, but he had met many members during his police career. He knew their passion, their weaknesses, their blindness to others, and at times their extraordinary courage. Forcible interruption of one of the great events of the year was not the way to persuade them of anything. Surely any serious revolutionary had long ago learned that.

But what was?

"Meister's style, maybe," Pitt said aloud. "But not Linsky's. Something far more violent. And more effective."

Gower shivered very slightly. "I wish you hadn't said that. It rather takes the edge off the idea of a week or two in the sun, eating French food and watching the ladies going about their shopping. Have you seen the girl from number sixteen, with the red hair?"

"To tell you the truth, it wasn't her hair I noticed," Pitt admitted, grinning broadly.

Gower laughed outright. "Nor I," he said. "I rather like that apricot jam, don't you? And the coffee! Thought I'd miss a decent cup of tea, but I haven't yet." He was silent again for a few minutes, then turned his head. "What do you really think they have planned in England, sir — beyond a show of power? What do they want in the long run?"

The *sir* reminded Pitt of his seniority,

and therefore responsibility. It gave him a sharp jolt. There were scores of possibilities, a few of them serious. There had been a considerable rise in political power of left-wing movements in Britain recently. They were very tame compared with the violence of their European counterparts, but that did not mean they would remain that way.

Gower was still staring at Pitt, waiting, his face puzzled and keen.

"I think a concerted effort to bring about change would be more likely," Pitt said slowly, weighing the words as he spoke.

"Change?" Gower said quizzically. "Is that a euphemism for overthrowing the government?"

"Yes, perhaps it is," Pitt agreed, realizing how afraid he was as he said it. "An end to hereditary privilege, and the power that goes with it."

"Dynamiters?" Gower's voice was a whisper, the amusement completely vanished. "Another blowing up, like the gunpowder plot of the early 1600s?"

"I can't see that working," Pitt replied. "It would rally everyone against them. We don't like to be pushed. They'll need to be a lot cleverer than that."

Gower swallowed hard. "What, then?" he

said quietly.

"Something to destroy that power permanently. A change so fundamental it can't be undone." As he said the words they frightened him. Something violent and alien waited ahead of them. Perhaps they were the only ones who could prevent it.

Gower let out his breath in a sigh. He looked pale. Pitt watched his face, obliquely, as if he were still more absorbed in enjoying the sun, thinking of swiveling around to watch the sailing boats in the harbor again. They would have to rely on each other totally. It was going to be a long, tedious job. They dare not miss anything. The slightest clue could matter. They would be cold at night, often hungry or uncomfortable. Always tired. Above all they must not look suspicious. He was glad he liked Gower's humor, his lightness of touch. There were many men in Special Branch he would have found it much harder to be with.

"That's Linsky now, coming out of the door!" Gower stiffened, and then deliberately forced his body to relax, as if this sharp-nosed man with the sloping forehead and stringy hair were of no more interest than the baker, the postman, or another tourist.

Pitt straightened up, put his hands in his

pockets quite casually, and went down the
steps to the square after him.

CHAPTER 2

On the late afternoon of the day that Pitt and Gower had followed Wrexham to Southampton, Victor Narraway was sitting in his office at Lisson Grove. There was a knock on his door, and as soon as he answered one of his more junior men, Stoker, came in.

"Yes?" Narraway said with a touch of impatience. He was waiting for Pitt to report on the information from West, and the man was late. Narraway had no wish to speak to Stoker now.

Stoker closed the door behind him and came to stand in front of Narraway's desk. His lean face was unusually serious. "Sir, there was a murder in a brickyard off Cable Road in Shadwell in the middle of the day —"

"Are you sure I care about this, Stoker?" Narraway interrupted.

"Yes, sir," Stoker said without hesitation.

50

"The victim had his throat cut, and the man who did it was caught almost in the act, knife still in his hand. He was chased by two men who seem to have followed him to Limehouse, according to the investigation by the local police. Then —"

Narraway interrupted him again impatiently. "Stoker, I'm waiting for information about a major attack of some sort by socialist revolutionaries, possibly another spate of dynamitings." Then suddenly he was chilled to the bone. "Stoker . . ."

"West, sir," Stoker said immediately. "The man with his throat cut was West. It looks as if Pitt and Gower went after the man who did it, at least as far as Limehouse, probably across the river to the railway station. From there they could have gone anywhere in the country. There's been no word. No telephone call."

Narraway felt the sweat break out on his body. It was almost a relief to hear something. But where the hell was Pitt now? Why had he not at least placed a telephone call? The train could have gone anywhere. Even on an all-night train to Scotland he could have gotten off at one of the stations and called.

Then another thought occurred to him: Dover — or any of the other seaports.

Folkestone, Southampton. If he were on a ship, then calls would be impossible. That would explain the silence.

"I see. Thank you," he said aloud.

"Sir."

"Say nothing to anyone, for the time being."

"Yes, sir."

"Thank you. That's all."

After Stoker had gone Narraway sat still for several minutes. To have lost West, with whatever information he had, was serious. There had been increased activity lately, known troublemakers coming and going more often than usual, a charge of expectancy in the air. He knew all the signs; he just did not know what the target was this time. There were so many possibilities. Specific assassination, such as a government minister, an industrialist, a foreign dignitary on British soil — that would be a serious embarrassment. Or the dynamiting of a major landmark. He had relied on Pitt to find out. Perhaps he still might, but without West it would be more difficult.

And of course it was not the only issue at hand. There were always whispers, threats, the air breathing of suspicion and betrayal. It was the purpose of Special Branch to detect such things before they happened, and prevent at least the worst.

But if Pitt had gone to Scotland after the murderer of West, or worse still, across the channel, and had had no time to tell Narraway, then certainly he would not have had time to tell his wife either. Charlotte would be at home in Keppel Street waiting for him, expecting him, and growing more and more afraid with each passing hour as the silence closed in on her.

Narraway glanced at the longcase clock standing against the wall of his office. Its ornate hands pointed at quarter to seven. On a usual day Pitt would be home by now.

He thought of her in the kitchen, preparing the evening meal, probably alone. Her children would be occupied with studies for the following day's school. He could picture her easily; in fact the picture was already there in his mind, unbidden.

Some would not have found Charlotte beautiful. They might have preferred a face more traditional, daintier, less challenging. Narraway found such faces boring. There was a warmth in Charlotte, a laughter he could never quite forget — and he had tried. She was quick to anger at times, far too quick to react. Many of her judgments were flawed, in his opinion, but never her courage, never her will.

Someone must tell her that Pitt had gone in hot pursuit of West's murderer — no, better leave out the fact that West had been murdered. Pitt had gone in hot pursuit of a man with vital information, possibly across the channel, and had been unable to telephone her to let her know. He could call Stoker back and send him, but she did not know him. She did not know anyone else at Lisson Grove Headquarters. It would be the courteous thing to tell her himself. It would not be far out of his way. Well, yes it would, but it would still be the better thing to do.

Pitt, for all his initial ignorance of Special Branch ways, and his occasional political naïveté, was one of the best men Narraway had ever known. A gamekeeper's son, he had been educated in the household of the manor, which had produced a man who was by nature a gentleman, and yet possessing an anger and a compassion Narraway admired. He found himself puzzlingly protective of Pitt. Now he must tell Charlotte that her husband had disappeared, probably to France. He tidied his desk, locked away anything that might be confidential, left his office, and caught a hansom within minutes. He gave him Pitt's address on Keppel Street.

Narraway saw the fear in Charlotte's eyes

54

as soon as she opened the door to him. He would never have called merely socially, and she knew that. The strength of her emotion gave him a startling twinge of envy. It was a long time since there had been anyone who would have felt that terror for him.

"I'm sorry to disturb you," he said with rather stiff formality. "Events did not go according to plan today, and Pitt and his assistant were obliged to pursue a suspected conspirator without the opportunity to inform anyone of what was happening."

Warmth returned to her face, flushing the soft honey color of her skin. "Where is he?" she asked.

He decided to sound more certain than he was. West's murderer might have fled to Scotland, but France was far more likely. "France," he replied. "Of course he could not telephone from the ferry, and he would not have dared leave in case the man got off as well, and he lost him. I'm sorry."

She smiled. "It was very thoughtful of you to come tell me. I admit, I was beginning to be concerned."

The April evening was cold, a sharp wind carrying the smell of rain. He was standing on the doorstep staring at the light beyond. He stepped back, deliberately, his thoughts, the temptation, the quickening of his heart frightening him.

"There is no need," he said hastily. "Gower is with him; an excellent man, intelligent and quite fluent in French. And I daresay it will be warmer there than it is here." He smiled. "And the food is excellent." She had been preparing dinner. That was clumsy. Thank goodness he was far enough into the darkness that she could not see the blush rise up his face. "I will let you know as soon as I hear from him. If this man they are following goes to Paris, it may not be easy for them to be in contact, but please don't fear for him."

"Thank you. I won't now."

He knew that was a polite lie. Of course she would fear for Pitt, and miss him. Loving always included the possibility of loss. But the emptiness of not loving was even greater.

He nodded very slightly, just an inclination of his head, then wished her good night. He walked away, feeling as if he were leaving the light behind him.

It was the middle of the following morning when Narraway received the telegram from Pitt in St. Malo. He immediately forwarded him sufficient money to last both men for at least two weeks. He thought about it as

56

soon as it had been sent, and knew he had been overgenerous. Perhaps that was an indication of the relief he felt to know Pitt was safe. He would have to go back to Keppel Street to tell Charlotte that Pitt had been in touch.

He had returned to his desk after lunch when Charles Austwick came in and closed the door behind him. He was officially Narraway's next in command, although in practical terms it had come to be Pitt. Austwick was in his late forties with fair hair that was receding a little, and a good-looking but curiously unremarkable face. He was intelligent and efficient, and he seemed to be always in control of whatever feelings he might have. Now he looked very directly at Narraway, deliberately so, as if he was uncomfortable and attempting not to show it.

"An ugly situation has arisen, sir," he said, sitting down before he was invited to. "I'm sorry, but I have no choice but to address it."

"Then do so!" Narraway said a little hastily. "Don't creep around it like a maiden aunt at a wedding. What is it?"

Austwick's face tightened, his lips making a thin line.

"This has to do with informers," Austwick

said coldly. "Do you remember Mulhare?"

Narraway recognized the name with a rush of sadness. Mulhare had been an Irishman who risked his life to give information to the English. It was dangerous enough that he would have to leave Ireland, taking his family with him. Narraway had made sure there were funds provided for him.

"Of course I do," he said quietly. "Have they found who killed him? Not that it'll do much good now." He knew his voice sounded bitter. He had liked Mulhare, and had promised him that he'd be safe.

"That is something of a difficult question," Austwick replied. "He never got the money, so he couldn't leave Ireland."

"Yes, he did," Narraway contradicted him. "I dealt with it myself."

"That's rather the point," Austwick said. He moved position slightly, scuffing the chair leg on the carpet.

Narraway resented being reminded of his failure. It was a loss that would continue to hurt. "If you don't know who killed him, why are you spending time on that now, instead of current things?" he asked abruptly. "If you have nothing to do, I can certainly find you something. Pitt and Gower are away for a while. Somebody'll have to pick up Pitt's case on the docks."

"Oh really?" Austwick barely masked his surprise. "I didn't know. No one mentioned it!"

Narraway gave him a chill look and ignored the implied rebuke.

Austwick drew in his breath. "As I said," he resumed, "this is something I regret we have to deal with. Mulhare was betrayed —"

"We know that, for God's sake!" Narraway could hear his own voice thick with emotion. "His corpse was fished out of Dublin Bay."

"He never got the money," Austwick said again.

Narraway clenched his hands under the desk, out of Austwick's sight. "I paid it myself."

"But Mulhare never received it," Austwick replied. "We traced it."

Narraway was startled.

"To whom? Where is it?"

"I have no idea where it is now," Austwick answered. "But it was in one of your bank accounts here in London."

Narraway froze. Suddenly, with appalling clarity, he knew what Austwick was doing here, and held at least a hazy idea of what had happened. Austwick suspected, or even believed, that Narraway had taken the

59

money and intentionally left Mulhare to be caught and killed. Was that how little he knew him? Or was it more a measure of his long-simmering resentment, his ambition to take Narraway's place and wield the razor-edged power that he now held?

"And out again," he said aloud to Austwick. "We had to move it around a little, or it would have been too easily traceable to Special Branch."

"Oh yes," Austwick agreed bleakly. "Around to several places. But the trouble is that in the end it went back again."

"Back again? It went to Mulhare," Narraway corrected him.

"No, sir, it did not go to Mulhare. It went back into one of your special accounts. One that we had believed closed," Austwick said. "It is there now. If Mulhare had received it, he would have left Dublin, and he would still be alive. The money went around to several places, making it almost untraceable, as you said, but it ended up right back where it started, with you."

Narraway drew in his breath to deny it, and saw in Austwick's face that it would be pointless. Whoever had put it there, Austwick believed it was Narraway himself, or he chose to pretend he believed it.

"I did not put it there," Narraway said,

not because he thought it would change anything, but because he would not admit to something of which he was not guilty. The betrayal of Mulhare was repugnant to him, and *betrayal* was not a word he used easily. "I paid it to Terence Kelly. He was supposed to have paid it to Mulhare. That was his job. For obvious reasons, I could not give it directly to Mulhare, or I might as well have painted a bull's-eye on his heart."

"Can you prove that, sir?" Austwick asked politely.

"Of course I can't!" Narraway snapped. Was Austwick being deliberately obtuse? He knew as well as Narraway himself that one did not leave trails to prove such things. What he would be able to prove now, to justify himself, anyone else could have used to damn Mulhare.

"You see it calls into question the whole subject of your judgment," Austwick said half apologetically, his bland face grave. "It would be highly advisable, sir, for you to find some proof of this, then the matter could be let go."

Narraway's mind raced. He knew what was in his bank accounts, both personal and for Special Branch use. Austwick had mentioned one that had been presumed closed.

No money had passed through it for some time, but Narraway had deliberately left a few pounds in it, in case he ever wished to use it again. It was a convenience.

"I'll check the account," he said aloud, his voice cold.

"That would be a good idea, sir," Austwick agreed. "Perhaps you will be able to find some proof as to why it came back to you, and a reason poor Mulhare never received it."

Narraway realized that this was not an invitation, but rather a warning. It was even possible that his position at Special Branch was in jeopardy. Certainly he had created enemies over the years, both in his rise to leadership and even more so in the time since then. There were always hard decisions to make; whatever you did could not please everyone.

He had employed Pitt as a favor, when Pitt had challenged his own superiors and been thrown out of the Metropolitan Police. And initially he had found Pitt unsatisfactory, lacking the training or the inclination for Special Branch work. But the man had learned quickly, and he was a remarkably good detective: persistent, imaginative, and with a moral courage Narraway admired. And he liked the man, despite his own resolution not to allow personal feelings into anything professional.

He had protected Pitt from the envy and the criticism of others in the branch. That was partly because Pitt was more than worthy of the place, but also to defend Narraway's own judgment. Yet — he admitted it now — it was also for Charlotte's sake. Without Pitt, he would have no excuse to see her again.

"I'll attend to it," he answered Austwick at last. "As soon as I have a few more answers on this present problem. One of our informants was murdered, which has made things more difficult."

Austwick rose to his feet. "Yes, sir. That would be a good idea. I think the sooner you put people's minds at rest on the issue, the better it will be. I suggest before the end of this week."

"When circumstances allow," Narraway replied coolly.

Circumstances did not allow. Early the following morning Narraway was sent for to report to the Home Office, directly to Sir Gerald Croxdale, his political superior, the one man to whom he was obliged to answer without reservation.

Croxdale was in his early fifties, a quiet,

persistent politician who had risen in the ranks of the government with remarkable swiftness, not having made great speeches or introduced new laws, nor apparently having used the benefit of patronage from any of the more noted ministers. Croxdale seemed to be his own man. Whatever debts he collected or favors he owed were too discreet for even Narraway to know of, let alone the general public. He had made no individual initiatives that were remarkable but — probably far more important — he had also made no visible mistakes. Insiders spoke his name with respect.

Narraway had never seen in him the passion that marked an ambitious man, but he noted the quick rise to greater power and it earned in him a deeper, if reluctant, respect.

"Morning, Narraway," Croxdale said with an easy smile as he waved him to a brown leather armchair in his large office. Croxdale was a big man, tall and solid. His face was far from handsome in any traditional sense, but he was imposing. His voice was soft, his smile benign. Today he was wearing his usual well-cut but unostentatious suit, and perfectly polished black leather boots.

Narraway returned the greeting and sat down, not comfortably, but a little forward, listening.

"Bad business about your informant West being killed," Croxdale began. "I presume he was going to tell you a great deal more about whatever it is building up among the militant socialists."

"Yes, sir," Narraway said bleakly. "Pitt and Gower were only seconds too late. They saw West, but he was already terrified of something and took to his heels. They caught up with him in a brickyard in Shadwell, only moments after he was killed. The murderer was still bending over him." He could feel the heat of the blood in his cheeks as he said it. It was partly anger at having been so close, and yet infinitely far from preventing the death. One minute sooner and West would have been alive, and all his information would be theirs. It was also a sense of failure, as if losing him were an incompetence on the part of his men, and so of himself. Deliberately he met Croxdale's eyes, refusing to look away. He never made excuses, explicit or implicit.

Croxdale smiled, leaning back and crossing his long legs. "Unfortunate, but luck cannot always be on our side. It is the measure of your men that they kept track of the assassin. What is the news now?"

"I've had a couple of telegrams from Pitt in St. Malo," Narraway answered. "Wrexham, the killer, seems to have more or less gone to ground in the house of a British expatriate there. The interesting thing is that they have seen other socialist activists of note."

"Who?" Croxdale asked.

"Pieter Linsky and Jacob Meister," Narraway replied.

Croxdale stiffened, straightening up a little, his face keen with interest. "Really? Then perhaps not all is lost." He lowered his voice. "Tell me, Narraway, do you still believe there is some major action planned?"

"Yes," Narraway said without hesitation. "I think West's murder removes any doubt. He would have told us what it was, and probably who else was involved."

"Damn! Well you must keep Pitt there, and the other chap, what's his name?"

"Gower."

"Yes, Gower too. Give them all the funds they need. I'll see to it that that meets no opposition."

"Of course," Narraway said with some surprise. He had always had complete authority to disburse the funds in his care as he saw fit.

Croxdale pursed his lips and leaned farther forward. "It is not quite so simple, Narraway," he said gravely. "We have been looking into the matter of past funds and their use, in connection with other cases, as I daresay you know." He interlaced his fingers and looked down at them a moment, then up again quickly. "Mulhare's death has raised some ugly questions, which I'm afraid have to be answered."

Narraway was stunned. He had not realized the matter had already gone as far as Croxdale, and before he had even had a chance to look into it more deeply, and prove his own innocence. Was that Austwick's doing again? Damn the man.

"It will be," he said now to Croxdale. "I kept certain movements of the funds secret, to protect Mulhare. They'd have killed him instantly if they'd known he received English money."

"Isn't that rather what happened?" Croxdale asked ruefully.

Narraway thought for a moment of denying it. They knew who had killed Mulhare, but it was only proof they lacked; the deduction was certain in his own mind. But he did not need another moral evasion. His life was too full of shadows. He would not allow Croxdale to provoke him into another. "Yes."

"We failed him, Narraway," Croxdale said sadly.

"Yes."

"How did that happen?" Croxdale pressed.

"He was betrayed."

"By whom?"

"I don't know. When this socialist threat is dealt with, I shall find out, if I can."

"If you can," Croxdale said gently. "Do you doubt it? You have no idea who it was here in London?"

"No, I haven't."

"But you used the word *betrayed*," Croxdale persisted. "I think advisedly so. Does that not concern you urgently, Narraway? Whom can you trust, in any Irish issue? — of which, God knows, there are more than enough."

"The European socialist revolutionaries are our most urgent concern now, sir." Narraway also leaned forward. "There is a high degree of violence threatened. Men like Linsky, Meister, la Pointe, Corazath, are all quick to use guns and dynamite. Their philosophy is that a few deaths are the price they have to pay for the greater freedom and equality of the people. As long, of course, as the deaths are not their own," he added drily.

"Does that take precedence over treachery among your own people?" He left it hanging in the air between them, a question that demanded answering.

Narraway had seen the death of Mulhare as tragic, but less urgent than the threat of the broader socialist plot that loomed. He knew how he had guarded the provenance of the money, and did not know how someone had made the funds appear to return to Narraway's own personal account. Above all he did not know who was responsible, or whether it was done through incompetence — or deliberately in order to make him look a thief.

"I'm not yet certain it was betrayal, sir. Perhaps I used the word hastily." He kept his voice as level as he could; still, there was a certain roughness to it. He hoped Croxdale's less sensitive ear did not catch it.

Croxdale was staring at him. "As opposed to what?"

"Incompetence," Narraway replied. "And this time we covered the tracks of the transfers very carefully, so no one in Ireland would be able to trace it back to us. We made it seem like legitimate purchases all the way."

"Or at least you thought so," Croxdale amended. "But Mulhare was still killed. Where is the money now?"

Narraway had hoped to avoid telling him, but perhaps it had always been inevitable that Croxdale would have to know. Maybe he did, and this was a trap. "Austwick told me it was back in an account I had ceased using," he replied. "I don't know who moved it, but I shall find out."

Croxdale was silent for several moments. "Yes, please do, and with indisputable proof, of course. Quickly, Narraway. We need your skills on this wretched socialist business. It seems the threat is real."

"I'll look into the money as soon as we have learned what West's killers are planning," Narraway answered. "With a little luck, we'll even catch some of them and be able to put them away."

Croxdale looked up, his eyes bright and sharp. Suddenly he was no longer an amiable, rather bearlike man but tigerish, the passion in him like a coiled spring, masked only by superficial ease. "Do you imagine that a few martyrs to the cause will stop anything, Narraway? If so, I'm disappointed in you. Idealists thrive on sacrifice, the more public and the more dramatic the better."

"I know that." Narraway was stung by the misjudgment. "I have no intention of giving them martyrs. Indeed, I have no intention of denying them social reform and a good deal of change, but in pace with the will of the majority of the people in the country, not ahead of it, and not forced on them by a few fanatics. We've always changed, but slowly. Look at the history of the revolutions of 1848. We were about the only major country in Europe that didn't have an uprising. And by 1850, where were all the idealists from the barricades? Where were all the new freedoms so bloodily won? Every damn one of them gone, and all the old regimes back in power."

Croxdale was looking at him intensely, his expression unreadable.

"We had no uprising," Narraway went on, his voice dropped a level but the heat still there. "No deaths, no grand speeches, just quiet progress, a step at a time. Boring, perhaps unheroic, but also bloodless — and more to the point, sustainable. We aren't back under the old tyrannies. As governments go, ours is not bad."

"Thank you," Croxdale said drily.

Narraway gave one of his rare, beautiful smiles. "My pleasure, sir."

Croxdale sighed. "I wish it were so simple. I'm sorry, Narraway, but you will solve this miserable business of the money that should have gone to Mulhare immediately. Austwick will take over the socialist affair until you have it dealt with, which includes inarguable proof that someone else placed it in your account, and you were unaware of it until Austwick told you. It will also include the name of whoever is responsible for this, because they have jeopardized the effectiveness of one of the best heads of Special Branch that we have had in the last quarter century, and that is treason against the country, and against the queen."

For a moment Narraway did not grasp what Croxdale was saying. He sat motionless in the chair, his hands cold, gripping the arms as if to keep his balance. He drew in his breath to protest but saw in Croxdale's face that it would be pointless. The decision was made, and final.

"I'm sorry, Narraway," Croxdale said quietly. "You no longer have the confidence of Her Majesty's government, or of Her Majesty herself. I have no alternative but to remove you from office until such time as you can prove your innocence. I appreciate that that will be more difficult for you without access to your office or the papers in it, but you will appreciate the delicacy of my position. If you have access to the papers, you also have the power to alter them, destroy them, or add to them."

Narraway was stunned. It was as if he had

been dealt a physical blow. Suddenly he could barely breathe. It was preposterous. He was head of Special Branch, and here was this government minister telling him he was dismissed, with no warning, no preparation: just his decision, a word and it was all over.

"I'm sorry," Croxdale repeated. "This is a somewhat unfortunate way of having to deal with it, but it can't be helped. You will not go back to Lisson Grove, of course."

"What?"

"You cannot go back to your office," Croxdale said patiently. "Don't oblige me to make an issue of it."

Narraway rose to his feet, horrified to find that he was a trifle unsteady, as if he had been drinking. He wanted to think of something dignified to say, and above all to make absolutely certain that his voice was level, completely without emotion. He drew in his breath and let it out slowly.

"I will find out who betrayed Mulhare," he said a little hoarsely. "And also who betrayed me." He thought of adding something about keeping this as a Special Branch fit to come back to, but it sounded so petty he let it go. "Good day."

Outside in the street everything looked just as it had when he went in: a hansom cab drawn up at the curb, half a dozen men here and there dressed in striped trousers.

He started to walk without a clear idea of where he intended to go. His lack of direction was immediate, but he thought with a sense of utter emptiness that perhaps it was eternal as well. He was fifty-eight. Half an hour ago he had been one of the most powerful men in Britain. He was trusted absolutely; he held other men's lives in his hands, he knew the nation's secrets; the safety of ordinary men and women depended on his skill, his judgment.

Now he was a man without a purpose, without an income — although that was not an immediate concern. The land inherited from his father supported him, not perhaps in luxury, but at least adequately. He had no family alive now, and he realized with a gathering sense of isolation that he had acquaintances, but no close friends. His profession had made it impossible during the years of his increasing power. Too many secrets, too much need for caution.

It would be pathetic and pointless to indulge in self-pity. If he sank to that, what better would he deserve? He must fight back. Someone had done this to him. The only person he would have trusted to help was Pitt, and Pitt was in France.

He was walking quickly up Whitehall, looking neither right nor left, probably passing people he knew and ignoring them. No one would care. In time to come, when it was known he was no longer in power, they would probably be relieved. He was not a comfortable man to be with. Even the most innocent tended to attribute ulterior motive to him, imagining secrets that did not exist.

Whitehall became Parliament Street, then he turned left and continued walking until he was on Westminster Bridge, staring eastward across the wind-ruffled water.

He could not even return to his office. He could not properly investigate who had betrayed Mulhare. Then another thought occurred to him, which was far uglier. Was Mulhare the one who was incidental damage, and Narraway himself the target of the treachery?

As that thought took sharper focus in his mind he wondered bitterly if he really wanted to know the answer. Who was it that he had trusted, and been so horribly mistaken about?

He turned and walked on over the bridge to the far side, and then hailed a hansom, giving the driver his home address.

When he reached his house he poured himself a quick shot of single-malt whiskey, his favorite Macallan. Then went to the safe and took out the few papers he had kept there referring to the Mulhare case. He read them from beginning to end and learned nothing he did not already know, except that the money for Mulhare had been returned to the account within two weeks. He had not known because he had assumed the account closed. There was no notification from the bank.

It was close to midnight and he was still sitting staring at the far wall without seeing it when there came a sharp double tap on the window of the French doors opening onto the garden. It startled him out of his reverie, and he froze for an instant then got to his feet.

The tap came again, and he looked at the shadow outside. He could just see the features of a man's face beyond, unmoving, as if he wished to be recognized. Narraway thought for a moment of Pitt, but he knew it was not him. He was in France, and this man was not as tall.

It was Stoker. He should have known that straightaway. It was ridiculous to be standing here in the shadows as if he were afraid. He went forward, unlocked the French doors, and opened them wide.

Stoker came in, holding a bundle of

papers in a large envelope, half hidden under his jacket. His hair was damp from the slight drizzle outside, as if he had walked some distance. Narraway hoped he had, and taken more than one cab, to make following or tracing him difficult.

"What are you doing here, Stoker?" he said quietly, for the first time this evening drawing the curtains closed. It had not mattered before, and he liked the presence of the garden at twilight, the birds, the fading of the sky, the occasional movement of leaves.

"Brought some papers that might be useful, sir," Stoker replied. His voice and his eyes were perfectly steady, but the tension in his body, in the way he held his hands, betrayed to Narraway that he knew perfectly well the risk he was taking.

Narraway took the envelope from him, pulled out the papers, and glanced down at them, riffling through the pages swiftly to see what they were. Then he felt the breath tighten in his chest. They referred to an old case in Ireland, twenty years ago. The memory of it was powerful, for many reasons, and he was surprised how very sharply it returned.

It was as if he had last seen the people only a few days ago. He could remember the smell of the peat fire in the room where he and Kate had talked long into the night about the planned uprising. He could almost bring back the words he had used to persuade her it could only fail, and bring more death and more bitterness with it.

Even with his eyes open in his mind he could see Cormac O'Neil's fury, and then his grief. He understood it. But for all its vividness, it had been twenty years ago.

He looked up at Stoker. "Why these?" he asked. "This case is old, it's finished."

"The Irish troubles are never finished," Stoker said simply.

"Our more urgent problem is here now," Narraway replied. "And possibly in Europe."

"Socialists?" Stoker said drily. "They're always grumbling on."

"It's a lot more than that," Narraway told him. "They're fanatic. It's the new religion, with all the fire and evangelism of a holy cause. And just like Christianity in its infancy, it has its apostles and its dogma — and its splinter groups, quarrels over what is the true faith."

Stoker looked puzzled, as if this were all true but irrelevant.

"The point," Narraway said sharply, "is that they each consider the others to be heretics. They fight one another as much as they fight anyone else."

"Thank God," Stoker said with feeling.

"So when we see disciples of different factions meeting in secret, working together, then we know it is something damn big that has patched the rifts, temporarily." Narraway heard the edge in his own voice, and saw the sudden understanding in Stoker's eyes.

Stoker let out his breath slowly.

"How close are we to knowing what they're planning, sir?"

"I don't know," Narraway admitted. "It all rests on Pitt now."

"And you," Stoker said softly. "We've got to sort this money thing out, sir, and get you back."

Narraway drew in his breath to answer, and felt a sudden wave of conviction, a helplessness, a loss, an awareness of fear so profound that no words were adequate.

Stoker held out the papers he had brought. "We can't afford to wait," he said urgently. "I looked through everything I could that had to do with informants, money, and Ireland, trying to work out who's behind this. This case seemed the most likely. Also, I'm pretty sure someone else has had these papers out recently."

"Why?"

"Just the way they were put back," Stoker answered.

"Untidy?"

"No, the opposite. Very neat indeed."

Now Narraway was afraid for Stoker. He would lose his job for this; indeed, if he were caught, he could even be charged with treason himself. Regardless, he wanted to read the pages, but not with Stoker present. If this were the act of personal loyalty it seemed, or even loyalty to the truth, he did not want Stoker to take such a risk. It would be better for both of them not to be caught.

"Where did you get them?" he asked.

Stoker looked at him with a very slight smile. "Better you don't know, sir."

Narraway smiled back. "Then I can't tell," he agreed wryly.

Stoker nodded. "That too, sir."

There was something about Stoker calling him *sir* that was stupidly pleasing, as if he were still who he had been this morning. Did he value such respect so much? How pathetic!

He swallowed hard and drew in his breath. "Leave them with me. Go home, where everyone expects you to be. Come back for them when it's safe."

"Sorry, sir, but they have to be back by

dawn," Stoker replied. "In fact, the sooner the better."

"It will take me all night to read these and make my own notes," Narraway argued, knowing even as he said it that Stoker was right. To have them absent from Lisson Grove, even for one day, was too dangerous. Then they could never be returned. Anyone with two wits to rub together would look to Narraway for them, and then to whoever had brought them to him. He had no right to jeopardize Stoker's life with such stupidity.

"All right," he said, "I'll have them read before dawn. Three o'clock. You can return then and I'll give them to you. You can be at the Grove before light, and away again. Or you can go and sleep in my spare room, if you prefer. It would be wiser. No chance then of being caught in the street."

Stoker did not move.

"I'll stay here, sir. I'm pretty good at not being seen, but no risk at all is better. Wouldn't do if I couldn't get back."

Narraway nodded. "Up the stairs, across the landing to the left," he said aloud. "Help yourself to anything you need."

Stoker thanked him and left, closing the door softly.

Narraway turned up the gas a little more

brightly, then sat down in the big armchair by the fireplace and began to read.

The first few pages were about the Mulhare case: the fact that a large sum of money had been promised to Mulhare if he cooperated. It was paid not as reward so much as a means for him to leave Ireland and go — not as might be expected, to America, but to Southern France, a less likely place for his enemies to seek him.

As Narraway was painfully aware, Mulhare had not received the money. Instead he had remained in Ireland and been killed. Narraway still did not know exactly what had gone wrong. He had arranged the money, passed it through one of his own accounts. It had been kept in a different name so that it could not be traced back to him, and thus to Special Branch.

But now, inexplicably, it had reappeared.

The papers Stoker had brought referred to a twenty-year-old case that Narraway would like to have forgotten. It was at a time when the passion and the violence were even higher than usual.

Charles Stewart Parnell had just been elected to Parliament. He was a man of fire and eloquence, a highly active member in the council of the Irish Home Rule League, and everything in his life was dedicated to that cause. Indeed, if he'd had his way, Ireland might at last throw off the yoke of domination and govern itself again. The horrors of the great potato famine could be put behind them. Freedom beckoned.

Of course 1875 was before Narraway had become head of Special Branch. He was simply an agent in the field at that time, in his mid-thirties; wiry, strong, quick thinking, and with considerable charm. With his black hair and eyes, and his dry wit, he could easily have passed for an Irishman himself. When that assumption was made, as it often was, he did not deny it.

One of the leaders of the Irish cause then had been a man called Cormac O'Neil. He had a dark, brooding nature, like an autumn landscape, full of sudden shadows, storms on the horizon. He loved history, especially that handed down by word of mouth or immortalized in old songs. He was a man built to yearn for what he could not have.

Narraway thought of that wryly, remembering still with regret and guilt Cormac's brother Sean, and more vividly Kate. Beautiful Kate, so fiercely alive, so brave, so quick to see reason, so blind to the wounded and dangerous emotions of others.

In the silence of this comfortable London room with its very English mementos,

Ireland seemed like the other side of the world. Kate was dead; so was Sean. Narraway had won, and their planned uprising had failed without bloodshed on either side.

Even Charles Stewart Parnell was dead now, just three and a half years ago, October 1891, of a heart attack.

And Home Rule for Ireland was still only a dream, and the anger remained.

Narraway shivered here in his warm, familiar sitting room with the last of the embers still glowing, the pictures of trees on the wall, and the gas lamp shedding a golden light around him. The chill was inside, beyond the reach of any physical ease, perhaps of any words either, any thoughts or regrets now.

Was Cormac O'Neil still alive? There was no reason why he should not be. He would barely be sixty, perhaps less. If he were, he could be the one behind this. God knew, after the failed uprising and Sean's and Kate's deaths, he had cause enough to hate Narraway, more than any other man on earth.

But why wait twenty years to do it? Narraway could have died of an accident or of natural causes anytime between then and now, and robbed the man of his revenge.

Could something have prevented him in

the meantime? A debilitating illness? Not twenty years long. Time in prison? Surely Narraway would have heard of anything serious enough for such a term. And even from prison there was communication.

Perhaps this case had nothing to do with the past. Or perhaps it was simply that this was the time when Special Branch would be most vulnerable if Narraway was taken from it and his work discredited?

He closed the papers and put them back in the envelope Stoker had brought, then sat quietly in the dark and thought about it.

The old memories returned easily to his mind. He was walking again with Kate in the autumn stillness, fallen leaves red and yellow, frozen and crunching under their feet. She had no gloves, and he had lent her his. He could feel his hands ache with the cold at the memory. She had laughed at him for it, smiling, eyes bright, all the while making bitter jokes about warming the hands of Ireland with English wool.

When they had returned to the tavern Sean and Cormac had been there, and they had drunk rye whiskey by the fire. He could recall the smell of the peat, and Kate saying it was a good thing he didn't want vodka because potatoes were too scarce to waste on making it.

There were other memories as well, all sharp with emotion, torn loyalties, and regret. Wasn't it Wellington who had said that there was nothing worse than a battle won — except a battle lost? Or something like that.

Was the record accurate, as far as he had told anyone? Sanitized, of course, robbed of its passion and its humanity, but the elements that mattered to Special Branch were correct and sufficient.

Then something occurred to him, maybe an anomaly. He stood up, turned the gaslight higher again, and took the papers back out of the envelope. He reread them from beginning to end, including the marginal notes from Buckleigh, his superior then.

Narraway found what he feared. Something had been added. It was only a word or two, and to anyone who did not know Buckleigh's turn of phrase, his pedantic grammar, it would be undetectable. The hand looked exactly the same. But the new words added altered the meaning. Once it was only the addition of a question mark that had not been there originally, another time it was a few words that were not grammatically exact, a phrase ending with a preposition. Buckleigh would have included it in the main sentence.

Who had done that, and when? The why was not obscure to him at all: It was to raise the question of his role in this again, to cause the old ghosts to be awakened. Perhaps this was the deciding factor that had forced Croxdale to remove him from office.

He read through the papers one more time, just to be certain, then replaced them in the envelope and went upstairs to waken Stoker so he could leave well before dawn.

By the time he had opened the door Stoker was standing beside the bed. In the light from the landing it was clear that the quilt was barely ruffled. One swift movement of the hand and it was as if he had never been there.

Stoker looked at Narraway questioningly.

"Thank you," Narraway said quietly, the emotion in his voice more naked than he had meant it to be.

"It told you something," Stoker observed.

"Several things," Narraway admitted. "Someone else has been judiciously editing it since Buckleigh wrote his marginal notes, altering the meaning very slightly, but enough to make a difference."

Stoker came out of the room, and Narraway handed him the envelope. Stoker put it under his jacket where it could not be seen, but he did not fold it, or tuck it into his belt so the edges could be damaged. It was a reminder of the risk he was taking in having it at all. He looked very directly at Narraway.

"Austwick has taken your place, sir."

"Already?"

"Yes, sir. Mr. Pitt's over the channel, and you've no friends at Lisson Grove anymore. At least not who'll risk anything for you. It's every man for himself," Stoker said grimly. "I'm afraid there's no one for sure who'll help Mr. Pitt either, if he gets cut off or in any kind of trouble."

"I know that," Narraway said with deep unhappiness.

Stoker hesitated as if he would say something else, then changed his mind. He nodded silently and went down the stairs to the sitting room. He felt his way across the floor without lighting the gas lamps. He opened the French doors and slipped out into the wind and the darkness.

Narraway locked the door behind him and went back upstairs. He undressed and went to bed but lay awake staring up at the ceiling. He had left the curtains open, and gradually the faintest softening of the spring night made a break in the shadows across the ceiling. The glimmer was almost invisible, just enough to tell him there was movement, light beyond.

Only a matter of hours had passed since Austwick had come into Narraway's office. Narraway had thought little enough of it: a nuisance, no more. Then Croxdale had sent for him, and everything had changed. It was like going down a steep flight of stairs, only to find that the last one was not there.

He lay until daylight, realizing with a pain that amazed him how much of himself he had lost. He was used to getting up whether he had slept or not. Duty was a relentless mistress, but suddenly he knew also that she was a constant companion, loyal, appreciative, and above all, never meaningless.

Without her he was naked, even to himself. Narraway was accustomed to not particularly being liked. He'd had too much power for that, and he knew too many secrets. But never before had he not been needed.

CHAPTER 3

Charlotte sat by the fire in the parlor alone in her armchair opposite Pitt's. It was early evening. The children were in bed. There was no sound except now and then the settling of ashes as the wood burned through. Occasionally she picked up a piece of the mending that was waiting to be done — a couple of pillowcases, a pinafore of Jemima's. More often she simply stared at the fire. She missed Thomas, but she understood the necessity of his having pursued whoever it was to France. She also missed Gracie, the maid who had lived with them since she was thirteen and now, in her twenties, had finally married the police sergeant who had courted her so diligently for years.

Charlotte picked up the pinafore and began stitching up the hem where it had fallen, doing it almost as much by feel as by sight. The needle clicked with a light, quick sound against her thimble. Jemima was thirteen and growing tall very quickly. One could see the young woman that she would shortly become. Daniel was nearly three years younger, and desperate to catch up.

Charlotte smiled as she thought of Gracie, so proud in her white wedding gown, walking down the aisle on Pitt's arm as he gave her away. Tellman had been desperately nervous waiting at the altar, then so happy he couldn't control the smile on his face. He must have thought that day would never come.

But Charlotte missed Gracie's cheerfulness, her optimism, her candor, and her courage. Gracie never admitted to being beaten in anything. Her replacement, Mrs. Waterman, was middle-aged and dour as a walk in the sleet. She was a decent woman, honest as the day, kept everything immaculately clean, but she seemed to be content only if she was miserable. Perhaps in time she would gain confidence and feel better. It was sincerely to be hoped.

Charlotte did not hear the doorbell ring and was startled when Mrs. Waterman knocked on the parlor door. The older woman immediately came in, her face pinched with displeasure.

"There's a gentleman caller, ma'am. Shall I tell him that Mr. Pitt is not at home?"

Charlotte was startled, and her first thought was to agree to the polite fiction. Then her curiosity intruded. Surely at this hour it must be someone she knew?

"Who is it, Mrs. Waterman?"

"A very dark gentleman, ma'am. Says his name is Narraway," Mrs. Waterman replied, lowering her voice, although Charlotte could not tell if it were in disgust or confidentiality. She thought the former.

"Show him in," she said quickly, putting the mending out of sight on a chair behind the couch. Without thinking, she straightened her skirt and made sure she had no badly straying hairs poking out of her rather loose coiffure. Her hair was a rich dark mahogany color, but it slithered very easily out of control. As the pins dug into her head during the day, she was apt to remove them, with predictable results.

Mrs. Waterman hesitated.

"Show him in, please," Charlotte repeated, a trifle more briskly.

"I'll be in the kitchen if you need me," Mrs. Waterman said with a slight twist of her mouth that was definitely not a smile. She withdrew, and a moment later Narraway came in. When Charlotte had seen him a few days ago he had looked tired and a little concerned, but that was not unusual. This evening he was haggard, his lean face hollow-eyed, his skin almost without color.

Charlotte felt a terrible fear paralyze her, robbing her of breath. He had come to tell her terrible news of Pitt; even in her own mind she could not think the words.

"I'm sorry to disturb you so late," he said. His voice was almost normal, but she heard in its slight tremor the effort that it cost him. He stood in front of her. She could see from his eyes that he was hurt; there was an emptiness inside him that had not been there before.

He must have read her fear. How could he not? It filled the room.

He smiled thinly. "I have not heard from Thomas, but there is no reason to believe he is other than in excellent health, and probably having better weather than we have," he said gently. "Although I daresay he finds it tedious hanging about the streets watching people while trying to look as if he is on holiday."

She swallowed, her mouth dry, relief making her dizzy. "Then what is it?"

"Oh dear. Am I so obvious?"

It was more candid than he had ever been with her, yet it did not feel unnatural.

"Yes," she admitted. "I'm afraid you look dreadful. Can I get you something? Tea, or whiskey? That is, if we have any. Now that I've offered it, I'm not sure we do. The best of it might have gone at Gracie's wedding."

"Oh yes, Gracie." This time he did smile, and there was real warmth in it, changing his face. "I shall miss seeing her here. She was magnificent, all five feet of her."

"Four feet eleven, if we are honest," Charlotte corrected him with answering warmth. "Believe me, you could not possibly miss her as much as I do."

"You do not care for Mrs. . . . Lemon?"

"Waterman," she corrected him. "But Lemon would suit her. I don't think she approves of me. Perhaps we shall become accustomed to each other one day. She does cook well, and you could eat off the floors when she has scrubbed them."

"Thank you, but the table will do well enough," Narraway observed.

She sat down on the sofa. Standing so close to him in front of the fire was becoming uncomfortable. "You did not come to inquire after my domestic arrangements. And even if you had known Mrs. Waterman, she is not sufficient to cause the gravity I see in your face. What has happened?" She was holding her hands in her lap, and realized that she was gripping them together hard enough to hurt. She forced herself to let go.

There was a moment or two with no sound in the room but the flickering of the fire.

Narraway drew in his breath, then changed his mind.

"I have been relieved of my position in Special Branch. They say that it is temporary, but they will make it permanent if they can." He swallowed as if his throat hurt, and turned his head to look at her. "The thing concerning you is that I have no more access to my office at Lisson Grove, or any of the papers that are there. I will no longer know what is happening in France, or anywhere else. My place has been taken by Charles Austwick, who neither likes nor trusts Pitt. The former is a matter of jealousy because Pitt was recruited after him, and has received preferment in fact, if not in rank, that has more than equaled his. The latter is because they have little in common. Austwick comes from the army, Pitt from the police. Pitt has instincts Austwick will never understand, and Pitt's untidiness irritates Austwick's orderly, military soul." He sighed. "And of course Pitt is my protégé . . . was."

Charlotte was so stunned her brain did

not absorb what he had said, and yet looking at his face she could not doubt it.

"I'm sorry," he said quietly.

She understood what he was apologizing
for. He had made Pitt unpopular by singling
him out, preferring him, confiding in him.
Now, without Narraway, he would be vulnerable. He had never had any other profession but the police, and then Special
Branch. He had been forced out of the
police and could not go back there. It was
Narraway who had given him a job when he
had so desperately needed it. If Special
Branch dismissed him, where was there for
him to go? There was no other place where
he could exercise his very particular skills,
and certainly nowhere he could earn a
comparable salary.

They would lose this house in Keppel
Street and all the comforts that went with
it. Mrs. Waterman would certainly no longer
be a problem. Charlotte might well be
scrubbing her own floors; indeed, it might
even come to scrubbing someone else's as
well. She could imagine it already, see the
shame in Thomas's face for his own failure
to provide for her, not the near luxury she
had grown up in, nor even the amenities of
a working-class domesticity.

She looked up at Narraway, wondering

now about him. She had never considered before if he was dependent upon his salary or not. His speech and his manner, the almost careless elegance of his dress, said that he was born to a certain degree of position, but that did not necessarily mean wealth. Younger sons of even the most aristocratic families did not always inherit a great deal.

"What will you do?" she asked.

"How like you," he replied. "Both to be concerned for me, and to assume that there is something to be done."

Now she felt foolish.

"What are you going to do?" she asked again.

"To help Pitt? There's nothing I can do," he replied. "I don't know the circumstances, and to interfere blindly might do far more harm."

"Not about Thomas, about yourself." She had not asked him what the charge was, or if he was wholly or partially guilty.

The ashes settled even further in the fire.

Several seconds passed before he answered. "I don't know," he admitted, his voice hesitant for the first time in her knowledge. "I am not even certain who is at the root of it, although I have at least an idea. It is all . . . ugly."

She had to press onward, for Pitt's sake. "Is that a reason not to look at it?" she said quietly. "It will not mend itself, will it?"

He gave the briefest smile. "No. I am not certain that it can be mended at all."

"Would you like a cup of tea?" she asked.

He was startled. "I beg your pardon?"

"I don't have anything better," she apologized. "But you look uncomfortable standing there in front of the fire. Wouldn't sitting down with a hot cup of tea be better?"

He turned slightly to look behind him at the hearth and the mantel. "You mean I am blocking the heat," he said ruefully.

"No," she replied with a smile. "Actually I meant that I am getting a crick in my neck staring up and sideways at you."

For a moment the pain in his face softened. "Thank you, but I would prefer not to disturb Mrs. . . . whatever her name is. I can sit down without tea, unnatural as that may seem."

"Waterman," she supplied.

"Yes, of course."

"I was going to make it myself, provided that she would allow me into the kitchen. She doesn't approve. The ladies she is accustomed to working for do not even know where the kitchen is. Although how I could lose it in a house this size, I have no idea."

"She has come down in the world," Narraway observed. "It can happen to the best of us."

She watched as he sat down, elegantly as always, crossing his legs and leaning back as if he were comfortable.

"I think it may concern an old case in Ireland," he began, at first meeting her eyes, then looking down awkwardly. "At the moment it is to do with the death of a present-day informant there, because the money I paid did not reach him in time to flee those he had . . . betrayed." He said the word crisply and clearly, as if deliberately exploring a wound: his own, not someone else's. "I did it obliquely, so it could not be traced back to Special Branch. If it had been it would have cost him his life immediately."

She hesitated, seeking the right words, but watching his face, she had no impression that he was being deliberately obscure. She waited. There was silence beyond the room, no sound of the children asleep upstairs, or of Mrs. Waterman, who was presumably still in the kitchen. She would not retire to her room with a visitor still in the house.

"My attempts to hide its source make it impossible to trace what actually happened to it," Narraway continued. "To the superficial investigation, it looks as if I took it myself."

He was watching her now, but not openly.

"You have enemies," she said.

"Yes," he agreed. "I have. No doubt many. I thought I had guarded against the possibility of them injuring me. It seems I overlooked something of importance."

"Or someone is an enemy whom you did not suspect," she amended.

"That is possible," he agreed. "I think it is more likely that an old enemy has gained a power that I did not foresee."

"You have someone in mind?" She leaned forward a little. The question was intrusive, but she had to know. Pitt was in France, relying on Narraway to back him up. He would have no idea Narraway no longer held any office.

"Yes." The answer seemed to be difficult for him.

Again she waited.

He leaned forward and put a fresh log on the fire. "It's an old case. It all happened more than twenty years ago." He had to clear his throat before he went on. "They're all dead now, except one."

She had no idea what he was referring to, and yet the past seemed to be in the room with them.

"But one is alive?" she probed. "Do you

know, or are you guessing?"

"I know Kate and Sean are dead," he said so quietly she had to strain to hear him. "I imagine Cormac is still alive. He would be barely sixty."

"Why would he wait this long?"

"I don't know," he admitted.

"But you believe he hates you enough to lie, to plan and connive to ruin you?" she insisted.

"Yes. I have no doubt of that. He has cause."

She realized with surprise, and pity, that he was ashamed of his part in whatever had happened.

"So what will you do?" she asked again. "You have to fight. Nurse your wound for a few hours, then gather yourself together and think what you wish to do."

Now he smiled, showing a natural humor she had not seen in him before. "Is that how you speak to your children when they fall over and skin their knees?" he asked. "Quick sympathy, a hug, and then briskly get back up again? I haven't fallen off a horse, Charlotte. I have fallen from grace, and I know of nothing to get me back up again."

The color was hot in her cheeks. "You mean you have no idea what to do?"

He stood up and straightened the shoulders of his jacket. "Yes, I know what to do. I shall go to Ireland and find Cormac O'Neil. If I can, I shall prove that he is behind this, and clear my name. I shall make Croxdale eat his words. At least I hope I will."

She stood also. "Have you anyone to help you, whom you can trust?"

"No." His loneliness was intense. Just the one, simple word. Then it vanished, as if self-pity disgusted him. "Not here," he added. "But I may find someone in Ireland."

She knew he was lying.

"I'll come with you," she said impulsively. "You can trust me because our interests are the same."

His voice was tight with amazement, as if he did not dare believe her. "Are they?"

"Of course," she said rashly, although she knew it was the absolute truth. "Thomas has no other friend in Special Branch than you. The survival of my family may depend upon your being able to prove your innocence."

The color was warm in his cheeks also, or perhaps it was the firelight. "And what could you do?" he asked.

"Observe, ask questions, go where you will be recognized and cannot risk being seen. I am quite a good detective — at least I was in the past, when Thomas was in the police force and his cases were not so secret. At least I am considerably better than nothing."

He blushed and turned away. "I could not allow you to come."

"I did not ask your permission," she retorted. "But of course it would be a great deal pleasanter with it," she added.

He did not answer. It was the first time she had seen him so uncertain. Even when she had realized some time ago, with shock, that he found her attractive, there had always been a distance between them. He was Pitt's superior, a seemingly invulnerable man: intelligent, ruthless, always in control, and aware of many things that others knew nothing about. Now he was unsure, able to be hurt, no more in control of everything than she was. She would have used his Christian name if she had dared, but that would be a familiarity too far.

"We need the same thing," she began. "We have to find the truth of who is behind this fabrication and put an end to it. It is survival for both of us. If you think that because I am a woman I cannot fight, or that I will not, then you are a great deal more naïve than I assumed, and frankly I do not believe that. You have some other reason. Either you are afraid of something I will find out, some lie you need to protect; or else your pride is more important to you than your survival. Well, it is not more important to me." She took a deep breath. "And should I be of assistance, you will not owe me anything, morally or otherwise. I care what happens to you. I would not like to see you ruined, because you helped my husband at a time when we desperately needed it."

"Every time I think I know something about you, you surprise me," he observed. "It is a good thing you are no longer a part of high Society; they would never survive you. They are unaccustomed to such ruthless candor. They would have no idea what to do with you."

"You don't need to be concerned for them. I know perfectly well how to lie with the best, if I have to," she retorted. "I am coming to Ireland with you. This needs to be done, and you cannot do it alone because too many people already know you. You said as much yourself. But I had better have some reasonable excuse to justify traveling with you, or we shall cause an even greater scandal. May I be your sister, for the occasion?"

"We don't look anything alike," he said with a slightly twisted smile.

"Half sister then, if anybody asks," she amended.

"Of course you are right," he conceded. His voice was tired, the banter gone from it. He knew it was ridiculous to deny the only help he had been offered. "But you will listen to me, and do as I tell you. I cannot afford to spend my time or energy looking after you or worrying about you. Is that understood, and agreed?"

"Certainly. I want to succeed, not prove some kind of point."

"Then I shall be here at eight o'clock in the morning the day after tomorrow to take us to the train, and then the boat. Bring clothes suitable for walking, for discreet calling upon people in the city, and at least one gown for evening, should we go to the theater. Dublin is famous for its theaters. No more than one case."

"I shall be waiting."

He hesitated a moment, then let out his breath. "Thank you."

After he had gone Charlotte went back to the front parlor. A moment later there was a knock on the door.

"Come in," she said, expecting to thank Mrs. Waterman for waiting up, tell her that nothing more was needed and she should go to bed.

Mrs. Waterman came in and closed the door behind her. Her back was ramrod-stiff, her face almost colorless and set in lines of rigid disapproval. One might imagine she had found a blocked drain.

"I'm sorry, Mrs. Pitt," she said before Charlotte had had time to say anything. "I cannot remain here. My conscience would not allow it."

Charlotte was stunned. "What are you talking about? You've done nothing wrong."

Mrs. Waterman sniffed. "Well, I daresay I have my faults. We all do. But I've always been respectable, Mrs. Pitt. There wasn't ever anyone who could say different."

"Nobody has." Charlotte was still mystified. "Nobody has even suggested such a thing."

"And I mean to keep it like that, if you understand me." Mrs. Waterman stood, if possible, even straighter. "So I'll be going in the morning. I'm sorry, about that. I daresay it'll be difficult for you, which I regret. But I've got my name to think of."

"What are you talking about?" Charlotte was growing annoyed. Mrs. Waterman was not particularly agreeable, but they might learn to accept each other. She was certainly hardworking, diligent, and totally reliable — at least she had been so far. With Pitt away for an indefinite period of time, and now this disastrous situation with Narraway, the last thing Charlotte needed was a domestic crisis. She had to go to Ireland. If Pitt were without a job they would lose the house and in quite a short time possibly find themselves scraping for food. He might have to learn a new trade entirely, and that would be difficult for a man in his forties. Even with all the effort he would put into it, it would still take time. It was barely beginning to sink in. How on earth would Daniel and Jemima take the news? No more pretty dresses, no more parties, no more hoping for a career for Daniel. He would be fortunate not to start work at anything he could find, in a year or two. Even Jemima could become somebody's kitchen maid.

"You can't leave," Charlotte said, her tone angry now. "If you do, then I cannot give you a letter of character." That was a severe threat. Without a recommendation no servant could easily find another position. Their reason for leaving would be unexplained, and most people would put the unkindest interpretation on it.

Mrs. Waterman was unmoving. "I'm not sure, ma'am, if your recommendation would be of any service to me, as to character, that is — if you understand me."

"No, I do not understand you," she said tartly.

"I don't like having to say this," Mrs. Waterman replied, her face wrinkling with distaste. "But I've never before worked in a household where the gentleman goes away unexpectedly, without any luggage at all, and the lady receives other gentlemen, alone and after dark. It isn't decent, ma'am, and that's all there is to it. I can't stay in a house with 'goings-on.'"

Charlotte was astounded. " 'Goings-on'! Mrs. Waterman, Mr. Pitt was called away on urgent business, without time to come home or pack any luggage. He went to France in an emergency, the nature of which is not your business. Mr. Narraway is his superior in the government, and he came to tell me, so I would not be concerned. If you see it as something else, then the 'goings-on,' as you put it, are entirely in your own imagination."

"If you say so, ma'am," Mrs. Waterman answered, her eyes unwavering. "And what did he come for tonight? Did Mr. Pitt give a message to him, and not to you, his lawful wedded wife — I assume?"

Charlotte wanted to slap her. With a great effort she forced herself to become calm.

"Mrs. Waterman, Mr. Narraway came to

tell me further news concerning my husband's work. If you choose to think ill of it, or of me, then you will do so whatever the truth is, because that is who you are . . ."

Now it was Mrs. Waterman's face that flamed. "Don't you try to cover it with nice words and high-and-mighty airs," she said bitterly. "I know a man with a fancy for a woman when I see one."

It was on the edge of Charlotte's tongue to ask sarcastically when Mrs. Waterman had ever seen one, but it was perhaps an unnecessarily cruel thought. Mrs. Waterman was exactly what her grandmama used to call a vinegar virgin, despite the courteous *Mrs.* in front of her name.

"You have an overheated and somewhat vulgar imagination, Mrs. Waterman," she said coldly. "I cannot afford to have such a person in my household, so it might be best for both of us if you pack your belongings and leave first thing in the morning. I shall make breakfast myself, and then see if my sister can lend me one of her staff until I find someone satisfactory of my own. Her husband is a member of Parliament, and she keeps a large establishment. I shall see you to say good-bye in the morning."

"Yes, ma'am." Mrs. Waterman turned for the door.

"Mrs. Waterman!"

"Yes, ma'am?"

"I shall say nothing of you to others, good or ill. I suggest that you return that courtesy and say nothing of me. You would not come out of it well, I assure you."

Mrs. Waterman's eyebrows rose slightly.

Charlotte smiled with ice in her eyes. "A servant who will speak ill of one mistress will do so of another. Those of us who employ servants are well aware of that. Good night."

Mrs. Waterman closed the door without replying.

Charlotte went to the telephone to speak to Emily and ask for her help, immediately. She was a little surprised to see her hand shaking as she reached for the receiver.

When the voice answered she gave Emily's number.

It rang at the other end several times before the butler picked it up.

"Mr. Radley's residence. May I help you?" he said politely.

"I'm sorry to disturb you so late," Charlotte apologized. "It is Mrs. Pitt calling. Something of an emergency has arisen. May I speak with Mrs. Radley, please?"

"I'm very sorry, Mrs. Pitt," he replied with sympathy. "Mr. and Mrs. Radley have gone to Paris and I do not expect them back until next weekend. Is there something I may do to assist you?"

Charlotte felt a sort of panic. Who else could she turn to for help? Her mother was also out of the country, in Edinburgh, where she had gone with her second husband, Joshua. He was an actor, and had a play running in the theater there.

"No, no thank you," she said a little breathlessly. "I'm sure I shall find another solution. Thank you for your trouble. Good night." She hung up quickly.

She stood in the quiet parlor, the embers dying in the fire because she had not re-stoked it. She had until tomorrow evening to find someone to care for Daniel and Jemima, or she could not go with Narraway. And if she did not, then she could not help him. He would be alone in Dublin, hampered by the fact that he was known there, by friend and enemy alike.

Pitt had been Narraway's man from the beginning, his protégé and then his second in command — perhaps not officially, that was Austwick, but in practice. It had bred envy, and in some cases fear. With Narraway gone it would be only a matter of time before Pitt too was dismissed, demoted to an intolerable position, or — worse than that — met with an accident.

Then another thought occurred to her, ugly and even more imperative. If Narraway was innocent, as he claimed, then someone had deliberately reorganized evidence to make him look guilty. They could do the same to Pitt. In fact it was quite possible that if Pitt had had anything whatever to do with the case, he might already be implicated. As soon as he was home from France he would walk straight into the trap. Only a fool would allow him time to mount a defense, still less to find proof of his innocence and, at the same time, presumably their guilt.

But why? Was it really an old vengeance against Narraway? Or did Narraway know something about them that they could not afford to have him pursue? Whatever it was, whatever Narraway had done or not done, she must protect her husband. Narraway could not be guilty, that was the only thing of which she had no doubt.

Now she must find someone to look after Jemima and Daniel while she was away. Oh, damn Mrs. Waterman! The stupid creature!

Charlotte was tired enough to sleep quite well, but when she woke in the morning it all flooded back to her. Not only did she have to make breakfast herself — not an unfamiliar task — but she also had to see Mrs. Waterman on her way, and explain to Daniel and Jemima at least something of what had happened. It might be easier for Jemima, since she was thirteen, but how would Daniel, at ten, grasp enough of the idea at least to believe her? She must make sure he did not imagine it was in any way his fault.

Then she must tackle the real task of the day: finding someone trustworthy with whom to leave her children. Put in such simple words, the thought overwhelmed her. She stood in her nightgown in the center of the bedroom floor, overcome with anxiety.

Still, standing here stalling would achieve nothing. She might as well get dressed while she weighed it up. A white blouse and a plain brown skirt would be fine. She was going to do chores, after all.

When she went down the stairs Mrs. Waterman was waiting in the hall, her one suitcase by the door. Charlotte was tempted to be sorry for her, but the moment passed. There was too much to do for her to relent, even if Mrs. Waterman wanted her to. This was an inconvenience. There were disasters on the horizon.

"Good morning, Mrs. Waterman," she

said politely. "I am sorry you feel it necessary to go, but perhaps in the circumstances it is better. You will forgive me if I do not draw this out. I have to find someone to replace you by this evening. I hope you find yourself suited very soon. Good day to you."

"I'm sure I will, ma'am," Mrs. Waterman replied, and with such conviction that it flashed across Charlotte's mind to wonder if perhaps she already had. Sometimes domestic staff, especially cooks, found a cause to give notice in order to avail themselves of a position they preferred, or thought more advantageous for themselves.

"Yes, I imagine you will land on your feet," Charlotte said a trifle brusquely.

Mrs. Waterman gave her a cold look, drew breath to respond, then changed her mind and opened the front door. With some difficulty she dragged her case outside, then went to the curb to hail a cab.

Charlotte closed the door as Jemima came down the stairs. She was getting tall. From the looks of it, she would grow to her mother's height, with Charlotte's soft lines and confident air. The day was not far off.

"Where's Mrs. Waterman going?" she asked. "It's breakfast time."

There was no point in evading it. "She is leaving us," Charlotte replied quietly.

"At this time in the morning?" Jemima's eyebrows rose. They were elegant, slightly winged, exactly like Charlotte's own.

"It was that, or last night," Charlotte answered.

"Did she steal something?" Jemima reached the bottom stair. "Are you sure? She's so terribly good I can't believe she'd do that. She'd never be able to face herself in the glass. Come to think of it, perhaps she doesn't anyway. She might crack it."

"Jemima! That is rude, and most unkind," Charlotte said sharply. "But true," she added. "I did not ask her to leave. It is actually very inconvenient indeed . . ."

Daniel appeared at the top of the stairs, considered sliding down the banister, saw his mother at the bottom, and changed his mind. He came down the steps in a self-consciously dignified manner, as if that had always been his intention.

"Is Mrs. Waterman going?" he asked hopefully.

"She's already gone," Charlotte answered.

"Oh good. Is Gracie coming back?"

"No, of course she isn't," Jemima put in. "She's married. She's got to stay at home and look after her husband. We'll get someone else, won't we, Mama?"

"Yes. As soon as we've had breakfast and

you've gone to school, I shall begin looking."

"Where do you look?" Daniel asked curiously as he followed her down the passage to the kitchen. It was shining clean after last night's dinner. Mrs. Waterman had left it immaculate, but not a thing was started for breakfast. Not even the stove was lit. It was still full of yesterday's ashes and barely warm to the touch. It would take some time to rake it out and lay it, light it, and wait for it to heat — too long for a hot breakfast of any sort before school. Even tea and toast required the use of the stove.

Charlotte controlled her temper with difficulty. If she could have been granted one wish, other than Pitt being home, it would have been to have Gracie back. Just her cheerful spirit, her frankness, her refusal ever to give in, would have made things easier.

"I'm sorry," she said to Daniel and Jemima, "but we'll have to wait until tonight for something hot. It'll be bread and jam for us all this morning, and a glass of milk." She went to the pantry to fetch the milk, butter, and jam without waiting for their response. She was already trying to find words to tell them that she had to leave and go to Ireland. Except that she couldn't, if she didn't find someone totally trustworthy to care for them, and how could she do that in half a day? As an absolutely final resort she knew she could take them to Emily's home for the servants to look after.

She came back with the milk, butter, and jam, and put them on the table. Jemima was setting out the knives and spoons; Daniel was putting the glasses out one at a time. She felt a sudden tightening in her chest. How could she have contemplated leaving them with the disapproving Mrs. Waterman? Blast Emily for being away now, when she was so badly needed!

She turned and opened the bread bin, took out the loaf, and set it on the board with the knife.

"Thank you," she said, accepting the last glass. "I know it's a little early, but we had better begin. I knew Mrs. Waterman was going. I should have been up sooner and lit the stove. I didn't even think of it. I'm sorry." She cut three slices of bread and offered them. They each took one, buttered it, and chose the jam they liked best: gooseberry for Jemima, blackcurrant for Daniel — like his father — and apricot for Charlotte. She poured the milk.

"Why did she go, Mama?" Daniel asked.

For once Charlotte did not bother to tell

him not to speak with his mouth full. His question deserved an honest answer, but how much would he understand? He was looking at her now with solemn gray eyes exactly like his father's. Jemima waited with the bread halfway to her mouth. Perhaps the whole truth, briefly and without fear, was the only way to avoid having to lie later, as more and more emerged. If they ever found her lying to them, even if they understood the reason, their trust would be broken.

"Mr. Narraway, your father's superior, called a few evenings ago to tell me that your father had to go to France, without being able to let us know. He didn't want us to worry when he didn't come home . . ."

"You told us," Jemima interrupted. "Why did Mrs. Waterman go?"

"Mr. Narraway came again yesterday evening, quite late. He stayed for a little while, because something very bad had happened to him. He has been blamed for something he didn't do, and he is no longer your father's superior. That matters rather a lot, so he had to let me know."

Jemima frowned. "I don't understand. Why did Mrs. Waterman go? Can't we pay her anymore?"

"Yes, certainly we can," Charlotte said

quickly, although that might not always be true. "She went because she didn't approve of Mr. Narraway coming here and telling me in the evening."

"Why not?" Daniel put his bread down and stared at her. "Shouldn't he have told you? And how does she know? Is she in the police as well?"

Pitt had not explained to his children the differences between the police, detecting any type of crime, and Special Branch, a force created originally to deal with violence, sometimes treason, or any other threat to the safety of the country. This was not the time to address it.

"No," she said. "It is not her concern at all. She thought I should not have received any man after dark when your father was not here. She said it wasn't decent, and she couldn't remain in a house where the mistress did not behave with proper decorum. I tried to explain to her that it was an emergency, but she did not believe me." If she did not have more urgent problems, that would still have rankled.

Daniel still looked puzzled, but it was clear that Jemima understood.

"If she hadn't left anyway, then you should have thrown her out," she said angrily. "That's impertinent." She was immediately defensive of her mother, and *impertinent* was her new favorite word of condemnation.

"Yes it was," Charlotte agreed. She had been going to tell them about her need to go to Ireland, but changed her mind. "But since she did leave of her own will, it doesn't matter. May I have the butter, please, Daniel?"

He passed it to her. "What's going to happen to Mr. Narraway? Is Papa going to help him?"

"He can't," Jemima pointed out. "He's in France." She looked questioningly at Charlotte to support her, if she was right.

"Well, who is, then?" Daniel persisted.

There was no escape, except lies. Charlotte took a deep breath. "I am, if I can think of a way. Now please finish your breakfast so I can get you on your way to school, and begin looking for someone to replace Mrs. Waterman."

But when she put on an apron and knelt to clear the ashes out of the grate in the stove, then laid a new fire ready to light when she returned, finding a new maid did not seem nearly as simple a thing to accomplish as she had implied to Daniel and Jemima. It was not merely a woman to cook and clean that she required. It was someone who would be completely reliable, kind, and, if any emergency arose, would know what to do.

If she were in Ireland, who would they ask for help? Was she even right to go? Which was the greater emergency? Should she ask any new maid, if she could find one, to call Great-Aunt Vespasia, if she needed help? Vespasia was close to seventy, although she might not look it, and certainly had not retired from any part of life. Her passion, courage, and energy would put to shame many a thirty-year-old, and she had always been a leader in the highest Society. Her great beauty had changed, but not dimmed. But was she the person to make decisions should a child be ill, or there be some other domestic crisis such as a blocked drain, a broken faucet, a shortage of coal, a chimney fire, and so on?

Gracie had risen to all such occasions, at one time or another.

Charlotte stood up, washed her hands in water that was almost cold, and took off her apron. She would ask Gracie's advice. It was something of a desperate step to disturb her newfound happiness so soon, but it was a desperate situation.

It was an omnibus ride, but not a very long one, to the small red-brick house where

Gracie and Tellman lived. They had the whole of the ground floor to themselves, including the front garden. This was quite an achievement for a couple so young, but then Tellman was twelve years older than Gracie, and had worked extremely hard to gain promotion to sergeant in the Metropolitan Police. Pitt still missed working with him.

Charlotte walked up to the front door and knocked briskly, holding her breath in anticipation. If Gracie was not in, she had no idea where she could turn next.

But the door opened and Gracie stood just inside, five feet tall with her smart boots on, and wearing a dress that for once was nobody else's cast-off taken up and in to fit her. There was no need to ask if she was happy; it radiated from her face like heat from a stove.

"Mrs. Pitt! Yer come ter see me! Samuel in't 'ere now, 'e's gorn already, but come in an 'ave a cup o' tea." She pulled the door open even wider and stepped back.

Charlotte accepted, forcing herself to think of Gracie's new house, her pride and happiness, before she said anything of her own need. She followed Gracie inside along the linoleum-floored passage, polished to a gleaming finish, and into the small kitchen at the back. It too was immaculately clean and smelled of lemon and soap, even this early in the morning. The stove was lit and there was well-kneaded bread sitting in pans on the sill, rising gently. It would soon be ready to bake.

Gracie pulled the kettle over onto the hob and set out a teapot and cups, then opened the pantry cupboard to get milk.

"I got cake, if yer like?" she offered. "But mebbe yer'd sooner 'ave toast an' jam?"

"Actually, I'd rather like cake, if you can spare it," Charlotte replied. "I haven't had good cake for a while. Mrs. Waterman didn't approve of it, and the disfavor came through her hands. Heavy as lead."

Gracie turned around from the cupboard where she had been getting the cake. Plates were on the dresser. Charlotte noted with a smile that it was set out exactly like the one in her own kitchen, which Gracie had kept for so long: cups hanging from the rings, small plates on the top shelf, then bowls, dinner plates lowest.

"She gorn, then?" Gracie said anxiously.

"Mrs. Waterman? Yes, I'm afraid so. She gave notice and left all at the same time, yesterday evening. Or to be exact, she gave notice late yesterday evening, and was in the hall with her case when I came down this morning."

Gracie was astounded. She put the cake — which was rich and full of fruit — on the table, then stared at Charlotte in dismay. "Wot she done? Yer din't never throw 'er out fer nothin'!"

"I didn't throw her out at all," Charlotte answered. "She really gave notice, just like that —"

"Yer can't do that!" Gracie waved her hands to dismiss the idea. "Yer won't never get another place, not a decent one."

"A lot has happened," Charlotte said quietly.

Gracie sat down sharply in the chair opposite and leaned a little across the small wooden table, her face pale. "It in't Mr. Pitt . . ."

"No," Charlotte assured her hastily. "But he is in France on business and cannot come home until it is complete, and Mr. Narraway has been thrown out of his job." There was no use, and no honor, in concealing the truth from Gracie. After all, it was Victor Narraway who had placed her as a maid in Buckingham Palace when Pitt so desperately needed help in that case. The triumph had been almost as much Gracie's as his. Narraway himself had praised her.

Gracie was appalled. "That's wicked!"

"He thinks it is an old enemy, perhaps hand in glove with a new one, possibly someone after his job," Charlotte told her. "Mr. Pitt doesn't know, and is trusting Mr. Narraway to support him in his pursuit now and do what he can to help from here. He doesn't know he will be relying on someone else, who may not believe in him as Mr. Narraway does."

"Wot are we goin' ter do?" Gracie said instantly.

Charlotte was so overwhelmed with gratitude, and with emotion at Gracie's passionate and unquestioning loyalty, that she felt the warmth rise up in her and the tears prickle her eyes.

"Mr. Narraway believes that the cause of the problem lies in an old case that happened twenty years ago in Ireland. He is going back there to find his enemy and try to prove his own innocence."

"But Mr. Pitt won't be there to 'elp 'im," Gracie pointed out. " 'Ow can 'e do that by 'isself? Don't this enemy know 'im, never mind that 'e'll expect 'im ter do it?" She looked suddenly quite pale, all the happy flush gone from her face. "That's just daft. Yer gotter tell 'im ter think afore 'e leaps in, yer really 'ave!"

"I must help him, Gracie. Mr. Narraway's

enemies in Special Branch are Mr. Pitt's as well. For all our sakes, we must win."

"Yer goin' ter Ireland? Yer goin' ter 'elp 'im . . ." She reached out her hand, almost as if to touch Charlotte's where it lay on the table, then snatched it back self-consciously. She was no longer an employee, but it was a liberty too far, for all the years they had known each other. She took a deep breath. "Yer 'ave gotta!"

"I know. I mean to," Charlotte assured her. "But since Mrs. Waterman has walked out — in disgust and outraged morality, because Mr. Narraway was alone in the parlor with me after dark — I have to find someone to replace her before I can leave."

A succession of emotions passed across Gracie's face: anger, indignation, impatience, and a degree of amusement. "Stupid ol' 'aporth," she said with disgust. "Got minds like cesspits, some o' them ol' vinegar virgins. Not that Mr. Narraway don't 'ave a soft spot for yer, an' all." The smile lit her eyes for an instant, then was gone again. She might not have dared say that when she worked for Charlotte, but she was a respectable married woman now, and in her own kitchen, in her own house. She wouldn't have changed places with the queen — and she had met the queen, which was more than most could say.

"Gracie, Emily is away and so is my mother," Charlotte told her gravely. "I can't go and leave Jemima and Daniel until I find someone to look after them, someone I can trust completely. Where do I look? Who can recommend someone without any doubt or hesitation at all?"

Gracie was silent for so long that Charlotte realized she had asked an impossible question.

"I'm sorry," she said quickly. "That was unfair."

The kettle was boiling and began to whistle. Gracie stood up, picked up the cloth to protect her hands, and pulled it away from the heat. She swirled a little of the steaming water around the teapot to warm it, emptied it down the sink, and then made the tea. She carried the pot carefully over to the table and set it on a metal trivet to protect the wood. Then she sat down again.

"I can," she said.

Charlotte blinked. "I beg your pardon?"

"I can recommend someone," Gracie said. "Minnie Maude Mudway. I knowed 'er since before I ever met you, or come to yer 'ouse. She lived near where I used ter, in Spitalfields, just 'round the corner, couple o' streets along. 'Er uncle were killed. I 'elped 'er find 'oo done it, 'member?"

Charlotte was confused, trying to find the memory, and failing.

"You were riding the donkey, for Christmas," Gracie urged. "Minnie Maude were eight then, but she's growed up now. Yer can trust 'er, 'cos she don't never, ever give up. I'll find 'er for yer. An' I'll go ter Keppel Street meself an' check on them every day."

Charlotte looked at Gracie's small, earnest face, the gently steaming teapot, and the homemade cake with its rich sultanas, the whole lovingly immaculate kitchen.

"Thank you," she said softly. "That would be excellent. If you call in every day then I shan't worry."

Gracie smiled widely. "Yer like a piece o' cake?"

"Yes please," Charlotte accepted.

By three o'clock in the afternoon, Charlotte was already packed to leave with Narraway on the train the following morning, should it prove possible after all. She could not settle to anything. One moment she wanted to prepare the vegetables for dinner, then she forgot what she was intending to cook, or thought of something else to pack. Twice she imagined she heard someone at the door, but when she looked there was no one. Three times she went to check that Daniel and Jemima were doing their homework.

Then at last the knock on the door came, familiar in the rhythm, as if it were a person she knew. She turned and almost ran to open it.

On the step was Gracie, her smile so wide it lit her whole face with triumph. Next to her stood another young woman, several inches taller, slender, and with unruly hair she had done her best to tame, unsuccessfully. But the thing that caught Charlotte's attention was the intelligence in her eyes, even though now she looked definitely nervous.

"This is Minnie Maude," Gracie announced, as if she were a magician pulling a rabbit out of a top hat.

Minnie Maude dropped a tiny curtsy, obviously not quite sure enough to do it properly.

Charlotte could not hide her smile — not of amusement, but of relief. "How do you do, Minnie Maude. Please come in. If Gracie has explained my difficulty to you, then you know how delighted I am to see you." She opened the door more widely and turned to lead the way. She took them into the kitchen because it was warmer, and it would be Minnie Maude's domain, if she accepted the position.

"Please sit down," Charlotte invited them. "Would you like tea?" It was a rhetorical question. One made tea automatically.

"I'll do it," Gracie said instantly.

"You will not!" Charlotte told her. "You don't work here, you are my guest." Then she saw the startled look on Gracie's face. "Please," she added.

Gracie sat down suddenly, looking awkward.

Charlotte set about making the tea. She had no cake to offer, but she cut lacy-thin slices of bread and butter, and there was fine-sliced cucumber and hard-boiled egg. Of course there was also jam, although it was a little early in the afternoon for anything so sweet.

"Gracie tells me that you have known each other for a very long time," Charlotte said as she worked.

"Yes, ma'am, since I were eight," Minnie Maude replied. "She 'elped me when me uncle Alf were killed, an' Charlie got stole." She drew in her breath as if to say something more and then changed her mind.

Charlotte had her back to the table, hiding her face and her smile. She imagined that Gracie had schooled Minnie Maude well in not saying too much, not offering what was not asked for.

"Did she also explain that my husband is in Special Branch?" she asked. "Which is a sort of police, but dealing with people who are trying to cause war and trouble of one sort or another to the whole country."

"Yes, ma'am. She said as 'e were the best detective in all England," Minnie Maude replied. There was a warmth of admiration in her voice already.

Charlotte brought the plate of bread and butter over and set it on the table.

"He is very good," she agreed. "But that might be a slight exaggeration. At the moment he has had to go abroad on a case, unexpectedly. My previous maid left without any notice, because she misunderstood something that happened, and felt she could not stay. I have to leave tomorrow morning very early, because of another problem that has arisen." It sounded peculiar, even to her own ears.

"Yes, ma'am." Minnie Maude nodded seriously. "A very important gentleman, as Gracie speaks very 'ighly of too. She said as someone is blaming 'im fer summink as 'e didn't do, an' you're going to 'elp 'im, 'cos it's the right thing ter do."

Charlotte relaxed a little. "Exactly. I'm afraid we are a household of unexpected events, at times. But you will be in no danger at all. However, your job will involve considerable responsibility, because although I am here most of the time, I am not always."

"Yes, ma'am. I bin in service before, but the lady I were with passed on, an' I in't found a new place yet. But Gracie said as she'll come by every day, just ter make certain as everything's all right, like." Minnie Maude's face was a little tense, her eyes never leaving Charlotte's face.

Charlotte looked at Gracie and saw the confidence in her eyes, because she was sitting at the table sideways to her, the small hands knotted, knuckles white, in her lap. She made her decision.

"Then Minnie Maude, I would be very happy to engage you in the position of housemaid, starting immediately. I apologize for the urgency of the situation, and you will be compensated for the inconvenience by a double salary for the first month, to reflect also the fact that you will be alone at the beginning, which is always the most difficult time in a new place."

Minnie Maude gulped. "Thank you,

ma'am."

"After tea I shall introduce you to Jemima and Daniel. They are normally well behaved, and the fact that you are a friend of Gracie's will endear you to them from the beginning. Jemima knows where most things are. If you ask her, she will be happy to help you. In fact she will probably take a pride in it, but do not allow her to be cheeky. And that goes for Daniel as well. He will probably try your patience, simply to test you. Please do not let him get away with too much."

The kettle was boiling and she made the tea, bringing it over to the table to brew. While they were waiting she explained some of the other household arrangements, and where different things were kept.

"I shall leave you a list of the tradesmen we use, and what they should charge you, although I daresay you are familiar with prices. But they might take advantage, if they think you don't know." She went on to tell her of the dishes Daniel and Jemima liked best, and the vegetables they were likely to refuse if they thought they could get away with it. "And rice pudding," she finished. "That is a treat, not more than twice a week."

"Wi' nutmeg on the top?" Minnie Maude asked.

Charlotte glanced at Gracie, then smiled, the ease running through her like a warmth inside. "Exactly. I think this is going to work very well."

CHAPTER 4

Gracie and Minnie Maude returned early in the evening, accompanied by Tellman, who carried Minnie Maude's luggage. He took it up to the room that not long ago had been Gracie's, then excused himself to take Gracie home. Minnie Maude began to unpack her belongings and settle in, helped by Jemima, and watched from a respectful distance by Daniel. Clothes were women's business.

Once she had made certain that all was well, Charlotte telephoned her great-aunt Vespasia. Immensely relieved to find her at home, she asked if she might visit.

"You sound very serious," said Vespasia across the rather crackly wire.

Charlotte gripped the instrument more tightly in her hand. "I am. I have a great deal to tell you, and some advice to seek. But I would much prefer to tell you in person rather than this way. In fact some of it is most confidential."

"Then you had better come to see me," Vespasia replied. "I shall send my carriage for you. Are you ready now? We shall have supper. I was going to have Welsh rarebit on toast, with a little very good Hock I have, and then apple flan and cream. Apples at this time of year are not fit for anything except cooking."

"I would love it," Charlotte accepted. "I shall just make certain that my new maid is thoroughly settled and aware of what to cook for Daniel and Jemima, then I shall be ready."

"I thought you had had her since Gracie's wedding," Vespasia exclaimed. "Is she still not able to decide what to prepare?"

"Mrs. Waterman gave notice last night and left this morning," Charlotte explained. "Gracie found me someone she has known for years, but the poor girl has only just arrived. In fact she is still unpacking."

"Charlotte?" Now Vespasia sounded worried. "Has something happened that is serious?"

"Yes. Oh . . . we are all alive and well, but yes, it is serious, and I am in some concern as to whether the course of action I plan is wise or not."

"And you are going to ask my advice? It

must be serious indeed if you are willing to listen to someone else." Vespasia was vaguely mocking, though anxiety clearly all but overwhelmed her.

"I'm not," Charlotte told her. "I have already given my word."

"I shall dispatch my coachman immediately," Vespasia responded. "If Gracie recommends this new person then she will be good. You had better wear a cape. The evening has turned somewhat cooler."

"Yes, yes I will," Charlotte agreed, then she said good-bye and replaced the receiver on its hook.

Half an hour later Vespasia's coachman knocked on the door. Minnie Maude seemed confident enough for Charlotte to leave her, and Daniel and Jemima were not in the least concerned. Indeed, they seemed to be enjoying showing her the cupboards and drawers, and telling her exactly what was kept in each.

Charlotte answered the door, told the coachman that she would be ready in a moment, then went to the kitchen. She stopped for a moment to stare at Jemima's earnest face explaining to Minnie Maude which jugs were used to keep the day's milk and where the milkman was to be found in the morning. Daniel was moving from foot to foot in his urgency to put in his advice as well, and Minnie Maude was smiling at first one, then the other.

"I may be late back," Charlotte interrupted. "Please don't wait up for me."

"No, ma'am," Minnie Maude said quickly. "But I'll be happy to, if you wish?"

"Thank you, but please make yourself comfortable," Charlotte told her. "Good night."

She went straight out to the carriage, and for the next half hour rode through the streets to Vespasia's house in Gladstone Park — which was really not so much a park as a small square with flowering trees. She sat and tried to compose in her mind exactly how she would tell Vespasia what she meant to do.

At last Charlotte sat in Vespasia's quiet sitting room. The colors were warm, muted to a familiar gentleness. The curtains were drawn across the window onto the garden, and the fire burned in the hearth with a soft whickering of flames. She looked into Vespasia's face, and it was not so easy to explain to her the wild decision to which Charlotte had already committed herself.

Vespasia had been considered by many to be the most beautiful woman of her generation, as well as the most outrageous in her wit and her political opinions — or maybe *passions* would be a more fitting word. Time had marked her features lightly and, if anything, liberated her temperament even more. She was secure enough in her financial means and her social preeminence not to have to care what other people thought of her, as long as she was certain in her own mind that a course of action was for the best. Criticism might hurt, but it was a long time since it had deterred her.

Now she sat stiff-backed — she had never lounged in her life — her silver hair coiffed to perfection. A high lace collar covered her throat, and the lamplight gleamed on the three rows of pearls.

"You had better begin at the beginning," she told Charlotte. "Supper will be another hour."

At least Charlotte knew what the beginning was. "Several evenings ago Mr. Narraway came to see me at home, to tell me that Thomas had been in pursuit of a man who had committed a murder, almost in front of him. He and his junior had been obliged to follow this person and had not had the opportunity to inform anyone of what they were doing. Mr. Narraway knew that they were in France. They sent a telegram. He told me of it so that I would not worry when

139

Thomas did not come home or call me."

Vespasia nodded. "It was courteous of him to come himself," she observed a trifle drily.

Charlotte caught the tone in her voice, and her eyes widened.

"He is fond of you, my dear," Vespasia responded. Her amusement was so slight it could barely be seen, and was gone again the second after. "What has this to do with the maid?"

Charlotte looked at the drawn curtains, the pale design of flowers on the carpet. "He came again last evening," she said quietly. "And stayed for much longer."

Vespasia's voice changed almost imperceptibly. "Indeed?"

Charlotte raised her eyes to meet Vespasia's. "There appears to have been a conspiracy within Special Branch to make it look as if he embezzled a good deal of money." She saw Vespasia's look of disbelief. "They have dismissed him, right there on the spot."

"Oh dear," Vespasia said. "I see why you are distressed. This is very serious indeed. Victor may have his faults, but financial dishonesty is not one of them. Money does not interest him. He would not even be tempted to do such a thing."

Charlotte did not find that comforting.

What faults was Vespasia implying? It seemed she knew him better than Charlotte had appreciated, even though Vespasia had interested herself in many of Pitt's cases, and therefore Narraway's. Then the moment after, studying Vespasia's expression, Charlotte realized that Vespasia was deeply concerned for him and believed in his innocence.

Charlotte found the tension in her body easing, and she smiled. "I did not believe it of him either, but there is something in the past that troubles him very much."

"There will be a good deal," Vespasia said with the ghost of a smile. "He is a man of many sides, but the most vulnerable one is his work, because that is what he cares about."

"Then he wouldn't jeopardize it, would he?" Charlotte pointed out.

"No. Someone finds it imperative that Victor Narraway be driven out of office, and out of credit with Her Majesty's government. There are many possible reasons, and I have no idea which of them it is, so I have very little idea where to begin."

"We have to help him." Charlotte hated asking this of Vespasia, but the need was greater than the reluctance. "Not only for his sake, but for Thomas's. In Special

Branch, Thomas is regarded as Mr. Narraway's man. I know this because, apart from my own sense, Thomas has told me so himself, and so has Mr. Narraway. Aunt Vespasia, if Mr. Narraway is gone, then whoever got rid of him may try to get rid of Thomas as well —"

"Of course," Vespasia cut across her. "You do not need to explain it to me, my dear. And Thomas is in France, not knowing what has happened, or that Victor can no longer give him the support from London that he needs."

"Have you friends —" Charlotte began.

"I do not know who has done this, or why," Vespasia answered even before the question was finished. "So I do not know whom I can trust."

"Victor . . . Mr. Narraway . . ." Charlotte felt a faint heat in her cheeks. ". . . said he believed it was an old case in Ireland, twenty years ago, for which someone now seeks revenge. He didn't tell me much about it. I think it embarrassed him."

"No doubt." Vespasia allowed a bleak spark of humor into her eyes for an instant. "Twenty years ago? Why now? The Irish are good at holding a grudge, or a favor, but they don't wait on payment if they don't have to."

" 'Revenge is a dish best served cold'?" Charlotte suggested wryly.

"Cold, perhaps, my dear, but this would be frozen. There is more to it than a personal vengeance, but I do not know what. By the way, what has this to do with your maid leaving? Clearly there is something you have . . . forgotten . . . to tell me."

Charlotte found herself uncomfortable. "Oh . . . Mr. Narraway called after dark, and clearly since the matter was of secrecy, for obvious reasons he closed the parlor door. I'm afraid Mrs. Waterman thought I was . . . am . . . a woman of dubious morals. She doesn't feel she can remain in a household where the mistress has 'goings-on,' as she put it."

"Then she is going to find herself considerably restricted in her choice of position," Vespasia said waspishly. "Especially if her disapproval extends to the master as well."

"She didn't say." Charlotte bit her lip, but couldn't conceal her smile. "But she would be utterly scandalized, so much so that she might have left that night, out into the street alone, with her suitcase in her hand, if she had known that I promised Mr. Narraway that I would go to Ireland with him, to do whatever I can to find the truth and help him clear his name. I have to. His enemies are Thomas's enemies, and Thomas will have no defense against them without Mr. Narraway there. Then what shall we do?"

Vespasia was silent for several moments. "Be very careful, Charlotte," she said gravely. "I think you are unaware of how dangerous that could become."

Charlotte clenched her hands. "What would you have me do? Sit here in London while Mr. Narraway is unjustly ruined, and then wait for Thomas to be ruined as well? At best he will be dismissed because he was Mr. Narraway's man, and they don't like him. At worst he may be implicated in the same embezzlement, and end up charged with theft." Her voice cracked a little and she realized how tired she was, and how very frightened. "What would you do?"

Vespasia reached across and touched her very gently, just fingertip-to-fingertip. "Just the same as you, my dear. That's not the same thing as saying that it is wise. It is simply the only choice you can live with."

There was a tap on the door, and the maid announced that supper was ready. They ate in the small breakfast room. Slender-legged Georgian mahogany furniture glowed dark amid golden-yellow walls, as if they were dining in the sunset, although the curtains were closed and the only light came from the mounted gas brackets.

They did not resume the more serious conversation until they had returned to the sitting room and were assured of being uninterrupted.

"Do not forget for a moment that you are in Ireland," Vespasia warned. "Or imagine it is the same as England. It is not. They wear their past more closely wound around themselves than we do. Enjoy it while you are there, but don't let your guard down for a second. They say you need a long spoon to sup with the devil. Well, you need a strong head to dine with the Irish. They'll charm the wits out of you, if you let them."

"I won't forget why I'm there," Charlotte promised.

"Or that Victor knows Ireland very well, and the Irish also know him?" Vespasia added. "Do not underestimate his intelligence, Charlotte, or his vulnerability. By the way, you have not mentioned how you intend to carry this off without causing a scandal that might not damage Narraway's good name any further, but would certainly ruin yours. I assume your sense of fear and injustice did not blind you to that?" There was no criticism in her voice, only concern.

Charlotte felt the blood hot in her face.

"Of course not. I can't take a maid, I don't

have one, or the money to pay her fare if I did. I am going to say I am Mr. Narraway's sister — half sister. That will make it decent enough."

A tiny smile touched the corners of Vespasia's lips. "Then you had better stop calling him *Mr. Narraway* and learn to use his given name, or you will certainly raise eyebrows." She hesitated. "Or perhaps you already do."

Charlotte looked into Vespasia's steady silver-gray eyes, and chose not to respond.

Narraway came early the following morning in a hansom cab. When she answered the door he hesitated only momentarily. He did not ask her if she were certain of the decision. Perhaps he did not want to give her the chance to waver. He called the cabdriver to put her case on the luggage rack.

"Do you wish to go and say good-bye?" he asked her. His face looked bleak, with shadows under his eyes as if he had not slept in many nights. "There is time."

"No thank you," she answered. "I have already done so. And I hate long good-byes. I am quite ready to go."

He nodded and walked behind her across the footpath. Then he helped her up onto the seat, going around to the other side to sit next to her. The cabbie apparently knew the destination.

She had already decided not to tell him that she had visited Vespasia. He might prefer to think Vespasia did not know of his dismissal. She also chose not to let him know of Mrs. Waterman's suspicions. It could prove embarrassing, even as if she herself had considered the journey as something beyond business herself.

"Perhaps you would tell me something about Dublin," she requested. "I have never been there, and I realize that beyond the fact that it is the capital of Ireland, I know very little."

The idea seemed to amuse him. "We have a long train journey ahead of us, even on the fast train, and then a crossing of the Irish Sea. I hear that the weather will be pleasant. I hope so, because if it is rough, then it can be very violent indeed. There will be time for me to tell you all I know, from 7500 BC until the present day."

She was amazed at the age of the city, but she would not allow him to see that he had impressed her so easily. It might look as if she were being deliberately gentle with the grief she knew he must be feeling.

"Really? Is that because our journey is enormously long after all, or because you know less than I had supposed?"

"Actually there is something of a gap between 7500 BC and the Celts arriving in 700 BC," he said with a smile. "And after that not a great deal until the arrival of Saint Patrick in AD 432."

"So we can leap eight thousand years without further comment," she concluded. "After that surely there must be something a little more detailed?"

"The building of Saint Patrick's Cathedral in AD 1192?" he suggested. "Unless you want to know about the Vikings, in which case I would have to look it up myself. Anyway, they weren't Irish, so they don't count."

"Are you Irish, Mr. Narraway?" she asked suddenly. Perhaps it was an intrusive question, and when he was Pitt's superior she would not have asked it, but now the relationship was far more equal, and she might need to know. With his intensely dark looks he easily could be.

He winced slightly. "How formal you are. It makes you sound like your mother. No, I am not Irish, I am as English as you are, except for one great-grandmother. Why do you ask?"

"Your precise knowledge of Irish history," she answered. That was not the real reason. She asked because she needed to know more about his loyalties, the truth about what had happened in the O'Neil case twenty years ago.

"It is my job to know," he said quietly. "As it was. Would you like to hear about the feud that made the King of Leinster ask Henry the Second of England to send over an army to assist him?"

"Is it interesting?"

"The army was led by Richard de Clare, known as Strongbow. He married the king's daughter and became king himself in 1171, and the Anglo-Normans took control. In 1205 they began to build Dublin Castle. 'Silken' Thomas led a revolt against Henry the Eighth in 1534, and lost. Do you begin to see a pattern?"

"Of course I do. Do they burn the King of Leinster in effigy?"

He laughed, a brief, sharp sound. "I haven't seen it done, but it sounds like a good idea. We are at the station. Let me get a porter. We will continue when we are seated on the train."

The hansom pulled up as he spoke, and he alighted easily. There was an air of command in him that attracted attention within seconds, and the luggage was unloaded into a wagon, the driver paid, and Charlotte walked across the pavement into the vast

Paddington railway station for the Great Western rail to Holyhead.

It had great arches, as if it were some half-finished cathedral, and a roof so high it dwarfed the massed people all talking and clattering their way to the platform. There was a sense of excitement in the air, and a good deal of noise and steam and grit.

Narraway took her arm. For a moment his grasp felt strange and she was about to object, then she realized how foolish that would be. If they were parted in the crowd they might not find each other again until after the train had pulled out. He had the tickets, and he must know which platform they were seeking.

They passed groups of people, some greeting one another, some clearly stretching out a reluctant parting. Every so often the sound of belching steam and the clang of doors drowned out everything else. Then a whistle would blast shrilly, and one of the great engines would come to life beginning the long pull away from the platform.

It was not until they had found their train and were comfortably seated that they resumed any kind of conversation. She found him courteous, even considerate, but she could not help being aware of his inner tensions, the quick glances, the concern, the way his hands were hardly ever completely still.

It would be a long journey to Holyhead on the west coast. It was up to her to make it as agreeable as possible, and also to learn a good deal more about exactly what he wanted her to do.

Sitting on the rather uncomfortable seat, upright, with her hands folded in her lap, she realized she must look very prim. It was not an image she liked, and yet now that they were embarked on this adventure together, each for their own reasons, she must be certain not to make any irretrievable mistakes, first of all in the nature of her feelings. She liked Victor Narraway. He was highly intelligent, and he could be very amusing at rare times, but she knew only one part of his life.

Still, she knew that there must be more, the private man. Somewhere beneath the pragmatism there had been dreams.

"Thank you for the lesson on ancient Irish history," she began, feeling clumsy. "But I need to know far more than I do about the specific matter that we are going to investigate; otherwise I may not recognize something important if I hear it. I cannot possibly remember everything to report it accurately to you."

"Of course not." He was clearly trying to keep a straight face, and not entirely succeeding. "I will tell you as much as I can. You understand there are aspects of it that are still sensitive . . . I mean politically."

She studied his face, and knew that he also meant they were personally painful. "Perhaps you could tell me something of the political situation?" she suggested. "As much as is public knowledge — to those who were interested," she added. Now it was her turn to mock herself very slightly. "I'm afraid I was more concerned with dresses and gossip at the time of the O'Neil case." She would have been about fifteen. "And thinking whom I might marry, of course."

"Of course," he nodded. "A subject that engages most of us, from time to time. All you need to know of the political background is that Ireland, as always, was agitating for Home Rule. Various British prime ministers had attempted to put it through Parliament, and it proved their heartbreak, and for some their downfall. This is the time of the spectacular rise of Charles Stewart Parnell. He was to become leader of the Home Rule Party in '77."

"I remember that name," she agreed.

"Naturally, but this was long before the

scandal that ruined him."

"Did he have anything to do with what happened with the O'Neil family?"

"Nothing at all, at least not directly. But the fire and hope of a new leader was in the air, and Irish independence at last, and everything was different because of it." He looked out the window at the passing countryside, and she knew he was seeing another time and place.

"But we had to prevent it?" she assumed.

"I suppose it came to that, yes. We saw it as the necessity to keep the peace. Things change all the time, but how its done must be controlled. There is no point in leaving a trail of death behind you in order merely to exchange one form of tyranny for another."

"You don't have to justify it to me," she told him. "I am aware enough of the feeling. I only wish to understand something of the O'Neil family, and why one of them should hate you personally so much that twenty years later you believe he would stoop to manufacturing evidence that you committed a crime. What sort of a man was he then? Why has he waited so long to do this?"

Narraway turned his head away from the sunlight coming through the carriage window. He spoke reluctantly. "Cormac? He

153

was a good-looking man, very strong, quick to laugh, and quick to anger — but it was usually only on the surface, and gone before he would dwell on it. But he was intensely loyal, to Ireland above all, then to his family. He and his brother Sean were very close." He smiled. "Quarreled like Kilkenny cats, as they say, but let anyone else step in and they'd turn on them like furies."

"How old was he then?" she asked.

"Close to forty," he replied without hesitation.

She wondered if he knew that from records, or if he had been close enough to Cormac O'Neil that such things were open between them. She had the increasing feeling that this was far more than a Special Branch operation. There was deep, many-layered personal emotion as well, and Narraway would only ever tell her what he had to.

"Were they from an old family?" she pursued. "Where did they live, and how?"

He looked out the window again. "Cormac had land to the south of Dublin — Slane. Interesting place. Old family? Aren't we all supposed to go back to Adam?"

"He doesn't seem to have bequeathed the heritage to us equally," she answered.

"I'm sorry. Am I being evasive?"

"Yes," she replied.

"Cormac had enough means not to have to work more than in an occasional overseeing capacity. He and Sean between them owned a brewery as well. I daresay you know the waters of the Liffey River are famous for their softness. You can make ale anywhere, but nothing else has quite the flavor of that made with Liffey water. But you want to know what they were like."

"Yes," she answered. "Don't you need me to seek him out? Because if he hates you as deeply as you think, he will tell you nothing that could help."

The light vanished from his face. "If it's Cormac, he's thought this out very carefully. He must have known all about Mulhare and the whole operation: the money, the reason for paying it as I did, and how any interference would cost Mulhare his life."

"And he must also have been able to persuade someone in Lisson Grove to help him," she pointed out.

He winced. "Yes. I've thought about that a lot." Now his face was very somber indeed. "I've been piecing together all I know: Mulhare's connections; what I did with the money to try to make certain it would never be traced back to Special Branch, or to me

155

personally, all the past friends and enemies I've made, where it happened. It always comes back to O'Neil."

"Why would anyone at Lisson Grove be willing to help O'Neil?" she asked. It was like trying to take gravel out of a wound, only far deeper than a scraped knee or elbow. She thought of Daniel's face as he sat on one of the hard-backed kitchen chairs, dirt and blood on his legs, while she tried to clean where he had torn the skin off, and pick out the tiny stones. There had been tears in his eyes and he had stared resolutely at the ceiling, trying to stop them from spilling over and giving him away.

"Many reasons," Narraway replied. "You cannot do a job like mine without making enemies. You hear things about people you might very much prefer not to know, but that is a luxury you sacrifice when you accept the responsibility."

"I know that," she told him.

His eyes wandered a little. "Really? How do you know that, Charlotte?"

She saw the trap and slipped around it. "Not from Thomas. He doesn't discuss his cases since he joined Special Branch. And anyway, I don't think you can explain to someone else such a complicated thing."

He was watching her intently now. His

eyes were so dark it was hard to read the expression in them. The lines in his face showed all the emotions that had passed over them through the years: the anxiety, the laughter, and the grief.

"My eldest sister was murdered, many years ago now," she explained. "But perhaps you know that already. Several young women were at that time. We had no idea who was responsible. In the course of the investigation we learned a great deal about each other that would have been far more comfortable not to have known, and we cannot unlearn such things." She remembered it with pain now, even though it was fourteen years ago.

She looked up at him and saw his surprise. The only way to cover the discomfort was to continue talking.

"After that, when Thomas and I were married, I am afraid I meddled a good deal in many of his cases, particularly those where Society people were involved. I had an advantage in being able to meet them socially, and observe things he never could. One listens to gossip as a matter of course. It is largely what Society is about. But when you do it intelligently, actually trying to learn things, comparing what one person says with what another does, asking questions obliquely, weighing answers, you cannot help but learn much that is private to other people, painful, vulnerable, and absolutely none of your affair."

He moved his head very slightly in assent, but he knew it was not necessary to speak.

For a little while they rode in silence. The rhythmic clatter of the wheels over the railway ties was comfortable, almost somnolent. It had been a difficult and tiring few days and she found herself drifting into a daze, then woke with a start. She hoped she had not been lolling there with her mouth open!

Still, she did not yet know enough about what she could do to help and asked, "Do you know who it was at Lisson Grove who betrayed you?"

"No, I don't," he admitted. "I have considered several possibilities. In fact the only people I am certain it is not are Thomas and a man called Stoker. It makes me realize how incompetent I have been that I suspected nothing. I was always looking outward, at the enemies I knew. In this profession I should have looked behind me as well."

She did not argue. "So we can trust no one in Special Branch, apart from Stoker," she concluded. "Then I suppose we need to concentrate on Ireland. Why does Cormac O'Neil hate you so much? If I am to learn anything, I need to know what to build upon."

This time he did not look away from her, but she could hear the reluctance in his voice. He told her only because he had to. "When he was planning an uprising I was the one who learned about it and prevented it. I did it by turning to his sister-in-law, Sean's wife, and using the information she gave me to have his men arrested and imprisoned."

"I see."

"No, you don't," he said quickly, his voice tight. "And I have no intention of telling you any further. But because of it Sean killed her, and was hanged for her murder. It is that which Cormac cannot forgive. If it had simply been a battle he would have considered it the fortunes of war. He might have hated me at the time, but it would have been forgotten, as old battles are. But Sean and Kate are still dead, still tarred as a betrayer and a wife murderer. I just don't know why he waited so long. That is the one piece of it I don't understand."

"Perhaps it doesn't matter," she said somberly. It was a tragic story, ugly even, and she was certain he had edited it very

159

heavily in the telling. "What do you want me to do?"

"I still have friends in Dublin, I think," he answered. "I cannot approach Cormac myself. I need someone I can trust, who looks totally innocent and unconnected with me. I . . . I can't even go anywhere with you, or he would suspect you immediately. Bring me the facts. I can put them together." He seemed about to add something more, then changed his mind.

"Are you worried that I won't know what is important?" she asked. "Or that I won't remember and tell you accurately?"

"No. I know perfectly well that you can do both."

"Do you?" She was surprised.

He smiled, briefly. "You tell me about helping Pitt when he was in the police, as if you imagined I didn't know."

"You said you didn't know about my sister Sarah," she pointed out. "Or was that . . . discretion rather than truth?"

"It was the truth. But perhaps I deserved the remark. I learned about you mostly from Vespasia. She did not mention Sarah, perhaps out of delicacy. And I had no need to know."

"You had some need to know the rest?" she said with disbelief.

160

"Of course. You are part of Pitt's life. I had to know exactly how far I could trust you. Although given my present situation, you cannot be blamed for doubting my ability in that."

"That sounds like self-pity," she said tartly. "I have not criticized you, and that is not out of either good manners or sympathy — neither of which we can afford just at the moment, if they disguise the truth. We can't live without trusting someone. It is an offense to betray, not to be betrayed."

"As I said, it is a good thing you did not marry into Society," he retorted. "You would not have survived. Or on the other hand, perhaps Society would not have, and that might not have been so bad. A little shake-up now and then is good for the constitution."

Now she was not sure if he was laughing at her or defending himself. Or possibly it was both.

"So you accepted my assistance because you believe I can do what you require?" she concluded.

"Not at all. I accepted it because you gave me no alternative. Also, since Stoker is the only other person I trust, and he did not offer, nor has he the ability, I had no alternative in any case."

"Touché," she said quietly.

They did not speak again for quite some time, and when they did it was about the differences between Society in London and Dublin. He described the city and surrounding countryside with such vividness that she began to look forward to seeing it herself. He even spoke of the festivals, saints' days, and other occasions people celebrated.

When the train drew into Holyhead they went straight to the boat. After a brief meal, they returned to their cabins for the crossing. They would arrive in Dublin before morning, but were not required to disembark until well after daylight.

Dublin was utterly different from London, but at least to begin with Charlotte was too occupied with getting ashore at Dun Laoghaire to have time to stare about her. Then there was the ride into the city itself, which was just waking up to the new day; the rain-washed streets were clean and filling with people about their business. She saw plenty of horse traffic — mostly trade at this hour; the carriages and broughams would come later. The few women were laundresses, maids going shopping, or factory workers wearing thick skirts and with heavy shawls wrapped around them.

Narraway hailed a cab, and they set out to look for accommodation. He seemed to know exactly where he was going and gave very precise directions to the driver, but he did not explain them to her. They rode in silence. He stared out the window and she watched his face, the harsh early-morning light showing even the smallest lines around his eyes and mouth. It made him seem older, far less sure of himself.

She thought of Daniel and Jemima, and hoped Minnie Maude was settling in. They had seemed to like her, and surely anyone Gracie vouched for would be good. She could not resent Gracie's happiness, but she missed her painfully at times like this.

That was absurd. There had never been another time like this, when a case took her out of London and away from her children. Here she was in a foreign country, with Victor Narraway, riding around the streets looking for lodgings. Little wonder Mrs. Waterman was scandalized. Perhaps she was right to be.

And Pitt was in France pursuing someone who thought nothing of slitting a man's throat in the street and leaving him to die as if he were no more than a sack of rubbish. Pitt didn't even have a clean shirt, socks, or personal linen. Narraway had sent him money, but he would need more. He would need help, information, probably the assistance of the French police. Would Narraway's replacement provide all this? Was he loyal? Was he even competent?

And worse than any of that, if he was Narraway's enemy, then he was almost certainly Pitt's enemy as well, only Pitt would not know that. He would go on communicating as if it were Narraway at the other end.

She turned away and looked out the window on her own side. They were passing handsome Georgian houses and every now and then public buildings and churches of classical elegance. There were glimpses of the river, which she thought did not seem to curve and wind as much as the Thames. She saw several horse-drawn trams, not unlike those in London, and — in the quieter streets — children playing with spinning tops, or jumping rope.

Twice she drew in breath to ask Narraway where they were going, but each time she looked at the tense concentration on his face, she changed her mind.

Finally they stopped outside a house in Molesworth Street in the southeastern part of the city.

"Stay here." Narraway came suddenly to attention. "I shall be back in a few moments." Without waiting for her acknowledgment he got out, strode across the footpath, and rapped sharply on the door of the nearest house. After less than a minute it was opened by a middle-aged woman in a white apron, her hair tied in a knot on top of her head. Narraway spoke to her and she invited him in, closing the door again behind him.

Charlotte sat and waited, suddenly cold now and aware of how tired she was. She had slept poorly in the night, aware of the rather cramped cabin and the constant movement of the boat. But far more than anything physical, it was the rashness of what she was doing that kept her awake. Now alone, waiting, she wished she were anywhere but here. Pitt would be furious. What if he had returned home to find the children alone with a maid he had never seen before? They would tell him Charlotte had gone off to Ireland with Narraway, and of course they would not even be able to tell him why!

She was shivering when Narraway came out again and spoke to the driver, then at last to her.

"There are rooms here. It is clean and

quiet and we shall not be noticed, but it is perfectly respectable. As soon as we are settled I shall go to make contact with the people I can still trust." He looked at her face carefully. She was aware that she must look rumpled and tired, and probably ill-tempered into the bargain. A smile would help, she knew, but in the circumstances it would also be idiotic.

"Please wait for me," he went on. "Rest if you like. We may be busy this evening. We have no time to waste."

He held out his arm to assist her down, meeting her eyes earnestly, questioningly, before letting go. He was clearly concerned for her, but she was glad that he did not say anything more. Though they would both feel terrible doubt and strain in the days to come, she should not forget that, after all, it was his career that was ruined, not hers. It was he who would in the end have to bear it alone; he was the one accused of theft and betrayal. No one would blame her for any of this.

But of course there was every likelihood that they would blame Pitt.

"Thank you," she said with a quick smile, then turned away to look at the house. "It seems very pleasant."

He hesitated, then with more confidence

he went ahead of her to the front door. When the landlady opened it for them, he introduced Charlotte as Mrs. Pitt, his half sister, who had come to Ireland to meet with relatives on her mother's side.

"How do you do, ma'am," Mrs. Hogan said cheerfully. "Welcome to Dublin, then. A fine city it is."

"Thank you, Mrs. Hogan. I look forward to it very much," Charlotte replied.

Narraway went out almost immediately. Charlotte began by unpacking her case and shaking the creases out of the few clothes she had brought. There was only one dress suitable for any sort of formal occasion, but she had some time ago decided to copy the noted actress Lillie Langtry and add different effects to it each time: two lace shawls, one white, one black; special gloves; a necklace of hematite and rock crystals; earrings; anything that would draw the attention from the fact that it was the same gown. At least it fit remarkably well. Women might be perfectly aware that it was the same one each time she wore it, but with luck men would notice only that it became her.

As she hung it up in the wardrobe along with a good costume with two skirts, and a

167

lighter-weight dress, she remembered the days when Pitt had still been in the police, and she and Emily had tried their own hands at helping with detection. Of course that had been particularly when the victims had been from high Society, to which they had access, and Pitt could observe them only as a police officer, when behavior was unnatural and everyone very much on their guard.

At that time his cases had been rooted in human passions, and occasionally social ills, but never secrets of state. There had been no reason why he would not discuss them with her and benefit from her greater insight into Society's rules and structures, and especially the subtler ways of women whose lives were so different from his own he could not guess what lay behind their manners and their words.

At times it had been dangerous. But she had loved the adventure of both heart and mind, the cause for which to fight. She had never for an instant been bored, or suffered the greater dullness of soul that comes when one does not have a purpose one believes in passionately.

Charlotte laid out her toiletries both on the dressing table and in the very pleasant bathroom that she shared with another female guest. Then she took off her traveling skirt and blouse, removed the pins from her hair, and lay down on the bed in her petticoat.

She must have fallen asleep because she woke to hear a tap on the door. She sat up, for a moment completely at a loss as to where she was. The furniture, the lamps on the walls, the windows were all unfamiliar. Then it came back to her and she rose so quickly she was dragging the coverlet with her.

"Who is it?" she asked.

"Victor," he replied quietly, perhaps remembering he was supposed to be her brother, and Mrs. Hogan might have excellent hearing.

"Oh." She looked down at herself in her underclothes, hair all over the place. "A moment, please," she requested. There was no chance in the world of redoing her hair, but she must make herself decent. She was suddenly self-conscious about her appearance. She seized her skirt and jacket and pulled them on, misbuttoning the latter in her haste and having then to undo it all and start anew. He must be standing in the corridor, wondering what on earth was the matter with her.

"I'm coming," she repeated. There was no

time to do more than put the brush through her hair, then pull the door open.

He looked tired, but it did not stop the amusement in his eyes when he saw her, or a flash of appreciation she would have preferred not to be aware of. Perhaps she was not beautiful — certainly not in a conventional sense — but she was a remarkably handsome woman with fair, warm-toned skin and rich hair. And she had never, since turning sixteen, lacked the shape or allure of womanhood.

"You are invited to dinner this evening," he said as soon as he was inside the room and the door closed. "It is at the home of John and Bridget Tyrone, whom I dare not meet yet. My friend Fiachra McDaid will escort you. I've known him a long time, and he will treat you with courtesy. Will you go . . . please?"

"Of course I will," she said instantly. "Tell me something about Mr. McDaid, and about Mr. and Mrs. Tyrone. Any advantage I can have, so much the better. And what do they know of you? Will they be startled that you suddenly produce a half sister?" She smiled slightly. "Apart from someone looking for distant family in Ireland. And how well do you and I know each other? Do I know you work with Special Branch?

170

We had better have grown up quite separately, because we know too little of each other. Even one mistake would arouse suspicion."

He leaned against the doorjamb, hands in his pockets. He looked completely casual, nothing like the man she knew professionally. She had a momentary vision of how he must have been twenty years ago: intelligent, elusive, unattainable — but to some women that in itself was an irresistible temptation. Before her marriage, and occasionally since, she had known women for whom that was an excitement far greater than the thought of a suitable marriage, even than a title or money.

She stood still, waiting for his reply, conscious of her traveling costume and extremely untidy hair.

"My father married your mother after my mother died," he began.

She was about to express sympathy, then realized she had no idea whether it was true, or if he was making it up for the story they must tell. Perhaps better she was not confused with the truth, whatever that was.

"By the time you were born," he continued. "I was already at university — Cambridge — you should know that. That is why we know each other so little. My father is from Buckinghamshire, but he could perfectly well have moved to London, so you may have grown up wherever you did. Always better to stay with the truth where you can. I know that area. I would have visited."

"What did he do — our father?" she asked. This all had an air of unreality about it, even ridiculousness, but she knew it mattered, perhaps vitally.

"He had land in Buckinghamshire," he replied. "He served in the Indian army. You don't need to have known him well. I didn't."

She heard the sharpness of regret in his voice. "He died some time ago. Keep the mother you have. You and I have become acquainted only recently. This trip is in part for that purpose."

"Why Ireland?" she asked. "Someone is bound to ask me."

"My mother was Irish," he replied.

"Really?" She was surprised, but perhaps she should have known it.

"No." This time he smiled fully, with both sweetness and humor. "But she's dead too. She won't mind."

She felt a strange lurch of pity inside her, an intimate knowledge of loneliness.

"I see," she said quietly. "And these relatives I am looking for — how is it that I remain here without finding them? In fact, why do I think to find them anyway?"

"Perhaps it is best if you don't," he answered. "You merely want to see Dublin. I have told you stories about it, and we have seized the excuse to visit. That will flatter them, and be easy enough to believe. It's a beautiful city and has a character that is unique."

She did not argue, but she felt that nothing very much would happen if she did not ask questions. Polite interest could be very easily brushed aside and met with polite and uninformative answers.

Charlotte collected her cape. They left Molesworth Street and in the pleasant spring evening walked in companionable silence the half mile to the house of Fiachra McDaid.

Narraway knocked on the carved mahogany door, and after a few moments it was opened by an elegant man wearing a casual velvet jacket of dark green. He was quite tall, but even under the drape of the fabric Charlotte could see that he was a little plump around the middle. In the lamplight by the front door his features were melancholy, but as soon as he recognized

173

Narraway, his expression lit with a vitality that made him startlingly attractive. It was difficult to know his age from his face, but he had white wings to his black hair, so Charlotte judged him to be close to fifty.

"Victor!" he said cheerfully, holding out his hand and grasping Narraway's fiercely. "Wonderful invention, the telephone, but there's nothing like seeing someone." He turned to Charlotte. "And you must be Mrs. Pitt, come to our queen of cities for the first time. Welcome. It will be my pleasure to show you some of it. I'll pick the best bits, and the best people; there'll be time only to taste it and no more. Your whole life wouldn't be long enough for all of it. Come in, and have a drink before we start out." He held the door wide and, after a glance at Narraway, Charlotte accepted.

Inside, the rooms were elegant, very Georgian in appearance. Their contents could easily have been found in a home in any good area of London, except perhaps for some of the pictures on the walls, and a certain character to the silver goblets on the mantel. She was interested in the subtle differences, but had no time to indulge in such trivial matters anyway.

"You'll be wanting to go to the theater," Fiachra McDaid went on, looking at Char-

174

lotte. He offered her sherry, which she merely sipped. She needed a very clear head, and she had eaten little.

"Naturally," she answered with a smile. "I could hardly hold my head up in Society at home if I came to Dublin and did not visit the theater." With a touch of satisfaction she saw an instant of puzzlement in his eyes. What had Narraway told this man of her? For that matter, what did Fiachra McDaid know of Narraway?

The look in McDaid's eyes, quickly masked, told her that it was quite a lot. She smiled, not to charm but in her own amusement.

He saw it and understood. Yes, most certainly he knew quite a lot about Narraway.

"I imagine everybody of interest is at the theater, at one time or another," she said.

"Indeed." McDaid nodded. "And many will be there at dinner tonight at the home of John and Bridget Tyrone. It will be my pleasure to introduce you to them. It is a short carriage ride from here, but certainly too far to return you to Molesworth Street on foot, at what may well be a very late hour."

"It sounds an excellent arrangement," she said, accepting. She turned to Narraway. "I shall see you at breakfast tomorrow? Shall we say eight o'clock?"

Narraway smiled. "I think you might prefer we say nine," he replied.

Charlotte and Fiachra McDaid spoke of trivial things on the carriage ride, which was, as he had said, quite short. Mostly he named the streets through which they were passing, and mentioned a few of the famous people who had lived there at some time in their lives. Many she had not heard of, but she did not say so, although she thought he guessed. Sometimes he prefaced the facts with "as you will know," and then told her what indeed she had not known.

The home of John and Bridget Tyrone was larger than McDaid's. It had a splendid entrance hall with staircases rising on both sides, which curved around the walls and met in a gallery arched above the doorway into the first reception room. The dining room was to the left beyond that, with a table set for above twenty people.

Charlotte was suddenly aware that her inclusion, as an outsider, was a privilege someone had bought through some means of favor. There were already more than a dozen people present, men in formal black and white, women in exactly the same variety of colors one might have found at any fashionable London party. What was different was the vitality in the air, the energy of emotion in the gestures, and now and then the lilt of a voice that had not been schooled out of its native music.

She was introduced to the hostess, Bridget Tyrone, a handsome woman with very white teeth and the most magnificent auburn hair, which she hardly bothered to dress. It seemed to have escaped her attempts like autumn leaves in a gust of wind.

"Mrs. Pitt has come to see Dublin," McDaid told her. "Where better to begin than here?"

"Is it curiosity that brings you, then?" John Tyrone asked, standing at his wife's elbow, a dark man with bright blue eyes.

Sensing rebuke in the question, Charlotte seized the chance to begin her mission. "Interest," she corrected him with a smile she hoped was warmer than she felt it. "Some of my mother's family were from this area, and spoke of it with such vividness I wanted to see it for myself. I regret it has taken me so long to do so."

"I should have known it!" Bridget said instantly. "Look at her hair, John! That's an Irish color if you like, now, isn't it? What were their names?"

Charlotte thought rapidly. She had to invent, but let it be as close to the truth as possible, so she wouldn't forget what she had said or contradict herself. And it must be useful. There was no point in any of this if she learned nothing of the past. Bridget Tyrone was waiting, eyes wide.

Charlotte's mother's mother had been Christine Owen. "Christina O'Neil," she said with the same sense of abandon she might have had were she jumping into a raging river.

There was a moment's silence. She had an awful thought that there might really be such a person.

"O'Neil," Bridget repeated. "Sure enough there are O'Neils around here. Plenty of them. You'll find someone who knew her, no doubt. Unless, of course, they left in the famine. Only God Himself knows how many that'd be. Come now, let me introduce you to our other guests, because you'll not be knowing them."

Charlotte accompanied her obediently and was presented to one couple after another. She struggled to remember unfamiliar names, trying hard to say something reasonably intelligent and at the same time gain some sense of the gathering, and whom she should seek to know better. She must tell Narraway something more useful than that she had gained an entry to Dublin Society.

She introduced her fictitious grandmother again.

"Really?" a women named Talulla Lawless said with surprise, raising her thin black eyebrows as soon as Charlotte mentioned the name. "You sound fond of her," Talulla continued. Talulla was a slender woman, almost bony, but with marvelous eyes, wide and bright, and of a shade neither blue nor green.

Charlotte thought of the only grandmother she knew, and found impossibly cantankerous. "She told me wonderful stories," she lied confidently. "I daresay they were a little exaggerated, but there was a truth in them of the heart, even if events were a trifle inaccurate in the retelling."

Talulla exchanged a brief glance with a fair-haired man called Phelim O'Conor, but it was so quick that Charlotte barely saw it.

"Am I mistaken?" Charlotte asked apologetically.

"Oh no," Talulla assured her. "That would be long ago, no doubt?"

Charlotte swallowed. "Yes, about twenty years, I think. There was a cousin she wrote to often, or it may be it was her cousin's wife. A very beautiful woman, so my grand-mama said." She tried rapidly to calculate the age Kate O'Neil would be were she still alive. "Perhaps a second cousin," she amended. That would allow for a consider-able variation.

"Twenty years ago," Phelim O'Conor said slowly. "A lot of trouble then. But you wouldn't be knowing that — in London. Might have seemed romantic, to your grand-mother, Charles Stewart Parnell and all that. God rest his soul. Other people's griefs can be like that." His face was smooth, almost innocent, but there was a darkness in his voice.

"I'm sorry," Charlotte said quietly. "I didn't mean to touch on something painful. Do you think perhaps I shouldn't ask?" She looked from Phelim to Talulla, and back again.

He gave a very slight shrug. "No doubt you'll hear anyway. If your cousin's wife was Kate O'Neil, she's dead now, God forgive her . . ."

"How can you say that?" Talulla spat the words between her teeth, the muscles in her thin jaw clenched tight. "Twenty years is nothing! The blink of an eye in the history of Ireland's sorrows."

Charlotte tried to look totally puzzled, and

guilty. But in truth she was beginning to feel a little afraid. Rage sparked in Talulla as if she'd touched an exposed nerve.

"Because there's been new blood, and new tears since then," Phelim answered, speaking to Talulla, not Charlotte. "And new issues to address."

Good manners might have dictated that Charlotte apologize again and withdraw, leaving them to deal with the memories in their own way, but she thought of Pitt in France, alone, trusting in Narraway to back him up. She feared there were only Narraway's enemies in Lisson Grove now, people who might easily be Pitt's enemies too. Good manners were a luxury for another time.

"Is there some tragedy my grandmother knew nothing of?" she asked innocently. "I'm sorry if I have woken an old bereavement, or injustice. I certainly did not mean to. I'm so sorry."

Talulla looked at her with undisguised harshness, a slight flush in her sallow cheeks. "If your grandmother's cousin was Kate O'Neil, she trusted an Englishman, an agent of the queen's government who courted her, flattered her into telling him her own people's secrets, then betrayed her to be murdered by those whose trust she gave away."

O'Conor winced. "I daresay she loved him. We can all be fools for love," he said wryly.

"I daresay she did!" Talulla snarled. "But that son of a whore never loved her, and with half a drop of loyalty in her blood she'd have known that. She'd have won his secrets, then put a knife in his belly. He might have been able to charm the fish out of the sea, but he was her people's enemy, and she knew that. She got what she deserved." She turned and moved away sharply, her dark head high and stiff, her back ramrod-straight, and she made no attempt to offer even a glance backward.

"You'll have to forgive Talulla," O'Conor said ruefully. "Anyone would think she'd loved the man herself, and it was twenty years ago. I must remember never to flirt with her. If she fell for my charm I might wake up dead of it." He shrugged. "Not that it'd be likely, God help me!" He did not add anything more, but his expression said all the rest.

Then with a sudden smile, like spring sun through the drifting rain, he told her about the place where he had been born and the little town to the north where he had grown up and his first visit to Dublin when he had been six.

"I thought it was the grandest place I'd ever seen," he said. "Street after street of buildings, each one fit to be the palace of a king. And some so wide it was a journey just to cross from one side to another."

Suddenly Talulla's hatred seemed no more than a lapse in manners. But Charlotte did not forget it. O'Conor's charm was clearly masking great shame. She was certain that he would find Talulla afterward and, when they were alone, berate her for allowing a foreigner — an Englishwoman at that — to see a part of their history that should have been kept private.

The party continued. The food was excellent, the wine flowed generously. There was laughter, sharp and poignant wit, even music as the evening approached midnight. But Charlotte did not forget the emotion she had seen, and the hatred.

She rode home in the carriage with Fiachra McDaid, and despite his gentle inquiries she said nothing except how much she had enjoyed the hospitality.

"And did anyone know your cousin?" he asked. "Dublin's a small town, when it comes to it."

"I don't think so," she answered easily. "But I may find trace of her later. O'Neil is not a rare name. And anyway, it doesn't

183

matter very much."

"Now, there's something I doubt our friend Victor would agree with," he said candidly. "I had the notion it mattered to him rather a lot. Was I wrong, then, do you suppose?"

For the first time in the evening she spoke the absolute truth. "I think maybe you know him a great deal better than I do, Mr. Mc-Daid. We have met only in one set of circumstances, and that does not give a very complete picture of a person, don't you think?"

In the darkness inside the carriage she could not read his expression.

"And yet I have the distinct idea that he is fond of you, Mrs. Pitt," McDaid replied. "Am I wrong in that too, do you suppose?"

"I don't do much supposing, Mr. Mc-Daid . . . at least not aloud," she said. And as she spoke, her mind raced, remembering what Phelim O'Conor had said of Narraway, and wondering how much she really knew him. The certainty was increasing inside her that it was Narraway of whom Talulla had been speaking when she referred to Kate O'Neil's betrayal — both of her country, and of her husband — because she had loved a man who had used her, and then he allowed her to be murdered for it.

184

Pitt had believed in Narraway; she knew that without doubt. But she also knew that Pitt thought well of most people, even if he accepted that they were complex, capable of cowardice, greed, and violence. But had he ever understood any of the darkness within Narraway, the human man beneath the fighter against his country's enemies? They were so different. Narraway was subtle, where Pitt was instinctive. He understood people because he understood weakness and fear; he had felt need and knew how powerful it could be.

But Pitt also understood gratitude. Narraway had offered him dignity, purpose, and a means to feed his family when he had desperately needed it. He would never forget that.

Was he also just a little naïve?

She remembered with a smile how disillusioned her husband had been when he had discovered the shabby behavior of the Prince of Wales. She had felt his shame for a man he thought should have been better. He had believed more in the honor of his calling than the man did himself. She loved Pitt intensely for that, even in the moment she understood it.

Narraway would never have been misled; he would have expected roughly what he eventually found. He might have been disappointed, but he would not have been hurt.

Had he ever been hurt?

Could he have loved Kate O'Neil, and still used her? Not as Charlotte understood love.

But then perhaps Narraway always put duty first. Maybe he was feeling a deep and insuperable pain for the first time, because he was robbed of the one thing he valued: his work, in which his identity was so bound up.

Why on earth was she riding through the dark streets of a strange city, with a man she had never seen before tonight, taking absurd risks, telling lies, in order to help a man she knew so little? Why did she ache with a loss for him?

Because she imagined how she would feel if he were like her — and he was not. She imagined he cared about her, because she had seen it in his face in unguarded moments. It was probably loneliness she saw, an instant of lingering for a love he would only find an encumbrance if he actually had it.

"I hear Talulla Lawless gave you a little display of her temper," McDaid said, interrupting her thoughts. "I'm sorry for that. Her wounds are deep, and she sees no need

186

to hide them; it is hardly your fault. But then there are always casualties of war, the innocent often as much as the guilty."

She turned to look at his face in the momentary light of a passing carriage's lamp. His eyes were bright, his mouth twisted in a sad little smile. Then the darkness shadowed him again and she was aware of him only as a soft voice, a presence beside her, the smell of fabric and a faint sharpness of tobacco.

"Of course," she agreed very quietly.

They reached Molesworth Street and the carriage stopped.

"Thank you, Mr. McDaid," she said with perfect composure. "It was most gracious of you to have me invited, and to accompany me. Dublin's hospitality is all that has been said of it, and believe me, that is high praise."

"We have just begun," he replied warmly. "Give Victor my regards, and tell him we shall continue. I won't rest until you think this is the fairest city on earth, and the Irish the best people. Which of course we are, despite our passion and our troubles. You can't hate us, you know." He said it with a smile that was wide and bright in the lamplight.

"Not the way you hate us, anyway," she

187

agreed gently. "But then we have no cause. Good night, Mr. McDaid."

CHAPTER 5

Charlotte faced Narraway across the breakfast table in Mrs. Hogan's quiet house the
next morning, still in conflict as to what she
would say to him.

"Very enjoyable," she answered his inquiry
as to the previous evening. And she realized
with surprise how much that was true. It
was a long time since she had been at a
party of such ease and sophistication.
Although this was Dublin, not London,
Society did not differ much.

There were no other guests in the dining
room this late in the morning. Most of the
other tables had already been set with clean,
lace-edged linen ready for the evening. She
concentrated on the generous plate of food
before her. It contained far more than she
needed for good health. "They were most
kind to me," she added.

"Nonsense," he replied quietly.

She looked up, startled by his abruptness.

He was smiling, but the sharp morning light showed very clearly the tiredness in his face. Her resolve to lie to him wavered. There were many ways in which he was unreadable, but not in the deep-etched lines in his face or the hollows around his eyes.

"All right," she conceded. "They were hospitable and a certain glamour in it was fun. Is that more precise?"

He was amused. He gave nothing so obvious as a smile, but it was just as plain to her.

"Whom did you meet, apart from Fiachra, of course?"

"You've known him a long time?" she asked, remembering McDaid's words with a slight chill.

"Why do you say that?" He took more toast and buttered it. He had eaten very little. She wondered if he had slept.

"Because he asked me nothing about you," she answered. "But he seems very willing to help."

"A good friend," he replied, looking straight at her.

She smiled. "Nonsense," she said with exactly the same inflection he had used.

"Touché," he acknowledged. "You are right, but we have known each other a long time."

"Isn't Ireland full of people you have known a long time?"

He put a little marmalade on his toast.

She waited.

"Yes," he agreed. "But I do not know the allegiances of most of them."

"If Fiachra McDaid is a friend, what do you need me for?" she asked bluntly. Suddenly an urgent and ugly thought occurred to her: Perhaps he did not want her in London where Pitt could reach her. Just how complicated was this, and how ugly? Where was the embezzled money now? Was it really about money, and not old vengeances at all? Or was it both?

He did not answer.

"Because you are using me, or both of us, with selected lies?" she suggested.

He winced as if the blow had been physical as well as emotional. "I am not lying to you, Charlotte." His voice was so quiet, she had to lean forward a little to catch his words. "I am . . . being highly selective about how much of the truth I tell you . . ."

"And the difference is?" she asked.

He sighed. "You are a good detective — in your own way almost as good as Pitt — but Special Branch work is very different from ordinary domestic murder."

"Domestic murder isn't always ordinary,"

she contradicted him. "Human love and hate very seldom are. People kill for all sorts of reasons, but it is usually to gain or protect something they value passionately. Or it is in outrage at some violation they cannot bear. And I do not mean necessarily a physical one. The emotional or spiritual wounds can be far harder to recover from."

"I apologize," he responded. "I should have said that the alliances and loyalties stretch in far more complicated ways. Brothers can be on opposite sides, as can husband and wife. Rivals can help each other, even die for each other, if allied in the cause."

"And the casualties are the innocent as well as the guilty," she said, echoing McDaid's words. "My role is easy enough. I would like to help you, but I am bound by everything in my nature to help my husband, and of course myself . . ."

"I had no idea you were so pragmatic," he said with a slight smile.

"I am a woman, I have a finite amount of money, and I have children. A degree of pragmatism is necessary." She spoke gently to take the edge from her words.

He finished spreading his marmalade. "So you will understand that Fiachra is my friend in some things, but I will not be able to count on him if the answer should turn out to be different from the one I suppose."

"There is one you suppose?"

"I told you: I think Cormac O'Neil has found the perfect way to take revenge on me, and has taken it."

"For something that happened twenty years ago?" she questioned.

"The Irish have the longest memories in Europe." He bit into the toast.

"And the greatest patience too?" she said with disbelief. "People take action because something, somewhere has changed. Crimes of state have that in common with ordinary, domestic murders. Something new has caused O'Neil, or whoever it is, to do this now. Perhaps it has only just become possible. Or it may be that for him, now is the right time."

He ate the whole of his toast before replying. "Of course you are right. The trouble is that I don't know which of those reasons it is. I've studied the situation in Ireland and I can't see any reason at all for O'Neil to do this now."

She ignored her tea. An unpleasant thought occurred to her, chilling and very immediate. "Wouldn't O'Neil know that this would bring you here?" she asked.

Narraway stared at her. "You think O'Neil wants me here? I'm sure if killing me were his purpose, he would have come to London and done it. If I thought it was simply murder I wouldn't have let you come with me, Charlotte, even if Pitt's livelihood rests on my return to office. Please give me credit for thinking that far ahead."

"I'm sorry," she said. "I thought bringing someone that nobody would see as assisting you might be the best way of getting around that. You never suggested it would be comfortable, or easy. And you cannot prevent me from coming to Ireland if I want to. You could simply have let me do it alone, which would be inefficient, and unlike you."

"It would have been awkward," he conceded. "But not impossible. I had to tell you something of the situation, for Pitt's sake. For your own, I cannot tell you everything. I don't know any reason why O'Neil should choose now. But then I don't know any reason why anyone should. It is unarguable that someone with strong connections in Dublin has chosen to steal the money I sent for Mulhare, so to bring about the poor man's death. Then they made certain it was evident first to Austwick, and then to Croxdale, and so brought about my dismissal."

He poured more tea for himself. "Perhaps it was not O'Neil who initiated it; he may simply have been willingly used. I've made many enemies. Knowledge and power both make that inevitable."

"Then think of other enemies," she urged. "Whose circumstances have changed? Is there anyone you were about to expose?"

"My dear, do you think I haven't thought of that?"

"And you still believe it is O'Neil?"

"Perhaps it is a guilty conscience." He gave a smile so brief it reached his eyes and was gone again. " 'The guilty flee where no man pursueth,' " he quoted. "But there is knowledge in this that only people familiar with the case could have."

"Oh." She poured herself fresh tea. "Then we had better learn more about O'Neil. He was mentioned yesterday evening. I told them that my grandmother was Christina O'Neil."

He swallowed. "And who was she really?"

"Christine Owen," she replied.

He started to laugh. She said nothing, but finished her toast and then the rest of her tea.

Charlotte spent the morning and most of the afternoon quietly reading as much as she could of Irish history, realizing the vast gap in her knowledge and becoming a little ashamed of it. Because Ireland was geographically so close to England, and because the English had occupied it one way or another for so many centuries, in their minds its individuality had been swallowed up in the general tide of British history. The empire covered a quarter of the world. Englishmen tended to think of Ireland as part of their own small piece of it, linked by a common language — disregarding the existence of the Irish tongue.

So many of Ireland's greatest sons had made their names on the world stage indistinguishably from the English. Everyone knew Oscar Wilde was Irish, even though his plays were absolutely English in their setting. They probably knew Jonathan Swift was Irish, but did they know it of Bram Stoker? Did they know it of the great duke of Wellington, victor of Waterloo, and later prime minister? The fact that these men had left Ireland in their youth did not in any way alter their heritage.

Her own family was not Anglo-Irish, but in pretending to have a grandmother who was, perhaps she should be a little more sensitive to people's feelings and treat the whole subject less casually.

By evening she was again dressed in her one black gown, this time with different jewelry and different gloves, and her hair decorated with an ornament given to her years ago. She was off to the theater, and quite suddenly worried that she was over-dressed. Perhaps other people would be far less formal. After all, they were a highly literate culture, educated in words and ideas but also very familiar with them. They might consider an evening at the theater not a social affair but rather an intellectual and emotional one.

She took the ornament out of her hair, and then had to restyle it accordingly. All of which meant she was late, and flustered, when Narraway knocked on the door to tell her that Fiachra McDaid was there to escort her for the evening again.

"Thank you," she said, putting the comb down quickly and knocking several loose hairpins onto the floor. She ignored them.

He looked at her with anxiety. "Are you all right?"

"Yes! It is simply an indecision as to what to wear." She dismissed it with a slight gesture.

He regarded her carefully. His eyes traveled from her shoes, which were visible beneath the hem of her gown, all the way to the crown of her head. She felt the heat burn up her face at the candid appreciation in his eyes.

"You made the right decision," he pronounced. "Diamonds would have been inappropriate here. They take their drama very seriously."

She drew in breath to say that she had no diamonds, and realized he was laughing at her. She wondered if he would have given a woman diamonds, if he loved her. She thought not. If he were capable of that sort of love, it would have been something more personal, more imaginative. A cottage by the sea, however small, perhaps; something of enduring meaning that would add joy to its owner's life.

"I'm so glad," she said, meeting his eyes. "I thought diamonds were too trivial." She accepted his arm, laying her fingers so lightly on the fabric of his jacket that he could not have felt her touch.

Fiachra McDaid was as elegant and graceful as the previous evening, although on this occasion dressed less formally. He greeted Charlotte with apparent pleasure at seeing her again, even so soon. He expressed his willingness to help her to understand as much of Irish theater as was possible for an Englishwoman to grasp. He smiled at Charlotte as he said it, as if it were some secret aside that she already understood.

It was some time since she had been to the theater at all. It was not an art form Pitt was particularly fond of, and she did not like going without him.

Here in Dublin the event was quite different. The theater building itself was smaller; indeed there was an intimacy to it that made it less an occasion to be seen, and more of an adventure in which to participate.

McDaid introduced her to various of his own friends who greeted him. They varied in age and apparent social status, as if he had chosen them from as many walks of life as possible.

"Mrs. Pitt," he explained cheerfully. "She is over from London to see how we do things here, mostly from an interest in our fair city, but in part to see if she can find some Irish ancestry. And who can blame her? Is there anyone of wit or passion who wouldn't like to claim a bit of Irish blood in their veins?"

She responded warmly to the welcome extended her, finding the exchanges easy, even comfortable. She had forgotten how interesting it was to meet new people, with new ideas. But she did wonder exactly what Narraway had told McDaid.

She searched his face and saw nothing in it but good humor, interest, amusement, and a blank wall of guarded intelligence intended to give away nothing at all.

They were very early for the performance, but most of the audience were already present. While McDaid was talking she had an opportunity to look around and study faces. They were different from a London audience only in subtle ways. There were fewer fair heads, fewer blunt Anglo-Saxon features, a greater sense of tension and suppressed energy.

And of course she heard the music of a different accent, and now and then people speaking in a language utterly unrecognizable to her. There was in them nothing of the Latin or Norman-French about the words, or the German from which so much English was derived. She assumed it was the native tongue. She could only guess at what they said by the gestures, the laughter, and the expression in faces.

She noticed one man in particular. His hair was black with a loose, heavy wave streaked with gray. His head was narrow-boned, and it was not until he turned toward her that she saw how dark his eyes were. His nose was noticeably crooked, giving his whole aspect a lopsided look, a kind of wounded intensity. Then he turned away, as if he had not seen her, and she was relieved. She had been staring, and that was ill-mannered, no matter how interesting a person might seem.

"You saw him," McDaid observed so quietly it was little more than a whisper.

She was taken aback. "Saw him? Who?"

"Cormac O'Neil," he replied.

She was startled. Had she been so very obvious? "Was that . . . I mean the man with the . . ." Then she did not know how to finish the sentence.

"Haunted face," he said for her.

"I wasn't going to . . ." She saw in his eyes that she was denying it pointlessly. Either Narraway had told him, or he had pieced it together himself. It made her wonder how many others knew, indeed if all those involved might well know more than she, and her pretense was deceiving no one.

"Do you know him?" she asked.

"I?" McDaid raised his eyebrows. "I've met him, of course, but know him? Hardly at all."

"I didn't mean in any profound sense," she parried. "Merely were you acquainted."

"In the past, I thought so." He was watching Cormac while seeming not to. "But tragedy changes people. Or then on the other hand, perhaps it only shows you what was always there, simply not yet uncovered.

201

How much does one know anybody? Most of all oneself."

"Very metaphysical," she said drily. "And the answer is that you can make a guess, more or less educated, depending on your intelligence and your experience with that person."

He looked at her steadily. "Victor said you were . . . direct."

She found it odd to hear Narraway referred to by his given name, instead of the formality she was used to, the slight distance that leadership required.

Now she was not sure if she was on the brink of offending McDaid. On the other hand, if she was too timid even to approach what she really wanted, she would lose the chance.

She smiled at him. "What was O'Neil like, when you knew him?"

His eyes widened. "Victor didn't tell you? How interesting."

"Did you expect him to have?" she asked.

"Why is he asking, why now?" He sat absolutely still. All around him people were moving, adjusting position, smiling, waving, finding seats, nodding agreement to something or other, waving to friends.

"Perhaps you know him well enough to ask him that?" she suggested.

Again he countered. "Don't you?"

She kept her smile warm, faintly amused. "Of course, but I would not repeat his answer. You must know him well enough to believe he would not confide in someone he could not trust."

"So perhaps we both know, and neither will trust the other," he mused. "How absurd, how vulnerable and incredibly human; indeed, the convention of many comic plays."

"To judge by Cormac O'Neil's face, he has seen tragedy," she countered. "One of the casualties of war that you referred to."

He looked at her steadily, and for a moment the buzz of conversation around them ceased to exist. "So he has," he said softly. "But that was twenty years ago."

"Does one forget?"

"Irishmen? Never. Do the English?"

"Sometimes," she replied.

"Of course. You could hardly remember them all!" Then he caught himself immediately and his expression changed. "Do you want to meet him?" he asked.

"Yes — please."

"Then you shall," he promised.

There was a rustle of anticipation in the audience and everyone fell silent. After a moment or two the curtain rose and the play began. Charlotte concentrated so that she could speak intelligently when she was introduced to people at the intermission.

But she found following it difficult. There were frequent references to events she was not familiar with, even words she did not know, and there was an underlying air of sadness.

Was that how Cormac O'Neil felt: helpless, predestined to be overwhelmed? Everybody lost people they loved. Bereavement was a part of life. The only escape was to love no one. She stopped trying to understand the drama on the stage and, as discreetly as she could, she studied O'Neil.

He seemed to be alone. He looked neither right nor left, and the people on either side seemed to be with others.

The longer she watched him, the more totally alone did he seem to be. But she was equally sure that he was never bored. His eyes never strayed from the stage, yet at times his expression did reflect the drama.

By the time the intermission came Charlotte felt herself moved by the passion emanating from players and audience alike. But she was also confused by it. It made her feel more sharply than the lilt of a different accent, or even the sound of another language, that she was in a strange place, teeming with emotions she caught and lost again.

"May I take you to get something to drink?" McDaid asked her when the curtain fell and the lights were bright again. "And perhaps to meet one or two more of my friends? I'm sure they are dying of curiosity to know who you are, and of course how I know you."

"I would be delighted," she answered. "And how do you know me? We had better be accurate, or it will start people talking." She smiled to rob the words of offense.

"But surely the sole purpose of coming to the theater with a beautiful woman is to start people talking?" He raised his eyebrows. "Otherwise one would be better to come alone, like Cormac O'Neil, and concentrate on the play, without distraction."

"Thank you. I'm flattered to imagine I could distract you." She inclined her head a little, enjoying the trivial play of words. "Especially from so intense a drama. The actors are superb. I have no idea what they are talking about at least half the time, and yet I am conquered by their emotions."

"Are you sure you are not Irish?" he pressed.

"Not sure at all. Perhaps I am, and I should simply look harder. But please do not tell Mr. O'Neil that my grandmother's name was O'Neil also, or I shall be obliged to admit that I know very little about her, and that would make me seem very discourteous, as if I did not wish to own that part of my heritage. The truth is I simply did not realize how interesting it would be."

"I shall not tell him, if you don't wish me to," he promised.

"But you have not told me how we met," she reminded him.

"I saw you across a room and asked a mutual acquaintance to introduce us," he said. "Is that not always how one meets a woman one sees, and admires?"

"I imagine it is. But what room was it? Was it here in Ireland? I imagine not, since I have been here only a couple of days. But have you been to London lately?" She smiled at him. "Or ever, for that matter?"

"Of course I've been to London. Do you think I am some provincial bumpkin?" He shrugged. "Only once, mind you. I did not care for it — nor it for me. It was so huge, so crowded with people, and yet at the same time anonymous. You could live and die there, and never be seen."

"But I have been in Dublin only a couple of days," she said to fill the silence.

"Then I was bewitched at first sight," he

said reasonably, suddenly smiling again. "I'm sorry I insulted your home. It was unforgivable. Call it my own inadequacy in the midst of three million English."

"Oh quite a few Irishmen, believe me," she said with a smile. "And none of them in the least inadequate."

He bowed.

"And I accepted your invitation because I was flattered, and irresponsible?" she challenged.

"You are quite right," he conceded. "We must have mutual friends — some highly respectable aunt, I daresay. Do you have any such relations?"

"My great-aunt Vespasia, by marriage. If she recommended you I would accompany you anywhere on earth," she responded unhesitatingly.

"She sounds charming."

"She is. Believe me, if you had met her really, you would not dare to treat me other than with the utmost respect."

"Where did I meet this formidable lady?"

"Lady Vespasia Cumming-Gould. It doesn't matter. Any surroundings would be instantly forgotten once you had seen her. But London will do."

"Vespasia Cumming-Gould." He turned the name over on his tongue. "It seems to find an echo in my mind."

"It has set bells ringing all over Europe," she told him. "You had better be aware that she is of an indeterminate age, but her hair is silver and she walks like a queen. She was the most beautiful and most outrageous woman of her generation. If you don't know that, they will know that you never met her."

"I am now most disappointed that I did not." He offered her his arm, and they began to descend the stairway.

Together they walked down to the room where refreshments were already being served, and the audience had gathered to greet friends and exchange views on the performance.

It was several minutes of pleasant exchange before McDaid introduced her to a woman with wildly curling hair named Dolina Pearse and a man of unusual height whom he addressed as Ardal Barralet. Beside them, but apparently not with them, was Cormac O'Neil.

"O'Neil!" McDaid said with surprise. "Haven't seen you for some time. How are you?"

Barralet turned as if he had not noticed O'Neil standing so close as to brush coattails with him.

" 'Evening, O'Neil. Enjoying the performance? Excellent, don't you think?" he said casually.

O'Neil had either to answer or offer an unmistakable rebuff.

"Very polished," he said, looking straight back at Barralet. His voice was unusually deep and soft, as if he too were an actor, caressing the words. He did not even glance at Charlotte. "Good evening, Mrs. Pearse." He acknowledged Dolina.

"Good evening, Mr. O'Neil," she said coldly.

"You know Fiachra McDaid?" Barralet filled in the sudden silence. "But perhaps not Mrs. Pitt? She is newly arrived in Dublin."

"How do you do, Mrs. Pitt," O'Neil said politely, but without interest. McDaid he looked at with a sudden blaze of emotion.

McDaid stared back at him calmly, and the moment passed.

Charlotte wondered if she had seen it, or merely imagined it.

"What brings you to Dublin, Mrs. Pitt?" Dolina inquired, clearly out of a desire to change the subject. There was no interest in either her voice or her face.

"Good report of the city," Charlotte replied. "I have made a resolution that I will no longer keep on putting off into the future the good things that can be done today."

"How very English," Dolina murmured. "And virtuous." She added the word as if it were insufferably boring.

Charlotte felt her temper flare. She looked straight back at Dolina. "If it is virtuous to come to Dublin, then I have been misled," she said drily. "I was hoping it was going to be fun."

McDaid laughed sharply, his face lighting with sudden amusement. "It depends how you take your pleasures, my dear. Oscar Wilde, poor soul, is one of us, of course, and he made the world laugh. For years we have tried to be as like the English as we can. Now at last we are finding ourselves, and we take our theater packed with anguish, poetry, and triple meanings. You can dwell on whichever one suits your mood, but most of them are doom-laden, as if our fate is in blood. If we laugh, it is at ourselves, and as a stranger you might find it impolite to join in."

"That explains a great deal." She thanked him with a little nod of her head. She was aware that O'Neil was watching her, possibly because she was the only one in the group he did not already know, but she wanted to engage in some kind of conversation with him. This was the man Narraway believed had contrived his betrayal. What on earth could she say that did not sound forced? She looked directly at him, obliging him either to listen or to deliberately snub her.

"Perhaps I sounded a bit trivial when I spoke of fun," she said half apologetically. "I like my pleasure spiced with thought, and even a puzzle or two, so the flavor of it will last. A drama is superficial if one can understand everything in it in one evening, don't you think?"

The hardness in his face softened. "Then you will leave Ireland a happy woman," he told her. "You will certainly not understand us in a week, or a month, probably not in a year."

"Because I am English? Or because you are so complex?" she pursued.

"Because we don't understand ourselves, most of the time," he replied with the slightest lift of one shoulder.

"No one does," she returned. Now they were speaking as if there were no one else in the room. "The tedious people are the ones who think they do."

"We can be tedious by perpetually trying to, aloud." He smiled, and the light of it utterly changed his face. "But we do it poetically. It is when we begin to repeat ourselves that we try people's patience."

"But doesn't history repeat itself, like variations on a theme?" she said. "Each generation, each artist, adds a different note, but the underlying tune is the same."

"England's is in a major key." His mouth twisted as he spoke. "Lots of brass and percussion. Ireland's is minor, woodwind, and the dying chord. Perhaps a violin solo now and then." He was watching her intently, as if it were a game they were playing and one of them would lose. Did he already know who she was, and that she had come with Narraway, and why?

She tried to dismiss the thought as absurd, then remembered that someone had already outwitted Narraway, which was a considerable feat. It required not only passion for revenge, but a high level of intelligence as well. Most frightening of all, it needed connections in Lisson Grove sufficiently well placed to have put the money in Narraway's bank account.

Suddenly the game seemed a great deal more serious. She was aware that because of her hesitation, Dolina was watching her curiously as well, and Fiachra McDaid was standing at her elbow.

"I always think the violin sounds so much like the human voice," she said with a smile.

"Don't you, Mr. O'Neil?"

Surprise flickered for a moment in his eyes. He had been expecting her to say something more defensive, no doubt.

"Did you not expect the heroes of Ireland to sound human?" he asked her.

"Not entirely." She avoided looking at Mc-Daid, or Dolina, in case their perception brought them back to reality. "I had thought of something heroic, even supernatural."

"Touché," McDaid said softly. He took Charlotte by the arm, holding her surprisingly hard. She could not have shaken him off even had she wished to. "We must take our seats." He excused them and led her away after only the briefest farewell. She nearly asked him if she had offended someone, but she did not want to hear the answer. Nor did she intend to apologize.

As soon as she resumed her seat she realized that it offered her as good a view of the rest of the audience as it did of the stage. She glanced at McDaid, and saw in his expression that he had arranged it so intentionally, but she did not comment.

They were only just in time for the curtain going up, and immediately the drama recaptured their attention. Charlotte, lost in the many allusions to history and legends with which she was not familiar, began to look at

213

the audience again, to catch something of their reaction and follow a little more.

John and Bridget Tyrone were in a box almost opposite. With the intimate size of the theater she could see their faces quite clearly. He was watching the stage, leaning a little forward as if not to miss a word. She glanced at him, then — seeing his absorption — turned away. Her gaze swept around the audience. Charlotte put up the opera glasses McDaid had lent her, not to see the stage but to hide her own eyes, and to keep watching Mrs. Tyrone.

Bridget's searching stopped when she saw a man in the audience below her, to her left. To Charlotte all that was visible was the back of his head, but she was certain she had seen him before. She could not remember where.

Bridget continued staring at him, as if willing him to look back at her.

On the stage the drama heightened. Charlotte was only dimly aware of it, for her emotional concentration was upon the audience. John Tyrone was still watching the players. At last the man Bridget was watching turned and looked back up at the boxes. It was Phelim O'Conor. As soon as she saw his profile Charlotte knew him. He remained with his eyes fixed on Bridget, his face unreadable.

Bridget looked away just as her husband became aware of her again, and switched his attention from the stage. They spoke to each other briefly.

In the audience below, O'Conor turned back to the stage. His neck was stiff, his head unmoving.

During the second intermission, McDaid took Charlotte back outside to the bar where once more refreshments were liberally served. The conversation buzzed about the play. Was it well performed? Was it true to the intention of the author? Had the main actor misinterpreted his role?

Charlotte listened, trying to fix her expression in an attitude of intelligent observation. But really she was watching to see whom else she recognized among those queueing for drinks or talking excitedly to people they knew. All of them were strangers to her, and yet in a way they were familiar. Many were so like those she had known before her marriage that she half expected them to recognize her. It was an odd feeling, pleasant and nostalgic, even though she would have changed nothing of her present life.

"Are you enjoying the play?" McDaid asked her. They drifted toward the bar counter, where Cormac O'Neil had a glass of whiskey in his hand.

"I am enjoying the whole experience," she replied. "I am most grateful that you brought me. I could not have come alone, nor would I have found it half so pleasant."

"I am delighted you enjoy it," McDaid replied with a smile. "I was not sure that you would. The play ends with a superb climax, all very dark and dreadful. You won't understand much of it at all."

"Is that the purpose of it?" she asked, looking from McDaid to O'Neil and back again. "To puzzle us all so much that we will be obliged to spend weeks or months trying to work out what it really means? Perhaps we will come up with half a dozen different possibilities?"

For a moment there was surprise and admiration in McDaid's eyes; then he masked it and the slightly bantering tone returned. "I think perhaps you overrate us, at least this time. I rather believe the playwright himself has no such subtle purpose in mind."

"What meanings did you suppose?" O'Neil asked softly.

"Oh, ask me in a month's time, Mr. O'Neil," she said casually. "There is anger in it, of course. Anyone can see that. There seems to me also to be a sense of predestination, as if we all have little choice, and birth determines our reactions. I dislike that. I don't wish to feel so . . . controlled by fate."

"You are English. You like to imagine you are the masters of history. In Ireland we have learned that history masters us," he responded. The bitterness in his tone was laced with irony and laughter, but the pain was real.

It was on her tongue to contradict him, until she realized her opportunity. "Really? If I understand the play rightly, it is about a certain inevitability in love and betrayal that is quite universal — a sort of darker and older Romeo and Juliet."

O'Neil's face tightened, and even in the lamplight of the crowded room Charlotte could see his color pale. "Is that what you see?" His voice was thick, almost choking on the words. "You romanticize, Mrs. Pitt." Now the bitterness in him was overwhelming. She was as aware of it as if he had touched her physically.

"Do I?" she asked him, moving aside to allow a couple arm in arm to pass by. In so doing she deliberately stepped close to O'Neil, so he could not leave without pushing her aside. "What harder realities should

I see? Rivalry between opposing sides, families divided, a love that cannot be fulfilled, betrayal and death? I don't think I really find that romantic, except for us as we sit in the audience watching. For the people involved it must be anything but."

He stared at her, his eyes hollow with a kind of black despair. She could believe very easily that Narraway was right, and O'Neil had nursed a hatred for twenty years, until fate had given him a way to avenge it. But what was it that had changed?

"And what are you, Mrs. Pitt?" he asked, standing close to her and speaking so McDaid almost certainly would not hear him. "Audience or player? Are you here to watch the blood and tears of Ireland, or to meddle in them, like your friend Narraway?"

She was stunned. So he did know that she was linked to Narraway. The hushed anger with which he now confronted her seemed on the verge of boiling over at last. Surely to feign innocence would be ridiculous?

"I would like to be a deus ex machina," she replied. "But I imagine that's impossible."

"God in the machine?" he said with an angry shrug. "You want to descend at the last act and arrange an impossible ending that solves it all? How very English. And

218

how absurd, and supremely arrogant. You are twenty years too late. Tell Victor that, when you see him. There's nothing left to mend anymore." He turned away before she could answer again, pushing past her and spilling what was left of his whiskey as he bumped into a broad man in a blue coat. The moment after, he was gone.

Charlotte was aware of McDaid next to her, and a certain air of discomfort about him.

"I'm sorry," she said. There was no point in trying to explain. "I allowed myself to express my opinions too freely."

He bit his lip. "You couldn't know it, but the subject of Irish freedom, and traitors to the cause, is painfully close to O'Neil. It was through his family that our great plan was betrayed twenty years ago." He winced. "We never knew for sure by whom. Sean O'Neil murdered his wife, Kate, and was hanged for it. Even though it was because she was the one who told the English our plans, some thought it was because Sean found her with another man. Either way, we failed again, and the bitterness still lasts."

"It was an uprising that you intended?" she asked quietly. She heard the chatter around her.

"Of course," McDaid replied flatly.

"Home Rule was in the very air we breathed then. We could have been ourselves, without the weight of England around our necks."

"Is that how you see it?" She turned as she spoke and looked at him, searching his face.

His expression softened. He smiled back at her, rueful and a little self-deprecating. "I did at the time. Seeing Cormac brings it back. But I'm cooler-headed now. There are better places to put one's energy — causes less narrow." She was aware of the color and whisper of fabric around them, silk against silk. They were surrounded by people in one of the most interesting capital cities in the world, come out to an evening at the theater. Some of them, at least, were also men and women who saw themselves living under a foreign oppression in their own land, and some of them at least were willing to kill and to die to throw it off. She looked just like them, cast of feature, tone of skin and hair, and yet she was not; she was different in heart and mind.

"What causes?" she asked with interest.

His smile widened, as if to brush it aside. "Social injustices, old-fashioned laws to reform," he replied. "Greater equality. Exactly the same as, no doubt, you fight for at home. I hear there are some great women

220

in London battling for all manner of things. Perhaps one day you will tell me about some of them?" He made it a question, as if he were interested enough to require an answer.

"Of course," she said lightly, trying to master facts in her mind so she could answer sensibly, if the necessity arose.

He took her arm as people milled around her, returning to their seats, courteous, hospitable, full of dry wit and a passion for life. How easy, and dangerous, it would be for her to forget that she did not belong here.

Narraway was uncertain what Charlotte would learn at the theater. As he walked along Arran Quay, on the north bank of the Liffey, his head down into the warm, damp breeze off the water, he was afraid that she would discover a few things about him that he would very much rather she not know, but he knew no way to help that.

He smiled bitterly as he pictured her probing relentlessly for the facts behind the pain. Would she be disillusioned to hear his part in it all? Or was that his vanity, his own feelings — that she cared enough for him that disillusion was even possible, let alone something that would wound her?

He would never forget the days after Kate's death. Worst was the morning they hanged Sean. The brutality and the grief of that had cast a chill over all the years since.

But he did not want Charlotte's grief for him, particularly if it was based on a misconception of who he was.

He laughed at himself; it was just a faint sound, almost drowned by his quick footsteps along the stones of the quayside. Why, at this time in his life, did he care so much for the opinion of another man's wife?

He forced his attention to where he was going, and why. If he did not learn who had diverted the money meant for Mulhare, anything else he learned about O'Neil was pointless. Someone in Lisson Grove had been involved. He blamed none of the Irish. They were fighting for their own cause, and at times he even sympathized with it. But the man in Special Branch who had done this had betrayed his own people, and that was different. He wanted to know who it was, and prove it. The damage he could cause would have no boundary. If he hated England enough to plan and execute a way of disgracing Narraway, then what else might he do? Was his real purpose to replace him? This whole business of Mulhare might be no more than a means to that end. But

222

was it simply ambition, or was there another, darker purpose behind it as well?

Without realizing it he increased his pace, moving so softly he almost passed the alley he was looking for. He turned and fumbled in the dark. He had to feel his way along one of the walls. Third door. He knocked sharply, a quick rhythm.

He had brought Charlotte because he wanted to, but she had her own compelling reasons to be here. If he was right, that there was a traitor in Lisson Grove, then one of the first things that person would do would be to get rid of Pitt. If Pitt was fortunate, he would simply be dismissed. There were much worse possibilities.

The door opened. He was let into a small, extremely stuffy office piled high with ledgers, account books, and sheaves of loose papers. A striped cat had claimed itself a space in front of the hearth and did not stir when Narraway came in and took a seat on a chair opposite the cluttered desk.

O'Casey sat in the chair behind it, his bald head gleaming in the gaslight.

"Well?" Narraway asked, masking his eagerness as closely as he could.

O'Casey hesitated.

Narraway considered threatening him. He still had power, albeit illegal now. He drew in his breath. Then he looked at O'Casey's face again and changed his mind. He had few enough friends; he could not afford to alienate any of them.

"So what is it you expect of me, then?" O'Casey asked, cocking his head a little to one side. "I'll not help you, not more than I owe. For old times' sake. And that's little enough."

"I know," Narraway agreed. There were wounds and debts between them, some still unpaid. "I need to know what's changed for Cormac O'Neil —"

"For God's sake, leave the poor man alone! Have you not already taken all he has?" O'Casey exclaimed. "You'll not be after the child, will you?"

"The child?" For a moment Narraway was at a loss. Then memory flooded back. Kate's daughter by Sean. She had been only a child, six or seven years old when her parents died. "Did Cormac raise her?" he asked.

"A little girl?" O'Casey squinted at him contemptuously. "Of course he didn't, you fool. And what would Cormac O'Neil do with a six-year-old girl, then? Some cousin of Kate's took her, Maureen, I think her name was. She and her husband. Raised her as their own."

Narraway felt a stab of pity for the child — Kate's child. That should never have happened.

"But she knows who she is?" he said aloud.

"Of course. Cormac would have told her, if no one else." O'Casey lifted one shoulder slightly. "Although, of course, it might not be the truth as you know it, poor child. There are things better left unsaid."

Narraway felt chilled. He had not thought of Kate's daughter.

Looking back, even weeks afterward, he had known that Kate had crossed sides because she believed it was a doomed rising, and more Irishmen would die in it than English, far more. But she knew Sean as well. He had been willing enough to use her beauty to shame Narraway, even lead him to his death, but in his wildest imagination he had never considered that she might give herself willingly to Narraway or, worse, care for him.

And when she did, it was beyond Sean's mind or heart to forgive. He had said he killed her for Ireland, but Narraway knew it was for himself, just as in the end Sean knew it too.

And Cormac? He had loved Kate also. Did he feel an Irishman bested in deviousness by an Englishman, in a fight where no one was fair? Or a man betrayed by a woman he wanted and could never have: his brother's wife, who had sided with the enemy — for her own reasons, political or personal?

What had he told Talulla?

Could it possibly be anything new in the last few months? And if it were, how could she have moved the money from Mulhare's account back to Narraway's, using some traitor in Lisson Grove? Not by herself. Then with whom?

"Who betrayed Mulhare?" he asked O'Casey.

"No idea," O'Casey answered. "And if I did know, I wouldn't tell you. A man who'll sell his own people deserves to have his thirty pieces of silver slip out of his hands. Deserves to have it put in a bag o' lead around his neck, before they throw him into Dublin Bay."

Narraway rose to his feet. The cat by the fire stretched out and then curled up on the other side.

"Thank you," he said.

"Don't come back," O'Casey replied. "I'll not harm you, but I'll not help you either."

"I know," Narraway replied.

■ ■ ■ ■

Charlotte did not have the opportunity to speak at any length with Narraway after returning from the theater that night. She had hoped to tell him all that she had seen and learned there the following morning, but when they met for breakfast, the presence of others eating at nearby tables kept her from revealing what had transpired. Narraway said he had business to attend to, that he had heard from Dolina Pearse that Charlotte would be most welcome to attend the opening of an art exhibition, if she cared to, and to take tea with Dolina and her friends afterward. He had accepted on her behalf.

"Thank you," she said a little coolly.

He caught the intonation, and smiled. "Did you wish to decline?" he asked, eyebrows raised.

She looked at his dark face. To have taken the slightest notice of his pride now would be idiotic. He was facing disgrace, and further, his own downfall would destroy his friend's life. If he failed to exonerate himself, Pitt too might lose all the worldly possessions he had; cutting most deeply would be the loss of his ability to support his family, most particularly the wife who had stepped down so far from financial and social comfort to marry him.

"No, of course not," she replied, smiling at Narraway. "I am just a little nervous about it. I met some of them at Bridget Tyrone's party, and I am not sure that the encounter was entirely amicable."

"I can imagine," he said wryly. "But I know you, and I know something of Dolina. Tea should be interesting. And you'll like the art. It is impressionist, I think." He rose from the table.

"Victor!" She used his name for the first time without thinking, until she saw his face, the quickening, the sudden vulnerability. She wanted to apologize, but that would only make it worse. She forced herself to smile up at him where he stood, half turned to leave. He was naturally elegant; his jacket perfectly cut, his cravat tied with care.

She hardly knew how to begin, and yet certain necessity compelled her.

He was waiting.

"If I am to go to the exhibition I would like to purchase a new blouse." She felt the flush of embarrassment hot in her face. "I did not bring . . ."

"Of course," he said quickly. "We will go

as soon as you have finished your breakfast. Perhaps we should get two. You cannot be seen in precisely the same costume at every function. Will you be ready in half an hour?" He glanced at the clock on the mantel.

"Good heavens! I could have luncheon as well in that time. I shall be ready in ten minutes," she exclaimed.

"Really? Then I shall meet you at the front door." He looked surprised, and quite definitely pleased.

They walked perhaps three hundred yards then quite easily found a hansom to take them into the middle of the city. Narraway seemed to know exactly where he was going and stopped at the entrance to a very elegant couturier.

Charlotte imagined the prices, and knew that they would be beyond her budget. Surely Narraway must know what Pitt earned? Why was he bringing her here?

He opened the door for her and held it.

She stood where she was. "May we please go somewhere a little less expensive? I think this is beyond what I should spend, particularly on something I may not wear very often."

He looked surprised.

"Perhaps you have never bought a woman's blouse before," she said a little tartly, humiliation making her tongue sharp. "They can be costly."

"I wasn't proposing that you should buy it," he replied. "It is necessary in pursuit of my business, not yours. It is rightly my responsibility."

"Mine also . . . ," she argued.

"May we discuss it inside?" he asked. "We are drawing attention to ourselves standing in the doorway."

She moved inside quickly, angry with both him and herself. She should have foreseen this situation and avoided it somehow.

An older woman came toward them, dressed in a most beautifully cut black gown. It had no adornment whatever; the sheer elegance of it was sufficient. She was the perfect advertisement for her establishment. Charlotte would have loved a gown that fitted so exquisitely. She still had a very good figure, and such a garment would have flattered her enormously. She knew it, and the temptation was so sharp she could feel it like a sweet taste in her mouth.

"May we see some blouses, please?" Narraway asked. "Suitable for attending an exhibition of art, or an afternoon soirée."

"Certainly, sir," the woman agreed. She regarded Charlotte for no more than a minute, assessing what might both fit and suit her, then another mere instant at Narraway, perhaps judging what he would be prepared to pay.

Looking at his elegant and clearly expensive clothes, Charlotte's heart sank. The woman had no doubt jumped to the obvious conclusion that they were husband and wife. Who else would a respectable woman come shopping with, for such intimate articles as a blouse? She should have insisted that he take her somewhere else and wait outside. Except that she would have to borrow the money from him anyway.

"Victor, this is impossible!" she said under her breath as soon as the woman was out of earshot.

"No it isn't," he contradicted. "It is necessary. Do you want to draw attention to yourself by wearing the same clothes all the time? People will notice, which you know even better than I do. Then they will wonder what our relationship is — that I do not take better care of you."

She tried to think of a satisfactory argument, and failed.

"Or perhaps you want to give up the whole battle?" he suggested.

"No, of course I don't!" she retaliated. "But —"

"Then be quiet and don't argue." He took her arm and propelled her forward, holding her firmly. If she had pulled back she would have bumped into him, and the pressure of his fingers on her arm would have hurt. She determined to have words with him later, in no uncertain fashion.

The woman returned with several blouses, all of them beautiful.

"If madame would care to try them, there is a room available over here," she offered.

Charlotte thanked her and followed immediately. Every one of them was ravishing, but the most beautiful was one in black and bronze stripes that fitted her as if it had been both designed and cut for her personally; and one in white cotton and lace with ruffles and pearl buttons that was outrageously feminine. Even as a girl, in the days when her mother was trying to marry her to someone suitable, she had never felt so attractive, even verging on the really beautiful.

Temptation to have them both ached inside her.

The woman returned to see if Charlotte had made a decision, or if perhaps she wished for a further selection.

"Ah!" she said, drawing in her breath. "Surely madame could not wish for anything lovelier."

Charlotte hesitated, glancing at the striped blouse on its hanger.

"An excellent choice. Perhaps you would like to see which your husband prefers?" the woman suggested.

Charlotte started to say that Narraway was not her husband, but she wanted to phrase it graciously and not seem to correct the woman. Then she saw Narraway just beyond the woman's shoulder, and the admiration in his face. For an instant it was naked, vulnerable, and completely without guard. Then he must have realized, and he smiled.

"We'll take them both," he said decisively, and turned away.

Unless she should contradict him in front of the saleswoman, embarrassing them all, Charlotte had no alternative but to accept. She stepped back, closed the door, and changed into her own very ordinary blouse.

"Victor, you shouldn't have done that," she said as soon as they were outside in the street again. "I have no idea how I am going to repay you."

He stopped and looked at her for a moment.

Suddenly his anger evaporated and she remembered the expression in his eyes only a few moments before.

He reached up and with his fingertips touched her face. It was only her cheek, but it was an extraordinarily intimate gesture, with a great tenderness.

"You will repay me by helping me to clear my name," he replied. "That is more than enough."

To argue would be pointlessly unkind, not only to his very obvious emotion but also to the hope of the success they both needed so much.

"Then we had better set about it," she agreed, then moved a step away from him and started walking along the pavement again.

The art exhibition was beautiful, but Charlotte could not turn her attention to it and knew that to Dolina Pearse she must have appeared terribly ignorant. Dolina seemed to know each artist at least by repute, and be able to say for what particular technique he was famous. Charlotte simply listened with an air of appreciation, and hoped she could remember enough of it to recite back later.

While they walked around the rooms looking at one picture after another, Charlotte watched the other women, who were fashionably dressed exactly as they would have been in London. Sleeves were worn large at the shoulder this season, and slender from the elbow down. Even the most unsophisticated were puffed, or flying like awkward wings. Skirts were wide at the bottom, padded and bustled at the back. It was very feminine, like flowers in full bloom — large ones, magnolias or peonies.

Tea reminded her of the days before she was married, accompanying her mother on suitable "morning calls," which were actually always made in the afternoon. Behavior was very correct, all the unwritten laws obeyed. And beneath the polite exchanges the gossip was ruthless, the cutting remark honed to a razor's edge.

"How are you enjoying Dublin, Mrs. Pitt?" Talulla Lawless asked courteously. "Do have a cucumber sandwich. Always so refreshing, don't you think?"

"Thank you," Charlotte accepted. It was the only possible thing to do, even if she had not liked them. "I find Dublin fascinating. Who would not?"

"Oh, many people," Talulla replied. "They think us very unsophisticated." She smiled. "But perhaps that is what you enjoy?"

Charlotte smiled back, utterly without warmth. "Either they were not serious, or if they were, then they missed the subtlety of

235

your words," she replied. "I think you anything but simple," she added for good measure.

Talulla laughed. It was a brittle sound. "You flatter us, Mrs. Pitt. It is *Mrs.,* isn't it? I do hope I have not made the most awful mistake."

"Please don't concern yourself, Miss Lawless," Charlotte replied. "It is very far from the most awful mistake. Indeed, were it a mistake, which it isn't, it could still quite easily be put right. Would that all errors were so simply mended."

"Oh dear!" Talulla affected dismay. "How much more exciting your life must be in London than ours is here. You imply dark deeds. You have me fascinated."

Charlotte hesitated, then plunged in. "I daresay the grass is always greener on the other side of the fence. After watching the play last night I imagined life was full of passion and doom-laden love here. Please don't tell me it is all just the fervor of a playwright's imagination. You will entirely ruin the reputation of Ireland abroad."

"I didn't know you had such influence," Talulla said drily. "I had better be more careful of what I say." There was mocking and anger in her face.

Charlotte cast her eyes down toward the

floor. "I am so sorry. I seem to have spoken out of turn, and struck some feeling of pain. I assure you, it was unintentional."

"I can see many of your actions are unintentional, Mrs. Pitt," Talulla snapped. "And cause pain."

There was a rustle of silk against silk as a couple of the other women moved slightly in discomfort. Someone drew breath as if to speak, glanced at Talulla, and changed her mind.

"Just as I am sure yours are not, Miss Lawless," Charlotte replied. "I find it easy to believe that every word you say is entirely both foreseen, and intended."

There was an even sharper gasp of breath. Someone giggled nervously.

"May I offer you more tea, Mrs. Pitt?" Dolina asked. Her voice was quivering, but whether with laughter or tears it was impossible to say.

Charlotte held out her cup. "Thank you. That is most kind."

"Don't be ridiculous," Talulla said tartly. "For heaven's sake, it's a pot of tea!"

"The English answer to everything," Dolina ventured. "Is that not so, Mrs. Pitt?"

"You would be surprised what can be done with it, if it is hot enough." Charlotte looked straight at her.

"Scalding, I shouldn't wonder," Dolina muttered.

Charlotte relayed it to Narraway later that night, after dinner. They were alone in Mrs. Hogan's sitting room with the doors open onto the garden, which was quite small, and overhung with trees. It was a mild evening, and a moon cast dramatic shadows. In unspoken agreement they stood up and walked outside into the balmy air.

"I didn't learn anything more," she admitted finally. "Except that we are still disliked. But how could we imagine anything else? At the theater Mr. McDaid told me something of O'Neil. And O'Neil himself implied that I was here to meddle in Irish affairs — 'like your friend Narraway,' as he said. It is time you stopped skirting around it and told me what happened. I don't want to know, but I have to."

He was silent for a long time. She was acutely aware of him standing perhaps a yard away from her, half in the shadow of one of the trees. He was slender, not much taller than she, but she had an impression of physical strength, as if he were muscle and bone, all softness worn away over the years. She did not want to look at his face, partly to allow him that privacy, but just as much because she did not want to see what was there.

"I can't tell you all of it, Charlotte," he said at last. "There was quite a large uprising planned. We had to prevent it."

"How did you do that?" She was blunt.

Again he did not answer. She wondered how much of the secrecy was to protect her, and how much was simply that he was ashamed of his role in it, necessary or not.

Why was she standing out here shivering? What was she afraid of? Victor Narraway? It had not occurred to her before that he might hurt her. She was afraid that she would hurt him. Perhaps that was ridiculous. If he had loved Kate O'Neil, and still been able to sacrifice her in his loyalty to his country, then he could certainly sacrifice Charlotte. She could be one of the unintended victims that Fiachra McDaid had referred to — just part of the price. She was Pitt's wife, and Narraway had shown a loyalty to Pitt, in his own way. She was also quite certain now that he was in love with her. But how naïve of her to imagine that it would change anything he had to do in the greater cause.

She thought of Kate O'Neil, wondering what she had looked like, how old she had been, if she had loved Narraway. Had she betrayed her country and her husband to him? How desperately in love she must have been. Charlotte should have despised her for that, and yet all she felt was pity. She could imagine herself in Kate's place. If she herself hadn't loved Pitt, she could easily have believed herself in love with Narraway.

"You used Kate O'Neil, didn't you?" she said.

"Yes." His voice was so soft she barely heard it.

She turned quietly and walked back the few steps into Mrs. Hogan's sitting room. There wasn't anything more to say, not here, in the soft night wind and the scents of the garden.

CHAPTER 6

Pitt was troubled. He stood in the sun in St. Malo, leaning against the buttress edge of the towering wall, and stared out over the sea. It was vivid blue, the light so dazzling that he found himself squinting. Out in the bay a sailboat heeled far over.

The town was ancient, beautiful, and at any other time he would have found it interesting. Were he here on holiday with his family, he would have loved to explore the medieval streets and alleys, and learn more of its history, which was peculiarly dramatic.

As it was he had the strong feeling that he and Gower were wasting time. They had watched Frobisher's house for nearly a week and seen nothing that led them any closer to the truth. Visitors came and went; not only men but women also. Neither Pieter Linsky nor Jacob Meister had come again, but there had been dinner parties where at least a dozen people were present. Delivery-men had come with baskets of the shellfish for which the area was famous. Scores of oysters had come, shrimp and larger crusta-ceans like lobsters, and bags of mussels. But then the same could be said of any of the houses in the area.

Gower wandered along the path, his face sunburned, his hair flopping forward. He stopped just inside the wall, a yard or two short of Pitt. He too leaned against the ledge as if he were watching the sailing boat.

"Where did he go?" Pitt asked quietly, without looking at him.

"Only to the same café as usual," Gower answered, referring to Wrexham, whom one or the other of them had followed every day. "I didn't go in because I was afraid he'd notice me. But I saw the same thin man with the mustache go in, then come back out again in about half an hour."

There was a slight lift in his voice, a quickening. "I watched them through the window for a few minutes as if I were wait-ing for someone. They were talking about more people coming, quite a lot of them. They seemed to be ticking them off, as if from a list. They're definitely planning something."

Pitt would like to have felt the same stir of

excitement, but the whole week seemed too careful, too halfhearted for the passion that inspires great political change. He and Narraway had studied revolutionaries, anarchists, firebrands of all beliefs, and this had a different feel to it. Gower was young. Perhaps he attributed to them some of the vivacity he still felt himself. And he did feel it. Pitt smiled as he thought of Gower laughing with their landlady, complimenting her on the food and letting her explain to him how it was cooked. Then he told her about such English favorites as steak-and-kidney pudding, plum duff, and pickled eels. She had no idea whether to believe him or not.

"They've delivered more oysters," Pitt remarked. "It's probably another party. Whatever Frobisher's political beliefs about changing conditions for the poor, he certainly doesn't believe in starving himself, or his guests."

"He would hardly go around letting everyone know his plans . . . sir," Gower replied quickly. "If everyone thinks he's a rich man entertaining his friends in harmless idealism he never intends to act on, then nobody will take him seriously. That's probably the best safety he could have."

Pitt thought about it for a while. What Gower said was undoubtedly true, and yet he was uneasy about it. The conviction that they were wasting time settled more heavily upon him, yet he could find no argument that was pure reason rather than a niggling instinct born of experience.

"And all the others who keep coming and going?" he asked, at last turning and facing Gower, who was unconsciously smiling as the light warmed his face. Below him in the small square a woman in a fashionable dress, wide-sleeved and full-skirted, walked from one side to the other and disappeared along the narrow alley to the west. Gower watched her all the way, nodding very gently in approval.

Gower turned to Pitt, his fair face puzzled. "Yes, about a dozen of them. Do you think they're really harmless, sir? Apart from Wrexham, of course?"

"Are they all wild revolutionaries pretending very successfully to be ordinary citizens living satisfied and rather pedestrian lives?" Pitt pressed.

It was a long time before Gower answered, as if he were weighing his words with intense care. He turned and leaned on the wall, staring at the water. "Wrexham killed West for a reason," he said slowly. "He was in no present danger, except being exposed as an anarchist, or whatever he would call himself. Perhaps he doesn't want chaos, but a specific order that he considers fairer, more equal to all people. Or it may be a radical reform he's after. Exactly what it is the socialists want is one of the things we need to learn. There may be dozens of different goals —"

"There are," Pitt interrupted. "What they have in common is that they are not prepared to wait for reform by consent; they want to force it on people, violently if necessary."

"And how long will they have to wait for anyone to hand it over voluntarily?" Gower said with an edge of sarcasm. "Who ever gave up power if they weren't forced to?"

Pitt scanned his memory for the history he could recall. "None that I can think of," he admitted. "That's why it usually takes awhile. But the abolition of slavery was passed through Parliament without overt violence. Certainly without revolution."

"I'm not sure the slaves would agree with that assessment," Gower said with a twist of bitterness.

"It's time we found out what we are looking at," Pitt conceded.

Gower straightened up. "If we ask open questions it's bound to get back to him, and he may take a great deal more care. The one advantage we have, sir, is that he doesn't know we're watching him. Can we afford to lose that?" He looked anxious, his fair brows drawn together, the sunburn flushing his cheeks.

"I've been making a few inquiries," Pitt said.

"Already?" Suddenly there was an edge of anger in Gower's voice.

Pitt was surprised. It seemed Gower's easy manner hid an emotional commitment he had not seen. He should have. They had worked together for more than two months, even before the hectic chase that had brought them here.

"As to who I can ask for information without it being obvious," he replied levelly.

"Who?" Gower said quickly.

"A man named John McIver. He's another expatriate Englishman who's lived here for twenty years. Married to a Frenchwoman."

"Are you positive he's trustworthy, sir?" Gower was still skeptical. "It'll only take one careless word, one remark made idly, and Frobisher will know he's being watched. We could lose the big ones, the people like Linsky and Meister."

"I didn't choose him blindly," Pitt replied. He did not intend to tell Gower that he had encountered McIver before, on a quite different case.

Gower drew in his breath, and then let it out again. "Yes, sir. I'll stay here and watch Wrexham, and whoever he meets with." Then he flashed a quick, bright smile. "I might even go down into the square and see the pretty girl with the pink dress again, and drink a glass of wine."

Pitt shook his head, feeling the tension ease away. "I think you'll do better than I will," he said ruefully.

McIver lived some five miles outside St. Malo in the deep countryside. He was clearly longing to speak to someone in his native tongue and hear firsthand the latest news from London. Pitt's visit delighted him.

"Of course I miss London, but don't misunderstand me, sir," he said, leaning back in the garden chair in the sun. He had offered Pitt wine and little sweet biscuits, and — when he declined those — fresh crusty bread and a soft country cream cheese, which he accepted with alacrity.

Pitt waited for him to continue.

"I love it here," McIver went on. "The French are possibly the most civilized nation on earth — apart from the Italians, of course. Really know how to live, and do it with a certain flair that gives even mundane things a degree of elegance. But there are parts of English life that I miss. Haven't had a decent marmalade in years. Sharp, aromatic, almost bitter." He sighed. "The morning's *Times,* a good cup of tea, and a manservant who is completely unflappable. I used to have a fellow who could have announced the Angel of Doom with the same calm, rather mournful air that he announced the duchess of Malmsbury."

Pitt smiled. He ate a whole slice of bread and sipped his wine before he pursued the reason he had come.

"I need to make some very discreet inquiries: government, you understand?"

"Of course. What can I tell you?" McIver nodded.

"Frobisher," Pitt replied. "Expatriate Englishman living here in St. Malo. Would he be the right man to approach to ask a small service to his country? Please be candid. It is of . . . importance, you understand?"

"Oh quite — quite." McIver leaned forward a little. "I beg you, sir, consider very carefully. I don't know your business, of course, but Frobisher is not a serious man." He made a slight gesture of distaste. "He likes to cultivate some very odd friends. He pretends to be a socialist, you know, a man of the people. But between you and me, it is entirely a pose. He mistakes untidiness and a certain levity of manner for being an ordinary man of limited means." He shook his head. "He potters around and considers it to be working with his hands, as if he had the discipline of an artisan who must work to live, but he has very substantial means, which he has no intention of sharing with others, believe me."

"Are you sure?" Pitt said as politely as he could. However he said it, he was still questioning McIver's judgment.

"As sure as anyone can be," McIver replied. "Made a lot of noise about getting things done, but never done a thing in his life."

"He had some very violent and well-known people visiting him." Pitt clung to the argument, unwilling to concede that they had spent so many days here for nothing.

"See 'em yourself?" McIver asked.

"Yes. One of them in particular is very distinctive," Pitt told him. Then even as he said it, he realized how easy it would be to pretend to be Linsky. After all, he had never seen Linsky except in photographs, taken at a distance. The hatchet features, the greasy hair would not be so hard to copy. And Jacob Meister was also ordinary enough.

But why? What was the purpose of it all?

That too was now hideously clear — to distract Pitt and Gower from something else entirely.

"I'm sorry," McIver said sadly. "But the man's an ass. I can't say differently. You'd be a fool to trust him in anything that matters. And I hardly imagine you'd have come this far for something trivial. I'm not as young as I used to be, and I don't get into St. Malo very often, but if there's anything I can do, you have only to name it, you know."

Pitt forced himself to smile. "Thank you, but it would really need to be a resident of St. Malo. But I'm grateful to you for saving me from making a bad mistake."

"Think nothing of it." McIver brushed it away with a gesture. "I say, do have some more cheese. Nobody makes a cheese like the French — except perhaps the Wensleydale, or a good Caerphilly."

Pitt smiled. "I like a double Gloucester, myself."

"Yes, yes," McIver agreed. "I forgot that. Well, we'll grant the cheese equal status. But you can't beat a good French wine!"

"You can't even equal it."

McIver poured them both some wine,

then leaned back in his chair. "Do tell me, sir, what is the latest news on the cricket? Here I hardly ever get the scores, and even then they're late. How is Somerset doing?"

Pitt walked back along the gently winding road as the sun dropped toward the horizon. The air glowed with that faint gold patina that lends unreality to old paintings. Farmhouses looked huge, comfortable, surrounded by barns and stables. It was too early for the trees to be in full leaf, but clouds of blossom mounded like late snow, taking the delicate colors of the coming sunset. There was no wind, and no sound across the fields but the occasional movement of the huge, patient cows.

In the east, the purple sky darkened.

He went over what they knew in his mind again, carefully, all he had seen or heard himself, and all that Gower had seen and reported.

A carter passed him on the road, the wheels sending up clouds of dust, and he smelled the pleasant odor of horses' sweat and fresh-turned earth. The man grunted at Pitt in French, and Pitt returned it as well as he could.

The sun was sinking rapidly now, the sky filling with hot color. The soft breeze whispered in the grass and the new leaves on the willows, always the first to open. A flock of birds rose from the small copse of trees a hundred yards away, swirled up into the sky, and circled.

Between them Pitt and Gower had seen just enough to believe it was worth watching Frobisher's house. If they arrested Wrexham now, it would unquestionably show everyone that Special Branch was aware of their plans, so they would automatically change them.

They should have arrested Wrexham in London a week ago. He would have told them nothing, but they had learned nothing anyway. All they had really done was waste seven days.

How had he allowed that to happen? West had arranged the meeting, promising extraordinary information. Pitt could see the letter in his mind, the scrawled, misspelled words, the smudged ink.

No one else knew of it, except himself and Gower. So how had Wrexham learned of it? Who had betrayed West? It had to be one of the men plotting whatever it was that poor West had been going to reveal.

But this person had not followed West. Pitt and Gower were on his heels from the minute he began to run. If there had been anyone else running they would have seen him. Whoever it was must have been waiting for West. How had they known he would run that way? It was pure chance. He could as easily have gone in any other direction. Pitt and Gower had cornered him there, Pitt along the main street, Gower circling to cut him off.

Had West run into Wrexham by the most hideous mischance?

Pitt retraced in his mind the exact route they had taken. He knew the streets well enough to picture every step, and see the map of it in his mind. He knew where they had first spotted West, where he had started to run, and which way he had gone. There had been no one else in the crowd running. West had darted across the street and disappeared for an instant. Gower had gone after him, jabbing his arm to indicate which way Pitt should go, the shorter way, so they could cut him off.

Then West had seen Gower and swerved. Pitt had lost them both for a few minutes, but he knew the streets well enough to know which way West would go, and had been there within seconds . . . and Gower had raced up from the right to come up beside Pitt.

But the right doglegged back to the street

where Pitt had run the minute before, not the way Gower had gone. Unless he had passed Wrexham? Wrexham had come from the opposite way, not following West at all. So why had West run so frantically, as if he knew death was on his heels?

Pitt stumbled and came to a stop. Because it was not Wrexham whom West was afraid of, it was either Pitt himself, or Gower. He had had no reason to fear Pitt, but Gower was a superb runner. In an uncrowded alley he could break into a full sprint in seconds. He could have been there before, ducked back into the shelter of the alley entrance, and then burst out of it again as Pitt arrived. It was he who had killed West, not Wrexham. West's blood was already pooled on the stones. Pitt could see it in his mind's eye. Wrexham was the harmless man he appeared to be, the decoy to lure Pitt to St. Malo, and keep him here, while whatever was really happening came to its climax somewhere else.

It had to be London, otherwise it was pointless to lure Pitt away from it.

Gower. In fifteen or twenty minutes Pitt would be inside the walls of St. Malo again, back to their lodgings. Almost certainly Gower would be there waiting for him. Suddenly he was no longer the pleasant, ambitious young man he had seemed only this morning. Now he was a clever and extremely dangerous stranger, a man Pitt knew only in the most superficial way. He knew that Gower slept well, that his skin burned in the sun, that he liked chocolate cake, that he was occasionally careless when he shaved himself. He was attracted to women with dark hair and he could sing rather well. Pitt had no idea where he came from, what he believed, or even where his loyalties lay — all the things that mattered, that would govern what he would do when the mask was off.

Now suddenly Pitt must wear a mask as well. His own life might depend on it. He remembered with a chill how efficiently Gower had killed West, cut his throat in one movement, and left him on the stones, bleeding to death. One error and Pitt could end the same way. Who in St. Malo would think it more than a horrific street crime? No doubt Gower would be first on the scene again, full of horror and dismay.

There was no one Pitt could turn to. No one in France even knew who he was, and London could be in another world for any help it could offer now. Even if he sent a telegram to Narraway it would make no difference. Gower would simply disappear, anywhere in Europe.

He started to walk again. The sun was on the horizon and within minutes it would be gone. It would be almost dark by the time he was within the vast city walls. He had perhaps fifteen minutes to make up his mind. He must be totally prepared once he reached the house. One mistake, one slip, and it would be his last.

He thought of the chase to the East End, and finally the railway station. He realized with acute self-blame how easily Gower had led him, always making sure they did not lose Wrexham completely, and yet the chase seemed natural enough to be real. They lost him momentarily, and it was always Gower who found him. It was Gower who stopped Pitt from arresting him, pointing out the use of watching him and learning more. Gower had had enough money in his pocket to buy tickets on the ferry.

Come to that, it was Gower who said he had seen Linsky and Meister, and Pitt who had believed it.

What was this plan that used Wrexham to lure Pitt away from London? Of course Pitt must go back, knowing now as he did that Wrexham was not West's killer. The question was what to say to Gower. What reason should he give? He would know there was no message from Lisson Grove. Had there been, it would have been delivered to the house, and simple enough to check on anyway. All Gower would have to do was ask at the post office.

The sun was already half gone, a burning orange semicircle above the purple horizon. Shadows were deepening right across the road.

Should Pitt try to elude him, simply go straight to the harbor now and wait for the next boat to Southampton? But that might not be till tomorrow morning; Gower would realize what had happened, and come after him, sometime during the night. Pitt didn't even have the rest of his clothes with him. He was wearing only a light jacket in the warm afternoon.

The idea of fighting Gower here was not to be considered. Even if he could subdue him — and that was doubtful; Gower was younger and extremely fit — what would Pitt do with him? He had no power to arrest him. Could he leave him tied up, and then escape — assuming he was successful anyway?

But Gower would not be alone here. That thought sobered him like a drench of cold water, raising goose bumps on his skin. How many of the people at Frobisher's house

257

were part of his plan? The only answer was for Pitt to deceive him, make him believe that he had no suspicions at all, and that would not be easy. The slightest change in manner and Gower would know. Even a self-consciousness, a hesitation, a phrase too carefully chosen, and he would be aware.

How could Pitt tell him they were returning to London? What excuse would he believe?

Or should he suggest he himself return, and Gower stay here and watch Frobisher and Wrexham, just in case there was something after all? In case Meister or Linsky came back? Or anyone else they would recognize? The thought was an immense relief. A weight lifted off him as if it were a breathtaking escape, a flight into freedom. He would be alone — safe. Gower would stay here in France.

A second later he despised himself for his cowardice. When he had first gone on the beat in London, as a young man, he had expected a certain amount of violence. Indeed, now and then he had met with it. There had been a number of wild chases, with a degree of brawling at the end. But after promotion, as a detective he had almost exclusively used his mind. There had been long days, even longer nights. The emotional horror had been intense, the pressure to solve a case before a killer struck again, before the public were outraged and the police force disgraced. And after arrest there was testimony at the trial. Worst of all was the fear, which often kept him awake at night, that he had not caught the real criminal. Perhaps he had made a mistake, drawn a wrong conclusion, and it was an innocent person who was going to face the hangman.

But it was not physical violence. The battle of wits had not threatened his own life. He was chilled in the first darkness of the early evening. The sunset breeze was cold on his skin, and yet he was sweating. He must control himself. Gower would see nervousness; he would be watching for it. The suspicion that he had been found out would be the first thing to leap to his mind, not the last.

Before he reached the house, Pitt must have thought of what he would say, and then he must do it perfectly.

Gower was already in when Pitt arrived. He was sitting in one of the comfortable chairs reading a French newspaper, a glass of wine on the small table beside him. He seemed very English, very sunburned — or perhaps it was more windburn from the breeze off the sea. He looked up and smiled at Pitt, glanced then at Pitt's dirty boots, and rose to his feet.

"Can I get you a glass of wine?" he offered. "I expect you're hungry?"

For a moment Pitt was attacked by doubt. Was he being ridiculous thinking that this man had swiftly and brutally killed West, and then turned with an innocent face and helped Pitt pursue Wrexham all the way to Southampton, and across the channel to France?

He mustn't hesitate. Gower was expecting an answer, an easy and natural response to a very simple question.

"Yes I am," he said with slight grimace as he sank into the other chair and realized how exhausted he was. "Haven't walked that far in a while."

"Eight or nine miles?" Gower raised his eyebrows. He set the wine down on the table near Pitt's hand. "Did you have any luncheon?" He resumed his own seat, looking at Pitt curiously.

"Bread and cheese, and a good wine," Pitt answered. "I'm not sure red is the thing with cheese, but it was very agreeable. It wasn't Stilton," he added, in case Gower should think him ignorant of gentlemen's habit of taking port with Stilton. They were sitting with wine, like friends, and talking about etiquette, as if no one were dead and they were on the same side. He must be careful never to allow the absurdity of it to blind him to its lethal reality.

"Worth the walk?" Gower inquired. There was no edge to his voice; his lean brown hand holding the glass was perfectly steady.

"Yes," Pitt said. "Yes it was. He confirmed what I suspected. It seems Frobisher is a poseur. He has talked about radical social reform for years, but still lives in more or less luxury himself. He gives to the occasional charity, but then so do most people of means. Talking about action seems to be his way of shocking people, gaining a degree of attention for himself while remaining perfectly comfortable."

"And Wrexham?" Gower asked.

There was a moment's silence in the room. Somewhere outside a dog was barking, and much farther away someone sang a bawdy song and there was a bellow of laughter. Pitt knew it was vulgar because the intonation of the words was the same in any language.

"Obviously a different matter," Pitt replied. "We know that for ourselves, unfortunately. What he is doing here I have no idea. I hadn't thought he knew we were after him, but perhaps I was wrong in that." He let the suggestion hang in the air.

"We were careful," Gower said, as if turning the idea over in his mind. "But why stay here with Frobisher if all he is doing is trying to escape from us? Why not go on to Paris, or anywhere?" He put down his glass and faced Pitt. "At best he's a revolutionary, at worst an anarchist wanting to destroy all order and replace it with chaos." There was stinging contempt in his voice. If it was false then he belonged on the stage.

Pitt rethought his plan. "Perhaps he's waiting here for someone, and he feels safe enough not to care about us?" he suggested.

"Or whoever's coming is so important he has to take the risk?" Gower countered.

"Exactly." Pitt settled himself more comfortably in his chair. "But we could wait a long time for that, or possibly fail to recognize it when it happens. I think we need a great deal more information."

"French police?" Gower said doubtfully. He moved his position also, but to one less comfortable, as if any moment he might stand up again.

Pitt forced himself not to copy him. He must appear totally relaxed.

"Their interests might not be the same as ours," Gower went on. "Do you trust them, sir? In fact, do you really want to tell them what we know about Wrexham, and why we're here?" His expression was anxious, bordering on critical, as if it were only his junior rank that held him from stronger comment.

Pitt made himself smile. "No I don't," he answered. "To all your questions. We have no idea what they know, and no way of checking anything they may tell us. And of course our interests may very well not be the same. But most of all, as you say, I don't want them to know who we are."

Gower blinked. "So what are you suggesting, sir?"

Now was the only chance Pitt was going to have. He wanted to stand up, to have the advantage of balance, even of weight, if Gower moved suddenly. He had to stiffen his muscles and then deliberately relax to prevent himself from doing it. Carefully he slid a little farther down in the seat, stretching his legs as if they were tired — which was not difficult after his eight-mile walk. Thank heaven he had good boots, although they looked dusty and scuffed now.

"I'll go back to London and see what they have at Lisson Grove," he answered. "They

263

may have much more detailed information they haven't given us. You stay here and watch Frobisher and Wrexham. I know that will be more difficult on your own, but I haven't seen them do anything after dark other than entertain a little." He wanted to add more, to explain, but it would cause suspicion. He was Gower's superior. He did not have to justify himself. To do so would be to break the pattern, and if Gower was clever that in itself would alarm him.

"Yes, sir, if you think that's best. When will you be back? Shall I keep the room on here for you?" Gower asked.

"Yes — please. I don't suppose I'll be more than a couple of days, maybe three. I feel we're working in the dark at the moment."

"Right, sir. Fancy a spot of dinner now? I found a new café today. Has the best mussel soup you've ever tasted."

"Good idea." Pitt rose to his feet a little stiffly. "I'll leave first ferry in the morning."

The following day was misty and a lot cooler. Pitt deliberately chose the first crossing to avoid having to breakfast with Gower. He was afraid in the affected casualness of it he might try too hard, and make some slip so small Gower picked it up — while

Pitt had no idea anything had changed.

Or had Gower suspected something already? Did he know, even as Pitt walked down to the harbor along ancient, now-familiar streets, that the pretense was over? He had a desperate instinct to swing around and see if anyone were following him. Would he pick out Gower's fair head, taller than the average, and know it was he? Or might he already have changed his appearance and be yards away, and Pitt had no idea?

But his allies, Frobisher's men, or Wrexham's, could be anyone: the hold man in the fisherman's jersey lounging in a doorway taking his first cigarette of the day; the man on the bicycle bumping over the cobbles; even the young woman with the laundry. Why suppose that Gower himself would follow him? Why suppose that he had noticed anything different at all? The new realization loomed gigantic to him, filling his mind, driving out almost everything else. But how self-centered to suppose that Gower had nothing more urgent to consume his thoughts! Perhaps Pitt and what he knew, or believed he knew, were irrelevant anyway.

He increased his pace and passed a group of travelers heaving along shopping bags and tightly packed portmanteaux. On the dockside he glanced around as if to search for someone he knew, and was flooded with relief when he saw only strangers.

He stood in the queue to buy his ticket, and then again to get on board. Once he felt the slight sway of the deck under his feet, the faint movement, even here in the harbor, it was as if he had reached some haven of safety. The gulls wheeled and circled overhead, crying harshly. Here on the water the wind was sharper, salt-smelling.

Pitt stood on the deck by the railing, staring at the gangway and the dockside. To anyone else, he hoped he looked like someone looking back at the town with pleasure, perhaps at a holiday well spent, possibly even at friends he might not see again for another year. Actually he was watching the figures on the quay, searching for anyone familiar, any of the men he had seen arriving or leaving Frobisher's house, or for Gower himself.

Twice he thought he saw him, and it turned out to be a stranger. It was simply the fair hair, an angle of shoulder or head. He was angry with himself for the fear; he knew the danger was largely in his mind. Perhaps it was so deep because until the walk back to the town yesterday evening it had never entered his mind that Gower had killed West, and Wrexham was either a co-conspirator or even a perfectly innocent man, a tissue-paper socialist posing as a fanatic, like Frobisher himself. It was his own blindness that dismayed him. How stupid he had been, how insensitive to possibilities. He would be ashamed to tell Narraway, but he would have to; there would be no escaping it.

At last they cast off and moved out into the bay. Pitt remained where he was at the rail, watching the towers and walls of the city recede. The sunlight was bright on the water, glittering sharp. They passed the rocky outcrops, tide slapping around the feet of the minor fortress built there, guarding the approaches. There were few sailing boats this early: just fishermen pulling up the lobster pots that had been out all night.

He tried to imprint it on his mind. He would tell Charlotte about it, how beautiful it was, how it was like stepping back in time. He should bring her here one day, take her to dine where the shellfish was so superb. She hardly ever left London, let alone England. It would be fun, different. He imagined seeing her again so vividly he could almost smell the perfume of her hair, hear her voice in his mind. He would tell her about the city, the sea, the tastes and the sounds of it all. He wouldn't have to dwell on the events that had brought him to France, only on the good.

Someone bumped against him, and for a moment he forgot to be startled. Then the chill ran through him, and he realized how his attention had wandered.

The man apologized.

Pitt spoke with difficulty, his mouth dry. "It's nothing."

The man smiled. "Lost my balance. Not used to the sea."

Pitt nodded, but he moved away from the rail and went back into the main cabin. He stayed there for the rest of the crossing, drinking tea and having a breakfast of fresh bread, cheese, and a little sliced ham. He tried to look as if he were at ease.

When they reached Southampton he went ashore carrying the light case he had bought in France and looking like any other holidaymaker returning home. It was midday. The quayside was busy with people disembarking, or waiting to take the next ferry out.

He went straight to the railway station, eager to catch the first train to London. He would go home, wash, and dress in clean clothes. Then if he were lucky, he'd just have time to catch Narraway before he left Lisson Grove for the evening. Thank heaven for the telephone. At least he would be able to call and arrange to meet with him wherever was convenient. Maybe with his news about Gower, a rendezvous at Narraway's home would be better.

He felt easier now. France seemed very far away, and he had had no glimpse of Gower on the boat. He must have satisfied him with his explanation.

The station was unusually busy, crowded with people all seemingly in an ill humor. He discovered why when he bought his ticket for London.

"Sorry, sir," the ticket seller said wearily. "We got a problem at Shoreham-by-Sea, so there's a delay."

"How long a delay?"

"Can't say, sir. Maybe an hour or more."

"But the train is running?" Pitt insisted. Suddenly he was anxious to leave Southampton, as if it was still dangerous.

"Yes, sir, it will be. D'yer want a ticket fer it or not?"

"Yes I do. There's no other way to London, is there?"

"No, sir, not unless yer want ter take a different route. Some folk are doing that, but it's longer, an' more expensive.

269

Trouble'll be cleared soon, I daresay."

"Thank you. I'll have one ticket to London, please."

"Return, sir? Would you like first, second, or third class?"

"Just one way, thank you, and second class will be fine."

He paid for it and went back toward the platform, which was getting steadily more and more crowded. He couldn't even pace backward and forward to release some of the tension that was mounting inside him, as it seemed to be for everyone else. Women were trying to comfort fretful children; businessmen pulled pocket watches out of their waistcoats and stared at the time again and again. Pitt kept glancing around him, but there was no sign of Gower, although he was not sure if he would have noticed him in the ever-increasing crowd.

He bought a sandwich and a pint of cider at two o'clock, when there was still no news. At three he eventually took the train to Worthing, and hoped to catch another train from there, perhaps to London via a different route. At least leaving Southampton gave him an illusion of achieving something. As he made his way toward a seat in the last carriage, again he had the feeling of having escaped.

The carriage was nearly full. He was fortunate there was room for him to sit. Everyone else had been waiting for some time and they were all tired, anxious, and looking forward to getting home. Even if this train did not take them all the way, at least they were moving.

One woman held a crying two-year-old, trying to comfort her. The little girl was rubbing her eyes and sniffing. It made him think of Jemima at that age. How long ago that seemed. Pitt guessed this girl had been on holiday and was now confused as to where she was going next, and why. He had some sympathy for her, and it made him engage the mother in conversation for the first two stops. Then the movement of the train and the rhythmic clatter over the connections on the rail lulled the child to sleep, and the mother finally relaxed.

Several people got off at Bognor Regis, and more at Angmering. By the time they reached Worthing and stopped altogether, there were only half a dozen people left in Pitt's carriage.

"Sorry, gents," the guard said, tipping his cap back a little and scratching his head. "This is as far as we go, till they get the track cleared at Shoreham."

There was a lot of grumbling, but the few

passengers remaining got out of the carriage. They walked up and down the platform restlessly, bothered the porters and the guard asking questions to which no one had an answer, or went into the waiting room with passengers from the other carriages.

Pitt picked up someone else's discarded newspaper and glanced through it. Nothing in particular caught his eye, and he kept looking up every time someone passed, in the hope that it was news of the train leaving again.

Once or twice as the long afternoon wore on, he got up and walked the length of the platform. With difficulty he resisted the temptation to pester the guard, but he knew that the poor man was probably as frustrated as everyone else, and would have been only too delighted to have news to give people.

Finally, as the sun was on the horizon, they boarded a new train and slowly pulled out of the station. The relief was absurdly out of proportion. They had been in no hardship and no danger, yet people were smiling, talking to one another, even laughing.

The next stop was Shoreham-by-Sea, where the trouble had been, then Hove. By then it was dusk, the light golden and casting heavy shadows. For Pitt this hour of the evening had a peculiar beauty, almost with a touch of sadness that sharpened its emotional power. He felt it even more in the autumn, when the harvest fields in the country were stubble gold, the stooks like some remnant of a forgotten age that was earlier, more barbaric, without the inroads of civilization on the land. He thought of his childhood at the big house where his parents had worked, of the woods and fields, and a sense of belonging.

Suddenly the carriage enclosed him. He stood up and went to the end and through the door onto the small platform before the next carriage. It was mostly for men to light cigars without the smoke being unpleasant to other passengers, but it was a good place to stand and feel the rush of air and smell the plowed earth and the damp of the woods as they passed. Not many trains had these spaces. He had heard somewhere that it was an American invention. He liked it very much.

The air was quite cold, but there was a sweetness to it and he was happy to remain there, even though it grew darker quickly, heavy clouds rolling in from the north.

Probably sometime in the night it would rain.

He considered what he would tell Narraway of what now seemed to be an abortive trip to France, and how he would explain his conclusions about Gower and his own blindness in not having understood the truth from the beginning. Then he thought with intense pleasure of seeing Charlotte, and of being at home where he had only to look up and she would be there, smiling at him. If she thought he had been stupid, she would not say so — at least not at first. She would let him say it, and then ruefully agree. That would take away most of the sting.

It was nearly dark now; the clouds had brought the night unnaturally soon.

Without any warning he was aware of it: someone behind him. With the rattle of the wheels he had not heard the carriage door open. He half turned, and was too late. The weight was there in the middle of his back, his right arm was locked in a fierce grip, his left pinned against the rail by his own body.

He tried to step backward onto the instep of the man, shock him with the pain of it. He felt the man wince, but there was no easing of the hold of him. He was being pushed forward, twisted a little. His arm was crushed on the rail and he gasped to get his breath. He was pushed so his head was far out over the speeding ground. The wind was cold on his face, smuts from the engine striking him, stinging. Any minute he was going to lose his balance and then it would be a second, two, and he would be over the edge and down onto the track. At this speed he would be killed. It would probably snap his spine. The man was strong and heavy. The weight of him was driving the breath out of Pitt's chest, and he had no leverage to fight back. It would be over in seconds.

Then there was a slam of carriage doors, and a wild shout. The pressure on Pitt's back was worse, driving the last bit of air out of his lungs. He heard a cry, and realized it was himself. The weight lifted suddenly and he gasped, hanging on to the rail, scrambling to turn around, coughing violently. The man who had attacked him was struggling with someone else, who was portly, thick-waisted. He could see only shadows and outlines in the dark. The man's hat flew off and was carried away. He was already getting the worst of the fight, backing toward the rail at the other side. In the momentary light from the door his face was contorted with anger and the beginning of terror as he realized he was losing.

Pitt straightened up and threw himself at the attacker. He had no weapon except his fists. He struck the man low in the chest, as hard as he could, hoping to wind him. He heard him grunt and he pitched forward, but only a step. The fat man slithered sideways and down onto one knee. At least that way he would not overbalance across the rail and onto the track.

Pitt followed his attacker, striking again, but the man must have expected it. He went down also, and Pitt's blow only caught the edge of his shoulder. The man twisted with it, but for no more than a moment. Then he lunged back at Pitt, his head down, catching Pitt in the stomach and sending him sprawling. The carriage door was slamming open and closed.

The fat man scrambled to his feet and charged, his face red, shouting something indistinguishable over the howl of the wind and roar and clatter of the train. He dived at Pitt's attacker, who stepped out of the way, and then swiveled around and raised himself. He grasped the fat man and heaved him over the rail to fall, screaming, arms flailing helplessly, out onto the track.

For a second Pitt was frozen with horror. Then he turned and stared at the man who had attacked him. He was only an outline in the dark, but he did not need to hear him speak to recognize him.

"How did you know?" Gower asked, curiosity keen, his voice almost normal.

Pitt was struggling to get his breath. His lungs hurt, his ribs ached where the rail had bruised him, but all he could think of was the man who had tried to rescue him, and whose broken body was now lying on the track.

Gower took a step toward him. "The man you walked eight miles to see, did he tell you something?"

"Only that Frobisher was a paper tiger," Pitt replied, his mind racing now. "Wrexham can't have taken a week to work that out, so maybe he always knew it. Then I thought perhaps he was just the same. I thought I saw him cut West's throat, but when I went over it step by step, I didn't. It just looked like it. Actually West's blood was already pooled on the stones. You were the one who had the chase, all the way to the ferry. I thought you were clever, but then I realized how easy it had been. It was always you who found him when we lost him, or who stopped us actually catching him. The whole pursuit was performed for my benefit, to get me away from London."

Gower gave a short burst of laughter. "The great Pitt, whom Narraway sets so much store by. Took you a week to work that out! You're getting slow. Or perhaps you always were. Just lucky." Then suddenly he flung himself forward, arms outstretched to grasp Pitt by the throat, but Pitt was ready this time. He ducked and charged, low, with his head down. He caught Gower in the belly just above the waist, and heard him gasp. He straightened his legs, lifting Gower off the ground. His own impetus carried him on, high over the rail and into the darkness. Pitt did not even see him land, but he knew with a violent sorrow that it had to kill him instantly. No one could survive such an impact.

He straightened up slowly, his legs weak, his body shaking. He had to cling to the rail to support himself.

The carriage door slammed shut again, then opened. The guard stood there, wide-eyed, terrified, the lantern in his hand, the carriage lights yellow behind him.

"Ye're a lunatic!" he cried, stuttering over his words.

"He was trying to kill me!" Pitt protested, taking a step forward.

The guard jerked the lantern up as if it were some kind of shield. "Don't you touch me!" His voice was shrill with terror. "I got 'alf a dozen good men 'ere 'oo'll tie yer down, so I 'ave. Ye're a bleedin' madman. Yer killed poor Mr. Summers as well, 'oo only came out there ter 'elp the other gent."

"I didn't —" Pitt began, but he didn't get to finish the sentence. Two burly men were crowding behind the guard, one of them with a walking stick, the other with a sharp-ended umbrella, both held up as weapons.

"We're gonna put yer in my van," the guard went on. "An' if we 'ave ter knock yer senseless ter do it, just gimme the excuse is all I ask. I liked Mr. Summers. 'E were a good man, an' all."

Pitt had no wish to be beaten into submission. Dazed, aching, and appalled at what he had done, he went without resisting.

CHAPTER 7

"You can't come," Charlotte said vehemently. It was early afternoon and she was standing in the dining room of Mrs. Hogan's lodging house, dressed in her best spring costume, wearing the magnificent blouse. She was rather uncomfortably aware of how well it suited her. With a plain dark skirt the effect was dramatic, to say the very least. "Someone is bound to know you," she added, forcing her attention to the matter in hand.

Narraway had obviously taken care to prepare himself for the occasion also. His shirt was immaculate, his cravat perfectly tied, his thick hair exactly in place.

"I have to," he replied. "I must see Talulla Lawless. I can only see her in a public place, or she will accuse me of assaulting her. She has already tried it once, and warned me she will do it again if I attempt to see her alone. I know she is going to be there this afternoon. It's a recital. Most people will be watching the musicians."

"It will only need one person to recognize you and they will tell the others," she pointed out. "Then what will I be able to do of any value? They'll know the reason behind everything I say."

"I will not go with you. The charade of your being my sister is for Mrs. Hogan." He smiled bleakly. "You will go to the recital with Fiachra McDaid. He's coming to meet you here —" He glanced at the clock on the mantel shelf. "— in ten minutes or so. I'll go alone. I have to, Charlotte. I think Talulla is crucial to this. Too many of my investigations come back to her. She is the one thread that connects everyone involved."

"Can't I do it?" she persisted.

He smiled briefly. "Not this time, my dear."

She did not argue any further, even though she was sure he was not telling her the entire truth. But it was foolish to come here at all if they were unprepared to take any risks. She smiled back at him, just in a very tiny gesture, and gave a little nod. "Then be careful."

His eyes softened. He seemed to be about to say something half mocking, but there

281

was a sharp tap on the door. Mrs. Hogan came in, her hair as usual falling out of its pins, her white apron crisply starched.

"Mr. McDaid is here for you, Mrs. Pitt." It was impossible to tell from her expression what her thoughts were, except that she was having an effort keeping them under control.

"Thank you, Mrs. Hogan," Charlotte said politely. "I shall be there immediately." She met Narraway's eyes. "Please be careful," she said again. Then, before he could respond, she picked up her skirt perhaps half an inch and swept out the door Mrs. Hogan was holding open for her.

Fiachra McDaid was standing in the hall next to the longcase clock, which read five minutes ahead of the one in the dining room. He was smartly dressed, but he could not manage the same casual elegance as Narraway.

"Good afternoon, Mrs. Pitt," he said pleasantly. "I hope you'll enjoy the music. It'll be another side of Dublin for you to see, and a fine day for it. And talking of the weather, have you been outside the city yet? While it's so agreeable, how about a trip to Droghada, and the ruins of Mellifont, the oldest abbey in Ireland — 1142, it was, on the orders of Saint Malachy. Or if that is too recent for you, how about the Hill of Tara? It was the center of Ireland under the High Kings, until the eleventh century when Christianity came and brought an end to their power."

"It sounds marvelous," she said with as much enthusiasm as she could manage, taking his arm and walking toward the front door. She did not look back to see if Narraway was watching her. "Are they far from the city?"

"A little distance, but it's well worth it," McDaid replied. "There's far more to Ireland than Dublin, you know."

"Of course. I appreciate your generosity in sharing it. Do tell me more about these places."

He accepted, and on the short journey to the hall where the recital was to take place, she listened with an air of complete attention. Indeed, at any other time she would have been as interested as she now pretended to be. The pride in his voice was unmistakable, and the love for his people and their history. He had a remarkable compassion for the poor and the dispossessed, which she could not help but admire.

When they arrived, the crowds were already beginning to gather, and they were obliged to find their seats if they wished to be well placed toward the front. Charlotte was pleased to do so, in order to be as far from Narraway as possible, so no one might think they were with each other — except McDaid, of course, and she had to trust in his discretion.

The other ladies were dressed very fashionably, and in the bronze-and-black-striped blouse she felt the equal of any of them. It still gave her a twinge of guilt that Narraway had paid for it, and she had no idea what words she would use to explain it to Pitt. But for the moment she indulged the pleasure of seeing both men and women glance at her, then look a second time with appreciation, or envy. She smiled a little, not too much, in case it looked like self-satisfaction, just enough to lift the corners of her mouth into a pleasant expression and return the nods of greeting from those she had met before.

She chose a chair, then sat as straight-backed as she could and affected an interest in the arrangements of the seats where the musicians were to play.

She noticed Dolina Pearse and only just avoided meeting her eyes. Next to her, Talulla Lawless was discreetly surveying the room, apparently looking for someone. Charlotte tried to follow her direction, and felt her breath catch in her throat as she saw Narraway arrive. The light was bright for a moment on the silver at his temples as he leaned forward to listen to someone. Talulla stiffened, her face set rigid. Then she smiled and turned back to the man beside her. It was a moment before Charlotte recognized him as Phelim O'Conor. He moved away and took his seat, and Talulla returned to hers.

The master of ceremonies appeared, and the babble of talk died away. The performance had begun.

For just over an hour they sat absorbed in the sound and the emotion of the music. It had a sweetness and a lilt that made Charlotte smile, and it was no effort at all to appear as if she were totally happy.

But the moment it ceased and the applause was finished, her mind returned to the reason she was here — and, more urgently, why Narraway was. She remembered the look on Talulla's face. Perhaps the greatest purpose Charlotte would serve would not be anything to do with Cormac O'Neil, but to support Narraway if Talulla should begin to create a scene.

Giving McDaid no more than a quick smile, she rose to her feet and headed for Talulla, trying to think of something reasonable to say, true or not. She reached her just as Talulla turned to walk away, and only just managed to save her balance. She looked instantly amazed.

"Oh, I am sorry," Charlotte apologized, although actually it had been Talulla who had nearly bumped into her. "I am afraid my enthusiasm rather got the better of me."

"Enthusiasm?" Talulla said coldly, her face reflecting complete disbelief.

"For the harpist," Charlotte said quickly. "I have never heard more delightful music." She was fishing desperately for anything to say.

"Then don't let me stop you from speaking to her," Talulla retorted. "I'm sure you'll find her agreeable."

"Do you know her?" Charlotte asked eagerly.

"Only by repute, and I shouldn't wish to trouble her," Talulla responded sharply. "There must be so many people eager to speak with her."

"I would be so grateful if you would introduce me," Charlotte asked, ignoring the rebuff.

"I'm afraid I cannot help you," Talulla was making it impossible to conceal her impatience. "I am not acquainted with her. Now, if you don't —"

"Oh!" Charlotte assumed an expression of dismay. "But you said she was most agreeable." She made it a challenge, not daring to look toward where she had seen Narraway talking to Ardal Barralet.

"It was the polite thing to say," Talulla snapped. "Now really, Mrs. Pitt, there is someone I wish to speak to, and I must hurry or he may leave. Excuse me." And she all but pushed Charlotte out of the way, obliging her to step aside.

Charlotte could see Narraway still talking to Barralet at the far end of the room. Talulla was heading directly toward them. Charlotte went after her, but several steps behind. They were halfway down the aisle between the chairs when Talulla stopped abruptly.

Then Charlotte saw why. A little knot of people had gathered around where Narraway had turned from Ardal Barralet and was facing Cormac O'Neil across a short open space of floor. Phelim O'Conor was looking from one to the other of them and Bridget Tyrone was just to his right.

For seconds they stood frozen. Then Cormac drew in his breath. "I never thought you'd dare show your face in Ireland again," he said between his teeth, staring at Narraway. "Who've you come back to betray this time? Mulhare is dead, or didn't you know that?" The hatred trembled in his voice; his whole body shook and his words were slurred.

A ripple of emotion ran through the gathering crowd like the passage of a storm through a field of barley.

"Yes, I know Mulhare is dead," Narraway replied, not moving backward despite Cormac's closeness to him. "Someone embezzled the money he should have had so he could go abroad and start a new life."

"Someone?" Cormac sneered. "And I suppose you have no idea who?"

"I hadn't," Narraway answered, still not moving, although Cormac was within two feet of him now. "I'm beginning to find out."

Cormac rolled his eyes. "If I didn't know you, I'd believe that. You stole the money yourself. You betrayed Mulhare just as you betrayed all of us."

Narraway was white-faced, eyes brilliant. "It was a war, Cormac. You lost, that's all —"

"All!" Cormac's face was now contorted with hate. "I lost my brother, and my sister-in-law, and my country, and you stand here and say *that's all* . . ." His voice choked.

There was a mutter from everyone around the group closest to him. Charlotte winced.

She knew what Narraway meant, but he was rattled and being clumsy. He knew they were against him, and he could prove nothing. He had no backing from London now; he was alone, and losing.

"We couldn't both win." Narraway regained his self-control with an effort. "That time it was me. You wouldn't have shouted *betrayal* if it had been you."

"It's my bloody country, you arrogant ape!" Cormac shouted. "How many more of us have to be robbed, cheated, and murdered before you get some shadow of a conscience and get the hell out of Ireland?"

"I'll go as soon as I prove who took Mulhare's money," Narraway answered. "Did you sacrifice him to get your revenge on me? Is that how you know all about it?"

"Everybody knows all about it," Cormac snarled. "His body was washed up on the steps of Dublin Harbor, God damn you!"

"I didn't betray him!" Narraway's voice was shaking and growing louder despite his efforts to keep it down. "If I'd done it I'd have made a better job. I wouldn't have left the money in my own damn account for others to find it. Whatever you think of me, Cormac, you know I'm not a fool."

Cormac was stunned into momentary silence.

It was Talulla who stepped forward. Her face was white to the lips, her eyes sunken like holes in her head.

"Yes, you are a fool," she said between her teeth, facing Narraway, her back to Cormac. "An arrogant English fool who thinks we can't ever get the better of you. Well, one of us did this time. You say you didn't put the money in your own bank? Apparently someone did, and you got the blame. Your own people think you're a thief, and no one in Ireland will ever give you information again, so you'll be no use to London anymore. You have Cormac O'Neil to thank for that."

She drew in her breath, all but choking on it. "Don't you have a saying in England — 'He who laughs last, laughs longest'? Well, we'll be laughing after you are a broken old man with nothing to do and no one who gives a damn about you! Remember it was an O'Neil who did that to you, Narraway!" She laughed with a brief, jagged sound, like something tearing inside her. Then she turned and pushed her way through the crowd until she disappeared.

Charlotte stared at Cormac, and Phelim O'Conor, and then at Narraway. They stood pale and shaking. It was Ardal Barralet who spoke.

"How unfortunate," he said drily. "I think,

Victor, it would have been better if you had not come. Old memories die hard. It seems from what has been said as if this is one part of the war you lost. Accept it with as much grace as you expected of us, and take your leave while you can."

Narraway did not even glance at Charlotte, not drawing her into the embarrassment. He bowed very stiffly. "Excuse me." He turned and left.

McDaid took Charlotte's arm, holding her surprisingly hard. She had not even known he was near her. Now she had no choice but to leave with him.

"He's a fool," McDaid said bitterly as soon as they were sufficiently far from the nearest people that he could speak without being overheard. "Did he think anyone would forget his face?"

She knew he was right, but she was angry with him for saying so. She did not know the details of Narraway's part in the old betrayal, whether he had loved Kate O'Neil, or used her, or even both, but he was the one betrayed this time — and by a lie, not by the truth.

She was allowing emotion and instinct to replace reason in her judgment. Or maybe her belief in him was a return for the loyalty Narraway had shown to Pitt. Pitt was not here to help, to offer any support or advice, so it was necessary that she do it for him.

Then another thought came to her, a moment of recollection as clear as lightning in a black storm. Talulla had said that Mulhare's money had been returned to Narraway's own bank in London, and now no one in London would trust him. How could she know, unless she were intimately involved in having brought that about? She was in her late twenties. At the time of Kate and Sean O'Neil's deaths she was no more than a child, perhaps six or seven years old.

Was that what Narraway had come here for: to provoke her, unrealizingly, into such self-revelation? What a desperate step to take.

She tried to free her arm from McDaid's grip, pulling sharply, but he held on.

"You're not going after him," he said firmly. "He did at least do one thing decently: He didn't involve you. As far as Talulla is concerned, you could be total strangers. Don't spoil that."

His words made it worse. It increased her debt; and to deny Narraway that would be pointless and desperately ungracious. She snatched her arm from McDaid, and this time he let go.

"I wasn't going to go after him," she said

angrily. "I'm going home."

"To London?" he said incredulously.

"To Mrs. Hogan's house in Molesworth Street," she snapped. "If you would be so kind as to take me. I do not wish to have to look for an omnibus. I've no idea where I am, or where I'm going."

"That I know," McDaid agreed ruefully.

However, as soon as McDaid had left her at Mrs. Hogan's door, she waited until he had gotten back into the carriage and it was around the corner out of sight, then walked briskly in the opposite direction and hailed the first carriage for hire that she saw. She knew Cormac O'Neil's town address from Narraway, and she gave it to the driver. She would wait for O'Neil to return, for as long as was necessary.

As it transpired, it was shortly after dusk when she saw Cormac O'Neil climb out of a carriage a hundred yards down the street. He made his way a trifle unsteadily along the footpath toward his front door.

She moved out of the shadows. "Mr. O'Neil?"

He stopped, blinking momentarily.

"Mr. O'Neil," she repeated. "I wonder if I may speak with you, please? It is very important."

"Another time," he said indistinctly. "It's late." He started forward to go past her to the door, but she took a step in front of him.

"No, it's not late, it's barely supper time, and this is urgent. Please?"

He looked at her. "You're a handsome enough girl," he said gently. "But I'm not interested."

Suddenly she realized that he assumed her to be a prostitute. It was too absurd for her to take offense. But if she laughed she might sound too close to hysteria. She swallowed hard, trying to control the nervous tension all but closing her throat.

"Mr. O'Neil." She had prepared the lie. It was the only way she could think of that might make him tell her the truth. "I want to ask you about Victor Narraway . . ."

O'Neil jerked to a stop and swung around to stare at her.

"I know what he did to your family," she went on a little desperately. "At least I think I do. I was at the recital this afternoon. I heard what you said, and what Miss Lawless said too."

"Why did you come here?" he demanded. "You're as English as he is. It's in your voice, so don't try to sympathize with me." Now his tone was stinging with contempt.

She matched his expression just as harshly.

"And you think the Irish are the only people who are ever victims?" she said with amazement. "My husband suffered too. I might be able to do something about it, if I know the truth."

"Something?" he said contemptuously. "What kind of something?"

She knew she must make this passionate, believable; a wound deep enough that he would see her as a victim like himself. Mentally she apologized to Narraway. "Narraway's already been dismissed from Special Branch," she said aloud. "Because of the money that was supposed to go to Mulhare. But he has everything else: his home, his friends, his life in London. My family has nothing, except a few friends who know him as I do, and perhaps you? But I need to know the truth . . ."

He hesitated a moment, then wearily, as if surrendering to something, he fished in his pocket for a key. Fumbling a little, he inserted it in the lock and opened the door for her.

They were greeted immediately by a large dog — a wolfhound of some sort, who gave her no more than a cursory glance before going to O'Neil, wagging its tail and pushing against him, demanding attention.

O'Neil patted its head, talking gently.

Then he led the way into the parlor and lit the gas lamps, the dog on his heels. The flames burned up to show a clean, comfortable room with a window onto the area way and then the street. He pulled the curtain across, more for privacy than to keep out the cold, and invited her to sit down.

She did so, soberly thanking him, then waiting for him to compose himself before she began her questions. She was acutely aware that if she made even one ill-judged remark, one clumsy reaction, she could lose him completely, and there would be no opportunity ever to try again.

"It was all over twenty years ago," he said, looking at her gravely. He sat opposite her, the dog at his feet. In the gaslight it was easy to see that he was laboring to keep some control of his feelings, as if seeing Narraway again had stirred emotions he had struggled hard to bury. His eyes were red-rimmed, his face haggard. His hair stood up on end, crookedly at one side, as though he had run his fingers through it repeatedly. She could not fail to be aware that he had been drinking; these sorrows were not of the kind that drown easily.

"Yes, I know, Mr. O'Neil." She spoke quietly. "But do you find that time heals? I would like to think so, but I see no evidence of it."

She settled herself a little more comfortably in the chair and waited for his reply.

"Heals?" he said thoughtfully. "No. Grows a seal over, maybe, but it's still bleeding underneath." He looked at her curiously. "What did he do to you?"

She leapt to the future she feared, creating in her mind the worst of it.

"My husband worked in Special Branch too," she replied. "Nothing to do with Ireland. Anarchists in England, people who set off bombs that killed ordinary women and children, old people, most of them poor."

O'Neil winced, but he did not interrupt her.

"Narraway sent him on a dangerous job, and then when it turned ugly, and my husband was far from home, Narraway realized that he had made a mistake, a misjudgment, and he let my husband take the blame for it. My husband was dismissed of course, but that's not all. He was accused of theft as well, so he can't get any other position at all. He's reduced to laboring, if he can even find that. He's not used to it. He has no skills, and it's hard to learn in your forties. He's not built for it." She heard the thickening in her own voice, as if she were fighting tears. It was fear, but it sounded like distress, grief, perhaps outrage at injustice.

"How is my story going to help?" O'Neil asked her.

"Narraway denies it, of course," she replied. "But if he betrayed you as well, that makes a lot of difference. Please — tell me what happened?"

"Narraway came here twenty years ago," he began slowly. "He pretended to have sympathy with us, and he fooled some people. He looked Irish, and he used that. He knows our culture, and our dreams, our history. But we weren't fooled. You're born Irish, or you're not. But we pretended to go along with it — Sean and Kate and I." He stopped, his eyes misty, as if he were seeing something far from this quiet, sparse room in 1895. The past was alive for him, the dead faces, the unhealed wounds.

She was uncertain if she should acknowledge that she was listening, or if it would distract him. She ended up saying nothing.

"We found out who he was, exactly," Cormac went on. "We were planning a big rebellion then. We thought we could use him, give him a lot of false information, turn the tables. We had all sorts of dreams. Sean was the leader, but Kate was the fire. She was beautiful, like sunlight on autumn leaves, wind and shadow, the sort of loveliness you can't hold on to. She was alive the way other women never are." He stopped again, lost in memory, and the pain of it was naked in his face.

"You loved her," she said gently.

"Every man did," he agreed, his eyes meeting hers for an instant, as if he had only just remembered that she was there. "You remind me of her, a little. Her hair was about the same color as yours. But you're more natural, like the earth. Steady."

Charlotte was not sure if she should be insulted. There was no time now, but she would think of it later, and wonder.

"Go on," she prompted. He had not told her anything yet, except that he had been in love with his brother's wife. Was that really why he hated Narraway?

As if he had seen her thought in her eyes, he continued. "Of course Narraway saw the fire in her too. He was fascinated, like any man, so we decided to use that. God knows, we had few enough weapons against him. He was clever. Some people think the English are stupid, and surely some of them are, but not Narraway, never him."

"So you decided to use his feelings for Kate?"

"Yes. Why not?" he demanded, his eyes angry, defending that decision so many years ago. "We were fighting for our land, our right to govern ourselves. And Kate agreed. She would have done anything for Ireland." His voice caught and for a moment he could not go on.

She waited. There was no sound outside, no wind or rain on the glass, no footsteps, no horses in the road. Even the dog at Cormac's feet did not stir. The house could have been anywhere — out in the countryside, miles from any other habitation. The present had dissolved and gone away.

"They became lovers, Kate and Narraway," Cormac said bitterly. "She told us what he was planning, he and the English. At least that's what she said." His voice was thick with grief.

"Wasn't it true?" she said when he did not continue.

"He lied to her," Cormac answered. "He knew what she was doing, what we all were. Somewhere she made a mistake." The tears were running down his face and he made no effort to check them. "He fed us all lies, but we believed him. The uprising was betrayed. Stupid, stupid, stupid! They blamed Kate!" He gulped, staring at the wall as if he could see all the players in that tragedy parading in front of him.

"They saw she had led us astray," he went on. "Narraway did that to her, used her against her own people. That's why I'd see him in hell. But I want him to suffer further, here on earth, where I know it for certain. Can you make that happen, Mrs. Pitt? For Kate?"

She was appalled by the rage in him. It shook his body like a disease. His skin was blotchy, the flesh of his face wasted. He must once have been handsome.

"What happened to her?" It was cruel of Charlotte to ask, but she knew it was not the end of the story yet, and she needed to hear it from him, not just from Narraway.

"She was murdered," he replied. "Strangled. Beautiful Kate."

"I'm sorry." She meant it. She tried to imagine the woman, all passion and dreams, as Cormac had painted her, but that vision was of a man in love with an image.

"They said it was Sean who killed her," he went on. "But it couldn't have been. He knew better than to believe she would have betrayed the cause. That was Narraway again. He killed her, because she would have told them what he had done. He would never have left Ireland alive." He stared at Charlotte, his eyes brimming with tears, waiting for her to respond.

She forced herself to speak. "Why would he? Can you prove that?" she asked. "I mean, can you give me anything I can take back to London that would make them listen to me?" She was cold now too, dreading what he might say. What if he could? What would she do then? Narraway would excuse himself, of course. He would say he had had to kill her, or she would have exposed him and the uprising might have succeeded. Perhaps that was even true? But it was still ugly and terrible. It was still murder.

"He killed her because she wouldn't tell him what he wanted to know. But if I could prove it do you think he'd be alive?" Cormac asked harshly. "They'd have hanged him, not poor Sean, and Talulla'd not be an orphan, God help her."

Charlotte gasped. "Talulla?"

"She's Kate's daughter," he said simply. "Kate and Sean's. Did you not know that? After Sean and Kate died she was cared for by a cousin, so she could be protected as much as possible from the hatred against her mother. Poor child."

The dreadful, useless tragedy of it overwhelmed Charlotte. She wanted to say something that would redeem any part of the loss, but everything that came to her mind was banal.

"I'm sorry," she said. "I'm . . ."

He looked up at her. "So are you going back to London to tell someone?"

"Yes . . . yes I am."

"Be careful," he warned. "Narraway won't go down easily. He'll kill you too, if he thinks he has to, to survive."

"I will be careful," she promised him. "I think I have a little more to learn yet, but I promise I'll be . . . careful." She stood up, feeling awkward. There was nothing to say that completed their conversation. They moved from the desperate to the mundane as if it were completely natural, but what words were there that could be adequate for what either of them felt? "Thank you, Mr. O'Neil," she said gravely.

He took her to the door and opened it for her, but he did not offer to find her any transport, as if for him she ceased to be real the moment she stepped out onto the pavement.

"Where have you been?" Narraway demanded as soon as she came into Mrs. Hogan's sitting room. He had been standing

303

by the window, or perhaps pacing. He looked exhausted and tense, as if his imagination had plagued him with fear. His eyes were hollow, and the lines in his face were deeper than she had ever seen them before. "Are you all right? Who's with you? Where is he?"

"Nobody is with me," she answered. "But I am perfectly all right —"

"Alone?" His voice shook. "You were out on the street alone, in the dark? For God's sake, Charlotte, what's the matter with you? Anything could have happened. I wouldn't even have known!" He put out his hand and gripped her arm. She could feel the strength of him, as if he were quite unaware how tightly he held her.

"Nothing happened to me, Victor. I wasn't very far away. And it isn't late. There are plenty of people about," she assured him.

"You could have been lost . . ."

"Then I would have asked for directions," she said. "Please . . . there is no need to be concerned. If I'd had to walk a little out of my way to get here it wouldn't have hurt me."

"You could have . . . ," he began, then stopped, perhaps realizing that his fear was disproportionate. He let go of her. "I'm sorry. I . . ."

She looked at him. It was a mistake. For an instant his emotion was too plain in his eyes. She did not want to know that he cared so much. Now it would be impossible for either of them to pretend he did not love her, and she could not pretend she did not know.

She turned away, feeling the color burning on her skin. All words would be belittling the truth.

He stood still.

"I went to see Cormac O'Neil," she said after a moment or two.

"What?"

"I was perfectly safe. I wanted to hear from him exactly what happened, or at least what he believes."

"And what did he say?" he asked quickly, his voice cracking with tension.

She did not want to look at him, to intrude into old grief that was still obviously so sharp, but evasion was cowardly. She met his eyes and repeated to him what Cormac had said, including the fact that Talulla was Kate's daughter.

"That's probably how he sees it," Narraway answered when she had finished. "I daresay he couldn't live with the truth. Kate was beautiful." He smiled briefly. In that moment she could imagine the man he had been twenty years earlier: younger, more virile, perhaps less wise.

"Few men could resist her," he went on. "I didn't try. I knew they were using her to trap me. She was brave, passionate . . ." He smiled wryly. "Perhaps a little short on humor, but far more intelligent than they realized. It sometimes happens when women are beautiful. People don't see any further than that, especially men. It's uncomfortable. We see what we want to see."

Charlotte frowned, suddenly thinking of Kate, a pawn to others, an object of both schemes and desires. "Why do you say intelligent?" she asked.

"We talked," he replied. "About the cause, what they planned to do. I persuaded her it would rebound against them, and it would have. The deaths would have been violent and widespread. Attacks like that don't crush people and make them surrender. They have exactly the opposite effect. They would have united England against the rebels, who could have lost all sympathy from everyone in Europe, even from some of their own. Kate told me what they were going to do, the details, so I could have it stopped."

Charlotte tried to imagine it, the grief, the cost.

"Who killed her?" she asked. She felt the loss touch her, as if she had known Kate more deeply than simply as a name, an imagined face.

"Sean," he replied. "I don't know whether it was for betraying Ireland, as he saw it, or betraying him."

"With you?"

Narraway colored, but he did not look away from her. "Yes."

"Do you know that, beyond doubt?"

"Yes." His throat was so tight his voice sounded half strangled. "I found her body. I think he meant me to."

She could not afford pity now. "Why are you sure it was Sean who killed her?" She had to be certain so she could get rid of the doubt forever. If Narraway himself had killed her it might, by some twisted logic of politics and terror, be what he had to do to save even greater bloodshed. She looked at him now with a mixture of new understanding of the weight he carried, and sorrow for what it had cost him: whether that was now shame, or a lack of it — which would be worse.

"Why are you sure it was Sean?" she repeated.

He looked at her steadily. "What you really mean is, how can I prove I didn't kill her myself."

She felt a heat of shame in her own face. "Yes."

He did not question her.

"She was cold when I found her," he replied. "Sean tried to blame me. The police would have been happy to agree, but I was with the viceroy in the residence in Phoenix Park at the time. Half a dozen staff saw me there, apart from the viceroy himself, and the police on guard duty. They didn't know who I was, but they would have recognized me in court, if it had been necessary. The briefest investigation showed them that I couldn't have been anywhere near where Kate was killed. It also proved that Sean lied when he said he saw me, and that by his own admission he was there." He hesitated. "If you need to, you can check it." His smile was there for a moment, then gone. "Don't you think they'd have loved to hang me for it, if they'd had the ghost of a chance?"

"Yes," she agreed, feeling the weight ease from her. Grief was one thing, but without guilt it was a passing wound, something that would heal. "I'm . . . I'm sorry I needed to ask. Perhaps I should have known you wouldn't have done it."

"I would like you to think well of me,

Charlotte," he said quietly. "But I would rather you saw me as a real person, capable of good and ill, and of pity, and shame . . ."

"Victor . . . don't . . ."

He turned away slowly, staring at the fire. "I'm sorry. It won't happen again."

She left quietly, going up to her room. She needed to be alone, and there was nothing either of them could say that would do anything but make it worse.

They were at breakfast the following morning: she with a slight headache after sleeping badly; he weary, but with the mark of professionalism so graciously back in place that yesterday could have been a dream.

They were eating toast and marmalade when the messenger arrived with a letter for Narraway. He thanked Mrs. Hogan, who had brought it to him, then tore it open.

Charlotte watched his face but she could not read anything more than surprise. When he looked up she waited for him to speak.

"It's from Cormac," he said gently. "He wants me to go and see him, at midday. He will tell me what happened, and give me proof."

She was puzzled, remembering Cormac's hate, the pain that seemed as sharp as it must have been the day it happened. She leaned forward. "Don't go. You won't, will you?"

He put the letter down. "I came for the truth, Charlotte. He may give it to me, even if it is not what he means to do. I have to go."

"He still hates you," she argued. "He can't afford to face the truth, Victor. It would place him in the wrong. All he has left is his illusions of what really happened, that Kate was loyal to Ireland and the cause, and that it would all have worked, except for you. He can't give that up."

"I know," he assured her, reaching out his lean hand and touching her gently, for an instant, then withdrawing it again. "But I can't afford not to go. I have nothing left to lose either. If it was Cormac who created the whole betrayal of Mulhare, I need to know how he did it, and be able to prove it to Croxdale." His face tightened. "Rather more than that, I need to find out who is the traitor in Lisson Grove. I can't let that go."

He did not offer any rationalization, taking it for granted that she understood.

It gave her an odd feeling of being included, even of belonging. It was frightening for the emotional enormity of it, and yet there was a warmth to it she would not willingly have sacrificed.

She did not argue any further, but nodded, and decided to follow after him and stay where she could see him.

Narraway went out of the house quite casually, as if merely to look at the weather. Then, as she came to the door, he turned and walked quickly toward the end of the road.

Charlotte followed after him, barely having time to close the door behind her, and needing to run a few steps to keep up. She had a shawl on and her reticule with her, and sufficient money for as long a fare as she would be likely to need.

He disappeared around the corner into the main street. She had to hurry to make sure she saw which way he went. As she had expected, he went straight to the first carriage waiting, spoke to the driver, then climbed in.

She swung around with her back to the road and pretended to look in a shop window. As soon as he had passed she darted out into the street to look for a second carriage. It was long, desperate moments before she found one. She gave the driver the address of Cormac O'Neil's house and urged him to go as fast as pos-

sible. She was already several minutes behind.

"I'll pay you an extra shilling if you catch
up with the carriage that just left here," she
promised. "Please hurry. I don't want to
lose him."

She sat forward, peering out as the carriage careered down the street, swung
around the corner, and then set off again at
what felt like a gallop. She was tossed
around, bruised, and without any sense of
where she was for what felt like ages, but
was probably no more than fifteen minutes.
Then finally they lurched to a stop outside
the house where she had been the previous
evening.

She stepped out, taking a moment to find
her balance after the hectic ride. She paid
him more than he had asked for, and an
extra shilling.

"Thank you," she said. "Please wait."
Then without ensuring that he did, she
walked up the same path she had trod in
the evening light such a short time ago.
Somehow at midday the path looked longer,
the bushes more crowding in, the trees
overhead cut out more of the sunlight.

She had not reached the front door when
she heard the dog barking. It was an angry,
frightening sound, with a note of hysteria to

it, as if the wag were out of control. It had certainly not been like that yesterday evening. It had been calm, resting its head on O'Neil's feet and barely noticing her.

She was surprised Cormac did not come to see what the fuss was. He could not possibly be unaware of the noise.

She touched the door with her fingers and it opened.

Narraway was standing in the hall. He swung around as the light spread across the floor. For a moment he was startled, then he regained his presence of mind.

"I should have known," he said grimly. "Wait here."

The dog was now throwing itself at whatever barrier held it in check. Its barking was high in its throat, as if it would rip someone to shreds the moment it could reach them.

Charlotte would not leave Narraway alone. She stepped inside and looked for the umbrella stand she had noticed yesterday. She saw it, picked out a sharp-ferruled black umbrella, and held it as if it were a sword.

The barking was reaching a crescendo.

Ahead of her Narraway went to the sitting room door, to the right of where the dog was hurling itself at another door, snarling in a high, singing tone as if it scented prey close at last.

Narraway opened the sitting room door then stopped motionless. She could see over his shoulder that Cormac O'Neil was lying on the floor on his back, a pool of blood spreading on the polished wood around what was left of his head.

Charlotte gulped, trying to stop herself from being sick. Yesterday evening he had been alive, angry, weeping with passion and grief. Now there was nothing left but empty flesh lying waiting to be found.

Narraway went over and bent down, touching the skin of Cormac's face with his fingers.

"He's still warm," he said, turning back to look at Charlotte. He had to raise his voice above the noise of the dog. "We must call the police."

He had barely finished speaking when there came the bang of the front door swinging open again and hitting the wall, then footsteps.

There was no time to wonder who it was. A woman screamed with a short, shrill sound, and then seemed to choke. Charlotte swiveled to stare at Talulla Lawless. She was ashen-faced, her hand to her mouth, black eyes staring wildly past Charlotte and Narraway to the figure of Cormac on the floor.

Behind her a policeman tried to catch his breath as a wave of horror overtook him.

Talulla glared at Narraway. "I warned him," she gasped. "I knew you'd kill him, after yesterday. But he wouldn't listen. I told him! I told him!" Her voice was getting higher and higher and her body was shaking.

The policeman regained control of himself and stepped forward, looking at Charlotte, then at Narraway. "What happened here?" he asked.

"He murdered my uncle, can't you see that?" Talulla shouted at him. "Listen to the dog, damn it! For God's sake don't let it out, it'll tear that murderer apart! That's what brought me here. I heard it, poor creature."

"He was dead when we got here!" Charlotte shouted back at her. "We don't know what happened any more than you do!"

Narraway stepped forward to the policeman. "I came in first," he said. "Mrs. Pitt waited outside. She has nothing to do with this. She never met Mr. O'Neil until very recently. I've known him for twenty years. Please allow her to leave."

Talulla thrust out her hand, finger pointing. "There's the gun! Look, it's lying right there on the floor. He hasn't even had time to take it away."

"Of course he hasn't," Charlotte retorted. "We only just got here! If you ask the . . ."

"Charlotte, be quiet," Narraway said with such force that she stopped speaking. He faced the policeman. "I came into the house first. Please allow Mrs. Pitt to leave. As I said before, she had no acquaintance with Mr. O'Neil, beyond a casual introduction. I have known him for years. We have an old enmity that has finally caught up with us. Is that not true, Miss Lawless?"

"Yes!" she said vehemently. "The dog just started to bark. I can hear it from my house. I live only a few yards away, over there. If there'd been anybody else, she'd have raised this row before. Ask anyone."

The policeman looked at Cormac on the floor, at Narraway, and the blood on his shoes, then at Charlotte, white-faced by the door. The dog was still barking and trying to break down the barrier that held it in check.

"Sir, I'm sorry, but you'll have to come with me. It'll be best for you if you don't give me any trouble."

"I have no intention of giving you trouble," Narraway told him. "None of this is your fault. Will you permit me to make certain that Mrs. Pitt has sufficient funds to pay a cabdriver? She has had a very ugly shock."

The policeman looked confused. "She was with you, sir," he pointed out.

"No," Narraway corrected him. "She came after me. She was not here when I arrived. I went in and O'Neil and I quarreled. He attacked me, and I had no choice but to defend myself."

"You came deliberately to kill," Talulla accused. "He showed you for the liar and the cheat you are. He got you dismissed from your position and you wanted your revenge. You came here and shot him." She looked at Charlotte. "Can you deny that?"

"Yes, I can," Charlotte responded heatedly. "I did arrive after Mr. Narraway was already here, but only seconds behind him. He had not gone farther than the hallway. The sitting room door was closed. We discovered Mr. O'Neil's body at the same moment."

"Liar!" Talulla shouted. "You're his mistress. You'd say anything."

Charlotte gasped.

A look at once of humor and pain flickered in Narraway's eyes. He turned to the policeman. "That is not true. Please allow her to go. If you can find the cabbie who brought her, he will affirm that Mrs. Pitt arrived after I did, and he must have seen her come into the house. O'Neil was shot, as you observe. Ask the driver if he heard the shot."

The policeman nodded. "You're right, sir. Don't take the lady down with you." He turned to Talulla. "And if you'd go back home, ma'am, I'll take care o' this. An' you, ma'am." He looked at Charlotte. "You'd better go an' find a cab back to your lodgings. But don't leave Dublin, if you please. We'll be wishing to talk to you. Where are you staying?"

"Number twelve, Molesworth Street."

"Thank you, ma'am. That'll be all. Now, don't stop me doing my duty, or it'll be the worse for you."

Charlotte could do nothing but watch helplessly as another policeman arrived. Narraway was manacled and led away, to Talulla's intense delight.

Charlotte walked back down the pathway and along the road, dazed and alone.

CHAPTER 8

Pitt ceased to struggle. At first, in the heat of the moment, there was no point. He was in the grasp of two burly constables, both convinced they had apprehended a violent lunatic who had just hurled two men, possibly strangers to him, off a fast-moving train.

The irate and terrified passengers who had witnessed half the events had seen Pitt on the platform with the first man who had gone over, and then alone with Gower just before he had been pitched over as well.

"I know what I saw!" one of them stated. He stood as far away from Pitt as he could, his face a mask of horror in the railway platform gaslight. "He threw them both over. You want to watch yourselves or he'll have you too! He's insane! He has to be. Threw them over, one after the other."

"We were fighting!" Pitt protested. "He attacked me, but I won!"

"Which one of them would that be, sir?" one of the constables asked him. "The first one, or the second one?"

"The second one," Pitt answered but he heard the note of desperation in his own voice. It sounded ridiculous, even to him.

"Maybe he didn't like it that you'd thrown the first man off the train," the constable said reasonably. " 'E was tryin' to arrest you. Good citizen doin' 'is duty."

"He attacked me the first time," Pitt tried to explain. "The other man was trying to rescue me, and he lost the fight!"

"But when this second man attacked you, you won, right?" the constable said with open disbelief.

"Obviously, since I'm here," Pitt snapped. "If you undo the manacles, I'll show you my warrant card. I'm a member of Special Branch."

"Yes, sir," the constable said sarcastically. "They always go around throwin' people off trains. Very special, they are."

Pitt barely controlled his temper. "Look in my pocket, inside my coat, up at the top," he said between his teeth. "You'll find my card."

The constables looked at each other. "Yeah? An' why would you be pitchin' people off trains, sir?"

"Because the man attacked me," Pitt said again. "He is a dangerous man planning violence here." He knew as he spoke how absurd that sounded, considering that Gower was dead on the track, and Pitt was standing here alive and unhurt, apart from a few bruises. "Look," he went on, trying anew. "Gower attacked me. The stranger came to my rescue, but Gower was stronger and he lost the fight. I couldn't save him. Then Gower attacked me, but this time I was ready. I won. Look for my warrant card. That'll prove who I am."

The constables exchanged glances again. Then one of them very gingerly approached Pitt and held his coat open with one hand, while the other felt inside his inner pocket.

"There in't nothin' there, sir," he said, removing his hand quickly.

"There's my warrant card and my passport," Pitt said with a sense of rising panic. It had to be. He had had them both when he got onto the train at Shoreham. He remembered putting them back, as always.

"No, sir," the constable repeated. "Your pocket's empty, sir. There in't nothin' in it at all. Now, why don't you come quietly? No use in causing a lot o' fuss. Just gets people 'urt, as I can promise you, sir, it'll be you as comes off worst." He turned to the other passenger. "Thank you for yer trouble, sir. We got yer name and address. We'll be in touch with yer when we needs more."

Pitt drew in his breath to try reasoning further, and realized the futility of it. He knew what must have happened. Either his warrant card and passport had fallen out of his pocket in the fight, which didn't seem likely — not from a deep pocket so well concealed — or else Gower had taken the precaution of picking it during the struggle. They had stood very close, struggling together. He had been thinking of saving his own life, not being robbed. He turned to the constable closest to him.

"I've just come in from France, through Southampton," he said with sudden hope. "I had to have my passport then, or they wouldn't have let me in. My warrant card was with it. Can't you see that I've been robbed?"

The constable stared at him, shaking his head. "I only know as you're on the train, sir. I don't know where you got on, or where you was before that. You just come quietly, and we'll get you sorted at the police station. Don't give us any more trouble, sir. Believe me, yer got enough already."

"Do you have a telephone at the police

station?" Pitt asked, but he made no protest as they led him away. It would be pointless. As it was, a crowd was gathering watching him. At this moment it was impossible for him to feel sorry Gower was dead. The other passenger he grieved for with a dull, angry pain. "Do you have a telephone?" he demanded.

"Yes, sir, o' course we do. If yer got family, we'll call them for yer an' let 'em know where you are," he promised.

"Thank you."

But when they arrived at the police station and Pitt was led in, a constable closely at either side of him, he was put straight into a cell and the door locked.

"My phone call!" he persisted.

"We'll make it for yer, sir. 'Oo shall we call, then?"

Pitt had considered it. If he called Charlotte she would be frightened and very distressed, and there was nothing she could do. Far better he call Narraway, who would straighten out the whole hideous mess, and could tell Charlotte about it afterward. "Victor Narraway," he answered.

" 'E related to yer?" the constable asked suspiciously.

"Brother-in-law," Pitt lied quickly. He gave them the Lisson Grove number.

"That's his work. It's where he'll be, or they'll know where to find him."

"At this time o' night, sir?"

"There's always someone there. Please, just call."

"If that's what yer want, we'll call."

"Thank you." Pitt sat down on the hard wooden bench in the cell and waited. He must stay calm. It would all be explained in a matter of minutes. This part of the nightmare would be over. There was still Gower's treachery and his death; now, in the silence of the cell, he had time to think of it more deeply.

He should not have been surprised that Gower came after him. The pleasant, friendly face Gower had shown in France, indeed all the time they had worked together over the last few months, might have been part of his real character, but it was superficial, merely a skin over a very different man beneath.

Pitt thought of his quick humor, how he had watched the girl in the red dress, admiring her, taking pleasure in her easy walk, the swing of her skirt, imagining what she would be like to know. He remembered how Gower liked the fresh bread. He drank his coffee black, even though he pulled his mouth at its bitterness, and still went back for more. He pictured how he stood smiling with his face to the sun, watched the sailing boats on the bay, and knew the French names for all the different kinds of seafood.

People fought for their own causes for all kinds of reasons. Maybe Gower believed in his goal as much as Pitt did; they were just utterly different. Pitt had liked him, even enjoyed his company. How had he not seen the ruthlessness that had let him kill West, and then turn on Pitt so stealthily?

Except perhaps it had not been easy? Gower might have lain awake all night wretched, seeking another way and not finding it. Pitt would never know. It was painful to realize that so much was not as he had trusted, and his own judgment was nowhere near the truth. He could imagine what Narraway would have to say about that.

The constable came back, stopping just outside the bars. He did not have the keys in his hand.

Pitt's heart sank. Suddenly he felt confused and a little sick.

"Sorry, sir," the constable said unhappily. "I called the number you gave. It was a branch o' the police all right, but they said as they'd got no one there called Narraway, an' they couldn't 'elp yer."

"Of course Narraway's there!" Pitt said

desperately. "He's head of Special Branch! Call again. You must have had the wrong number. This is impossible."

"It were the right number, sir," the constable repeated stolidly. "It was Special Branch, like you said. An' they told me they got no one there called Victor Narraway. I asked 'em careful, sir, an' they were polite, but very definite. There in't no Victor Narraway there. Now you settle down, sir. Get a bit o' rest. We'll see what we can do in the morning. I'll get you a cup o' tea, an' mebbe a sandwich, if yer like?"

Pitt was numb. The nightmare was getting worse. His imagination created all kinds of horror. What had happened to Narraway? How wide was this conspiracy? Perhaps he should have realized that if they removed Pitt himself to France on a pointless errand, then of course they would have gotten rid of Narraway as well. There was no purpose in removing Pitt otherwise. He was only a kind of backup: a right-hand man possibly, but not more than that. Narraway was the real threat to them.

"Yer want a cup o' tea, sir?" the constable repeated. "Yer look a bit rough, sir. An' a sandwich?"

"Yes . . . ," Pitt said slowly. The man's humanity made it all the more grotesque, yet he was grateful for it. "I would. Thank you, Constable."

"Yer just rest, sir. Don't give yerself so much trouble. I'll get yer a sandwich. Would 'am be all right?"

"Very good, thank you." Pitt sat down on the cot to show that he had no intention of causing any problem for them. He was numb anyway. He did not even know whom to fight: certainly not this man who was doing his best to exercise both care and a degree of decency in handling a prisoner he believed had just committed a double murder.

It was a long and wretched night. He slept little, and when he did his dreams were full of fear, shifting darkness, and sudden explosions of sound and violence. When he woke in the morning his head throbbed, and his whole body was bruised and aching from the fight. It was painful to stand up when the constable came back again with another cup of tea.

"We'll take yer ter the magistrate later on," he said, watching Pitt carefully. "Yer look awful!"

Pitt tried to smile. "I feel awful. I need to wash and shave, and I look as if I've slept in my clothes, because I have."

"Comes with being in jail, sir. 'Ave a cup

o' tea. It'll 'elp."

"Yes, I expect it will, even if not much," Pitt accepted. He stood well back from the door so the constable could place it inside without risking an attack. It was the usual way of doing things.

The constable screwed up his face. "Yer bin in the cells before, in't yer," he observed.

"No," Pitt replied. "But I've been on your side of them often enough, as I told you. I'm a policeman myself. I have another number I would like you to call, seeing that Mr. Narraway doesn't seem to be there. Please. I need to let someone know where I am. My wife and family, at least."

" 'Oo would that be, sir?" The constable put down the tea and backed out of the cell again, closing and locking the door. "You give me the number and I'll do it. Everyone deserves that much."

"Lady Vespasia Cumming-Gould," Pitt replied. "I'll write the number down for you, if you give me a pencil."

"You jus' tell me, sir. I'll write it down."

Pitt obeyed. There was no point in arguing.

The man returned ten minutes later, his face wide-eyed and a trifle pale.

"She says as she knows yer, sir. Described yer to a T, she did. Says as ye're one o' the best policemen in London, an' Mr. Narra-way's 'oo yer said 'e were, but summink's 'appened to 'im. She's sending a Member o' Parliament down ter get yer out of 'ere, an' as we'd better treat yer proper, or she'll be 'avin' a word wi' the chief constable. I dunno if she's real, sir. I 'ope yer understand I gotter keep yer in 'ere till this gentleman comes, wi' proof 'e's wot 'e says 'e is, an' all. 'E could be anyone, but I know I got two dead bodies on the tracks."

"Of course," Pitt said wearily. He would not tell him that Gower was Special Branch, and Pitt had not known that he was a traitor until yesterday. "Of course I'll wait here," he said aloud. "I'd be obliged if you didn't take me before the magistrate until the man arrives that Lady Vespasia sends."

"Yes, sir, I think as we can arrange that." He sighed. "I think as' we'd better. Next time yer come from Southampton, sir, I'd be obliged if yer'd take some other line!"

Pitt managed a lopsided smile. "Actually I'd prefer this one. Given the circumstances, you've been very fair."

The constable was lost for words. He struggled, but clearly nothing he could think of seemed adequate.

It was nearly two hours later that Mr. Somerset Carlisle, MP, came sauntering into the police station, elegantly dressed, his curious face filled with a rueful amusement. Many years ago he had committed a series of outrages in London, to draw attention to an injustice against which he had no other weapon. Pitt had been the policeman who led the investigation. The murder had been solved, and he had seen no need to pursue the man who had so bizarrely brought it to public attention. Carlisle had remained grateful, becoming an ally in several cases since then.

On this occasion he had with him all his identification verifying the considerable office he held. Within ten minutes Pitt was a free man, brushing aside the apologies of the local police and assuring them that they had performed their duties excellently, and he found no fault with them.

"What the devil's going on?" Carlisle asked as they walked outside into the sun and headed in the direction of the railway station. "Vespasia called me in great agitation this morning, saying you had been charged with a double murder! You look like hell. Do you need a doctor?" There was laughter in his voice, but his eyes reflected a very real anxiety.

"A fight," Pitt explained briefly. He found walking with any grace very difficult. He had not realized at the time how bruised he was. "On the platform at the back of a railway carriage traveling at considerable speed." He told Carlisle very briefly what had happened.

Carlisle nodded. "It's a very dark situation. I don't know the whole story, but I'd be very careful what you do, Pitt. Vespasia told me to get you to her house, not Lisson Grove. In fact she advised me strongly against letting you go there at all."

Pitt was cold. The sunlit street, the clatter of traffic all seemed unreal. "What's happened to Narraway?"

"I don't know. I've heard whispers, but I don't know the truth. If anyone does, it'll be Vespasia. But I'll take you to my flat first. Clean you up a bit. You look as if you've spent the night in jail!"

Two hours later, he was washed, shaved, and dressed in a clean shirt, provided by Carlisle, as well as clean socks and underwear. Pitt alighted from the hansom cab outside Vespasia's house and walked up to the front door. She was expecting him, and he was taken straight to her favorite sitting room, which looked onto the garden. There was a bowl of fresh narcissi on the table, their scent filling the air. Outside the breeze very gently stirred the new leaves on the trees.

Vespasia was dressed in silver-gray, with the long ropes of pearls he was so accustomed to seeing her wear. She looked calm, as she always did, and her beauty still moved him with a certain awe. However, he knew her well enough to see the profound anxiety in her eyes. It alarmed him, and he was too tired to hide it.

She looked him up and down. "I see Somerset lent you a shirt and cravat," she observed with a faint smile.

"Is it so obvious?" he asked, standing in front of her.

"Of course. You would never choose a shirt of that shade, or a cravat with a touch of wine in it. But it becomes you very well. Please sit down. It is uncomfortable craning my neck to look up at you."

He would never have seated himself before she gave her permission, but he was glad to do so, in the chair opposite her. The formalities were over, and they would address the issues that burdened them both.

"Where have you been?" she asked. Her imperious tone swept aside the possibility that the answer was confidential even though she knew more about the power and danger of secrets than most ministers of government.

"In St. Malo," he replied. He was embarrassed now by his prior failure to see through the subterfuge more rapidly. However, he did not avoid her eyes as he told her about himself and Gower chasing through the streets, their brief parting, then their meeting and almost instantly finding Wrexham crouched over the corpse of West, his neck slashed open and blood covering the stones.

Vespasia winced but did not interrupt him.

He described their pursuit of Wrexham to the East End, and then the train to Southampton, and the ferry across to France. He found himself explaining too fully why they had not arrested Wrexham until it sounded miserably like excuses.

"Thomas," she interrupted gently. "Common sense justifies your actions, as seen at the time. You were aware of a socialist conspiracy, and you believed it to be more important than one grisly murder in London. What did you learn in St. Malo?"

"Very little," he replied. "We saw one or two known socialist agitators in the first couple of days . . . at least I think we did."

"You think?" she questioned.

He explained to her that it was Gower who had made the identification, and he had accepted it.

"I see. Who did he say they were?"

He was about to say that she would not know their names, then remembered her own radical part in the revolutions of 1848 that had swept across every country in Western Europe, except Britain. She had been in Italy, manning the barricades for that brief moment of hope in a new freedom. It was possible she had not lost all interest. "Jacob Meister and Pieter Linsky," he replied. "But they didn't come back again."

She frowned. Pitt noticed how she tensed her shoulders involuntarily, the way her hands in her lap gripped each other.

"You know of them?" he concluded.

"Of course," she said drily. "And many others. They are dangerous, Thomas. There is a new radicalism awakening in Europe. The next insurrections will not be like '48. They will be of a different breed. There will be more violence; I think perhaps it will be much more. The Russian monarchy cannot last a much longer in its current state. The oppression is fearful. I have a few friends left who are able to write occasionally, old friends, who tell me the truth. There is desperate poverty. The tsar has lost all sense of reality and is totally out of touch with his people — as are all his ministers and advisers. The gulf between the obscenely rich and the starving is so great it will eventually swallow them all. The only question is when."

The thought was chilling, but he did not argue, or even question it.

"And I am afraid the news is not good here," Vespasia continued. "But you already know something of it."

"Only that Narraway is out of Lisson Grove," he replied. "I have no idea why, or what happened."

"I know why." She sighed, and he saw the sadness in her eyes. She looked pale and tired. "He has been charged with the embezzlement of a considerable amount of money, which —"

"What?" It was absurd. Ordinarily he would not have dreamed of interrupting her — it was a breach of courtesy unimaginable to him — but Pitt's disbelief was too urgent to be stifled.

A flicker of amusement sparkled in her eyes, and vanished as quickly. "I am aware of the absurdity, Thomas. Victor has several faults, but petty theft is not among them."

"You said a large amount."

"Large to steal. It cost a man's life because he did not have it. Someone engineered this very astutely. I have my ideas as to who it may have been, but they are no more than ideas, insubstantial, and quite possibly mistaken."

"Where is Narraway?" he demanded.

"In Ireland," she told him.

"Why Ireland?" he asked.

"Because he believes that whoever was the author of his misfortune is Irish, and that the culprit is to be found there." She bit her lip very slightly. It was a gesture of anxiety so deep, he could not recall having seen her do it before.

"Aunt Vespasia?" He leaned forward a little.

"He believed it personal," she continued. "An act of revenge for an old injury. At the time I thought he might have been correct, although it was a long time to wait for such perceived justice, and the Irish have never been noted for their patience, especially for revenge. I assumed some new circumstance must have made it possible . . ."

"You said *assumed* — were you wrong?" he asked.

"After what you have told me of your experience in France, and of this man Gower, who was your assistant, and of whom neither you nor anyone else in Special Branch appeared to have any suspicions, I think Victor was mistaken," she said gravely. "I fear it may have had nothing to do with personal revenge, but have been a means of removing him from command of the situation in London, and replacing him with someone either of far less competence or — very much worse — of sympathy with the socialist cause. It looks as if you were removed to France for the same reason."

He smiled with a bitter humor. "I am not of Narraway's experience or power," he told her honestly. "I am not worth their trouble to remove."

"You are too modest, my dear." She regarded him with amused affection. "Surely you would have fought for Victor. Even if you were not as fond of him as I believe you to be, you would do it out of loyalty. He took you into Special Branch when the Metropolitan Police dismissed you, and you had too many enemies to return there. He took some risk doing so, and made more enemies of his own. Most of those men are gone now, but at the time it was a dangerous act. You have more than repaid him with your ability, but you can now repay the courage. I do not imagine you think differently."

Her eyes were steady on his. "Added to which, you have enemies in Special Branch yourself, because of the favor he showed you, and your somewhat rapid rise. With Victor gone, you will be very fortunate indeed if you survive him for long. Even if you do, you will be forever watching over your shoulder and waiting for the unseen blow. If you do not know that, you are far more naïve than I think you."

"My loyalty to Narraway would have been enough, to bring me to his aid," he told her. "But yes, of course I am aware that without his protection I won't last long."

Her voice was very gentle. "My dear, it is imperative, for many reasons, that we do what we can to clear Victor's name. I am glad you see it so clearly."

He felt a sudden chill, a warning.

She inclined her head in assent. "Then you will understand why Charlotte has gone to Ireland with Victor to help him in any way she can. He will find it hard enough on his own. She may be his eyes and ears in places he is unable to go himself."

For a moment he did not even understand, as if her words were half in a foreign language. The key words were plain enough — *Charlotte, Narraway,* and *Ireland* — but the whole of it made no sense.

"Charlotte's gone to Ireland?" he repeated. "She can't have! What on earth could she do? She doesn't know Ireland, and she certainly doesn't know anything about Narraway's past, his old cases, or anyone else in Special Branch." He hesitated to tell her she had misunderstood. It would sound so rude, but it was the only explanation.

"Thomas," Vespasia said gravely. "The situation is very serious. Victor is helpless. He is closed out of his office and all access to any assistance from Special Branch. We know that at least one person there, highly placed, is a thief and a traitor. We do not know who it is. Charles Austwick is in charge . . ."

"Austwick?"

"Yes. You see how serious it is? Do you imagine that without your help he will find the traitor? Apparently none of you, including Victor, were aware of Gower's treason. Who else would betray you? Charlotte is at least in part aware of the danger, including the danger to you personally. She went with Victor partly out of loyalty to him, but mostly to save his career because she is very sharply aware that yours depends upon it also. And another element that you may not yet have had time to consider: If Victor can be made to appear guilty of theft, how difficult would it be for the same people to make you appear guilty with him?"

It was a nightmare again: frightening, irrational. Pitt was exhausted, aching with the pain of disillusion and the horror of his own violence. His body was bruised and so tired he could sleep sitting in this comfortable chair, if only he could relax long enough. And yet fear knotted the muscles in his back, his shoulders, and his neck, and his head throbbed. This last piece of news made the situation immeasurably worse. He struggled to make sense of it.

"Where is she? Is she safe . . . ?" *Safe* was a stupid word to use if she was in Ireland with Narraway.

"Thomas, Victor is out there with her. He won't let any harm come to her if he can prevent it," Vespasia said softly.

Pitt knew Narraway was in love with her, but he did not want to hear it. "If he cared, he wouldn't have . . . ," he began.

"Allowed her to go?" she finished for him. "Thomas, she has gone in order to honor her friendship and loyalty, and above all to protect her husband's career, and therefore the family's means of survival. What do you imagine he could have said or done that would have stopped her?"

"Not told her he was going in the first place!" he snapped.

"Really?" She raised her silver eyebrows. "And left her wondering why you did not come home after chasing your informant through the streets? Not that night, or the entire following week? She might have gone to Lisson Grove and asked, by which time she would be frantic with fear. And she would have been met with the news that Narraway was gone and you were nowhere to be found, and there was no one in Lisson Grove to help or support you. Do you feel that would have been preferable?"

"No . . ." He felt foolish — panicky. What should he do? He wanted to go immediately to Ireland and make sure Charlotte was safe, but even an instant's reflection told him that it was an irresponsible, hotheaded thing even to think of. By reacting thoughtlessly, he would likely be playing directly into the hands of his enemies.

"I'll go home and see Daniel and Jemima," he said more calmly. "If they have had a week of Mrs. Waterman, they may be feeling pretty desperate. She is not an easy woman. I must speak to Charlotte about that, when she gets home."

"You don't need to concern yourself —" Vespasia began.

"You don't know the woman — " he started.

"She is irrelevant," Vespasia told him. "She left."

"What? Then . . ."

Vespasia raised her hand. "That is the other thing I was going to tell you. She has been replaced by a new maid, on the recommendation of Gracie. She seems a very competent girl, and Gracie looks in on them every day. Her reports of this new girl are glowing. In fact I must say that I rather like the sound of young Minnie Maude. She has character."

Pitt was dizzy. Everything seemed to be shifting. The moment he looked at it, it changed, as if someone had struck the kaleidoscope and all the pieces had shattered and re-formed in a different pattern.

"Minnie Maude?" he said stumblingly. "For God's sake, how old is she?" To him, Gracie herself was little more than a child, despite the fact that he had known her since she was thirteen.

"About twenty," Vespasia replied. "Gracie has known her since she was eight. She has courage and sense. There is nothing to concern yourself about, Thomas. As I said — I have been there myself, and everything was satisfactory. Perhaps just as important, both Daniel and Jemima like her. Do you imagine I would allow the situation to remain if that were not so?"

Now he felt clumsy and deeply ungracious. He knew an apology was appropriate; his fear had made him foolish and rude. "Of course not. I'm sorry. I . . ." He hunted for words.

She smiled. It was a sudden, beautiful gesture that lit her face and restored everything of the beauty that had made her famous. "I would think less of you were you to take it for granted," she said. "Now, before you leave, would you like tea? And are you hungry? If you are I shall have whatever you care for prepared. In the meantime we need to discuss what is to be done next. It is now up to you to address the real issue behind all this ploy and counterploy by whoever is the traitor at Lisson Grove."

Her words were sobering. How like Vespasia to discuss the fate of revolution, murder, and treason in high places over tea and a plate of sandwiches in the withdrawing room. It restored a certain sanity to the world. At least something was as it should be. He drew in a deep breath and let it out slowly, steadying himself.

"Thank you. I should very much like a good cup of tea. The prison in Shoreham had only the most moderate amenities. And a sandwich would be excellent."

Pitt arrived home at Keppel Street in the early afternoon. Both Daniel and Jemima were still at school. He knocked on the door, rather than use his key and startle this Minnie Maude in whom Vespasia seemed to have so much confidence.

He stood on the step shifting his weight from one foot to the other, his mind racing over what changes he might find: what small things uncared for, changed so it was no longer the home he was used to, and which he realized he loved fiercely, exactly as it was. Except, of course, Charlotte should be there. Without her nothing was more than a shell.

The door opened and a young woman stood just inside, her expression guarded.

"Yes, sir." She said it politely, but stood squarely blocking the way in. "Can I 'elp yer?" She was not pretty but she had beautiful hair: thick and curling and of a rich, bright color. And she had the freckles on her face that so often went with such vividness. She was far taller than Gracie and slender; however, she had the same direct, almost defiant gaze.

"Are you Minnie Maude?" he asked.

"Beggin' yer pardon, sir, but that in't yer

business," she replied. "If yer want the master, yer gimme a card, an' I'll ask 'im to call on yer."

He could not help smiling. "I'll give you a card, by all means." He fished for one in his pocket and passed it to her, then wondered if she could read. He had become used to Gracie reading, since Charlotte had taught her.

Minnie Maude looked at the card, then up at him, then at the card again.

He smiled at her.

The blush spread up her cheeks in a hot tide. "I'm sorry, sir." She stumbled over the words. "I din't know yer."

"Don't be sorry," he said quickly. "You shouldn't allow anyone in unless you know who they are, and not just because they say so."

She stood back, allowing him to pass. He went into the familiar hallway, and immediately smelled the lavender floor polish. The hall mirror was clean, the surfaces free of dust. Jemima's shoes were placed neatly side by side under the coat stand.

He walked down to the kitchen and looked around. Everything was as it should be: blue-and-white-ringed plates on the Welsh dresser, copper pans on the wall, kitchen table scrubbed, the stove burning warm but not overhot. He could smell newly baked bread and the clean, comfortable aroma of fresh laundry hanging from the airing rail up near the ceiling. He was home again. There was nothing wrong, except that his family was not there. But he knew where Charlotte was, and the children were at school.

"Would you like a cup o' tea, sir?" Minnie Maude asked in an uncertain voice.

He did not really need one so soon after leaving Vespasia's, but he felt she would like to do something familiar and useful.

"Thank you," he accepted. He had been obliged to buy several necessities for the days he had been in France, including the case in which he now carried them. "I have a little laundry in my bag, but I don't know whether I shall be home for dinner or not. I'm sorry. If I am, something cold to eat will do very well."

"Yes, sir. Would you like some cold mutton an' 'ot bubble and squeak? That's wot Daniel an' Jemima'll be 'avin', as it's wot they like. 'Ceptin' they like eggs wif it."

"Eggs will be excellent, thank you." He meant it. Eggs sounded familiar, comfortable, and very good.

Vespasia had warned Pitt not to go to Lisson Grove, but he had no choice; he could do nothing to help Narraway and Charlotte, without information held there.

Of course there was the question of explaining what had happened to Gower. Pitt had no idea how badly he had been disfigured by the fall from the train, but every effort would be made to identify him. Indeed, by the time Pitt reached Lisson Grove he might find that it had already been done.

What should his story be? How much of the truth could he tell without losing every advantage of surprise that he had? He did not know who his enemies were, but they certainly knew him. His instinct was to affect as much ignorance as possible. The less they considered him a worthwhile opponent, the less likely they'd be to eliminate him. Feigning ignorance would be a manner of camouflage, at least for a while.

He should be open and honest about the attack on the train. It was a matter of record with the police. But it would be easy enough, highly believable in fact, to claim that he had no idea who the man was. Remove every thought that it was personal.

He had last seen Gower in St. Malo, when they agreed that Pitt should come home to see what Lisson Grove knew of any conspiracy, and Gower should remain in France and watch Frobisher and Wrexham, and anyone else of interest. Naturally he would know nothing of Narraway's disgrace, and be thoroughly shocked.

He arrived just before four o'clock. He went in through the door, past the man on duty just inside, and asked to see Narraway.

He was told to wait, as he had expected, but it was a surprisingly short time before Charles Austwick himself came down and conducted Pitt up to what used to be Narraway's office. Pitt noticed immediately that all signs of Narraway were gone: his pictures, the photograph of his mother that used to sit on top of the bookcase, the few personal books of poetry and memoirs, the engraved brass bowl from his time in North Africa.

Pitt stared at Austwick, allowing his sense of loss to show in his face, hoping Austwick would see it as confusion.

"Sit down, Pitt." Austwick waved him to the chair opposite the desk. "Of course you're wondering what the devil's going on. I'm afraid I have some shocking news for you."

Pitt forced himself to look alarmed, as if his imagination were racing. "Something has happened to Mr. Narraway? Is he hurt? Ill?"

"I'm afraid in some ways it is worse than that," Austwick said somberly. "Narraway appears to have stolen a rather large amount of money, and — when faced with the crime — he disappeared. We don't know where he is. Obviously he has been dismissed from the service, and at least for the time being I have replaced him. I am sure that is temporary, but until further notice you will report to me. I'm sorry. It must be a great blow to you, indeed it is to all of us. I don't think anyone imagined that Narraway, of all people, would give in to that kind of temptation."

Pitt's mind raced. How should he respond? He had thought it was all worked out in his mind, but sitting here in Narraway's office, subtly but so completely changed, he was uncertain again. Was Austwick the traitor? If so then he was a far cleverer man than Pitt had thought. But Pitt had had no idea that there was a traitor at all, and he had trusted Gower. What was his judgment worth?

"I can see that you're stunned," Austwick said patiently. "We've had a little while to get used to the idea. We knew almost as soon as you had gone. By the way, where is Gower?"

Pitt inhaled deeply, and plunged in. "I left

him in France, in St. Malo," he replied. He watched Austwick's face as closely as he dared, trying to read in his eyes, his gestures, if he knew that that was only half true.

Austwick spoke slowly, as if he also was measuring what he said, and he seemed to be watching Pitt just as closely. Had he noticed Somerset Carlisle's beautifully cut shirt? Or his wine-colored cravat?

Pitt repeated exactly what he believed had happened at the time he had first notified Narraway that he had to remain in France.

Austwick listened attentively. His expression did not betray whether he knew anything further or not.

"I see," he said at last, drumming his fingers silently on the desktop. "So you left Gower there in the hope that there might yet be something worthwhile to observe?"

"Yes . . . sir." He added the *sir* with difficulty. There was a slowly mounting rage inside him that this man was sitting there in Narraway's chair, behind his desk. Was he also a pawn in this game, or was he the one playing it with the opposing pieces?

"Do you think that is likely?" Austwick asked. "You say you saw nothing after that first sighting of . . . who did you say? Meister and Linsky, was it?"

"Yes," Pitt agreed. "There were plenty of

people coming and going all the time, but neither of us recognized anyone else. It's possible that was coincidence. On the other hand, West was murdered, and the man who killed him, very brutally and openly, fled to that house. There has to be a reason for that."

Austwick appeared to consider it for several moments. Finally he looked up, his lips pursed. "You're right. There is certainly something happening, and there is a good chance it concerns violence that may affect us here in England, even if it begins in France. We have our allies to consider, and what our failure to warn them may do to our relationship. I would certainly feel a distinct sense of betrayal if they were to have wind of such a threat against us, and keep silent about it."

"Yes, sir," Pitt agreed, although the words all but stuck in his throat. He rose to his feet. "If you'll excuse me, I have several matters to attend to."

"Yes, of course," Austwick agreed. He seemed calm, even assured. Pitt found himself shaking with anger as he left the room, making an effort to close the door softly.

That evening he went to see the minister,

Sir Gerald Croxdale. Croxdale himself had suggested that he come to the house. If the matter were as private and as urgent as Pitt had said, then it would be better if their meeting were not observed by others.

Croxdale's home in Hampstead was old and very handsome, overlooking the heath. The garden trees were coming into leaf, and the air seemed to be full of birdsong.

Pitt was shown in by the butler. He found Croxdale standing in his library, which had long windows onto the lawn at the back of the house. At present the curtains were open; the evening sky beyond was pale with the last light. Croxdale turned from gazing at it as Pitt came in. He offered his hand.

"Miserable time," he said sympathetically. "Pretty bad shock to all of us. I've known Narraway for years. Difficult man, not really a team player, but brilliant, and I'd always thought he was sound. But it seems as if a man can never entirely leave his past behind." He gestured to one of the armchairs beside the fire. "Do sit down. Tell me what happened in St. Malo. By the way, have you had any dinner?"

Pitt realized with surprise that he had not. He had not even thought of eating, and his body was clenched with anxiety as different possibilities poured through his mind. Now he was fumbling for a gracious answer.

"Sandwich?" Croxdale offered. "Roast beef acceptable?"

Experience told Pitt it was better to eat than try to think rationally on an empty stomach. "Thank you, sir."

Croxdale rang the bell, and when the butler appeared again he requested roast beef sandwiches and whiskey.

"Now." He sat back as soon as the door was closed. "Tell me about St. Malo."

Pitt offered him the same edited version he had given Austwick. He was not yet ready to tell anyone the whole truth. Croxdale had known Victor Narraway far longer than he had known Pitt. If he would believe that Narraway had stolen money, why should he think any better of Pitt, who was Narraway's protégé and closest ally?

The butler brought the sandwiches, which were excellent. Pitt took an unaccustomed glass of whiskey with it, but declined a second. To have the fire inside him was good, his heart beating a little faster. However, to be fuzzy-headed could be disastrous.

Croxdale considered in silence for some time before he replied. Pitt waited him out.

"I am certain you have done the right thing," Croxdale said at length. "The situation requires very careful watching, but at this point we cannot afford your absence from Lisson Grove. This fearful business with Narraway has changed all our priorities."

Pitt was aware that Croxdale was watching him far more closely than at a glance it might seem. He tried to keep his expression respectful, concerned, but not as if he were already aware of the details.

Croxdale sighed. "I imagine it comes as a shock to you, as it does to me. Perhaps we should all have seen some warning, but I admit I did not. Of course we are aware of people's financial interests — we would be remiss not to be. Narraway has no urgent need of money, as far as we know. This whole business with O'Neil is of long standing, some twenty years or more." He looked closely at Pitt, his brows drawn together. "Did he tell you anything about it?"

"No, sir."

"Old case. All very ugly, but I thought it was over at the time. We all did. Very briefly, Narraway was in charge of the Irish situation, and we knew there was serious trouble brewing. As indeed there was. He foiled it so successfully that there was never any major news about it. Only afterward did we learn what the price had been."

Pitt did not need to pretend his ignorance,

or the growing fear inside him, chilling his body.

Croxdale shook his head minutely, his face clouded with unhappiness. "Narraway used one of their own against them, a woman named Kate O'Neil. The details I don't know, and I prefer to be able to claim ignorance. The end of it was that the woman's husband killed her, rather messily, and was tried and hanged for it."

Pitt was stunned. Was Narraway really as ruthless as that story implied? He pictured Narraway's face in all the circumstances they had known each other through: success and failure; exhaustion, fear, disappointment; the conclusion of dozens of battles, won or lost. Reading Narraway defied reason: It was instinct, the trust that had grown up over time in all sorts of ways. It took him a painful and uncertain effort to conceal his feelings. He tried to look confused.

"If all this happened twenty years ago, what is it that has changed now?" he asked.

Croxdale was only momentarily taken aback. "We don't know," he replied. "Presumably something in O'Neil's own situation."

"I thought you said he was hanged?"

"Oh yes, the husband was; that was Sean

O'Neil. But his brother Cormac is still very much alive. They were unusually close, even for an Irish family," Croxdale explained.

"Then why did Cormac wait twenty years for his revenge? I assume you are saying that Narraway took the money in some way because of O'Neil?"

Croxdale hesitated, then looked at Pitt guardedly. "You know, I have no idea. Clearly we need to know a good deal more than we do at present. I assume it is to do with O'Neil because Narraway went almost immediately to Ireland."

This question nagged at Pitt, but Croxdale cleared his throat and continued on, once again in his usual tones of assuredness.

"This regrettable defection of Narraway's has astounded us all, but at the same time, we must keep sight of the greater threat: the ominous socialist activity cropping up. There seem to be plots on all sides. I'm sure what you and Gower were witness to is part of some larger and possibly very dangerous plan. The socialist tide has been rising for some time in Europe, as we are all aware. I can no longer have Narraway in charge, obviously. I need the very best I can find, a man I can trust morally and intellectually, whose loyalty is beyond question and who has no ghosts from the past to sabotage our present attempts to safeguard our country, and all it stands for."

Pitt blinked. "Of course." Did that mean that Croxdale knew Austwick was the traitor? Pitt had been avoiding the issue, waiting, judging pointlessly. It was a relief. Croxdale was clever, more reliable than he had thought. Then how could he think such things of Narraway?

But what was Pitt's judgment to rely on? He had trusted Gower!

Croxdale was still looking at him intently.

Pitt could think of nothing to say.

"We need a man who knows what Narraway was doing and can pick up the reins he dropped," Croxdale said. "You are the only man who fits that description, Pitt. It's a great deal to ask of you, but there is no one else, and your skills and integrity are things about which I believe Narraway was both right and honest."

"But . . . Austwick . . . ," Pitt stammered. "He . . ."

"Is a good stopgap," Croxdale said coolly. "He is not the man for the job in such dangerous times as these. Frankly, he has not the ability to lead, or to make the difficult decisions of such magnitude. He was a good enough lieutenant."

Pitt's head swam. He had none of his

predecessor's nerve, confidence, political savvy, or decision-making experience.

"Neither have I the skills," he protested. "And I haven't been in the service long enough for the other men to have confidence in me. I will support Austwick as best I can, but I haven't the abilities to take on the leadership."

Croxdale smiled. "I thought you would be modest. It is a good quality. Arrogance leads to mistakes. I'm sure you will seek advice, and take it — at least most of the time. But you have never lacked judgment before, or the courage to go with your own beliefs. I know your record, Pitt. Do you imagine you have gone unnoticed in the past?" He asked it gently, as if with a certain degree of amusement.

"I imagine not," Pitt conceded. "You will know a good deal about anyone, before taking them into the service at all. But —"

"Not in your case," Croxdale contradicted him. "You were Narraway's recruit. But I have made it my business to learn far more about you since then. Your country needs you now, Pitt. Narraway has effectively betrayed our trust and has likely fled the country. You were Narraway's second in command. This is your duty as well as your privilege to serve." He held out his hand.

Pitt was overwhelmed, not with pleasure or any sense of honor, but with great concern for Narraway, fear for Charlotte, and the knowledge that he did not want this weight of command. It was not in his nature to act with certainty when the balance of judgment was so gray, and the stakes were the lives of other men.

"We look to you, Pitt," Croxdale said again. "Don't fail your country, man!"

"No, sir," Pitt said unhappily. "I will do everything I can, sir . . ."

"Good." Croxdale smiled. "I knew you would. That is one thing Narraway was right about. I will inform the necessary people, including the prime minister, of course. Thank you, Pitt. We are grateful to you."

Pitt accepted: He had little choice. Croxdale began to outline to him exactly what his task would be, his powers, and the rewards.

It was midnight when Pitt walked outside into the lamplit night and found Croxdale's own carriage waiting to take him home.

CHAPTER 9

Charlotte walked away from Cormac O'Neil's home with as much composure as she could muster, but she had the sinking fear inside her that she looked as afraid and bewildered as she felt, and as helplessly angry. Whatever else Narraway might have been guilty of — and it could have been a great deal — she was certain that he had not killed Cormac O'Neil. She had arrived at the house almost on his heels. She had heard the dog begin to bark as Narraway went into the house, and continue more and more hysterically, knowing there was an intruder, and perhaps already aware of O'Neil's death.

Had Cormac cried out? Had he even seen his killer, or had he been shot in the back? She had not heard a gun fire, only the dog barking. That was it, of course! The dog had barked at Narraway, but not at whoever had fired the shot.

She stopped in the street, standing rooted to the spot as the realization shook her with its meaning. Narraway could not possibly have shot Cormac. Her certainty was not built on her belief in him but on evidence: facts that were not capable of any other reasonable interpretation. She turned on her heel and stepped out urgently, striding across the street back toward O'Neil's house, then stopped again just as suddenly. Why should they believe her? She knew that what she said was true, but would anyone else substantiate it?

Of course not! Talulla would contradict it because she hated Narraway. With hindsight, that had been perfectly clear, and predictable. She would be only too delighted if he were hanged for Cormac's murder. To her it would be justice — the sweeter now after the long delay. She must know he was not guilty because she had been close enough to have heard the dog start to bark herself, but she would be the last person to say so.

Narraway would know that. She remembered his face as he allowed the police to handcuff him. He had looked at Charlotte only once, concentrating everything he had to say in that one glance. He needed her to understand.

He also needed her to keep a very calm

361

mind and to think: to work it out detail by detail and not act before she was certain — not only of the truth, but that she could prove it so it could not be ignored. It is very difficult indeed to make people believe what is against all their emotions: the conviction of friend and enemy years-deep, paid for in blood and loss.

She was still standing on the pavement. A small crowd had gathered because of the violence and the police just over a hundred yards away. They were staring, wondering what was the matter with her.

She swallowed, straightened her skirt, then turned yet again and walked back toward where she judged to be the best place to find a carriage to take her to Molesworth Street. There were many practical considerations to weigh very carefully. She was completely alone now. There was no one at all she could trust. She must consider whether to remain at Mrs. Hogan's or if it would be safer to move somewhere else where she would be less exposed. Everyone knew she was Narraway's sister.

But where else could she go? How long would it take anyone to find her again in a town the size of Dublin? She was a stranger, an Englishwoman, on her own. She knew no one except those Narraway had introduced her to. A couple of hours' inquiries would find her again, and she would merely look ridiculous, and evasive, as if she had something of which to be ashamed.

She was walking briskly along the pavement, trying to appear to know precisely where she was going and to what purpose. The former was true. There was a carriage ahead of her setting down a fare, and she could hire it if she was quick enough. She reached the carriage just as it began to move.

"Sir!" she called out. "Will you be good enough to take me to Molesworth Street?"

"Sure, an' I'll be happy to," the driver responded, completing his turn and pulling the horse up.

She thanked him and climbed up into the carriage, feeling intensely grateful as the wheels rumbled over the cobbles and they picked up speed. She did not turn to look behind her; she could picture the scene just as clearly as if she were gazing upon it. Narraway should still be in the house, manacled like any other dangerous criminal. He must feel desperately alone. Was he frightened? Certainly he would never show any such weakness.

She told herself abruptly to stop being so useless and self-indulgent. Pitt was somewhere in France with nobody else to rely on, believing Narraway was still at Lisson Grove. Not even in his nightmares would he suppose Narraway could be in Ireland under arrest for murder, and Lisson Grove in the hands of traitors. Whatever she felt was irrelevant. The only task ahead was to rescue Narraway, and to do that she must find the truth and prove it.

Talulla Lawless knew who had killed Cormac because it had to be someone the dog would not bark at: therefore someone who had a right to be in Cormac's home. The clearest answer was Talulla herself. Cormac lived alone; he had said so the previous evening when Charlotte had asked him. No doubt a local woman would come in every so often and clean for him, and do the laundry.

Why would Talulla kill him? He was her uncle. But then how often was murder a family matter? She knew from Pitt's cases in the past, very much too often. The next most likely answer would be a robbery, but any thief breaking in would have set the dog into a frenzy.

Still, why would Talulla kill him, and why now? Not purely to blame Narraway, surely? How could she even know that he would be there to be blamed?

The answer to that was obvious: It must have been she who had sent the letter luring Narraway to Cormac's house. She of all people would be able to imitate his hand. Narraway might recall it from twenty years ago, but not in such minute detail that he would recognize a good forgery.

That still left the question as to why she had chosen to do it now. Cormac was her uncle; they were the only two still alive from the tragedy of twenty years ago. Cormac had no children, and her parents were dead. Surely both of them believed Narraway responsible for that? Why would she kill Cormac?

Was Narraway on the brink of finding out something Talulla could not afford him to know?

That made incomplete sense. If it were true, then surely the obvious thing would be to have killed Narraway?

She recalled the look on Talulla's face as she had seen Narraway standing near Cormac's body. She had been almost hysterical. She might have a great ability to act, but surely not great enough to effect the sweat on her lip and brow, the wildness in her eyes, the catch in her voice as it soared out of control? And yet never once had she looked at Cormac's body — perhaps she already knew exactly what she would see? She had not gone to him even to assure herself that he was beyond help. There had been nothing in her face but hate — no grief, no denial.

Charlotte was oblivious to the handsome streets of Dublin as the carriage drove on. It could have been any city on earth, so absorbed was she in thought. She was startled by a spatter of cold rain through the open window that wet her face and shoulder.

How much of this whole thing was Talulla responsible for? What about the issue of Mulhare and the embezzled money? She could not possibly have arranged that.

Or was someone in Lisson Grove using Irish passion and loyalties to further their own need to remove Narraway? Whom could she ask? Were any of Narraway's supposed friends actually willing to help him? Or had he wounded or betrayed them all at one time or another, so that when it came to it they would take their revenge? He was totally vulnerable now. Could it be that at last they had stopped quarreling with one another long enough to conspire to ruin him?

Perhaps Charlotte had no right to judge Narraway's Irish enemies. What would she have felt, or done, were it all the other way around: if Ireland were the foreigner, the occupier in England? If someone had used and betrayed her family, would she be so loyal to her beliefs in honesty or impartial justice? Perhaps — but perhaps not. It was impossible to know without one's having lived that terrible reality.

Yet Narraway was innocent of killing Cormac — and she realized as she said this to herself that she thought he was no more than partially responsible for the downfall of Kate O'Neil. The O'Neils had tried to use him, turn him to betray his country. They might well be furious that they had failed, but had they the right to exact vengeance for losing?

She needed to ask help from someone, because alone she might as well simply give up and go back to London, leaving Narraway to his fate, and eventually Pitt to his. Before she reached Molesworth Street and even attempted to explain the situation to Mrs. Hogan, which she must do, she had decided to ask Fiachra McDaid for help.

"What?" McDaid said incredulously when she found him at his home and told him what had happened.

"I'm sorry." She gulped and tried to

regain her composure. She had thought herself in perfect control, and realized she was much farther from it than she'd imagined. "We went to see Cormac O'Neil. At least Victor said he was going alone, but I followed him, just behind . . ."

"You mean you found a carriage able to keep up with him in Dublin traffic?" Mc-Daid frowned.

"No, no I knew where he was going. I had been there the evening before myself . . ."

"To see O'Neil?" He looked incredulous.

"Yes. Please . . . listen." Her voice was rising again, and she made an effort to calm it. "I arrived moments after he did. I heard the dog begin to bark as he went in, but no shot!"

"It would bark." The frown deepened on his brow. "It barks for anyone except Cormac, or perhaps Talulla. She lives close by and looks after it if Cormac is away, which he is from time to time."

"Not the cleaning woman?" she said quickly.

"No. She's afraid of it." He looked at her more closely, his face earnest. "Why? What does it matter?"

She hesitated, still uncertain how far to trust him. It was the only evidence she had that protected Narraway. Perhaps she should keep it to herself.

"I suppose it doesn't," she said, deliberately looking confused. Then, as coherently as she could, but missing out any further reference to the dog, she told him what had happened. As she did, she watched his face, trying to read the emotions in it, the belief or disbelief, the confusion or understanding, the loss or triumph.

He listened without interrupting her. "They think Narraway shot Cormac? Why would he, for God's sake?"

"In revenge for Cormac having ruined him in London," she answered. "That's what Talulla said. It makes a kind of sense."

"Do you think that's what happened?" he asked.

She nearly said that she knew it was not, then realized her mistake just in time. "No." She spoke guardedly now. "I was just behind him, and I didn't hear a shot. But I don't think he would do that anyway. It doesn't make sense."

He shook his head. "Yes it does. Victor loved that job of his. In a way it was all he had." He looked conflicted, emotions twisting his features. "I'm sorry. I don't mean to imply that you are not important to him, but I think from what he said that you do not see each other so often."

369

Now she was angry. She felt it well up inside her, knotting her stomach, making her hands shake, her voice thick as if she were a little drunk. "No. We don't. But you've known Victor for years. Was he ever a fool?"

"No, never. Many things good and bad, but never a fool," he admitted.

"Did he ever act against his own interest, hotheadedly, all feelings and no thought?" She could not imagine it, not the man she knew. Had he once had that kind of runaway passion? Was his supreme control a mask?

McDaid laughed abruptly, without joy. "No. He never forgot his cause. Hell or heaven could dance naked past him and he would not be diverted. Why?"

"Because if he really thought Cormac O'Neil was responsible for ruining him in London, for setting up what looked like embezzlement and seeing that he was blamed, the last thing he would want was Cormac dead," she answered. "He would want Cormac's full confession, the proof, the names of those who aided —"

"I see," he interrupted. "I see. You're right. Victor would never put revenge ahead of getting his job and his honor back."

"So someone else killed Cormac and made it look like Victor," she concluded.

"That would be their revenge, wouldn't it." It was a statement, not a question.

"Yes," he agreed, his eyes bright, his hands loosely beside him.

"Will you help me find out who?" she asked.

He gestured to one of the big leather chairs in his gracious but very masculine sitting room. She imagined wealthy gentlemen's clubs must be like this inside: worn and comfortable upholstery, lots of wood paneling, brass ornaments — except these were silver, and uniquely Celtic.

She sat down obediently.

He sat opposite her, leaning forward a little. "Have you any idea who already?"

Her mind raced. How should she answer, how much of the truth? Could he help at all if she lied to him?

"I have lots of ideas, but they don't add up," she replied, hoping to conceal her knowledge of the facts. "I know who hated Victor, but I don't know who hated Cormac."

A moment of humor touched his face, and then vanished. It looked like self-mockery.

"I don't expect you to know," she said quietly. "Or you would have warned him. But perhaps with hindsight you might understand something now. Talulla is Scan

371

and Kate's daughter, brought up away from Dublin after her parents' deaths." She saw instantly in his eyes that he had known that.

"She is, poor child," he agreed.

"You didn't warn Victor of that, did you?" It sounded more like an accusation than she had intended it to.

McDaid looked down for a moment, then back up at her. "No. I thought she had suffered enough."

"Another one of your innocent casualties," she observed, remembering what he had said during their carriage ride in the dark. Something in that had disturbed her, a resignation she could not share. All casualties still upset her; but then her country was not at war, not occupied by another people.

"I don't make judgments as to who is innocent and who guilty, Mrs. Pitt, just what is necessary, and that only when I have no choice."

"Talulla was a child!"

"Children grow up."

Did he know, or guess, whether Talulla had killed Cormac? She looked at him steadily and found herself a little afraid. The intelligence in him was overwhelming, rich with understanding of terrible irony. And it was not himself he was mocking: it was her, and her naïveté. She was quite certain of that now. He was a thought, a word ahead of her all the time. She had already said too much, and he knew perfectly well that she was sure Talulla had shot Cormac.

"Into what?" she said aloud. "Into a woman who would shoot her uncle's head to pieces in order to be revenged on the man she thinks betrayed her mother?"

That surprised him, just for an instant. Then he covered it. "Of course she thinks that," he replied. "She can hardly face thinking that Kate went with him willingly. In fact if he'd asked her, maybe she would have gone to England with him. Who knows?"

"Do you?" she said immediately.

"I?" His eyebrows rose. "I have no idea."

"Is that why Sean killed her, really?"

"Again, I have no idea."

She did not know whether to believe him or not. He had been charming to her, generous with his time and excellent company, but behind the smiling façade he was a complete stranger. She had no idea what was going on in his thoughts.

"More incidental damage," she said aloud. "Kate, Sean, Talulla, now Cormac. Incidental to what, Mr. McDaid? Ireland's freedom?"

"Could we have a better cause, Mrs. Pitt?" he said gently. "Surely Talulla can be understood for wanting that? Hasn't she paid enough?"

But it didn't make sense, not completely. Who had moved the money meant for Mulhare back into Narraway's account? Was that done simply in order to lure him to Ireland for this revenge? Wouldn't Talulla's rage have been satisfied by killing Narraway herself? Why on earth make poor Cormac the sacrifice? If she wanted Narraway to suffer, she could have shot him somewhere uniquely painful, so he would be disabled, mutilated, die slowly. There were plenty of possibilities.

And why now? There had to be a reason.

McDaid was still watching her, waiting.

"Yes, I imagine she has paid enough," she said, answering his question. "And Cormac? Hasn't he too?"

"Ah yes . . . poor Cormac," McDaid said softly. "He loved Kate, you know. That's why he could never forgive Narraway. She cared for Cormac, but she would never have loved him . . . mostly I suppose because he was Sean's brother. Cormac was the better man, I think. Maybe in the end, Kate thought so too."

"That doesn't answer why Talulla shot him," Charlotte pointed out.

"Oh, you're right. Of course it doesn't . . ."

"Another victim of incidental damage?" she said with a touch of bitterness. "Whose freedom do you fight for at such a cost? Is that not a weight of grief to carry forever?"

His eyes flashed for a moment, then the anger was gone again. But it had been real.

"Cormac was guilty too," he said grimly.

"Of what? Surviving?" she asked.

"Yes, but more than that. He didn't do much to save Sean. He barely tried. If he'd told the truth, Sean might have been a hero, not a man who murdered his wife in a jealous rage."

"Perhaps to Cormac he *was* a man who murdered his wife in a jealous rage," she pointed out. "People react slowly sometimes when they are shattered with grief. Cormac might have been too shocked to do anything useful. What could it have been anyway? Didn't Sean himself tell the truth as to why he killed Kate?"

"He barely said anything," McDaid admitted, this time looking down at the floor, not at her.

"Stunned too," she said. "But someone told Talulla that Cormac should have saved her father, and she believed them. Easier to think of your father as a hero betrayed than as a jealous man who killed his wife in a rage because she cuckolded him with his enemy, and an Englishman at that."

McDaid looked at her with another momentary flare of anger. Then he masked it so completely she might almost have thought it was her imagination.

"It would seem so," he agreed. "But how do we prove any of that?"

She felt the coldness sweep over her. "I don't know. I'm trying to think."

"Be careful, Mrs. Pitt," he said gently. "I would not like you to be incidental damage as well."

She managed to smile just as if she did not even imagine that his words could be as much a threat as a warning. She felt as if it were a mask on his face: transparent, ghostly. "Thank you. I shall be cautious, I promise, but it is kind of you to care." She rose to her feet, vigilant not to sway. "Now I think I had better go back to my lodgings. It has been a . . . a terrible day."

When she reached Molesworth Street again, Mrs. Hogan came out to see her immediately. She looked awkward, her hands winding around each other, twisting her apron.

Charlotte addressed the subject before Mrs. Hogan could search for the words.

"You have heard about Mr. O'Neil," she said gravely. "A very terrible thing to have happened. I hope Mr. Narraway will be able to help them. He has some experience in such tragedies. But I quite understand if you would prefer that I move out of your house in the meantime. I will have to find something, of course, until I get my passage back home. I daresay it will take me a day or two. In the meantime I will pack my brother's belongings and put them in my own room, so you may let his rooms to whomsoever you wish. I believe we are paid for another couple of nights at least?" Please heaven within a couple of days she would be a great deal further on in her decisions, and at least one other person in Dublin would know for certain that Narraway was innocent.

Mrs. Hogan was embarrassed. The issue had been taken out of her hands and she did not know how to rescue it. As Charlotte had hoped, she settled for the compromise. "Thank you, that would be most considerate, ma'am."

"If you will be kind enough to lend me the keys, I'll do it straightaway." Charlotte held out her hand.

Reluctantly Mrs. Hogan passed them over.

Charlotte unlocked the door and went inside, closing it behind her. Instantly she felt intrusive. She would pack his clothes, of course, and have someone take the case to her room, unless she could drag it there herself.

But far more important than shirts, socks, personal linen, were whatever papers he might have. Had he committed anything to writing? Would it even be in a form she could understand? If only she could at least ask Pitt! She had never missed him more. But then of course if he were here, she would be at home in London, not trying desperately to carry out a task for which she was so ill suited. She was in a foreign country where she was considered the enemy, and justly so. The weight of centuries of history was against her.

She opened the case, then went to the wardrobe and took out Narraway's suits and shirts, folded them neatly, and packed them. Then, feeling as if she were prying, she opened the drawers in the chest. She took out his underwear and packed it also, making sure she had his pajamas from under the pillow on the bed. She included his extra pair of shoes, wrapped in a cloth to keep them from marking anything, and put them in as well.

She collected the toiletries, a hairbrush, a toothbrush, razor, and small clothes brush. He was an immaculate man. How he would hate being locked up in a cell with no privacy, and probably little means to wash.

The few papers there were in the top drawer of the dresser. Thank heaven they were not locked in a briefcase. But that probably indicated that they would mean nothing to anyone else.

Back in her own room, with Narraway's case propped in the corner, she looked at the few notes he had made. They were a curious reflection on his character, a side of him she had not even guessed at before. They were mostly little drawings, very small indeed, but very clever. They were little stick men, but imbued with such movement and personality that she recognized instantly who they were.

There was one little man with striped trousers and a banknote in his hat, and beside him a woman with chaotic hair. Behind him was another woman, even thinner, her limbs poking jaggedly.

Even with arms and legs merely suggested, Charlotte knew they were John and Bridget Tyrone, and that Tyrone's being a banker was important. The other woman had such a savagery about her it immediately suggested Talulla. Beside her was a question mark. There was no more than that, except a man of whom she could see only the top half, as if he was up to his arms in something. She stared at it until it came to her with a shiver of revulsion. It was Mulhare, drowning — because the money had not been paid.

The little drawing suggested a connection between John Tyrone and Talulla. He was a banker — was he the link to London? Had he the power, through his profession, to move money around from Dublin to London and, with the help of someone in Lisson Grove, to place it back in Narraway's account?

Then who in Lisson Grove? And why? No one could tell her that but Tyrone himself.

Was it dangerous, absurd, to go to him? She had no one else she could turn to, because she did not know who else was involved. Certainly she could not go back to McDaid. She was growing more and more certain within herself that his remarks about accidental damage to the innocent were statements of his philosophy, and also a warning to her.

Was Talulla the prime mover in Cormac's death, or only an instrument, used by someone else? Someone like John Tyrone, so harmless seeming, but powerful enough in Dublin and in London even to create a traitor in Lisson Grove?

There seemed to be two choices open to her: go to Tyrone himself; or give up and go home, leaving Narraway here to answer whatever charge they brought against him, presuming he lived long enough to face a trial. Would it be a fair trial, even? Possibly not. The old wounds were raw, and Special Branch would not be on his side. So Charlotte really had no choice at all.

The maid who answered the door let her in somewhat reluctantly.

"I need to speak with Mr. Tyrone," Charlotte said as soon as she was into the large, high-ceilinged hall. "It is to do with the murder of Mr. Mulhare, and now poor Mr. O'Neil. It is most urgent."

"I'll ask him, ma'am," the maid replied. "Who shall I say is calling?"

"Charlotte Pitt." She hesitated only an instant. "Victor Narraway's sister."

"Yes, ma'am." She went across the hall and knocked on a door at the far side. It opened and she spoke for a moment, then returned to Charlotte. "If you'll come with me, ma'am."

Charlotte followed her, and the maid knocked on the same door again.

"Come in." Tyrone's voice was abrupt.

The maid opened it for Charlotte to go

past her. Tyrone had obviously been working — there were papers spread across the
surface of the large desk.

He stood impatiently, making no attempt
to hide the fact that she had interrupted
him.

"I'm sorry," she began. "I know it is late
and I have come without invitation, but the
matter is urgent. Tomorrow may be impossible for me to rescue what is left of the situation."

He moved his weight from one foot to the
other. "I am very sorry for you, Mrs. Pitt,
but I have no idea how I can help. Perhaps
I should send the maid to see where my wife
is." It was offered more as an excuse than a
suggestion. "She is calling on a neighbor.
She cannot be far."

"It is you I need to see," she told him.
"And it might be more suitable for your
reputation if the maid were to remain,
although my inquiries are confidential."

"Then you should call at my place of business, within the usual hours," he pointed
out.

She gave him a brief, formal smile. "Confidential to you, Mr. Tyrone. That is why I
came here."

"I don't know what you are talking about."
It was still only a deduction from Narra-

way's drawings, but it was all she had left.

She plunged in. "The money for Mulhare that you transferred back into my brother's account in London, which was responsible for Mulhare's death, and my brother's professional ruin, Mr. Tyrone."

He might have intended to deny it, but his face gave him away. The shock drained the blood from his skin, leaving him almost gray. He drew in his breath sharply, then changed his mind and said nothing. His eyes flickered; and for an instant Charlotte wondered if he was going to call for some kind of assistance and have her thrown out. Probably no servant would attack her, but if any other of the people involved in the plan were — it would only increase her danger. McDaid had warned her.

Or did Tyrone imagine she had even had some hand in murdering Cormac O'Neil?

Now her own voice was shaking. "Mr. Tyrone, too many people have been hurt already, and I'm sure you know poor Cormac was killed this morning. It is time for this to end. I would find it easy to believe that you had no idea what tragedies would follow the transfer of that money. Nor do I find it hard to sympathize with your hatred of those who occupy a country that is rightfully yours. But by using personal murder and betrayal you win nothing. You only bring more tragedy on those you involve. If you doubt me, look at the evidence. All the O'Neils are dead now. Even the loyalty that used to bind them is destroyed. Kate and Cormac have both been murdered, and by the very ones they loved."

"Your brother killed Cormac," he said at last.

"No, he didn't. Cormac was already dead by the time we got there."

He was startled. "We? You went with him?"

"Just after him, but only moments after . . ."

"Then he could have killed him before you got there!"

"No. I was on his heels. I would have heard the shot. I heard the dog begin to bark as Victor entered."

He let out a long, slow sigh, as if at last the pieces had settled into a dark picture that, for all its ugliness, still made sense to him. His face looked bruised, as if some familiar pain had returned inside him.

"You had better come into the study," he said wearily. "I don't know what you can do about any of it now. The police believe Narraway shot O'Neil because they want to believe it. He's earned a long, deep hatred here. They caught him all but in the act.

They won't look any further. You would be wise to go back to London while you can." He led the way across the floor into the study and closed the door. He offered her one of the leather-seated chairs and took the other himself.

"I don't know what you think I can do to change anything." There was no lift in his voice, no hope.

"Tell me about transferring the money," she answered.

"And how will that help?"

"Special Branch in London will know that Victor did not steal it." She must remember always to refer to him by his given name. One slip calling him *Mr. Narraway* and she would betray both of them.

He gave a sharp bark of laughter. "And when he's hanged in Dublin for murdering O'Neil, what will that matter to him? There's a poetic justice to it, but if it's logic you're after, the fact that he didn't steal the money won't help. O'Neil had nothing to do with it, but Narraway didn't know that."

"Of course he did!" she retorted instantly. "How do you think I know?"

That caught him off guard; she saw it instantly in his eyes.

"Then what is it you want me to tell you?" he asked.

"Who helped you? Someone in Lisson Grove gave you the account information so you could have it done. And it was nothing to do with helping you. It was to get Victor out of Special Branch. You just served their purpose." She had not thought what she was going to say until the words were on her lips. Did she really mean that it was Charles Austwick? It didn't have to be; there were a dozen others who could have done it, for a dozen other reasons, even one as simple as being paid to. But again that came back to Ireland, and who would pay, and for what reason — just revenge, or an enemy who wanted their own man in Narraway's place? Or was it simply an ambitious man, or one Narraway suspected of treason or theft, and they struck before he could expose them?

She watched Tyrone, waiting for him to respond.

He was trying to judge how much she knew, but there was also something else in his eyes: a hurt that so far made no sense as part of this old vengeance.

"Austwick?" she guessed, before the silence allowed the moment to slip.

"Yes," he said quietly.

"Did he pay you?" She could not keep the contempt from her voice.

His head came up sharply. "No he did

386

not! I did it because I hate Narraway, and Mulhare, and all other traitors to Ireland."

"Victor is not a traitor to Ireland," she pointed out. "He's as English as I am. You're lying." She picked a weapon out of her imagination. "Did he have an affair with your wife, as well as with Kate O'Neil?"

Tyrone's face flamed, and he half rose from his chair. "If you don't want me to throw you out of my house, woman, you'll apologize for that slur on my wife! Your mind's in the gutter. But then I daresay you know your brother a great deal better than I do. If he is your brother, that is?"

Now Charlotte felt her own face burn. "I think perhaps it is your mind that is in the gutter, Mr. Tyrone," she said with a tremor in her voice, and perhaps guilt, because she knew what Narraway felt for her.

Unable to piece together a defense, she attacked. "Why do you do this for Charles Austwick? What is he to you? An Englishman who wants to gain power and office? And in the very secret service that was formed to defeat Irish hopes of Home Rule." That was an exaggeration, she knew. It was formed to combat the bombings and murders intended to terrorize Britain into granting Home Rule to Ireland, but the difference hardly mattered now.

Tyrone's voice was low and bitterly angry. "I don't give a tinker's curse who runs your wretched services, secret or open. It was my chance to get rid of Narraway. Whatever else Austwick is, he's a fool by comparison."

"You know him?" She seized the only part of what he was saying that seemed vulnerable, even momentarily.

There was a tiny sound behind her; just the brushing of a silk skirt against the door-jamb.

She turned around and saw Bridget Tyrone standing a yard from her. Suddenly she was horribly, physically afraid. She could scream her lungs out here and no one would hear her, no one would know . . . or care. It took all the strength she had to stand still, and command her voice to be level — or at least something like it.

It would be absurd to pretend Bridget had not overheard the conversation.

Charlotte was trapped, and she knew it. The fury in Bridget's face was unmistakable. Just as Bridget moved forward, Charlotte did also. She had never before struck another woman. However, when she turned as if to say something to Tyrone and saw him also moving toward her, she swung back, her arm wide. She put all her weight behind it, catching Bridget on the side of the head just as she lunged forward.

Bridget toppled sideways, catching at the small table with books on it and sending it crashing, herself on top of it. She screamed, as much in rage as pain.

Tyrone was distracted, diving to help her. Charlotte ran past, out of the door and across the hall. She flung the front door open, hurtling out into the street without once looking behind her. She kept on running, both hands holding her skirts up so she did not trip. She reached the main crossroads before she was so out of breath she could go no farther.

She dropped her skirt out of shaking hands and started to walk along the dimly lit street with as much dignity as she could muster, keeping an eye to the roadway for carriage lights in the hope of getting one to take her home as soon as it could. She would prefer to be far away from the area.

When she saw an unoccupied cab, she gave the driver the Molesworth Street address before climbing in and settling back to try to arrange her thoughts.

The story was still incomplete: bits and pieces that only partially fit together. Talulla was Sean and Kate's daughter. When had she known the truth of what had happened, or at least something like it? Perhaps more important, who had told her? Had it been with the intention that she should react violently? Did they know her well enough, and deliberately work on her loneliness, her sense of injustice and displacement, so that she could be provoked into murdering Cormac and blaming Narraway? To her it could be made to seem a just revenge for the destruction of her family. Sometimes rage is the easiest answer to unbearable pain. Charlotte had seen that too many times before, even been brushed by it herself long ago, at the time of Sarah's death. It is instinctive to feel that someone must be made to pay.

Who could have used Talulla that way? And why? Was Cormac the intended victim? Or was he a victim of incidental damage, as Fiachra McDaid had said — one of the fallen in a war for a greater purpose — and Narraway the real victim? It would be a poetic justice if he were hanged for a murder he did not commit. Since Talulla believed Sean innocent of killing Kate, and Narraway guilty, for her that would be elegant, perfect.

But who prompted her to it, gave her the information and stoked her passions, all but guided her hand? And why? Obviously not Cormac. Not John Tyrone, because he seemed to know nothing about it, and Charlotte believed that. Bridget? Perhaps. Certainly she was involved. Her reaction to Charlotte that evening had been too immediate and too violent to spring from ignorance. In fact, looking back at it now, perhaps she had known more than Tyrone himself. Was Tyrone, at least in part, another victim of incidental damage? Someone to use, because he was vulnerable, more in love with his wife than she was with him, and because he was a banker and had the means?

She could no longer evade the answer — Fiachra McDaid. Perhaps he had nothing to do with the past at all, or any of the old tragedy, except to use it. And for him winning was all, the means and the casualties nothing.

How did getting Narraway out of Special Branch help the cause of Ireland, though? He would only be replaced. But perhaps that was it. Replaced with a traitor, bought and paid for. She was still working on this train of thought when she arrived at Mrs. Hogan's door. She had promised Mrs. Hogan she would be gone by the next day. It would be very difficult to manage her own luggage and Narraway's as well, and there were other practical considerations to be taken in mind, such as the shortage of money to remain much longer away from home. She had still her tickets to purchase, for the boat and for the train.

When everything was weighed, she had little choice but to go to the police station in the morning and tell them, carefully, all that she believed. However, she had no proof she could show them. That she had arrived at Cormac's house just after Narraway but had heard no gunshot, just the dog barking — why should her story convince them?

The police would ask her why she had not given this account at the time. Should she admit that she had not thought they would believe her? Is that what an innocent person would do?

She went to sleep uneasily, waking often with the problem still unsolved.

Narraway sat in his cell in the police station less than a mile from where Cormac O'Neil had been murdered. He maintained a motionless pose, but his mind was racing. He must think — plan. Once they moved him to the main prison he would have no chance. He might be lucky to survive long enough to come to trial. And by that time memories would be clouded, people persuaded to forget, or to see things differently. But far worse even than that, whatever was being planned and for which he had been lured to Ireland, and Pitt to France, would have happened, and be irretrievable.

He sat there and remained unmoving for more than two hours. No one came to speak to him or give him food or drink. Slowly a desperate plan took shape in his mind. He would like to wait for nightfall, but he could not take the risk that they would take him into the main prison before that. Daylight would be much more dangerous, but perhaps that too was necessary. He might have only one chance.

He listened intently for the slightest sound beyond the cell door, any movement at all. He had decided exactly what to do when at last it came. It would have to, eventually.

When they put the heavy key in the lock and swung the door open Narraway was lying on the floor, sprawled in a position that looked as if he had broken his neck. His beautiful white shirt was torn and hanging from the bars on the window above him.

"Hey! Flaherty!" the guard called. "Come, quick! The stupid bastard's hung himself!" He came over to Narraway and bent to check his pulse. "Sweet Mother of God, I think he's dead!" he breathed. "Flaherty, where the devil are you?"

Before Flaherty could come, and there

would be two of them to fight, Narraway snapped his body up and caught the guard under the chin so hard his head shot back. Narraway hit him again, sideways, so as to knock him unconscious, but very definitely not kill him. In fact he intended him to be senseless for no more than fifteen or twenty minutes. He needed him alive, and able to walk.

He moved the inert body to the exact spot where he himself had been lying, all but tore the man's jacket off him, and left him in his shirt. He took his keys and barely managed to get behind the door when Flaherty arrived.

Narraway held his breath in case Flaherty had the presence of mind to come in and lock the door or, even worse, stay out and lock it. But he was too horrified by the sight of the other guard on the floor to think so rationally. He covered the few paces to the fallen man, calling his name, and Narraway took his one chance. He slipped around the door, slammed it shut, and locked it. He heard Flaherty yelling almost immediately. Good. Someone would let him out within minutes. He needed them in hot pursuit.

He was very careful indeed going out of the police station, twice standing motionless on corners while people moved past him,

following the shouting and the hurried footsteps.

Outside in the street, he ran. He wanted
to draw attention to himself, to be remembered. Someone had to tell them which way
he had gone.

He could afford no delay, no hesitation.

It was wet. The rain came down in a
steady drizzle. The gutters were awash and
very quickly he was soaked, his hair sticking
to his brow, his bare neck cold without his
shirt. People looked at him but no one stood
in his way. Perhaps they thought he was
drunk.

He had to go around Cormac's house, in
case there were still police there. He could
not be stopped now. He slowed to a walk
and crossed the road away from it, then
back again, without seeing anyone, and in
at the gate of Talulla's house and up to the
front door. If she did not answer he would
have to break a window and force his way
in. His whole plan rested on confronting
her when the police caught up with him.

He knocked loudly.

There was no answer. What if she were
not here, but with friends? Could she be, so
soon after killing Cormac? Surely she would
need to be alone? And she had to take care
of the dog. Wouldn't she be waiting until

the police left so she could take whatever she wanted, or needed to protect, of the records of her parents that Cormac had kept?

He banged again.

Again — silence.

Was she there already? He had seen no police outside. She might be upstairs here in her own house, lying down, emotionally exhausted from murder and the ultimate revenge.

He took off the jacket. Standing in the rain, bare-chested, he wrapped the jacket around his fist and with as little noise as possible broke a side window, unlocked it, and climbed inside. He put the jacket on again and walked softly across the floor to look for her.

He searched from top to bottom. There was no one there. He had not expected a maid. Talulla would have given her the day off so she could not witness anything to do with Cormac's murder, not hear any shots, any barking dog.

He let himself out of the back door and ran swiftly to Cormac's house. Time was getting short. The police could not be far behind him. Hurry! Hurry!

He wasted no time knocking on the door. She would almost certainly not answer. And he had no time to wait.

He took off the jacket again, shivering with cold now, and perhaps also with fear. He smashed another window and within seconds was inside. At once the dog started barking furiously.

He looked around him. He went into some kind of pantry. He must get as far as the kitchen before she found him. If she let the dog attack him he had to be ready. And why would she not? He had broken into the house. He was already accused of Cormac's murder. She would have every possible justification.

He opened the door quickly and found himself in the scullery, the kitchen beyond. He darted forward and grabbed at a small, hard-backed wooden chair just as Talulla opened the door from the farther side and the dog leapt forward, still barking hysterically.

She stopped, stunned to see him.

He lifted the chair, its thin, sharp legs pointed toward the dog.

"I don't want to hurt the animal," he said, having to raise his voice to be heard above it. "Call it off."

"So you can kill me too?" she shouted back at him.

"Don't be so damn stupid!" He heard the

rage trembling in his own voice, abrasive, almost out of control. "You killed him yourself, to get your revenge at last."

She smiled, a hard, glittering expression, vibrant with hate. "Well, I have, haven't I? They'll hang you, Victor Narraway. And the ghost of my father will laugh. I'll be there to watch you — that I swear." She turned to the dog. "Quiet, girl," she ordered. "Don't attack him. I want him alive to suffer trial and disgrace. Ripping his throat out would be too quick, too easy." She looked back at him.

But the dog was distracted by something else now. It swung its head around and stared toward the front door, hackles raised, a low growl in its throat.

"Too easy?" Narraway heard his voice rising, the desperation in it palpable. She must hear it too.

She did, and her smile widened. "I want to see you hang, see your terror when they put the noose around your neck, see you struggle for breath, gasping, your tongue purple, filling your mouth and poking out. You won't charm the women then, will you? Do you soil yourself when you hang? Do you lose all control, all dignity?" She was screeching now, her face twisted with the pain of her own imagination.

"Actually the function of the noose and the drop of the trapdoor is to break your neck," he replied. "You are supposed to die instantly. Does that take the pleasure away for you?"

She stared at him, breathing heavily. The dog now was fully concentrated on the front door, the growl low in its throat, lips curled back off the teeth.

If she realized there was someone at the front, please God in heaven, the police, then she would stop, perhaps even claim he had attacked her. But this was the moment of her private triumph, when she could tell him exactly how she had brought about his ruin.

He made a sudden movement toward her.

The dog swung around, barking again.

He raised the chair, legs toward it, just in case it leapt.

"Frightened, Victor?" she said with relish.

"Why now?" he asked, trying to keep his voice level. He nearly succeeded, but she must have seen the sheen of sweat on his face. "It was McDaid, wasn't it? He told you something? What? Why does he want all this? He used to be my friend."

"You're pathetic!" she said, all but choking over her words. "He hates you as much as we all do!"

"What did he tell you?" he persisted.

"How you seduced my whore of a mother and then betrayed her. You killed her, and let my father hang for it!" She was sobbing now.

"Then why kill poor Cormac?" he asked. "Was he expendable, simply to create a murder for which you could blame me? It had to be you who killed him, you're the only one the dog wouldn't bark at, because you feed her when Cormac's away. She's used to you in the house. She'd have raised the roof if it had been me."

"Very clever," she agreed. "But by the time you come to trial, no one else will know that. And no one will believe your sister, if that's who she is, because they'll all know she would lie for you."

"Did you kill Cormac just to get me?" he asked again.

"No! I killed him because he didn't raise a hand to save my father! He did nothing! Absolutely nothing!"

"You were only a child, not even eight years old," he pointed out.

"McDaid told me!" she sobbed.

"Ah yes, McDaid — the Irish hero who wants to turn all Europe upside down in a revolution to change the social order, sweep away the old, and bring in the new. And do you imagine that will bring Ireland freedom? To him you are expendable, Talulla, just as I am, or your parents, or anyone else."

It was at that point that she let go of the dog's collar and shrieked at it to attack, just as the police threw open the door to the hall and Narraway raised the chair as the dog leapt and sent him flying to land hard on his back, half winding him.

One of the policemen grabbed the animal by its collar, all but choking it. The other seized hold of Talulla.

Narraway climbed to his feet, coughing and gasping to get his breath.

"Thank you," he said hoarsely. "I hope you have been here rather longer than it would appear."

"Long enough," the elder of the two responded. "But there'll still be one or two charges for you to answer, like assaulting a policeman while in custody, and escaping custody. If I were you, I'd run like hell and never come back to Ireland, Mr. Narraway."

"Very good advice." Narraway stood to attention, gave the man a smart salute, then turned and ran, exactly as he had been told.

In the morning there was no alternative for Charlotte but to have a hasty breakfast, pay Mrs. Hogan the last night for which she owed her. Then, with Mrs. Hogan's assistance, she sent for a carriage to take her and all the baggage as far as the police station where Narraway was held.

It was a miserable ride. She had come up with no better solution than simply to tell the police that she had further information on the death of Cormac O'Neil, and hope that she could persuade someone with judgment and influence to listen to her.

As she drew closer and closer the idea seemed to grow even more hopeless.

The carriage was about a hundred yards away from the police station. She was dreading being put out on the footpath with more luggage than she could possibly carry, and a story she was already convinced no one would believe. Then abruptly the carriage pulled up short and the driver leaned down to speak to someone Charlotte could only partially see.

"We are not there yet!" she said desperately. "Please go farther. I cannot possibly carry these cases so far. In fact I can't carry them at all."

"Sorry, miss," the driver said sadly, as if he felt a real pity for her. "That was the police. Seems there's been an escape of a very dangerous prisoner in the night. They just discovered it, an' the whole street's blocked off."

"A prisoner?"

"Yes, miss. A terrible, dangerous man, they say. Murdered a man yesterday, near shot his head off, an' now he's gone like magic. Just disappeared. Went to see him this morning, and his cell is empty. They're not allowing any carriages through."

Charlotte stared at him as if she could barely understand his words, but her mind was racing. Escape. Murdered a man yesterday. It had to be Narraway, didn't it? He must have known even more certainly than she did just how much people hated him, how easy it would be for them to see all the evidence the way they wished to. Who would believe him — an Englishman with his past — rather than Talulla Lawless, who was Sean O'Neil's daughter and, perhaps even more important, Kate's daughter? Who would want to believe she shot Cormac?

The driver was still staring at Charlotte, waiting for her decision.

"Thank you," she said, fumbling for words. She did not want to leave Narraway alone and hunted in Ireland, but there was no way in which she could help him. She had no idea which way he would go, north or south, inland, or even across the country to the west. She did not know if he had friends, old allies, anyone to turn to.

Then another thought came to her with a new coldness. When they arrested him, they would have taken his belongings, his money. He would be penniless. How would he survive, let alone travel? She must help him.

Please heaven he did not trust any of the people he knew in Dublin! Every one of them would betray him. They were tied to one another by blood and memory, old grief too deep to forget.

"Miss?" The driver interrupted her thoughts.

Charlotte had little money either. She was marked as Narraway's sister. She would be a liability to him. There was nothing she could do to help here. Her only hope was to go back to London and somehow find Pitt or, at the very least, Aunt Vespasia.

"Please take me to the dock," she said as steadily as she could. "I think it would be better if I caught the next steamer back to England. Whatever dock that is, if you please."

"Yes, miss." He climbed back over the box again and urged his horse forward and around. They made a wide turn in the street heading away from the police station.

The journey was not very long, but to Charlotte it seemed to take ages. They

404

passed down the wide, handsome streets. Some of the roads would have taken seven or eight carriages abreast, but they seemed half deserted compared with the noisy, crushing jams of traffic in London. She was desperate to leave, and yet also torn with regrets. One day she wanted to come back, anonymous and free of burdens, simply to enjoy the city. Now she could only lean forward, peering out and counting the minutes until she reached the dock.

The whole business of alighting with the luggage and the crowds waiting to board the steamer was awkward and very close to desperate. She tried to move the cases without leaving anything where it could be taken, and at the same time keep hold of her reticule and pay for a ticket. In the jostling of people she was bumped and knocked. Twice she nearly lost her own case while trying to move Narraway's and find money ready to pay the fare.

"Can I help you?" a voice said close to her.

She was about to refuse when she felt his hand over hers and he took Narraway's case from her. She was furious and ready to cry with frustration. She lifted her foot with its nicely heeled boot and brought it down sharply on his instep.

He gasped with pain, but he did not let go of Narraway's case.

She lifted her foot to do it again, harder.

"Charlotte, let the damn thing go!" Narraway hissed between his teeth.

She let not only his case go but her own also. She was so angry she could have struck him with an open hand, and so relieved she felt the tears prickle in her eyes and slide down her cheeks.

"I suppose you've no money!" she said tartly, choking on the words.

"Not much," he agreed. "I borrowed enough from O'Casey to get as far as Holyhead. But since you have my luggage, we'll manage the rest. Keep moving. We need to buy tickets, and I would very much like to catch this steamer. I might not have the opportunity to wait for the next. I imagine the police will think of this. It's the obvious way to go, but I need to be back in London. I have a fear that something very nasty indeed is going to happen."

"Several very nasty things already have," she told him.

"I know. But we must prevent what we can."

"I know what happened with Mulhare's money. I'm pretty sure who was behind it all."

"Are you?" There was an eagerness in his voice that he could not hide, even now in this pushing, noisy crowd.

"I'll tell you when we are on board. Did you hear the dog?"

"What dog?"

"Cormac's dog."

"Of course I did. The poor beast hurled itself at the door almost as soon as I was in the house."

"Did you hear the shot?"

"No. Did you?" He was startled.

"No," she said with a smile.

"Ah!" He was level with her now, and they were at the ticket counter. "I see." He smiled also, but at the salesman. "Two for the Holyhead boat, please."

CHAPTER 10

Pitt was overwhelmed with the size and scope of his new responsibilities. There was so much more to consider than the relatively minor issues of whether the socialist plot in Europe was something that could be serious, or only another manifestation of the sporadic violence that had occurred in one place or another for the last several years. Even if some specific act were planned, very possibly it did not concern England.

The alliance with France required that he pass on any important information to the French authorities, but what did he know that was anything more than speculation? West had been killed before he could tell him whatever it was he knew. With hindsight now, it had presumably been Gower who was a traitor. But had there been more to it than that? Had West also known who else in Lisson Grove was — what? A socialist conspirator? To be bought for money, or power? Or was it not what they wished to gain so much as what they were afraid to lose? Was it blackmail over some real or perceived offense? Was it someone who had been made to appear guilty, as Narraway had, but this person had yielded to pressure in order to save himself?

Had Narraway been threatened, and defied them? Or had they known better than to try, and he had simply been professionally destroyed, without warning?

He sat in Narraway's office, which was now his own: a cold and extraordinarily isolating thought. Would he be ousted next? It was hard to imagine he posed the threat to them that Narraway had, whoever they were. He looked around the room. It was so familiar to him from the other side of the desk that even with his back to the wall he could see in his mind's eye the pictures Narraway used to have there. They were mostly pencil drawings of bare trees, the branches delicate and complex. There was one exception: an old stone tower by the sea, but again the foreground was in exquisite detail of light and shadow, the sea only a feeling of distance without end.

He would ask Austwick where they were, and put them back where they belonged. If Narraway ever returned, then Pitt would

give them back to him. Narraway's belongings were part of the furniture of his mind,
of his life. They would give Pitt a sense of
his presence, and it was both sad and
comforting at the same time.

Narraway would have known what to do
about these varied and sometimes conflict-
ing remnants of work that scattered the desk
now. Pitt was familiar with some of them,
but he had only a vague knowledge of others. They were cases Narraway had dealt
with himself.

Austwick had left him notes, but how
could he trust anything Austwick had said?
He would be a fool to, without corrobora-
tion from someone else, and that would take
time he could not afford now. And whom
could he trust? There was nothing but to go
on. He would have to compare one piece of
information with another, canceling out the
impossible and then weighing what was left.

As the morning wore on, and assistants of
one sort or another came with new papers,
more opinions, he became painfully aware
of how isolated Narraway must have been.
He was commander now; he was not permitted to reveal vulnerability or confusion.
He was not expected to consult. But he
badly needed to — and recognized no one
he could trust with certainty.

He looked in the faces of his juniors and saw courtesy, respect for his new position. In a few he also saw envy. Once he recognized an anger that he, such a relative newcomer, should have been promoted before them. In none did he see the kind of respect he needed in order to command their personal loyalty beyond their commitment to the task. That could only exist when it had been earned.

He would have given most of what he possessed to have Narraway back. Knowing that one misjudgment could now cost him his life, Pitt desperately craved his colleague's steady, quick-thinking presence and his quiet support.

Where was Narraway now? Somewhere in Ireland, trying to clear his name of a crime he did not commit? Pitt realized with a chill that he was not certain that Narraway was innocent. Could he have lied, embezzled, betrayed his country, and broken the trust of all he knew? Pitt would never before have believed that Narraway would commit *any* crime, even out of desperation. But perhaps he would if his life were in jeopardy, or Charlotte's. That thought hurt Pitt in a way that he could not fight.

Why had she gone with him? To help fight against injustice, out of loyalty to a friend in desperate need? How like her! But Narraway was Pitt's friend, not really hers. And yet, remembering a dozen small things, he knew that Narraway was in love with her, and had been for some time.

He knew exactly when he had first realized it. He had seen Narraway turn to look at her. They had been standing in the kitchen in his own house in Keppel Street. It had been during a bad case, a difficult one. Narraway had come to see him late in the evening over something or other, a new turn in events. They had had tea. The kettle was steaming on the hob. Charlotte had been standing waiting for it to boil again. She had been wearing an old dress, not expecting anyone except Pitt. The lamplight had shone on her hair, bringing up the warm, deep color of it, and on the angle of her cheek. He could see her in his mind's eye picking up the mitt so as not to burn her hands on the kettle.

Narraway had said something, and she had looked at him and laughed. In an instant his face had given him away.

Did she know? It had taken her what seemed like ages to realize that Pitt was in love with her, years ago, in the beginning. But since then they had all changed. She had been awkward, the middle sister of three, the one her mother found so difficult to match with an acceptable husband. Now she knew she was loved. But Pitt knew that her righteous indignation over the injustice against Narraway may have spurred Charlotte to impulsive actions.

She would be furiously angry that Narraway's reputation had been damaged, and she would still feel a gratitude to Narraway for having taken Pitt into Special Branch when he so badly needed it. Life could have become very bleak indeed. And if she knew that Narraway loved her that could be an added sense of responsibility, even of debt. To think of it as a debt was ridiculous — she had not asked for his regard, but Pitt knew the fierce protectiveness she felt toward the vulnerable. It was instinctive, defensive, like an animal with cubs. She would act first and think afterward. He loved her for it. He would lose something of infinite value if she were different, more guarded, more sensible. But it was still a liability.

There were papers piled on the desk in front of him, reports waiting to be made sense of, but still his mind was on Charlotte.

Where was she? How could he find out without placing her in further danger? Who was he absolutely certain he could trust? A week ago, he would have sent Gower. Unwittingly he would have been giving them the perfect hostage.

Should he contact the Dublin police? How could he be sure that he could trust them either, in light of all the schemes and plots that seemed to be under way right in his own government branch?

Perhaps anonymity was her best defense, but his own helplessness was almost like a physical pain. He had all the forces of Special Branch at his fingertips, but no idea whom he could trust.

There was a knock on his door. The moment he answered it Austwick came in, looking grave and slightly smug. He had more papers in his hand.

Pitt was glad to be forced back into the present. "What have you?" he asked.

Austwick sat down without being asked. Pitt realized he would not have done that with Narraway.

"More reports from Manchester," Austwick replied. "It does begin to look as if Latimer is right about this factory in Hyde. They are making guns, despite their denials. And then there's the mess-up in Glasgow. We need to pay more attention to that, before it gets any bigger."

"Last report said it was just young people protesting," Pitt reminded him. "Narraway had it marked as better left alone."

Austwick pulled his face into a grimace of distaste. "Well I think Narraway's mind was hardly on the country's interests over the last while. Unfortunately we don't know how long his . . . inattention had been going on. Read it yourself and see what you think. I've been handling it since Narraway went, and I think he may have made a serious misjudgment. And we can't afford to ignore Scotland either."

Pitt swallowed his response. He did not trust Austwick, but he must not allow the man to see his doubt. All this felt like wasting time, of which he had far too little.

"What about the other reports from Europe on the socialists?" he asked. "Anything from Germany? And what about the Russian émigrés in Paris?"

"Nothing significant," Austwick replied. "And nothing at all from Gower." He looked at Pitt steadily, concern in his eyes.

Pitt kept his expression perfectly composed. "He won't risk communication unless he has something of value to report. It all has to go through the local post office."

Austwick shook his head. "I think it's of secondary importance, honestly. West may

415

have been killed simply on principle when they discovered he was an informant. He may not have possessed the crucial information we assumed he did."

Austwick shifted his position a little and looked straight at Pitt. "There have been rumblings about great reform for years, you know. People strike postures and make speeches, but nothing serious happens, at least not here in Britain. I think our biggest danger was three or four years ago. There was a lot of unrest in the East End of London, which I know you are aware of, though much of it took place just before you joined the branch."

That was a blatant reminder of how new Pitt was to this job. He saw the flicker of resentment in Austwick's eyes as he said it. He wondered for a moment if the hostility he sensed was due to Austwick's personal ambition having been thwarted. Then he remembered Gower bending over West's body on the ground, and the blood. Either Austwick had nothing to do with it, or he was better at masking his emotions than Pitt had judged. He must be careful.

"Perhaps we'll escape it," he offered.

Austwick shifted in his chair again. "These are the reports in from Liverpool, and you'll see some of the references to Ireland. Nothing dangerous as yet, but we need to make note of some of these names, and watch them." He pushed across more papers, and Pitt bent to read them.

The afternoon followed the same pattern: more reports both written and verbal. A case of violence in a town in Yorkshire looked as if it was political and turned out not to be. A government minister was robbed in Piccadilly; and investigating it took up the rest of the day. The minister had been carrying sensitive papers. Fortunately it was not Pitt's decision as to how seriously he should be reprimanded for carelessness. It was, however, up to him to decide with what crime the thief should be charged.

He weighed it with some consideration. He questioned the man, trying to judge whether he had known his victim was in the government, and if so that his attaché case might contain government papers. He was uncertain, even after several hours, but Narraway would not have asked advice, and neither would he.

Pitt decided that the disadvantages of letting the public know how easy it was to rob an inattentive minister outweighed the possible error of letting a man be charged with a lesser crime than the one he had intended to commit.

He went home in the evening tired and with little sense of achievement.

It changed the moment he opened the front door and Daniel came racing down the hall to greet him.

"Papa! Papa, I made a boat! Come and look." He grasped Pitt's hand and tugged at him.

Pitt smiled and followed him willingly down to the kitchen, where the rich smell of dinner cooking filled the air. Something was bubbling in a big pan on the stove and the table was littered with pieces of newspapers and a bowl of white paste. Minnie Maude was standing with a pair of scissors in her hands. As usual, her hair was all over the place, pinned up over and over again as she had lost patience with it. In pride of place in the center of the mess was a rather large papier-mâché boat, with two sticks for masts and several different lengths of tapers for bowsprit, yardarms, and a boom.

Minnie Maude looked abashed to see him, clearly earlier than she had expected.

"See!" Daniel said triumphantly, pointing to the ship. "Minnie Maude showed me how to do it." He gave a little shrug. "And Jemima helped a bit . . . well . . . a lot."

Pitt felt a sudden and overwhelming

warmth rush up inside him. He looked at Daniel's face shining with pride, and then at the boat.

"It's magnificent," he said, emotion all but choking his voice. "I've never seen anything better." He turned to Minnie Maude, who was standing wide-eyed. She was clearly waiting to be criticized for playing when she should have been working, and having dinner on the table for him.

"Thank you," he said to her sincerely. "Please don't move it until it is safe to do so without risk of damage."

"What . . . what about dinner, sir?" she asked, beginning to breathe again.

"We'll clear the newspapers and the paste, and eat around it," he answered. "Where's Jemima?"

"She's reading," Daniel answered instantly. "She took my *Boys' Own!* Why doesn't she read a girls' book?"

" 'Cos they're boring," Jemima answered from the doorway. She had slipped in without anyone hearing her come along the corridor. She looked past Pitt at the table, and the ship at the center. "You've got the masts on! That's beautiful." She gave Pitt a radiant smile. "Hello, Papa. Look what we made."

"I see it," he replied, putting his arm

around her shoulder. "It's magnificent."

"How is Mama?" she asked, an edge of worry in her voice.

"Well," he answered, lying smoothly and holding her a little closer. "She's helping a friend in bad trouble, but she'll be home soon. Now let's help clear the table and have dinner."

Afterward he sat alone in the parlor as silence settled over the house. Daniel and Jemima had gone up to bed. Minnie Maude had finished in the kitchen and went up as well. He heard every creak of her tread on the stairs. Far from being comforting, the absence of all voices or movement made the heaviness swirl back in again like a fog. The islands of light from the lamps on the wall made the shadows seem deeper than they were. He knew every surface in the room. He also knew they were all immaculately clean, as if Charlotte had been there to supervise this new girl whose only fault was that she was not Gracie. She was good; it was only the familiarity she lacked. The papier-mâché ship made him smile. It wasn't a trivial thing; it was very important indeed. Minnie Maude Mudway was a success.

He sat in the armchair, thinking of Jemima's pride and Daniel's happiness for as long as he could. Finally he turned his mind to the following day and to the fact that he must go and tell Croxdale the truth about Gower, and the betrayal that might run throughout the service.

The following day at Lisson Grove was filled with the same necessary trivia as the one before. There was news from Paris that was only vaguely disturbing: a definite increase in activity among the people Special Branch was watching, though if it had any meaning he was unable to determine what it was. It was much the same sort of thing he might have done had Narraway been there, and he in his own job. The difference was the weight of responsibility, the decisions that he could no longer refer upward. Now they all came to him. Other men who had previously been his equals were now obliged to report to him, for Pitt needed to know of anything at all that might threaten the safety of Her Majesty's realm, and her government, the peace and prosperity of Britain.

Late that morning he finally obtained an interview with Sir Gerald Croxdale. He felt the urgent need to tell Croxdale of Gower's death, and how it had happened. No report had come in yet, as far as he knew, but it could not be long now.

Pitt arrived at Whitehall late in the afternoon. The sun was still warm and the air was soft as he walked across from the park and along the street to the appropriate entrance. Several carriages passed him, the women in them wearing wide hats to protect their faces from the light, their muslin sleeves drifting in the breeze. Horse brasses winked with bright reflections, and some doors carried family crests painted on them.

He was admitted without question. Apparently the footman knew who he was. He was taken straight to Croxdale's rooms and ushered into his presence after only a matter of moments.

"How are you, Pitt?" Croxdale said warmly, rising from his seat to shake Pitt's hand. "Sit down. How is it at Lisson Grove?" His voice was pleasant, almost casual, but he was watching Pitt intently. There was a gravity in him as if he already knew that Pitt had ugly news to tell him.

It was the opening Pitt needed without having to create it himself.

"I had hoped to tell you more, sir," he began. "But the whole episode of seeing West murdered and following Frobisher to France was far more serious than I thought at first."

Croxdale frowned, sitting a little more

upright in his chair. "In what way? Have you learned what he was going to tell you?"

"No, sir, I haven't. At least, I am not certain. But I have a strong idea, and everything I have discovered since returning supports it, but does not provide a conclusion."

"Stop beating around the bush, man!" Croxdale said impatiently. "What is it?"

Pitt took a deep breath. "We have at least one traitor at Lisson Grove . . ."

Croxdale froze, his eyes hard. His right hand on top of the desk suddenly became rigid as if he were deliberately forcing himself not to clench it.

"I presume you mean other than Victor Narraway?" he said quietly.

Pitt made another decision. "I don't and never have believed that Narraway was a traitor, sir. Whether he is guilty of a misjudgment, or a carelessness, I don't yet know. But regrettably we all misjudge at times."

"Explain yourself!" Croxdale said between his teeth. "If not Narraway, and I reserve judgment on that, then who?"

"Gower, sir."

"Gower?" Croxdale's eyes opened wide. "Did you say *Gower*?"

"Yes, sir." Pitt could feel his own temper rising. How could Croxdale accept so easily that Narraway was a traitor, yet be so incredulous that Gower could be? What had Austwick told him? How deep and how clever was this web of treason? Was Pitt rushing in where a wiser, more experienced man would have been careful, laying his ground first? But there was no time to do that. Narraway was considered a fugitive by his former colleagues in the Special Branch and heaven only knew if Charlotte was safe, or where she was and in what circumstances. Pitt could not afford to seek their enemies cautiously.

Croxdale was frowning at him. Should he tell him the whole story, or simply the murder of West? Any of it made Pitt look like a fool! But he had been a fool. He had trusted Gower, even liked him. The memory of it was still painful.

"Something happened in France that made me realize it only appeared that Gower and I arrived together as Wrexham killed West," he said. "Actually Gower had been there moments before and killed him himself."

"For God's sake, man! That's absurd," Croxdale exploded, almost rising from his seat. "You can't expect me to believe that! How did you fail . . ." He sat back again, composing himself with an effort. "I'm

424

sorry. This comes as an appalling shock to me. I . . . I know his family. Are you certain? It all seems very . . . flimsy."

"Yes, sir, I'm afraid I am certain." Pitt felt a stab of pity for him. "I made an excuse to leave him in France and return by myself —"

"You left him?" Again Croxdale was stunned.

"I couldn't arrest him," Pitt pointed out. "I had no weapon, and he was a young and very powerful man. The last thing I wanted to do was inform the local police of who we were, and that we were there without their knowledge or permission, watching French citizens . . ."

"Yes, of course. I see. I see. Go on." Croxdale was flushed and obviously badly shaken. Pitt could have sympathized at another time.

"I told him to remain watching Wrexham and Frobisher . . ."

"Who's Frobisher?" Croxdale demanded.

Pitt told him what they knew of Frobisher, and the other men they had seen coming and going from his house.

Croxdale nodded. "So there was some truth to this business of socialists meeting, and possibly planning something?"

"Possibly. Nothing conclusive yet."

"And you left Gower there?"

"I thought so. But when I reached Southampton I took the train to London. On that train I was attacked, twice, and very nearly lost my life."

"Good God! By whom?" Croxdale was horrified.

"Gower, sir. The first time he was interrupted, and the man who did so paid for his courage with his life. Then Gower renewed his attack on me, but this time I was ready for him, and it was he who lost."

Croxdale wiped his hand across his brow. "What happened to Gower?"

"He went over onto the track," Pitt replied, his stomach knotting at that memory and the sweat breaking out on his skin again. He decided not to mention his own arrest, because then he would have to explain how Vespasia had rescued him, and he preferred to keep her name out of it altogether.

"He was . . . killed?" Croxdale said.

"At that speed, sir, there can be no doubt."

Croxdale leaned back. "How absolutely fearful." He let out his breath slowly. "You are right, of course. We had a traitor at Lisson Grove. I am profoundly grateful that it was he and not you who went over onto the tracks. Why on earth did you not tell me

426

this as soon as you returned?"

"Because I hoped to learn who was the man behind Gower before I told you," Pitt answered.

Croxdale's face went white. "Behind . . . Gower?" he said awkwardly.

"I don't yet know," Pitt admitted. "Not for certain. I never found evidence one way or the other whether Frobisher was the power behind a new socialist uprising, perhaps violent, or only a dilettante playing on the edge of the real plot."

"We don't assume it is trivial," Croxdale said quickly. "If Gower . . . I still find it hard to credit . . . but if Gower murdered two people, and attempted to murder you also, then it is very real indeed." He bit his lip. "I assume from what you say that you did not tell Austwick this?"

"No. I believe someone made it appear that Narraway was guilty of embezzlement in order to get him out of the way, discredit him so deeply that anything he said against them would be disbelieved."

"Who? Someone to do with Frobisher? Or Gower again?"

"Neither Frobisher nor Gower had the ability," Pitt pointed out. "That has to be someone in Lisson Grove, someone with a considerable amount of power in order to have access to the details of Narraway's banking arrangements."

Croxdale was staring at him, his face drawn, cheeks flushed. "I see. Yes, of course you are right. Then this socialist plot seems very deep. Perhaps this Frobisher is as dangerous as you first thought, and poor West was killed to prevent you from learning the full extent of it. No doubt Gower kept you along with him when he went to France so you could be duped into believing Frobisher harmless, and sending that misinformation back to London." He smiled bleakly, just for an instant. "Thank God you were clever enough to see through it, and agile enough to survive his attack on you. You are the right man for this job, Pitt. Whatever else he may be guilty of, Narraway did well when he brought you into the service."

Pitt felt he should thank him for the compliment, and for his trust, but he wanted to argue and say how little he was really suited to it. He ended by inclining his head, thanking him briefly, and moving on to the more urgent problem of the present.

"We need to know very urgently, sir, what information Gower himself may have passed back to London, and — more specifically — to whom. I don't know who I can trust."

"No," Croxdale said thoughtfully, now leaning back again in his chair. "No, neither do I. We need to look at this a great deal more closely, Pitt. Austwick has reported to me at least three times since Narraway left. I have the papers here. We need to go through all this information and you must tell me what you know to be accurate, or inaccurate, and what we still need to test. Some picture should emerge. I'm sorry, but this may very well require all night. I'll have someone fetch us supper." He shook his head. "God, what a miserable business."

There was no question of argument.

Croxdale had other notes not only of what Austwick had reported to him but, going back farther, of what Narraway also had written. It was curious looking at the different papers. Austwick's writing was neat, his notes carefully thought out and finely presented. Narraway's Pitt saw with a jolt of familiarity, and a renewed sense of his friend's absence. Narraway's penmanship was smaller, more flowing than his successor's. There was no hesitation. He had written his note with forethought, and there was no attempt to conceal the fact that he was giving Croxdale only the minimum. Was that an agreement between them, and Croxdale could read between the lines? Or

429

had Narraway simply not bothered to conceal the fact that he was telling only part of what he knew?

Pitt studied Croxdale's face, and did not know the answer.

They read them carefully. A servant brought in a tray of light toast and pâté, then cheese and finally a heavy fruitcake — along with brandy, which Pitt declined.

It was now totally dark outside. The wind was rising a little, spattering rain against the windows.

Croxdale put down the last paper. "Narraway obviously thought there was something to this business in St. Malo, but not major. Austwick seems to disagree, and thinks that it is nothing but noise and posturing. Unlike Narraway, he believes it will not affect us here in Britain. What do you think, Pitt?"

It was the question Pitt had dreaded, but it was inevitable that it would come. There was no room for excuses, no matter how easy to justify. He would be judged on the accuracy of his answer. He had lain awake weighing everything he knew, hoping Croxdale's information would tip the balance one way or the other.

Again he answered with barely a hesitation. "I think that Narraway was on the brink of finding out something crucial, and he was gotten rid of before he could do so."

Croxdale waited a long time before he answered.

"Do you realize that if that is true, then you are also saying that Austwick is either incompetent to a most serious degree, or else — far worse than that — he is complicit in what is going on?"

"Yes, sir, I'm afraid that has to be the case," Pitt agreed. "But Gower was reporting to someone, so we know that at least one person within the service is a traitor."

"I've known Charles Austwick for years," Croxdale said softly. "But perhaps we don't know anyone as well as we imagine." He sighed. "I've sent for Stoker. Apparently he's newly back from Ireland. He may be able to throw some light on things. Do you trust him?"

"Yes. But I trusted Gower as well," Pitt said ruefully. "Do you?"

Croxdale gave him a bleak smile. "Touché. Let's at least see what he has to say. And the answer is no, I trust no one. I am painfully aware that we cannot afford to. Not after Narraway, and not it would seem Gower also. Are you sure you won't have a brandy?"

"I'm quite sure, thank you, sir."

There was a knock on the door and, at

431

Croxdale's word, Stoker came in. He looked tired. There were shadows around his eyes, and his face was pinched with fatigue. However, he stood to attention until Croxdale gave him permission to sit. Stoker acknowledged Pitt, but only so much as courtesy demanded.

"When did you get back from Ireland?" Croxdale asked him.

"About two hours ago, sir," Stoker replied. "Weather's a bit poor."

"Mr. Pitt doesn't believe the charge of embezzlement against Narraway," Croxdale went on. "He thinks it is possibly false, manufactured to get rid of him because he was on the verge of gaining information about a serious socialist plot of violence that would affect Britain." He was completely ignoring Pitt, his eyes fixed on Stoker so intently they might have been alone in the room.

"Sir?" Stoker said with amazement, but he did not look at Pitt either.

"You worked with Narraway," Croxdale continued. "Does that seem likely to you? What is the news from Ireland now?"

Stoker's jaw tightened as if he were laboring under some profound emotion. His face was pale as he leaned forward a little into the light. He seemed leached of color by

432

exhaustion. "I'm sorry, sir, but I can't see any reason to question the evidence. It's amazing what lack of money can do, and how it can change your view of things."

Pitt felt as if he had been struck. The sting of Stoker's words was hard enough to have been physical. He would rather it had been.

Stoker continued, a grim weariness in his voice. "Sir, there is more. I deeply regret that I must bear this grave news, gentlemen, but yesterday O'Neil was murdered, and the police immediately arrested Narraway. He was on the scene and practically caught red-handed. He had the grace not to deny it. He is now in prison in Dublin awaiting trial."

Pitt felt as if he had been sandbagged. He struggled to keep any sense of proportion, even of reality. He stared at Stoker, then turned to Croxdale. Their faces wavered and the room seem to swim in and out of his focus.

"My word," Croxdale said slowly. "This comes as a terrible shock." He turned to Pitt. "You could have had no idea of this side of Narraway, and I admit, neither had I. I feel remiss to have had such a man in charge of our most sensitive service during my period of office. His extraordinary skill completely masked this darker, and clearly very violent side of his nature."

Pitt refused to believe it, partly because he could not bear it. Charlotte was in Ireland with Narraway. What had happened to her? How could he find out without admitting that he knew this? He would not draw Vespasia into it. She was one element he had in his favor, perhaps the only one.

Stoker gazed downward, his voice quieter, as though he too were stunned. "I am afraid it's true, sir. We were all deceived as to his character. The case against him is as plain as day. It seems Narraway quarreled with O'Neil rather publicly, making no secret of the fact that he believed O'Neil to be responsible for creating the evidence that made it seem he was guilty of embezzling the money intended for Mulhare. And to be honest, that could well be true."

"Could it? Croxdale asked, a slight lift of hope in his voice."

"From what I can make out, yes, sir, it could," Stoker replied. "Only problem is how he got the information he'd need to get it into Mr. Narraway's account. I've been trying to find the answer to that, and I think I'll get there."

"Someone at Lisson Grove?" Croxdale said.

"No, sir," Stoker answered without a

flicker in his face. "Not as far as I can see."

Croxdale's eyes narrowed. "Then who? Who else would be able to do that?"

Stoker did not hesitate. "Looks like it could be someone at Mr. Narraway's bank, sir. I daresay one time and another, he's made some enemies. Or it could just be someone willing to be paid. Nice to think that wouldn't happen, but maybe a bit innocent. There'd be those with enough money to buy most things."

"I suppose so," Croxdale replied. "Perhaps Narraway found out already? That would explain a great deal. What other news have you from Ireland?"

Stoker told him about Narraway's connections, whom he had spoken to and their reactions, the confrontation with O'Neil at the soirée. Never once did he mention Charlotte. At least some of what he described was so unlike Narraway, panicky and protective, that it seemed as if his whole character had fallen apart.

Pitt listened with disbelief and mounting anger at what he felt had to be a betrayal.

"Thank you, Stoker," Croxdale said sadly. "A tragic end to what was a fine career. Give your report on Paris to Mr. Pitt."

"Yes, sir."

Stoker left, and Croxdale turned to Pitt.

"I think that makes the picture clearer. Gower was the traitor, which I admit I still find hard to credit, but what you say makes it impossible to deny. We may have the disaster contained, but we can't take it for granted. Make as full an investigation as you can, Pitt, and report to me. Keep an eye to what's going on in Europe and if there is anything we should inform the French of, then we'll do so. In the meantime there's plenty of other political trouble to keep us busy, but I'm sure you know that." He rose to his feet, extending his hand. "Take care of yourself, Pitt. You have a difficult and dangerous job, and your country needs you more than it will ever appreciate."

Pitt shook his hand and thanked him, going out into the night without any awareness of the sudden chill. The coldness was already inside him. What Stoker had said of Narraway's bank betraying him could be true, although he did not believe it. The rest seemed a curious set of exaggerations and lies. Pitt could not accept that Narraway had fallen apart so completely, either to steal anything in the first place, or to so lose the fundamental values of his past as to behave in the way Stoker had described. Pitt could not possibly believe that Narraway was a cold-blooded murderer. And surely Stoker must at the very least have noticed Charlotte?

Or was Stoker the traitor at Lisson Grove?

He was floundering, like a man in quicksand. None of his judgments was sound. He had trusted Stoker, he had even liked Gower. Narraway he would have sworn his own life on . . . He admitted, he still would. Something had to be amiss. The Narraway that Pitt had known would never kill for any reason other than self-defense.

Croxdale's carriage was waiting to take him home. He half saw the shadow of a man on the pavement who moved toward him, but he ignored it. The coachman opened the door for him and he climbed in, sitting miserable and shivering all the way back to Keppel Street. He was glad it was late. He did not want to make the intense effort it would cost to hide his disillusion from Daniel and Jemima. If he was fortunate, even Minnie Maude would be asleep.

In the morning he was halfway to Lisson Grove when he changed his mind and went instead to see Vespasia. It was too early for any kind of social call, but if he had to wait until she rose, then he was willing to. His need to speak with her was so urgent he was prepared to break all the rules of etiquette, even of consideration, trusting that she would see his purpose beyond his discourtesy.

In fact she was already up and taking breakfast. He accepted tea, but he had no need to eat.

"Is your new maid feeding you properly?" Vespasia asked with a touch of concern.

"Yes," he answered, his own surprise coming through his voice. "Actually she's perfectly competent, and seems very pleasant. It wasn't . . ." He saw her wry smile and stopped.

"It wasn't to seek recommendation for a new maid that you came at this hour of the morning," she finished for him. "What is it, Thomas? You look very troubled indeed. I assume something new has occurred?"

He told her everything that had happened since they last spoke, including his dismay and disappointment over Stoker's sudden change of loyalties, and the brutal details with which he had described Narraway's falling apart.

"I seem to be completely incompetent at judging anyone's character," he said miserably. He would like to have been able to say it with some dry wit, but he felt so inadequate that he was afraid he sounded self-pitying.

She listened without interrupting. She poured him more tea, then grimaced that the pot was cold.

"It doesn't matter," he said quickly. "I don't need more."

"Let us sum up the situation," she said gravely. "It would seem inarguable that you were wrong about Gower, as was everyone else at Lisson Grove, including Victor Narraway. It does not make you unusually fallible, my dear. And considering that he was your fellow in the service, you had a right to assume his loyalty. At that point it was not your job to make such decisions. Now it is."

"I was wrong about Stoker," he pointed out.

"Possibly, but let us not leap to conclusions. You know only that what he reported to Gerald Croxdale seemed to blame Victor, and also was untrue in other respects. He made no mention of Charlotte, as you observed, and yet he must have seen her. Surely his omission is one you are grateful for?"

"Yes . . . yes, of course. Although I would give a great deal to know she is safe." That was an understatement perhaps only Vespasia could measure.

"Did you say anything to Croxdale about your suspicions of Austwick?" she asked.

"No." He explained how reluctant he had been to give any unnecessary trust. He had guarded everything, fearing that because Croxdale had known Austwick a long time perhaps he would be more inclined to trust him than to trust Pitt.

"Very wise," she agreed. "Is Croxdale of the opinion that there is something very serious being planned in France?"

"I saw nothing except a couple of faces," he answered. "And when I look back, it was Gower who told me they were Meister and Linsky. There was talk, but no more than usual. There was a rumor that Jean Jaures was coming from Paris, but he didn't."

Vespasia frowned. "Jacob Meister and Pieter Linsky? Are you sure?"

"Yes, that's what Gower said. I know the names, of course. But only for one day, maybe thirty-six hours, then they left again. They certainly didn't return to Frobisher's."

Vespasia looked puzzled. "And who said Jean Jaures was coming?"

"One of the innkeepers, I think. The men in the café were talking about it."

"You think? A name like Jaures is mentioned and you don't remember by whom?"

she said incredulously.

Again he was struck by his own foolishness. How easily he was duped. He had not heard it himself, Gower had told him. He admitted it to Vespasia.

"Did he mention Rosa Luxemburg?" she asked with a slight frown.

"Yes, but not that she was coming to St. Malo."

"But he mentioned her name?"

"Yes. Why?"

"Jean Jaures is a passionate socialist, but a gentle man," she explained. "He was campaigner for reform. He sought office, and on occasion gained it, but he fights for change, not for overthrow. As far as I know, he is content to keep his efforts within France. Rosa Luxemburg is different. She is Polish, now naturalized German, and of a much more international cast of mind. I have Russian émigré friends who fear that one day she will cause real violence. In some places I'm afraid real violence is almost bound to happen. The oppression in Russia will end in tragedy."

"Stretching as far as Britain?" he said dubiously.

"No, only insofar as the world is sometimes a far smaller place than we think. There will be refugees, however. Indeed,

441

London is already full of them."

"What did Gower want?" he asked. "Why did he kill West? Was West going to tell me Gower was a traitor?"

"Perhaps. But I admit, none of it makes sufficient sense to me so far, unless there is something a great deal larger than a few changes in the laws for French workers, or a rising unease in Germany and Russia. None of this is new, and none of it worries Special Branch unduly."

"I wish Narraway were here," he said with intense feeling. "I don't know enough for this job. He should have left it with Austwick — unless he knows Austwick is a traitor too?"

"I imagine that is possible." She was still lost in thought. "And if Victor is innocent, which I do not doubt, then there was a very clever and carefully thought-out plan to get both you and him out of London. Why can we not deduce what it is, and why?"

Pitt went to his office in Lisson Grove, aware as he walked along the corridors of the eyes of the other men on him, watching, waiting: Austwick particularly.

"Good morning," Austwick said, apparently forgetting the *sir* he would have added for Narraway.

"Good morning, Austwick," Pitt replied a little tartly, not looking at him but going on until he reached Narraway's office door. He realized he still thought of it as Narraway's, just as he still thought of the position as his.

He opened the door and went inside. There was nothing of Pitt's here yet — no pictures, no books — but Narraway's things were returned, as if he were still expecting the man himself to come back. When that happened he would not have to pretend to be pleased, and it would not be entirely for unselfish reasons either. He cared for Narraway, and he had at least some idea of how much the job meant to him: It was his vocation, his life. Pitt would be immensely relieved to give it back to him. It was not within Pitt's skill or his nature to perform this job. He regretted that it was now his duty.

He dealt with the most immediate issues of the day first, passing on all he could to juniors. When that was done, he told them not to interrupt him. Then he went through all Narraway's records of every crime Gower had been involved with over the past year and a half. He read all the documents, getting a larger picture concerning European revolutionary attempts to improve the lot of workingmen. He also read Stoker's latest report from Paris.

As he did so, the violence proposed settled over him like a darkness, senseless and destructive. But the anger at injustice he could not help sharing. It grieved him that it had oppressed people and denied them a reasonable life for so long that the change, when it came — and it must — would be fueled by so much hatred.

The more he read, the greater a tragedy seemed to him that the high idealism of the revolution of '48 had been crushed with so little legacy of change left behind.

Gower's own reports were spare, as if he had edited out any emotive language. At first Pitt thought that was just a very clear style of writing. Then he began to wonder if it was more: a guarding of Gower's own feelings, in case he gave something away unintentionally, or Narraway himself picked up a connection, an omission, even a false note.

Then he took out Narraway's own papers. He had read most of them before, because it was part of his duty in taking over the position. Many of the cases he was familiar with anyway, from general knowledge within the branch. He selected three specifically to do with Europe and socialist unrest, those associated with Britain, memberships of socialist political groups such as the Fabian Society. He compared them with the cases in which Gower had worked, and looked for any notes that Narraway might have made.

What were the facts he knew, personally? That Gower had killed West and made it appear it was Wrexham who had done so. All doubt left him that it had been extremely quick thinking on Gower's part. Had it been his intention all the time — with Wrexham's collaboration? Pitt recalled the chase across London and then on to Southampton. He was bitterly conscious that it had been too easy. On the rare occasions when it seemed Wrexham had eluded them, it was Gower and not Pitt who had found the trail again. The conclusion was inevitable — Gower and Wrexham were working together. To what end? Again, looked at from the result, it could only have been to keep Pitt in St. Malo — or more specifically, to keep him from being in London, and aware of what was happening to Narraway.

But to what greater purpose? Was it to do with socialist uprisings? Or was that also a blind, a piece of deception?

Who was Wrexham? He was mentioned briefly, twice, in Gower's reports. He was a young man of respectable background who had been to university and dropped out of a modern history course to travel in Europe. Gower suggested he had been to Germany and Russia, but seemed uncertain. It was all very vague, and with little substantiation. Certainly there was nothing to cause Narraway to have him watched or inquired into any further. Presumably it was just sufficient information to allow Gower to say afterward that he was a legitimate suspect.

Had he intended to turn on him in France?

The more he studied what was there, the more Pitt was certain that there had to be a far deeper plan behind the random acts he had connected in bits and pieces. The picture was too sketchy, the rewards too slight to make sense of murder. It was all random, and too small.

The most urgent question was whether Narraway had been very carefully made to look guilty of theft in order to gain some kind of revenge for old defeats and failures, or whether the real intent was to get him dismissed from Lisson Grove and out of England. The more Pitt looked at it, the more he believed it was the latter.

If Narraway had been here, what would he have made of the information? Surely he would have seen the pattern. Why could Pitt not see it? What was he missing?

He was still comparing one event with another and searching for links when there was a sharp knock on the door. He had asked not to be interrupted. This had better be something of importance, or he would tear a strip off the man, whoever he was.

"Come in," he said sharply.

The door opened and Stoker came in, closing it behind him.

Pitt stared at him coldly.

Stoker ignored his expression. "I tried to speak to you last night," he said quietly. "I saw Mrs. Pitt in Dublin. She was well and in good spirits. She's a lady of great courage. Mr. Narraway is fortunate to have her fighting his cause, although I daresay it's not for his sake she's doing it."

Pitt stared at him. He looked subtly quite different from the way he had when standing in front of Croxdale the previous evening. Was that a difference in respect? In loyalty? Personal feeling? Or because one was the truth and the other lies?

"Did you see Mr. Narraway?" Pitt asked him.

"Yes, but not to speak to. It was the day O'Neil was shot," Stoker answered.

"By whom?"

"I don't know. I think probably Talulla Lawless, but whether anyone will ever prove that, I don't know. Mr. Narraway's in trouble, Mr. Pitt. He has powerful enemies —"

"I know that," Pitt interrupted. "Apparently dating back twenty years."

"Not that," Stoker said impatiently. "Now, here in Lisson Grove. Someone wanted him discredited and out of England, and wanted you in France, gone in the other direction, where you wouldn't know what was going on here and couldn't help."

"Tell me all you know of what happened in Ireland," Pitt demanded. "And for heaven's sake sit down!" It was not that he wanted the information in detail so much as he needed the chance to weigh everything Stoker said, and make some judgment as to the truth of it, and exactly where Stoker's loyalties lay.

Stoker obeyed without comment. Possibly he knew the reason Pitt asked, but if so there was nothing in his face to betray it. "I was only there two days," he began.

"Who sent you?" Pitt interrupted.

"No one. I made it look like it was Mr. Narraway, before he went."

"Why?"

"Because I don't believe he's guilty any more than you do," Stoker said bitterly. "He's a hard man, clever, cold at times in his own way, but he'd never betray his country. They got rid of him because they knew he'd see what was going on here, and stop it. They thought you might too, in loyalty to Mr. Narraway, even if you didn't spot what they're doing. No offense, sir, but you don't know enough yet to see what it is."

Pitt winced, but he had no argument. It was painfully true.

"Mr. Narraway seemed to be trying to find out who set him up to look like he took the money meant for Mulhare, probably because that would lead back to whoever it is here in London," Stoker went on. "I don't know whether he found out or not, because they got him by killing O'Neil. They set that up perfectly. Fixed a quarrel between them in front of a couple o' score of people, then somehow got him to go alone to O'Neil's house, and had O'Neil shot just before he got there.

"By all accounts, Mrs. Pitt was right on his heels, but he swore to the police that she wasn't there at the time, so they didn't bother her. She went back to Dublin where she was staying, and that's the last I know of it. Mr. Narraway was arrested and no doubt if we don't do anything, they'll try him and hang him. But we'll have a week or two before that." He stopped, meeting Pitt with steady, demanding eyes.

The weight of leadership settled on Pitt like a leaden coat. There was no one beyond himself to turn to, no one else's opinion to listen to and use as a balance. Whoever had designed this so that it was he, and not Narraway, that they had to face, was supremely clever.

He must trust Stoker. The advantage outweighed the risk.

"Then we have ten days in which to rescue Narraway," he replied. "Perhaps whoever it is will be as aware of that as we are. It is safe to assume that by that time they will have achieved whatever it is they plan, and for which they needed him gone."

Stoker sat up a little straighter. "Yes, sir."

"And we have no idea who it is planning it," Pitt continued. "Except that they have great power and authority within the branch, so we dare not trust anyone. Even Sir Gerald himself may choose to trust this person rather than trust you or me."

Stoker allowed himself a slight smile. "You're right, sir. And that could be the end of everything, probably of you an' me, and certainly of Mr. Narraway."

"Then we are alone in working out what it is." Pitt had already made up his mind that if he were to trust Stoker at all, then it might as well be entirely. This was not the time to let Stoker believe he was only half relied on.

Pitt pulled out the papers he had been studying and placed them sideways on the desk so they could both see them.

"This is the pattern I found so far." He pointed to communications, the gun smuggling, the movements of known radicals both in Britain and on the continent of Europe.

"Not much of a pattern," Stoker said grimly. "It looks pretty much like always to me." He pointed. "There's Rosa Luxemburg in Germany and Poland in that part, but she's been getting noisier for years. There's Jean Jaures in France, but he's harmless enough. Your basic socialist reformer. Bit hard now and then, but what he's saying is fair enough, if you look at it. Nothing to do with us, though. He's as French as frog's legs."

"And here?" Pitt pointed to some Fabian Society activity in London and Birmingham.

"They'll get changes through Parliament, eventually," Stoker said. "That Keir Hardie'll do a thing or two, but that's not our bother either. Personally I wish him good luck. We need a few changes. No, sir, there is something big planned, and pretty bad, an' we haven't worked out what it is yet."

Pitt did not reply. He stared at the reports yet again, rereading the text, studying the geographic patterns of where they originated, who was involved.

Then he saw something curious. "Is that Willy Portman?" he asked Stoker, pointing to a report of known agitators observed in Birmingham.

"Yes, sir, seems like it. What's he doing here? Nasty piece of work, Willy Portman. Violent. Nothing good, if he's involved."

"I know," Pitt agreed. "But that's not it. This report says he was seen at a meeting with Joe Gallagher. Those two have been enemies for years. What could bring them together?"

Stoker stared at him. "There's more," he said very quietly. "McLeish was seen in Sheffield with Mick Haddon."

Pitt knew the names. They were both extremely violent men, and again known to hate each other.

"And Fenner," he added, putting his finger on the page where that name was noted. "And Guzman, and Scarlatti. That's the pattern. Whatever it is, it's big enough to bring these enemies together in a common cause, and here in Britain."

There was a shadow of fear in Stoker's eyes. "I'd like reform, sir, for lots of reasons. But I don't want everything good thrown out at the same time. And violence isn't the way to do anything, because no matter what you need to do in the first place, it never ends there. Seems to me that if you execute the king, either you end up with a religious dictator like Cromwell who rules over the people more tightly than any king ever did, and then you only have to get rid of him anyway — or else you end up with a monster like Robespierre in Paris, and the Reign of Terror, then Napoleon after that. Then you get a king back in the end anyway. At least for a while. I prefer us as we are, with our faults, rather than all that."

"So do I," Pitt agreed. "But we can't stop it if we don't know what it is, and when and how it will strike. I don't think we have very long."

"No, sir. And if you'll excuse me spelling it out, we haven't any allies either, least of all here in Lisson Grove. Whoever blackened Mr. Narraway's name did a very good job of it, and nobody trusts you, because you're his man."

Pitt smiled grimly. "It's a lot more than

that, Stoker. I'm new to this job and I don't know the history of it and none of the men will trust me above Austwick, for which you can hardly blame them."

"Is Austwick a traitor, sir?"

"I think so. But he may not be the only one."

"I know that," Stoker said very quietly.

CHAPTER 11

Narraway was intensely relieved to see the familiar coast of Ireland slip away over the horizon with no coast guard or police boat in pursuit of them. At least for a few hours he could turn his attention to what he should do once he arrived at Holyhead. The obvious thing would be to catch the next train to London. Would it be so obvious a move that he might be apprehended? On the other hand, a delay might give anyone still bent on catching him a better chance to cross the Irish Sea in a lighter, perhaps faster boat, and arrest him before he could get any help.

He was standing on the deck gazing westward. Charlotte was beside him. She looked weary, and the marks of fear were still drawn deep into her face. Even so, he found her beautiful. He had long ago grown tired of unspoiled perfection. If that was what one hungered for — the color, the proportion, the smooth skin, the perfect balance of feature — there were works of art all over the world to stare at. Even the poorest man could find a copy for himself.

A real woman had warmth, vulnerability, fears, and blemishes of her own — or else how could she have any gentleness toward those of her mate? Without experience, one was a cup waiting to be filled — well crafted perhaps, but empty. And to a soul of any courage or passion, experience also meant a degree of pain, false starts, occasional bad judgments, a knowledge of loss. Young women were charming for a short while, but very soon they bored him.

He was used to loneliness, but there were times when its burden ached so deeply he could never be unaware of it. Standing on the deck with Charlotte, watching the wind unravel her hair and blow it across her face, was one such time.

She had already told him what she had learned of Talulla, of John Tyrone and the money, and of Fiachra McDaid. It was complicated. Some of the situation he had guessed from what O'Casey had told him, but he had not understood Talulla's place in it. Had Fiachra not convinced her that her parents were innocent, she would not have blamed Cormac. She would still have blamed Narraway, of course, but that was fair. Kate's death was as much his fault as anyone's, insofar as it was foreseeable. He had known how Sean felt about her.

What did Talulla imagine Cormac could have done to save Sean? Sean was a rebel whose wife gave him up to the English. Was that betrayal treason to the spirit of Ireland, or just a practical decision to avoid more pointless, heartbreaking bloodshed? How many people were still alive who would not have been if it had happened? Perhaps half the people she knew.

But of course she wouldn't see it that way. She couldn't afford to. She needed her anger, and it was justified only if her parents were the victims.

And Fiachra? Narraway winced at his own blindness. How desperately he had misread him! He had concealed the passion of his Irish nationalism inside what had seemed to be a concern for the disenfranchised of all nations. The more Narraway thought about it, the more it made sense. Odd how often a sweeping love for all could be willing to sacrifice the one, or the ten, or the score, almost with indifference. Fiachra would see the glory of greater social justice, freedom for Ireland — and the price would slip through his fingers uncounted. He was a dreamer who stepped over the corpses without even seeing them. Under the charm there was ice — and by God he was clever. In law he had committed no crime. If justice ever reached him, it would be for some other reason, at another time.

Narraway looked at Charlotte again. She became aware of his gaze and turned to him.

"There's no one anywhere on the whole sea," she said with a slightly rueful smile. "I think we're safe."

The inclusion of herself in his escape gave him a sort of warmth that he was aware was ridiculous. He was behaving like a man of twenty.

"So far," he agreed. "But when we get on the train at Holyhead you would be safer in a different carriage. I doubt there will be anyone looking for me, but it's not impossible."

"Who?" she said, as if dismissing the idea. "No one could have gotten here ahead of us." Before he could answer she went on. "And don't tell me they anticipated your escape. If they had, they'd have prevented it. Don't be naïve, Victor. They wanted you hanged. It would be the perfect revenge for Sean."

He winced. "You're very blunt."

"I suppose you just noticed that!" She

gave a tiny, twisted smile.

"No, of course not. But that was unusual, even for you."

"This is an unusual situation," she said. "At least for me. Should I be trite if I asked you if you do it often?"

"Ah, Charlotte!" He brushed his hand through his heavy hair and turned away, needing to hide the emotion in his face from her. He needed it to be private, but — far more than that — he knew that it would embarrass her to realize how intense were his feelings for her.

"I'm sorry," she said quickly.

Hell, he swore to himself. He had not been quick enough.

"I know it's serious," she went on, apparently meaning something quite different.

A wave of relief swept over him, and, perversely, of disappointment. Did some part of him want her to know? If so, it must be suppressed. It would create a difficulty between them that could never be forgotten.

"Yes," he agreed.

"Will you go to Lisson Grove?" Now she sounded anxious.

"No. I'd rather they didn't even know I was back in England, and certainly not where." He saw the relief in her face.

"There's only one person I dare trust totally, and that is Vespasia Cumming-Gould. I shall get off the train one or two stops before London and find a telephone. If I'm lucky I'll be able to get hold of her straightaway. It'll be long after dark by then. If not, I'll find rooms and wait there until I can."

His voice dropped to a more urgent note. "You should go home. You won't be in any danger. Or else you could go to Vespasia's house, if you prefer. Perhaps you should wait and see what she says." He realized as he spoke that he had no idea what had happened to Pitt, even if he was safe. To send Charlotte back to a house with no one there but a strange maid was possibly a cruel thing to do. She had said before that her sister Emily was away somewhere, similarly her mother. God! What a mess. But if anything had happened to Pitt, no one would be able to comfort her. He could not bear to think of that.

Please heaven whoever was behind this did not think Pitt a sufficient danger to have done anything drastic to him. "We'll get off a couple of stops before London," he repeated. "And call Vespasia."

"Good idea," she agreed, turning back to watch the gulls circling over the white wake of the ship. The two of them stood side by side in silence, oddly comforted by the endless, rhythmic moving of the water and the pale wings of the birds echoing the curved line of it.

Narraway was connected with Vespasia immediately. Only when he heard the sound of her voice, which was thin and a little crackly over the line, did he realize how overwhelmingly glad he was to speak with her.

"Victor! Where on earth are you?" she demanded. Then an instant later: "No. Do not tell me. Are you safe? Is Charlotte safe?"

"Yes, we are both safe," he answered her. She was the only woman since his childhood who had ever made him feel as if he were accountable to her. "We are not far away, but I thought it better to speak to you before coming the rest of the journey."

"Don't," she said simply. "It would be far better if you were to find some suitable place, which we shall not name, and we shall meet there. A very great deal has happened since you left, but there is far more that is about to happen. I do not know what that is, except that it is of profound importance, and it may be tragically violent. But I daresay you have deduced that for yourself. I

461

rather fear that your whole trip to Ireland was designed to take you away from London. Everything else was incidental."

"Who's in charge now?" he asked, the chill seeping into him, even though he was standing in a very comfortable hotel hallway, looking from left to right every few moments to make sure he was still alone and not overheard. "Charles Austwick?"

"No," she answered, and there was a heaviness in her voice, even over the wires. "That was only temporary. Thomas is back from France. That trip was entirely abortive. He has replaced Austwick, and is now in your office, and hating it."

Narraway was so stunned for a moment he could think of no words adequate to his emotions — certainly none that he could repeat in front of Vespasia, or Charlotte, were she close enough to hear.

"Victor!" Vespasia said sharply.

"Yes . . . I'm here. What . . . what is going on?"

"I don't know," she admitted. "But I have a great fear that he has been placed there precisely because he cannot possibly cope with whatever atrocity is being planned. He has no experience in this kind of leadership. He has not the deviousness nor the subtlety of judgment to make the necessary unpleasant decisions. And there is no one there whom he can trust, which at least he knows. I am afraid he is quite appallingly alone, exactly as someone has designed he should be. His remarkable record of success as a policeman, and as a solver of crimes within Special Branch jurisdiction, will justify his being placed in your position. No one will be held to blame for choosing him . . ."

"You mean he's there to take the blame when this storm breaks," Narraway said bitterly.

"Precisely." Her voice cracked a little. "Victor, we must beat this, and I have very little idea how. I don't even know what it is they plan, but it is something very, very wrong indeed."

She was brave; no one he knew had ever had more courage; she was clever and still beautiful . . . but she was also growing old and at times very much alone. Suddenly he was aware of her vulnerability: of the friends, and even the loves she had cared for passionately, and lost. She was perhaps a decade or so older than he. Suddenly he thought of her not as a force of society, or of nature, but as a woman, as capable of loneliness as he was himself.

"Do you remember the hostelry where we met Somerset Carlisle about eight years ago? We had the most excellent lobster for luncheon?" he asked.

"Yes," she said unhesitatingly.

"We should meet there as soon as possible," he told her. "Bring Pitt . . . please."

"I shall be there by midnight," she replied.

He was startled. "Midnight?"

"For heaven's sake, Victor!" she said tartly. "What do you want to do, wait until breakfast? Don't be absurd. You had better reserve us three rooms, in case there is any of the night left for sleeping." Then she hesitated.

He wondered why. "Lady Vespasia?"

She gave a little sigh. "I dislike being offensive, but since I assume that you escaped from . . . where you were, you have little money, and I daresay are in less than your usually elegant state. You had better give my name, as if you were booking it for me, and tell them that I shall settle when I arrive. Better if you do not give anyone else's name, your own, or Thomas's."

"Actually Charlotte had the foresight to pack my case for me, so I have all the respectable attire I shall need," he replied with the first flash of amusement he had felt for some time.

"She did what?" Vespasia said coolly.

"She was obliged to leave the lodgings,"

he exclaimed, still with a smile. "She did not wish to abandon my luggage, so she took it with her. If you don't know me better than that, you should at least know her!"

"Quite so," she said more gently. "I apologize. Indeed, I also know you. I shall see you as close to midnight as I am able to make it. I am very glad you are safe, Victor."

That meant more to him than he had expected, so much more that he found himself suddenly unable to answer. He replaced the receiver on its hook in silence.

Pitt was at home, sitting at the kitchen table beginning his supper when Minnie Maude came into the room. Her face was pink, her eyes frightened, her usually untamed hair pulled even looser and badly pinned up at one side.

"What's the matter?" Pitt said, instantly worried as well.

Minnie Maude took a deep breath and let it out shakily. "There's a lady 'ere ter see yer, sir. I mean a real lady, like a duchess, or summink. Wot shall I do wif' 'er, sir?"

"Oh." Pitt felt a wave of relief wash over him, like warmth from a fire on cold flesh. "Show her in here, and then put the kettle on again."

Minnie Maude held her guard. "No, sir, I

mean a real lady, not jus' some nice person, like."

"Tall and slender, and very beautiful, despite the fact that she isn't young anymore," Pitt agreed. "And eyes that could freeze you at twenty paces, if you step out of line. Lady Vespasia Cumming-Gould. Please ask her to come into the kitchen. She has been in here before. Then make her a cup of tea. We have some Earl Grey. We keep it for her."

Minnie Maude stared at him as if he had lost his wits.

"Please," he added.

"Yer'll pardon me, sir," Minnie Maude said shakily. "But yer look like yer bin dragged through an 'edge backward."

Pitt pushed his hand through his hair. "She wouldn't recognize me if I didn't. Don't leave her standing in the hall. Bring her here."

"She in't in the 'all, sir. She's in the parlor," Minnie Maude told him with disgust at his imagining she would do anything less.

"I apologize. Of course she is. Bring her here anyway."

Defeated, she went to obey.

Pitt ate the last mouthful of his supper and cleared the table as Vespasia arrived in the doorway.

"I always liked this room," she observed. "Thank you, Minnie Maude. Good evening, Thomas. I am sorry to have interrupted your dinner, but it is unavoidable."

Behind him Minnie Maude skirted her and put the kettle onto the hob. Then she began to wash out the teapot in which Pitt's tea had been, and prepare it to make a different brew for Vespasia. Her back was very straight, and her hands shook just a little.

Pitt did not interrupt Vespasia. He held one of the hard-backed kitchen chairs for her to be seated. She declined to take off her cape.

"I have just heard from Victor," she told him. "On the telephone, from a railway station not far from the city. Charlotte was with him, and perfectly well. You have no need to concern yourself about her health, or anything else. However there are other matters of very great concern indeed. Matters that require your immediate and total attention."

"Narraway?" His mind raced. She was being discreet, no doubt aware that Minnie Maude could hear all they said. It would be cruel, pointless, and possibly even dangerous to frighten her unnecessarily. Certainly she did not deserve it, apart from the very practical matter that he needed her common sense to care for his household and, most important, his children — at least until Charlotte returned. And, he admitted, he rather liked her. She was good-natured and not without spirit. There was something about her not totally unlike Gracie.

"Indeed." Vespasia turned to Minnie Maude. "When you have made the tea, will you please go and pack a small case for your master, with what he will need for one night away from home. Clean personal linen and a clean shirt, and his customary toiletries. When you have it, bring it downstairs and leave it in the hall by the bottom step."

Minnie Maude's eyes widened. She blinked, as if wondering whether she dare confirm the orders with Pitt, or if she should simply obey them. Who was in charge?

They were giving the poor girl a great deal to become accustomed to in a very short while. He smiled at her. "Please do that, Minnie Maude. It appears I shall have to leave you. But also, I shall return before too long."

"You may be extremely busy for some time," Vespasia corrected him. "It is a very good thing that Minnie Maude is a responsible girl. You will need her. Now let us have tea and prepare to leave."

As soon as the tea was poured and Minnie Maude was out of the room Pitt turned to Vespasia. The look on his face demanded she explain.

"It is a conclusion no longer avoidable that both you and Victor were drawn away from London for a very specific purpose," she said, sipping delicately at her tea. "Victor was put out of office, with an attempt to have him at least imprisoned in Ireland, possibly hanged. You were lured away from London before that, so you, as the only person at Lisson Grove with an unquestionable personal loyalty to him, and the courage to fight for him, would not be there. He would be friendless, as indeed he was."

Pitt would have interrupted Narraway to ask why, but he would not dare interrupt Vespasia.

"It appears that Charles Austwick is involved," she continued. "To what degree, and for what purpose, we do not yet know, but the plot is widespread, dangerous, and probably violent."

"I know," he said quietly. "I think I can rely on Stoker, but so far as I can see, at the moment, he is the only one. There will be more, but I don't know who they are, and I can't afford any mistakes. Even one could be fatal. What I don't understand is why Austwick made so little fuss at being removed from the leadership. It makes me fear that there is someone else who knows every move I make and who is reporting to him."

She set her cup down. "The answer is uglier than that, my dear," she said very quietly. "I think that what is planned is so wide and so final in its result that they wish you to be there to take the blame for Special Branch's failure to prevent it. Then the branch can be re-created from the beginning with none of the experienced men who are there now, and be completely in the control of those who are behind this. Or alternatively, it might be disbanded altogether, as a force that has served its purpose in the past but is now manifestly no longer needed."

The thought was so devastating that it took him several moments to grasp the full import of it. He was not promoted for merit, but as someone completely dispensable, a Judas goat to be sacrificed when Special Branch took the blame for failing to prevent some disaster. He should have been furiously angry, and he would be, eventually, when he absorbed the enormity of it and had time to think of himself. Now all he could deal with was the nature of the plot, and who was involved. How could they ever begin to fight against it?

He looked at Vespasia. He was startled to see the gentleness in her face, a deep and hurting compassion.

He forced himself to smile at her. In the same circumstances she would never have spent time pitying herself. He would not let her down by doing so.

"I'm trying to think what I would have been working on had I not gone to St. Malo," he said aloud. "I don't know if poor West was actually going to tell me anything that mattered, such as that Gower was a traitor, or if he was killed only to get me chasing Wrexham to France. I thought it was the former, but perhaps it wasn't. Certainly that was the end of my involvement over here."

"If you had been here you might have prevented Victor from having been removed from office," she concluded. "On the other hand, you might have been implicated in the same thing, and removed also . . ." She stopped.

He shrugged. "Or killed." He said what he knew she was thinking. "Sending me to France was better, much less obvious. Also, it seems they wanted me here now, to take the blame for this failure that is about to descend on us. I've been trying to think what cases we were most concerned with, what we may have learned had we had time."

"We will consider it in my carriage on the way to our appointment," she said, finishing her tea. "Minnie Maude will have your case packed any moment, and we should be on our way."

He rose and went to say good night and — for the very immediate future — good-bye to his children. He gave Minnie Maude last instructions, and a little more money to ascertain that she had sufficient provisions. Then he collected his case and went outside to Vespasia's carriage where it was waiting in the street. Within seconds they were moving briskly.

"I've already looked over everything that happened shortly before I left, and in Austwick's notes since," he began. "And in the reports from other people. I did it with Stoker. We saw something that I don't yet understand, but it is very alarming."

"What is it?" she asked quickly.

He told her about the violent men who had been seen in several different parts of England, and watched her face grow pale and very grave as he told her how old enemies had been seen together, as if they had a common cause.

"This is very serious," she agreed. "There is something I also have heard whispers of while you have been away. I dismissed it at first as being the usual idealistic talk that has always been around among dreamers, always totally impractical. For example, certain social reformers seem to be creating plans as if they could get them through the House of Commons without difficulty. Some of the reforms were radical, and yet I admit there is a certain justice to them. I assumed they were simply naïve, but perhaps there is some major element that I have missed."

They rode in silence for the length of Woburn Place toward Euston Road, then turned right with the stream of traffic and continued north until it became the Pentonville Road.

"I fear I know what element you have missed," Pitt said at last.

"Violence?" she asked. "I cannot think of any one man, or even group of men, who would pass some of the legislation they are proposing. It would be pointless anyway. It would be sent back by the House of Lords, and then they would have to begin again. By that time the opposition would have collected its wits, and its arguments. They must know that."

"Of course they do," he agreed. "But if there were no House of Lords . . ."

The street lamps outside seemed harsh, the rattle of the carriage wheels unnaturally loud. "Another gunpowder plot?" she asked. "The country would be outraged. We hung, drew, and quartered Guy Fawkes and his conspirators. We might not be quite so barbaric this time, but I wouldn't risk all I valued on it." Her face was momentarily in the shadows as a higher, longer carriage passed between them and the nearest street lamps.

Nearly an hour later they arrived at the hostelry Narraway had chosen, tired, chilly, and uncomfortable. They greeted one another briefly, with intense emotion, then allowed the landlord to show them to the rooms they would occupy for the night. Then they were offered a private lounge where they might have whatever refreshments they wished, and be otherwise uninterrupted.

Pitt was filled with emotion to see Charlotte; joy just at the sight of her face, anxiety that she looked so tired. He was relieved that she was safe when she so easily might not have been; frustrated that he had no opportunity to be alone with her, even for a moment; and angry that she had been in such danger. She had acted recklessly and with no reference to his opinion or feelings. He felt painfully excluded. Narraway had been there and he had not. His reaction was childish; he was ashamed of it, but that did nothing to lessen its sharpness.

Then he looked at Narraway, and despite himself his anger melted. The man was exhausted. The lines in his face seemed more deeply cut than they had been just a week or two before; his dark eyes were bruised around the sockets, and he brushed his hair back impatiently with his thin, strong hands as if it were in his way.

They glanced at each other, no one knowing who was in command. Narraway had led Special Branch for years, but it was Pitt's job now. And yet neither of them would preempt Vespasia's seniority.

Vespasia smiled. "For heaven's sake, Thomas, don't sit there like a schoolboy waiting for permission to speak. You are the commander of Special Branch. What is your judgment of the situation? We will add to it, should we have something to offer."

Pitt cleared his throat. He felt as if he were usurping Narraway's place. Yet he was also aware that Narraway was weary and beaten, betrayed in ways that he had not foreseen, and accused of crimes where he could not prove his innocence. The situation was harsh; a little gentleness was needed in the few places where it was possible.

Carefully he repeated for Narraway what had happened from the time he and Gower had seen West murdered until he and Stoker had put together as many of the pieces as they could. He was aware that he was speaking of professional secrets in front of both Vespasia and Charlotte. It was something he had not done before, but the gravity of the situation allowed no luxury of exclusion. If they failed to restore justice, it would all become desperately public in a very short time anyway. How short a time he could only guess.

When he had finished he looked at Narraway.

"The House of Lords would be the obvious and most relevant target," Narraway said slowly. "It would be the beginning of a revolution in our lives, a very dramatic one. God only knows what might follow. The French throne is already gone. The Austro-Hungarian is shaking, especially after that wretched business at Mayerling." He glanced at Charlotte and saw the puzzlement in her face. "Six years ago, in '89," he explained, "Crown Prince Rudolf and his mistress shot themselves in a hunting lodge. All very messy and never really understood." He leaned forward a little, his face resuming its gravity. "The other thrones of Europe are less secure than they used to be, and Russia is careering toward chaos if they don't institute some sweeping reforms, very soon. Which is almost as likely as daffodils in November. They're all hanging on with their fingers."

"Not us," Pitt argued. "The queen went through a shaky spell a few years ago, but her popularity's returning."

"Which is why if they struck here, at our hereditary privilege, the rest of Europe would have nothing with which to fight back," Narraway responded. "Think about it, Pitt. If you were a passionate socialist and you wanted to sweep away the rights of a privileged class to rule over the rest of us, where would you strike? France has no ruling nobility. Spain isn't going to affect the rest of us anymore. They used to be related to half Europe in Hapsburg times, but not now. Austria? They're crumbling anyway. Germany? Bismarck is the real power. All the great royal houses of Europe are related to Victoria, one way or the other. If Victoria gets rid of her House of Lords, then it will be the beginning of the end for privilege by birth."

"One cannot inherit honor or morality, Victor," Vespasia said softly. "But one can learn from the cradle a sense of the past, and gratitude for its gifts. One can learn a responsibility toward the future, to guard and perhaps improve on what one has been given, and leave it whole for those who follow."

His face pinched as he looked at her. "I am speaking their words, not my own, Lady Vespasia." He bit his lip. "If we are to defeat them, we must know what they believe, and what they intend to do. If they can gain the power they will sweep away the good with the bad, because they don't understand what it is to answer only to your conscience rather than to the voice of the people, which comes regardless whether or not they have the faintest idea what they are talking about."

"I'm sorry," she said very quietly. "I think perhaps I am frightened. Hysteria appalls me."

"It should," he assured her. "The day there is no one left to fear it we are all lost." He turned to Pitt. "Have you any idea as to what specific plans anyone has?"

"Very little," Pitt admitted. "But I know

who the enemy is." He relayed to Narraway what he had told Vespasia about the different violent men who loathed one another, and yet appeared to have found a common cause.

"Where is Her Majesty now?" Narraway asked.

"Osborne," Pitt replied. He felt his heart beating faster, harder. Other notes he had seen from various people came to mind: movements of men that were small and discreet, but those men's names should have given pause to whoever was reading the reports. Narraway would have seen it. "I believe that's where they'll strike. It's the most vulnerable and most immediate place."

Narraway paled even further. "The queen?" He gave no exclamation, no word of anger or surprise; his emotion was too consuming. The thought of attacking Victoria herself was so shocking that all words were inadequate.

Pitt's mind raced to the army, the police on the Isle of Wight, all the men he himself could call from other duties. Then another thought came to him: Was this what they were supposed to think? What if he responded by concentrating all his resources on Osborne House, and the actual attack came somewhere else?

"Be careful," Narraway said quietly. "If we cause public alarm it could do all the damage they need."

"I know." Pitt was aware of Charlotte and Vespasia watching him as well. "I know that. I also know that they have probably a large space of time in which to strike. They could wait us out, then move as soon as we have relaxed."

"I doubt it." Narraway shook his head. "They know I escaped and they know you are back from France. I think it's urgent, even immediate. And the men you named here in England, together, won't wait. You should go back to Lisson Grove and —"

"I'm going to Osborne," Pitt said, cutting across him. "I don't have anyone else I can send, and if you're right, we could already be late."

"You're going to Lisson Grove," Narraway repeated. "You are head of Special Branch, not a foot soldier to be going into battle. What happens to the operation if you are shot, captured, or simply where no one can reach you? Stop thinking like an adventurer and think like a leader. You need to find out exactly whom you can trust, and you need to do it by the end of tomorrow." He glanced at the ormolu clock on the mantel. "Today," he corrected. "I'll go to Osborne.

480

I can at least warn them, perhaps find a way of holding off whatever attack there is until you can send men to relieve us."

"You may not be let in," Vespasia pointed out to him. "You have no standing now."

Narraway winced. Clearly he had forgotten that aspect of his loss of office.

"I'll come with you," Vespasia said, not as an offer but as a statement. "I am known there. Unless I am very unfortunate, they will admit me, at least to the house. If I explain what has happened, and the danger, the butler will give me audience with the queen. I still have to decide what to tell her once I am in her company."

Pitt did not argue. The logic of it was only too clear. He rose to his feet. "Then we had better return and begin. Charlotte, you will come with me as far as Keppel Street. Narraway and Aunt Vespasia had better take the carriage and set out for the Isle of Wight."

Vespasia looked at Pitt, then at Narraway. "I think a couple of hours' sleep would be wise," she said firmly. "And then breakfast before we begin. We are going to make some very serious judgments, and perhaps fight some hard battles. We will not do it well if we are mentally or physically so much less than our best."

Pitt wanted to argue with her, but he was exhausted. If it was in any way acceptable he would like to lie down for an hour or two and allow his mind to let go of everything. He couldn't remember when he had last relaxed totally, let alone had the inner peace of knowing that Charlotte was beside him, that she was safe.

He looked at Narraway.

Narraway gave a bleak smile. "It's good advice. We'll get up at four, and leave at five." He glanced toward Vespasia to see that it met with her agreement.

She nodded.

"I'm coming with you," Charlotte said. There was no question in her voice, just a simple statement. She turned to Pitt. "I'm sorry. It is not a question of not wanting to be left out, or of any idea that I am indispensable. But I can't let Aunt Vespasia travel alone. It would be remarked on, for a start. Surely the servants at Osborne would consider it very odd?"

Of course she was right. Pitt should have thought of it himself. It was a large omission on his part that he had not. "Of course," he agreed. "Now let's retire while we still have a couple of hours left."

When they were upstairs and the door closed Charlotte looked at him with gentleness and intense apology. "I'm sorry . . . ," she began.

"Be quiet," he answered. "Let's just be together, while we can."

She walked into his arms and held him close. He was so tired that he was almost asleep on his feet. Moments later, when they lay down, he was dimly aware that she was still holding him.

In the morning Pitt left to return to Lisson Grove. Charlotte, Vespasia, and Narraway took the coach south along the main road to the nearest railway station to catch the next train to Southampton, and from there the ferry to the Isle of Wight.

"If nothing is happening yet we may have a little trouble in gaining an audience with the queen," Narraway said when they were sitting in a private compartment in the train. The soothing rattle of the wheels over the rails rhythmically clattered at every joint. "But if the enemy are there already, we will have to think of a better way of getting inside."

"Can we purchase a black Gladstone bag in Southampton?" Charlotte suggested. "With a few bottles and powders from an apothecary, Victor could pose as a doctor, I shall be his nurse." She glanced at Vespasia.

"Or your lady's maid. I have no skills in either, but am sufficiently plainly dressed to pass, at least briefly."

Vespasia considered for only a moment. "An excellent idea," she agreed. "But we should get you a plainer gown, and an apron. A good white one, without ornament, should serve for either calling. I think Victor's nurse would be better. The staff will be very familiar with lady's maids; nurses they might know less. Do you agree, Victor?"

There was a flash of amusement in his eyes. "Of course. We will arrange it all as soon as we arrive at the station."

"You think we are late already, don't you?" Charlotte said to him.

He made no pretense. "Yes. If I were they, I would have acted by now."

An hour and a half later they approached the spacious, comfortable house in which Queen Victoria had chosen to spend so many years of her life, particularly since the death of Prince Albert. Osborne seemed to offer her a comfort she found nowhere else in the more magnificent castles and palaces that were also hers.

The house looked totally at peace in the fitful spring sun. Most of the trees were in leaf, in a clean, almost gleaming translucency. The grass was vivid green. There was blossom on the blackthorn, and the hawthorn was in heavy bud.

Osborne was set in the gently rolling parkland that one would expect of any family mansion of the extremely wealthy. Much of the land was wooded, but there were also wide, well-kept sweeps of grass that gave it a feeling of great space and light. The house had been designed by Prince Albert himself, who had clearly much admired the opulent elegance of the Italian villas. It had two magnificent square towers, which were flat-topped and had tall windows on all sides. The main building copied the same squared lines, and the sunlight seemed to reflect on glass in every aspect. One could only imagine the beauty of the inside.

Their carriage pulled up and they alighted, thanking the driver and paying him.

"You'll be wanting me to wait," the cabbie said with a nod. "You can look, but that's all. Her Majesty's in residence. You don't get no closer than this."

Vespasia paid him generously. "No thank you. You may leave us."

He shrugged and obeyed, turning his vehicle around and muttering to the horse about tourists with no sense.

"There is nothing for us to wait for either,"

Narraway said ruefully. "I can't tell anything from the outside, can you? It all looks just as I imagine it should. There's even a gardener at work over there." He did not point but inclined his head.

Charlotte glanced in the direction he indicated and saw a man bent over a hoe, his attention apparently on the ground. The scene looked rural and pleasantly domestic. Some of her anxiety eased. Perhaps they had been more frightened than necessary. They were in time. Now they must avoid looking foolish, not only for the sake of pride, but so that when they gave the warning the royal household staff would take them seriously. Anyway, it would not be long before Pitt would send reinforcements who were trained for just this sort of duty, and the danger would be past.

Unless, of course, they were mistaken, and the blow would strike somewhere else. Was this yet another brilliant diversion? Narraway forced himself to smile in the sunlight. "I feel a trifle ridiculous carrying this case now."

"Hold on to it as if it were highly valuable to you," Vespasia said very quietly. "You will need it. That man is no more a gardener than you are. He doesn't know a weed from a flower. Don't look at him, or he will become alarmed. Doctors called out to the queen are not concerned with men hoeing the heads off petunias."

Charlotte felt the sun burn in her eyes. The huge house in front of them seemed to blur and go fuzzy in her vision. Ahead of her, Vespasia's back was ruler-straight. Her head with its fashionable hat was as high and level as if she were sailing into a garden party as an honored guest.

They were met at the door by a butler whose white hair was scraped back from the high dome of his forehead as if he had run his hands through it almost hard enough to pull it out. He recognized Vespasia immediately.

"Good afternoon, Lady Vespasia," he said, his voice shaking. "I am afraid Her Majesty is a little unwell today, and is not receiving any callers whatever. I'm so sorry we didn't know in time to advise you. I would invite you in, but one of our housemaids has a fever that we would not wish anyone else to catch. I'm so sorry."

"Most unpleasant for the poor girl," Vespasia sympathized. "And for all the rest of you also. You are quite correct to take it seriously, of course. Fortunately I have brought Dr. Narraway with me and I'm sure he would be happy to see the girl and do

487

whatever can be done for her. Sometimes a little tincture of quinine helps greatly. It might be wise for Her Majesty's sake as well. It would be dreadful if she were to catch such a thing."

The butler was lost for words. He drew in his breath, started to speak, and stopped again. The sweat stood out on his brow and his eyes blinked rapidly.

"I can see that you are distressed for her." Vespasia spoke as reassuringly as she could, although her voice wavered a trifle also. "Perhaps in humanity, as well as wisdom, we should have Dr. Narraway look at her. If all your staff became infected you will be in a serious and most unpleasant situation."

"Lady Vespasia, I cannot . . ."

Before he could finish, another, younger man appeared, also dressed as a servant. He was dark-haired, perhaps in his mid-thirties, and heavier set.

"Sir," he said to the butler. "I think perhaps the lady is right. I just had word poor Mollie is getting worse. You'd better accept their offer and have them in."

The butler looked at the man with loathing, but after one desperate glance at Vespasia, he surrendered.

"Thank you." Vespasia stepped across the

threshold; Charlotte and Narraway followed her.

The moment they were inside and the front door closed, it was apparent that they were prisoners. There were other men at the foot of the sweeping staircase and at the entrance to the kitchens and servants' quarters.

"You didn't have to do that!" the butler accused the other man.

"Oh, decidedly, we did," the other contradicted. "They'd 'ave gone away knowing there was something wrong. Best we keep all this quiet. Don't want the old lady upset."

"No you don't," Vespasia agreed tartly. "If she has an attack and dies, you will be guilty not only of murder but of regicide. Do you imagine there is anywhere in the world that you could hide from that? Not that you would escape. We may have many ideas about the liberty or equality that we aspire to, even fight for, but no one will countenance the murder of the queen who has been on our throne longer than the lifetime of most of her subjects around the face of the earth. You would be torn apart, although I daresay that matters less to you than the complete discrediting of all your ideas."

"Lady, keep a still tongue in yer head, or

I'll still it for yer. Whatever people feel about the queen, no one cares a jot if yer survive this or not," the man said sharply. "Yer pushed yer way in here. Yer've no one but yerself to blame if it turns bad for yer."

"This is . . . ," the butler began. Then, realizing he was only offering another hostage to fate, he bit off his words.

"Is anyone sick?" Vespasia inquired of no one in particular.

"No," the butler admitted. "It's what they told us to say."

"Good. Then will you please conduct us to Her Majesty. If she is being held with the same courtesy that you are offering us, it might still be as well for Dr. Narraway to be close to her. You don't want her to suffer any unnecessary ill effects. If she is not alive and well I imagine she will be of little use to you as a hostage."

"How do I know ye're a doctor?" the man said suspiciously, looking at Narraway.

"You don't," Narraway replied. "But what have you to lose? Do you think I mean her any harm?"

"What?"

"Do you think I mean her any harm?" Narraway repeated impatiently.

"Of course not! What kind of a stupid question is that?"

"The only kind that needs an answer. If I mean her no harm then it would be of less trouble to you to keep us all in the same room rather than use several. This is not so very large a house, for all its importance. I will at least keep her calm. Is that not in your interest?"

"What's in that bag? Yer could have knives, even gas for all I know."

"I am a physician, not a surgeon," Narraway said tartly.

"Who's she?" the man glanced at Charlotte.

"My nurse. Do you imagine I attend female patients without a chaperone?"

The man took the Gladstone bag from Narraway and opened it up. He saw only the few powders and potions they had bought from the apothecary in Southampton, all labeled. They had been careful, for precisely this reason, not to purchase anything that was an obvious weapon, not even small scissors for the cutting of bandages. Everything was exactly what it purported to be.

The man shut the bag again and turned toward his ally at the foot of the stairs. "Yer might as well take 'em up. We don't want the old lady passing out on us."

"Not yet, anyway," the other man agreed.

He jerked his hand toward the flight of stairs. "Come on, then. Yer wanted to meet Her Majesty — this is yer lucky day."

It was the butler who conducted them up and then across the landing and knocked on the upstairs sitting room door. At the order from inside, he opened it and went in. A moment later he came out again. "Her Majesty will receive you, Lady Vespasia. You may go in."

"Thank you," Vespasia accepted, leading the way while Narraway and Charlotte followed a couple of steps behind her.

Victoria was seated in one of the comfortable, homely chairs in the well-used, very domestic living room. Only the height and ornate decoration of the ceiling reminded one that this was the home of the queen. She herself was a small, rather fat, elderly woman with a beaky nose and a very round face. Her hair was screwed back in an unflatteringly severe style. Her large eyes were pale and she was dressed entirely in black, which drained every shred of color from her skin. When she saw Vespasia for a second she blinked, and then she smiled.

"Vespasia. How very agreeable to see you. Come here!"

Vespasia went forward and dropped a graceful curtsy, her head slightly bowed, her back perfectly straight. "Your Majesty."

"Who are these?" Victoria inquired, looking beyond Vespasia to Narraway and Charlotte. She lowered her voice only slightly. "Your maid, presumably. The man looks like a doctor. I didn't send for a doctor. There's nothing the matter with me. Every fool in this household is treating me as if I'm ill. I want to go for a walk in the garden, and I am being prevented. I am empress of a quarter of the world, and my own household won't let me go for a walk in the garden!" Her voice was petulant. "Vespasia, come for a walk with me." She made to rise to her feet, but she was too far back in the chair to do so without assistance, and rather too fat to do it with any grace.

"Ma'am, it would be better if you were to remain seated," Vespasia said gently. "I am afraid I have some very harsh news to tell you . . ."

"Lady Vespasia!" Narraway warned.

"Be quiet, Victor," Vespasia told him without turning her eyes away from the queen. "Her Majesty deserves to know the truth."

"I demand to know it!" Victoria snapped. "What is going on?"

Narraway stepped back, surrendering with as much dignity as possible.

"I regret to say, ma'am," Vespasia said frankly, "that Osborne House has been surrounded by armed men. Of what number I do not know, but several of them are inside and have taken your household prisoner."

Victoria stared at her, then glanced past her at Narraway. "And who are you? One of those . . . traitors?"

"No, ma'am. Until very recently I was head of your Special Branch," he replied gravely.

"Why are you not still so? Why did you leave your post?"

"I was dismissed, ma'am, by traitors within. But I have come now to be of whatever service I may until help arrives, as it will do. We have seen to it."

"When?"

"I hope by nightfall, or shortly after," Narraway replied. "First the new head of the branch must be absolutely certain whom he can trust."

She sat very still for several moments. The ticking of the long-case clock seemed to fill the room.

"Then we had best wait with some composure," Victoria said at last. "We will fight if necessary."

"Before that we may have some chance to attempt escape . . . ," Narraway began.

Victoria glared at him again. "I am Queen of England and the British Empire, young man. In my reign we have stood our ground and won wars in every corner of the earth. Am I to run away from a group of hooligans in my own house? In Osborne!"

Narraway stood a little more uprightly.

Vespasia held her head high.

Charlotte found her own back ramrod-straight.

"I should think so!" Victoria said, regarding them with a very slight approval. "To quote one of my greatest soldiers, Sir Colin Campbell, who said at the battle of Balaclava, 'Here we stand, and here we die.' She smiled very slightly. "But since it may be some time, you may sit, if you wish."

CHAPTER 12

Pitt returned to Lisson Grove knowing that he had no allies there except probably Stoker, and that the safety of the queen, perhaps of the whole royal house, depended upon him. He was surprised, as he walked up the steps and in through the doorway, how intensely he felt about his responsibility. There was a fierce loyalty in him, but not toward an old woman sitting in lonely widowhood in a house on the Isle of Wight, nursing the memories of the husband she had adored.

It was the ideal he cared about, the embodiment of what Britain had been all his life. It was the whole idea of unity greater than all the differences in race, creed, and circumstance that bound together a quarter of the earth. The worst of society was greedy, arrogant, and self-serving, but the best of it was supremely brave, it was generous, and above all it was loyal. What was anybody worth if they had no concept of a purpose greater than themselves?

This was very little to do with Victoria herself, and most certainly nothing to do with the Prince of Wales. The murder at Buckingham Palace was very recent in his mind. He could not forget the selfishness of the prince, his unthinking arrogance, and the look of hatred he had directed at Pitt, nor should he. Soon the prince would be King Edward VII, and Pitt's career as a servant of the Crown would rest at least to some degree in his hands. Pitt would have wished him a better man, but his own loyalty to the throne was something apart from any personal disillusionment.

All his concentration now was bent on controlling Austwick. Whom did he dare to trust? He could not do this alone, and he must force himself not to think of Charlotte or Vespasia, or even of Narraway, except insofar as they were allies. Their danger he must force from all his conscious thoughts. One of the burdens at the core of leadership was that you must set aside personal loyalties and act in the good of all. He made himself think of how he would feel if others in command were to save their own families at the cost of his, if Charlotte were sacrificed because another leader put his wife's safety ahead of his duty. Only then could he dismiss all questions from his mind.

As he passed along the familiar corridors he had to remind himself again not to go to his old office, which was now occupied by someone else, but to go back to the one that used to be Narraway's, and would be again as soon as this crisis was past. As he closed the door and sat at the desk, he was profoundly glad that he had retrieved Narraway's belongings and never for a moment behaved as if he believed this was permanent. The drawings of trees were back on the walls, and the tower by the sea, even the photograph of Narraway's mother, dark and slender as he was, but more delicate, the intelligence blazing out of her eyes.

Pitt smiled for a moment, then turned his attention to the new reports on his desk. There were very few of them, just pedestrian comments on things that for the most part he already knew. There was no information that changed the circumstances.

He stood up and went to find Stoker rather than sending for him, because that would draw everyone's attention to the fact that he was singling him out. Even with Stoker's help, success would be desperately difficult.

"Yes, sir?" Stoker said as soon Pitt had

closed the door and was in front of him. He stared at Pitt's face, as if trying to read in it what he was thinking.

Pitt hoped that he was a little less transparent than that. He remembered how he had tried to read Narraway, and failed, at least most of the time.

"We know what it is," he said quietly. There was no point in concealing anything, and yet even now he felt as if he were standing on a cliff edge, about to plunge into the unknown.

"Yes, sir . . ." Stoker froze, his face pale. On the desk, still holding the paper he had been reading, his hands were stiff.

Pitt took a breath. "Mr. Narraway is back from Ireland." He saw the relief in Stoker's eyes, too sharp to hide, and went on more easily, a darkness sliding away from him also. "It seems we are right in thinking that there is a very large and very violent plan already begun. There is reason to believe that the people we have seen together, such as Willy Portman, Fenner, Guzman, and so on, intend to attack Her Majesty at Osborne House —"

"God Almighty!" Stoker gasped. "Regicide?"

Pitt grimaced.

"Not intentionally. We think they mean to

hold her ransom in return for a bill to abolish the hereditary power of the House of Lords — a bill that of course she will sign before, I imagine, her own abdication . . ."

Stoker was ashen. He looked at Pitt as if he had turned into some nightmare in front of his eyes. He swallowed, then swallowed again. "And then what? Kill her?"

Pitt had not taken it that far in his mind, but perhaps it was the logical end, the only one they could realistically live with. In the eyes of Britain, and most of the world, as long as Victoria was alive she would be queen, regardless of what anyone else said or did. He had thought things could not get worse, but in one leap they had.

"Yes, I imagine so," he agreed. "Narraway and Lady Vespasia Cumming-Gould have gone to Osborne, to do what they can, until we can send reinforcements to deal with whatever we find."

Stoker half rose in his seat.

"But not until we know whom we can trust," Pitt added. "The group must be small enough to be discreet. If we go in with half an army it will be far more likely to provoke them to violence immediately. If they know they are cornered and cannot escape, they'll hold her for ransom — their freedom for her life." He felt his throat tighten as he said it. He was fighting an enemy of unknown size and shape. Moreover, elements of it were secret from him, and lay within his own men. For a moment he was overwhelmed. He had no idea even where to begin. Every possibility seemed to carry its own failure built into it.

"A few men, well armed and taking them by surprise," Stoker said quietly.

"That's our only hope, I think," Pitt agreed. "But before we do that, we need to know who is the traitor here in Lisson Grove, and who else is with him. Otherwise they may sabotage any effort we make."

Stoker's hand on the desk clenched into a fist. "You mean you think there's more than one?"

"Don't you?"

"I don't know." Stoker pushed his hand through his hair, scraping it back off his forehead. "God help me, I don't know. And there's no time to find out. It could take us weeks."

"It's going to have to take us a lot less than that," Pitt replied, pulling out the hard-backed chair opposite the desk and sitting on it. "In fact we must make a decision by the end of today."

Stoker's jaw dropped. "And if we're wrong?"

501

"We mustn't be," Pitt told him. "Unless you want a new republic born in murder, and living in fear. We'll start with who set up the fraud that got rid of Narraway and made it all connect up with Ireland, so he would be in an Irish prison when all this happened."

Stoker took a deep breath. "Yes, sir. Then we'd better get started. And I'm sorry to say this, but we'll have to consider whoever Gower worked with as well, because getting you out of the way has to be part of it."

"Of course it has," Pitt agreed. "But Gower worked with me, and I reported to Narraway."

"That's the way it looked to all of us," Stoker agreed. "But it can't be what it was. I'll get his records from the officer who keeps all the personal stuff. We'll have to know who he worked with before you. You don't happen to know, do you?"

"I know what he said," Pitt replied with a twisted smile. "I'd like to know rather more than that. I think we'd better take as close a look as we can at everyone."

They spent the rest of the day going through all the records they could find going back a year or more, having to be discreet as to why.

"What are you looking for, sir?" one man

502

asked helpfully. "Perhaps I can find it. I know the records pretty well."

Pitt had his answer prepared. "It's a pretty serious thing that we were caught out by Narraway," he replied grimly. "I want to be sure, beyond any doubt at all, that there's nothing else of that kind, in fact nothing at all that can catch us out again."

The man swallowed, his eyes wide. "There won't be, sir."

"That's what we thought before," Pitt told him. "I don't want to leave it to trust — I want to know."

"Yes, sir. Of course, sir. Can I help . . . or . . ." He bit his lip. "I see, sir. Of course you can't trust any of us."

Pitt gave him a bleak smile. "I don't mind your help, Wilson. I need to trust all of you, and equally you need to trust me. It was Narraway who embezzled the money, after all, not one of the juniors here. But I have to know who helped him, if anyone, and who else might have had similar ideas."

Wilson straightened up. "Yes, sir. Is anyone else allowed to know?"

"Not at the moment." Pitt was taking a chance, but time was growing short, and if he caught Wilson in a lie, it would at least tell him something. In fact perhaps fear would be a better ally than discretion, as long as that too was used secretly.

He loathed this. At least in the police he had always known that his colleagues were on the same side as he. He had not realized then how infinitely valuable that was. He had taken it for granted.

By the middle of the afternoon, they had found the connection between Gower and Austwick. They discovered it more by luck than deduction.

"Here," Stoker held out a piece of paper with a note scrawled across the bottom.

Pitt read it. It was a memorandum of one man, written to himself, saying that he must see Austwick at a gentlemen's club, and report a fact to him.

"Does this matter?" he asked, puzzled. "It's nothing to do with socialists or any kind of violence or change, it's just an observation of someone that turned out to be irrelevant."

"Yes, sir," Stoker agreed. "But it's this." He handed another note with something written on the bottom in the same hand.

Gave the message on Hibbert to Gower to pass on to Austwick at the Hyde Club. Matter settled.

The place was a small, very select gentlemen's club in the West End of London. He looked up at Stoker. "How the devil did Gower get to be a member of the Hyde Club?"

"I looked at that, sir. Austwick recommended him. And that means that he must know him pretty well."

"Then we'll look a lot more closely at all the cases Gower's worked on, and Austwick as well," Pitt replied.

"But we already know they're connected," Stoker pointed out.

"And who else?" Pitt asked. "There are more than two of them. But with this we've got a better place to start. Keep working. We can't afford even one oversight."

Silently Stoker obeyed. He concentrated on Gower while Pitt looked at every record he could find of Austwick.

By nine o'clock in the evening they were both exhausted. Pitt's head thumped and his eyes felt hot and gritty. He knew Stoker must feel the same. There was little time left.

Pitt put down the piece of paper he had been reading until the writing on it had blurred in front of his vision.

"Any conclusions?" he asked.

"Some of these letters, sir, make me think Sir Gerald Croxdale was just about on to him. He was pretty close to putting it together," Stoker replied. "I think that might be what made Austwick hurry it all up and act when he did. By getting rid of Narraway he shook everybody pretty badly. Took the attention away from himself."

"And also put him in charge," Pitt added. "It wasn't for long, but maybe it was long enough." The last paper he had read was a memorandum from Austwick to Croxdale, but it was a different thought that was in his mind.

Stoker was waiting.

"Do you think Austwick is the leader?" he asked. "Is he actually a great deal cleverer than we thought? Or at any rate, than I thought?"

Stoker looked unhappy. "I don't think so, sir. It seems to me like he's not making the decisions. I've read a lot of Mr. Narraway's letters, and they're not like this. He doesn't suggest, he just tells you. And it isn't that he's any less of a gentleman, just that he knows he's in charge, and he expects you to know it too. Maybe that wasn't how he spoke to you, but it's how he did to the rest of us. No hesitation. You ask, you get your answer. I reckon that Austwick's asking someone else first."

That was exactly the impression Pitt had

had: a hesitation, as if checking with the man in control of the master plan.

But if Croxdale was almost on to him, why was Narraway not?

"Who can we trust?" he asked aloud. "We have to take a small force, no more than a couple of dozen men at the very most. Any more than that and we'll alert them. They'll have people watching for exactly that."

Stoker wrote a list on a piece of paper and passed it across. "These I'm sure of," he said quietly.

Pitt read it, crossed out three, and put in two more. "Now we must tell Croxdale and have Austwick arrested." He stood up and felt his muscles momentarily lock. He had forgotten how long he had been sitting, shoulders bent, reading paper after paper.

"Yes, sir. I suppose we have to?"

"We need an armed force, Stoker. We can't go and storm the queen's residence, whatever the reason, without the minister's approval. Don't worry, we've got a good enough case here." He picked up a small leather satchel and put into it the pages vital to the conclusions they had reached. "Come on."

At Osborne, Charlotte, Vespasia, and Narraway were kept in the same comfortable sitting room with the queen. One terrified lady's maid was permitted to come and go in order to attend to the queen's wishes. They were given food by one of the men who kept them prisoner, and watched as they availed themselves of the necessary facilities for personal relief.

The conversation was stilted. In front of the queen no one felt able to speak naturally. Charlotte looked at the old lady. This close to her, with no distance of formality possible, she was not unlike Charlotte's own grandmother, someone she had loved and hated, feared and pitied over the years. As a child she had never dared to say anything that might be construed as impertinent. Later, exasperation had overcome both fear and respect, and she had spoken her own mind with forthrightness. More recently she had learned terrible secrets about that woman, and loathing had melted into compassion.

Now she looked at the short, dumpy old lady whose skin showed the weariness of age, whose hair was thin and almost invisible under her lace cap. Victoria was in her seventies, and had been on the throne for nearly half a century. To the world she was queen, empress, defender of the faith, and her numerous children had married into

508

half the royal houses of Europe. However, it was not the responsibility to her country that wore her down; it was the bitter loneliness of widowhood.

Here at Osborne, standing looking out of the upstairs window across the fields and trees in the waning afternoon light, she was a tired old woman who had servants and subjects, but no equals. She would probably never know if any of them would have cared a jot for her if she were a commoner. The loneliness of it was unimaginable.

Would they kill her, those men in the hallway with guns and violent dreams of justice for people who would never want it purchased this way? If they did, would Victoria mind so very much? A clean shot through the heart, and she would join her beloved Albert at last.

Would they kill the rest of them too: Narraway and Vespasia, and Charlotte herself? What about all the servants? Or did the hostage-takers consider the servants to be ordinary people like themselves? Charlotte was sure the servants didn't think anything of the sort.

Charlotte had been sitting quietly on a chair at the far side of the room. On a sudden impulse she stood up and walked over toward the window. She stopped several feet

short of the queen. It would be disrespectful to stand beside her. Perhaps it was
disrespectful to stand here at all, but she
did so anyway.

The view was magnificent. She could even
see a bright glint of sunlight on the sea in
the distance.

The hard light picked out every line on
Victoria's face: the marks of tiredness, sorrow, ill temper, and perhaps also the inner
pain of emotional isolation. Was she afraid?

"It is very beautiful, ma'am," Charlotte
said quietly.

"Where do you live?" Victoria asked.

"In London, in Keppel Street, ma'am."

"Do you like it?"

"I have always lived in London, but I think
I might like it less if I had the choice of living where I could see something like this,
and just hear the wind in the trees, instead
of the traffic."

"Can you not be a nurse in the country?"
Victoria asked, still staring straight ahead of
her.

Charlotte hesitated. Surely this was a time
for the truth? It was only conversation. The
queen did not care in the slightest where
she lived. Any answer would do. If they were
all to be shot, what sort of an answer mattered? An honest one? No, a kind one.

She turned and looked quickly at Vespasia.

Vespasia nodded.

Charlotte moved half a step closer to the queen. "No, ma'am. I'm afraid I'm not a nurse at all. I told the man at the door that I was in order for them to allow me in."

Victoria twisted her head to stare at Charlotte with cold eyes. "And why was that?"

Charlotte found her mouth dry. She had to lick her lips before she could speak. "My husband is in Special Branch, ma'am. Yesterday he became aware what these men planned to do. He returned to London to get help from among those we can trust. Lady Vespasia, Mr. Narraway, and I came here to warn you, hoping we were in time. Clearly we were not, but now that we are here, we will do all we can to be of help."

Victoria blinked. "You knew that those . . . creatures were here?" she said incredulously.

"Yes, ma'am. Lady Vespasia realized that the man pretending to be a gardener was actually taking the heads off the petunias. No real gardener would do that."

Victoria looked beyond Charlotte to Vespasia, still at the far side of the room.

"Yes, ma'am." Vespasia answered the unspoken question.

Narraway moved at last. He came forward,

bowed very slightly, just an inclination of his head. "Ma'am, these men are violent and we believe they are seeking reform of all hereditary privilege in Europe —"

"All hereditary privilege?" she interrupted. "You mean . . ." Her voice faltered. ". . . like the French?" From the pallor of her face she had to be thinking of the guillotine, and the execution of the king.

"Not as violently as that, ma'am," Narraway told her. "We believe that when they are ready they will ask you to sign a bill abolishing the House of Lords . . ."

"Never!" she said vehemently. Then she gulped. "I do not mind dying so much, for myself, if that is what they have in mind. But I do not wish it for my household. They have been loyal, and do not deserve this repayment. Some of them are . . . young. Can you negotiate . . . something . . . that will spare them?"

"With your permission, ma'am, I will attempt to prevaricate long enough for help to arrive," he replied.

"Why does Special Branch not call in the army or, at the very least, the police?" she asked.

"Because if they come in with force, these people may react violently," he explained. "They are tense now. In their own way they are frightened. They know the cost of losing. They will certainly be hanged. We cannot afford to panic them. Whatever we do, it must be so stealthy that they are unaware of it. Everything must appear normal, until it is too late."

"I see," she said quietly. "I thought I was being brave when I said *Here we die.* It looks as if I was more accurate than I intended. I will remain here in this room, where I have been so happy in the past." She gazed out of the window. "Do you suppose heaven is like that, Mr. . . . what is your name?"

"Narraway, ma'am. Yes, I think it may well be. I hope so."

"Don't humor me!" she snapped.

"If God is an Englishman, ma'am, then it certainly will be," he said drily.

She turned and gave him a slow, careful look. Then she smiled.

He bowed again, then turned away and walked to the door.

Outside in the landing he saw one of the armed men halfway down the stairs.

The man must have caught the movement in the corner of his vision. He spun around, raising the gun.

Narraway stopped. He recognized Gallagher from Special Branch photographs, but he did not say so. If any of them realized who he was they might shoot him, on principle.

"Get back there!" Gallagher ordered.

Narraway stood where he was. "What do you want?" he asked. "What are you waiting for? Is it money?"

Gallagher gave a snort of contempt. "What do you think we are — bloody thieves? Is that as far as your imagination goes? That's all your sort thinks of, isn't it! Money, all the world's money, property. You think that's all there is, property and power."

"And what's yours?" Narraway asked, keeping his voice level, and as emotionless as he could.

"Get back in there!" Gallagher jerked the gun toward the upstairs sitting room again.

Again Narraway remained where he was. "You're holding Her Majesty hostage, you must want something. What is it?"

"We'll tell you that when we're ready. Now unless you want to get shot, get back in there!"

Reluctantly Narraway obeyed. There was an edge of fear in Gallagher's voice, a jerkiness in his movements that said he was as tight as a coiled spring inside. He was playing for the highest stakes he could imagine, and this was the only chance they would have. This was win, or lose it all.

Back in the sitting room Vespasia looked at Narraway the moment the door was closed.

"They're waiting for something," he said quickly. "Whoever it is here, he's not in charge. Someone will come with a proclamation for Her Majesty to sign, or something of the sort." He gritted his teeth. "We may be here for some time — this has been put to the prime minister — if they are arguing this thing in the cabinet. We'll have to keep our heads. Try to keep them calm, and possibly even convince them they have a hope of success. If they lose that, they may just kill us all. They'll have nothing to lose." He looked at her white face. "I'm sorry. I would prefer not to have had to tell you that, but I can't do this alone. We must all stay steady — the household staff as well. I wish I could get to them to persuade them of the need for calm. One person in hysterics might be enough to panic them all."

Vespasia rose to her feet a trifle unsteadily. "Then I will ask this lunatic on the stairs for permission to go and speak with the household staff. Perhaps you will be good enough to help me persuade him of the necessity. Charlotte will manage here very well."

Narraway took her arm, holding it firmly.

He turned to Victoria.

"Ma'am, Lady Vespasia is going to speak with your staff. It is imperative that no one loses control or behaves with rashness. I shall try to persuade the men who hold us hostage to permit her to do this, for all our sakes. I am afraid we may be here for some little time."

"Thank you." Victoria spoke more to Vespasia than to Narraway, but the comment included them both.

"Perhaps they could serve everyone food?" Charlotte suggested. "It is easier to be busy."

"An excellent idea," Vespasia agreed. "Come, Victor. If they have any sense at all, they will see the wisdom of it."

They went to the door, and he held it open for her.

Charlotte watched them go with her heart pounding and her stomach clenched tight. She turned to Victoria, who was staring at her with the same fear bright in her eyes.

Out on the landing there was still silence . . . no sound of gunfire.

A little before midnight Pitt and Stoker sat in a hansom cab on its way to the home of Sir Gerald Croxdale. With them in the satchel was the main evidence to prove Austwick's complicity in the movement of the money that had made Narraway appear guilty of theft and had resulted in the murder of Mulhare. Also included were the reports of the leading revolutionary socialists prepared to use violence to overthrow governments they believed to be oppressive, who were now gathered together in England, and had been seen moving south toward Osborne House and the queen. Also, of course, were the names of the traitors with Special Branch.

It took nearly five minutes of ringing and knocking before they heard the bolts drawn back in the front door. It was opened by a sleepy footman wearing a coat over his nightshirt.

"Yes, sir?" he said cautiously.

Pitt identified himself and Stoker. "It is an extreme emergency," he said gravely. "The government is in danger. Will you please waken the minister immediately." He made it a request, but his tone left no doubt that it was an order.

They were shown to the withdrawing room. Just over ten minutes later Croxdale himself appeared, hastily dressed, his face drawn in lines of anxiety. As soon as he had closed the door, he spoke, looking from Pitt to Stoker and back again.

"What is it, gentlemen?"

There was no time for any more explanation than necessary to convince him. "We have traced the money that was placed in Narraway's account," Pitt said briefly. "It was Charles Austwick behind it, and the consequent murder of Mulhare, and also behind Gower's murder of West. Far more important, we know the reason for both. It was to place Austwick in charge of Special Branch, so no one else would notice the violent radical socialists coming into Britain, men who have been idealogical enemies until now, suddenly cooperating with one another and all moving down toward the Isle of Wight."

Croxdale looked startled. "The Isle of Wight? For God's sake, why?"

"Osborne House," Pitt said simply.

"God Almighty! The queen!" Croxdale's voice was all but strangled in his throat. "Are you sure? No one would . . . why? It makes no sense. It would unite the world against them." He waved one hand and shook his head, as if to push away the whole idea.

"Not to kill her," Pitt told him. "At least not to start with, perhaps not at all."

"Then what?" Croxdale peered at him as if he had never really seen him before. "Pitt, are you sure you know what you are talking about?"

"Yes, sir," Pitt said firmly. He was not surprised Croxdale doubted him. If he had not seen the proof himself he would not have believed it. "We traced the money that was supposed to go to Mulhare. The information he gave was very valuable. He gave up Nathaniel Byrne, one of the key men responsible for several bombings in Ireland and in London. Very few people knew that, even in Special Branch, but Austwick was one of them. Narraway arranged the payment so Mulhare could escape. That was a condition of his giving the information."

"I knew nothing about it!" Croxdale said sharply. "But why would Austwick do such a thing? Did he take some of it himself?"

"No. He wanted Narraway out of Special Branch, and me too, in case I knew enough of what Narraway had been working on to piece it together."

"Piece what?" Croxdale said sharply. "You haven't explained anything yet. And what has this to do with socialist violence against the queen?"

"Passionate idealism gone mad," Pitt answered. "Hold the queen for ransom to abolish the House of Lords, and then probably to abdicate. The end of rule by hereditary privilege, then likely a republic, with only elected representation of the people."

"Good God." Croxdale sank into the nearest armchair, his face ashen, his hands shaking. "Are you certain, man? I can't act on this without absolute proof. If I have to mount a force of armed men to take Osborne House, I'd better be bloody sure I'm doing the right thing — in fact the only thing. If you're wrong, I'll end up in the Tower, and it'll be my head on the block."

"Mr. Narraway is already at Osborne, sir," Pitt told him.

"What?" Croxdale sat up with a jerk. "Narraway's in . . ." He stopped, rubbing his hand over his face. "Do you have proof of all this, Pitt? Yes or no? I have to explain this to the prime minister before I act: immediately, tonight. I can have Austwick arrested — I'll do that first, before he gets any idea that you know what he's done. I'll do that now. But you must give me more than your word to take to the prime minister."

"Yes, sir." Pitt indicated the case he had with him. "It's in here. Reports, instructions, letters. It takes a bit of piecing together, but it's all there."

"Are you certain? My God, man, if you're wrong, I'll see you go down with me!" Croxdale rose to his feet. "I'll get it started.

There's obviously no time to waste." He walked slowly from the room, closing the door behind him.

Stoker was standing where he had been throughout the conversation. There was a very slight frown on his face.

"What is it?" Pitt asked.

Stoker shook his head. "I don't know, sir."

Pitt had the case in his hand with the papers. Why had Croxdale not asked to see them, at least check over them? With the possibility of treachery inside Special Branch, and his belief earlier that Narraway himself was a thief, why had he not asked to see it? Pitt was known to be Narraway's man. In his place, Pitt would have been skeptical, at the very least.

"Do you think he suspected Austwick all along?" Stoker asked.

"Of what? If he was part of setting up the forgeries to blame Narraway, then he was part of the plot to attack the queen. If Croxdale knew that, then he's part of it too." As he spoke the pieces fell together in his mind. Austwick was reporting to someone else, they were certain of that. Croxdale himself?

Then he remembered something else: Croxdale had said he did not know about Austwick sending the money for Mulhare

— but Croxdale had had to countersign it. It was too large an amount for one signature alone.

He turned to Stoker. "He's going to get rid of Austwick, and blame him for all of it," he said. "Then the queen."

Stoker was hollow-eyed in the lamplight; Pitt knew he must look the same. Could they possibly be right? The price would be total ruin if they were wrong. And ruin for the country if they were right, and did nothing.

Pitt nodded.

Stoker went to the door and opened it very quietly, not allowing the latch to click back. Pitt came behind him. Across the hallway the study door was ajar and there was a crack of light across the dark floor.

"Wait till he comes out," Stoker said under his breath. "I'll get over the far side, in the other doorway. You hold his attention, I'll be behind him. Be prepared. He'll fight."

Pitt could feel his heart pounding so hard his whole body must be shaking with it. Had his promotion gone to his head? He was doing the wildest thing of his life, perhaps throwing away everything he had in a gesture that in the light of day would look like the act of a madman, or a traitor. He should wait, act with moderation, ask someone else's opinion.

What if Stoker was the traitor, and deliberately provoking Pitt to this? What if he was Austwick's man, about to arrest the one person who stood in their way?

What if it were all a plan to ruin Special Branch? Discredit it into oblivion?

He froze.

Ahead of him Stoker tiptoed across the hall to stand, little more than a shadow, in the doorway next to the study, where Croxdale would have his back to him when he came out to go back to Pitt.

The seconds ticked by.

Was Croxdale speaking to the prime minister? What could he tell him over a telephone? Would he have to go and see him in person in order to raise a force of men to relieve Osborne House? No — this was an emergency, no time to argue, or plead a case. Was he arranging to have Austwick arrested?

The study door opened and Croxdale came out. Now was the time for decision, as Croxdale walked across the unlit hall, before he reached the sitting room door.

Pitt stepped forward. "Sir Gerald, Austwick is not the leader in the attempted coup."

Croxdale stopped. "What the devil are you talking about? If there's somebody else, why in God's name didn't you tell me before?"

"Because I didn't know who it was," Pitt said honestly.

Croxdale was in the shadow, his face all but invisible. "And now you do?" His voice was soft. Was it in disbelief, or understanding at last?

"Yes," Pitt said.

Stoker moved silently forward until he was a yard behind Croxdale. He had deliberately chosen an angle from which he cast no shadow.

"Indeed. And who is it?" Croxdale asked.

"You," Pitt answered.

There was total silence.

Croxdale was a big man, heavy. Pit wondered if he and Stoker would be able to take him, if he fought back, if he called for the footman who must be waiting somewhere. Please God he was in the kitchen where he would only hear a bell. But he would not go back to bed while his master was up and there were visitors in the house.

"You made a mistake," Pitt pointed out, as much to hold Croxdale's attention from any slight sound Stoker might make as for any reasoning.

"Really? What was that?" Croxdale did not

sound alarmed. In seconds he had regained his composure.

"The amount of money you paid Mulhare."

"He was worth it. He gave us Byrne," Croxdale replied, the contempt undisguised in his voice. "If you were up to your job, you would know that."

"Oh, I do know it," Pitt answered, keeping his eyes on Croxdale so he did not waver even once and glance at Stoker behind him. "The point is not whether Mulhare was worth it, it is that that amount had to be authorized by more than one man. It has your signature on it."

"What of it?" Croxdale asked. "It was a legitimate payment."

"It was used to get rid of Narraway — and you said you didn't know anything about it," Pitt reminded him.

Croxdale brought his hands out of his pockets. In the left one there was a small gun. The light from the sitting room behind Pitt gleamed on the metal of the barrel as Croxdale raised it.

Pitt swung around as if Stoker were behind him, just as Stoker slammed into Croxdale, kicking high and hard at his left elbow.

The gun flew in the air. Pitt lunged for it, just catching it as it arced over to his left.

Croxdale swung around and grabbed at Stoker, twisting his arm and turning him so he half fell and Croxdale had him in a stranglehold.

"Give me back the gun, or I'll break his neck!" Croxdale said in a grating voice, just a little high-pitched.

Pitt had no doubt whatever that he would do it. The mask was off: Croxdale had nothing to lose. Pitt looked at Stoker's face, which was already turning red as his neck was crushed by Croxdale's hold. There was no choice. Stoker was still only half in front of Croxdale, but slipping forward and sideways. A minute more and he would be unconscious and form a perfect shield. He aimed the gun and cocked the trigger.

Pitt shot Croxdale in the head, making a single wound.

Croxdale fell backward. Stoker, sprayed with blood, staggered and collapsed onto the floor. Pitt was alarmed by his own accuracy, though the distance to his target had been short enough. Of course he was surprised; he had never shot a man to death before.

He dropped the gun and held out his hand, hauling Stoker to his feet again.

Stoker looked at the gun.

"Leave it!" Pitt said, startled to find his

voice almost level. "The minister shot himself when he realized we had proof of his treason. We didn't know he had a gun, so we weren't able to prevent him from doing it." Now he was shaking, and it took all his control to keep even reasonably steady. "What the hell did you think you were doing?" he snarled at Stoker suddenly. "He would have killed you, you fool!"

Stoker coughed and rubbed his hand over his throat. "I know that," he said huskily. "Just as well you shot him, or I'd have been the one on the floor. Thank you, sir."

Pitt was about to tell Stoker that he was incompetent to have allowed Croxdale to grasp hold of him like that. However, with a shock like a physical blow, he realized that Stoker had done it on purpose, risking his own life to force Pitt to shoot Croxdale. He stared at him as if seeing him for the first time.

"What could we have done with him, sir?" Stoker said pragmatically. "Tie him up here, for his servants to find and let go? Take him with us, in a hansom cab or one of us stay and sit —"

"All right!" Pitt cut in. "Now we have to get to the Isle of Wight and rescue the queen — and Narraway and Lady Vespasia, and my wife." His mind raced, picturing the men he knew were going to be there: violent, fanatical men like Portman, Gallagher, Haddon, Fenner, and others with the same distorted idealism, willing to kill and to die for the changes they believed would bring a new era of social justice.

Then another idea came to him. "If he had Austwick arrested, where would he be taken to? Quickly?"

"Austwick?" Stoker sounded confused.

"Yes. Where would he be now? Where does he live, do you know? How can we find out?"

"Kensington, sir, not far from here," Stoker replied. "It'd be the Kensington police — if Croxdale really called anyone."

"If he didn't, we will," Pitt said, now knowing exactly what he was going to do. "Come on, we've got to hurry. We don't know who Croxdale actually spoke to. It won't have been the prime minister." He started toward Croxdale's study.

"Sir!" Stoker said, bewildered.

Pitt turned. "If one of the servants comes down, tell him Sir Gerald shot himself. Do what you can to make it look right. I'm going to call the Kensington police." In Croxdale's study there was no time to search. He picked up the receiver and asked the operator to connect him, as an emergency. Perhaps Croxdale had done the same.

As soon as they answered he identified himself and said that there had been a practical joke suggested concerning the arrest of Mr. Austwick. It should be disregarded.

"Are you sure, sir?" the man at the other end said doubtfully. "We've 'ad nothing 'ere."

"Mr. Austwick lives in your area?" Pitt had a sudden sinking in the pit of his stomach.

"Oh yes, sir."

"Then we'd better make certain he's safe. What is his address?"

The man hesitated a moment, then told him. "But we'll send men there ourselves, sir, if you'll pardon me, seein' as 'ow I don't really know 'oo you are."

"Good. Do that," Pitt agreed. "We'll be there as soon as I can get a cab." He replaced the receiver and went to find Stoker. The other man was waiting by the front door, anxiously moving his weight from one foot to the other.

"Right, find a hansom," Pitt told him.

"We'll have to walk as far as the main road," Stoker warned, opening the door and slipping out with immense relief. They strode along at as rapid a pace as possible, short of breaking into a run.

It was still several minutes before they found a cab. They gave Austwick's address, with orders to make the best speed possible.

"What are we going to do with Austwick, sir?" Stoker asked. He had to raise his voice above the clatter of the hooves and the rattle and hiss of wheels over the cobbles.

"Get him to help us," Pitt replied. "They're his men down there. He's the one person who might be able to call them off without an all-out shooting battle. We won't have achieved much in capturing them if they kill the queen in the process." He did not mention Narraway or Vespasia, or Charlotte.

"Do you think he'll do that?" Stoker asked.

"It's up to us to persuade him," Pitt said grimly. "Croxdale's dead, Narraway's alive. I doubt the queen will sign anything that reduces the power or dignity of the Crown, even in fear of her life."

Stoker did not reply, but in the light of the next street lamp they passed, Pitt saw that he was smiling.

When they reached Austwick's house there were police outside it, discreetly, well in the shadows.

Pitt identified himself, showing them his new warrant card, and Stoker did the same.

"Yes, sir," the sergeant said smartly. "How can we help, sir?"

Pitt made an instant decision. "We are going to collect Mr. Austwick, and we are all going to travel to Portsmouth, as rapidly as possible."

The sergeant looked bemused.

"Use Austwick's telephone. Hold the night train," Pitt told him. "It's imperative we get to the Isle of Wight by morning."

The sergeant came to attention. "Yes, sir. I'll . . . I'll call immediately."

Pitt smiled at him. "Thank you." Then he nodded to Stoker. They went to the front door of Austwick's house and knocked hard and continuously until a footman in his nightshirt opened it, blinking and drawing in breath to demand an explanation.

Pitt told him sharply to step back.

The man saw the police beyond Pitt, and Stoker at his elbow, and did as he was told. Ten minutes later Austwick was in the hall, hastily dressed, unshaven, and very angry.

"What the hell is going on?" he said furiously. "Do you know what time it is, man?"

Pitt looked at the long-case clock at the far side of the hall. "Coming up to quarter to two," he answered. "And we must make Portsmouth by dawn."

Austwick paled visibly, even in the dim

531

light of the hall with its main chandelier unlit. If anything could tell Pitt that he knew of Croxdale's plan, it was the fear in his face now.

"Croxdale is dead," Pitt said simply. "He shot himself when we faced him with his plans. It's all over. Narraway's back. He's at Osborne now, with the queen. You've got two choices, Austwick. We can arrest you now, and you'll be tried as a traitor. You'll hang, and your family will never live it down. Your grandchildren, if you have any, will still carry the stigma of your name." He saw Austwick's horror, but could not afford to pity him. "Or you can come with us and call off your men from Osborne," he went on. "You have two minutes to choose. Do you wish to hang as a traitor, or come with us, to live or die as a hero?"

Austwick was too paralyzed with fear to speak.

"Good," Pitt said decisively. "You're coming with us. I thought you'd choose that. We're going for the night train to Portsmouth. Hurry."

Stoker grasped Austwick by the arm, holding him hard, and they stumbled out into the night.

They half heaved him into the waiting hansom, then sat with one on either side of

532

him. Two uniformed police followed in another cab, ready to clear traffic if there should be any and to confirm that the night train was held.

They raced through the streets in silence toward the river and the railway station beyond, where they could catch the mail train to the coast. Pitt found his fists clenched and his whole body aching with the tension of not knowing whether the sergeant he had instructed had been able to hold the train there. It could only have taken a telephone call from Austwick's house to his own police station, and then a call from there to the railway. What if the station master on night duty did not believe them, or realize the urgency of it? What if he was simply incompetent for such a crisis?

They swayed and lurched along the all-but-deserted streets, then over the river at the Battersea Bridge, and sharp west along the High Street. One moment he was desperate that they were going too slowly, the next, as they slewed around a corner, that they were going too fast and would tip over.

At the station they leapt out, Pitt wildly overpaying the driver because he could not wait for change. They ran into the station, dragging Austwick with them. The sergeant showed his warrant card and shouted at the stationmaster to direct them to the train.

The man obeyed with haste, but was clearly unhappy about it all. He looked at Austwick's ashen face and dragging feet with pity. For a moment Pitt feared he was going to intervene.

The train was waiting, the engine belching steam. A very impatient guard stood at the door of his van, his whistle in one hand ready to be raised to his lips.

Pitt thanked the sergeant and his men, happy to be able to give them some idea of how intensely grateful he was. He made a mental note to commend the sergeant if they survived the night. He was doubly glad that his own reputation was such that his appreciation was a blessing, not a curse.

As soon as they were in the guard's van, the whistle blew. The train lurched forward like a horse that had been straining at the bit.

The guard was a small, neat man with bright blue eyes.

"I hope all this is worth it," he said looking at Pitt dubiously. "You've a lot of explaining to do, young man. Do you realize you have kept this train waiting ten minutes?" He glanced at his pocket watch and then replaced it. "Eleven minutes," he corrected himself. "This train carries the

Royal Mail. Nobody holds us up. Not rain nor floods nor lightning storms. And here we stood around the platform for the likes of you."

"Thank you," Pitt said a little breathlessly.

The guard stared at him. "Well . . . nice manners are all very good, but you can't hold up the Royal Mail, you know. While it's in my care, it belongs to the queen."

Pitt drew in his breath to reply, and then the irony of the situation struck him. Smiling, he said nothing.

They continued on to the rear carriage and found seats. Stoker remained next to Austwick, as if he feared the man might make a run for it, although there was nowhere for him to go.

Pitt sat silently trying to make the best plans possible for when they arrived. They would have to commandeer a boat — any sort would do — to get them across the narrow strip of water to the Isle of Wight.

He was still thinking of it when about fifteen minutes into the journey the train slowed. Then, with a great panting of steam, it stopped altogether. Pitt shot to his feet and went back to the guard's van.

"What's the matter?" he demanded. "Why have we stopped? Where are we?"

"We stopped to put off the mail, o'

course," the guard said with elaborate patience. "That's what we came for. Now you just go an' sit down in your seat and be quiet, sir. We'll be on our way when we're ready."

"How many places do you stop?" Pitt asked. His voice was louder and harsher than he meant it to be, but it was sliding out of his control.

The guard stood very straight, his face grim.

"Every place where we got to pick up mail, or set it down, sir. Like I said, that's what we do. Jus' you go an' sit back down, sir."

Pitt pulled out his warrant card and held it for the guard to see. "This is an emergency. I'm on the queen's business, and I need to get to the Isle of Wight by sunrise. Drop off the mail on the way back, or let the next train through pick it up."

The guard stared at Pitt with both pride and disgust. "I'm on the queen's business too, sir. I carry the Royal Mail. You'll get to Portsmouth when we've done our job. Now, like I said, go an' sit down an' we'll get on with the mail. Ye're just holding us up, sir, an' I won't have that. You've caused enough trouble already."

Pitt felt exasperation well up inside him

so he could almost have hit the man. It was unfair; the guard was doing his duty. He had no idea who Pitt was, other than some kind of policeman.

Could Pitt tell him any part of the truth? No. He would find himself held in charge as a lunatic. He could prove nothing, and it would only delay them even more. With a chill he remembered his helplessness on his last train ride, the horror and absurdity of it — and Gower's mangled body on the tracks. Thank God, at least he had not seen it.

He returned to the carriage and sat down in his seat.

"Sir?" Stoker said.

"We have to stop at all the stations," Pitt answered, keeping his voice level this time. "Without telling him the truth I can't persuade him not to." He smiled lopsidedly. "It's the Royal Mail. Nothing stands in its way."

Stoker started to say something, then changed his mind. Everything he meant to express was in the lines of his face.

The journey seemed achingly slow. None of them spoke again until finally they pulled into Portsmouth station as the dawn was lightening the eastern sky. Austwick caused no trouble as they went through the barely wakening streets and found a large rowing boat to take them across the water.

There was a brisk wind and the sea was choppy, the wave caps translucent, almost mirroring the high, rippling clouds shot through by the rising wind. It was hard work, and they were obliged to bend their backs to make headway.

They landed, shivering, at the wharf and set off toward Osborne House, which was just in sight above the tangle of the still-bare trees. They walked as fast as they could, since there was no one around from whom to beg or hire any kind of transport.

The sun was above the horizon and glittering sharp in a clear morning when they approached the boundaries. The rolling parkland and the splendid stone mansion were spread before them, broad and magnificent, as if still sleeping in the hushed land, which was silent but for the birdsong.

Pitt had a moment of terrible doubt. Was this whole thing no more than a vast nightmare, without reality at all? Had they misunderstood everything? Was he about to burst in on the queen and make the ultimate fool of himself?

Stoker strode forward, still gripping Austwick by the arm.

Nothing at Osborne stirred. Surely there had to be a guard of some sort, whatever the circumstances, even if the entire conspiracy was Pitt's delusion?

As they reached the gate, a man stepped forward. He was in livery, but it fitted him poorly. He stood straight, but not like a soldier. There was an arrogance in his eyes.

"You can't come in here," he said curtly. "This is the queen's house. You can look, of course, but no farther, understand?"

Pitt knew his face. He tried to remember his name, but it eluded him. He was so tired his vision swam a little. He must stay alert, keep his mind sharp, his judgment steady. He was a little behind Austwick, so he pushed him hard in the small of the back.

"It's all right, McLeish," Austwick said, his voice shaky and a little rough. "These gentlemen are with me. We need to come in."

McLeish hesitated.

"Quickly," Pitt added. "There are others behind us. It'll all be over in an hour or two."

"Right!" McLeish responded, turning on his heel and leading the way.

"Ask about the queen!" Pitt hissed at Austwick. "Don't slip up now. Hanging is not a nice way to die."

Austwick stumbled. Stoker yanked him up.

Austwick cleared his throat. "Is Her

Majesty still all right? I mean . . . I mean, will she be able to sign papers?"

"Of course," McLeish answered cheerfully. "Three people turned up unexpectedly. We had no choice but to let them in, or they'd have gone away and raised the alarm. A man and two women. But they're no trouble. It's all going well."

They were nearly at the front doors.

Austwick hesitated.

The sun was dazzling through a break in the trees. There was no sign of life inside, no sound, but then the weight of the doors would have muffled anything.

Someone must have been watching. The door opened and a heavyset man stood barring the way, a shotgun hanging on his arm.

Austwick stepped forward, his head high. His voice cracked at first, then gained strength.

"Good morning, Portman. My name is Charles Austwick. I represent Gerald Croxdale and the socialist people of Britain."

"About damn time you turned up!" Willy Portman said sharply. "Have you got the documents?"

"We're taking them to the queen," Pitt said quickly. "Get everybody in. It's nearly over." He tried to put some excitement in his voice.

Portman smiled. "Right. Yes!" He raised his arm with the gun in it, giving a salute of victory.

Stoker stepped forward and hit him as hard as he could, with all the force of his weight. He caught him in the vulnerable point of the solar plexus, driving him backward and inside. Portman doubled up in agony, the gun flying from his hand. Stoker spun around and picked it up.

Austwick stood as if paralyzed.

Pitt started up the stairs as another man came out of the servants' quarters with a gun at the ready.

Narraway emerged onto the landing and struck the man at the top of the stairs, sending him pitching forward and down, his gun flying out of his grasp. He landed at the bottom, his neck broken.

The man in the hall raised his gun and aimed at Pitt.

Austwick stepped in front of him. There was the roar of an explosion and Austwick collapsed slowly, crumpling to the ground in a sea of blood.

Stoker shot the man with the gun.

Narraway came down the stairs and picked up the gun from the man at the bottom.

"There are five more," he said calmly. "Let's see if we can get them without any further bloodshed."

Pitt looked at him. Narraway sounded totally in control, but his face was haggard, hollow-eyed. There was a rough edge to his voice as if he held it level with an effort that cost him all he had.

Pitt glanced at Stoker, who was now armed with the gun that had killed Austwick.

"Yes, sir," Stoker said obediently, and set off toward the servants' quarters.

Narraway looked at Pitt. He smiled very slightly, but there was a warmth in his eyes Pitt had never seen before, even in the best of their past triumphs. "Would you like to go up and tell Her Majesty that order is restored?" he said. "There will be no papers to sign."

"Are you . . . all right?" Pitt asked. Suddenly he found he cared very much.

"Yes, thank you," Narraway replied. "But this business is not quite finished yet. Is that Charles Austwick on the floor?"

"Yes," Pitt answered. "I think it might be better all around if we say he died giving his life for his country."

"He was the head of this God damn

conspiracy," Narraway said between his teeth.

"Actually he wasn't," Pitt told him. "Croxdale was."

Narraway looked startled. "Are you sure?"

"Absolutely. He more or less admitted it."

"Where is he?"

"Dead. We'll say he took his own life." Pitt found he was shivering. He tried to control it, and couldn't.

"But he didn't?"

"I shot him. He had Stoker by the neck. He was going to break it." Pitt passed him on the stairs.

"I see," Narraway said slowly. He broke into a companionable smile. "Croxdale underestimated you, didn't he?"

Pitt found himself blushing. Embarrassed, he turned and went on up the stairs. At the top he crossed the landing and knocked on the door.

"Come!" a quiet voice commanded.

He turned the handle and went inside. Victoria was standing in the middle of the room, Charlotte to one side of her, Vespasia to the other. As Pitt looked at them, the emotion welled up inside him until he felt the tears of relief prickle in his eyes. His throat was so tight the words were difficult to say.

"Your Majesty." He cleared his throat. "I am pleased to inform you that Osborne House is now back in the hands of those to whom it belongs. There will be no further trouble, but I would advise you to remain here until a little clearing up has been done."

Vespasia's face was radiant with relief, all the past weariness slipping from her.

Charlotte smiled at him, too happy, too proud even to speak.

"Thank you, Mr. Pitt," Victoria said a trifle hoarsely. "We are most obliged to you. We shall not forget."

ABOUT THE AUTHOR

Anne Perry is the bestselling author of two acclaimed series set in Victorian England: the Charlotte and Thomas Pitt novels, most recently *Buckingham Palace Gardens* and *Long Spoon Lane,* and the William Monk novels, most recently *Dark Assassin* and *Execution Dock.* She is also the author of the World War I novels *No Graves As Yet, Shoulder the Sky, Angels in the Gloom, At Some Disputed Barricade,* and *We Shall Not Sleep,* as well as nine Christmas novels, most recently *A Christmas Odyssey.* Her stand-alone novel *The Sheen on the Silk,* set in the Byzantine Empire, was a *New York Times* bestseller. Anne Perry lives in Scotland.

www.anneperry.net

The employees of Thorndike Press hope you have enjoyed this Large Print book. All our Thorndike, Wheeler, and Kennebec Large Print titles are designed for easy reading, and all our books are made to last. Other Thorndike Press Large Print books are available at your library, through selected bookstores, or directly from us.

For information about titles, please call:
(800) 223-1244

or visit our Web site at:
http://gale.cengage.com/thorndike

To share your comments, please write:
Publisher
Thorndike Press
10 Water St., Suite 310
Waterville, ME 04901

The Book of Negro Folklore

A SELECTED LIST OF BOOKS BY LANGSTON HUGHES

The Weary Blues

The Big Sea

Simple Stakes a Claim

The Langston Hughes Reader

Famous Negro Music Makers

Tambourines to Glory

A SELECTED LIST OF BOOKS BY ARNA BONTEMPS

Chariot in the Sky

Lonesome Boy

Sad-Faced Boy

Black Thunder

God Sends Sunday

EDITED BY LANGSTON HUGHES AND ARNA BONTEMPS

Poetry of the Negro

The Book of

Negro Folklore

EDITED BY

LANGSTON HUGHES AND ARNA BONTEMPS

DODD, MEAD & COMPANY · NEW YORK · 1965

Thanks are due to the following for permission to use the material indicated: George
C. S. Adams and Stephen B. Adams: for The Animal Court, Big Swamps of the
Congaree, Tad's Advice to His Son, The Two Ducks, The Crow, Jack-Ma-Lantern,
Jeff's Funeral Sermon, Falling Stars, Old Sister's Advice to Her Daughter, Wild
Goose Nest, from *Congaree Sketches* by E. C. L. Adams (University of North Caro-
lina Press); An Escaped Convict, A Roost on the Rim of the Moon, Sister Lucy,
Silas, The Harps of God, God, Lula, Ruint, from *Nigger to Nigger* by E. C. L. Adams
(Charles Scribner's Sons); Captain Lord Welton. The American Folklore Society:
for Tar Baby, Rabbit Teaches Bear a Song, Playing Godfather, The Watcher Blinded,
The Fox and the Goose, T'appin, Wait Till Emmett Comes, Tailypo. The American
Mercury Magazine: for High John de Conquer by Zora Neale Hurston. Appleton-
Century-Crofts, Inc.: for The Gang from *The Pecking Order* by Mark Kennedy,
Copyright 1953 by Mark Kennedy. Ray B. Browne: for The Farmer and the G.P.C.
and The Superfluous Brains from *Negro Folktales from Alabama* (Southern Folk-
lore Quarterly, June 1954). Sterling A. Brown: for The Blues as Folk Poetry and
The Spirituals. Dan Burley: for First Steps in Jive, There Is a Square in My Hair,
Here I Come with My Hair Blowing Back, The Barefoot Boy from *Handbook of
Jive*. Carl Carmer: for Brer Rabbit and Sis Cow, Why Brer Rabbit Wears A'Round-
'Bout, Brer Fox and the Goobers, De Knee-High Man from *Stars Fell On Alabama*.
The Caxton Printers, Ltd.: for A Love Letter From De Lord by Ruth Rogers
Johnson from *Eve's Stepchildren* by Lealon N. Jones, by special permission of the
copyright owners. Cherio Music Publishers, Inc.: for Saturday Night Fish Fry by
Ellis Walsh and Louis Jordan. Alice Childress: for New York's My Home, originally
published by Independence Publishers. Edna Gallman Cooke: for Build Me a Cabin.
Crown Publishers: for Why the Fox's Mouth Is Sharp and The Hairy Toe, from
A Treasury of Southern Folklore edited by B. A. Botkin; Fish Fry from *Born To Be*
by Taylor Gordon, Copyright 1929 by Covici, Friede, Inc. Waring Cuney: for Right
Off-Right On and Lame Man and the Blind Man. Dodd, Mead & Company: for
Levee Life from *An American Miscellany* by Lafcadio Hearn; Li'l Gal, The Party,
Itching Heels, When Malindy Sings, At Candle-Lightin' Time, from *The Complete
Poems of Paul Laurence Dunbar;* John Henry in Harlem from *Rendezvous with Amer-
ica* by Melvin B. Tolson. Richard M. Dorson: for The Three Preachers, from *Negro
Tales from Bolivar County, Mississippi* (Southern Folklore Quarterly, 1955). Duell,
Sloan & Pearce, Inc.: for South Carolina Superstitions, from *Thursday's Child* by
Eartha Kitt; Jelly Roll Morton Remembers, from *Mister Jelly Roll* by Alan Lomax.
Duke University Press: for The Headless Hant, from *Bundle of Troubles and Other
Tarheel Tales* edited by W. C. Hendricks. Ralph Ellison: for Harlem Children's
Rhymes and Gags. Farrar, Straus & Cudahy, Inc.: for Baptism and Lodge Sisters
at a Funeral, from *The Boy at the Window* by Owen Dodson, Copyright 1951 by
Owen Dodson; Jam Session from *South Street* by William Gardner Smith, Copy-
right 1954 by William Gardner Smith. Fisk University, Source Documents of the
Social Science Department: for Unwritten History, from *The Unwritten History of
Slavery*, Social Science Source Document No. 1; Hooked in the Heart, My Jaws
Became Unlocked, God Struck Me Dead, The Lord Spoke Peace to My Soul, from
God Struck Me Dead, Social Science Source Document No. 2. Harry Fox: for I Ain't
Gonna Be No Topsy, words and music by Reginald Beane and Avon Long, Copy-

INTRODUCTION

THE lore of the Negro turned out to be a deeper vein than was at
first suspected. Once represented principally by Uncle Remus and
the Brer Rabbit tales, it has since found its way into such enter-
tainments as the minstrel shows of the late nineteenth and early
twentieth centuries and the monologues of Bert Williams (on
phonograph records as well as in vaudeville and the *Ziegfield Follies*), not to mention recent characterizations like those projected
by *Stepin Fetchet, Rochester,* and the *Amos n' Andy* ensemble. A
carry-over from Negro folktales into the American writing by and
about Negroes, from Mark Twain to William Faulkner and Ralph
Ellison, is also conspicuous.

But the tales, as varied and intriguing as they are, give only a
partial indication of the range and capacity of the folk who created
them. For many Americans these are still apt to evoke memories
of favored house servants, trusting and trusted Aunties, Uncles,
and Grannies. But a less cozy, less contented side of folk life is
recaptured by ballads like "John Henry," by work and prison songs,
by the blues, and even by the spirituals. Still another mood of the
folk may be detected in sermons, prayers, and testimonials. These
expressions of life's hardship, its stress and strain, did not lend
themselves so quickly to exploitation, but ways were eventually
found. The blues provided a tap-root of tremendous vitality for
season after season, vogue after vogue of popular music, and became
an American idiom in a broad sense. A time came when even
"Dry Bones," "When the Saints go Marching In," and "He's Got
the Whole World in His Hand" seemed to express a national mood.
Nor was the art of the old-time Negro preacher overlooked in the
scramble.

Interestingly, too, folk expression of this kind continues. The
"Black and Unknown Bards," eulogized by James Weldon Johnson
as creators of the spirituals, have now come out as the composers

of gospel songs such as those sung by Mahalia Jackson, but their intimate links with the folk, personal as well as musical, remain intact. Louis Armstrong is himself a bridge between the sporting houses in which Jelly Roll Morton introduced his special piano style and "invented" jazz for seduction and the era of television, goodwill tours, and jazz as a secret weapon of diplomacy. Uncle Remus finds a very hep Harlem counterpart in Langston Hughes' "Simple Minded Friend."

Close reading, so called, can become a bad habit, possibly a vice, where simple appreciation is concerned, but never does it start more quarrels than when the folk are involved. So let it be said quickly that Negro folklore, like almost any other kind, can be traced in its origins to a dim past when it drew on a common cultural heritage, which most of the folk of the world appear to have shared. In any case, the telling of tales is a time honored custom in Africa. By what steps the FABLES OF AESOP (Ethiop) became the animal stories of West Africa, of the West Indies, and of the slaves states of the U.S.A. is a lively question but not to the point here. What does concern us is that the slaves brought with them to the New World their ancient habit of story telling as pastime, together with a rich bestiary.

While the masters of slaves went to some length to get rid of tribal languages and some tribal customs, like certain practices of sorcery, they accepted the animal stories as a harmless way to ease the time or entertain the master's children. That the folk tales of these Negro slaves were actually projections of personal experiences and hopes and defeats in terms of symbols appears to have gone unnoticed.

In the African prototypes of the American Negro tales the heroes were generally the jackal, the hare, the tortoise, and the spider. The African jackal survived as the American fox, the African hare as the American rabbit, and the African tortoise as the American dry-land turtle or terrapin. The spider came only as near as the West Indies, where it reappeared in the Anansi tales of Jamaica. As a villain the African hyena was replaced by the American wolf, but that role is sometimes assigned to the fox or the bear in the American tale. The rest of the cast of characters, the lions, leopards, tigers, and monkeys was safely transported.

Much has sometimes been made of the fact that a study of some three hundred versions of "The Tar Baby" story tends to leave the impression that its origin was in India, or that the well-liked "Playing Godfather," for example, is in the Reynard cycle and reappears in Grimm's FAIRY TALES. This, however, is not true of the great majority of the tales brought over from Africa, and even where it is, the American Negro fables, as has been pointed out by anthropologists, "have been so modified with new beasts and local color added, different themes, and different experiences, that an almost new, certainly a quite different thing results." Written literature, of course, does the same thing.

The American Negro slave, adopting Brer Rabbit as hero, represented him as the most frightened and helpless of creatures. No hero-animals in Africa or elsewhere were so completely lacking in strength. But the slaves took pains to give Brer Rabbit other significant qualities. He became in their stories by turn a practical joker, a braggart, a wit, a glutton, a lady's man, and a trickster. But his essential characteristic was his ability to get the better of bigger and stronger animals. To the slave in his condition the theme of weakness overcoming strength through cunning proved endlessly fascinating.

Also satisfying, for related reasons, were accounts of the defeat, if not destruction, of the powerful Brer Wolf, the stupid Brer Bear, and the sly Brer Fox. Variations on these themes permitted the story tellers to invest Brer Squirrel, Sis Goose, Brer Rooster, Brer Alligator, and the rest with traits equally recognizable, equally amusing, and equally instructive.

The Brer Rabbit lore owes its wide vogue among Americans in general to the Uncle Remus stories of Joel Chandler Harris, but his were not the first or the last collections of these tales. Much of the special appeal of his versions may be attributed to the setting in which the old Uncle entertains the Young Master. To this extent they do not conform as fully to the definition of a folktale as one *by the folk for the folk* as do versions like "Brer Rabbit Fools Buzzard," collected by Arthur Huff Fauset, or "Brer Fox and the Goobers," collected by Carl Carmer. Such a story as "Ole Sis Goose," collected by A. W. Eddins, appears to belong to a time more recent than the Joel Chandler Harris tales and to suggest, by its

reference to the problem of justice in the courts, that the possibilities of this genre have not even yet been exhausted by the Negro folk.

Another body of Negro folktales, equally dear to the slaves themselves, stemmed from the familiar trickster theme. In slavery the trickster, most frequently called John or Jack, had a made-to-order setting. Surprised in his folly or his wrong-doing by Ole Master, Old Miss, the "patterollers," or even the devil, he would attempt to clear himself by his wit. He did not always succeed, but the happy ending was when he avoided a whipping or, better still, obtained his freedom. In the course of the tales the story tellers poked as much fun at themselves as they did at their masters, but pretentiousness was unfailingly exposed.

Stories of enormous exaggeration, sometimes called "lies" by the folk themselves, a large body of "why" stories, accounting humorously for the beginnings of almost everything, from the creation of man and beast to explanations of the peculiar ways of women, together with humanized accounts of heaven, continue to amuse the folk after nearly a century of Emancipation. Equally durable is the preacher story, likewise of slavery time origin.

The Negro "preacher tale" is in the tradition of the religious tales of antiquity and the "exempla" of medieval Europe, as well as of the anecdotes used so effectively by Lorenzo Dow and other Methodist and Baptist preachers in proclaiming protestant religion to the plantation folk in the latter part of the 18th century. While frequently failing to moralize and generally taking off into directions not suggested by their respected predecessors, the Negro religious tales retained at least one important characteristic of the genre: they aimed to entertain.

To the folk the Negro "preacher tale" included both the stories told by their preachers in the pulpit and the stories told *about* their preachers when not in the pulpit. In either case, whether borrowed or adapted originally, they took root in one section of the South or another and became a part of the cultural heritage of the local folk. Sometimes a popular preacher tale was *no lie,* as in the case of the story told about the Reverend L. K. Williams, later pastor of the huge Olivet Baptist Church in Chicago and vice-president of the Baptist World Alliance.

In the Brazos Bottoms of Texas, where he was born and raised, L. K. was known as a gambler in his youth. His father, a deacon in the church, did all he could to make a Christian of the boy, but to no avail. Young L. K. went right on shooting dice on the banks of the Brazos River while the good folk of the Bottom were in church singing hymns on Sunday morning. But a time came, as the old folks used to say, and as J. Mason Brewer has recorded, when the spirit overcame him, and young L. K. Williams gave up his "worldly ways" and "put on de armuh of de Lawd." Here is how it was remembered by one of his contemporaries:

"We was all listenin' to de preachuh an' jes' beginnin' to feel de sperrit movin' in our haa'ts, when all of a sudden we heahs a hoss gallopin' up to'a'ds de chu'chhouse es fas' ez he kin trot. Evuhbody wonder what de trouble be an' staa't lookin' outen de windows. Putty soon dey seed a roan hoss stop out at de fence roun' de chu'chhouse an a boy git offen 'im. De boy staa'ted runnin' up to de chu'chhouse an' when he gits close 'nuff we seed dat hit was L. K. Williams. He had on his duckins an' dey was dirty ez dey could be an' his hair ain't been combed, but he runned in de do' straight up to whar de preachuh was preachin' say, 'Elduh, ah wants to jine de chu'ch an' be a Christun.' His pappy was settin' on de front row an' soon as L. K. said dis his pappy grab 'im an' staa't cryin' an' say, 'Bless de Lawd! Bless de Lawd.' Mah prayers done been answered.' From dat day on L. K. comed to chu'ch all day evuh Sunday, an' putty soon he come to be a exhorter (dat's a preachuh tryin' to git on foot preachin', you know). So putty soon dey calls 'im to pastuh a li'l ole chu'ch, and he comed to be one of de bes' preachuhs in de Bottoms. Dey say dat de why he comed an' jined de chu'ch dat Sunday was 'caze he losed all his money in a dice game down to Falls on de Brazos, and de Lawd meck hit come to 'im to git shed of his sinful ways an' live a good life."

While life has changed a great deal down on the Brazos since L. K. Williams was a crap-shooting boy, and many of the folk have gone away, as he himself did long ago, his kind and theirs survive, and many of them are never more delighted than when they have a chance to tell you about what happened to their preacher or the story he told in a recent sermon. This should not surprise. Writing about the Negro church in the United States in 1903, W. E. B. Du-

Bois observed that "there is a church organization for every sixty Negro families. This institution, therefore, naturally assumed many functions which the harshly suppressed social organ had to surrender; the church became the center of amusements, of what little spontaneous economic activity remained, of education and of all social intercourse." The picture is still recognizable.

The tempo of the singing, as represented by the Negro spirituals, has been stepped up and a jazz note added to make the gospel songs, and the "moaning" of the preacher has given way (well, more or less) to a more ordered discourse, but the "gravy" is still there, as the folk themselves would testify.

James Weldon Johnson recognized in the sermons of the old-time Negro preacher an important form of folk expression. He reproduced a number of these as poetry. Other folklorists have gone to the same sources and made literal transcriptions or prose adaptations. All have confirmed one point. There was a wonderful creativity behind this preaching, which fully warrants the esteem in which it was held by its rapt, hand-clapping, foot-patting, and vocally responsive hearers.

Many of the more successful sermons of the old-time Negro preacher were repeated time and again and gradually took on the set pattern of a work of folk art. John Jasper of Richmond became famous for his "De Sun Do Move," and thousands of people, white and black, flocked to his church to hear it. Other old-time preachers imitated it, adapted it, and added it to their own repertories. The same happened with such numbers as "Dry Bones in the Valley," "The Heavenly March," and the "Train Sermon," sometimes called "The Black Diamond Express, running between here and hell, making thirteen stops and arriving in hell ahead of time."

The old-time Negro preacher himself belonged to a unique breed. Entertaining, comic when comedy was needed, he was in every sense the shepherd of the flock. It was he who gave the slave hope and inspiration. It was he who eased the hard journey with the comforting sentiment, "You may have all dis world, but give me Jesus." It was he who created the setting in which the spirituals were born.

Before the Revolutionary War the Negroes George Liele and Andrew Bryan were preaching to whites and blacks alike in

Augusta and Savannah, Georgia, respectively. John Ledman in his HISTORY OF THE RISE OF METHODISM IN AMERICA tells about Black Harry who preached from the same platform with the other founders of that church in the United States and concludes, "The truth was that Harry was a more popular speaker than Mr. Asbury (Bishop Francis Asbury) or almost anyone else in his day." The old-time preacher was among the first slaves to learn to read and write. He became a teacher. When the time came for courageous action, he took a hand in the Underground Railroad, while his counterpart in the North became an effective Abolitionist speaker. So the tradition to which Martin Luther King of Montgomery, Alabama, belongs is a long one. The Negro preacher has had a vital role, not the least important aspect of which has been the awakening and encouragement of folk expression. He is forever memorialized in the spirituals, the preacher stories, and to a lesser extent, since the whole setting cannot be recaptured (the moaning and the hand-clapping and the responses of the audience, for example), in the sermons themselves.

As an indication of the kind of backing the old-time preacher could count on, we have the testimonials and remembrances of his members. The church folk answered him back, and the answer was strong and affirmative. What he gave, and what they picked up was hope, confidence, a will to survive. The lore that stemmed from the religious experiences of the Negro in slavery, like that which found expression in the animal tales and the pastime rhymes, was always fundamentally optimistic. But this is not the whole story.

Just as sure as God had his heaven, the devil had his hell. And the box (guitar), as all the older folk know, has always been a special device of the devil's. I can remember what happened to one of these careless minstrels who made the mistake of wandering onto the church grounds during an intermission between services back in my childhood. The sisters of the church lit into him like a flock of mother hens attacking a garter snake. He protested. He was just fixing to play a couple of hymns, he explained. But this did not save him. He was obliged to leave in a hurry. The deaconesses knew from bitter experience, no doubt, that the church yard was no place

for a box. They also knew that the songs with which the guitar was associated were not for the ears of children.

The blues, like the work and prison songs and most of the folk ballads, seemed at first shockingly incompatable with the new condition and aspirations of freedmen. But this was not actually the case. Behind these earthy lyrics was the beginning of a new racial consciousness and self conception. It recognized difference but without the usual connotations of disparity. It made no apology, asked no pity, offered no defense. It insisted only on being itself, as the young poets of the Harlem Renaissance loved to say.

Because of this a distinguished sociologist could observe some thirty years ago that "Who would know something of the core and limitations of this life (Negro folk) should go to the *Blues*. In them is the curious story of disillusionment without a saving philosophy and yet without defeat. They mark these narrow limits of life's satisfactions, its vast treacheries and ironies. Stark, full human passions crowd themselves into an uncomplex expression, so simple in their power that they startle. If they did not reveal a fundamental and universal emotion of the human heart, they would not be noticed now as the boisterous and persistent intruders in the polite society of lyrics that they are. . . . Herein lies one of the richest gifts of the Negro to American life. . . . These are the *Blues,* not of the Negro intellectuals any more than of the white ones, but, of those who live beneath the range of polite respect."

Ellison has called the blues "an autobiographical chronicle of personal catastrophe expressed lyrically" and added, "Their attraction lies in this, that they at once express both the agony of life and the possibility of conquering it through sheer toughness of spirit. They fall short of tragedy only in that they provide no solution, offer no scapegoat but the self."

It is not surprising, under the circumstances, that Negro writers, and the many others who have used the Negro as a subject, should continue to dip into the richness of Negro folk life. The novelist and the sociologist just quoted were born into a folk culture. The same was true of Paul Laurence Dunbar, James Weldon Johnson, Jean Toomer, Sterling Brown, Zora Neale Hurston, Richard Wright, Margaret Walker, Gwendolyn Brooks, and James Baldwin,

to name but a few. It shows, indeed it is conspicuous, in their writing. But does this fact, this tendency to lean more heavily on Negro folk tradition than on "standard" or "white" models, set the Negro writer of the United States outside the main stream of Western literature?

It should not. Stanley Edgar Hyman has noted that in this matter contemporary Negro writers, employing what we have called the folk manner, are in line with Aristophanes, Shakespeare, and St. Paul, all of whom drew similarly from *their* folk sources in myth and ritual. So, Mr. Hyman concludes, correctly, I believe, "High Western culture and the Negro folk tradition thus do not appear to pull the writer in opposite directions, but to say the same thing in their different vocabularies, to come together and reinforce insight with insight."

ARNA BONTEMPS

Contents

III. MEMORIES OF SLAVERY

IV. SOMETIMES IN THE MIND

V. GOD, MAN AND THE DEVIL

VI. DO YOU CALL THAT A PREACHER?

VII. GHOST STORIES

VIII. BLACK MAGIC AND CHANCE

XII. GOSPEL SONGS

XIII. PASTIME RHYMES

XIV. BALLADS

XV. BLUES

XVI. WORK SONGS

XVII. STREET CRIES

XVIII.   PLAYSONGS AND GAMES

XIX.   THE JAZZ FOLK

XX.   HARLEM JIVE

XXI.   THE "PROBLEM"

XXII.   SONGS IN THE FOLK MANNER

XXIII.   POETRY IN THE FOLK MANNER

XXIV. PROSE IN THE FOLK MANNER

Animal Tales

TAR BABY

Rabbit says to himself, "Gee, it's gittin' dry here; can't git any mo' water. Git a little in the mornin' but that ain't enough." So he goes along an' gits the gang to dig a well. So the Fox goes roun' an' calls all the animals together to dig this well. He gits Possum, Coon, Bear, an' all the animals an' they start to dig the well. So they come to Rabbit to help. Rabbit he sick. They say, "Come on, Brother Rabbit, help dig this well; we all need water." Rabbit say, "Oh the devil, I don't need no water; I kin drink dew." So he wouldn't go. So when the well was done Rabbit he was the first one to git some of the water. He went there at night an' git de water in jugs. The other animals see Rabbit's tracks from gittin' water in jugs. So all the animals git together an' see what they goin' to do about Brother Rabbit. So Bear say, "I tell you, I'll lay here an' watch for it. I'll ketch that Rabbit." So Bear watched but Rabbit was too fast for him. So Fox said, "I tell you, let's study a plan to git Brother Rabbit." So they all sit together an' study a plan. So they made a tar baby an' put it up by the well. So Brother Rabbit come along to git some water. He see the tar baby an' think it is Brother Bear. He say, "Can't git any water tonight; there's Brother Bear layin' for me." He looked some more, then he said. "No, that ain't Brother Bear, he's too little for Brother Bear." So he goes up to the tar baby an' say, "Whoo-oo-oo-oo." Tar Baby didn't move. So Rabbit got skeered. He sneaked up to it an' said, "Boo!" Tar

Baby didn't move. Then Rabbit run all aroun' an' stood still to see did he move. But Tar Baby kept still. Then he moved his claw at him. Tar Baby stood still. Rabbit said, "That must be a chunk o' wood." He went up to see if it was a man. He said, "Hello, old man, hello, old man, what you doin' here?" The man didn't answer. He said again, "Hello, old man, hello, old man, what you doin' here?" The man didn't answer. Rabbit said, "Don't you hear me talkin' to you? I'll slap you in the face." The man ain't said nothin'. So Rabbit hauled off sure enough an' his paw stuck. Rabbit said, "Turn me loose, turn me loose or I'll hit you with the other paw." The man ain't said nothin'. So Rabbit hauled off with his other paw an' that one stuck too. Rabbit said, "You better turn me loose, I'll kick you if you don't turn me loose." Tar Baby didn't say anything. "Bup!" Rabbit kicked Tar Baby an' his paw stuck. So he hit him with the other an' that one got stuck. Rabbit said, "I know the things got blowed up now; I know if I butt you I'll kill you." So all the animals were hidin' in the grass watchin' all this. They all ran out an' hollered, "Aha, we knowed we was gonna ketch you, we knowed we was gonna ketch you." So Rabbit said, "Oh, I'm so sick." So the animals said, "Whut we gonna do?" So they has a great meetin' to see what they gonna do. So someone said, "Throw him in the fire." But the others said, "No, that's too good; can't let him off that easy." So Rabbit pleaded an' pleaded, "Oh, please, please throw me into the fire." So someone said, "Hang him." They all said, "He's too light, he wouldn't break his own neck." So a resolution was drawed up to burn him up. So they all went to Brother Rabbit an' said, "Well, today you die. We gonna set you on fire." So Rabbit said, "Aw, you couldn't give me anything better." So they all say, "We better throw him in the briar patch." Rabbit cry out right away, "Oh, for God's sake, don't do dat. They tear me feet all up; they tear me behind all up; they tear me eyes out." So they pick him up an' throw him in the briar patch. Rabbit run off an' cry, "Whup-pee, my God, you couldn't throw me in a better place! There where my mammy born me, in the briar patch."

RABBIT TEACHES BEAR A SONG

BR'ER RABBIT. . . . This rabbit an' Bear goin' to see a Miss Reyford's daughter. N'Br'er Rabbit been killin' Miss Reyford's hogs. Miss Reyford didn't know he was killin' her hogs. She said to him, "If you tell me who been killin' my hogs I'll give you my daughter." N' so he said he'd go an' find out. He went to Mr. Bear an' said, "They's some ladies down here an' they're givin' a social. Y'know, you have a wonderful voice, an' they want you to sing a bass solo." So Bear he felt real proud an' he said, "All right." So Rabbit said, "I'm gonna try to train your voice. Now you just listen to me an' do everything I tell you." So Bear said, "All right." So Rabbit said, "Now I'm gonna sing a song. Listen to me. When I say these lines:

"Who killed Mr. Reyford's hogs,
Who killed Mr. Reyford's hogs?"

you just sing back:

"Nobody but me."

So Brer Rabbit started singing:

"Who killed Mr. Reyford's hogs,
Who killed Mr. Reyford's hogs?"

Then Bear answered back:

"Nobody but me."

Rabbit said, "That's right, Br'er Bear, that's fine. My, but you got one fine voice." So ol' Bear he felt real good, 'cause Rabbit flatterin' him, tellin' him that his voice was such a wonderful one. So they went up there to Miss Reyford's party an' pretty soon Rabbit an' Bear commence to sing. Rabbit sang:

"Who killed Mr. Reyford's hogs,
Who killed Mr. Reyford's hogs?"

an' Bear sang out:

"Nobody but me."

So Mr. Reyford shot Bear. Then Rabbit said to Miss Reyford, "I told you Mr. Bear killed your hogs." Bear said to Rabbit, "All right, I'll git you." Ol' Rabbit jes' grin. So later Bear caught him n' tol' him he was gonna kill him. So Rabbit said, "Please don't kill me, please don't kill me." So Rabbit said he'd show him some honey. So Rabbit carried Bear to some honey. He said, "Here's the honey." The bees started on Bear an' Bear started hollerin', but Rabbit he yelled, "Taint nothin' but the briars, 'taint nothin' but the briars." So Bear got killed by the bees.

BRER RABBIT AND SIS COW

BRER RABBIT see Sis Cow an' she have a bag plumb full of milk, an' it's a hot day an' he ain't had nothin' to drink fur a long time. He know 'tain't no use askin' her fur milk 'cause las' year she done 'fused him onct, and when his ole 'oman was sick, too.

Brer Rabbit begun thinkin' mighty hard. Sis Cow is grazin' under a persimmon tree, an' de persimmons is turned yellow, but they ain't ripe enough yit to fall down.

So Brer Rabbit, he say: 'Good mornin', Sis Cow.'

'Good mornin', Brer Rabbit.'

'How is you feelin' dis mornin', Sis Cow?'

'Poly, thank God, Brer Rabbit, I'se jest sorter haltin' 'twix a balk and a breakdown, Brer Rabbit.'

Brer Rabbit express his sympathy and then he say: 'Sis Cow, would you do me the favor to hit this here persimmon tree with yore head an' shake down a few of dem persimmons?'

Sis Cow say 'Sure' an' she hits the tree, but no persimmons come down. They ain't ripe enough yit.

So den Sis Cow git mad an' she go to the top of de hill an' she hists her tail over her back and here she come a bilin'. She hit dat tree so hard dat her horns go right into the wood so fur she can't pull 'em out.

Brer Rabbit,' say Sis Cow, 'I implores you to help me git a-loose.' But Brer Rabbit say: 'No, Sis Cow. I can't git you a-loose. I'm a

mighty weakly man, Sis Cow. But I kin 'suage your bag, Sis Cow, and I'm goin' to do it fur you.'

Then Brer Rabbit he go home for his ole 'oman and de chillun an' dey come back to de persimmon tree an' milk Sis Cow and have a big feastin'.

WHY BRER RABBIT WEARS A 'ROUND-'BOUT

BRER RABBIT wa'n't al'a's de prankin' tricky fellow he is now; not him, he was rankin' wid de biggoty onct. He didn't wear no short tail 'round-'bout dem days. Not him, he was buttoned up befo' and swingin' round de behime same as any longtail broadcloth preacher is now. He was a good un to rise and foller den. He special lay down de law to his family and his folks.

One night Miss Rabbit she done stepped crost Quarters to beg Miss Goat fer a pail er fresh milk. Mist' Rabbit he had all his chillun settin' in a row befo' him tellin' 'em how dey bes' do to live long and get wise besides.

He stan' wid his back to de fire, he done made 'em chillun cut a big back log and put in de light 'ood chunks a-top dat back log. He wa'n't no worker even den. He stan' frontin' dem little rabbits tellin' 'em dey gotter live to thrive. He say: 'Chillun, Al'a's you do dis, think twict befo' yuh speak onct. Lil' rabbits all settin' wid de goose-flesh risin' on 'em foh lack er de heat dey pa keep off 'em standin' befo' 'em.

He say: 'Dar was Sis Mole; she speak fust 'fo' she think, an' she say she too proud to walk on de groun', she was put under de groun'.' He say: 'Dar was Mist' Mockin' Bird, he speak onct'fo' he think twict, and he up and sing de birds' notes—he keepin' up de interest on dem notes twell yit.' He say: 'Dar was Mist' Robin say he choose a red breast, 'fo' he know what choice was de best.'

All dem lil' rabbits set des as solumn thinkin' twict, 'bout what dey pa say. Miss Rabbit she come er runnin' home crost de Quarters, she say: 'I see smoke! I smell fire!' she burst into de do'. Old Brer Rabbit he yit standin' 'fo' de fire. Brer Rabbit coat tail burnt off

clean 'round de crock, er rim er fire, still creepin' up an' 'round. Miss Rabbit she say: 'Chillun, didn' yuh smell smoke? Chillun, why didn't yuh spoke?'

Lil' rabbits say: 'Us thinkin' 'case Dad tells us to think twict 'fo' us spoke onct.'

Brer Rabbit been wearin' a 'round-'bout ever sence. Chillun, it's might' bad when yo' own advice turn agin you.

PLAYING GODFATHER

RABBIT an' Fox make a proposition once to start farmin', Dey bought lot of groceries for the year, butter, coffee, everything you could mention. So the butter was the most important. So they all went out in the field to work. Rabbit studied a plan to leave Possum an' Fox in the field an' make believe that some one was callin' him away. So he let on some one callin' him, "Y-hoo-y hoo!" So Fox an' Possum said, "What's that?" Rabbit said, "Aw, I can't work here for bein' bothered by these people. I'm goin' this time but I won't go no more." So Rabbit goes to the house an' sees the bucket o' butter. He ate some of the butter. Pretty soon he come back. Pretty soon somebody callin', "Y-hoo-y-hoo-y-hoo!" So they all said, "What's the matter, Brother Rabbit?" Rabbit said, "Aw, they want me to christen another baby. These people are botherin' me too much. I'm not goin'." So they all said, "You better go ahead. Hurry on." So he went an' got another stomach full o' butter. So when he come back they said, "Well, what did you name the baby?" He said, "Just begun." So he went an' got another stomach full o' butter. So pretty soon they heard somebody callin', "Y-hoo-y-hoo-y-hoo." So they all said, "What's the matter, Brother Rabbit?" Rabbit said, "Aw, those people just won't let me alone. They want me to christen another child. I'm not goin' this time, tho, deed I'm not." But they all said, "You better go ahead." So he went an' got some more butter. So he come back an' they asked him what name the baby had. He said, "Pretty Well On The Way." He comes back an' works a little while an' somebody yells, "Y-hoo-y-hoo-y-hoo."

They all said, "What's that?" So Rabbit said, "Aw, it's them same people want me to come christen another baby. I'm not goin', I tell you." They said, "You better go ahead." So he went off an' eat some more butter. When he come back they asked him what the baby's name was. He said, "About Quarter Gone." So he went on workin' some more an' somebody yelled, "Y-hoo-y-hoo-y-hoo." They said, "What's that?" He said, "It's those same people again. I tell you I just won't go an' christen any more of their children." But they said, "You better go on ahead." So he went off an' eat some more of the butter. When he returned they asked him what was the child's name. He said, "Half Gone." So he went on back to work. This time somebody yelled, "Y-hoo-y-hoo-y-hoo." So they all said, "What's that?" He said, "Doggone the luck, you know that's rotten. A fellow can't work here for those people callin' on you to christen their children." So they all said, "You better go on ahead." He went on an' eat some more of the butter. When he come back he said, "Well I christened another child." They said, "What you name him?" He said, "Quarter Lef." So he come on back, work awhile, an' pretty soon somebody cry, "Heh-h-h-h-h-h-h." Rabbit say, "Doggone the luck. I aint goin' this time. By God they want to run a fellow to death." So they all said, "You better go on ahead." So he went this time an' eat all the butter. When he come back they said, "What happened this time?" He said, "I had another child to christen." They said, "What did you name him?" He said, "All Gone." Well about the middle o' June they was gonna open the keg of butter. The crops were half grown. So when they got there the butter was all gone. They all said, "Who stole the butter?" Rabbit didn't know; Fox didn't know; Possum didn't know. So Rabbit say, "I tell you, Possum, he been layin' around dat house all time. I believe he must o' done it." So he said, "Let's build a big fire. Then all three of us will lay aroun' the fire, an' whoever et the butter the grease will come out o' his stomach." So they made a big fire an' everybody went to sleep but Rabbit. So he peeped. Everybody sound asleep. So Rabbit say, "All right, I got him now." So he took his tail an' greased it an' his belly right good. He oiled Fox up too. So pretty soon Fox woke up. He spied Possum an' cried, "Dah, dah, I tol' you, Possum done it!" Possum woke up an' looked aroun'. He say, "Hey there, Fox, you had some too; look

at your belly." Fox made for Rabbit but Rabbit got away. So Fox
struck Possum a lick an' Possum went through the blaze of fire.
That's why his tail is bare of hair today.

WHY THE FOX'S MOUTH IS SHARP,
WHY THE POSSUM HAS NO HAIR ON HIS TAIL,
AND WHY THE RABBIT HAS A SHORT TAIL
AND A WHITE SPOT ON HIS FOREHEAD

ONE day de fox, de 'possum and Brer Rabbit was gwine down in
Sister Dimsey' corn field. Dere was a grave-yard in de corn field
dat had a hant in it. Brer Possum ask Brer Fox, was he 'fraid o'
hants. Brer Fox say dat if de odder gentermens will stan' dey base,
he will hang on till de las' corn was off de stalk. "All right, den,"
say Brer Possum, "I'se got my bag an' I'se gwine to make corn
fly tonight." Brer Rabbit he lay low, 'kase he knowed how Brer
Possum was 'fraid o' hant.

Atter a while, Brer Rabbit 'lowed dat dey better start, Brer Fox
he led de way. Dey all went tho de grave-yard an' got ober de
fence in de corn field. Brer Fox, he start to fill his bag fust. When
he begin to pull de corn de hant say, "Macaroni, macaroni, pull
down you wine." De Fox look up an' say, "I ain't pullin' wine; I
pullin' corn." Bimeby de hant come jumpin' up an' down de row
atter Brer Fox. Brer Fox he got skeered, he did, and took out for
de fence. When he got dere he stick he mouf thoo de wrong hole
in de fence an' mash he mouf right sharp.

Den Brer Possum thought he would try, dat he wasn't afraid.
But no sooner dan he begin to pull de corn de hant say, "Macaroni,
macaroni, pull down you wine." Brer Possum say, "I ain't pull
wine, I pull corn." When Brer Possum got his bag half full, de
hant jumped down in front of him. Brer Possum drop de bag an'
run for de fence. When he went to jump ober de fence de hant
cotch him by de tail an' skinned all de hair off, but he got away.

Now Brer Rabbit say he gwine to try, an' dat he gwine to get de corn, fedder or no. So when Brer Rabbit got his bag mos' full, de hant say, "Macaroni, macaroni, pull down you wine." Brer Rabbit say, "I ain't pullin' wine, I pullin' corn," an' dat he was gwine to get his bag full or bus' dat hant wide open. De hant went off an' come back lookin' like a man wid a long knife in his han'. When Brer Rabbit seed dat, he grab he bag up on he shoulders an' laid out for de fence. Ka-blim! An' when he went to go ober, he skin he head agains' de fence, and when he got all over but de tail, de hant chopped at him and cut de tail right off short.

THE WATCHER BLINDED

Once upon a time there was a rabbit an' a wolf, an' the rabbit an' the wolf was workin' for a man. They were drivin' oxens. So the wolf an 'rabbit decided to steal one. The wolf had children an' the rabbit didn't. So they stole the ox an' they killed it. They skinned it an' they cleaned it. Then they cut it into four parts; that was to get it out of the way quick. So when they got it killed Rabbit asked Wolf what would he do if some ladies came an' asked him for some meat. Wolf said he wouldn't do anything, he'd just give the ladies some. Old Rabbit told Wolf to stay till he came back. The rabbit borrowed four suits an' the rabbit come back all dressed up as a lady an' asked the wolf would he sell her a piece of meat. The wolf said, "Oh no, lady, I'll give you a piece," as he gave her a hind quarter. The rabbit went back an' dressed again an' when he come back he asked for another hind quarter. But the wolf didn't know she carried that on her back. Rabbit came back. He asked the wolf to sell some meat. He gave the rabbit a full quarter. He went back home an' dressed again and asked to sell some meat for her supper. Then he went back home an' stored it all. He came back as a man from work. He said to Wolf, "Oh Mr. Wolf, where's all the meat?" Wolf said, "Oh, man, some ladies called to buy an' I give them the meat an' there is nothin' left but the head an' the guts. You take the head an' I'll take the guts." So the next day Wolf

goes by the rabbit's house. Rabbit saw him comin' an' got his fiddle an' began to play:

> Folly-rolly day,
> You eat the meat an' I eat the guts,
> Folly-rolly day,
> You eat the meat an' I eat the guts,
> Folly-rolly day.

An' the wolf asked Rabbit to play it again. Wolf began to run the rabbit. He runned him till he reached a hollow tree. When they reached the tree Rabbit run into the hollow part. The wolf couldn't git him out. He saw a frog an' asked the frog to watch the tree till he come back. Frog said, "What for?" He told him the rabbit was up there an' if he git the rabbit he kill him an' give him one half. He went home an' got his ax. He cut the tree down; limb by limb he split it. The rabbit was up in the hollow tree. He pretended as if he was eatin'. The frog heard him. The frog asked him what he was eating. Rabbit said, "Oh, man good t'ing!" He asked him did he want some of it. He says, "Yes." The rabbit told him to look up de tree. He filled the frog's eyes full of pepper an' the frog began to git the pepper from his eyes. Rabbit got away. When the wolf couldn't git the rabbit he asked the frog had he been away. The frog told him no he hadn't closed his eyes an' neither been away. Frog began to get close to the water, an' when the frog began to leap the wolf cut the frog's tail off, an' the frog been bumpin' ever since and hasn't had no tail.

BRER FOX AND THE GOOBERS

BRER RABBIT seen Brer B'ar one day a-settin' out to dig goobers wid de donkey draggin' de dump cart. Brer Rabbit say me an' Miss Rabbit an' all them little rabbits sho' is hungry fo goobers. So he go home an' fin' him a red string an' tie it 'roun' his neck an' he run an' lay down in de road where Brer B'ar would be com'n by wid de cart carryin' his sack filled up wid goobers.

By'n by Brer B'ar come along an' de donkey shy so he 'most upset de cart. Brer B'ar git out an' he say: 'If'n it ain't Brer Rabbit as dead as a doornail wid his throat cut. Make good rabbit stew foh me an' Miss B'ar. So he pick up Brer Rabbit an' fling him in de cart an' go on. Soon's his back is turned Brer Rabbit fling out de bag o' goobers an' jump out heself an' run home. On de way he meet Brer Fox an' Brer Fox say: 'Where you git dat bag o' goobers?' an' Brer Rabbit tell him.

Soon's Brer B'ar come in sight er his house, way behime dem dark pines, he holler to his ole 'oman:

> 'Hello dar. Come heah, Miss B'ar:
> Goobers heah; rabbits dar!'

Miss B'ar she run out de cabin. She run 'roun' de dump cart. She look in. Des a lil' rattlin' load o' goobers in de bottom er de cart. She say:

> 'Goobers gone, rabbit gone, bag gone!'

Brer B'ar tu'n 'roun' an' look, he scratched his head, he say: 'Dat 'ar rabbit done left me bar.'

Nex day he hitch up de donkey to de dump cart an' start to de patch to haul up mo' goobers. His ole 'oman, she tell him: 'Watch out, don' drap noddin' on de big road wid dis nex' load.'

Dis time Brer Fox he 'low he'll git his winter's pervisions by speculatin' wid Brer B'ar's load, labor and land.

Brer Fox git a red string, he do. He tie hit 'roun' his neck. He go to de big road. Same place what Brer Rabbit done lay down, Brer Fox he done lay down. He keep des' as still. D'reckly heah come Brer B'ar wid 'noder heapin' load o' goobers.

De donkey he shy agin at de same place. Brer B'ar he git off de cart, he look at Brer Fox, he say: 'What dis mean? Un-hum! Maybe perhaps de same thief what stole my goobers yestiddy. You got de same like red 'roun' your th'oat. Maybe perhaps you dead too. He feel Brer Fox, he say: 'You good weight too, I take you to my ole 'oman, maybe you'll make er good stew.'

Wid dat Brer Fox think he sho' goin' git good chance to git his fill er goobers.

Brer B'ar he lif' Brer Fox by de behime legs, he say:

'Maybe you be dead, er maybe no,
But I will make you dead fer sho'!'

And wid dat he swing Brer Fox 'roun' and lam his head 'ginst de wheel er de cart.

Dat lick like to kilt Brer Fox. Hit all he can do to jerk his behime legs loose from Brer B'ar and run home t'rough de dark pines. He had de swole head some seasons frum dat lick. Chillum, de same cunnin' trick ain't apt to work twict.

THE FOX AND THE GOOSE

One day a Fox was going down the road and saw a Goose. "Good-morning, Goose," he said; and the Goose flew up on a limb and said, "Good-morning, Fox."

Then the Fox said, "You ain't afraid of me, is you? Haven't you heard of the meeting up at the hall the other night?"

"No, Fox. What was that?"

"You haven't heard about all the animals meeting up at the hall! Why, they passed a law that no animal must hurt any other animal. Come down and let me tell you about it. The hawk mustn't catch the chicken, and the dog mustn't chase the rabbit, and the lion mustn't hurt the lamb. No animal must hurt any other animal."

"Is that so!"

"Yes, all live friendly together. Come down, and don't be afraid."

As the Goose was about to fly down, way off in the woods they heard a "Woo-wooh! woo-wooh!" and the Fox looked around.

"Come down, Goose," he said.

And the Dog got closer. "Woo-wooh!"

Then the Fox started to sneak off; and the Goose said, "Fox, you ain't scared of the Dog, is you? Didn't all the animals pass a law at the meeting not to bother each other any more?"

"Yes," replied the Fox as he trotted away quickly, "the animals passed the law; but some of the animals round here ain't got much respec' for the law."

OLE SIS GOOSE

OLE SIS GOOSE wus er-sailin' on de lake, and ole Br'er Fox wus hid in de weeds. By um by ole Sis Goose swum up close to der bank and ole Br'er Fox lept out an cotched her.

"O yes, ole Sis Goose, I'se got yer now, you'se been er-sailin' on der lake er long time, en I'se got yer now. I'se gwine to break yer neck en pick yer bones."

"Hole on der', Br'er Fox, hold on, I'se got jes' as much right to swim in der lake as you has ter lie in der weeds. Hit's des' as much my lake es hit is yours, and we is gwine to take dis matter to der cotehouse and see if you has any right to break my neck and pick my bones."

And so dey went to cote, and when dey got dere, de sheriff, he wus er fox, en de judge, he wus er fox, and der tourneys, dey wus fox, en all de jurymen, dey was foxes, too.

En dey tried ole Sis Goose, en dey 'victed her and dey 'scuted her, and dey picked her bones.

Now, my chilluns, listen to me, when all de folks in de cotehouse is foxes, and you is des' er common goose, der ain't gwine to be much jestice for you pore cullud folks.

SHEER CROPS

BR'ER BEAR en Br'er Rabbit dey wuz farmers. Br'er Bear he has acres en acres uf good bottom land, en Br'er Rabbit has des' er small sandy-land farm. Br'er Bear wuz allus er "raisin' Cain" wid his neighbors, but Br'er Rabbit was er most engenerally raisin' chillun.

After while Br'er Rabbit's boys 'gun to git grown, en Br'er Rabbit 'lows he's gwine to have to git more land if he makes buckle en tongue meet.

So he goes ober to Br'er Bear's house, he did, en he say, sez he, "Mo'nin', Br'er Bear. I craves ter rent yer bottom field nex' year."

Br'er Bear he hum en he haw, en den he sez, "I don't spec I kin 'commodate yer, Br'er Rabbit, but I moughten consider hit, bein's hit's yer."

"How does you rent yer land, Br'er Bear?"

"Well," said Br'er Bear, "I takes der top of de crop fer my sheer, en yer takes de rest fer yer sheer."

Br'er Rabbit thinks erbout it rale hard, en he sez, "All right, Br'er Bear, I took it; we goes ter plowin' ober dare nex' week."

Den Br'er Bear goes back in der house des' er-laughin'. He sho is tickled ez to how he hez done put one by ole Br'er Rabbit dat time.

Well, 'long in May Br'er Rabbit done sont his oldest son to tell Br'er Bear to come down to the field to see erbout dat are sheer crop. Br'er Bear he comes er-pacin' down to de field en Br'er Rabbit wuz er-leanin' on de fence.

"Mo'nin', Br'er Bear. See what er fine crop we hez got. You is to hab de tops fer yer sheer. Whare is you gwine to put 'em? I wants ter git' em off so I kin dig my 'taters."

Br'er Bear wuz sho hot. But he done made dat trade wid Br'er Rabbit, en he had to stick to hit. So he went off all huffed up, en didn't even tell Br'er Rabbit what to do wid de vines. But Br'er Rabbit perceeded to dig his 'taters.

'Long in de fall Br'er Rabbit lows he's gwine to see Br'er Bear ergin en try to rent der bottom field. So he goes down to Br'er Bear's house en after passin' de time of day en other pleasant sociabilities, he sez, sez he, "Br'er Bear, how erbout rentin' der bottom field nex' year? Is yer gwine ter rent hit to me ergin?"

Br'er Bear say, he did, "You cheat me out uf my eyes las' year, Br'er Rabbit. I don't think I kin let yer hab it dis year."

Den Br'er Rabbit scratch his head er long time, en he say, "Oh, now, Br'er Bear, yer know I ain't cheated yer. Yer jes' cheat yerself. Yer made de trade yerself en I done tuck yer at yer word. Yer sed yer wanted der tops fer yer sheer, en I gib um ter yer, didn't I? Now yer jes' think hit all ober ergin and see if yer can't make er new deal fer yerself."

Den Br'er Bear said, "Well, I rents to yer only on dese perditions:

dat yer hab all de tops fer yer sheer en I hab all de rest fer my sheer."

Br'er Rabbit he twis' en he turn en he sez, "All right, Br'er Bear, I'se got ter hab more land fer my boys. I'll tuck hit. We go to plowin' in dare right erway."

Den Br'er Bear he amble back into de house. He wuz shore he'd made er good trade dat time.

Way 'long in nex' June Br'er Rabbit done sont his boy down to Br'er Bear's house ergin, to tell him to come down ter de field ter see erbout his rent. When he got dare, Br'er Rabbit say, he did: "Mo'nin', Br'er Bear. See what er fine crop we hez got? I specks hit will make forty bushels to der acre. I'se gwine ter put my oats on der market. What duz yer want me ter do wid yer straw?"

Br'er Bear sho wuz mad, but hit wa'nt no use. He done saw whar Br'er Rabbit had'im. So he lies low en 'lows to hisself how he's gwine to git eben wid Br'er Rabbit yit. So he smile en say, "Oh, der crop is all right, Br'er Rabbit. Jes' stack my straw anywheres around dare. Dat's all right."

Den Br'er Bear smile en he say, "What erbout nex' year, Br'er Rabbit? Is yer cravin' ter rent dis field ergin?"

"I ain't er-doin nothin' else but wantin' ter rent hit, Br'er Bear," sez Br'er Rabbit.

"All right, all right, yer kin rent her ergin. But dis time I'se gwine ter hab der tops fer my sheer, en I'se gwine ter hab de bottoms fer my sheer too."

Br'er Rabbit wuz stumped. He didn't know whatter do nex'. But he finally managed to ask, "Br'er Bear, ef yer gits der tops en der bottoms fer yer sheer, what will I git fer my sheer?"

Den ole Br'er Bear laff en say, "Well yer would git de middles."

Br'er Rabbit he worry en he fret, he plead en he argy, but hit do no good.

Br'er Bear sez, "Take hit er leave hit," en jes' stand pat.

Br'er Rabbit took hit.

Way 'long nex' summer ole Br'er Bear 'cided he would go down to der bottom field en see erbout dat dare sheer crop he had wid Br'er Rabbit. While he wuz er-passin' through de woods on hiz way, he sez to himself, he did:

"De fust year I rents to de ole Rabbit, I makes de tops my sheer,

en ole Rabbit planted 'taters; so I gits nothin' but vines. Den I rents ergin, en der Rabbit is to hab de tops, en I de bottoms, en ole Rabbit plants oats; so I gits nothin' but de straw. But I sho is got dat ole Rabbit dis time. I gits both de tops en de bottoms, en de ole Rabbit gits only de middles. I'se bound ter git' im dis time."

Jes' den de old Bear come ter de field. He stopped. He look at hit. He shet up his fist. He cuss en he say, "Dat derned little scoundrel! He done went en planted dat fiel' in corn."

JOHN AND THE LION

WELL, John was ridin' long one day straddle of his horse when de grizzly bear come pranchin' out in de middle of de road and hollered: "Hold on a minute! They tell me you goin' 'round strowin' it dat youse de King of de World."

John stopped his horse: "Whoa! Yeah, Ah'm de King of de World, don't you b'lieve it?" John told him.

"Naw, you ain't no King. Ah'm de King of de World. You can't be no king till you whip me. Git down and fight."

John hit de ground and de fight started. First, John grabbed him a rough-dried brick and started to work de fat offa de bear's head. De bear just fumbled 'round till he got a good holt, then he begin to squeeze and squeeze and squeeze. John knowed he couldn't stand dat much longer, do he'd be jus' another man wid his breath done give out. So he reached into his pocket and got out his razor and slipped it between dat bear's ribs. De bear turnt loose and reeled on over in de bushes to lay down. He had enough of dat fight.

John got back on his horse and rode on off.

De lion smelt de bear's blood and come runnin' to where de grizzly was layin' and started to lappin' his blood.

De bear was skeered de lion was gointer eat him while he was all cut and bleedin' nearly to death, so he hollered and said: "Please don't touch me, Brer Lion. Ah done met de King of de World and he done cut me all up."

De lion got his bristles all up and clashed down at de bear: "Don't

you lay there and tell me you done met de King of de World and not be talkin' 'bout me! Ah'll tear you to pieces!"

"Oh, don't tetch me, Brer Lion! Please lemme alone so Ah kin git well."

"Well, don't you call nobody no King of de World but me."

"But Brer Lion, Ah done met de King sho' nuff. Wait till you see him and you'll say Ah'm right."

"Naw, Ah won't, neither. Show him to me and Ah'll show you how much King he is."

"All right, Brer Lion, you jus' have a seat right behind dese bushes. He'll be by here befo' long."

Lion squatted down by de bear and waited. Fust person he saw goin' up de road was a old man. Lion jumped up and ast de bear, "Is dat him?"

Bear say, "Naw, dat's Uncle Yestiddy, he's a useter-be!"

After while a li'l boy passed down de road. De lion seen him and jumped up agin. "Is dat him?" he ast de bear.

Bear told him, "Naw, dat's li'l Tomorrow, he's a gointer-be, you jus' lay quiet. Ah'll let you know when he gits here."

Sho nuff after while here come John on his horse but he had done got his gun. Lion jumped up agin and ast, "Is dat him?"

Bear say: "Yeah, dat's him! Dat's de King of de World."

Lion reared up and cracked his tail back and forwards like a bull-whip. He 'lowed, "You wait till Ah git thru wid him and you won't be callin' him no King no mo'."

He took and galloped out in de middle of de road right in front of John's horse and laid his ears back. His tail was crackin' like torpedoes.

"Stop!" de lion hollered at John. "They tell me you goes for de King of de World!"

John looked him dead in de ball of his eye and told him, "Yeah, Ah'm de King. Don't you like it, don't you take it. Here's mah collar, come and shake it!"

De lion and John eye-balled one another for a minute or two, den de lion sprung on John.

Talk about fightin'! Man, you ain't seen no sich fightin' and wrasslin' since de mornin' stars sung together. De lion clawed and bit John and John bit him right back.

Way after while John got to his rifle and he up wid de muzzle right in ole lion's face and pulled de trigger. Long, slim black feller, snatch 'er back and hear 'er beller! Dog damn! Dat was too much for de lion. He turnt go of John and wheeled to run to de woods. John levelled down on him agin and let him have another load, right in his hind-quarters.

Dat ole lion give John de book; de bookity book.[1] He hauled de fast mail back into de woods where de bear was laid up.

"Move over," he told de bear. "Ah wanta lay down too."

"How come?" de bear ast him.

"Ah done met de King of de World, and he done ruint me."

"Brer Lion, how you know you done met de King?"

"Cause he made lightnin' in my face and thunder in my hips. Ah know Ah done met de King, move over."

THE ANIMAL COURT

". . . I been talkin' to ole man Robbin way back in slavery-time, 'en he tell me 'bout one night he been los' on de bee-tree track, an' when he find he-self he been in de bushes on the aige of de big sandbar, an' he set down on a log to res' heself, an' de moon been shinin' bright, an' while he settin' dere he look out on de sand-bar an' he seen a drove of owl walk out dere like a set of men, one big owl been wid dem. When dey got out a piece in de sand-bar dey all stan' up dere together, an' ain't move, an' atter while he seen a fox, seen a coon, seen a possum, an' seen a rabbit, all of 'em comin' dere an' get together nigh until dem owl, 'en crow, jay-bird, snake, crawl out de water all kinds of varmints been gathered around, an' while he settin' dere he say he see two woodpeckers come in wid a turkey buzzard an' dey march up dere in front of dem owl an' he set der an' watch 'em, an' dem owl helt a cote, just like people, an' dey 'scused de buzzard of eatin' bur rabbit brother. Bur Buzzard had been a undertaker an' went to de settin' up dat night all night long, an' he look like he guine shed tear an' stan' roun' dere an'

[1] Sound word meaning running.

look mournful, an' bow he ball head, like bur rabbit brother ain't been nobody brother but he own, he look like he fret so; next mornin' all de animals lef' to go to dey work an' lef' bur Buzzard to bury bur rabbit brother, an' when dey come back dey find out bur buzzard ain't bury him, but eat him. An' dey had a jay-bird 'scusin' bur buzzard, an' dey had varmint, an' had snake all for one kind of witness or anudder, an' lyin' every which-a-way, an' dey convict bur buzzard, an' dey pick out bur fox to execute him he got so much sharp ways an' he do so much low trick, but bur fox mighty perticular 'bout what he do an' what he put he mout' on. Bur Fox he start to lef' an' dey axe him wuh he guine, an' he say, "Ain't you hear dem dogs out dere in de woods, dat is wuh I guine."

An' nobody didn't do nuthen to bur buzzard, an' ain't never done nuthen to buzzard. Dat's why so much buzzard. Dey always gits off.

DE KNEE-HIGH MAN

"DE KNEE-HIGH man lived by de swamp. He wuz alwez a-wantin' to be big 'stead of little. He sez to hisself: 'I is gwinter ax de biggest thing in dis neighborhood how I kin git sizable.' So he goes to see Mr. Horse. He ax him: 'Mr. Horse, I come to git you to tell me how to git big like you is.'

Mr. Horse, he say: 'You eat a whole lot of corn and den you run round and round and round, till you ben about twenty miles and atter a while you big as me.'

So de knee-high man, he done all Mr. Horse tole him. An' de corn make his stomach hurt, and runnin' make his legs hurt and de trying make his mind hurt. And he gits littler and littler. Den de knee-high man he set in his house and study how come Mr. Horse ain't help him none. And he say to hisself: 'I is gwinter go see Brer Bull.'

So he go to see Brer Bull and he say: 'Brer Bull, I come to ax you to tell me how to git big like you is.'

And Brer Bull, he say: 'You eat a whole lot o' grass and den you

bellow and bellow and fust thing you know you gits big like I is.'

And de knee-high man he done all Brer Bull tole him. And de grass make his stomach hurt, and de bellowing make his neck hurt and de thinking make his mind hurt. And he git littler and littler. Den de knee-high man he set in his house and he stidy how come Brer Bull ain't done him no good. Atter wile, he hear ole Mr. Hoot Owl way in de swamp preachin' dat de bad peoples is sure gwinter have de bad luck.

Den de knee-high man he say to hisself: 'I gwinter ax Mr. Hoot Owl how I kin git to be sizable,' and he go to see Mr. Hoot Owl.

And Mr. Hoot Owl say: 'What for you want to be big?' and de knee-high man say: 'I wants to be big so when I gits a fight, I ken whup.'

And Mr. Hoot Owl say: 'Anybody ever try to pick a scrap wid you?'

De knee-high man he say naw. And Mr. Hoot Owl say: 'Well den, you ain't got no cause to fight, and you ain't got no cause to be mo' sizable 'an you is.'

De knee-high man says: 'But I wants to be big so I kin see a fur ways.' Mr. Hoot Owl, he say: 'Can't you climb a tree and see a fur ways when you is clim' to de top?'

De knee-high man, he say: 'Yes.' Den Mr. Hoot Owl say: 'You ain't got no cause to be bigger in de body, but you sho' is got cause to be bigger in de BRAIN.' "

T'APPIN (TERRAPIN)

IT WAS famine time an' T'appin had six chillun. Eagle hide behin' cloud an' he went crossed de ocean an' go gittin' de palm oil; got de seed to feed his chillun wid it. T'appin see it, say "hol' on, it har' time. Where you git all dat to feed your t'ree chillun? I got six chillun, can't you show me wha' you git all dat food?" Eagle say, "No, I had to fly 'cross de ocean to git dat." T'appin say, "Well, gimme some o' you wings an' I'll go wid you." Eagle say, "A' right. When shall we go?" T'appin say, "Morrow mornin' by de firs'

cock crow." So 'morrow came but T'appin didn' wait till mornin'. T'ree 'clock in de mornin' T'appin come in fron' Eagle's house say, "Cuckoo—cuckoo—coo." Eagle say, "Oh, you go home. Lay down. 'Taint day yit." But he kep' on, "Cuckoo—cuckoo—coo." An bless de Lor' Eagle got out, say, "Wha' you do now?" T'appin say, "You put t'ree wings on this side an' t'ree on udda side." Eagle pull out six feathers an' put t'ree on one side an' t'ree on de udda. Say, "Fly, le's see." So T'appin commence to fly. One o' de wings fall out. But T'appin said, "Da's all right, I got de udda wings. Le's go." So dey flew an' flew; but when dey got over de ocean all de eagle wings fell out. T'appin about to fall in de water. Eagle went out an' ketch him. Put him under his wings. T'appin say, "Gee it stink here." Eagle let him drop in ocean. So he went down, down, down to de underworl'. De king o' de underworl' meet him. He say, "Why you come here? Wha' you doin' here?" T'appin say, "King, we in te'bul condition on de earth. We can't git nothin' to eat. I got six chillun an' I can't git nothin' to eat for dem. Eagle he on'y got t'ree an' he go 'cross de ocean an' git all de food he need. Please gimme sumpin' so I kin feed my chillun." King say, "A' right, a' right," so he go an' give T'appin a dipper. He say to T'appin, "Take dis dipper. When you want food for your chillun say:

> Bakon coleh
> Bakon cawbey
> Bakon cawhubo lebe lebe."

So T'appin carry it home an' go to de chillun. He say to dem, "Come here." When dey all come he say:

> Bakon coleh
> Bakon cawbey
> Bakon cawhubo lebe lebe.

Gravy, meat, biscuit, ever'ting in de dipper. Chillun got plenty now. So one time he say to de chillun, "Come here. Dis will make my fortune. I'll sell dis to de King." So he showed de dipper to de King. He say:

> Bakon coleh
> Bakon cawbey
> Bakon cawhubo lebe lebe.

Dey got somet'ing. He feed ev'ryone. So de King went off, he call ev'ryboda. Pretty soon ev'ryboda eatin'. So dey ate an' ate, ev'ryt'ing, meats, fruits, all like dat. So he took his dipper an' went back home. He say, "Come, chillun." He try to feed his chillun; nothin' came. (You got a pencil dere, ain't you?) When it's out it's out. So T'appin say, "Aw right, I'm going back to de King an' git him to fixa dis up." So he went down to de underworl' an' say to de King, "King, wha' de matter? I can't feeda my chillun no mora." So de King say to him, "You take dis cow hide an' when you want somepin' you say:

> Sheet n oun
> n-jacko
> nou o quaako.

So T'appin went off an' he came to cross roads. Den he said de magic:

> Sheet n oun
> n-jacko
> nou o quaako.

De cowhide commence to beat um. It beat, beat. Cowhide said, "Drop, drop." So T'appin droup an' de cowhide stop beatin'. So he went home. He called his chillun in. He gim um de cowhide an' tell dem what to say, den he went out. De chillun say:

> Sheet n oun
> n-jacko
> nou o quaako.

De cowhide beat de chillun. It say, "Drop, drop." Two chillun dead an' de others sick. So T'appin say, "I will go to de King." He calls de King, he call all de people. All de people came. So before he have de cowhide beat, he has a mortar made an' gits in dere an' gits all covered up. Den de King say:

> Sheet n-oun
> n-jacko
> nou o quaako.

So de cowhide beat, beat. It beat everyboda, beat de King too. Dat cowhide beat, beat, beat right t'roo de mortar wha' was T'appin an'

beat marks on his back, an' da's why you never fin' T'appin in a clean place, on'y under leaves or a log.

Told by Cugo Lewis, Plateau, Alabama.
Brought to America from West Coast Africa, 1859.

WHY BR' GATOR'S HIDE IS SO HORNY

ONE time Br' Alligator's back used to be smooth an' white as a catfish-skin, so dat when he come out o' de water, an' lie down for sleep in de sun-hot on de mudbank, he shine like a piece o' silber. He been mighty proud o' he hide, an' mighty pleased wid heself nohow.

He an' his wife an' he fambly lib down in de ribber at de edge o' de rice fiel'. Dem hab plenty o' fish to nyam for dem bittle, an' nebber bodder wid none o' de creeter what been on de lan', lessn dem bog in de mud by de ribber-side, or fall in de water. Dem projeck roun' down in de bottom o' de ditch an' canal, an' eben if dey aint so smart, dem mek out alright. An' ebery year God sen', dey hab a gang o' chillen, so dey house is full-up widout axin' in no company. An' de whole dit an' bilin' been dat satisfy wid deyself dat dey t'ink dey ain' nobody quite like 'em. An' dey aint hab no notion how true dat is!

Well, suh, one hot day in de fall Br' Gator been res' heself 'pontop de rice-fiel' bank, a-lettin' de sun soak into dat bright back o' hisn, when along come Br' Rabbit.

Now Br' Rabbit ain' got a bit o' use for Br' Gator, but he stop all de same for pass de time o' day an' hab a little compersation wid him, 'cause Br' Rabbit too lub compersation! Rather dan keep he mout' shut he will eben gone out o' he way for talk, if tis only wid one o' dem ridic'lous creeter dat ain' know no better dan to lib in de water.

"Howdy, Br' Alligator. How is Sis' Alligator, an' all de young Alligator mekin' out?"

Br' Gator ain't bodder to speak to Br' Rabbit at de fus' goin' off. Seem like he ain' care what no other creeter t'ink 'bout him, nor how dey git 'long dey-self. But after while he fix he cat-eye on Br'

Rabbit, an' tell-him-say, "Please Gawd, I like you to know dat dey
gits on fine! But taint no wonder dat dem chillen is smart, an' purty,
an' rais' right, 'cause dey lib in de ribber. I swear-to-Gawd I can't
see how oonuh (you) mek out, a-libin' up 'pon-top o' dat dry,
drafty lan'. An' you, an' all de udder creeter dat ain' fitten to lib
in de water, seems to spen' all o' you' time a-skirmishin' roun', till
you must' be wore out 'fore de day is half done!"

Br' Rabbit is bex wid Br' Gator for bein' so set in he notions, till
he had a-mind to tell him what he t'ink o' dat kind o' talk, but he
been jis' so bex dat he lay low, an' 'tend like Br' Gator's is speakin'
de truth. He sigh an' he shake he head, an' say bery mou'nful-like,
"Mebbe so. We sho' is been seein' a heap o' trouble!"

"Who dat, you talk 'bout, Br' Rabbit—Trouble?"

Br' Rabbit s'pose dat Br' Gator mus' be jokin' him, 'cause he
'member too good 'bout dat trouble Br' Gator had wid Br' Dog.
"How, Br' Alligator! You aint nebber hear o' Trouble?"

Br' Gator shake he head. "No. I nebber yeddy 'bout him, needer
seen him. How he is stan'?"

Br' Rabbit ain' b'liebe he ears. "Oh, cry out, Br' Alligator! Old
as you is, an' ain' nebber seed Trouble yit?"

"I tell you, Br' Rabbit, I ain' nebber know nothin' 'bout dis here
Trouble. How is Trouble look?"

Br' Rabbit scratch he head. He figger if Br' Gator been so stupid,
an' so satisfy wid heself an' he own t'ing, an' so ridic'lous an'
onmannersable 'bout all dat lib on de lan', dat now here is he
chance for learn Br' Gator he right place. An' Br' Rabbit is so
mischiebous dat he scheme 'bout he he goin' to hab de mos' fun
out o' Br' Gator.

"I dunno dat I kin 'xactly tell you how Trouble stan'. But mebbe
you'd like for see him?"

"Sho' 'nough, Br' Rabbit, I like bery much for see him."

"O' cose I kin show him to you, Br' Alligator, but I dunno dat I
is a-goin' to. Mebbe you aint like him so good."

"Go'long, boy! I ain' scare' o' dat. I jis' want to see him. If I don'
like him, dat ain' goin' to be no matter to me."

"I is purty busy jis' now," Br' Rabbit 'tend.

"Do, Br' Rabbit! You gots time for a lot o' no-count t'ing, an'
after all, tis Me what ax you—don't forgit dat!"

"Sho! O' cose. How kin I forgit dat!" Br' Rabbit mock him, only Br' Gator ain' nebber see dat Br' Rabbit mean mischief. "But I gots to fix me house, an' Sis' Rabbit is poly, an' de chillen gotta be 'tend to, an'—"

"Tchk! All dat'll tek care o' itself!" An' Br' Alligator 'suade an' beg, an' beg an' 'suade, till at las' Br' Rabbit 'gree to show him Trouble.

"Meet me in dis same place soon as de jew dry up offn de grass nex' Saturday. Dat been a good day. Trouble mebbe hab some time off come Sunday." An' Br' Rabbit bid him good mawnin', an' gone 'long.

Come Saturday, Br' Gator git up befo' day-clean in de mornin', an' start for fix heself.

Sis' Alligator wake up, an' ax, "Whe' you gwine?"

Br' Gator aint crack he teet' at she, but gone 'long fixin' heself. Dat jis' set Sis' Alligator for bodder him. "Whe' is you gwine?" she ax again. An' she squestion an' she squestion, till after sich a lengt' o' time Br' Gator see dat de 'oman is jis' boun' for know.

He gi' up at las'. "I is goin' out wid Br' Rabbit."

"Whe' is you goin' to?"

Br' Alligator mek a long mout', an' try for pay no mo' 'tention. But Sis' Alligator know de ways for git roun' dat fellah! An' after such anudder length o' time, Br' Alligator tell she: "I is goin' for see Trouble."

"What Trouble is?"

"How I know? Dat's what I goin' for see."

"Kin I go 'long?" ax Sis' Alligator.

He say no, but after talk an' 'suade, an' talk an' 'suade, at las' Br' Alligator say, short-patience-like, "All right, you kin come 'long."

So she start for fix sheself. What wid all de talkin' an' goin' on, all de leetle alligators wake up by dis time. Dem look at dey pappy, an' dey mammy, fixin' deyself an' gittin' ready to gone out, an' dem run to Br' Gator an' ax him, "Whe' you gwine, Pappy?"

"None o' yo' business!"

Dem run den to Sis' Alligator, an' all cry out, one after anudder, "How! Where is you goin', Mammy?"

But all Sis' Alligator say is, "Git 'way, an' let me 'lone."

Den dey run to dey Pa, an' tease, "Pappy, Mammy say you is for tell we where you is goin'."

Br' Gator is bex but he see taint no use to try for hold back. "I go for see Trouble."

"Pappy! Kin we go? Kin we go?" An' dem chillen all jump up an' down, an' holler, an' beg him.

Br' Gator tell 'em, "No!"

So dem run to dey Ma, an' ax, "Mammy, kin we go?"

An' dey Ma tell-'em-say, "If you' Pa say you kin go, den you kin go."

So back dem gone at dey Pa. "Ma say we kin go if you jis' let we!"

By dis time Br' Gator is plumb wore out, so he say, "Well, den, yes! You kin go. But fix you'self nice an' purty. An' act manner-sable, now! You is to show Br' Rabbit how much better water-chillen behave dan woods-chillen!"

Dem run for fix deyself nice, an' turreckly dey is all dress up for gone out. Dey hab on dey bes', wid mud on dey head, an' marsh on dey back, an' moonshine on dey tails, an' dey t'ink dat dey jis' look fine.

'Bout dis time Br' Gator look out de do', an' see dat de jew is mos' off de grass. He call he wife an' he chillen, "Come on!"

An' dem come a-crowdin', an' all gone out on de rice fiel' bank to wait on Br' Rabbit.

Dey aint been there long, 'for here come Br' Rabbit, a-smokin' he pipe. When he git up wid dem, he been s'prise to see what a hebby haul he is mek—de whole dart fambly. He laugh to hisself, but he ain' say nothin' but jus' say, "Howdy," to Br' Gator an' he wife. An' he tell 'em, "How nice de chillen is all a-lookin'!" But all de time he say to heself, "Do Lord! Dis is a oagly gang o' people. An' how mean dey clo'es is! Dat "oman is a po' buckra hussy, for true."

Br' Gator aint eben 'pologize to him for fetch sich a crowd. All he say is, "Dey all beg me so dat I hab to giv in, an' let 'em come along."

Br' Rabbit say, "Plenty o' room for all. Hope you will all enjoy yo'self."

"T'enky!" dey all tell him. An' de chillen all been dat glad dat

Br' Rabbit ain' sen' 'em home dey all dance 'bout wid joy.

Dey look so comical, a-histin' dey nose an' dey tail, till Br' Rabbit mos' laugh in dey face. But 'stid o' dat he squinch up he eyebrow an' look at he watch, an' say, "Time to gone 'long, I reckin."

So dem all start down de rice fiel' bank, Br' Rabbit an' Br' Gator leadin' off, wid Sis' Alligator walkin' behin' to mek de leetle Alligator behave deyself'. But dey wouldn't hardlly mind she—dey played 'long, or dawdled, or fit, till dey 'most set her 'stracted.

Br' Rabbit lead dem up through a patch o' woods till he git to a ol' fiel' all growed up full o' broom-grass an' briar! De grass stan' so t'ick you hardly kin see roun' in it an' tis dry as tinder, an' yaller like de pure gol'. De path dem tek gone spang through de fiel', an' twas a big fiel' too. Br' Rabbit lead, an' after a while dem git to de middle o' de fiel', an' den he stop.

Br' Rabbit tek he pipe out he mout', an' he clap he han' to he ear, an' mek out like he listen. Seem like he hear somet'ing. "Sh! Sh!" he tell de chillen.

Sis' Alligator say, "Sh! Sh! Or I'll lick de tar out o' you!"

After Br' Rabbit listen some mo', he shout out, "Who dat a-callin' Br' Rabbit?"

Den he mek out like he yeddy somet'in' mo', an' yell back, "Yes. Tis me. What you want wid me?"

He clap he han' to he ear again, an' den he say, "I is comin' right now." An' he turn to Br' Gator an' tell him, "Ax you' pardon, but somebody is callin' me 'way a minute on a business. Please for 'scuse me. An' wait right whe' you is till I kin git back."

"We goin' to stay right here," Br' Gator promise.

Br' Rabbit mek him a low bow, an' run 'long de path, out o' sight. Dat 'ceitful debbil gone till he git to de edge o' de woods, an' set heself down an' snigger to heself like he was tastin' de fun before he started it. Den he gone to business.

He smell de wind an' look which way it is drivin'. Den he pull a handful o' dat long, dry broom-grass, an' he knock out de hot coal from he pipe on it, an' he blow till de grass catch fire good. Den he run long de edge o' de fiel' wid de fire, an' set de fiel' roun' an' roun'. When he is done dat, he git up on a safe high stump whe' he kin se good, an' he set down an' wait.

All dis time de Alligator been down in de middle o' de fiel'. Dey

been tired wid walkin' so far, an' mighty satisfy wid res' deyself awhile.

Sis' Alligator been jus' de kind dat like for know jis' what she is goin' for see, an' she pester an' bodder Br' Gator wid w'ich-an'-w'y talk, "W'ich way is we gwine for find Trouble? Whyn you mek Br' Rabbit tell you mo' 'bout dis t'ing you is a-lookin' for? How long we got to wait?"

He aint mek she no answer, but jus' set still an' grunt ebery now an' den.

Once in awhile Sis' Alligator call to de chillen dat been a-projeckin' aroun', "Stop dat rookus!"

An' dey set, an' dey set.

De fire burn an' burn. At last de wind catch it an' it flared up high, an' de spark an' flame flew up, 'way up, in de element. One o' de leetle Alligator see dat. An' he holler out, "Look-a'-dere! Look-a-dere!"

But jis den he Ma ax he Pa another squestion, an' she hesh de chillen right short.

But all de turrah res' o' dem leetle Alligators look de way dey bubbuh (brother) p'int, an' dey sing out too, "Look-a'-dere!"

An' one get a notion an' he holler out, "Mus' be dat is Trouble."

An' Sis' Alligator turn an' look, an' she squizzit Br' Gator, "Look, Pa! Is dat Trouble for true?"

Br' Gator been so ignorant he ain' know. He lib in water an' mud, an' he aint ebber see fire till now, but he ain' feel easy in he mind. "Reckin mebbe Br' Rabbit git los' or somepn?" he ax Sis' Alligator, widout answer de squestion.

Den one o' de chillen sing out, "Trouble is pretty!"

An' wid dat, all o' de brats h'ist dey tail an' dey voice, an' holler. "Trouble is pretty! Trouble is pretty! Trouble is pretty!"

Br' Gator say, "If dat is Trouble, he sho' nough is pretty! De chile speak de trut'." An' he an' he wife set a-gogglin' dey big eye up in de element, watchin' de fire come on, an' dey kind o' forgit all 'bout Br' Rabbit. An' all de chillen goggle dey eye too, same as dey Ma an' Pa, an' keep still, as if dey ben 'fraid dat dey might scare Trouble away.

At las' a hot spark lan' right on one o' dem leetle Alligator' back.

An' he squall, an' cry out, "Trouble hurt! O'hey! O'hey! O'hey!"

He Ma fetch him a smack in de jaw an' tell him to mind he manners an' shut up, an' look how pretty Trouble is. But jus' as she done so, a hebby spark light on she, an' burn she too bad. An' she start for jump 'bout, an' holler.

"Tis true Trouble hurt! Trouble hurt for true? O'hey! O'hey! O'hey!" An' dey 'member quick who dey is forgit! "Br' Rabbit! Br' Rabbit! We don't want to see no mo' o' Trouble, Br' Rabbit! Oh, Br' Rabbit!"

Well, my frien', 'bout dat time de spark begin for sweeten de whole lot o' dem. Dey is dat put to it dey don't know whaffor do. An' dey run 'bout an' run 'bout, dis way an' dat way, for git out; but eberywhere dem turn is de fire. An' dey holler out, an' holler out, "Br' Rabbit, whe' is you? Call to Trouble, Br' Rabbit! Come for we! Ooh, Br' Rabbit!"

But Br' Rabbit ain' come, an' he ain' say nothin'. An' mighty soon de fire git so close on dem Gator', dat dey can't hol' dey groun' no longer. Dey quit callin' on Br' Rabbit, an' jis' git ready for breck t'rough de best dey kin.

Dey ain' got no notion o' nothin' lef' in dey head but Git Home! Sis' Alligator holler, "Chillen, foller you' Pa."

An' right t'rough de scorchin' fire dey bus', Sis' Alligator a-herdin' dem. Dey don't walk so fas' ebery day, but dis been a special day, wid dat hot fire a-blisterin' an' a-frizzlin' 'em, an' dey gone a-runnin'. After dey git t'rough dey ain' slow up. Dey gone past Br' Rabbit just a-scuttlin'! An' dey look dat comical till Br' Rabbit most fall off de stump, he laugh so hard.

"Ki, Br' Alligator!" he shout, "I reckin you is seen Trouble now! Git 'long back in de water, where you belong. An' don't nebber, no mo', hunt Trouble!"

But dem Gator been too busy runnin' to stop to argue wid him.

Dem aint stop till dey git spang to de rice fiel' bank an' jump in de ribber. An' dey is still so hot from de fire when dey gone overboard an' de water hit dem, it gone "Swiish-sssssssssh-sh!" An' de pure steam rise up like a cloud.

Dey aint come out again de lib-long day, nor dat night needer; but when next dey git a chance to look upon one anudder dey find

dat de fire work on dem so bad dat dey white skin is just as black an' crinkly as a burnt log o' wood, an' rough as a libe-oak bark. Dat family done git swinged for bein' so fool. An' from dat day to dis Gator hab a horny hide.

· II ·

Animal Rhymes

THE ROOSTER AND THE CHICKEN

The rooster and the chicken had a fight,
The chicken knocked the rooster out of sight,
The rooster told the chicken, that's all right,
I'll meet you in the gumbo tomorrow night.

LITTLE ROOSTER

I had a little rooster.
He crowed befo' day.
Long come a big owl
And toted him away.

But the rooster fight hard,
And de owl let him go—
Now all de pretty hens
Wants dat rooster for their beau.

BUZZARD

Oh, Mr. Buzzard, don't yo' fly so high,
Yo' can't get yo' livin' flyin' in de sky.

SO IT HAPPENED

Way down yonder
In de fork of the branch
The old cow bellered
And the buzzard danced.

The bullfrog jumped
From bank to bank
Every time he jumped
He holler "Hank-de-hank!"

Jumped from the side bank
Into the holler
Wagon come along
And run over his collar.

MISS TERRAPIN AND MISS TOAD

As I went marchin' down de road,
I met Miss Tearpin an' I met Miss Toad.
An' ev'ry time Miss Toad would jump,
Miss Tearpin would peep from 'hind de stump.

I axed dem ladies fer to marry me,
An' bofe find fault wid de t'other, you see.
"If you marries Miss Toad," Miss Tearpin said,
"You'll have to hop 'round lak you'se been half dead!"

"If you combs yo' head wid a Tearpin comb,
You'll have to creep 'round all tied up at home."
I run'd away frum dar, my foot got bruise,
For I didn't know zactly which to choose.

FROG WENT A-COURTING

De frog went a-co'tin', he did ride. Uh-huh! Uh-huh!
De frog went a-co'tin', he did ride.
Wid a sword an' a pistol by 'is side. Uh-huh! Uh-huh!

He rid up to Miss Mousie's do'. Uh-huh! Uh-huh!
He rid up to Miss Mousie's do',
Whar he'd of'en been befo. Uh-huh! Uh-huh!

Says he: "Miss Mousie, is you in?" Uh-huh! Uh-huh!
Says he: "Miss Mousie, is you in?"
"Oh yes, Sugar Lump! I kyard an' spin." Uh-huh! Uh-huh!

He tuck dat Mousie on his knee. Uh-huh! Uh-huh!
He tuck dat Mousie on his knee,
An' he say: "Dear Honey, marry me!" Uh-huh! Uh-huh!

"Oh Suh!" she say, "I cain't do dat." Uh-huh! Uh-huh!
"Oh Suh!" she say, "I cain't do dat,
Widout de sayso o' uncle Rat." Uh-huh! Uh-huh!

Dat ole gray Rat, he soon come home. Uh-huh! Uh-huh!
Dat ole gray Rat, he soon come home,
Sayin': "Whose been here since I'se been gone?" Uh-huh! Uh-huh!

"A fine young gemmun fer to see." Uh-huh! Uh-huh!
"A fine young gemmun fer to see,
"An' one dat axed fer to marry me." Uh-huh! Uh-huh!

Dat Rat jes laugh to split his side. Uh-huh! Uh-huh!
Dat Rat jes laugh to split his side.
"Jes think o' Mousie's bein' a bride!" Uh-huh! Uh-huh!

Nex' day, dat rat went down to town. Uh-huh! Uh-huh!
Nex' day dat rat went down to town,
To git up de Mousie's Weddin' gown. Uh-huh! Uh-huh!

"What's de bes' thing fer de Weddin' gown?" Uh-huh! Uh-huh!
"What's de bes' thing fer de Weddin' gown?"—
"Dat acorn hull, all gray an' brown!" Uh-huh! Uh-huh!

"Whar shall de Weddin' Infar' be?" Uh-huh! Uh-huh!
"Whar shall de Weddin' Infar' be?"—
"Down in de swamp in a holler tree." Uh-huh! Uh-huh!

"What shall de Weddin' Infar' be?" Uh-huh! Uh-huh!
"What shall de Weddin' Infar' be"—
"Two brown beans an' a blackeyed pea." Uh-huh! Uh-huh!

Fust to come in wus de Bumblebee. Uh-huh! Uh-huh!
Fust to come in wus de Bumblebee.
Wid a fiddle an' bow across his knee. Uh-huh! Uh-huh!

De nex' dat come wus Khyernel Wren. Uh-huh! Uh-huh!
De nex' dat come wus Khyernel Wren,
An' he dance a reel wid de Turkey Hen. Uh-huh! Uh-huh!

De nex' dat come wus Mistah Snake. Uh-huh! Uh-huh!
De nex' dat come wus Mistah Snake,
He swallowed de whole weddin' cake! Uh-huh! Uh-huh!

De nex' come in wus Cap'n Flea. Uh-huh! Uh-huh!
De nex' come in wus Cap'n Flea,
An' he dance a jig fer de Bumblebee. Uh-huh! Uh-huh!

An' now come in ole Giner'l Louse. Uh-huh! Uh-huh!
An' now come in ole Giner'l Louse.
He danced a breakdown 'round de house. Uh-huh! Uh-huh!

De nex' to come wus Major Tick. Uh-huh! Uh-huh!
De nex' to come wus Major Tick,
An' he e't so much it make 'im sick. Uh-huh! Uh-huh!

Dey sent fer Mistah Doctah Fly. Uh-huh! Uh-huh!
Dey sent fer Mistah Doctah Fly.
Says he: "Major Tick, you's boun' to die." Uh-huh! Uh-huh!

Oh, den crep' in ole Mistah Cat. Uh-huh! Uh-huh!
Oh, den crep' in ole Mistah Cat,
An' chilluns, dey all hollered, "Scat!!" Uh-huh!!! Uh-huh!!!

It give dat frog a turble fright. Uh-huh! Uh-huh!
It give dat frog a turble fright,
An' he up an' say to dem, "Good-night!" Uh-huh! Uh-huh!

Dat frog, he swum de lake aroun'. Uh-huh! Uh-huh!
Dat frog, he swum de lake aroun',
An' a big black duck come gobble 'im down. Uh-huh! Uh-huh!

"What d'you say 'us Miss Mousie's lot?" Uh-huh! Uh-huh!
"What d'you say 'us Miss Mousie's lot?"—
"W'y—, she got swallered on de spot!" Uh-huh Uh-huh!

Now, I don't know no mo' 'an dat. Uh-huh! Uh-huh!
Now, I don't know no mo' 'an dat.
If you gits mo' you can take my hat. Uh-huh! Uh-huh!

An' if you thinks dat hat won't do. Uh-huh! Uh-huh!
An' if you thinks dat hat won't do,
Den you mought take my head 'long, too. Uh-huh!!! Uh-huh!!!

THE FROG

What a wonderful bird the frog are.
When he sit he stand almost.
When he hop he fly almost.
He ain't got no sense hardly.
He ain't got no tail hardly neither
Where he sit almost.

PERSIMMON TREE

Raccoon up the 'simmon tree,
Possum on the ground.
Raccoon shake them 'simmons down,
Possum pass 'em 'round.

TAILS

De coon's got a long ringed bushy tail,
De possum's tail is bare.
Dat rabbit hain't got no tail 'tall,
'Cept a liddle bunch o' hair.

De gobbler's got a big fan tail,
De pattridge's tail is small.
Dat peacock's tail's got *great* big eyes,
But dey don't see nothin' 'tall.

LUCKY FOOT

Ole Molly Cottontail,
Won't you be shore not to fail
To give me yo' right hin' foot?
My luck, it won't be fer sale.

RABBIT SOUP

Rabbit soup! Rabbit sop!
Rabbit et my turnip top!
Rabbit hop, rabbit jump,
Rabbit hide behind that stump.
Rabbit stop, twelve o'clock.
Killed dat rabbit with a rock.
Rabbit's mine. Rabbit's skint.
Clean him off and take him in.
Rabbit's on. Dance and whoop!
We gonna have some rabbit soup.

RABBIT HASH

Dere wus a big ole rabbit
Dat had a mighty habit
A-settin' in my gyardin,
An' eatin' all my cabbitch.
I hit 'im wid a mallet,
I tapped 'im wid a maul.

Sich anudder rabbit hash,
You's never tasted 'tall.

FOX AND RABBIT

Fox on de low ground,
Rabbit on de hill.
Says he: "I'll take a drink,
An' leave you a gill."

De fox say: "Honey,
(You sweet liddle elf!)
Jes hand me down de whole cup;
I wants it fer myself."

BAT

Bat! Bat! Come under my hat,
An' I'll give you a slish o' bacon,
But don't bring none yo' ole bedbugs,
If you don' want to get fersaken.

FISH

Little fishes in the brook,
Willie catch 'em with a hook,
Mama fry 'em in the pan,
Papa eat 'em like a man.

SHEEP AND GOAT

A sheep and a goat
Went a-walkin' through de pasture.

Says de sheep to de goat,
"Can't you walk a little faster?"

Says de goat to de sheep,
"My foot am sore."

"Oh, 'scuse me, goat,
I did not know your foot am sore."

GOAT AND SHEEP

Sheep an' goat
Gwine to de paster;
Says de goat to de sheep:
"Cain't you walk a liddle faster?"

De sheep says: "I cain't,
I's a liddle too full."
Den de goat says: "You can,
Wid my ho'ns in yo' wool."

But de goat fall down
An' skin his shin
An' de sheep split his lip
Wid a big broad grin.

WOODPECKER

Redhead woodpecker: "Chip! Chip! Chee!"
Promise dat he'll marry me.
Where shall de weddin' supper be?
Down in de lot in a holler tree.
What will de weddin' supper be?
A little green worm and a bumble bee.
'Way down yonder in de holler tree.
De redhead woodpecker: "Chip! Chip! Chee!"

LITTLE DOGS

I had a liddle dog,
His name was Pug.
Ever time he run
He went jug, jug, jug.

I had a little dog,
His name was Trot.
He helt up his tail
All tied in a knot.

I had a little dog,
His name was Ball.
W'en I give him a liddle
He want it all.

I had a little dog,
His name was Blue.
I put him on de road
And he almos' flew.

I had a little dog,
His name was Mack.
I rid his tail
Fer to save his back.

I had a little dog,
His name was Rover.
W'en he died
He died all over.

DID YOU FEED MY COW?

"Did you feed my cow?"
    "Yes, Mam!"
"Will you tell me how?"
    "Yes, Mam!"
"Oh, what did you give her?"
    "Corn an' hay."
"Oh, what did you give her?"
    "Corn an' hay."

"Did you milk her good?"
    "Yes, Mam!"
"Did you do like you should?"
    "Yes, Mam!"
"Oh, how did you milk her?"
    "Swish! Swish! Swish!"
"Oh, how did you milk her?"
    "Swish! Swish! Swish!"

"Did that cow die?"
    "Yes, Mam!"
"With a pain in her eye?"
    "Yes, Mam!"

"Oh, how did she die?"
"Uh! Uh! Uh!"
"Oh, how did she die?"
"Uh! Uh! Uh!"

"Did the buzzards come?"
"Yes, Mam!"
"For to pick her bones?"
"Yes, Mam!"
"Oh, how did they come?"
"Flop! Flop! Flop!"
"Oh, how did they come?"
"Flop! Flop! Flop!"
"Flop! Flop! Flop!"
"Flop! Flop! Flop!"
"Flop! Flop! Flop!"

· III ·

Memories of Slavery

UNWRITTEN HISTORY

I

OLD MRS. —— lived out on Granny White Pike, and she was so mean her husband couldn't stay with her. She had one old woman and a boy and a girl; they come to her by her husband and that was all the slaves he left her when he went off. She used to whip that old woman 'till she would run away, and they put a big iron bell on her and fixed it so she couldn get to the clapper and put it on her neck with an iron collar. Then when she would run away they could hear the bell and you could see her and her half-crazy sister riding horseback through the woods and listening to hear that bell. Just before the war they sent her to the greenhouse to make the fire —you see they had a sort of florist place, but they didn't sell flowers. People would just come there to look at them, but nobody ever visited her at all. Well, she stayed so long in the greenhouse that the old lady got the cowhide and went out to see what the trouble was, and there was the old lady bending down just like she was making the fire and old lady —— cut her a lick with the cowhide, and lo and behold she was dead. She come running over to our house to get someone to lay her out, and she was just crying like she had lost her best friend. Uh, crying because she didn't have nobody to whip no more.

When the War broke out her daughter was in Columbia in

45

school and she rode right through the lines with just a boy driving her—the boy was one of my brothers. We let him go with her to drive for her usually, and she got that girl and come on back. Governor Johnson would send guards there to guard her house and she said she didn't want them. She said, "Just send me some ammunition and I'll take care of myself. The Yankees walking 'round here with all that blue on gets on my nerves." She had a nice house. We would go there to see the girl. It was just her and the girl and her crazy sister there, and it was my idea of a beautiful house, but it got burnt down one night. They think somebody set it on fire, but they don't know who. It was way in the middle of the night and they had to run out in their night clothes. They didn't save a thing. She had a watch and she told the man where it was and said if he got it he could have it. Her husband had given it to her when they were engaged, and she didn't want it to burn up. He tried to get it, but the house started falling in before he could get to it and he had to give it up. She had some more little houses in the yard, and she moved in one of them, and somebody set that on fire; and she just moved into another one. That was just past Belmont College on the Granny White Pike. A house is still there on the place, but it doesn't look like nobody lives in it. I know she can't be living, but somebody might still live there. She was just so mean the white folks and nobody could stand her.

Mrs. Bradford lived up above us on the Granny White Pike. They were called Bradford's free Negroes because they was nice to them too. Old man Johnson—the man that carried so many to sell —had a nice time there too, but he'd just sell them, some one day and some another. But I can say one thing for him, there was never no half-white children among his group. All of them was colored. He would let them come home Christmas, and they would have candy pullings, and he'd just give them anything he could to make them have a good time, but they would be crying all the time because they knowed what they would get New Year's morning. That was their money, and after the War when their slaves were taken away, the whites were poor, some of them poorer than their slaves because if they had any money it was counterfeit.

When I was quite a girl I went to a colored person's wedding. She was as black as that thing there (card table top) but she was

her young master's woman and he let her marry because he could get her anyhow if he wanted her. He dressed her up all in red— red dress, red band and rosette around her head, and a red sash with a big red bow. She was so black that when we saw a person who was real black and we wanted to say how black he was, we would say "black as aunt Mary Jane," and you can imagine all that black and all that red; but they had a little ceremony and all the young white folks were there looking at them get married. It was the funniest looking sight I ever did see, black and all that red, and she married a yellow man and had two yellow girls to wait on her! After the ceremony, there was a dance. She and her husband belonged to the church and they didn't dance, but the rest of them did, and the white men and women were standing 'round looking at them dance all night.

We had dances often in the summer, down in the woods. They would have lanterns hanging out in the trees all around. In the winter they would have candy pullings, but some of them (slaves) didn't have any pleasure at all. They just had to work and go to bed. We could get a pass to go to any of them (parties). Jimmie Baxter's was a place that we could go and have a good time. There, the white folks would have a party and when they finished eating, they would set the things out on the table for the colored to eat. Some of them were right good to colored—no responsibility, and some of them had a better time than they do now. Of course they whipped them but some of them need it, and when I look around and see them doing some of the things they do now, I think it would be a good thing if some of them could be whipped now.

They taught us to be against one another and no matter where you would go you would always find one that would be tattling and would have the white folks pecking on you. They would be trying to make it soft for themselves. I had an aunt by marriage who would peep around and tell the women things. She wouldn't tell master because he always said he wouldn't have a tattler on his place, and if he found one he would sell her just as far as wind would carry.

Sho' nough rich white people, if they had a girl on the place and she had a baby, they would say, "Just do it again, and I'll sell you as far as water and wind will carry you. I'll sell you to Mississippi."

Yes, we had log rollings and house raisings. They would give a big dinner and put up the frame of a house in one day. It was just logs and they would daub it with dirt and when that dirt would fall off you could look out and see the snow falling. Sometimes you would get up out of your warm bed and the side towards the wall would be full of snow. They had great big grates with a big back log and a little log in front, and we would put chips in between. That fire would might nigh run you out.

No, they didn't tell you a thing. I was a great big girl twelve or thirteen years old, I reckon, and a girl two or three years older than that and we'd be going 'round to the parsley bed looking for babies; and looking in hollow logs. It's a wonder a snake hadn't bitten us. The woman that would wait on my mother would come back and tell us here's her baby; and that was all we knew. We thought she brought it because it was hers. I was twenty years old when my first baby came, and I didn't know nothing then. I didn't know how long I had to carry my baby. We never saw nothing when we were children.

In summer time we had all kinds of vegetables and bacon, but in the winter we had potatoes and sweet potatoes and turnips. We'd just eat the things in season. In the spring when turnip salad come in every body was just wild. Rice and light bread and things like that you never saw unless somebody was sick; and tea was another thing. They would kill a chicken and make a little soup for the sick and put a little rice in it, and you'd have some toast maybe, but that was all it was good for, and I think that's all it is good for now. We had three hot meals, breakfast at six, dinner at one and supper at six in the evening. For breakfast we'd have mush and gravy and meat. The children would just have mush, but the grown folks would have meat. On Saturday evening, they would take their pans and go to the big house to get the things to cook for Sunday. We'd get brown sugar, meat, flour, syrup, and on Sunday we'd get coffee with milk in it; the white folks had the cream. We'd have good things to eat too, out of that on Sunday.

When they would kill hogs, the chillen would have to pick up chips to smoke the meat. The colored had the heads and scraps like that and then they would have the fat part of the middling, but they would save the lean parts and the shoulders for the white folks.

Some wouldn't give their slaves enough to eat, but we had plenty, and my folks would steal meat and give it to those half starved slaves who would slip over for something to eat; but we were not supposed to see anything so we couldn't say nothing. They were afraid we would say something that would give them away.

If anybody would die, there was an old man on the place who would make a box. They had a graveyard for the colored and they would call in some people and have a short funeral service over the grave, then later on they would have a real funeral at the church. The first real coffin I saw was after the War. My mother had a little baby to die soon after the War and a friend of hers had a spring wagon, and he went to town and got a coffin. A lady made a winding sheet for the child, and it had lace on it.

There was an old man who belonged to Dr. Shelby, and he said if he ever got free he wasn't ever going to get up any more, and after he got free he really stayed there 'till he starved to death and died. He was an old man, too. He was just so happy to know that he could lay in bed and nobody could make him get up, he just wouldn't even get up to eat. You sho' couldn't do that (lie in bed) on old man Shelby's place. He'd whip slaves to death and then sell them before they died. The white folks got down on him for it and he was always in a lawsuit with somebody about selling a slave he had beat so bad that he died soon after the other man got him.

We'd sing "Steal Away to Jesus," "This World Is Not My Home." At corn shuckings they would sing, "Walk Jawbone, Come Jine the Re." I don't know what the "Re" was.

Our cabin was just a little weatherboard cabin with two rooms. My mother had so many chillen she had to have two rooms. It had old fashioned windows that you would just shut, no glass at all. There was a fireplace in each room that would come out on the inside. We called that the hob, and we chillen would climb up on it sometimes. For women that worked in the house, the cabin was whitewashed; it was closer to the house, you see, so the white folks could get to them easy if they wanted them; and they had to have it that way to keep from spoiling the looks of the big house.

Chillen couldn't sit in chairs; we had to sit on little blocks; you couldn't think you were grown and they said if you sit in chairs it would make you think you were grown and they said when I

was a child I was so long getting grown, I didn't know it. I used to say, Lord, if I ever had any chillen, I wouldn't treat them like I was treated. They would never ask you what you liked, they would just fix it and give it to you, and you had to eat it cause you were chillen. You'd see grown folks eating the best things! and you dasen't to look at it. In some places they had troughs for the chillen, and they had to eat just like hogs; but we didn't have that at our place.

My mother hired me out during the War, and I learned how to use a knife and fork by looking at the folks there. My folks were away during most of the War. In September they would always go South because it was warmer, and they went like this fall and in the spring the Battle of Ft. Donelson came off and the Yankees took Nashville, so they were cut off. Our young mistress was sick and they left her here. The day they took Ft. Donelson, the soldiers had a dress parade and a newsboy was running 'round with papers, hollering, "Extra! Extra! Fort Donelson has fallen and the enemy will be here tomorrow!" I remember young mistress took some table linen and started South to her folks. We could hear the Rebels singing as they retreated, "I Wish I was in Dixie," and right now at the reunions when those old soldiers start singing that, they just jump around and shout. And the Yankees were singing as they advanced, "It must be now the kingdom coming, in the year of jubilee; old marster run away and the darkies stay at home."

Yes, the slaves stayed and took care of the place 'til the white folks came back, and some of them stayed there 'till they died. Colonel McNairy—took charge of the place when our folks were away, but he had to go to War. He had been in West Point, and he said that before he'd let his mother bake bread and his sister wash and iron, he would wade in blood up to his stirrups, and he went off to war and he got blown to pieces in one of the first battles he fought in. They wasn't sure it was him but you know they had special kinds of clothes and they found pieces of his clothes and they thought he was blown to pieces from that. When he left, his brother looked after us. He would get the provisions and things like that. You see there wasn't many of us on the farm up here, so we never had a white overseer, we just had a foreman, you know, and he was colored.

We used to play a game we called "smut," but we would play it with corn spots instead of cards. We played it just like you would with cards only we would have grains of corn and call them hearts and spades, and so forth, and go by the spots on the corn. We would play marbles too, and this time of year our biggest amusement was running through the woods, climbing trees, hunting grapes and berries and so forth. We would play peeping squirrel too. We would say, "Peep, squirrel, peep dibble, dibble, dibble; walk, squirrel, walk, dibble, dibble, dibble, then run, squirrel, run, dibble, dibble, dibble;" and we would run after the squirrel (child).

Children never knew anything went on at night; all of their play was in the day. We played "Goosey, goosey, gander," too. We had a lots better time then than children have now, in our playing.

The white people in the summer time would sit out on the porch in the front of the house and the colored folks would sit on the kitchen porch. We didn't have porches to our cabins and we'd sing to the white folks. You know white folks always did like to hear slaves sing, "I'll court Miss Millie Simmons on a long summer's day."

We used to play Sugar and Tea too, and Frog in the middle and can't get out, and we would play songs like:

> "The Americans are gaining the day
> The British government beating,
> War's all over and we'll turn back;
> I'll make my way back home
> If the British guns don't kill me."

We would play them plays for games when we'd go to parties and get tired of dancing, then we would play with songs like that , . . I can't get all of that, but anyway, I know it was "Americans Are Gaining the Day." That was the play and we didn't know what "Americans" were.

We chillen would get in the woods and have meetings and sing them (spirituals), but we wouldn't sing them to the white folks. I remember another one we used to sing to the white folks:

> Bullfrog dies with the whooping cough
> Sparrow died with the colic
> Young ladies, ain't you sorry?

That was a Rebel song, and another one was, "I'll make my way back home again, if the Lincolnites don't kill me."

Oh, they tried to scare us; said they had horns (Yankees) but when we saw them with their blue clothes, brass spurs on their feet and their guns just shining, they just looked pretty to us.

None of our slaves went to war. They were all either too old or too young on our plantation. Some might have went from the Mississippi plantation.

II

They used to have prayer meetings. In some places that they have prayer meetings they would turn pots down in the middle of the floor to keep the white folks from hearing them sing and pray and testify, you know. Well, I don't know where they learned to do that. I kinda think the Lord put them things in their minds to do for themselves, just like he helps us Christians in other ways. Don't you think?

In them days the people professed religion just like they do now, but they was more ignorant, and yet I sometimes think they was more honest and sincere then they are now. I begin to think about religion right early; but I never professed till I come here and had chillen, too. I wanted to join St. Paul, and I begin to think about it a lot. I prayed and thought, and thought and prayed; I went to church and prayed, and come home and I got on my knees and I asked the Lord to tell me what church to join. Well, seem like he showed me the way. Seem like something kept telling me over my shoulder, "Go down yonder on Pearl Street and join Murray's church." The Lord sho' tole me that. I hadn't never been in that church then. It sounded like a natural man talking to me. I kept thinking about it. I said, "Lord, that's the Baptists what's always having a lot of fusses and rows in the church," but something just answered like a natural man, "don't make no difference; you go down on Pearl Street and join Murray's church." Well, for a while I didn't know what to do.

I was a wild thing when I was young. Why I was more on dancing than my Ole Missy, and she taught me to dance, too. Well,

after I joined the church, I didn't have no desire to dance no more. You know, I really object to Christians dancing. Now dancing don't bother me one bit, and it never did after I married. I see sin in dancing. I prayed to the Lord to take that off of me, and he sho' did. For a long time, you know, I could not git religion 'cause I wanted to dance, yessiree, I know what my religion done for me; it cleared my soul for all eternity. Dancing was an injury to me, I see it now.

We had a man named William—I can't think of that man's name to save my life. Anyway, he baptized my sister. I don't see how I forgot his name. Brother William—I don't see why I can't think of it; but my sister was baptized on the very same ground she was buried on. I went back there about twenty years ago; and all the folks that lived 'round there and knowed my sister and me was sho' nice to me. I stayed almost six weeks. All the white folks was so nice to me. 'Course, all my own old white people was dead 'cept just one family. He is a lawyer. His name was Howard. Me and him used to fuss and fight something awful when we was kids. When I went back there he said, "Lucy, I remember grandpa give me a good beating about you, didn't he?" I hadn't forgot it either, and we laughed about it a lot.

Well, they used to say when your right eye jump you was going to have good luck, and when your left eye jump, you going to cry. Then when the raincrow holler, it sho' going to rain. Why it hollered right out here in the front of the house yesterday, and it sho' rained before the day was over, didn't it? It used to be 'round here that it would be so dry; be six months before we have rain sometimes. Another thing, just as sho' as you born, when a bird comes in the house, it sho' going to be death right there in the family. Why a bird come in this here house, and flew right on my daughter's shoulder before she died. She was sixteen years old. I was so nervous from it. The bird had been eating polk berries and he left some on her dress. Well, she went on to church, and coming back she fell down, and she come on home to me, just about half crying, you know. She always in poor health. She come on home and went to school Monday, Tuesday and Wednesday; and I had just went to see a lady about giving her fancy work lessons. Well, she went to school on Wednesday morning; and in a little while Martha come

in. Martha was the youngest. I said, "Where is Lucy?" and then somebody come and told me my child had done got sick at school, and I said, "Lord, don't let my child die in school, please." I told Mr. King to go get a horse and buggy and go get her; and he was so nervous he couldn't hardly go; and so I sent for Dr. Hadley and Reverend Taylor, and they had done sent her home in a carriage. They didn't tell me for a long time that she done had a real heavy hemorrhage at school. She lived just three weeks, right to a day, poor child. And she was the only one named for me; her pa named her for me, and everybody said she looked like me, too. She had the prettiest hair; when she died she had a sick spell, and was gone just that quick.

No, I don't do much dreaming now. I'm too old; if I live to see the 27th day of next month I will be seventy-nine years old. I professed religion in 1866, and the Lord have taken good care of me, I think. The only real sin I committed, I was a dancer, that's all.

Yes, I was here in Nashville when they killed Grizzard. I remember those white people. They brought him and hung him over the bridge. The white people oughta been stoned to death for a trick like that. They brought that poor Negro up here from down in Tennessee. Well, after it happened the people said the girl's father give that old white girl to that man hisself. I remember there was a girl working at the hotel soon after that by the same name, and them old white folks and the steward asked her if she was any relation to them, and she said yes she was a sister; and they fired her at the hotel. Yessiree, they got rid of her right away; and that was the most disgraceful thing what ever happened in Nashville; and I tell you the real sho' nuff white folks was sick of it.

You know up there where Jubilee Hall is built; well, it's built right on Colonel Gillum's fort. There's a plate on that concrete wall right in the middle with his name on it.

III

I was a boy in slavery. I started plowing at eight years old. I served my old marster until freedom taken place—my mother, my father, and five or six children was there.

I was raised on pot-likker. I love it till today. I would take it and crumble a little bread in it. We never did get meat at night—mostly buttermilk.

Them times peoples children was lousy as a pet pig. Mothers would stay home on Sundays and look at their heads and kill them. I worked at herding of the cows. Every morning I would go into the woods and drive them up. I was bare-footed as a duck. Sometimes I would drive the hogs out of their warm place to warm my feet. I used to work in the tobacco patch catching worms off the leaves. Some of them worms was as big as my finger. Marster would come behind me and if he would find a worm I would have to bite his head off. That was done in order to make me more particular and not leave worms again.

You as teachers used to whip the children with a paddle or something, but my whip was a raw cowhide. I didn't see it but I used to hear my mother tell it at the time how they would whip them with a cowhide and then put salt and pepper in your skin until it burn. The most barbarous thing I saw with these eyes—I lay on my bed and study about it now—I had a sister, my oldest sister, she was fooling with the clock and broke it, and my old master taken her and tied a rope around her neck—just enough to keep it from choking her—and tied her up in the back yard and whipped her I don't know how long. There stood mother, there stood father, and there stood all the children and none could come to her rescue.

Now it is a remarkable thing to tell you, some people can't see into it, but I am going to tell you, you can believe it if you want to —some colored people at that wouldn't be whipped by their master. They would run away and hide in the woods, come home at night and get something to eat and out he would go again. Some of them stayed away until after the war was over. Some of them would run to the Yankees and would bring the Yankees back and take all the corn and meat they had.

Now I had a young master named Colonel Hale. All of them is dead but me. I seen the clod put on Mars Jim. After Freedom taken place we still called them Old Master and Old Miss, but they used to tell us not to call them that. Jim Hale before he died told me not to call him Mars, but Mr. Hale.

Time has been that they wouldn't let them have a meeting, but

God Almighty let them have it, for they would take an old kettle and turn it up before the door with the mouth of it facing the folks, and that would hold the voices inside. All the noise would go into that kettle. They could shout and sing all they wanted to and the noise wouldn't go outside.

The first Sunday school I went to was after the War. The house was an old oak tree. We used to carry our dinner and stay there from eight o'clock until four. In slavery they used to teach the Negro that they had no soul. They said all they needed to do was to obey their mistress. One old sister was shouting in the back of the church and her mistress was up in the front and she looked back and said, "Shout on old 'nig' there is a kitchen in heaven for you to shout in too." The people used to say "dis," "dat," and "tother," now they say "this," "that" and "the other." In all the books that you have studied you never have studied Negro history, have you? You studied about the Indians and white folks, what did they tell you about the Negro? If you want Negro history you will have to get from somebody who wore the shoe, and by and by from one to the other you will get a book.

I am going to tell you another thing. A Negro has got no name. My father was a Ransom and he had a uncle named Hankin. If you belong to Mr. Jones and he sell you to Mr. Johnson, consequently you go by the name of your owner. Now whar you get a name? We are wearing the name of our marster. I was first a Hale then my father was old and then I was named Reed. He was brought from old Virginia some place. I have seen my grandma and grandfather too. My grandfather was a preacher and didn't know *A* from *B*. He could preach. I had a uncle and he was a preacher. I had a cousin who was a preacher. I am no mathematician, no biologist, neither grammarian, but when it comes to handling the Bible I knocks down verbs, break up prepositions and jumps over adjectives. Now I tell you something—I am a God-sent man. But sometimes Jim calls and John answers. The children of Israel was four hundred years under bondage and God looked down and seen the suffering of the striving Israelites and brought them out of bondage. Young folks think old folks are fools, but old folks *know* young folks are fools. How many old folks do you find in prison?

I remember seeing my old mother spinning with tears running down her cheeks, crying about her brother who was sold and carried to Arkansas. She would sing,

> Oh, my good Lord, go low in the valley to pray,
> To ease my troubling mind.

Oh where else can we go but to the Lord. The young people don't live close to God now as they did in them times. God lived close to them, too. Some of them old slaves composed the songs we sing now like "I am bound for the promised land," "No more, no more, I'll never turn back no more," "Come on moaner, come on moaner, come on before the judgment day," "Run away to the snow field, run away to the snow field, my time is not long," "Moses smote the water and the children they crossed over, Moses smote the water and the children they crossed over, Moses smote the water and the sea gave away," "Quit this sinful army and your sins are washed away."

I didn't go to school until I was a man. I would go out and plow and take my book with me. We used to have spelling matches. If one would beat the other spelling he would turn him down.

Preachers used to get up and preach and call moaners up to the moaner's bench. They would all kneel down and sometimes they would lay down on the floor, and the Christians would sing:

> Rassal Jacob, rassal as you did in the days of old,
> Gonna rassal all night till broad day light
> And ask God to bless my soul.

They would call for moaners first night, and moaners would come up for two and three nights waiting to feel something, or to hear something. Sometimes they would walk way out in the woods after getting religion. They would get to rolling and shouting and tell everybody that they had found Jesus and they would shout and shout, and sometimes they would knock the preacher and deacon down shouting. But about a week after that they would go to a dance, and when the music would start they would get out there and dance and forget all about the religion.

Now I want to tell you all something about the Civil War. All the money was Confederate money then. After the war was over it

was worth about as much as this handkerchief is. After that come
the paper dimes and paper fifty cents, then the large paper dollars.
They had silver nickels. You don't see them today. I have seen
changes made in money three and four times.

After we was set free my father took charge of me. He told me I
was free but as long as I was under the roof of his house he was
boss. That was when I went out to find me a job. I went two miles
from home and got a job and worked all day for fifty cents. I was
paid off that night and I thought I was putting it in my pocket,
but when I got home I found that I had lost the money that I had
worked all day for. It was a paper fifty cents. I worried all night
about losing it, but the next morning I got up early and went back
and thar on the ground lay the money covered with dew, just where
I had dropped it. I been losing and finding money every since.

I remember just as well as if it was yesterday—my father give us
three boys a patch to make us a tobacco patch. We would take the
money and buy us clothes. I remember the first shirt I bought was
a pleated bosom shirt. I bought me some shoes and a hat. I tell you
I been a traveling man. Been getting up and falling down every
since.

One blessed thing, I got good religion and live close to the Lord.
When people 'fess religion in these days all you have to do is answer
a few questions. Do you believe that Jesus Christ is the Son of God,
and if so give me your hand. I don't believe in all that what the
people say about having to see a little white man. That is all
fogieism. What was it for them to see? Always a little *white* man.
Don't believe nothing like that. The Lord said, "Follow me," now
what else was for you to do but do that? A vast number of our
preachers still preach that kind of stuff.

IV

I'm 'bout played out now. Yes, I like to look at the ladies sometimes. I don't get out much now. Last night was a cold night,
wasn't it?

I was a young man when the stars fell; and you know that was a
long time ago. I seen them; they just fell and went out before they

hit the ground. How come me to see it, we had just killed hogs and had the meat hanging up on poles and I had to watch it all night. I had a fire out there, you know. It scared a lot of them, but it didn't do no good. Somebody started the blowing the horn what you call the dogs with, and they started hollering that Gabriel was blowing his trumpet. I never was a kind of man to worry about any one thing.

I was born right over yonder where Purdy had his school, right over there back of Jubilee Hall. It was woods around here then. My marster's oldest son was my father. My master never was very mean to me. He knocked me around once. I was driving the calves home, and I tied a can around their necks and made them holler. He whipped me about that. My mother cooked, washed and do things like that around the house. Mistress uster ask me what that was I had on my head and I would tell her, "Hair," and she said, "No that ain't hair, that's wool." They wan't mean to none of the slaves. He didn't have but 'bout ten or fifteen slaves. They lived in different little cabins around the yard. He didn't have no overseers. Way after while he had a overseer.

I uster drive my mistress to town, after freedom, and she give me a home back over there back of Meharry.

I uster live mighty bad sometimes—dance, drink whiskey, all night long. I could drink a pint of whiskey at a time. I uster play a fiddle for dance. Sometimes I would play from Saturday night to Sunday morning. They danced 'bout like they do now. They was "wild cats," I tell you. The slaves would get the 4th of July and part day on Saturday, and holidays like that.

I expect I am the oldest man in Nashville. Nearest we can come to making out my age, I am 'bout 120 years old. (A son says 110.) I don't know it exactly 'cause when the War broke out they lost the Bible.

I didn't do much when I was a boy; just played around all the time and pull a little grass out of the pavement. I had a easy time compared to some. Mother didn't have a husband till after the war. She stayed right in the house with the white folks. My wife had good folks, too.

I was out to Fort Negley, and they come and carried me to jail; and I stayed there eight weeks—that's how come I didn't have to

go to war. My mother come there and brought me some clothes and someting to eat, and the next day they come and carried me home. My mother didn't know where I was at first. I looked like a skallin (skeleton) when I first come out, I was so poor. I was weak and half starved too. Then it would a took me from now till night to walk to Jubilee Hall. (His owners contrived this means of preventing his running away to the Yankees.)

I don't like slavery nohow. They believe in tramping you like a dog. Just meanness, that's all. They did every kind of thing. They used to stand slaves up on a platform down on the public square, and sell them like they was dogs or horses—women and men. It was awful.

We used to raise oats, corn and things like that. Get up at daybreak, went out to feed the stock and come in, eat breakfast, and then out to the field. We used to have hog jowl, cabbage, potatoes and different things like that to eat. Sometimes we would have it for breakfast and dinner too. Mother worked for them a good while after the War. I didn't have sense enough to feel anyway about it. All I cared about was fiddling and dancing. It was "come day, go day, God send Sunday" with me.

In the summer time we would go around half naked. We didn't wear nothing but one piece—a shirt that come down below your knees. After freedom I used to go hunting a whole lot. Sometimes I would kill fifty rabbits. I wore them long boots, and sometimes I would be bare footed.

I waited on my master till he died. He took sick in Arkansas. He inhaled the scent of his brother who was dead, and he took sick and died. That was after freedom. A man killed his brother. They tried to press him in the Rebel army. He told them he wouldn't go and leave his wife and chillen; and they shot him down. It was awful to try to make a man leave his wife and family to go to the army. It's awful to think of slavery anyhow.

I pretended to profess religion one time. I don't hardly know what to think about religion. They say God killed the just and unjust; I don't understand that part of it. It looks hard to think that if you ain't done nothing in the world you be punished just like the wicked. Plenty folks went crazy trying to get that thing straightened out.

BIG SIXTEEN

It was back in slavery time when Big Sixteen was a man and they called 'im Sixteen 'cause dat was de number of de shoe he wore. He was big and strong and Ole Massa looked to him to do everything.

One day Ole Massa said, "Big Sixteen, Ah b'lieve Ah want you to move dem sills Ah had hewed out down in de swamp."

"I yassuh, Massa."

Big Sixteen went down in de swamp and picked up dem 12x12's and brought 'em on up to de house and stack 'em. No one man ain't never toted a 12x12 befo' nor since.

So Ole Massa said one day, "Go fetch in de mules. Ah want to look 'em over."

Big Sixteen went on down to de pasture and caught dem mules by de bridle but they was contrary and balky and he tore de bridles to pieces pullin' on 'em, so he picked one of 'em up under each arm and brought 'em up to Old Massa.

He says, "Big Sixteen, if you kin tote a pair of balky mules, you kin do anything. You kin ketch de Devil."

"Yassuh, Ah kin, if you git me a nine-pound hammer and a pick and shovel!"

Ole Massa got Sixteen de things he ast for and tole 'im to go ahead and bring him de Devil.

Big Sixteen went out in front of de house and went to diggin'. He was diggin' nearly a month befo' he got where he wanted. Then he took his hammer and went and knocked on de Devil's door. Devil answered de door hisself.

"Who dat out dere?"

"It's Big Sixteen."

"What you want?"

"Wanta have a word wid you for a minute."

Soon as de Devil poked his head out de door, Sixteen lammed him over de head wid dat hammer and picked 'im up and carried

'im back to Old Massa.

Ole Massa looked at de dead Devil and hollered, "Take dat ugly thing 'way from here, quick! Ah didn't think you'd ketch de Devil sho 'nuff."

So Sixteen picked up de Devil and throwed 'im back down de hole.

Way after while, Big Sixteen died and went up to Heben. But Peter looked at him and tole 'im to g'wan 'way from dere. He was too powerful. He might git outa order and there wouldn't be nobody to handle 'im. But he had to go somewhere so he went on to hell.

Soon as he got to de gate de Devil's children was playin' in de yard and they seen 'im and run to de house, says, "Mama, Mama! Dat man's out dere dat kilt papa!"

So she called 'im in de house and shet de door. When Sixteen got dere she handed 'im a li'l piece of fire and said, "You ain't comin' in here. Here, take dis hot coal and g'wan off and start you a hell uh yo' own."

So when you see a Jack O'Lantern in de woods at night you know it's Big Sixteen wid his piece of fire lookin' for a place to go.

ALL GOD'S CHILLEN HAD WINGS

ONCE all Africans could fly like birds; but owing to their many transgressions, their wings were taken away. There remained, here and there, in the sea islands and out-of-the-way places in the low country, some who had been overlooked, and had retained the power of flight, though they looked like other men.

There was a cruel master on one of the sea islands who worked his people till they died. When they died he bought others to take their places. These also he killed with overwork in the burning summer sun, through the middle hours of the day, although this was against the law.

One day, when all the worn-out Negroes were dead of overwork, he bought, of a broker in the town, a company of native Africans

just brought into the country, and put them at once to work in the cottonfield.

He drove them hard. They went to work at sunrise and did not stop until dark. They were driven with unsparing harshness all day long, men, women and children. There was no pause for rest during the unendurable heat of the midsummer noon, though trees were plenty and near. But through the hardest hours, when fair plantations gave their Negroes rest, this man's driver pushed the work along without a moment's stop for breath, until all grew weak with heat and thirst.

There was among them one young woman who had lately borne a child. It was her first; she had not fully recovered from bearing, and should not have been sent to the field until her strength had come back. She had her child with her, as the other women had, astraddle on her hip, or piggyback.

The baby cried. She spoke to quiet it. The driver could not understand her words. She took her breast with her hand and threw it over her shoulder that the child might suck and be content. Then she went back to chopping knot-grass; but being very weak, and sick with the great heat, she stumbled, slipped and fell.

The driver struck her with his lash until she rose and staggered on.

She spoke to an old man near her, the oldest man of them all, tall and strong, with a forked beard. He replied; but the driver could not understand what they said; their talk was strange to him.

She returned to work; but in a little while she fell again. Again the driver lashed her until she got to her feet. Again she spoke to the old man. But he said: "Not yet, daughter; not yet." So she went on working, though she was very ill.

Soon she stumbled and fell again. But when the driver came running with his lash to drive her on with her work, she turned to the old man and asked: "Is it time yet, daddy?" He answered: "Yes, daughter; the time has come. Go; and peace be with you!" . . . and stretched out his arms toward her . . . so.

With that she leaped straight up into the air and was gone like a bird, flying over field and wood.

The driver and overseer ran after her as far as the edge of the field; but she was gone, high over their heads, over the fence, and

over the top of the woods, gone, with her baby astraddle of her hip, sucking at her breast.

Then the driver hurried the rest to make up for her loss; and the sun was very hot indeed. So hot that soon a man fell down. The overseer himself lashed him to his feet. As he got up from where he had fallen the old man called to him in an unknown tongue. My grandfather told me the words that he said; but it was a long time ago, and I have forgotten them. But when he had spoken, the man turned and laughed at the overseer, and leaped up into the air, and was gone, like a gull, flying over field and wood.

Soon another man fell. The driver lashed him. He turned to the old man. The old man cried out to him, and stretched out his arms as he had done for the other two; and he, like them, leaped up, and was gone through the air, flying like a bird over field and wood.

Then the overseer cried to the driver, and the master cried to them both: "Beat the old devil! He is the doer!"

The overseer and the driver ran at the old man with lashes ready; and the master ran too, with a picket pulled from the fence, to beat the life out of the old man who had made those Negroes fly.

But the old man laughed in their faces, and said something loudly to all the Negroes in the field, the new Negroes and the old Negroes.

And as he spoke to them they all remembered what they had forgotten, and recalled the power which once had been theirs. Then all the Negroes, old and new, stood up together; the old man raised his hands; and they all leaped up into the air with a great shout; and in a moment were gone, flying, like a flock of crows, over the field, over the fence, and over the top of the wood; and behind them flew the old man.

The men went clapping their hands; and the women went singing; and those who had children gave them their breasts; and the children laughed and sucked as their mothers flew, and were not afraid.

The master, the overseer, and the driver looked after them as they flew, beyond the wood, beyond the river, miles on miles, until they passed beyond the last rim of the world and disappeared in the sky like a handful of leaves. They were never seen again.

Where they went I do not know; I never was told. Nor what it was that the old man said . . . that I have forgotten. But as he

went over the last fence he made a sign in the master's face, and cried "Kuli-ba! Kuli-ba!" I don't know what that means.

But if I could only find the old wood sawyer, he could tell you more; for he was there at the time, and saw the Africans fly away with their women and children. He is an old, old man, over ninety years of age, and remembers a great many strange things.

As told by Caesar Grant, of John's Island, carter and laborer.

ELIJAH'S LEAVING TIME

MASTER DAN WALLER was a very sympathetic master. He visited all the cabins on his plantation every night to see how the slaves were getting along, and to find out whether anyone was sick. The slaves all liked Master Dan and generally left his chickens and hogs alone.

One Saturday evening, however, Elijah, one of the slaves who had a family, decided he would like to have some pork chops for Sunday. About nine o'clock that night Elijah went down to the master's hog pen and stole a pig. Just about the time he got back inside his cabin, the master, on his customary round of evening visits, knocked at the door. Elijah, the pig still under his arm, hurriedly put it in the baby cradle and covered it over with a quilt. He was rocking the cradle backwards and forwards when the master entered.

"What's the matter?" asked the master as he entered.

"Mah po' baby's sick," answered Elijah, "an' Ah's tryin' to rock 'im to sleep."

"Well, I'm sorry," said the master, starting over to the cradle. "Let me see him. He may need some medicine."

"No, sah, no, sah. If you pulls de kivver offen 'im, he gonna die, Massa."

"Well," answered the master, "I am not going to let him suffer. I am going to pull the cover off him and see what the trouble is."

"Aw right, Massa, aw right," answered Elijah, sidling towards the door. "You kin pull de kivver offen 'im ef yuh wants ter, but Ah ain't gwine stay hyeah and see 'im die."

DEN TO DE FIAH

UNCLE JACK was the only man on the Sipsey plantation that the master could not catch to whip. All of the other slaves were kept at work without any trouble. The master had been trying so long to think of some way to catch Jack in order to whip him that he had just about decided to give the job up. As a last resort he consulted Jim, an old slave always faithful and always full of advice.

"Sho', Massa," said Jim. "Eb'ry night Ah goes down under uh big ole oak tree in de woods, Jack meets me dere, an' Ah plays de banjo fo' him. He is gwine be down dere tonight 'bout ha'f pas' eight. So Ah tells yer whut we'll do. Ah's gwine build uh fiah an' ef Uncle Jack's dere, you'll hyeah me sing dis li'l' tune: 'Oh, mah Massa, cum uh li'l' nyeah, fus' to de libe oak, den to de fiah.' Yer see, while Ah plays, Ah'll hab Uncle Jack dance back'a'ds an' fo'wa'ds f'om de libe oak to de fiah. Yuh be behin' de tree. Den when dat rascal gits close to it, you kin grab 'im."

"All right," said Master Sipsey, "we will try your plan this very night."

So, sure enough, that night about half past eight the master walked out into the yard and saw a light from a fire in the woods. Guided by this light, he started forward. As he neared the edge of the woods, he heard the strumming of a banjo and Jim's voice singing, "Oh, mah massa, cum uh li'l' nyeah, fus' to de libe oak, den to de fiah."

Finally the master reached the live oak tree under which Jim was playing and Jack dancing, and hid himself behind the trunk. Jim continued to play and sing, "Oh, mah massa, cum uh li'l' nyeah, fus' to de libe oak, den to de fiah."

The master was all ready and now Jack was starting back to the live oak.

Just as he reached the tree and was turning to dance back to "de fiah," the master jumped out and grabbed him. Jack was so scared that he did not have sense enough to see what or who had him.

He just picked up the master and threw him right in the middle of the fire. Master Sipsey never did try to catch Jack after that, but for three months he made Jim work two hours longer every day, because Jim had caused him to get such an awful singeing.

A LAUGH THAT MEANT FREEDOM

THERE were some slaves who had a reputation for keeping out of work because of their wit and humor. These slaves kept their masters laughing most of the time, and were able, if not to keep from working altogether, at least to draw the lighter tasks.

Nehemiah was a clever slave, and no master who had owned him had ever been able to keep him at work, or succeeded in getting him to do heavy work. He would always have some funny story to tell or some humorous remark to make in response to the master's question or scolding. Because of this faculty for avoiding work, Nehemiah was constantly being transferred from one master to another. As soon as an owner found out that Nehemiah was outwitting him, he sold Nehemiah to some other slaveholder. One day David Wharton, known as the most cruel slave master in Southwest Texas, heard about him.

"I bet I can make that rascal work," said David Wharton, and he went to Nehemiah's master and bargained to buy him.

The morning of the first day after his purchase, David Wharton walked over to where Nehemiah was standing and said, "Now you are going to work, you understand. You are going to pick four hundred pounds of cotton today."

"Wal, Massa, dat's aw right," answered Nehemiah, "but ef Ah meks you laff, won' yuh lemme off fo' terday?"

"Well," said David Wharton, who had never been known to laugh, "if you make me laugh, I won't only let you off for today, but I'll give you your freedom."

"Ah decla', Boss," said Nehemiah, "yuh sho' is uh goodlookin' man."

"I am sorry I can't say the same thing about you," retorted David

Wharton.

"Oh, yes, Boss, yuh could," Nehemiah laughed out, "yuh could, if yuh tole ez big uh lie ez Ah did."

David Wharton could not help laughing at this; he laughed before he thought. Nehemiah got his freedom.

HOW BUCK WON HIS FREEDOM

BUCK was the shrewdest slave on the big Washington plantation. He could steal things almost in front of his master's eyes without being detected. Finally, after having had his chickens and pigs stolen until he was sick, Master Harry Washington called Buck to him one day and said, "Buck, how do you manage to steal without getting caught?"

"Dat's easy, Massa," replied Buck, "dat's easy. Ah kin steal yo' clo'es right tonight, wid you a-guardin' 'em."

"No, no," said the master, "you may be a slick thief, but you can't do that. I will make a proposition to you: If you steal my suit of clothes tonight, I will give you your freedom, and if you fail to steal them, then you will stop stealing my chickens."

"Aw right, Massa, aw right," Buck agreed. "Dat's uh go."

That night about nine o'clock the master called his wife into the bedroom, got his Sunday suit of clothes, laid it out on the table, and told his wife about the proposition he had made with Buck. He got on one side of the table and had his wife get on the other side, and they waited. Pretty soon, through a window that was open, the master heard the mules and horses in the stable lot running as if some one were after them.

"Here, wife," said he, "you take this gun and keep an eye on this suit. I'm going to see what's the matter with those animals."

Buck, who had been out to the horse lot and started the stampede to attract the master's attention, now approached the open window. He was a good mimic, and in tones that sounded like his master's he called out, "Ol'lady, ol'lady, ol'lady, you better hand me that suit. That damn thief might steal it while I'm gone."

The master's wife, thinking that it was her husband asking for his suit, took it from the table and handed it out the window to Buck. This is how Buck won his freedom.

HOW UNCLE STEVE INTERPRETED SPANISH

DURING slavery times it was the custom among some of the owners of land and slaves to go every year or two on a horse-trading expedition into old Mexico across the border. If the owner could not speak Spanish, he usually carried along as interpreter some Mexican living in the vicinity.

Master Phil Potts had his plans all made to leave for the border on a horse-trading expedition the following Monday morning. On Sunday he received word that the Mexican he had engaged to go along as interpreter was sick and could not go. Without an interpreter the trip would be useless. An interpreter had to be found.

Now Steve, a sharp slave, had for a long time wanted to make a trip into Mexico. On more than one occasion he had maneuvered to be taken along as a hand, but had never succeeded in his purpose. Here, he thought, was his opportunity. He hunted up Master Phil an told him he could interpret Spanish. Master Phil was rather surprised to learn of Steve's linguistic accomplishments, but, as there was no choice, agreed to take him.

The expedition, everybody in it in high spirits excepting Steve, who was wondering what he was going to say when the test came, traveled all day and did not see a soul until close to sundown. Then, as they approached a water hole, they saw some Mexicans camped. One of the Mexicans had a very fine looking bay horse that at once caught the eye of Master Phil.

"Steve," he said, "ask that Mexican how much he will take for that horse."

"Boss," said Steve, "dat Mescan don't wanna sell dat hoss. Mescans don't trade on Monday, no-how."

"That's all right," answered his master, "go on and ask him what he wants for the horse."

"Aw right, Boss," agreed Steve, "but Ah jes' knows he ain't gonna sell 'im terday."

"Oh, hombre," called out Steve, "fo' how muchee you sellee de hossy?"

The Mexican, disgusted at Steve's attempt to speak Spanish, replied, "Usted no bueno," which means "you are no good."

"What did he say, Steve?" asked his master.

"He say," answered Steve, "that he did not want to sell 'im till Wednesday."

"Ah, go on," said the master. "Tell him we will give him a good price, that we really want the horse."

"Aw right, Boss," answered Steve, "Ah'll tell 'im, but Ah don' tol' yuh dat Mescans don' trade on Mondays."

"Oh, hombre," said Steve, "no sellee de hossy sho' nuffee?"

"No sabe," answered the Mexican, meaning "I do not understand."

"Well," asked the boss, "what did he say this time, Steve?"

"He sez he don' wanna sell 'im til Sat'day now, Boss. Ah done tol' yuh dese Mescans don' trade on Monday."

"Now," replied the master, "we have just got to have that horse. He is a wonderful animal. Go on and tell him that we will pay him a big price for the horse."

"Aw right, Boss. Yuh sho' is wastin' time though, 'case Ah knows dat Mescan ain't gwine trade on Monday."

"Oh, hombre," said Steve, "no sellee de hossy fo' biggee de mon?"

The Mexican, who had some wood piled up beside the road, now thought that Steve, who was pointing in its direction, was asking him the price of it, and replied, "Cinco pesos" (five dollars).

"What did he say this time, Steve?" asked his master.

"Boss, he sho' done gone an' talk foolish dis time. He sez sometime dat hoss is trottin' an' he thinks he's pacin'."

"All right," said his master, "let's go on to Mexico."

SWAPPING DREAMS

MASTER JIM TURNER, an unusually good-natured master, had a fondness for telling long stories woven out of what he claimed to be his dreams, and especially did he like to "swap" dreams with Ike, a witty slave who was a house servant. Every morning he would set Ike to telling about what he had dreamed the night before. It always seemed, however, that the master could tell the best dream tale, and Ike had to admit that he was beaten most of the time.

One morning, when Ike entered the master's room to clean it, he found the master just preparing to get out of bed. "Ike," he said, "I certainly did have a strange dream last night."

"Sez yuh did, Massa, sez yuh did?" answered Ike. "Lemme hyeah it."

"All right," replied the master. "It was like this: I dreamed I went to Nigger Heaven last night, and saw there a lot of garbage, some old torn-down houses, a few old broken-down, rotten fences, the muddiest, sloppiest streets I ever saw, and a big bunch of ragged, dirty Negroes walking around."

"Umph, umph, Massa," said Ike, "yuh sho' musta et de same t'ing Ah did las' night, 'case Ah dreamed Ah went up ter de white man's paradise, an' de streets wuz all ob gol' an' silvah, and dey wuz lots o' milk an' honey dere, an' putty pearly gates, but dey wuzn't uh soul in de whole place."

UNCLE ISRAEL AND THE LAW

EVERY week on the Hunter plantation five or six chickens would be missing, and the master couldn't find out what had become of them. At length he started a thorough investigation. After a good deal of questioning among the slaves, he found that Uncle Israel's wife had recently made some feather pillows and that chicken feathers had

been seen under Uncle Israel's cabin a few days before.

With this information, the master laid his trap. One evening a strange white man driving a wobbly old buggy with a chicken coop tied on the back end of it halted at Uncle Israel's cabin. He was a chicken buyer, he said, and was paying fancy prices. Uncle Israel was not long in suggesting that he might have a few very fat chickens to sell.

"All right," said the stranger, "bring them out."

"No, sah, no, sah," explained Uncle Israel, "Ah cain't ketch 'em till da'k."

The stranger went on to say that he didn't much want to hang around the plantation and be seen by Mr. Hunter and finally asked Uncle Israel point-blank where he was going to get his chickens.

"Wal, Ah tell yuh," chuckled Uncle Israel. "Ah's got uh hoodoo on dem chickens up dar in Massa's hen-house. Dey comes into mah sack after da'k lak crows flyin' to de roost-tree in de ebenin'."

"Aw," sneered the stranger, "you know you are afraid to go into your master's hen-house."

"Yuh jes' wait an' see," answered Uncle Israel. He was all eagerness. "Why, two of dem pullets flewed right into mah ol' 'oman's stew kittle las' night."

"You don't say," explained the stranger in a changed tone. "Do you know who I am?"

"No, sah, Boss, 'ceptin' yuh's a chicken buyah. Who else is yuh?"

"I'm the biggest constable in this county," answered the stranger.

"Sez yuh is, Boss?" said Uncle Israel. "Wal, Ah'll decla'. An' don' yuh know who Ah is? Ain't Massa and de oberseeah tol' yuh who Ah is? Wal, Ah's de bigges' liah in dis county."

DEY'S AUGANIZED

ONE day Ananias, tall, black coachman of the Kaufmans, was driving his master down a long lane on the way to a neighboring plantation when a horse-fly alighted on the mane of one of

the horses. "Massa," said Ananias, "you see dat hoss fly on dat hoss's mane? Watch me git 'im." Ananias had the reputation of being the most exact wielder of the coachwhip in the county, and his master always enjoyed watching him wield it. Ananias raised his whip and split the horse-fly into small pieces.

A little farther down the lane Ananias looked over and spied a bumblebee on a sunflower. "Massa," said Ananias, "yuh see dat bumblebee on dat sunflowah? Watch me git 'im." Ananias raised his whip again, and the bumblebee was torn into shreds by the snapper on the end of it.

After a little while the master noticed a hornets' nest hanging from the limb of a tree by the side of the road. "Look, Ananias," said he. "You see that hornets' nest hanging from the limb of that tree by the side of the road? You are such an expert with the coachwhip, let me see you cut that hornets' nest off the limb."

"No, sah, Massa," said Ananias, "Ah ain't gwine bothah dem hornets, 'case dey's auganized."

THE PROPHET VINDICATED

UNCLE Phimon was the most useful slave on the Pettus plantation. Master Tom Pettus did not have to worry about dissatisfaction among his slaves or their plans for rebelling; he had a way of knowing what was going on in the dark and of anticipating future events. Uncle Phimon prophesied for him, and he had for so long a time been so accurate in his predictions that Master Tom had actually come to take the old fellow for a fortune-teller endowed with some sort of supernatural power or foresight, though in fact Uncle Phimon gathered his information from eavesdropping.

One day while Master Tom was talking with some of the other plantation owners in the settlement, they expressed a great deal of concern over a vague kind of unrest working among their slaves. Master Tom, after listening a while, informed his neighbors that he owned a remarkable slave who always warned him of any

trouble brewing, and that, consequently, he could manage to head off trouble and keep his slaves pacified. The other men were in doubt about the prophetic powers of Uncle Phimon, but Master Tom was so confident that he invited them all to come over to his plantation the following Saturday morning to witness a demonstration of Uncle Phimon's powers of divination. They accepted the invitation.

Saturday came; it was summer-time; and not long after sunup not only the owners of neighboring plantations, but most of their slaves were gathered together to see Uncle Phimon demonstrate his magic powers of looking into the hidden world. A wooden box was provided for him to stand on. In front of this box was an old-fashioned wash-pot turned over. Under the pot one of the planters had placed something, the nature of which was unknown even to Master Tom Pettus. When all was ready, Master Tom led Uncle Phimon forth to the box blind-folded and mounted him. "Now, neighbors," Master Tom announced, "Uncle Phimon will tell us what is hidden under the pot."

For a long time Uncle Phimon stood on the box, working his hands through the air and over his face. He seemed to be in a kind of trance. He thought and he thought, and the longer he stood there blindfolded, the more uncertain he became as to what to say was under the pot. He was to have only one guess. Finally Uncle Phimon decided that it was no use for him to guess anything. He might as well give up and acknowledge that he was not a fortune-teller.

"Wal, Massa," he finally began, speaking very slowly, "de ol' coon run uh long time, but dey cotch 'im at las'." Of course, what he meant was that his claim to being a prophet had been exposed and now he was "fessing up."

At Uncle Phimon's announcement, two planters turned the pot up, and there under it was an old coon. Master Tom Pettus was more thoroughly convinced than ever that his prize slave was a prophet, and everybody else was convinced.

ABRAHAM EXPLAINS HIS MASTER'S SHOT

Deer hunting was a favorite sport of many planters in Texas during the days of slavery. Frequently the hunters made up a party, at which time each planter took along a slave to bag the game, tend the horses, and help with the work in the camp. The merriest part of the day was at meal time, when jokes and anecdotes were rife. Among the plantation hunters of Goliad County, Jim Fant was the king of story tellers. He was a magnificent liar and always had his slave Abraham bear him out in his lies. The day came for the big hunt, and, after a morning filled with good luck, the planters sat down to dinner, and the story-telling began. Jim Fant, as usual, was the last to tell his story.

"Well, fellers," he began, "Abraham and I just couldn't wait for our regular hunt. We couldn't keep from going out last week and hunting some deer. After we had hunted all day until it was almost sundown and not shot a thing and were just about ready to go home, a big buck rushed out of the woods and headed straight for Abraham and me. I drew down with my old rifle and fired. He fell dead, and, well, sir, when we got to him we found that the bullet had shot him first through the ear, then through the hind foot, and then through the head."

"How did you do all of that with one bullet?" the other plantation owners chimed in.

"Abraham," said Master Jim Fant, turning to his slave, "tell 'em how I did it."

Abraham scratched his head and thought for a moment, then said slowly, "Wal, yuh see, hit wuz lak dis. When Massa shot 'im, he wuz scratchin' 'is ear wid 'is hin' foot."

On the way home that evening Abraham said to his master, "Looka hyeah, Massa, yuh tell yo' lies a li'l' closer togedder f'om now on. Dat lie yuh tol' terday wuz uh li'l' too fer uh-paht."

UNCLE PLEAS'S PRAYER

PRAYER was one of the essential factors in the life of nearly all slaves. They prayed in public, and also they prayed in private. The woods near their cabins seemed to lure them after the day's work, and many stole away to some tree after nightfall to make their petitions to God. The Negroes on the Fant plantation were especially religious. They were especially prayerful, and they were especially prayerful in secret.

Among those who visited a favorite prayer spot each night was Uncle Pleas Brown. Pleas would leave his cabin each evening about dusk and make his way underneath a large live oak tree where he could be "alone with his Gawd," as he put it, and "talk to his Jesus." Pleas would always pray the same prayer: "Oh, Lawd, kill all de white fo'ks, and save all de black. Oh, Lawd, kill all de white fo'ks, and save all de black."

One night Master George Fant, who had become suspicious of Pleas's nocturnal trips away from the cabin, followed Pleas and found out where he went and what he was doing. The next night the master decided he would get to the tree first and hide in its branches so that he might hear exactly what Pleas said.

Incidentally the master carried four or five rocks up in the tree with him. Shortly after the master had hidden himself in the branches of the tree, Pleas appeared and, kneeling down beneath the tree, started to praying, "Oh, mah Gawd, kill all de white fo'ks, and save all de black. Oh, mah Gawd, kill all de white fo'ks, and save all de black."

Just as Pleas started to repeat this prayer the third time, the master let two or three rocks fall on his head. Pleas, frightened and thinking God was throwing the rocks, called out, "Look out dere, Gawd! Stop dat th'owin' dem rocks. Don' yuh know white from black."

LIAS' REVELATION

LIAS JONES was a praying slave. Lias would pray any time, but no matter what he was doing at twelve o'clock noon, he would stop short, kneel and pray to God. The prayer Lias prayed at this hour was a special one. "Oh, Lawd," he would pray, "won't yuh please gib us ouah freedom? Lawd, won't Yuh please gib us ouah freedom."

Yet Lias was not discouraged. Without variation he continued at high noon every day to pray that God would give him and his slave brothers freedom. Finally, one day the master sent for Lias to help clean the big house. Lias at twelve o'clock was starting in on the parlor, but had not been in the room long enough to examine the furnishings. Just then the big gong that called the Negroes to dinner started sounding. Lias stopped, as was his custom, to pray for freedom. So he knelt down in the parlor and began to pray: "Oh, Lawd, cum an' gib us all ouah freedom. Oh, Lawd, cum an' gib us all ouah freedom." When Lias got up, it happened that he was standing just opposite a lifesize mirror in the parlor, which reflected his image in it.

Since the slaves had no looking-glasses, Lias had never seen one before, and now he was amazed to see a black man gazing at him from the glass. The only thing he could think of in connection with the image was that God had come down in answer to his prayers; so he said, looking at the image in the mirror, "Ah decla', Gawd, Ah didn't know Yuh wuz black. Ah thought Yuh wuz uh white man. If Yuh is black, Ah's gwine make Yuh gib us ouah freedom."

HOLD THE BOOK UP HIGHER, JOHN

UNCLE JOHN was the smartest slave in seven counties. Slaves, not only on his master's plantation but in all the country around, marveled at his learning. He could read, at least all black people thought he could. Whenever the slaves were permitted to have prayer meeting, they always depended upon Uncle John to read the Bible for them.

Now, as a matter of fact, Uncle John could not read a line, but his master, James Buchanan, could, and master and slave had an agreement that worked. The prayer meetings were always in the master's barn, and Uncle John would always take a seat near the front window of the barn. After all the slaves had gathered together inside, Master James Buchanan would kneel down beneath the window just outside so that he could not be seen, but in a position to see the Bible which Uncle John, standing close to the window, help up high. Then, when the Bible was opened, Master James would whisper the words of the text, and Uncle John, his eyes glued to the page, would repeat them in a loud voice.

This went on for years. Finally one night, however, there was a hitch. The preacher opened the services and prayed as usual, and then, according to custom, asked Uncle John to read the Scriptures.

Uncle John took up his Bible as usual, but something appeared to be troubling him. He seemed nervous. He held the Bible so low that the master could not see to read. The master whispered, "Hold the book up higher, John."

"Hold the book up higher, John," repeated Uncle John aloud, thinking that the words were in the Bible.

The master whispered again, "Hold the book up higher, John."

Uncle John read aloud again, louder than the firnt time, "Hold the book up higher, John."

Exasperated at such stupidity, the master stuck his head inside the window and yelled as loud as he could, "John, I said for you to hold that Bible up higher."

This is the way the other slaves found out that Uncle John could not read.

BRINGING HOME THE BEAR

ALL of Uncle Jeremiah's five sons liked to hunt. Their master, Henry Jones, had the best hunting grounds in the country; and when on a Saturday afternoon or night they went to hunt, meat-in-the-pot for Sunday was almost a certainty. The five brothers usually hunted together, but one Saturday night while the older boys were gone to a plantation dance and only Rufus, the youngest son, and his father and mother remained at home, he decided that he would take the dogs and go hunting alone. Uncle Jeremiah wished him good luck, and with the eager dogs he disappeared into the woods.

After Rufus had been away from the cabin about two hours, Uncle Jeremiah heard the dogs barking loudly and some one running towards the cabin as fast as his feet could carry him. He went quickly to the door, and looking out into the moonlight, saw a big black bear chasing Rufus, who was now almost to the cabin.

"What yuh runnin' f'om dat beah fo'?" yelled Uncle Jeremiah.

"Ah ain't runnin' f'om no beah," yelled Rufus, rushing into the open door of the cabin. "Ah's jes 'bringin' 'im home."

VOICES IN THE GRAVEYARD

ONE night two slaves on the Byars plantation entered the potato house of the master and stole a sack of sweet potatoes. They decided that the best place to divide them would be down in the graveyard, where they would not be disturbed. So they went down there and started dividing the potatoes.

Another slave, Isom, who had been visiting a neighboring plantation, happened to be passing that way on the road home, and,

hearing voices in the graveyard, he decided to stop and overhear what was being said. It was too dark for him to see, but when he stopped he heard one of the thieves saying in a singsong voice, "Ah'll take dis un, an' yuh take dat un. Ah'll take dis un, an' yuh take dat un."

"Lawd, ha' mercy," said Isom to himself, "Ah b'lieve dat Gawd an' de debbil am down hyeah dividin' up souls. Ah's gwine an' tell ol' Massa."

Isom ran as fast as he could up to the master's house and said, "Massa, Ah's passin' th'oo de graveya'd jes' now, an' what yuh reckon Ah heerd? Gawd an' de debbil's down dar dividin' up souls. Ah sho' b'lieves de Day ob Jedgment am come."

"You don't know what you are talking about," said the master. "That's foolish talk. You know you are not telling the truth."

"Yas, sah, Massa, Yas, sah, Ah is. Ef yuh don' b'lieve hit, cum go down dar yo'se'f."

"All right," said the master, "and if you are lying to me I am going to whip you good tomorrow."

"Aw right, Massa," said Isom, "case Gawd an' de debbil sho' am down dere."

Sure enough, when Isom and the master got near the graveyard they heard the sing-song voice saying, "Yuh take dis un, an' Ah'll take dat un. Yuh take dis un, an' Ah'll take dat un."

"See dar, didn' Ah tell yuh, Massa?" said Isom.

In the meantime the two slaves had almost finished the division of the potatoes, but remembered they had dropped two over by the fence—where Isom and the master were standing out of sight. Finally when they had only two potatoes left, the one who was counting said, "Ah'll take dese two an' yuh take dem two over dere by de fence."

Upon hearing this, Isom and the master ran home as fast as they could go. After this the master never doubted Isom's word about what he saw or heard.

UNCLE BOB'S VOYAGE TO NEW ENGLAND

To NEGRO slaves the word New England meant escape from bondage. Many of them looked forward to some day getting to this promised land and there obtaining their freedom.

In Matagorda County, near the Gulf of Mexico, was a large plantation owned by Master George Kearnes. The oldest slave on this plantation was Uncle Bob Kennedy. Uncle Bob did not talk much but was always a very attentive listener, and he usually remembered what he heard. One time he overheard white people talking about how slaves had run away to the New England States and gained their freedom. Some of them, it seems, had made their escape in boats.

Since the Kearnes plantation was on the edge of the Gulf and had a small boat, Uncle Bob decided to take the water route to New England. One evening about dark he got a sack of meal and a jug of molasses and made his way down to the little cove where the master's boat was tied. He got in it with his meal and molasses. Uncle Bob had heard about low tide and high tide, and so he thought that some time during the night the high tide would take him and the boat out to sea and eventually land him somewhere in New England. Confident that the tides would take care of him, he lay down in the boat and soon was asleep.

The next morning early another slave on the plantation, Ezekiel, passed close to the boat, and, seeing Uncle Bob in it, shouted to wake him up. "Uncle Bob, Uncle Bob," he called, "wake up, wake up!"

On hearing his name called, Uncle Bob woke up, rubbing his eyes in a confused manner. Yes, the boat had carried him far away from the plantation to New England, but, still, there was something not just right about this foreign shore.

"Who is dat knowin' me up hyeah so early in New England?" he called out.

BUBBER'S 'RITHMETIC

ON THE Rogers plantation in Refugio County was a mulatto boy called Bubber. Bubber was considered by the other slaves as having the easiest job on the plantation. He never had been given any work to do in the fields, but had always worked up at the big house for "Ol' Missus." Bubber was well liked by the master and his family, and they treated him better than any other slave on the place. One of the master's boys who was about the same age liked Bubber so well that he undertook to teach him how to count. Bubber finally learned to count up to fifty.

One day soon after Bubber had learned to count to fifty, he found an old watch that had been thrown away by the master. Attaching it to a piece of wire, which he called a chain, he put it in his shirt pocket so that it would be conspicuous. As he strutted around among the other slaves, he was not disappointed in his intention to draw questions about the time. Every prayer meeting night after the slaves had been praying and shouting for a while, some of them would ask the time. These meetings were supposed to last only until nine o'clock. Bubber always replied that it was "gettin' close to nine o'clock."

One night, however, the slaves got to shouting and remained so long down in the grove that Bubber when asked the time, replied, "Hit's thirty-nine now; hit'll be forty in uh few minutes. Yuh bettah skee-daddle."

UNCLE JOHN'S PROPHETIC ERROR

ON the Pleasant plantation, a slave known as Uncle John could tell his master every morning what the master was going to do all that day. The manner in which Uncle John found out about Master

Tom Pleasant's plans was by hiding behind the chimney of the fire-place at the big house every evening. The master had a practice of telling his wife soon after supper each night what he planned to do the next day, and Uncle John had found this out.

After the evening eavesdropping, Uncle John was prepared the next morning to tell his master how many slaves were going to pick cotton, how many were going to chop cord wood, how many were going to husk corn, etc. He was often called upon to make such predictions, or rather, as it seemed, to read his master's mind. At length Master Tom Pleasant decided to make a thorough test of the slave's fortune-telling abilities. The Civil War had commenced, and he considered it dangerous to have a fortune-teller among the slaves.

One Saturday night, shortly after Texas joined the Confederacy, the master told his wife that he was going to whip Uncle John good the next night, and find out whether he was fooling him or not. Uncle John was behind the chimney as usual and heard what the master had to say. The next morning the master called him and said, "John, what am I going to do today?"

"Wal," said John, "Boss, yuh's gonna whip ol' John ternight."

"Yes," said the master, "tonight at nine o'clock you meet me out at the stable and get your whipping."

"Aw right Massa, aw right," said Uncle John.

The first thing Uncle John did was to go look for Uncle Jeremiah, his best friend. He asked him to get a lantern and an old bugle; to get high up in a tree near the stable shortly before nine o'clock that night, and wave the lantern and blow the trumpet every time he shouted to him to do so.

Uncle Jeremiah did as he was commanded and was in the tree at the hour appointed; Uncle John was at the back steps of the big house, where the master soon appeared.

"Don' whip me, Massa, don't whip me," pleaded Uncle John. "Ef yuh does, Ah's gwine call down Gab'ul f'om de heavens."

"Oh, yes," shouted the master, "I am going to beat you good. You know so much now, stop me from beating you."

"Flash yo' lightnin' Gab'ul, an' blow yo' trumpet!" shouted Uncle John. Uncle Jeremiah, hidden in the tree, started to waving the lantern and blowing the bugle.

"Stop! Stop!" shouted the master, seeing the light and hearing the

trumpet. "I'll give you a thousand dollars if you don't have Gabriel come down."

"Naw suh, naw suh," shouted Uncle John. "Flash yo' lightnin', Gab'ul, an' blow yo' trumpet."

"Stop! Stop!" cried the master. "I'll give you your freedom if you don't have Gabriel come down."

"Naw suh, naw suh. Flash yo' lightnin', Gab'ul, an' blow yo' trumpet." Uncle Jeremiah waved the lantern again and blew the trumpet.

"Stop! Stop!" shouted the master. "I will give all of the slaves their freedom if you don't have Gabriel come down."

"Naw suh, naw suh," shouted Uncle John. "Flash yo' lightnin', Gab'ul, an' blow yo' trumpet."

Uncle Jeremiah, who had been very faithful up to this time, but who had just heard the master offer the freedom of all the slaves to Uncle John, now refused to flash the lantern. Instead he shouted from the branches of the tree to Uncle John: "Dat's ernuf. He done offahed you all ouah freedom. Whut mo' does yuh want?"

The master, looking up into the tree, saw that he had been fooled, and, turning to Uncle John, gave him the worst whipping he had ever had.

POMPEY AN DE LAWD

I AIN'T been dere but I been told bout how hit was in de slavery days.

Mister Bird owned him a worker name Pompey an Pompey want to be free. "Ain't no free, Pomp," dey say, "less you dies and goes to heaven."

"Well," say Pompey, "I'll jes go and jump in de river an sink like a rock."

"Naw, Pomp," dey say, "dat ain't no free, neither, Aw, naw! Hit's a SIN, Pomp, an you's gwine to hot hell if you does dat. Ol Devil spread you out on de fiery coals an turn de blower on. Den you's damned in hell, Pompey, faw ever AN a day."

"I'll run away," say Pompey.

"Aw, naw, Pomp," dey say. "Don't you do hit. Paddroller git you faw sho. Dey bring you back an whup you to yo hide won't hold shucks. Now, Pompey, don't you do hit, boy."

So every night Pompey pray to de Lawd. "Oh Lawd," pray Pompey, "I wants to be free an dey ain't no free but sweet heaven."

But po Pompey never git no action. Pray AN pray an dere he still is, still Pompey livin an workin in de slavery days.

So he git down on his knees an pray harder an louder faw de Lawd to fetch him away from de slavery days. Dat de way Pompey run on every night of de world, but he never git no satisfaction.

Well, one night Pompey was prayin away. Mister Bird come wanderin down to de slave quarters, jes walking in de night air and worryin bout somethin. So whut do he hear but a lot of loud blimblam from Pompey's cabin. Mister Bird thought somebody's dyin, sho. He run to de cabin but he stop outside cause he can hear hit was only Pompey beggin de Lawd to take him away.

"Hunh," say Mister Bird. "Well now!" Den he kind of laugh an say, "I see where I has myself a little fun."

He sneak up to de window an pull his big black hat down over his haid and peep in.

Pompey's ol woman seed him an say, "Whut dat?"

All de chillun quit playin an say, "What dat, Pappy?"

Pompey quit prayin an look round. "Who dat at my window?"

Mister Bird he stick his haid in de empty rain barrel an yell, "Pompey, hit's me, hit's de Lawd. You ready to go to yo long home in sweet heaven, Pomp?"

He ask again, "I say you ready, Pomp?"

Reason Pompey ain't answer was he was behind de stove wid his head shove into de wood bin. He psst to his wife, he say, "Tell de Lawd I's gone possum huntin."

"Lawd," say de old woman, "Pomp ain't here. He gone possum huntin."

"Do tell," say de Lawd.

"Come back nother time," say de ol woman.

"Naw, ol woman, can't do dat. Hit costes heap of money to make dis trip. Can't afford to come down here an not bring nobody back wid me. Got to take SOMEBODY. Reckon I'll jes take you, ol

woman. Come on."

Ol woman jump out of her chair an howl, "Lawd, I's made a MIStake. Pompey he's right here, Lawd. Come out from behind dat stove, you nappy-haided scoundrel, yo'."

"Yas, Pompey," say de Lawd, "come on out! De heavenly choir waitin faw you to jine em. Dey needs a good tune-caller, an I hear you's as good as dey comes wid de fa-so-la."

"Lawd," say Pompey from behind de stove, "wait to I gits de spring plowin done."

"Naw, Pomp, can't do hit. You been beggin me to come git you, so come on now. Hit's gittin late."

"Lawd," say Pompey, "Mister Bird spect me to boss de other slaves when hit's time to top de cotton. I's de onliest one know how to do hit right."

"Roust out from behind dat stove, Pompey!" yell de Lawd. "I can't stand out here in dis here night air arguin wid you. You HEAR me!"

Ol woman say, "Pomp, do like he say fo he git mad an maybe hurt de chillun tryin to git at you!" So she take Pomp by de hind laig an pull him out.

"Lawd," say Pompey, "ol woman here she's de best alto we got at de Praise House. Take her, Lawd. I spect she help out de heavenly choir mo dan me. Anyhow, Mister Bird ain't gwine like hit if you take me, de best field hand on de place."

"You Pompey!" was all de Lawd say. But from de way he say hit, Pomp know hit mean business.

"All right, Lawd, I's comin," he say. "Jes give me time to put on my Sunday pants."

"Suits me," say de Lawd. "Might as well look good til dey can git you fit out wid dem snow white robes."

So Pompey got back to de far end of de room. "Ol woman," he say, "hold dat do open."

Well, ol woman she open de do an Pompey rared back an–zip! He went through de do an I MEAN he WENT through de do!

"Whoa, dere, Pomp!" say de Lawd, an taken out after him.

By time old woman an de chillun crept to de do, dey hear Pomp hit de canebrake, a good mile away, wid a sound like fire-crackers.

"Mammy," say de chillun, "de Lawd gwine catch Pappy, ain't he?"

Ol woman say, "Ain't NOBODY can catch yo pappy."
"Howcome?" de say.
She say, "Didn't you fool chillun see dat Pappy was barefooted?"

SLAVE SONG

We raise de wheat,
Dey gib us de corn.
We bake de bread,
Dey gib us de crust.
We sif de meal,
Dey gib us huss.
We peel de meat,
Dey gib us de skin.
And dat's de way
Dey take us in.

PROMISES OF FREEDOM

My ole Mistiss promise me,
W'en she died, she'd set me free,
She lived so long dat 'er head got bal',
An' she give out'n de notion a-dyin' at all.

My ole Mistiss say to me:
"Sambo, I'se gwine ter set you free."
But w'en dat head git slick an' bal',
De Lawd couldn't a' killed 'er wid a big green maul.

My ole Mistiss never die,
Wid 'er nose all hooked an' skin all dry.
But my ole Miss, she's somehow gone,
An' she lef' Uncle Sambo a-hillin' up co'n.

Ole Mosser lakwise promise me,
W'en he died, he'd set me free.
But ole Mosser go an' make his will
Fer to leave me a-plowin' ole Beck still.

Yes, my ole Mosser promise me;
But "his papers" didn' leave me free.
A dose of pizen he'ped 'm along.
May de Devil preach 'is funer'l song.

A SLAVE'S RIDDLE

Sambo lingo lang tang,
Chicken he flutter 'de do lang tang!
Ol' eighteen hundred and fifty-one,
As I went out and in again,
Out de dead de livin' came.

Under de gravel I do travel;
On de col' iron I do stan'.
I ride de filly never foaled,
An' hol' de damsel in me han'.

Water knee-deep in de clan,
Not a wiggle tail to be seen!
Seven dere were, but six dere be,
As I'm a virgin, set me free!

Since the master could not solve the slave's riddle, he gave him his freedom the very Christmas morning on which he told it, in "Ole Virginny."
The answer:
    First two lines: "Only de innerduction!"
    Third line: "The year it happen'."
    Fourth & fifth lines: "As Jim went out of his house he saw ole

hen partridge come out de skelekin of a hoss wid six little 'uns!"

Sixth line: "Jim had grabble (gravel) sewed in top of his hat. 'Course old Massa couldn' see 'em."

Seventh line: "Jim had his foots in de iron stirrups of de saddle as he ride de filly (colt)."

Eighth & ninth lines: "De mare she die', an' Jim he take de filly. Den he make a whip of her hide an' hol' it in his han'."

Tenth line: "Jim had his boots full of water. 'Course old Massa couldn' see wiggle tails!"

Eleventh line: "Hen partridge set on seven eggs. One spoil, and six hatch'."

Twelfth line: "As Jim done no wrong, ole Massa shoulda set him free. An' he did too!"

As told to William J. Faulkner by: Simon Brown,
of Society Hill, South Carolina, about 1905

MEMORIES OF SLAVERY

'I WAS borned back in the old country,' said Cecile, 'in South Carolina. My marse died, and me and my ma was shipped down the river to this heathen land. I was sold right at the French Market in New Orleans.'

'Lots of folks was real mean,' said Francis Doby. 'Like I said, they was always good to us at my place, but other places I knows it was just whippin', whippin', whippin' all the time. My ma once belonged to Massa De Gruy and he was sure a hard man. My ma was hardheaded and sassy, and she'd talk right back to anybody, massa or nobody. Lots of time she got a bullwhip on her nekkid back.'

'My ma died when I was about eleven years old,' said Janie Smith. 'Old Marse was mean to her. Whip her all the time. Made her work in the fields the very day she had a baby, and she borned the baby right out in the cotton patch and died. Old marse couldn't stand for his slaves gettin' educated, either. If he so much as caught one with

a paper or pencil, trying to learn how to write, he'd beat him half
to death. People didn't want us to learn nothin' in them days.'

When a pregnant woman was to be whipped it was the custom to
dig a hole in the ground, then spread-eagle her, face downward, so
that her abdomen would fit into the hole. Then the whip was
applied.

'I seen that lots of times,' said Odee Jackson, aged ninety-three.
'They'd dig a hole for that poor soul's belly 'cause they didn't want
her child to get hurted. It worth money. Then they would beat her
'til her back was a mass of blood. After that they'd rub salt into it,
or throw a bucket of salt and water over her. Sure they done that.
I seen 'em.'

But George Blisset said, 'Our marster couldn't stand noise. Us
slaves used to get together in one of the houses in the quarter and
take a big iron pot with three laigs—the kind you use for killin'
hawgs—and dance and sing around that, and there wouldn't be
no noise could be heard, 'cause all the noise go right into the pot.
Us held balls by candlelight, though they was strictly against
orders. If they catched us we got whipped. We couldn't look tired
next day, either. First thing ole driver's say was that we was up
late the night before, and he sure lay that bullwhip on our nekkid
skin.'

Charity Parker said, 'Saturday was our day. Sunday we had to go
to church. When I was young I didn't care 'bout no church, but
I could sure beat them feets on the floor. We had no music, but we
beat, "Boum! Coum! Doum! Doum!" One day a old man we
called Antoine say, "I'm gonna make you-all a drum what'll beat,
'Boum! Boum! Boum!' Wait 'til massa kill a cow." You see, they
only keep that old man 'round to play with the children, 'cause
he was too old to do any work. Well, he get that hide and he make
us a drum. He straddle that drum and beat on it and fust thing you
know we was all a-dancing and a-beating the floor with our feets.
Chile, we dance 'til midnight. To finish the ball we say, "Balancez
Calinda!", and turn 'round again. Then the ball was over.'

'Mind, what I tell you,' Cecile George said. 'I tell you what I seen
wit' my own two eyes. The people on the plantation they take sick
and die. Ain't no coffin for them. They take planks and nail them
together like a chicken coop. You could see through it. And it's too

short, the neck's too long. So a man stand up on the coffin, jump on the corpse, break his neck and his head fall on his chest. Then they nail the top and one nail go through the brain. You think I make that up or dream it? I seen that wit' mine own eyes. Then they put them in a wagon—the one they haul the manure in, nobody wit' them. The people have to go right on to work. Make no difference it your own father, you gotta go out in the fields that day. I seen that wit' my own eyes. It was wicked! Wicked! Wicked! And I seen it wit' my own eyes.'

'Sometimes,' said Annie Flowers, 'we still sets and talks of plantation days, and cuttin' the cane in the field; and we sings:

> Rains come wit' me,
> Sun come dry me.
> Stay back, boss man
> Don't come nigh me.

'Sometimes I thinks them days was happier, sometimes these. But so much trouble done gone over this old haid I ain't sure of nothin' no more. I jest don't know.'

Sometimes in the Mind

HIGH JOHN DE CONQUER

Maybe, now, we used-to-be black African folks can be of some help to our brothers and sisters who have always been white. You will take another look at us and say that we are still black and, ethnologically speaking, you will be right. But nationally and culturally, we are as white as the next one. We have put our labor and our blood into the common causes for a long time. We have given the rest of the nation song and laughter. Maybe now, in this terrible struggle, we can give something else—the source and soul of our laughter and song. We offer you our hopebringer, High John de Conquer.

High John de Conquer came to be a man, and a mighty man at that. But he was not a natural man in the beginning. First off, he was a whisper, a will to hope, a wish to find something worthy of laughter and song. Then the whisper put on flesh. His footsteps sounded across the world in a low but musical rhythm as if the world he walked on was a singing-drum. The black folks had an irresistible impulse to laugh. High John de Conquer was a man in full, and had come to live and work on the plantations, and all the slave folks knew him in the flesh.

The sign of this man was a laugh, and his singing-symbol was a drum-beat. No parading drum-shout like soldiers out for show. It did not call to the feet of those who were fixed to hear it. It was

an inside thing to live by. It was sure to be heard when and where the work was the hardest, and the lot the most cruel. It helped the slaves endure. They knew that something better was coming. So they laughed in the face of things and sang, "I'm so glad! Trouble don't last always." And the white people who heard them were struck dumb that they could laugh. In an outside way, this was Old Massa's fun, so what was Old Cuffy laughing for?

Old Massa couldn't know, of course, but High John de Conquer was there walking his plantation like a natural man. He was treading the sweat-flavored clods of the plantation, crushing out his drum tunes, and giving out secret laughter. He walked on the winds and moved fast. Maybe he was in Texas when the lash fell on a slave in Alabama, but before the blood was dry on the back he was there. A faint pulsing of a drum like a goat-skin stretched over the heart, that came nearer and closer, then somebody in the saddened quarters would feel like laughing, and say, "Now, High John de Conquer, Old Massa couldn't get the best of him. That old John was a case!" Then everybody sat up and began to smile. Yes, yes, that was right. Old John, High John could beat the unbeatable. He was top-superior to the whole mess of sorrow. He could beat it all, and what made it so cool, finish it off with a laugh. So they pulled the covers up over their souls and kept them from all hurt, harm and danger and made them a laugh and a song. Night time was a joke, because daybreak was on the way. Distance and the impossible had no power over High John de Conquer.

He had come from Africa. He came walking on the waves of sound. Then he took on flesh after he got there. The sea captains of ships knew that they brought slaves in their ships. They knew about those black bodies huddled down there in the middle passage, being hauled across the waters to helplessness. John de Conquer was walking the very winds that filled the sails of the ship. He followed over them like the albatross.

It is no accident that High John de Conquer has evaded the ears of white people. They were not supposed to know. You can't know what folks won't tell you. If they, the white people, heard some scraps, they could not understand because they had nothing to hear things like that with. They were not looking for any hope in those

days, and it was not much of a strain for them to find something
to laugh over. Old John would have been out of place for them.

Old Massa met our hope-bringer all right, but when Old Massa
met him, he was not going by his right name. He was traveling,
and touristing around the plantations as the laugh-provoking Brer
Rabbit. So Old Massa and Old Miss and their young ones laughed
with and at Brer Rabbit and wished him well. And all the time,
there was High John de Conquer playing his tricks of making a
way out of no-way. Hitting a straight lick with a crooked stick.
Winning the jack pot with no other stake but a laugh. Fighting a
mighty battle without outside-showing force, and winning his war
from within. Really winning in a permanent way, for he was winning with the soul of the black man whole and free. So he could
use it afterwards. For what shall it profit a man if he gain the whole
world, and lose his own soul? You would have nothing but a
cruel, vengeful, grasping monster come to power. John de Conquer
was a bottom-fish. He was deep. He had the wisdom tooth of the
East in his head. Way over there, where the sun rises a day ahead
of time, they say that Heaven arms with love and laughter those
it does not wish to see destroyed. He who carries his heart in his
sword must perish. So says the ultimate law. High John de Conquer
knew a lot of things like that. He who wins from within is in the
"Be" class. *Be* here when the ruthless man comes, and *be* here when
he is gone.

Moreover, John knew that it is written where it cannot be erased,
that nothing shall live on human flesh and prosper. Old Maker said
that before He made any more sayings. Even a man-eating tiger
and lion can teach a person that much. His flabby muscles and
mangy hide can teach an emperor right from wrong. If the emperor
would only listen.

II

There is no established picture of what sort of looking-man this
John de Conquer was. To some, he was a big, physical-looking
man like John Henry. To others, he was a little, hammered-down,

low-built man like the Devil's doll-baby. Some said that they never heard what he looked like. Nobody told them, but he lived on the plantation where their old folks were slaves. He is not so well known to the present generation of colored people in the same way that he was in slavery time. Like King Arthur of England, he has served his people, and gone back into mystery again. And, like King Arthur, he is not dead. He waits to return when his people shall call again. Symbolic of English power, Arthur came out of the water, and with Excalibur, went back into the water again. High John de Conquer went back to Africa, but he left his power here, and placed his American dwelling in the root of a certain plant. Only possess that root, and he can be summoned at any time.

"Of course, High John de Conquer got plenty power!," Aunt Shady Anne Sutton bristled at me when I asked her about him. She took her pipe out of her mouth and stared at me out of her deeply wrinkled face. "I hope you ain't one of these here smart colored folks that done got so they don't believe nothing, and come here questionizing me so you can have something to poke fun at. Done got shamed of the things that brought us through. Make out 'tain't no such thing no more."

When I assured her that that was not the case, she went on.

"Sho John de Conquer means power. That's bound to be so. He come to teach and tell us. God don't leave nobody ignorant, you child. Don't care where He drops you down, He puts you on a notice. He don't want folks taken advantage of because they don't know. Now, back there in slavery time, us didn't have no power of protection, and God knowed it, and put us under watch-care. Rattlesnakes never bit no colored folks until four years after freedom was declared. That was to give us time to learn and to know. 'Course, I don't know nothing about slavery personal like. I wasn't born till two years after the Big Surrender. Then I wasn't nothing but a infant baby when I was born, so I couldn't know nothing but what they told me. My mama told me, and I know that she wouldn't mislead me, how High John de Conquer helped us out. He had done teached the black folks so they knowed a hundred years ahead of time that freedom was coming. Long before the white folks knowed anything about it at all.

"These young Negroes reads they books and talk about the war

freeing the Negroes, but Aye, Lord! A heap sees, but a few knows. 'Course, the war was a lot of help, but how come the war took place? They think they knows, but they don't. John de Conquer had done put it into the white folks to give us our freedom, that's what. Old Massa fought against it, but us could have told him that it wasn't no use. Freedom just had to come. The time set aside for it was there. That war was just a sign and a symbol of the thing. That's the truth! If I tell the truth about everything as good as I do about that, I can go straight to Heaven without a prayer."

Aunt Shady Anne was giving the inside feeling and meaning to the outside laughs around John de Conquer. He romps, he clowns, and looks ridiculous, but if you will, you can read something deeper behind it all. He is loping on off from the Tar Baby with a laugh.

Take, for instance, those words he had with Old Massa about stealing pigs.

Old John was working in Old Massa's house that time, serving around the eating table. Old Massa loved roasted young pigs, and had them often for dinner. Old John loved them too, but Massa never allowed the slaves to eat any at all. Even put aside the left-over and ate it next time. John de Conquer got tired of that. He took to stopping by the pig pen when he had a strong taste for pig-meat, and getting himself one, and taking it on down to his cabin and cooking it.

Massa began to miss his pigs, and made up his mind to squat for who was taking them and give whoever it was a good hiding. So John kept on taking pigs, and one night Massa walked him down. He stood out there in the dark and saw John kill the pig and went on back to the "big house" and waited till he figured John had it dressed and cooking. Then he went on down to the quarters and knocked on John's door.

"Who dat?" John called out big and bold, because he never dreamed that it was Massa rapping.

"It's me, John," Massa told him. "I want to come in."

"What you want, Massa? I'm coming right out."

"You needn't do that, John. I want to come in."

"Naw, naw, Massa. You don't want to come into no old slave cabin. Youse too fine a man for that. It would hurt my feelings to see you in a place like this here one."

"I tell you I want to come in, John!"

So John had to open the door and let Massa in. John had seasoned that pig down, and it was stinking pretty! John knowed Old Massa couldn't help but smell it. Massa talked on about the crops and hound dogs and one thing and another, and the pot with the pig in it was hanging over the fire in the chimney and kicking up. The smell got better and better.

Way after while, when that pig had done simbled down to a low gravy, Massa said, "John, what's that you cooking in that pot?"

"Nothing but a little old weasly possum, Massa. Sickliest little old possum I ever did see. But I thought I'd cook him anyhow."

"Get a plate and give me some of it, John. I'm hungry."

"Aw, naw, Massa, you ain't hongry."

"Now, John, I don't mean to argue with you another minute. You give me some of that in the pot, or I mean to have the hide off of your back tomorrow morning. Give it to me!"

So John got up and went and got a plate and a fork and went to the pot. He lifted the lid and looked at Massa and told him, "Well, Massa, I put this thing in here a possum, but if it comes out a pig, it ain't no fault of mine."

Old Massa didn't want to laugh, but he did before he caught himself. He took the plate of brownded down pig and ate it up. He never said nothing, but he gave John and all the other house servants roast pig at the big house after that.

III

John had numerous scrapes and tight squeezes, but he usually came out like Brer Rabbit. Pretty occasionally, though, Old Massa won the hand. The curious thing about this is, that there are no bitter tragic tales at all. When Old Massa won, the thing ended up in a laugh just the same. Laughter at the expense of the slave, but laughter right on. A sort of recognition that life is not one-sided. A sense of humor that said, "We are just as ridiculous as anybody else. We can be wrong, too."

There are many tales, and variants of each, of how the Negro got his freedom through High John de Conquer. The best one deals

with a plantation where the work was hard, and Old Massa mean. Even Old Miss used to pull her maids' ears with hot firetongs when they got her riled. So, naturally, Old John de Conquer was around that plantation a lot.

"What we need is a song," he told the people after he had figured the whole thing out. "It ain't here, and it ain't no place I knows of as yet. Us better go hunt around. This has got to be a particular piece of singing."

But the slaves were scared to leave. They knew what Old Massa did for any slave caught running off.

"Oh, Old Massa don't need to know you gone from here. How? Just leave your old work-tired bodies around for him to look at, and he'll never realize youse way off somewhere, going about your business."

At first they wouldn't hear to John, that is, some of them. But, finally, the weak gave in to the strong, and John told them to get ready to go while he went off to get something for them to ride on. They were all gathered up under a big hickory nut tree. It was noon time and they were knocked off from chopping cotton to eat their dinner. And then that tree was right where Old Massa and Old Miss could see from the cool veranda of the big house. And both of them were sitting out there to watch.

"Wait a minute, John. Where we going to get something to wear like that. We can't go nowhere like you talking about dressed like we is."

"Oh, you got plenty things to wear. Just reach inside yourselves and get out all those fine raiments you been toting around with you for the last longest. They is in there, all right. I know. Get 'em out, and put 'em on."

So the people began to dress. And then John hollered back for them to get out their musical instruments so they could play music on the way. They were right inside where they got their fine raiments from. So they began to get them out. Nobody remembered that Massa and Miss were setting up there on the veranda looking things over. So John went off for a minute. After that they all heard a big sing of wings. It was John come back riding on a great black crow. The crow was so big that one wing rested on the morning, while the other dusted off the evening star.

John lighted down and helped them, so they all mounted on, and the bird took out straight across the deep blue sea. But it was a pearly blue, like ten squillion big pearl jewels dissolved in running gold. The shore around it was all grainy gold itself.

Like Jason in search of the golden fleece, John and his party went to many places, and had numerous adventures. They stopped off in Hell where John, under the name of Jack, married the Devil's youngest daughter and became a popular character. So much so, that when he and the Devil had some words because John turned the dampers down in old Original Hell and put some of the Devil's hogs to barbecue over the coals, John ran for High Chief Devil and won the election. The rest of his party was overjoyed at the possession of power and wanted to stay there. But John said no. He reminded them that they had come in search of a song. A song that would whip Old Massa's earlaps down. The song was not in Hell. They must go on.

The party escaped out of Hell behind the Devil's two fast horses. One of them was named Hallowed-Be-Thy-Name, and the other, Thy-Kingdom-Come. They made it to the mountain. Somebody told them that the Golden Stairs went up from there. John decided that since they were in the vicinity, they might as well visit Heaven.

They got there a little weary and timid. But the gates swung wide for them, and they went in. They were bathed, robed, and given new and shining instruments to play on. Guitars of gold, and drums, and cymbals and wind-singing instruments. They walked up Amen Avenue, and down Hallelujah Street and found with delight that Amen Avenue was tuned to sing base and alto. The west end was deep bass, and the east end alto. Hallelujah Street was tuned for tenor and soprano, and the two promenades met right in front of the throne and made harmony by themselves. You could make any tune you wanted to by the way you walked. John and his party had a very good time at that and other things. Finally, by the way they acted and did, Old Maker called them up before His great workbench, and made them a tune and put it in their mouths. It had no words. It was a tune that you could bend and shape in most any way you wanted to fit the words and feelings that you had. They learned it and began to sing.

Just about that time a loud rough voice hollered, "You Tunk!

You July! You Aunt Diskie!" Then Heaven went black before their eyes and they couldn't see a thing until they saw the hickory nut tree over their heads again. There was everything just like they had left it, with Old Massa and Old Miss sitting on the veranda, and Massa was doing the hollering.

"You all are taking a mighty long time for dinner," Massa said. "Get up from there and get on back to the field. I mean for you to finish chopping that cotton today if it takes all night long. I got something else, harder than that, for you to do tomorrow. Get a move on you!"

They heard what Massa said, and they felt bad right off. But John de Conquer took and told them, saying, "Don't pay what he say no mind. You know where you got something finer than this plantation and anything it's got on it, put away. Ain't that funny? Us got all that, and he don't know nothing at all about it. Don't tell him nothing. Nobody don't have to know where us gets our pleasure from. Come on. Pick up your hoes and let's go."

They all began to laugh and grabbed up their hoes and started out.

"Ain't that funny?" Aunt Diskie laughed and hugged herself with secret laughter. "Us got all the advantage, and Old Massa think he got us tied!"

The crowd broke out singing as they went off to work. The day didn't seem hot like it had before. Their gift song came back into their memories in pieces, and they sang about glittering new robes and harps, and the work flew.

IV

So after a while, freedom came. Therefore High John de Conquer has not walked the winds of America for seventy-five years now. His people had their freedom, their laugh and their song. They have traded it to the other Americans for things they could use like education and property, and acceptance. High John knew that that was the way it would be, so he could retire with his secret smile into the soil of the South and wait.

The thousands upon thousands of humble people who still believe

in him, that is, in the power of love and laughter to win by their subtle power, do John reverence by getting the root of the plant in which he has taken up his secret dwelling, and "dressing" it with perfume, and keeping it on their person, or in their houses in a secret place. It is there to help them overcome things they feel that they could not beat otherwise, and to bring them the laugh of the day. John will never forsake the weak and the helpless, nor fail to bring hope to the hopeless. That is what they believe, and so they do not worry. They go on and laugh and sing. Things are bound to come out right tomorrow. That is the secret of Negro song and laughter.

So the brother in black offers to these United States the source of courage that endures, and laughter. High John de Conquer. If the news from overseas reads bad, and the nation inside seems like it is stuck in the Tar Baby, listen hard, and you will hear John de Conquer treading on his singing-drum. You will know then, that no matter how bad things look now, it will be worse for those who seek to oppress us. Even if your hair comes yellow, and your eyes are blue, John de Conquer will be working for you just the same. From his secret place, he is working for all America now. We are all his kinfolks. Just be sure our cause is right, and then you can lean back and say, "John de Conquer would know what to do in a case like this, and then he would finish it off with a laugh."

White America, take a laugh out of our black mouths, and win! We give you High John de Conquer.

Zora Neale Hurston

CONJURATION

TIMES are not what they used to be for this old man, who has the unmistakable manner of one brought up by gentle folk. He is gentle and gracious and his quizzical smile hardly does justice to his sense of humor. Of late he never feels well. He is always "poorly, thank God," or feels "like old people," or "betwixt the sap and the bark." His mind dwells on days when he was young and free from care and worry. No "boll evils" pestered his cotton crop, then.

Shoats fattened in his barnyard to make plenty of meat for his family from Christmas to Christmas. Sweet potatoes and peanuts and sugar cane filled the patches around his cabin, and a few head of cattle to sell each year gave him money to bury for hard times. Plenty of "chicken and t'ing" throve in his yard, and the salt creeks nearby yielded fish, crabs, shrimp and oysters to eat and to sell to the canning factory. He had a good wife and flocks of willing women helped him pass the time whenever he got weary of staying too close around home. He could roam around much as he pleased, for he had enough children to help his wife do all the work without him, and to keep her company while he pleasured himself.

Those were good days, but now that they have "ceasted," he fears they are gone for good and all. His troubles came all at one time. Soon as his wife died, boll weevils began to destroy his cotton, and they have done this ever since. Just after the boll weevils started their deviltry, a tidal wave rose up out of the sea one night when he was away from home and drowned most of his children, most of his hogs and cattle; and everything growing in his field was ruined. He would have died from pure worryation except for the little whiskey he drank now and then to cheer himself up, but before long the white people made a law forbidding whiskey. After that a decent drink cost too dear to buy it. Plenty of white lightning was made by stills in the swamp, but it was raw and strong and made his head ache.

A few weeks ago he asked one of his white friends please to "lend him the loan" of a few dollars to buy a dress and a pair of ladies' shoes. He explained that since his only daughter had taken it into her head to marry and leave him for a no-count husband he had nobody to cook for him or scour his house or feed his fowls. He had made up his mind to "take wife," and a fine lady had agreed to marry him if he would buy her wedding dress and shoes.

When the loan was made he laughed at how the lady had won him by laying a cunjure bag right on his top step one night so his foot would step on it when he went inside the door. His foot might have done that very thing for true, but a full moon shone bright and he saw the cunjure tied up in a little white cloth that shone same like a hard-boiled egg. One mind told him to leave it right where it was, but another mind told him that the cloth might

be the very piece somebody cut off his Sunday shirt tail.

He rubbed both hands with ashes before he picked the cunjure bag up, and was careful not to touch the charm things inside it. They fell on the steps, but he let them be and hurried in to see if the cloth fitted the place where the shirt tail was cut. It did. It fitted exactly. Then he knew the lady who washed his clothes every week had a mind to marry him. One mind said, "You better not let no preacher read out o' de book over you, not no more in dis life." Another mind said, "You better thank God a smart lady wid a houseful o' smart chillen cut you shirt tail because 'e craves you for husband."

The cunjure bag stuff lay on the steps—a piece of dried snake skin, a small charred bone, a white feather—when he started to the lady's house. On the way he had to pass by her mother's house. The old lady was sitting in a rocking chair smoking her pipe, and he halted so he could tell her what her daughter had done. She looked powerful glad to see him, and acted like she expected him. She even had on her Sunday dress and her shoes, like she was wait-ing for company, and it late in the night, too. She laughed when he told her about the shirt-tail charm bag, then asked him to come in and sit with her a spell. She said she was too lonesome to have appetite for supper and was hoping some nice somebody would come by and cheer her up. She had coffee made and ash cake roasted to eat with the good fry meat in her skillet. Lord, they smelled good, and fast walking had made him hungry. He had aimed to go straight to her daughter's house and do some heavy courting, but his heavy appetite tricked him. He went inside, sat down, filled his empty belly with the lady's food, filled his pipe with the sweet plug-cut tobacco she had in a red tin can from the store. Bless God, before he finished smoking he was courting her.

Sweet-talk pure rolled off his tongue, but the more he begged her to marry to him, the more she said she could not. She said she had no frock, neither shoes, fitten for a bride, so he up and promised to buy them. She was not so young, but she was a fine woman, and he felt he had luck to get her for a wife.

He bought her dress and shoes, then stood up with her and let the preacher read out of the book over him before he found out that she and not her daughter laid the charm bag on his step and cut

off his Sunday shirt tail. What is done, is done, but the cunjure that made him want to marry her does not make him want to keep her.

The very day she became his lawful lady she gave every Gawd's thing she had to her grandchildren. She is trifling and goes to bed at first dark; if he much as wants to walk out after night, she threatens to tie the tail of his shirt to the tail of her night shift.

It's enough to make any man down in the heart to think on how he was once happy and prosperous, with plenty to eat and drink and willing young women right at his hand. Now he is old and poor, with no decent liquor to drink, and only one "scold gully" woman too old and too fat to work.

THE BURY LEAGUE

The Bury League is a cooperative society that grew out of the Negro's sincere desire for an elaborate and respectful funeral. Every neighborhood has a local chapter headed by a "Noble Shepherd," and the members pay a small sum each week to a common fund which provides for the next funeral. The Noble Shepherd keeps the "treasury," a black tin box with a lock and key, and once a month when the treasury is heavy with dues he takes it over the river and empties it into the hands of the Leader of the Flock, who owns and drives the automobile hearse and provides fine store-bought coffins and white stones to stand at the head of the graves.

Bury League members are required to attend every burial unless hindered by providence. They all wear white gloves, the women carry white paper flowers, and officers who carry the banners of the organization wear large badges.

The moderate dues must be paid promptly and every member must visit the sick and take presents of money or food. To fail in the least of these obligations means to be dropped from the League, but nobody fails. The reward for complying with them is a fine coffin, a journey to the grave in the automobile hearse, and a tombstone.

Before the Bury League was organized, coffins were simple pine boxes made by the plantation carpenter, and hearses were farm wagons drawn by mules. Nobody was buried before the sun had "set in the grave" to make it sweet for the last long sleep. The services were long with much mourning and praying and singing, and fat lightwood torches gave light for the burial and for marching round and round the grave.

All this had to be changed, for the Bury League's membership is large and the hearse has to travel all over the country. Roads are rough, the hearse gets weary and sometimes refuses to run, for it has taken as many as three people to their graves in one day. There is not time to wait on the sun to set in all the graves, and people have to trust to Jesus to make their graves sweet and restful, now that times have changed, and changed for the better, for poor people used to have it hard when death took those who were dear to them.

These Negroes are not alone in their attitude toward death. Most people crave a proper burial, and pride often plays its part in making funerals so expensive that families are left with uncomfortable debts. Unscrupulous undertakers of all races have made fortunes out of the attitude toward death that haunts every human creature when those near to him are stricken.

The Negroes delight in making a good appearance before their fellows, but when death takes one of them, their pride is accompanied with a fear that failure to give the departed a proper burial will result in disaster for the lonely spirit on its way to a final home. This fear is probably a lineal descendant of the old African belief that without proper rites for its protection a soul may be hindered by other spirits from finding its destination and become a pitiful wanderer on the face of the earth. A proper funeral ceremony is believed to be of great help in enabling a soul to find the right road to heaven and God, or to hell and Satan. Otherwise, it will haunt houses and burial grounds and lonely roads and frighten the very people it loved best on earth.

As a rule spirits resemble the bodies they occupied. The most unfortunate ones become plat-eyes and take on many shapes, changing quickly from one to another. Now a dog, then a horse, a man without a head, a warm cloud or a hot smoke that suffocates all

living creatures. Plat-eyes fear nothing and stop at nothing. Wise people and beasts flee from them, for "a coward never totes broke bones."

People with vivid imaginations are often terrified by apparitions that walk at night when the moon is young. The vicinity of cemeteries is carefully avoided after dark and so are places where people have met with fatal misfortune. Animals have "second sight" and can see spirits, but only people born with cauls over their faces have this keen vision.

One Saturday evening a plantation mother who had second sight sent her two small sons on a trustworthy mule to the crossroads store to fetch home the week's supply of groceries. She warned them to hurry home before sundown since a young moon was due to shine and set spirits to walking all over the country. The boys put the paper bags of rice, sugar, white flour and coffee all together in a large crocus sack so that none would be dropped on the way home.

The lonely road ran through thick woods that ever looked scary, but the mule walked along quietly until the sun dropped and a young moon showed in the sky. Then he began to back his ears and switch his tail. Just as they came in sight of the spot where a man had been mysteriously killed years ago, the mule stopped short in his tracks and would not budge. At first the boys thought he was being contrary so the older one got a stick and frailed his sides, then beat him on the head, but the beast only rolled his eyes and snorted like he smelt something dangerous. They did not know what to make of such carrying on, until a warm gust of air passed over their faces and a small white cloud floated across the road right in front of their eyes. The hair on their heads stood up and pushed off their hats, for the cloud smelled like smoke from burning sulphur. The mule shivered and leaped backward with hoarse hee-haws, and tried his best to talk. The boys fell off his back and the groceries tumbled into the road. They did not tarry to pick up the groceries or hats but scrambled onto the mule's back just as he struck out for home. He had always been too lame and broken-winded to go faster than a walk, but he galloped like a colt until he reached home, then he fell down flat in the yard where he laid all night gasping for breath. The mother did what she could

to comfort him, then she thanked God on her knees that the poor beast had sense like people and brought her sons home safe instead of letting them be smothered to death by the evil-smelling cloud. It was undoubtedly the spirit of the man who had been secretly killed years ago. His strange end was due to turn him into the most dangerous of all ghostly things, a plat-eye.

The groceries and hats stayed where they fell until the sun shone next morning, for spirits of all kinds, even plat-eyes and hags, dread sunlight and hide in dark places until first dark comes. The incident furnished the preacher with a subject for his sermon the next Sunday. He explained that if the dead man had been given a proper burial, instead of being hurried into the ground with not even a church deacon to pray over his body, he might have been a harmless "ha'nt" instead of a plat-eye which changes from one ugly thing to another as it strives to harm innocent people.

The dead are helped by thoughtfulness just as the living are, and the very poorest people must struggle to pay insurance dues to the Bury League, not only for themselves but for every member of their families.

Soon afterward, a black father came to get the plantation carpenter to make a box for his dead baby. He was pitifully grief-stricken because the child had not been "insured" in the Bury League, and since he lacked money to buy a nice coffin the baby was condemned to be laid away in a simple box of pine boards. As he helped to saw the short lengths and plane them smooth he sobbed over his "bad mistake" that kept the child from being put away right.

The carpenter tried to console him, for the child was too young to have sin and was bound to reach heaven; death levels everything and makes a home-made pine box as soft a bed as a Bury League Coffin. The father shook his head and sobbed as he explained that he and his wife and every other child in his house were Bury League members. Times were so hard and money so scarce, it pinched him to pay all their dues, but he did it. This baby was so healthy he never thought it would sicken and die. It was his only boy child, too, the flower of his flock, the child he ever loved best. Nobody ever saw a finer little boy child or one so smart for its age.

The mother took more pains with him than with any child she ever birthed. Three or four times every day she left her work in

the field and went home to suckle him. And now, this failure to provide a proper burial would work the child heavy harm. No common sickness killed him, for he was ailing only one day and night.

Some people thought the mother was to blame because she would not wean him when she started breeding again. Others thought maybe her breast milk was too hot or poisoned with weariness from hoeing grass so long in the sun. That could not be so. The mother was an able woman and never minded sun-hot or hard work when she was carrying a new child. Evil spirits must have killed the little boy child, for they saw how his parents loved him more than the little gal-children. They loved him more than life itself, and now their hearts were pure broken because he was dead and would be buried in a home-made box.

The mother believed some jealous-hearted woman with no child to equal him had put a "black hand" on him. A strong healthy child would not die so quick unless somebody cast a spell on him or a spirit tricked him into leaving this world. It was hard to think anybody could be mean enough to do such a damage to an innocent little baby, but evil spirits are all over the land. They know everything about everybody, and they pleasure themselves with causing sorrow.

Tears leaped out of the father's eyes as he lifted the little pine box and put it on his head to take home. Its small weight was slight for his strength, but his broad shoulders drooped and his feet stumbled along the smooth path as if they bore a heavy burden. The carpenter groaned with pity as the short, narrow box balanced on the father's head made a stark pattern against the sunset sky. Then he set about boiling water to scald the tools that had cut and nailed together the little coffin boards.

The earth from which people spring clings to their feet no matter where they go, and will try to fetch them back home. The Negroes delight in taking journeys, but a dread of being sent home "cold in a box" often keeps them from tarrying long when they go away. When a message came from a town some miles away saying "Diana dead. No insurance. Promised to send her home," everybody cheerfully contributed something to bring Diana's body home "right." The next day a fine hearse and automobiles filled with Diana's

friends made a long funeral procession that moved toward the river bridge which marks the town's limit. The elegant vehicles halted at the bridge, where they were met by a pitiful line of wagons and carts drawn by mules and oxen. Diana's body in a fine coffin was taken out of the hearse and put in one rickety wagon. The mourners got out of the automobiles and climbed into broken-down wagons and carts. The humble procession went slowly across the bridge and followed the highway until it reached the narrow winding road which led to the country graveyard where Diana wanted to lie.

These simple people could not afford the hearse and automobiles for the whole journey, but they had done the best they could to give Diana's soul a good start on the way to its eternal home.

When the old graveyard became too full and another one had to be started, the whole Bury League was terribly upset, for there is a powerful superstition that the first person buried in a graveyard never rests easy. Superstitions here are no light beliefs to be disregarded or laughed away, and this one involved everybody's peace of mind. Nobody knows what would have happened if an old woman who was respected by everybody in the community had not come forward and said that she was willing to lie first in the new graveyard. She had thought the matter over. She knew her time on this earth was almost out, for lately, one rainy day she was walking home and her dead husband came and held an umbrella over her. It meant he wanted her to come with him. She would trust the Master to take care of her. He knew she had tried to live a good life, and would see to it that her last long sleep would not be restless.

She had never joined the Bury League or accepted changes that crept into the plantation. Her old baptising robe, made when she was baptised many years ago, had been put away carefully in her trunk to serve as her shroud. Time had yellowed and weakened the cloth, so it was hardly fit to serve as a pattern, but she bought new white cloth, and asked a "seamster" to make a robe exactly like it.

When the shroud was made and pressed with a "laying-out head rag" to match it, she bought a pair of white gloves and new shoes to wear with them. She examined them all carefully, then put them in the trunk to wait. "I'm all ready for de journey now," she said

with a gentle smile.

She talked of this journey as if she were going home to live forever, not only with God and Jesus and the angels, but with her father and mother and husband and the children who had gone on before.

All her treasures were kept in the trunk where the shroud was laid. She took them out and gave all away except a pretty blue china mug wrapped in a clean white cloth. This was to be kept until a white lad whom she had nursed and tried to teach and train should marry and have a son. The mug had been saved for the little boy child she had hoped to nurse like his father and grandfather before him. As she unwrapped it her mind went away back into the gentle past, and she told how, forty years ago, when she was a middle-aged woman, a group of Polish people came to the neighborhood to farm. Only one was a woman and she had children, one of whom was a beautiful, red-cheeked blue-eyed girl child. Soon after they came, the girl child sickened and died. The mother mourned in a strange language, but her grief was something any mother could understand. She refused to have the child buried in the white people's graveyard, but laid her away in a shady spot on the edge of the woods near a little waterfall that made music day and night. A lonesome grave told where the child had so loved to wade in the clear water, and gather pebbles and pick white violets that bloomed along the banks. The poor woman would not believe the stream had stolen the child's spirit although it was plain enough to everybody else.

The child's death made the Polish people unhappy there and they decided to go away. When the mother said goodbye she left the china mug for a keepsake. It had been a parting gift to the little dead girl from an old grandmother in Poland.

The old trunk had held it for over forty years, and now it must be kept for the white lad's first boy child or for his first grandboy in case he got only girl children. No girl child must ever own it, for it brought bad luck to one and it might do the same thing again.

Trees and bushes hid the little Polish girl's grave long ago, but sometimes when a thin young moon shows in the west her singing can be heard above the music of the water, and the words of her song are strange, same like those of her mother.

When the story of the cup ended, the old woman slowly wrapped it up again, as she added, "When I first thought on leavin' dis world, one mind told me to stay until Christmas when my white baby will come home from school; but my other mind said I better go spend Christmas in heaven wid my own lil chillen. Maybe lil chillen don' grown up in heaven, but my white baby is done tall, like a man. I would like to look in his blue eyes one more time. I ever dream 'bout em same like I dream 'bout de chillen I birthed my own'self. I won' forget em when I get up yonder. I'll pray for em same like I pray for em here, Gawd bless em."

It was useless to argue with her about staying until her white baby came home. Her mind was made up.

Her last request was, "After I'm laid out do watch my eyes so dey won' crack open an' scare de lil chillen what comes to look a last look on my face." She refused to eat and drank only enough water to wet her dry lips, but she reached heaven in time for Christmas. Her burial was one of the greatest celebrations the plantation has ever known. She was not a Bury League member, but the Bury League hearse brought her coffin, and the Bury League members marched behind it carrying banners and white paper flowers. The sun set in her grave to make it sweet, and pine torches made light to fill the dirt in. When the low mound of earth was smoothed and the Bury League white paper flowers laid on it, things she prized on earth were put with them: a clock that had not ticked for many years, the cup and saucer she used, a glass lamp filled with kerosene, and a china vase holding fresh blossoms from those growing around her doorstep.

When the funeral sermon was preached, some months later, the church could not hold the congregation. Windows and doors were crowded with people who strained their ears to hear the preacher describe the welcome she received from God and Jesus, her parents and friends, her husband and children, when the angels flew through heaven's gate with her soul. People rocked their bodies from side to side and hummed the tune of "I'm gwine home to die no more" while the preacher told how she walked on golden streets, and flew down the sky on her strong white wings to watch over those she loved on earth.

Funeral sermons are never preached at a burial, but always after-

ward at the church on a Sunday, and the sermon tells with utter frankness whether the deceased is happy in heaven or wretched in hell, or driven by pains far worse than torment to roam through the air, without rest or peace day or night.

The old graveyard, unused and deserted, waits for Judgment Day on the edge of a hill that drops to the river with a steep fall called "Lover's Leap." Below it lie untamed miles of swamp where the river bends into Devil's Elbow, or swollen by rains, makes a vast yellow lake that uproots and drowns the swamp's undergrowth. Yellow stains high on the trunks of tall trees mark the height of its flood long after it has passed. But no flood can reach the old graveyard.

Spring shows early in the tender, misty green of willows that mark the river channel where strong roots clutch swamp mud and strive to hold the unruly stream to its rightful road. Maples flame scarlet, poplars make bright yellow splashes, wood ducks quack gaily, turkey hens call gobblers who deserted them and their children in the fall to gang together all winter like carefree bachelors. Then the old graves sunken with waiting so long for Gabriel to blow his trumpet and clothe old bones with living flesh are sprinkled with blue violets; tangles of yellow jessamine drop golden bells and crab apple thickets send down showers of fragrant pink petals to lie among carved wooden heads of wheat placed on some of the graves long ago. Nobody knows who carved them or why the wood lasts so long, but everybody knows they are symbols of eternal life carved by somebody who believed that some day "The trumpet shall sound and the dead shall be raised incorruptible . . . and this mortal must put on immortality."

BIG SWAMPS OF THE CONGAREE

TAD: Gentlemens, how is you-all?
VOICE: Howdy! how you been?
SECOND VOICE: Tolerable.
TAD: I been down in de big swamps on de Congaree.

VOICE: Tell us, brother?

TAD: I been down to de Congaree in de big swamps, where de trees is tall an' de moss long an' gray, where de Bullace grow, an' where I hear de tune of de bird in de mornin'; down wey de wild turkey gobbles, way down on de Congaree; wey God's mornin' leads to de devil's night; down on de river, where night make her sign, where owls on a dead limb talks of de dead, talks wid de dead an laughs like de dead, way down in de big swamps of de Congaree; down where de blunt-tailed moccasin crawls in de grass, where de air is stink wid he smell; where de water is green, where de worms is spewed out of de groun', where de groun' is mud, where de trees sweat like a man; down in de home of de varmint an' bugs, down in de slick yellow mud, de black mud an' de brown, way down in de big swamps of de Congaree; down in de land of pizen, where de yallow-fly sting, in de home of de fever an' wey death is de king. Dat wey I been, down in de big swamps. Down in de land of mosquito, way down in de big swamps, down on de Congaree.

AN ESCAPED CONVICT

Nothin' but a convict
Loosed from de chains,
Wid shackles left behind me,
Wid shackle scars upon me,
Wid a whip an' a chain
Waitin' ef dey ketch me,
Wid bloodhounds an' bullets
On my trail,
An' de dangers er de swamp
In front er me.
I'll take my chance, brother,
I'll take my chance.

De rattlesnake an' mocassin,
De mud an' de briar,

An' de pizen vine ain' nothin'
To de danger
Dat is left behind me.
Dere is striped clothes
An' double shackles
An' a rawhide whip
All behind me.
So I'll take my chance, brother,
I'll take my chance.

I know dere's a hard, hard road
Behind me,
An' der ain' no road in front;
Dat de mud is heavy,
An' dere ain' much food
To separate my backbone
From my belly.
For I ain' nothin' but a convict,
Wid de scars to prove it,
I'll take my chance, brother,
I'll take my chance.

FALLING STARS

BROTHER, don' pint you han' at a fallin' star. Jesus sets on he throne in heben, an' he watch all de night theu, an' he watch a sinful world, and den is de fallin' stars, an' Jesus weeps on he throne in heben, and dem is de tears of Jesus, fallin' for a sinful world. Dem is de sparks of heben, dem in de fallin' stars, and dem is de tears of Jesus, fallin' on a sinful world. Don' pint your han' brother, don' pint your han', for dem is de tears of Jesus, fallin' on a sinful world. Dem is de lights from de throne in heben, dem is de tears of Jesus. Don' pint your han', Brother, don' pint your han' at a fallin' star.

UGLY

It's woman's privilege to be ugly, but some take advantage of it.

She's ugly as home-made sin.

She's so ugly she scares herself.

That old woman's so old her futures (features) all run together, and she's so ugly she can't die. I reckon she'll just ugly away.

TAD'S ADVICE TO HIS SON

Don't trust a 'ooman,
She's a curious thing,
When she's right she'll die to save you,
An' when she's wrong she'll die to git you.

There's danger in de trut',
When a lie will do de work,
Tell it to a 'ooman,
Tell her what she loves to hear.

Tell her she's de only 'ooman,
Tell her dat your heart is bursting,
An' your head is swimmin',
An' dere ain't no other wimmens.

What a 'ooman loves to hear is soft and sweet,
Dere's danger in de trut',
An' a lie will do de work.
A lie will do de work wid a 'ooman,
An' de trut' is sure to hurt.

When you're talking to a 'ooman,
Talk as soft as a breath of air creepin' t'ru a crack.
Be as calm as a mouse crawlin' on a carpet.
An' when you're breakin' loose from her,
A lie will do de work.
Take her in your arms, and whisper in her ear.
Be gentle as a ray of moon-light fallin' on a flower.
Be tender as a mother' song floating on de air.
If you know'd it you'd be careful in a bed of rattle-snakes,
So be careful when a 'ooman's near.

Soft talk is cheap,
It ain't cost you nothen
An' when you dealin' wid a 'ooman,
Dere's danger in de trut',
An' a lie will do de work.

OLD SISTER'S ADVICE TO HER DAUGHTERS

Don't trus' mens,
But keep your feets flat,
Flat upon de groun'

Don't listen to no easy talk,
Don't l'em 'suade you,
For de worl' is full of lying mens,
Just keep your feets flat,
Flat upon de groun'.

De Bible says dey all is liars,
And Jesus knows 'tis true,
De more fair dey talk,
De worse dey is.
Sister, keep your feets flat,
Flat upon de groun'.

Don't l'em 'suade you,
Don't listen to no easy talk,
If dey axe a unfair question,
Keep your feets flat,
Flat upon de groun',
For dey is devils,
An' dey is atter you,
So keep your feets flat,
Flat upon de groun'.

Don't you rask 'em,
An' don't you trus' 'em,
For if you listen to dey honey
You might not keep your feets flat,
Flat upon de groun'.
For dey'll kiss you an dey'll love you,
An' talk as soft and pretty as de jue upon a flower,
But dey'll leaf' you wid a laugh,
If you don't keep your feets flat,
Flat upon de groun'.

PLANTATION PROVERBS

Big 'possum clime little tree.
Dem w'at eats kin say grace.
Ole man Know-All died las' year.
Better de gravy dan no grease 'tall.
Lazy fokes' stummucks don't git tired.
Mole don't see w'at his naber doin'.
Don't rain eve'y time de pig squeal.
Crow en corn can't grow in de same fiel'.
Tattlin' 'oman can't make de bread rise.
Rails split 'fo' brekfus' 'll season de dinner.
Hog dunner w'ich part un 'im'll season de turnip salad.
Mighty po' bee dat don't make mo' honey dan he want.

Kwishins on mule's foots done gone out er fashun.
Pigs dunno w'at a pen's fer.
Possum's tail good as a paw.
Dogs don't bite at de front gate.
Colt in de barley-patch kick high.
Jay-bird don't rob his own nes'.
Pullet can't roost too high for de owl.
De howlin' dog know w'at he sees.
Bline hoss don't fall w'en he follers de bit.
Don't fling away de empty wallet.
Settin' hens don't hanker arter fresh aigs.
Tater-vine growin' w'ile you sleep.
Hit take two birds fer to made a nes'.
Ef you bleedzd ter eat dirt, eat clean dirt.
Tarrypin walk fast 'nuff fer to go visitin'.
Empty smoke house makes de pullet holler.
W'en coon take water he fixin' fer ter fight.
Corn makes mo' at de mill dan it does in de crib.
Good luck say: "Op'n yo' mouf en shet yo' eyes."
Rooster makes mo 'racket dan de hin w'at lay de aig.
Meller mush-million hollers at you fum over de fence.
Rain-crow don't sing no chune, but youk'n 'pen' on 'im.
One-eyed mule can't be handled on de bline side.
Moon may shine, but a lightered knot's mighty handy.
Licker talks mighty loud w'en it git loose fum de jug.
De proudness un a man don't count w'en his head's cold.
Hongry rooster don't cackle w'en he fine a wum.
Youk'n hide de fier, but w'at you gwine do wid de smoke?
Ter-morrow may be de carridge-driver's day for ploughin'.
Hit's a mighty deaf field hand dat don't year de dinner ho'n.
Hit takes a bee fer ter git de sweetness out'n de hoar-houn' blossom.
You'd see mo' er de mink ef he know'd whar de yard dog sleeps.
Watch out w'en you'er gittin all you want. Fattenin' hogs ain't in
    luck.

APHORISMS

It's hard to make clothes fit a miserable man.

De stopper get de longest rest in de empty jug.

De church bells sometimes do better work dan de sermon.

De price of your hat ain't de measure of your brain.

Ef your coat-tail catch a-fire, don't wait till you kin see de blaze
'fo' you put it out.

De graveyard is de cheapes' boardin'-house.

Dar's a fam'ly coolness 'twix' de mule an' de single-tree.

It pesters a man dreadful when he git mad an' don' know who to
cuss.

Buyin' on credit is robbin' next year's crop.

Christmas without holiday is like a candle without a wick.

De crawfish in a hurry look like he tryin' to git dar yesterday.

Lean hound lead de pack when de rabbit in sight.

Little flakes make de deepest snow.

Knot in de plank will show through de whitewash.

Dirt show de quickest on de cleanest cotton.

De candy-pulling can call louder dan de log-rolling.

De right sort of religion heaps de half-bushel.

De stell hoe dat laughs at de iron one is like de man dat is shamed
of his grand-daddy.

A mule can tote so much goodness in his face that he don't have
none left for his hind legs.

De cow-bell can't keep a secret.

Ripe apples make de tree look taller.

Blind horse knows when de trough is empty.

De noise of de wheels don't measure de load in de wagon.

Last year's hot spell cools off mighty fast.

Little hole in your pocket is worse than a big one at de knee.

Appetite don't regulate de time of day.

He drinks so much whisky that he staggers in his sleep.

De rich git richer and de po 'git children.

Persimmons ain't no good until dey're frost-bit.

Man who gits hurt working oughta show de scars.

Life is short and full of blisters.

If you want to see how much folks is goin' to miss you, just stick your finger in de pond den pull it out and look at de hole.

De quagmire don't hang out no sign.

One person can thread a needle better than two.

De point of de pin is de easiest end to find.

Muzzle on de yard dog unlocks de smokehouse.

It's hard for de best and smartest folks in de world to git along without a little touch of good luck.

De billy-goat gets in his hardest licks when he looks like he's going to back out of de fight.

In God we trust, all others cash.

He may mean good, but he do' so doggone po'.

A whistling woman and a crowing hen,
Don't never come to no good end.

God, Man and the Devil

THE ROCK

CHRIST was walkin' long one day wid all his disciples and he said, "We're goin' for a walk today. Everybody pick up a rock and come along." So everybody got their selves a nice big rock 'ceptin' Peter. He was lazy so he picked up a li'l bit of a pebble and dropped it in his side pocket and come along.

Well, they walked all day long and de other 'leven disciples changed them rocks from one arm to de other but they kept on totin' 'em. Long towards sundown they come 'long by de Sea of Galilee and Jesus tole 'em, "Well, le's fish awhile. Cast in yo' nets right here." They done like he tole 'em and caught a great big mess of fish. Then they cooked 'em and Christ said, "Now, all y'all bring up yo' rocks." So they all brought they rocks and Christ turned 'em into bread and they all had a plenty to eat wid they fish exceptin' Peter. He couldn't hardly make a moufful offa de li'l bread he had and he didn't like dat a bit.

Two or three days after dat Christ went out doors and looked up at de sky and says, "Well, we're goin' for another walk today. Everybody git yo'self a rock and come along."

They all picked up a rock apiece and was ready to go. All but Peter. He went and tore down half a mountain. It was so big he couldn't move it wid his hands. He had to take a pinch-bar to move it. All day long Christ walked and talked to his disciples and Peter sweated and strained wid dat rock of his'n.

Way long in de evenin' Christ went up under a great big old tree and set down and called all of his disciples around 'im and said, "Now everybody bring up yo' rocks."

So everybody brought theirs but Peter. Peter was about a mile down de road punchin' dat half a mountain he was bringin'. So Christ waited till he got dere. He looked at de rocks dat de other 'leven disciples had, den he seen dis great big mountain dat Peter had and so he got up and walked over to it and put one foot up on it and said, "Why Peter, dis is a fine rock you got here! It's a noble rock! And Peter, on dis rock Ah's gointer build my church."

Peter says, "Naw you ain't neither. You won't build no church house on dis rock. You gointer turn dis rock into bread."

Christ knowed dat Peter meant dat thing so he turnt de hillside into bread and dat mountain is de bread he fed de 5,000 wid. Den he took dem 'leven other rocks and glued 'em together and built his church on it.

And that's how come de Christian churches is split up into so many different kinds—cause it's built on pieced-up rock.

THE WORD THE DEVIL MADE UP

OLE DEVIL looked around hell one day and seen his place was short of help so he thought he'd run up to Heben and kidnap some angels to keep things runnin' tell he got reinforcements from Miami.

Well, he slipped up on a great crowd of angels on de outskirts of Heben and stuffed a couple of thousand in his mouth, a few hundred under each arm and wrapped his tail 'round another thousand and darted off towards hell.

When he was flyin' low over de earth lookin' for a place to land, a man looked up and seen de Devil and ast 'im, "Ole Devil, Ah see you got a load of angels. Is you goin' back for mo'?"

Devil open his mouth and tole 'im, "Yeah," and all de li'l angels flew out his mouf and went on back to Heben. While he was tryin' to ketch 'em he lost all de others. So he went back after another load.

He was flyin' low agin and de same man seen him and says, "Ole Devil, Ah see you got another load uh angels."

Devil nodded his head and said "unh hunh," and dat's why we say it today.

CHRISTMAS GIFT

WELL, one Christmas time, God was goin' to Palatka. De Devil was in de neighborhood too and seen God goin' long de big road, so he jumped behind a stump and hid. Not dat he was skeered uh God, but he wanted to git a Christmas present outa God but he didn't wanta give God nothin'.

So he squatted down behind dis stump till God come along and then he jumped up and said, "Christmas gift!"

God just looked back over his shoulder and said, "Take de East Coast," and kept on walkin'. And dat's why we got storms and skeeters—it's de Devil's property.

FIGURE AND FANCY

GOD did not make folks all at once. He made folks sort of in His spare time. For instance one day He had a little time on his hands, so He got the clay, seasoned it the way He wanted it, then He laid it by and went on to doing something more important. Another day He had some spare moments, so He rolled it all out, and cut out the human shapes, and stood them all up against His long gold fence to dry while He did some important creating. The human shapes all got dry, and when He found time, He blowed the breath of life in them. After that, from time to time, he would call everybody up, and give them spare parts. For instance, one day He called everybody and gave out feet and eyes. Another time He give out toe-nails that Old Maker figured they could use. Anyhow,

they had all that they got up to now. So then one day He said, "Tomorrow morning, at seven o'clock sharp, I aim to give out color. Everybody be here on time. I got plenty of creating to do tomorrow, and I want to give out this color and get it over wid. Everybody be 'round de throne at seven o'clock tomorrow morning!"

So next morning at seven o'clock, God was sitting on His throne with His big crown on His head and seven suns circling around His head. Great multitudes was standing around the throne waiting to get their color. God sat up there and looked east, and He looked west, and He looked north and He looked Australia, and blazing worlds were falling off His teeth. So He looked over to His left and moved His hands over a crowd and said, "You's yellow people!" They all bowed low and said, "Thank you God," and they went on off. He looked at another crowd, moved His hands over them and said, "You'se red folks!" They made their manners and said, "Thank you, Old Maker," and they went on off. He looked towards the center and moved His hand over another crowd and said, "You's white folks!" They bowed low and said, "Much obliged, Jesus," and they went on off. Then God looked way over to the right and said, "Look here, Gabriel, I miss a lot of multitudes from around the throne this morning." Gabriel looked too, and said, "Yessir, there's a heap of multitudes missing from round de throne this morning." So God sat there an hour and a half and waited. Then He called Gabriel and said, "Looka here, Gabriel, I'm sick and tired of this waiting. I got plenty of creating to do this morning. You go find them folks and tell 'em they better hurry on up here if they expect to get any color. Fool with me, and I won't give out no more."

So Gabriel run on off and started to hunting around. Way after while, he found the missing multitudes lying around on the grass by the Sea of Life, fast asleep. So Gabriel woke them up and told them, "You better get up from there and come on up to the throne and get your color. Old Maker is mighty wore out from waiting. Fool with him and He won't give out no more color."

So as the multitudes heard that, they all jumped up and went running towards the throne hollering, "Give us our color! We want our color! We got just as much right to color as anybody else."

So when the first ones got to the throne, they tried to stop and be polite. But the ones coming on behind got to pushing and shoving so till the first ones got shoved all up against the throne so till the throne was careening all over to one side. So God said, "Here! Here! Git back! Git back!" But they was keeping up such a racket that they misunderstood Him, and thought He said, "Git black!" So they just got black, and kept the thing a-going.

THE MAN WHO WENT TO HEAVEN
FROM JOHNSTOWN

You know, when it lightnings, de angels is peepin' in de lookin' glass; when it thunders, they's rollin' out de rain barrels; and when it rains, somebody done dropped a barrel or two and bust it.

One time, you know, there was going to be big doin's in Glory and all de angels had brand new clothes to wear and so they was all peepin' in the lookin' glasses, and therefore it got to lightning all over de sky. God tole some of de angels to roll in all de full rain barrels and they was in such a hurry that it was thunderin' from the east to the west and the zigzag lightning went to join the mutterin' thunder and, next thing you know, some of them angels got careless and dropped a whole heap of them rain barrels, and didn't it rain!

In one place they call Johnstown they had a great flood. And so many folks got drownded that it looked jus' like Judgment day.

So some of de folks that got drownded in that flood went one place and some went another. You know, everything that happen, they got to be a colored man in it—and so one of de brothers in black went up to Heben from de flood.

When he got to the gate, Ole Peter let 'im in and made 'im welcome. De colored man was named John, so John ast Peter, says, "Is it dry in dere?"

Ole Peter tole 'im, "Why, yes it's dry in here. How come you ast that?"

"Well, you know Ah jus' come out of one flood, an Ah don't want to run into no mo'. Ooh, man! You ain't seen no water. You just oughter seen dat flood we had at Johnstown."

Peter says, "Yeah, we know all about it. Jus' go wid Gabriel and let him give you some new clothes."

So John went on off wid Gabriel and come back all dressed up in brand new clothes and all de time he was changin' his clothes he was tellin' Ole Gabriel all about dat flood, jus' like he didn't know already.

So when he come back from changin' his clothes, they give him a brand new gold harp and handed him to a gold bench and made him welcome. They was so tired of hearing about dat flood they was glad to see him wid his harp 'cause they figgered he'd get to playin' and forget all 'bout it. So Peter tole him, "Now you jus' make yo'self at home and play all de music you please."

John went and took a seat on de bench and commenced to tune up his harp. By dat time, two angels come walkin' by where John was settin' so he throwed down his harp and tackled 'em.

"Say," he hollered, "y'all want to hear 'bout de big flood Ah was in down on earth? Lawd, Lawd! It sho rained, and talkin' 'bout water!"

Dem two angels hurried on off from 'im jus' as quick as they could. He started to tellin' another one and he took to flyin'. Gabriel went over to 'im and tried to get 'im to take it easy, but John kept right on stoppin' every angel dat he could find to tell 'im about dat flood of water.

Way after while he went over to Ole Peter and said: "Thought you said everybody would be nice and polite?"

Peter said, "Yeah, Ah said it. Ain't everybody treatin' you right?"

John said, "Naw. Ah jus' walked up to a man as nice and friendly as Ah could be and started to tell 'im 'bout all dat water Ah left back there in Johnstown and instead of him turnin' me a friendly answer he said, 'Shucks! You ain't seen no water!' and walked off and left me standin' by myself."

"Was he a ole man wid a crooked walkin' stick?" Peter ast John. "Yeah."

"Did he have whiskers down to here?" Peter measured down to his waist.

"He sho did," John tol' 'im.

"Aw shucks," Peter tol' 'im. "Dat was Ole Nora. You can't tell him nothin' 'bout no flood."

LITTLE EIGHT JOHN

ONCE an long ago dey was a little black boy name of Eight John. He was a nice lookin little boy but he didn't act like he look. He mean little boy an he wouldn't mind a word de grown folks told him. Naw not a livin word. So if his lovin mammy told him not to do a thing, he go straight an do hit. Yes, spite of all de world.

"Don't step on no toad frawgs," his lovin mammy told him, "aw you bring de bad lucks on yo family. Yes you will."

Little Eight John he say, "No'm, I won't step on no toad frawgs. No ma'am!"

But jes as sho as anything, soon as he got out of sight of his lovin mammy, dat Little Eight John find him a toad frawg an squirsh hit. Sometime he squirsh a heap of toad frawgs.

An the cow wouldn't give no milk but bloody milk an de baby would have de bad ol colics.

But Little Eight John he jes duck his haid an laugh.

"Don't set in no chair backwards," his lovin mammy told Eight John. "It bring de weary troubles to yo family."

An so Little Eight John he set backwards in every chair.

Den his lovin mammy's cawn bread burn an de milk wouldn't churn.

Little Eight John jes laugh an laugh an laugh cause he know why hit was.

"Don't climb no trees on Sunday," his lovin mammy told him, "aw hit will be bad luck."

So dat Little Eight John, dat bad little boy, he sneak up trees on Sunday.

Den his pappy's taters wouldn't grow an de mule wouldn't go. Little Eight John he know howcome.

"Don't count yo teeth," his lovin mammy she tell Little Eight

John, "aw dey come a sad sickness in yo family."

But dat Little Eight John he go right ahaid an count his teeth. He count his uppers an he count his lowers. He count em on weekdays an Sundays.

Den his mammy she whoop an de baby git de croup. All on count of dat Little Eight John, dat badness of a little ol boy.

"Don't sleep wid yo haid at de foot of the baid aw yo family git de weary money blues," his lovin mammy told him.

So he do hit an do hit sho, dat cross-goin Little Eight John boy. An de family hit went broke wid no money in de poke.

Little Eight John he jes giggle.

"Don't have no Sunday moans, faw fear Ol Raw Haid Bloody Bones," his lovin mammy told him.

So he had de Sunday moans an he had de Sunday groans, an he moan an he groan and he moan.

An Ol Raw Haid Bloody Bones he come after dat little bad boy an change him to a little ol grease spot on de kitchen table an his lovin mammy wash hit off de next mawnin.

An dat was de end of Little Eight John.

An dat whut always happen to never-mindin little boys.

DE WAYS OF DE WIMMENS

Most folks say de six day was Satdy, cause on de SEVENTH day didn't de Lawd rest an look his creation over? Now hit MAY be Satdy dat he done de WORK of makin man an woman, but from all de signs, he must THOUGHT UP de first man an woman on ol unlucky FRIDAY.

Satdy AW Friday, de Lawd MADE em. Den he made a nice garden an a fine house wid a cool dogtrot faw dem to set in when de sun git hot. "Adam an Eve," he say, "here hit is. Git yo stuff together an move in."

"Thank you kindly, Lawd," say Eve.

"Wait a minute, Lawd," say Adam. "How we gwine pay de rent? You ain't create no money yet, is you?"

De Lawd say, "Don't worry yo haid 'bout dat, Adam. Hit's a free gift faw you an de little woman."

So de man and woman move in an start to red up de house to make hit comfortable to live in. And den de trouble begun.

"Adam," say de woman, "you git de stove put up while I hangs de curtains."

"Whyn't you put up de stove," say Adam, "an me hang de curtains? You's strong as me. De Lawd ain't make neither one of us stronger dan de other. Howcome you always shovin off de heavy stuff on me?"

"Cause dey's man's work and dey's woman's work, Adam," say Eve. "Hit don't look right faw me to do dat heavy stuff."

"Don't look right to who?" say Adam. "Who gwine see hit? You know de ain't no neighbors yet."

Eve stomp de flo. She say, "Jes cause hit ain't no neighbors yet ain't no reason faw us actin trashy behind dey backs, is hit?"

"Ain't dat jes like a woman!" say Adam. Den he sat down and fold his arms. "I ain't gwine put up no stove!" he say. "An dat DAT, woman!"

Next thing he know ol Eve lollop him in de talk-box wid her fist an he fell over backward like a calf hit by lightnin. Den he scramble up an was all over her like a wildcat. Dey bang an scuffle round dere till de house look like a cyclone wind been playin in hit. Neither one could whup, cause de Lawd had laid de same equal strength on dem both.

After while dey's both too wore out to scrap. Eve flop on de baid and start kickin her feets an bawlin. "Why you treat me so mean, Adam?" she holler. "Wouldn't treat a no-count ol hound like you does po me!"

Adam spit out a tooth an try to open de black eye she give him. He say, "If I had a hound dat bang into me like you does, I'd kill him."

But Eve start bawlin so loud, wid de tears jes sopping up de bedclose, dat Adam sneak out of de house. Feelin mighty mean an low, he set round awhile out behind de smokehouse studyin whut better he do. Den he go find de Lawd.

De Lawd say, "Well, Adam? Anything bout de house won't work? Hit's de first one I ever made an hit might have some faults."

Adam shake his head. "De house is prime, Lawd, de HOUSE couldn't be no better dan hit is."

"Whut den, Adam?" say de Lawd.

"To tell de truth," say Adam, "hit's dat Eve woman. Lawd, you made us wid de equal strength and dat's de trouble. I can't git de best of her nohow at all."

De Lawd frown den. "Adam!" he say. "Is you tryin to criticize de Lawd? Course you's of de equal strength. Dat de fair way to make a man an woman so dey both pull in de harness even."

Adam tremble an shake but he so upset an miserble he jes has to keep on. He say, "But Lawd, hit reely ain't equal tween de two of us."

Lawd say, "Be keerful dere, Adam! You is desputin de Lawd smack to de face!"

"Lawd," say Adam, "like you says, we is equal in de strength. But dat woman done found nother way to fight. She start howlin an blubberin to hit make me feel like I's a lowdown scamp. I can't stand dat sound, Lawd. If hit go on like dat, I knows ol Eve gwine always git her way an make me do all de dirty jobs."

"Howcome she learn dat trick?" say de Lawd, lookin like he thinkin hard. "Ain't seed no little ol red man wid hawns an a pitchfawk hangin round de place, is you, Adam?"

"Naw, Lawd. Though I heard Eve talkin wid somebody down in de apple orchard dis mawnin', but she say hit jes de wind blowin. Naw, I ain't seed no red man wid hawns. Who would dat be, anyhow, Lawd?"

"Never you mind, Adam," say de Lawd. "Hmmmmmmmm!"

"Well," say Adam, "dis woman trouble got me down. I sho be much oblige if you makes me stronger dan Eve. Den I can tell her to do a thing an slap her to she do. She do whut she told if she know she gwine git whupped."

"So be hit!" say de Lawd. "Look at yoself, Adam!"

Well Adam look at his arms. Where befo dey was smooth an round, now de muscle bump up like prize yams. Look like hit was two big cawn pones under de skin of his chest an dat chest hit was like a barrel. His belly hit was like a washboard an his laigs was so awful big an downright lumpy dey scared him.

"Thank you kindly, good Lawd!" say Adam. "Watch de woman

mind me now!" So dat Adam high-tail hit home an bust in de back do.

Eve settin down rockin in de rocker. Eve lookin mean. Didn't say a mumblin word when Adam come struttin in. Jes look at him, jes retch down in de woodbox faw a big stick of kindlin.

"Drap dat stick, woman!" say Adam.

"Say who?" say de woman! "Who dat talkin big round here?" Wid dat, she jump on him an try to hammer his haid down wid de stick.

Adam jes laugh an grab de stick an heave hit out de window. Den he give her a lazy little slap dat sail her clean cross de room. "Dat who sayin hit, sugar!" he say.

"My feets must slip aw somethin," say Eve. "An you de one gwine pay faw hit out of yo hide, Adam!"

So de woman come up clawin an kickin an Adam pick her up an whop her down.

"Feets slip agin, didn't dey?" say Adam.

"Hit must be I couldn't see good where you is in dis dark room," say Eve. She riz up an feather into him agin.

So Adam he pick her up an thow her on de baid. Fo she know whut, he start laying hit on wid de flat of his hand cross de big end of ol Eve. Smack her wid one hand, hold her down wid tother.

Fo long Eve bust out bawlin. She say, "Please quit dat whackin me, Adam honey! Aw please, honey!"

"Is I de boss round here?" say Adam.

"Yas, honey," she say. "You is de haid man boss."

"Aw right," he tell her. "I is de boss. De lawd done give me de mo power of us two. From now on an den some, you mind me, woman! Whut I jes give you ain't nothin but a little hum. Next time I turn de whole song loose on you."

He give Eve a shove an say, "Fry me some catfish, woman."

"Yas, Adam honey," she say.

But ol Eve was mad enough to bust. She wait till Adam catchin little nap. Den she flounce down to de orchard where dey's a big ol apple tree wid a cave tween de roots. She look round till she sho ain't nobody see her, den she stick her haid in de cave an holler.

Now, hit MAY be de wind blowin an hit MAY been a bird, but hit sho sound like somebody in dat cave talkin wid Eve. Eve

she sound like she sayin, "Yas-Yas-Yas. You means on which wall? De east wall? Oh! Aw right."

Anyhow, Eve come back to de house all smilin to herself like she know somethin. She powerful sweet to Adam de rest of de day.

So next mawnin Eve go an find de Lawd.

Lawd say, "You agin, Eve? Whut can I do faw you?"

Eve smile an drap a pretty curtsy. "Could you do me a little ol favor, Lawd?" say Eve.

"Name hit, Eve," say de Lord.

"See dem two little ol rusty keys hangin on dat nail on de east wall?" Eve say. "If you ain't usin em I wish I had dem little ol keys."

"I declare!" say de Lawd. "I done fawgot dey's hangin dere. But, Eve, dey don't fit nothin. Found em in some junk an think maybe I find de locks dey fit some day. Dey been hangin on dat nail ten million years an I ain't found de locks yet. If you want em, take em. Ain't doin me no good."

So Eve take de two keys an thank de Lawd an trot on home. Dere was two dos dere without no keys an Eve find dat de two rusty ones fit.

"Aaah!" she say. "Here's de locks de Lawd couldn't find. Now, Mister Adam, we see who de boss!" Den she lock de two dos and hide de keys.

Fo long Adam come out of de garden. "Gimme some food, woman!" he say.

"Can't Adam," say Eve. "De kitchen do's locked."

"I fix dat!" say Adam. So he try to bust de kitchen do down. But de Lawd bilt dat do an Adam can't even scratch hit.

Eve say, "Well, Adam honey, if you go out in de woods an cut some wood faw de fire, I maybe can git de kitchen do open. Maybe I can put one dem cunjur tricks on hit. Now, run long, honey, an git de wood."

"Wood choppin is yo work," say Adam, "since I got de most strenth. But I do hit dis once an see can you open de do."

So he git de wood an when he come back, Eve has de do open. An from den on out Eve kept de key to de kitchen and made Adam haul in de wood.

Well, after supper Adam say, "Come on honey, les you an me

hit de froghair."

"Can't," say Eve. "De baidroom do is locked."

"Dadblame!" say Adam. "Reckon you can trick dat do too, Eve?"

"Might can," say Eve. "Honey, you jes git a piece of tin an patch dat little hole in de roof an while you's doin hit, maybe I can git de baidroom do open."

So Adam patched de roof an Eve she unlocked de baidroom do. From den on she kept DAT key an used hit to suit herself.

So dat de reason, de very reason, why de mens THINKS dey is de boss an de wimmen KNOWS dey is boss, cause dey got dem two little keys to use in dat slippery sly wimmen's way. Yas, fawever mo an den some!

An if you dont' know DAT already, you ain't no married man.

HE HEARD THE BULLET TWICE

IN THE trial of a Negro for shooting at another, a lawyer examining one of the parties said, "You say that when the defendant pulled his gun you began to run. How did you know that he was shooting at you?"

"I heard de gun fire, en I heard de bullet when it passed me."

"Are you absolutely sure that you heard the bullet pass you?"

"Yes, I'm sure I heard dat bullet pass me, 'cause I heard it twice."

"You say you heard the bullet *twice*. How could that be possible?"

"Well, it was jes lack dis—I heard de bullet when it passed me, en I heard it again when I passed it."

MOTHER WIT

DURING a battle a general of a colored regiment noticed one of his men seemed to be devoted to him and followed him everywhere. At

length he remarked, "Well, my man, you have stuck by me well during this engagement."

"Yes, sir," said the soldier, "my mama back in Alabama told me to stick with the generals and I'd never get hurt."

WHO DAT DARKEN DE HOLE?

Two cullud gentlemens wuz er-walkin' through de big woods er-huntin' rabbits, en dey seed er little cub bear run in de holler uv er great big tree. Dey tried to git 'em out, but couldn't.

Den one uv de hunters sed, "You keep er watch-out en I'll crawl up in de holler uv de tree en fotch 'em out."

De udder one sed all right, en de fust one got down on his han's and knees en crawled up inside de tree. Jes' den ole mammy bear seed 'em en made er break for her den. De watcher seed her jes' in time to grab her by de tail jes' ez she got her head in de hole, en he wuz er-holdin' on wid all his might while de ole bear wuz er-tryin' her bes' to git in de tree.

Der hunter inside wuz skeered by the racket en said, "Who dat darken de hole?"

De udder one holdin' wid all his might answered, "Ef dis tail holt slip, yer will find out who darken de hole."

LULA

TAD: I 'clare to God, Lula tickled me today.

VOICE: How come?

TAD: She been to de doctor. Say she been ailin' a good while, an' she tell de doctor she wants a zamination. An' de doctor put her on a table an' zamine her an' tell her she need to be operate on. An' Lula say:

"How much is you charge me for tellin' me dis?"

An' de doctor tell her two dollars. An' she say:
"Here's you' money. Good day, sir."
An' de doctor tell her hold on, how 'bout de operation.
An' Lula say:
"I ain' guh hab no operation."
An' de doctor say:
"It is very important. You has a serious trouble."
An' Lula say:
"I ain' guh hab no operation."
An' de doctor say:
"Ef you ain' operate on, you guh die."
An' Lula say:
"Good day, sir. I reckon I'll hab to go to my Jesus by myself."
scip: Lula got more sense dan I gee her credit for.

RUINT

tad: Is you hear de tale 'bout Ella?
voice: Wuh Ella?
tad: Ella up to de white folks' yard.
voice: Wuh 'bout Ella?
tad: You know Ella been raise up mighty proper. She ain't run
'round wid no mens. Ack like she ain' got no use for 'em.
scip: I ain' never pay no 'tention to no lie like dat. She ooman,
ain' she? Mens is mens, ain' dey?
tad: Well, she ack dat er way.
scip: She ack dat er way.
voice: Wuh de tale?
tad: It ain' no tale. Ella been a apple in de white folks' yard.
Dey 'pend on her. An' atter she been dere God knows how long,
she disappear an' ain' say a word an ain't nobody know wey Ella.
Well, all dese colored folks had a excursion an' went to Wilming-
ton, an' Janey—you know old man Jube' gal Janey—say she went on
de excursion an' been standin' on de street cornder waitin' for de
street car. An' she say she see a ooman all dress up wid fine clothes

an' high-heel shoes wid ribbon all over her, an' more paint an' talcum powder 'an you ever heared of. An' she look at her an' she say it look like somebody she know. An' Janey say she walk up a little closer an' take her time an' look good. An' she say she walk up to de ooman an say:

"Ain't dis Ella?"

An' de gal say:

"Sho, dis Ella."

An' Janey say:

"In de name er God, wey you been? Everybody been axen 'bout you."

An' Ella say:

"Ain't you hear de news? I been ruint."

Do You Call That a Preacher?

Do you call that a preacher?
Oh, no!
Do you call that a preacher?
Oh, no!
Do you call that a preacher?
Oh, no!
Scandalize my name!

THE FARMER AND G.P.C.

ONE time dere was a man what was a farmer. One year he had a real good crop. But dis man was kinda lazy, and when it come time to gather de crop he tole ole lady dat he could not he'p gather de crop cause he felt de Lord was callin' him to go preach. He tole her to look up in de sky, and he pointed out de letters G P C, which he say meant, "Go Preach Christ" and he had to go.

139

But de ole lady she was too much fer him. "Dose letters don' mean, 'Go Preach Christ,' " she said. "Dey mean, 'Go Pick Cotton.' "

THE SUPERFLUOUS BRAINS

ONE time dare was a man studyin' to be a minister and he brain went bad. So he go to de doctor. De doctor 'vised dat he see a speshlist. De speshlist say dat he need a brain operation. He say dat de brain got to come out and be scraped and retimed. So de man he left de brain dare and went away. He 'sposed to come back in a few days for the brain, but he never come back. Few days later de speshlist see de man on de streets weavin' back an' fo'th. So de speshlist ast him why he never come back for he brain. Say it been ready for days now. De man say that he could keep it. Say when he come in with de bad brain he was studyin' to be a minister and he needed he brain, but now he's 'cided to be a doctor and he won't need it.

THE THREE PREACHERS

THERE was a big Baptist state convention. The delegates was so numerous they couldn't hardly take care of all of them. And there was three preachers left didn't have nowhere to stay, a Baptist preacher, a Methodist preacher, and a Presbyterian preacher. The lady told them she had fixed a room in a nearby house (she didn't tell them it was hanted), and they could take their meals with her.

They came for meeting that night and set down and begin to talk. Eventually the hants commenced to coming in. The Baptist preacher began singing. The more he sang the more the hants came in. The Presbyterian preacher he begin praying. And the more he prayed the more the hants come in. He says to the Methodist preacher, "Now doc, it's your floor." And the Methodist preacher, say, "Let's take up a collection," and the hants begin to leave.

THE PREACHER AND HIS FARMER BROTHER

OF OCCASION in de bottoms, in de same fam'ly you kin fin' some of de bestes' preachuhs dat done evuh grace a pulpit, an' a brothuh or a sistuh what ain't nevuh set foot in de chu'ch ez long ez dey live. Ah calls to min' Revun Jeremiah Sol'mon what pastuh de Baptis' chu'ch down to Egypt, on Caney Creek. He done put on de armuh of de Lawd when he rech fo'teen; he come to be a deacon when he rech sixteen, an' dey 'dained 'im for to preach de Word when he turnt to be eighteen. He one of de mos' pow'ful preachuhs dat done evuh grace a Texas pulpit an' he de moderatuh of de St. John's 'Sociation. But he hab a brothuh, what go by de name of Sid, what ain't nevuh set foot in a chu'ch house in his life.

Sid hab a good spot of lan' roun' bout Falls, on de Brazos, though; so one time Revun Jeremiah 'cide to pay Sid a visit. Hit been twenty yeah since he laid eyes on 'im; so he driv up to de house an' soon ez he gits thoo shakin' han's wid Sid's wife, Lulu Belle, an' de chilluns, he say, "Ah wants to see yo' fawm, Sid. Le's see what kinda fawmuh you is."

"Sho," say Sid. So he gits his hat on an' dey goes down to de cawn patch an' looks at de cawn Sid done planted an' what nelly 'bout grown, an' de Revun say, "Sid, youse got a putty good cawn crop by de he'p of de Lawd." Den dey goes on down to de cotton patch and de Revun looks at hit an' 'low, "Sid, youse got a putty good cotton crop by de he'p of de Lawd." Den dey moseys on down to de sugah cane patch an' when de Revun eye dis, he say, "Sid, youse got a putty good cane patch, by de he'p of de Lawd."

An' when he say dis, Sid eye 'im kinda disgusted lack, an' say, "Yeah, but you oughta seed hit when de Lawd had it by Hisse'f."

A JOB FOR GOD

AH CALLS to min' two han's on de old Babb planuhtation on de Lowuh Brazos what was cuttin' logs on de wes' side of de rivuh to buil' a bawn on de boss-man's premisus. Dey cut de cypress trees down on de wes' side an' brung de logs 'cross to de eas' side on a li'l' ole row boat. Hit wasn't far from de Gulf an' of occasion a alluhgattuh comed up in de back wattah, but de ain't seed one in dese paa'ts for quite a spell. Anyhow, dese two han's, Tim Groce an' Steve Risby, done been to chu'ch de Sunday 'fo' de staa't to bringing' de logs crost de rivuh, an' dey heahs Elduh Sample, de pastuh of Mothuh Mt. Zion Chu'ch, say, "Gawd so lacked de worl' in sich a way, dat he done sen' de onlies' son he got down to de urf so dat dem what believe on 'im gonna be saved."

Dat sermon stay on Steve's min'. He don' forgit hit. So Tim an' Steve been cuttin' down de cypress trees an' bringin' de logs 'cross de rivuh for four days now, an' dey ain't seed nor heerd tell of no alluhgatuh yit, but when dey staa't back crost de rivuh wid dey las' load dat Friday, what was de thirteenth of de mont'—dat's a bad luck day, you knows—anyways, dey spy sump'n or 'nothuh swimmin' to'a'ds 'em from de Gulf. "What's day?" say Tim. "Looks lack a allugattuh," say Steve. 'N' sho' nuff, 'fo' you c'd say, "amen," de allugattuh done rech de boat an' turn hit ovuh an' lit out to swimmin' attuh Steve an' Tim. Tim 'bout to git away, but de allugattuh gainin' on Steve all de time; so Steve calls to min' what de preachuh say, and he pray:

"Gawd, Ah knows youse got a habit of sen'in' you' son down heah to do yo' work, but Ah wanna tell you rat now, don' you come sen'in' yo' son down heah now, you come down heah you'se'f, 'caze savin' me from dis alluhgatttuh is a man's job."

LITTLE BILL'S CONVERSATION WITH GOD

DE YOUNGUNS on de planuhtations in de Bottoms was plenty smaa't. Dey take 'vantage of dey pappies an' mammies bein' so wropped up in de Word and de chu'ch till dey study all kinds of devulmint to git outen work by dey wits. When dey don' wanna work 'roun' de house, chop cordwood, dry dishes, feed de cows, or tote wattuh from de well, or de pump, dey allus go an' git de Bible an' staa't to readin' hit, or de Sunday School quarterly. Den when dey mammies ast 'em to do sump'n 'roun' de house, dey say, "Mammy, Ah's readin' de Word; Ah wanna be a good Christun lack you an' pappy an' work in de chu'ch, an' de Word'll gimme dat information to go thoo. Ah heerd de pastuh say evuhbody ought to set down an' keep comp'ny wid Gawd durin' of de weekadays ez well ez on a Sunday." Dis heah kind of talk allus meck dey mammies happy, 'cauze dey ain't nothin' dey lack bettuh 'n habin' dey chilluns hab a love for de chu'ch. So de younguns allus git out of work in dis wise.

Oncet dere was a li'l' yap down to Chinaberry Grove on de ole Lee fawm name' Bill what hab dis style down pat. He gib his pappy a hot time all de time by stealin' tea cakes outen de flow'r sack full dat his mammy done bake; an' he lie on de othuh li'l' chilluns in de house evuh day de Lawd sen' 'bout sump'n. Dey hab a ole rickety cawn crib next to his pappy's shack, so evuh time he lie his pappy tell 'im to go on up in de lof' of de cawn crib an 'ast de Lawd to forgib 'im. So Bill would go on up in de lof' in de cawn crib an' stay 'bout two or three hours at a time. Tom, his pappy, allus ast him huccome he stay up in de lof' so long. Den Bill would say, "Hit tuck a long time for me to git de message thoo. Gawd a busy man, ain't he, pappy?"

Bill allus lie de fuss thing in de mawnin' jes' 'fo' dey staa't to de fiel', 'caze he know his pappy gonna sen' 'im to de lof' to ast Gawd to forgib 'im for de lie he done tole, an' he kin dodge work dat mawnin'. He allus lolluhgag in de lof' long ez he kin. Dis sho'

'nuff Bad Religion li'l' Bill, practicin', but his pappy Tom jes' ez 'sponsibul as li'l' Bill be; he didn't oughta sen' 'im to de lof' to pray.

So when his pappy call 'im to come to breakfast, he comes on in an' staa't to soppin' his biscuit in his 'lasses an' one-eyed gravy, an' fin'ly he look up at his pappy an' say, "Pappy, one dem lions must of got loose up dere at de circus yestiddy; Ah looked outen de window jes' now an' seed a lion crossin' de lane goin' up to'a'ds de mule lot."

"You git rat up from heah," say Tom, his pappy, "An' go rat up in de lof' an' ast de Lawd to forgib you. You know dat ain't nuthin' but Ole Lady Jackson's shaggy dog you seed." So Bill gits up from de table an' goes up to de lof' in de cawn crib. He don' come down no mo' till de dinnuh time bell soun'. Den he come an' tuck his seat on de bench at de table 'side his ol'es' brothuh on one side an' his pappy on de othuh. When his pappy spy 'im, he say, "Bill, is you done gone up to de lof' an' ast de Lawd to forgib you lack Ah done tole you?"

"Yas, suh," say Bill.

"What'd he say?" asts Tom.

"What'd he say?" 'low Bill. "He say, 'Go 'long boy, Ah thought dat was a lion mahse'f.'"

REVEREND CARTER'S TWELFTH
ANNIVERSARY SERMON

'BOUT ten years attuh freedom done come in de Bottoms de membuhship gits pow'ful good to de pastuhs what done tuck 'em down from hangin' out on de promise limb an' brung 'em to dat condition whar dey git dat whole thing lack de Word say, an' de Lawd stick up to 'em, 'caze he glory in de style dey done tuck up wid.

Dey hab poun' paa'ties whar evuhbody brung a poun' o' victuals to de pastuh evuh mont', an' dey staa't de style of de annuhversury sermon, lackwise. De annuhversury sermon come oncet a yeah so de membuhship kin help de pastuh 'long wid his duds ez well ez

his grub. Dey 'low he haftuh hab sump'n nothuh on his back ez well ez in his stummick. Dey gibs 'im a li'l' money too, an' of occasion, he gits a right smaa't in de collection when dey pass de hat 'roun' mongst de membuhs.

One o'dese preachuhs in de Bottoms what been pastuhin' mought' nigh on to twelve yeahs when dey staa't off dis fashion was name Elduh Neal. He de pastuh of de Ball Hill Baptis' Chu'ch what hab a small membuhship, so he don' speck much outen de han's what b'long to his chu'ch. He got a good sermon though. So when de Sunday 'roll 'roun' for 'im to preach his twelfth annuhversury sermon he dike up in his frocktail coat, his stan'in' collar, an' his high silk hat an' staa'ts to walking thoo de thickets to de chu'ch house wid his Bible in his han'. He doin' what dey calls "cuttin' buddy short." (Dat mean, teckin' a short cut thoo de woods, so you git whar you goin' lots quicker'n goin' way 'roun' de dirt road). But he ain't done had bettuh tuck dis heah fashion of gittin' to chu'ch, 'caze 'fo' he trace his footsteps ver' far, he look up an' see a white man a straddle of de lane he walkin' down on a white hoss wid a cap an' ball in his han'. When Elduh Neal spy de man he try to dodge 'im an go thoo de cawn patch, but de white man call 'im back an' say, "Hol' on a minnit, Elduh; Ah wants you to dance a li'l' bit for me."

"Ah ain't gonna do no such thing," say Elduh Neal; "Ah done put away dem sinful things long time ago."

"Aw, come on," say de white man, slingin' two caps an' balls, one in one han' an' one in de othuh; "Ah'll gib you a ten dolluh bill if'n you do a li'l' step for me."

"Well, awright den," 'low Revun Neal, eyen' de caps and balls de man got pointed at 'im an' peekin' at de ten dolluh bill de white man holdin' tween his thumb. "Ah ain't got much for time though," say Elduh Neal, "but Ah'll do a li'l' step for you bein' dat's de case." So no quicker'n he say dis he clicks his heels togedduh an' do a li'l' jig.

De white man gib 'im de ten dolluh bill an' Revun Neal staa't on down de lane again to'a'ds de chu'ch house. He ain't gone ver' far though 'fo' he wheel 'roun' rail quick an' squall out to de white man to wait a minnit, he wanna tell 'im sump'n. So de white man stop his hoss smack dab in his tracks an' wait for Elduh Neal to

ketch up wid 'im.

"What you want?" say de white man when Revun Neal git 'longst 'side 'im.

"Ah jes' wanna tell you," say Revun Neal, "dat Ah'll be heah evuh Sunday at ten-thuhty from now on."

THE WRONG MAN IN THE COFFIN

You know de chu'ch folks in de Bottoms hab a love for big funerals. 'Reckly attuh freedom, dey hab de funerals on Sunday, 'caze de boss-mens don' 'low no funerals in de week-a-days. Nowadays, dey hab al funerals on a Sunday jes' for de sake of de love of big funerals.

In dem days comin' up, womens ain't gonna talk 'bout dey men folks while dey's livin'. Dey wanna keep folks thinkin' dey hab a good man for a husband, but dese days an' times hit's a lot diffunt. De gals what ma'ied nowadays talk 'bout dey husbands to any an' evuhbody. You can heah 'em all de time talkin' 'bout "dat ole scoun'al ain't no 'count." Dey say, "If'n you been ma'ied a yeah an' yo' husband ain't nevuh paid a light bill, ain't nevuh bought a sack of flour, ain't nevuh brung you a pair of stockin's, ain't never paid on de insu'ances, what you think 'bout a scoun'al lack dat?"

One time dere was a han' what died on de old McPherson fawm by de name of Ken Parker. De membuhship of de Salem Baptis' Chu'ch think Ken's a good man, 'caze he hab a fine big family an' he 'ten' chu'ch regluh as de Sundays come. De pastuh think he a Good Christun, too. So when he git up to preach Ken's funeral, he tell 'bout what a good man Brothuh Ken was, 'bout how true he was to his wife, an' what a good providuh he done been for his family an' all lack dat. He keep on an' keep on in dis wise, but Ken's wife Sadie know de pastuh done errored; so she turn to de ol'es' boy, Jim, an' say, "Jim, go up dere an' look in dat coffin an' see if'n dat's yo' pappy in dere."

WHAT MAJOR BUFORD KNEW

DE WORD ain't nothin' to joke wid, but some of de brothuhs an' sistuhs in de chu'ch so full of devulmint till dey allus meckin' light of de chu'ch in some fashion or nothuh. Ah calls to min' a ole man what use to come ovuh here constant to paa'lance wid me 'fo' his daughtuh move offen de plannuhtation dat's way yonnuh pas' de li'l' rivuh. Dat's de ole Bass plannuhtation, an' dis heah ole brothuh, what was called Major Buford, was allus doin' sump'n nothuh to tease de sistuhs, or to opset de pastuh an' de deacon boa'd of de Mt. Gilead Chu'ch ovuh to Satan, a li'l' ole community on de rivuh bed. Seem lack de Major got some of de name of dis place Satan in his bones. De place call Satan, an' de Major got de Devul in 'im all de time.

One Sunday he passes a bunch of li'l' ole boys on de planuhtation playin' marbles for keeps. So he ast 'em dey names an' writ 'em down on a paper bag he hab in his han' an' brung 'em fore de deacon boa'd for trial. De Major say de parent 'sponsible for de chile till he come to be sebun yeahs ole; so all dese li'l' boys was five an' six an' dey pappies had to 'ten' de meetin' wid dey chilluns. When dey all done 'sembled, Revun Galloway, de pastuh, say, "Brothuh Buford, what's de 'ditement 'gainst dese chillun?"

"Dey was playin' marbles on a Sunday for keeps," 'low de Major, "an' de Bible say, 'Don' do dat!'"

"Show us whar 'bouts in de Holy Writ do hit say not to play marbles," 'low one of de papies of de li'l' boys, name Silas Andrews.

"Awright," de Major reply, "Ah'm gonna turn to hit rat now." So he turns ovuh to a passage of Scriptur' an' han' hit to de pastuh an' tell 'im to read what hit say.

De pastuh tuck up de Bible an', lookin' at de passage de Major hab mark, turnt back 'round to'a'ds de Major an' say, "Look heah, Brothuh Buford, dis passage don't say 'Marble not,' dis heah passage say 'Marvel not.'"

"Huh, Ah knowed hit all de time," chuckled de Major. "Huccome

you didn' know?"

"Nothuh time we was all in a Sunday School teachuhs' meetin' an' evuhbody haftuh ast a question 'bout de Word. So when Major Buford's turn come, he say, "Who kin tell me de name of de dog what lick Lazarus' sores?" Dis heah puzzle evuhbody, ebun down to de pastuh. So fin'ly dey say, "We gibs up. What was his name?"

"Look a heah," say de Major openin' de Word an' p'intin' to a verse. "Don't you see whar hit say heah 'Mo Rover de dog lick Lazrus' sores'?"

But de Major git de bigges' kick outen teasin' de sistuhs. Dey 'low he bettuh stop playin' wid de Lawd's Word lack he do, too. If'n he don', sump'n gonna happen to 'im, but de Major he 'low dat he don' mean no haa'm.

One Sunday de Major cap de climax sho' nuff wid his foolishness. 'Twas attuh de lebun o'clock servus an' ez usual he walks ovuh to whar a big bunch of sistuhs am stan'in' 'roun', an' he say, "Gawd knows evuhthing an' Ah knows mo'."

De sistuhs look at 'im lack dey think he done lose his min'. Talkin' 'bout Gawd knows evuhthing an' he knows mo'; dat's de wus religion dey done evuh heerd of; so dey say, "Gawd know evuhthing an' you knows mo'?"

"Yeah," says de Major, "Gawd knows evuhthing an' Ah knows Mo'. Ah knows ole man Billy Mo'." An' when he say dis you could heah him laff plum on down to de commissary, clean on crost de big rivuh an' de li'l' rivuh, up to de Pos'-oak district.

HOW ELDER SAMUELS WAS SAVED

AH CALLS to min' a preachuh down to Eloise what allus tellin' his membuhship to ast de Lawd for evuh thing dey wants an' de Lawd'll gib hit to 'em. He been preachin' in dis heah fashion for ten yeahs now, but he ain't put his teachin' into practice, 'caze him an' de membuhship still worshipin' unnuh de same ole arbor what got a dirt floor an' no walls on de side. Hit do putty good for de summuh servuses, but when de fall of de yeah roll 'roun' an' de

northuhs staa't to blowin' dey cain't in no wise hab servuses in hit, 'caze dey ain't no place to put a wood heater.

De membuhship fin'ly gits tiahed of Elduh Samuels' (dat's de name de preachuh go by) trying to 'vise 'em to ast de Lawd for what dey wants an' he'll gib hit to 'em, 'caze he ain't yit ast de Lawd to build 'em no chu'ch house in de whole ten yeahs he been pastuhin' de chu'ch. So one night when dey was havin' boa'd meetin', one de deacons name Henry Sample say, "Look a heah, Elduh, you allus tellin' us to ast de Lawd for what we wants an' he'll gib hit to us. Huccome you don' ast de Lawd to gib us a new chu'ch house?"

"Dat sho' am de truf, Brothuh Sample," 'low de elduh, "so Ah'm gonna ast de Lawd rat now to gib us a chu'ch house." So Elduh Samuels gits down on his knees an' pray an' ast de Lawd to please gib 'em a chu'ch house to worship in. So dat same night he ast all de deacons to go 'roun' from membuh to membuh's house an' ast all of 'em to gib a piece of lumbuh, a package of shingles, a keg of nails, or sump'n 'nothuh to he'p staa't buildin' de chu'ch.

When de nex' boa'd meetin' rolled 'roun' de deacons hab 'nuff lumbuh, an' nails an' shingles to buil' putty nice li'l' ole chu'ch house; so dey 'cides to staa't buildin' de chu'ch house dat nex' comin' week. Dey ain't in no wise got 'nuff money to hire no carpenter, so dey 'sides to use all de men membuhs of de chu'ch to he'p wid de buildin'. Elduh Samuels 'low he ain't no jack-leg carpenter hisse'f, but he gonna do ez much work ez de nex' one on de chu'ch. He 'low, "Ain't Ah done tole y'all dat de Lawd allus gib you what you asts for an' allus tech keer of you in de time of trouble?"

"Sho' Elduh, sho'," say de deacons. "Evuhthing you say done come to pass."

So time rolled on an' rolled on till de li'l' ole chu'ch house almos' ready to go into. De onlies' thing lef' for de workers to do is to finish shinglin' de roof, an' Elduh Samuels workin' rat 'long wid 'em on de chu'ch puttin' on de shingles.

Evuhthing was goin' fine an' in tip-top shape till one day when Elduh Samuels was runnin' his mouf an' braggin' 'bout all you got to do is trus' Gawd an' He'll teck keer of you, he loosed his balance an' staa'ted fallin' off de roof of de chu'ch house. "He'p me, Lawd,

he'p me!" yelled Elduh Samuels ez he falled; "You knows Ah trus' you an' you knows Ah knows you'll tech keer of me." But 'fo' Elduh Samuels kin git de words outen his mouf good, a nail stickin' way far out on one de walls of de chu'ch ketches 'im in de seat of de pants an' hol's 'im. So Elduh Samuels looks up at de ceilin' of de chu'ch an' yells loud as he kin yell, "Nevuh min' Gawd; a nail's got me now."

SISTER LIZA AND THE NEW PASTOR

AH CALLS to min' Sistuh Liza Johnson, what b'longed to de Pilgrim Baptist Chu'ch, down on de ole Timson plannuhtation, on the Big Brazos. Sistuh Liza hab a husban' what go by de name of Mose, what used to backslide all de time, but Sistuh Liza don' in no wise 'low nobody to lay Ole Mose's race out to her. She a good payin' membuh, so de preachuhs don' nevuh chu'ch Ole Mose an' teck his name offen de books, don' give a nevuhmin' how much he cuss an' cavort an' shoot craps up an' down de Bottoms. De preachuhs pays heed to de money Sistuh Liza th'ows in de colleckshun plate evuh Sunday de Lord sen' an' dey 'lows Ole Mose to be sho' 'nuff gone to de Devul ez far ez dey is concerned.

Well, suh, things rolled on in dis wise for many a yeah till a rail young preachuh comed to pastuh de chu'ch. Dis rail young preachuh ain't in no wise sold on keepin' Ole Mose's name on de chu'ch rolls wid 'im gallavantin' up an' down de Bottoms gamblin' and cavortin' evuh day de Lawd sen's, so he sen's Ole Mose a letter puttin' 'im outen de chu'ch. Sistuh Liza so riled 'bout what de new preachuh done dat she don' jar loose from no money no mo' when dey passes de colleckshun plate 'roun', but she still 'tendin' de chu'ch servuses.

But hit so happen dat reckly aftuh de new preachuh done lit in de Bottoms an' chu'ched Ole Mose dat Mose came down wid de dropsy an' had to stay cooped up in de house, 'caze he done growed so big an' fat he can't ebun wobble 'roun' de room he's forced to set in all de time. He plagued wid de misery so bad 'till 'tain't long 'fo' he kicks de bucket. Sistuh Liza ast de new preachuh to preach Ole

Mose's funeral, but de preachuh, what go by de name of Elduh Freeman, don' in no wise want to falsify Ole Mose into heabun. But Sistuh Liza cry an' git down on her knees an' beg Elduh Freeman so ha'ad to preach de funeral, since Mose been livin' rat 'roun' heah in de Bottoms all his life, till Elduh Freeman give in to her an' say he'll do de job, but he ver' careful 'bout what he say 'bout Ole Mose. When hit comed time for 'im to put Ole Mose in heabun Elduh Freeman riz up his haid an' his hands an' say, "Brothuhs an' Sistuhs, Ah ain't been heahin' no good repo'ts 'bout de deceased since Ah's been down heah in de Bottoms, so Ah's jes' gonna put 'im on de Jordan, an' let whosoevuh wants 'im, Gawd or de Devul, come an' git 'im."

Dis meck Sistuh Liza pow'ful mad, an' she 'low dat if'n hit tecks her de res' of her nachul bawn days she gonna git ebun wid Elduh Freeman for what he done did to Ole Mose.

So time rolled on, an' rolled on till fin'ly one Sunday de haid-knocker of de Baptist convention comed to visit Elduh Freeman's Chu'ch to spy on 'im an' see how he feedin' de sheep in his flock. Sistuh Liza say to herself, "Now's de time for me to git ebun wid Elduh Freeman for what he done did to Mose, so rat aftuh Elduh Freeman done tuck his tex' for de mawnin' an' was gittin' all warmed up for de finishin' stretch of his sermon Sistuh Liza riz up outen her seat an' yelled, "Hol' on dere a minute Elduh! Ah wants to tell mah determination."

Elduh Freeman eye her lack he could tar her to pieces for stoppin' 'im rat in de middle of his message when he tryin' so ha'ad to show de big-shot preachuh from de convention what a big hol' he got on de membuhship, so he gits mad as a hornet an' yells, "Well, tell hit Sistuh! tell hit!"

"Ah cain't tell hit now," 'low Sistuh Liza; "Ah'm too full."

"You heerd what Ah said, didn't you, Sistuh Johnson?" yelled Elduh Freeman; "Now you go on an' tell hit."

"Ah done told you Ah too full to tell hit, too, ain't Ah?" 'low Sistuh Liza.

"Too full of what?" yelled Elduh Freeman, "De Holy Sperrit?"

"No Sirree Bob!" shouted Sistuh Liza loud as she kin holler; "too full of dat clabber milk Ah drunk dis mawnin!"

THE OLD PREACHER'S WILL AND
THE YOUNG WIFE

SOME of de ole time preachuhs in de Bottoms was good managers. Some of dem come to be well fixed wid lan' an' de lack. Dey do de membuhship some good an' deyse'f some good, lackwise. Lots of 'em bargained for de Bottom lan' when hit was sellin' for two an' three dollars a acre. Ah calls to min' Elduh Warren down to Mussel Run Creek. He de pastuh of de onlies' Foot Washin' Baptis' chu'ch in de Bottoms. So de han's what lack dis style of 'ligion comed from evuhwhichuhwhar to Revun Warren's chu'ch. Dis meck 'im hab a pow'ful big membuhship.

He staa't to preachin' when he in his late sixties, so 'tain't long 'fo his health staa't to failin' fas'. He hab a young wife for a secon' wife, an' she wan' im to be sicker'n he is. So she calls all de chilluns 'roun' Elduh Warren's bedside one day an' she say, "Youse sinkin' fas', Elduh Warren; you oughta meck yo' will."

"Awright, honey," say Revun Warren. "Git a pencil an' a tablet an' run an' git Deacon Moore to come ovuh heah rail quick." So de littles' boy runned an' got Deacon Moore an' Miz Warren gits a pencil an' a tablet an' Revun Warren staa'ts to meckin' his will. He say, "Oh, Lawd, Ah mecks dis as mah las' will an' testuhmint an' Ah hopes hit'll be mah las' will. Ah wants mah wife to hab de two hunnud an' fifty acres of black lan' on de hill; an' de two spans of black mules, Ah wants dem to go to mama, too. De five hunnud acres of Bottom lan' Ah wants mama to hab dat. Ah wants her to hab de chariot an' de two surreys."

"Chillun," say de young wife, "jes come heah an' lissen to yo' pappy; he's sho' dyin' wid his good senses."

"We's got lots of milk cows," say Revun Warren. "Ah wants mama to teck de ones dat's in de uppuh pasture, an' de chillun de ones in de lowuh pasture."

"Lissen, chillun, lissen," say de young wife. "Yo' pappy sho' is dyin' wid his good senses."

"Ah got three thousan' dollars in de bank," say Revun Warren. "Give de chilluns one thousan', an' Ah wants mama to hab two thousan'."

"Now, wife," say he, "Ah'm de one what's de writer of dis will; Ah hopes dis will be mah final an' las' will. An' now, mama, Ah don't nevuh wan' you to marry no mo'."

When Revun Warren say dis, Miz Warren jump straight up from de chair she settin' in an' yell loud as she kin, "Run an' git de Doctuh, chillun, quick! Yo' pappy's talkin' out of his haid again!"

FUTURE WORLD DIFFICULTIES

MANY preachers of a generation ago, and too many of those of the present generation, have spent most of their time and energy describing the beatitudes of heaven and the torments of hell. Some of the old-timers became so expert in their knowledge of the future world that they could even give details of its architecture and landscaping. Some wag facetiously suggested that such sermons accounted for the former high death rate of the colored population: that hearing such glowing accounts of "heaven," they were all making a grand rush to get there.

There was the old black parson who used to describe both heaven and hell in great detail, as a "four-square city wid de streets all gold, an' jasper walls, an' pearly gates, an' spires, an' temples, an' angels." His descriptions were so vivid that some of the sisters, going into various ecstacies and spasms and contortions, declared that they could fairly hear the flapping of the angels' wings.

And after the sermon was over and the collection was being taken, a devilish young fellow who had been seated in the rear of the church, came forward and dropped a "whole half" dollar into the collection. He seemed to think that this big donation gave him at least the right to ask the pastor a question. And so, stepping back a pace, he knitted his brow into a pretense of sincere puzzlement and said:

"Mr. Pastor, I sho' enj'yed yo' sermon dis mawnin', 'bout all dem anjuls wid all dem wings. But dere's one thing in yo' sermon what puzzles me, an' I wants to ax you 'bout it. Whut puzzles me, an' whut I wants to know, is: When I gits to hebben, how in de worl' is I ever gwine ter git my shirt on over all dem wings?"

But the old parson not only had a gift for humor but he was also a good sport. He therefore looked over his spectacles at the boy, and replied:

"Look hyeah, boy, don' you be axin' no sich fool questions as dat in dis church,—'cause in de fust place, when you dies, dat ain't a-gwine to be yo' problem nohow. When you dies, yo' problem's gwine to be: How in de worl' is you ever gwine to git yo' hat on over yo' horns! Dat's whut's gwine to be yo' problem."

PAYING AGAIN FOR THE SAME GOODS

IN THE days of Bookei T. Washington there was war in a colored church in the country near Tuskegee. As usual, they asked Washington to come out and act as judge and pacificator. After hearing a few speeches by members of the congregation, he discovered that the trouble had arisen over the refusal of the church to pay the pastor his salary.

"Now," said Washington, "the pastor's salary ought to be paid. That is just common morality. The rest of us get paid for our work: we who pick cotton, get pay; if we hire a lawyer or a teacher, we must pay him; the shoemaker, the cook, the washerwoman, all must be paid for their work and their time.—We ought to begin by deciding to pay the pastor all his back salary."—But as Washington spoke, he noticed one old deacon mumbling something to himself and shaking his head in the manner of an objection to what was being said. And so Washington pointed to him and asked:

"You, there, brother, don't you think the pastor ought to be paid like other people?"

"Yas, lak other people!" cut in the old deacon, "an' dat's de reason why we ain't gwine ter pay him nuthin dis year! Ain't

gwine ter pay him NUTHIN!"

"Well, I have tried to give you reasons," said Washington, "as to why you should pay your pastor. Won't you please give us the reason why you think he should not be paid?"

"We don't owe him nuthin!" said the old deacon with readiness, "cause we done paid him for dem same sermons las' year!"

ORIGIN OF RACES

THE question of which race existed first, the white or the black, and how the other finally developed from the original, has long agitated the scientific brain in vain. But this is how a Black Belt preacher disposed of the matter:

"Brudders an' sisters, de fust man whut de Lord made, been named Adam. De fust 'oman been named Eve. Dey had two chilluns, Cain an' Abel. De ma an' de pa an' all dem chilluns wuz black, wuz cullud fokes.

"Now, Cain wuz a bad Negro, allus shootin' an' cuttin' an' gamblin'. He wuz jealous uv his brudder Abel an' killed him one day in a 'spute ovah de bes' watermillon in de patch. Den de Lord come up behin' Cain and say, sez he: 'Cain whar am dy brudder?' Dat Cain wuz a sassy Negro, so he don't turn 'roun' to see who 'tis, but jes' ansers up biggity: 'Am I my brudder's keeper? I ain't got him in my pockets. I s'pose he's off somewhar shootin' craps.'

"Den de Lord he spoke more angry-like: 'Cain, whar am dy brudder?'—Den dat Negro turn 'roun' an' he see it wuz de Lord, an' he got so skeered dat his hair stan' up right straight an' his face turn right pale,—an' sisters an' brudders, dar am whar de fust white man come frum!"

GROUP PRIDE

THE old-fashioned Negro pastor had been taking his members and congregation to task for what he considered acts of dishonesty. He had used plain language; he had called a spade a spade. It seemed that some of the members had been trying to get more credit on the outside of their collection envelopes than they had money on the inside. The old man called this act by its right name.

But after abusing them for a while, he then desired to make peace again, so as to go ahead with the order of service, and the collection. Therefore he concluded thus, in a fatherly tone:

"Well, of co'se, our people is de bes' people in de worl'. But de trouble wid you is, dat de white man done been dealin' wid you so long, some uv you gittin' real tricky!"

DEMOCRATIZING HEAVEN

THE white parson, in his sermon to a colored congregation, seemed to hint that in heaven there must be some Jim Crow partition, with the white saints on one side and the black saints on the other. And after the sermon, when one of the black deacons was called on to pray, he got his chance to reply to this white preacher; for like many praying people, the old black man knew how to talk to the Lord and talk at other people, in the same phrases, and by attaching "riders" to privileged prayers. He therefore prayed as follows:

"And, O Lord, we thank thee fer the brother preacher who has spoke to us,—we thank thee for heaven,—we thank thee that we kin all go to heaven,—but as to that partition, O Lord, we thank thee that we'se a shoutin' people,—we thank thee that we kin shout so hard in heaven that we will break down that partition an' spread

all over heaven,—an' we thank thee that if the white fokes can't stand it, they can git on out of heaven an' go to elsewhere!"

DOCTRINE OF ELECTION

THE white bishop was doing his best to make clear to the Negro candidate for the ministry the important denominational doctrine of "election." The colored man seemed incapable of comprehending how any one could be "elected" to anything without ever having been a candidate for that thing, and even before that person was born or thought of. The doctrinal argument seemed to mean that if one were saved, he was born to be saved; if he were lost, he was born to be lost; if he became rich, or poor, he was born to be rich, or poor; if one died and went to heaven, he was born to go to heaven; while if one died and went to—Texas, he was born to go to that bad place.

The Negro janitor, who was sweeping the church aisles, noticed the despair of the white man at ever being able to make the black man comprehend this peculiar doctrine, and so he halted his sweeping and helpfully remarked: "I think I kin make him understan' dat 'lection doctrine. It's jes' like dis: dere's God,—he is allus votin' fer you. An' den dere's de Debbil,—he is allus votin' ag'inst you. An' so whichevah way you vote, dat's de way de 'lection goes!"

DENOMINATIONALISM

"CHILE, when is yo' gwine ter jine de army?" asked a devoted Methodist sister.

The other woman replied: "Lawsy, honey, I'se already in de army o' de Lord. Been a soljer o' de gospel fifteen years."

"Is dat so?" said the Methodist. "Whut chu'ch yo' b'longs ter?"

"Ter de Calvary Baptis' Chu'ch."

"Lawdy, honey, dat ain't no army an' yo' ain't no soljer,—dat's de navy an' you'se a merreen!"

A Baptist brother read from a Methodist hymnal a line which says: "We shall sail into the harbor on that day"—and remarked: "I have often wondered how them Methodists ever hoped to git to heaven, but now I see they mean to use the water route on the home stretch!"

A Baptist Negro was working for a white Methodist preacher, and they were on such good terms that the white man volunteered that if the Negro should die first, he would preach the funeral sermon.—Embarrassed, the black Baptist replied: "I highly appreciates yo' offer, an' I regards you as a good friend fer this worl', but when I dies I wants my funeral preached by a sho-nuff preacher."

The congregation of one church began to sing: "Will there be any stars, any stars in my crown?" And immediately the choir of another denomination, in the church next door struck up the song whose refrain is: "No, not one! No, not one!"

AN EXCLUSIVE CHURCH

A NEGRO in a northern community went to church one Sunday. It was a church of white people, and the minister was speaking from the text: "Come all ye that labor and are heavy laden." In the exaltation of feelings and rhetoric the minister had cried out: "Come! The Gospel is free! Free to all alike! Salvation is free, absolutely free, free to all, to all mankind, to every race, every class, every individual! Come! The church, this church is a brotherhood of men!"

Being a fundamentalist, the Negro interpreted this rhetoric

literally, and went up to join. The preacher quietly whispered to the Negro that he would see him in his study, after services.— In the study the Negro was asked: "Are you sure the Lord wants you to join this church? Don't you think it best to go and consult the Lord about the matter, and let him direct you?"

The black man thought this a bit strange, as the Lord had already given an urgent, general and unqualified invitation—thru this same preacher. But he left the pastor's study resolved to test the matter to the end. He therefore paid another visit to the preacher, indicating that the Lord was willing, and the white man said a little more fervently than before: "Consult the Lord a little further, —put the whole matter into the hands of the Lord,—and ask him whether you might not serve him better in some other church."

For a third time the Negro went. The pastor was chagrined, and became impatient: "My brother, you are not trusting in the Lord. I have put the matter before the Lord myself, and he has told me" . . .

"Wait a minute," said the black man, anticipating the white man, "cause I done seen de Lord, too, an' he tol' me all about it."

"Well, wh-what?" asked the anxious white man.

"I axed de Lord if I mus' keep tryin' to jine dis-yere church, an' he sez to me, sez he: 'Well, I hates awfully to discourage you, but I mus' tell you de trufe, fer you'se jes' wastin' yo' time on dat pertic'lar church. Fer de las' twenty years', sez de Lord, sez he, 'dat is, since de 'cumbency o' de present paster-in-charge, I'se tried repeatedly to git into dat church myself, an' I ain't made it yet!'"

THANKSGIVING

A MAN named Simon Suggs was sitting in church listening to the Thanksgiving sermon and hearing the minister tell about all the things there were to be thankful for—even though Simon Suggs and all the folks sitting around him did not have much, since luck that year had been unlucky, crops had been bad and weather awful.

When the minister got through preaching and asked for testi-

monials, this is what Simon Suggs got up and said: "Give thanks
for what? Me! The branch has flooded and washed away my barn.
My house roof leaks. My hound dog died, my mule broke his leg
and boll weevils et up my crops."

"Yes, brother," replied the minister, "I is heard—
And neither me nor God could doubt your word—
So let's bow down anyhow in all this muss
And thank the Lord it ain't no wuss."

CONFESSION

A COLORED preacher was hearing the confession of a young man.
In the middle of it he stopped the young sinner, saying: "Wait a
minute, young man, wait a minute. You ain't confessin'—you's
braggin'!"

THE TWO DUCKS

DERE was er ole man, you know, he had a daughter, and he tell
he daughter he had invited a preacher to he house, and he say,
"Daughter, I guine down to de train to meet de Reverend, and
bake two ducks and leave 'em dere for him, don't tech 'em." And
she said, "No, I ain't guh tech 'em." And he go to de train to meet
de Reverend, and de gal taste de ducks, and dey taste good, and
she taste 'em till she taste 'em all up.

And atter de ole man come, he never look in de place wey he
had he ducks, and he went in de other room to sharpen he knife
on the oil stove, and de preacher was settin' in de room wid de
gal. She knewed her papa was guine to whip her, and she started
snifflin' 'bout it, and de preacher say, "What is de matter, daughter?"
And she say, "Dat's all de fault I find wid papa,—papa go invite
preachers to he house and go sharpen he knife to cut off both dey

years." And de Reverend say, "What is dat, daughter?" And de gal say, "Yes, papa invite preachers here all de time and cut off both dey years." And he say, "Daughter, han' me my hat quick." And de gal guin him he hat and he run out. And she call her papa and say, "Papa, de preacher got both de ducks and gone." And he run to de door and holler to him and say, "Hey, hey, wey you guine? Come back here!" And de preacher answer him and say, "Damned ef you'll git either one of dese."

And he raise a dust de way he flewed down de road. And de ole tales tell you dat womens has always been sharper dan mens.

THE CROW

HE SET to preaching a text every night 'bout gainen sinners. And he was preaching several years and preaching one text, and said to the congregation, he says, "Sisters and brothers, dey come an' remark, 'Some people say you preach one text all of de time,' but when John was preaching on de river Jerden he didn't have but one text, and his text was, Repent and be baptized, an' dat was his one subject. Atter dat John would go preachin' and preachin' until Jesus, the Master, come to him to be baptized. An' my subject is one text, I don't preach but one text, Sisters and Brothers, and that is, Sinners, you want to find Jesus; go down below. My subject is, you want to find Jesus; go down below." Old Sister answered him in the corner, "Yes, Buddy, dat is de way I fine him I went down below. Dat is what I say. My standpoint is if you want Jesus, go down below! Go down below!"

And while he was preaching every night dere was a crow got familiar with de text, an' he flewed up in the loft over de pulpit, and he heard him preachin' his text dat night, "Sinners, if you want to find Jesus, go down below! Go down below!" After the crow got familiar with it the crow flewed out de loft of de church an' lit on de altar and turn he head one side an' look up at de preacher, an' say, "Go down below," an' de preacher went right down below. He jump over de altar and de people screamed an'

crowded one another, and in getting away dey jumped out of windows, so dat dey got all mixed up under de quire in front of de door, an' de crow got frightened hisself and flewed across de church an' lit on a old lady's shoulder, who could not get out, an' he look up in de old lady face an' say: "Go down below!" An' she said, "Do Bubber, I jest come here on a visit. Dis ain't my church."

Ghost Stories

GHOSTS

PERHAPS the simplest way for an ordinary person to see ghosts is to look back over his own left shoulder, though the same result may be accomplished by looking through a mule's ear; by punching a small hole in your own ear; by looking into a mirror with another person; by breaking a raincrow's egg into some water and washing your face in it, or by breaking a stick in two. Some say that if you go to the graveyard at twelve o'clock in the day and call the name of anyone you know, his spirit will answer you, though generally the procedure is more complicated. Some suggest that you go to a graveyard at twelve o'clock noon or midnight and take with you a piece of mirror and a pair of new steel scissors. At exactly twelve o'clock hold up the mirror before your eyes and drop the scissors on the ground. Call upon that person with whom you desire to talk. You will see his reflection in the mirror and can ask him what you please. The blades of the scissors of their own accord will begin to work, cutting away any doubt or fear that might arise in your mind. Another method used is to put half a dozen pure white dinner plates around the table at home, and then go to the graveyard at twelve noon, and call the name of some dead acquaintance. His spirit will answer you at once. Or else wipe off a rusty nail and put it in your mouth. The spirits will crowd about you. If you eat a little fat meat or grease at night you will be able to see witches, ghosts, and all sorts of half-visible occupants of the atmosphere.

Whenever you talk to such ghosts, however, you must say all you have to say in one breath. If you so much as gasp, or make the least indrawing through the lips, your slippery companion is gone forever.

THE HEADLESS HANT

A MAN and his wife was going along the big road. It was cold and the road was muddy and sticky red, and their feet was mighty nigh froze off, and they was hungry, and it got pitch dark before they got where they was going.

'Twan't long before they came to a big fine house with smoke coming outen the chimley and a fire shining through the winder. It was the kind of a house rich folks lives in, so they went round to the back door and knocked on the back porch. Somebody say, "Come in!" They went in but they didn't see nobody.

They looked all up and down and all round, but still they didn't see nobody. They saw the fire on the hearth with the skillets setting in it all ready for supper to be cooked in 'em. They saw there was meat and flour and lard and salsody and a pot of beans smoking and a rabbit a-biling in a covered pot.

Still they didn't see nobody, but they saw everything was ready for somebody. The woman took off her wet shoes and stockings to warm her feet at the fire, and the man took the bucket and lit out for the springhouse to get fresh water for the coffee. They 'lowed they was going to have them brown beans and that molly cottontail and that cornbread and hot coffee in three shakes.

The woman was toasting her feet when right through the shut door in walks a man and he don't have no head. He had on his britches and his shoes and his galluses and his vest and his coat and his shirt and his collar, but he don't have no head. Jes raw neck and bloody stump.

And he started to tell the woman, without no mouth to tell her with, how come he happened to come in there that a-way. She mighty nigh jumped outen her skin, but she said, "What in the name of the Lord do you want?" So he said he's in awful misery,

being dead and buried in two pieces. He said somebody kilt him for his money and took him to the cellar and buried him in two pieces, his head in one place and his corpse in 'nother. He said them robbers dug all round trying to find his money, and when they didn't find it they went off and left him in two pieces, so now he hankers to be put back together so's to get rid of his misery.

Then the hant said some other folks had been there and asked him what he wanted but they didn't say in the name of the Lord, and 'cause she did is how come he could tell her 'bout his misery.

'Bout that time the woman's husband came back from the springhouse with the bucket of water to make coffee with and set the bucket on the shelf before he saw the hant. Then he saw the hant with the bloody joint of his neck sticking up and he come nigh jumping outen his skin.

Then the wife told the hant who her husband is, and the hant begun at the start and told it all over agin 'bout how come he is the way he is. He told 'em if they'd come down into the cellar and find his head and bury him all in one grave he'd make 'em rich.

They said they would and that they'd get a torch.

The hant said, "Don't need no torch." And he went up to the fire and stuck his front finger in it and it blazed up like a lightwood knot and he led the way down to the cellar by the light.

They went a long way down steps before they came to the cellar. Then the hant say, "Here's where my head's buried and over here's where the rest of me's buried. Now yo' all dig right over yonder where I throw this spot of light and dig till you touch my barrels of gold and silver money."

So they dug and dug and sure 'nough they found the barrels of money he'd covered up with the thick cellar floor. Then they dug up the hant's head and histed the thing on the spade. The hant jes reached over and picked the head offen the spade and put it on his neck. Then he took off his burning finger and stuck it in a candlestick on a box, and still holding on his head, he crawled back into the hole that he had come out of.

And from under the ground they heard him a-saying, "Yo' all can have my land, can have my house, can have all my money and be as rich as I was, 'cause you buried me in one piece together, head and corpse."

Then they took the candlestick blazing with the hant's finger and went back upstairs and washed themselves with lye soap. Then the woman made up the cornbread with the spring water and greased the skillet with hogmeat and put in the hoecake and lifted the lid on with the tongs and put coals on fire on top of the lid and round the edges of the skillet, and cooked the hoecake done. Her man put the coffee and water in the pot and set it on the trivet to boil. Then they et that supper of them beans and that rabbit and that hoecake and hot coffee. And they lived there all their lives and had barrels of money to buy vittels and clothes with. And they never heard no more 'bout the man that came upstairs without no head where his head ought to be.

JACK-MA-LANTERN

JAKE: Who you reckon dat walk up and down dat ditch an' 'bout dat mash?

BRUZER: I ain't know.

JAKE: Ain't you see 'em wid dat light bob up and down like dey lost sumpen?

BRUZER: I ain't know who dey is, dey must be sumpen perticular make 'em walk all around in de rain an' brier. I see 'em but I ain't know wuh ail 'em.

HOOTEN: You sure God ain't know. Dat ain't no people. Dat's a Jack-ma-lantern an' you best l'um 'lone. You ain't know what kind of danger dey lead you in if you follow 'em.

JAKE: Wuh make dey lead you in danger. Ain't you kin stop follow 'em when you see danger.

HOOTEN: If dey gits a holt on you and you follow 'em, it don't lead you to no good. When you starts to follow, one mind will tell you l'um 'lone and turn back, and another mind will tell you follow 'em, and you follow 'em.

JAKE: What's a Jack-ma-lantern?

HOOTEN: A Jack-ma-lantern is a sperrit. It is a evil sperrit. It is ole folks. Sinful ole folks. It is folks wuh ain't 'lowed in heben and

can't get in hell, and dey punishment is to wander in de bad places and on de bad night, and dey business is enticing mens to follow 'em, an' dey ain't got no res', les' dey entice mens to lef' de right road. Is you 'member Ole man Lunnen? Well you know he been a ole man, and he been wise, and ole man Lunnen tell me, he say, one time he been walking down de road and he been wid dis same old man, July Uncle, dey call him "Hock," and say, him and Hock walk down dis road and dey see a light walking right out in dat dere mash and Hock say he guh see who it is and ole man Lunnen say he try to 'suade Hock to stay in de road. Hock say he ain't scared he guin dere and old man Lunnen say he ain't guh have nothin' to do wid it, and Hock left him, and old man Lunnen say de last time he see Hock dat night Hock been fallin' in de hole and scramblin' in de brier, and dat night Hock ain't come home and den dey search for him and dey find him that night back in de high grass and brier on Hog-Pen-Gut, and he stan' in de mud up to he knee, and he reared back wid he head pulled back holdin' both han' out in front of him like he tryin' to 'fend hisself and he look in he face and he eye wide open and de look on he face were terrible, like it were froze, and he put han' on him and war stiff dead.

HOLD HIM, TABB

BEFORE railroads were built in Virginia, goods were carried from one inland town to another on wagons. There were a great many men who did this kind of work from one end of the year to the other. One of them, "Uncle Jeter," tells the following story:—

"A number of wagons were travelling together one afternoon in December. It was extremely cold, and about the middle of the afternoon began to snow. They soon came to an abandoned settlement by the roadside, and decided it would be a good place to camp out of the storm, as there were stalls for their horses and an old dwelling-house in which they themselves, could stay. When they had nearly finished unhooking their horses a man came along and said that he was the owner of the place, and that the men were welcome to stay

there as long as they wanted to, but that the house was haunted, and not a single person had stayed in it alive for twenty-five years. On hearing this the men immediately moved their camp to a body of woods about one half mile further up the road. One of them, whose name was Tabb, and who was braver than the rest, said that he was not afraid of haunts, and that he did not mean to take himself and horses into the woods to perish in the snow, but that he'd stay where he was.

"So Tabb stayed in the house. He built a big fire, cooked and ate his supper, and rested well through the night without being disturbed. About daybreak he awoke and said: 'What fools those other fellows are to have stayed in the woods when they might have stayed in here, and have been as warm as I am!' Just as he had finished speaking he looked up to the ceiling, and there was a large man dressed in white clothes just stretched out under the ceiling and sticking up to it. Before he could get from under the man, the man fell right down upon him, and then commenced a great tussle between Tabb and the man. They made so much noise that the men in the woods heard it and ran to see what was going on. When they looked in at the window and saw the struggle, first Tabb was on top and then the other man. One of them cried, 'Hold him, Tabb, hold him!' 'You can bet your soul I got him!' said Tabb. Soon the man got Tabb out of the window. 'Hold him, Tabb, hold him!' one of the men shouted. 'You can bet your life I got him!' came from Tabb. Soon the man got Tabb upon the roof of the house. 'Hold him, Tabb, hold him!' said one of the men. 'You can bet your boots I got him!' answered Tabb. Finally the man got Tabb up off the roof into the air. 'Hold him, Tabb, hold him!' shouted one of the men. 'I got him and he got me, too!' said Tabb. The man, which was a ghost, carried Tabb straight up into the air until they were both out of sight. Nothing was ever seen of him again."

SOME NEW ORLEANS GHOSTS

GERTRUDE APPLE of New Orleans intends to be a ghost when she dies and she is going to haunt the white woman for whom she works.

'You better leave Gertrude alone,' the husband of her mistress told his wife, according to Gertrude. 'That dark gal's sure gonna haunt you when she dies.'

'And I sure is gonna haunt her,' Gertrude admits. 'I'm gonna haunt her very soul. She's nice in her way but pays cheap.'

One night a ghost came into Gertrude's room. He wore a flashy checked suit, carried a walking cane and he was black as ink.

'He come up to my bed,' Gertrude said, 'and dropped that cane on the floor and it didn't make no noise at all. Then he throwed one of his legs over me. I yelled, "Get away from me!" And he went.

'Another time,' said she, 'a rooster appeared in my room. That thing changed into a man, then into a cow. Then it disappeared—jest evapulated. Was I glad. Whew! Sometimes I'm sorry I can see spirits, they scare me so. Spirits is bad if you ain't a Christian, but if you is and you is borned with a veil over your face you ain't got nothin' to worry about.

'I seen plenty of witches, too. Them things ride you at night. They done tried to ride me, but I hollers, "In the name of my religion, help me, good spirits!" And the witches run. Witches don't mess with spirits. I think lots of white peoples is witches. Others is just plain bitches.'

Aunt Jessie Collins, an authority on supernatural manifestations, explained it all this way, 'Ghosts is liable to look like anything,' she said. 'Some comes back just like they was when they died, but others turns into animals and balls of fire or things with long teeth and hairy arms. You can just walk around all your life lookin' at things and you don't never know when you is lookin' at a ghost. My grandpa seen one once and it sure did him a lot of good. You see, my grandpa was a drinkin' man and you know how men sees

things when they is in their cups. Still, my grandpa didn't drink quite that much. We was livin' way out in the country then and he had to walk to town and back to get hisself his gin. Well, one night he come home, walkin' down that dark country road not studyin' about nothin' or nothin' and he heard somethin' walkin' behind him. My grandpa turned aroun' and seen it wasn't nothin' but a little old white dog. "Hello, little ole dog," my grandpa said. "Where you goin' at?" Outside of that he didn't pay it no mind. Jest kept walkin'. That little old dog followed him clean to his door.

'Now, when my grandpa reached his front door, he heard that dog paddin' up on the porch back of him and he heard my grandma breathin' mad like right inside, jest waitin' for him. He turned around and say, "Go 'way, little ole dog. You don't want to mess in this business."

'He went to say more but the words jest stuck in his throat, 'cause he seen now that that dog wasn't no dog at all, but a big white ghost fifteen feet tall with two heads and 'bout twelve arms. My grandpa jest fell right smack down on that porch and lay. My grandma run out when she heard the noise and drug him inside. She didn't hit him or nothing, 'cause he had plumb fainted. He was in bed nearly a week. No, my grandma didn't see no ghost. I always figured that ghost knowed my grandma and he run when he heard her comin' out. But you know after that my grandpa didn't touch no liquor for more than a month?'

'When my husband died I give him a fine funeral. I went in deep mourning and wore me a long widow's veil. Every day I'd go to the cemetery and cry all day by his grave. But his spirit started to haunt me somethin' terrible. I had chickens and every night he'd come back wearin' a white apron and shoo my chickens. Every mornin' some of 'em would be dead. We had a horse and that haunt done drove me and him both crazy. Then I got mad and I quit goin' to the cemetery and I took off that widow's veil. I put black pepper 'round the sills of all my doors. That stopped him; that always chases ghostses. You know I wouldn't go near no graveyard on All Saints' Day for nothin'. No, sir! Them evil spirits just whizzes by you like the wind and knocks you flat on the ground.'

THE HAIRY TOE

ONCE there was a woman went out to pick beans, and she found a Hairy Toe. She took the Hairy Toe home with her, and that night, when she went to bed, the wind began to moan and groan. Away off in the distance she seemed to hear a voice crying, "Who's got my Hair-r-ry To-o-oe? Who's got my Hair-r-ry To-o-oe?"

The woman scrooched down, 'way down under the covers, and 'bout that time the wind 'peared to hit the house, smoosh, and the old house creaked and cracked like somethin' was tryin' to get in. The voice had come nearer, almost at the door now, and it said, "Where's my Hair-r-ry To-o-oe? Who's got my Hair-r-ry To-o-oe?"

The woman scrooched further down under the covers and pulled them tight around her head. The wind growled around the house like some big animal and r-r-um-m-bled over the chimbley. All at once she heard the door cr-r-a-ack and Somethin' slipped in and began to creep over the floor. The floor would cre-e-eak, cre-e-eak at every step that thing took toward her bed. The woman could almost feel it bending over her bed. Then in a awful voice it said: "Where's my Hair-r-ry To-o-oe? Who's got my Hair-r-ry To-o-oe? You've got it!"

WAIT TILL EMMETT COMES

ONCE upon a time there was an old colored preacher who was riding to a church he served at some distance from his home when night overtook him and he got lost. As it grew darker and darker, he began to be afraid, but he bolstered up his courage by saying every little while, "De Lawd will sholy take care ob me." By and by he saw a light, and riding up to it, he discovered that it came from the cabin of another colored man. Getting off his horse and tying

it to a fence stake, he knocked at the cabin door. When the owner
opened it, the old preacher told his trouble and asked to stay all
night. The colored man replied, "Well, Pahson, I suttinly would
like ter keep yo' all night, but my cabin hain't got but one room in
it an' I got a wife an' ten chilluns. Dey jis' ain't no place fo' yo' ter
stay."

The old preacher leaned up against the side of the house and in a
woebegone voice said, "Well, I guess de Lawd will sholy take care
ob me." Then slowly untying his horse and getting on him, he
started to ride on. But the owner of the cabin stopped him and said,
"Pahson, yo' might sleep in de big house. Da' ain't nobody up da'
an de doo' ain't locked. Yo' can put yo' hoss in the ba'n an' give him
some hay an' den you can walk right in. You'll fin' a big fiahplace
in de big room an' de wood all laid fo' de fiah. Yo' can jis' tech a
match to it an' make yo' self cumfable." As the old preacher began to
disappear into the dark, the other called out, "But, Pahson, I didn't
tell you dat de house is hanted." The old man hesitated for a
moment, but finally rode away, saying, "Well, I guess de Lawd
sholy will take care ob me."

When he arrived at the place, he put his horse in the barn and
gave him some hay. Then he moved over to the house, and sure
enough, he found it unlocked. In the big room he found a great
fireplace with an immense amount of wood all laid ready to kindle.
He touched a match to it and in a few minutes had a big fire roaring. He lighted an oil lamp that was on a table and drawing up a
big easy chair, he sat down and began to read his Bible. By and by the
fire burnt down, leaving a great heap of red-hot coals.

The old man continued to read his Bible until he was aroused by
a sudden noise in one corner of the room. Looking up, he saw a
big cat, and it was a black cat, too. Slowly stretching himself, the
cat walked over to the fire and flung himself into the bed of red-hot-
coals. Tossing them up with his feet, he rolled over in them, then
shaking the ashes off himself, he walked over to the old man and
sat down to one side of him, near his feet, looked up at him with his
fiery-green eyes, licked out his long, red tongue, lashed his tail, and
said, "Wait till Emmett comes."

The old man kept on reading his Bible, when all at once he
heard a noise in another corner of the room, and looking up, he

saw another black cat, big as a dog. Slowly stretching himself, he walked over to the bed of coals, threw himself into them, tumbled all around, and tossed them with his feet. Then he got up, shook the ashes off himself, walked over to the old man, and sat down near his feet on the opposite side from the first cat. He looked up at him with his fiery-green eyes, licked out his long, red tongue, lashed his tail, and asked the first cat, "Now what shall we do wid him?" The first cat answered, "Wait till Emmett comes."

The old man kept on reading his Bible and in a little while he heard a noise in a third corner of the room, and looking up, he saw a cat black as night and as big as a calf. He, too, got up, stretched himself, walked over to the bed of coals, and threw himself into them. He rolled over and over in them, tossed them with his feet, took some into his mouth, chewed them up and spat them out again. Then shaking the ashes off himself, he walked over to the old colored man and sat down right in front of him. He looked up at him with his fiery-green eyes, licked out his long, red tongue, lashed his tail, and said to the other cats, "Now what shall we do wid him?" They both answered, "Wait till Emmett comes."

The old preacher looked furtively around, slowly folded up his Bible, put it into his pocket, and said, "Well, geman, I suttinly is glad to hab met up wid yo' dis ebenin', an' I sholy do admire fo' to had yo' company, but when Emmett comes, you tell him I done *been* heah an' hab done *went.*"

TAILYPO

ONCE upon a time, way down in de big woods ob Tennessee, dey lived a man all by hisself. His house didn't hab but one room in it, an' dat room was his pahlor, his settin' room, his bedroom, his dinin' room, an' his kitchen, too. In one end ob de room was a great, big, open fiahplace, an' dat's wha' de man cooked an' et his suppah. An' one night atter he had cooked an' et his suppah, dey crep' in troo de cracks ob de logs de curiestes creetur dat you ebber did see, an' it had a *great, big, long tail.*

Jis' as soon as dat man see dat varmint, he reached fur his hatchet, an' wid one lick, he cut dat thing's tail off. De creeter crep' out troo de cracks ob de logs an' run away, an' de man, fool like, he took an' cooked dat tail, he did, an' et it. Den he went ter bed, an' atter a while, he went ter sleep.

He hadn't been 'sleep berry long, till he waked up, an' heerd sumpin' climbin' up de side ob his cabin. It sounded jis' like a cat, an' he could hear it *scratch, scratch, scratch,* an' by-an'-by, he heerd it say, *"Tailypo, tailypo; all I want's my tailypo."*

Now dis yeer man had t'ree dogs: one wuz called Uno, an' one wuz called Ino, an' de udder one wuz called Cumptico-Calico. An' when he heerd dat thing he called his dawgs, huh! huh! huh! an' dem dawgs cum bilin' out from under de floo', an' dey chased dat thing way down in de big woods. An' de man went back ter bed an' went ter sleep.

Well, way long in de middle ob de night, he waked up an' he heerd sumpin' right above his cabin doo', tryin' ter git in. He listened, an' he could heer it *scratch, scratch, scratch,* an' den he heerd it say, *"Tailypo, tailypo; all I want's my tailypo."* An' he sot up in bed and called his dawgs, huh! huh! huh! an' dem dawgs cum bustin' round de corner ob de house an' dey cotched up wid dat thing at de gate an' dey jis' tore de whole fence down, tryin' ter git at it. An' dat time, dey chased it way down in de big swamp. An' de man went back ter bed agin an' went ter sleep.

Way long toward mornin' he waked up, an he heerd sumpin' down in de big swamp. He listened, an' he heerd it say, *"You know, I know; all I want's my tailypo."* An' dat man sot up in bed an' called his dawgs, huh! huh! huh! an' you know dat time dem dawgs didn' cum. Dat thing had carried 'em way off down in de big swamp an' killed 'em, or los' 'em. An' de man went back ter bed an' went ter sleep agin.

Well, jis' befo' daylight, he waked up an' he heerd sumpin' in his room, an' it sounded like a cat, climbin' up de civers at de foot ob his bed. He listened an' he could hear it scratch, scratch, scratch, an' he looked ober de foot ob his bed an' he saw two little pinted ears, an' in a minute, he saw two big roun', fiery eyes lookin' at him. He wanted to call his dawgs, but he too skeered ter holler. Dat thing kep' creepin' up until by-an-by it wuz right on top ob dat

man, an' den it said in a low voice, "Tailypo, tailypo; all I want's my tailypo." An' all at once dat man got his voice an' he said, "I hain't got yo' tailypo." An dat thing said, "Yes you has," an' it jumped on dat man an' scratched him all to pieces. An' sum folks say he got his tailypo.

Now dey ain't nothin' lef' ob dat man's cabin way down in de big woods ob Tennessee, 'ceptin' the chimbley, an' folks w'at lib in de big valley say dat when de moon shines bright an' de win' blows down de valley you can heer sumpin' say, "Tailypo. . . . . ," An' den, die away in de distance.

DAID AARON

AARON KELLY dead. So dey berry 'im. Fay-ye-well, Aaron Kelly!

Dat night dem all set roun' de fiah, hopin' dat the dead deceased is gone whun dey berry well know Aaron Kelly ain't got one uthly chance o' goin'. De widder say: "Ah hopes 'e gone whuh ah spec's 'e ain't!" When in walk de co'pse, lookin' dusty. *Oh, my Lawdy!*

He pick 'im a seat twix' de widder an' de lead mounah; an' sezzee: "Wut disyuh all about. You-all ack lak somebuddy dead. Who dead?"

De widder look at 'im. . . . She say: "Oh, my Gawd!"

Aaron say kina fretful: "Dammit, 'oman! Ah ax you, who dead?"

"You is," sez de widder, shakin' lak a cold dog in a wet sack.

"Me dead?" say Aaron. "Huccum? Ah don't feel dead." He tell 'em 'e don't belieb 'em, 'cuz 'e don't feel dead.

Dem tell 'im dey yent duh cayeh how 'e feel. . . . 'E dead.

"But," sezzee, "Ah don't feel dead a dam bit!"

"Orri," dem 'spond. "Oonah don't feel dead; but oonah look dead orri. Oonah bettah gone back tuh de grabe whuh oonah blongst."

"No," sezzee. "An ain't gwine back to no grabe twell ah feels dead. 'Top you-all oggyment. Ain't no use fuh oggyment. Ah ain't gwine back to no grabe twell ah feels dead fo' true."

"Oh, my Gawd!" sez de widder. "How long oonah spec' de co'pse gwine las'?"

"Not so long," say de lead. "Not in dis hot time. 'E cain't las' long."

Yut, spite de widder, de wedder, de hot, de rainy, an' all, Aaron las'. An' 'e ain't done one fo'm t'ing cep' set by de cookin' fiah wa'min' 'e han's an' 'e foots, an' chillin' off de room. 'E des set dey, sundown an' sunup, wa'min' 'e han's an' foots.

De 'surance 'sociation won't pay de 'surance cuz Aaron sway to Gawd 'e ain't dead. An' de fambly cain' pay de coffin, cuz dem ain't git de 'surance. An' de undehtakeh sez 'e gwine graff de coffin effen de dead deceased won't ockepy 'em; an' dey's de berry ol' debble to pay.

De widder 'puzent dese t'ing to Aaron; but Aaron des' say, sezzee: "Le' me be, 'oman! Ah ain't gwine back to no berr'in groun' twell ah dead. Don't oonah miss me?"

"My Gawd!" say de widder. "Miss oonah? How ah gwine miss oonah? Ah ain't had no chance fuh miss oonah. Oonah ain't gone. Ah could miss oonah dat easy."

"Ain't oonah goin' in mou'nin' fuh me?" sezzee, fretful an' grumblesome.

"Wut de use o' me goin' in mou'nin', when ah ain't lost oonah yet?"

"Oonah ain't pay no propah 'tention tuh me," sezzee.

"Ain't pay no propah 'tention? Oh, my Gawd! Ain't we took oonah out an' berrit oonah? Ain't de Reb'ren Rab'nel preach de funeral? Oonah t'ink us gwine berry oonah two time? Us ain't. Quit yo' complainin'."

Den Aaron des' set by de fiah, wa'min' 'e han's an' 'e foots, an' lookin' peevish. 'E des set by de fiah, an' creak an' crack. E' j'ints dry; 'e back stiff; an' ebry time 'e mobe 'eseff's crack an' creak lak dead tree in de wind.

One night de bes' fiddleh come a-cou'tin' de widder. 'E sot on one side de fiah; Aaron sot tudder side, wa'min' 'e han's an' foots, an' stretchin' 'e laigs fuh wa'm . . . an' all de tim creakin' an' crackin'.

De fiddleh him des' wore out hearin' 'im creak an' crack. 'E 'sid an' 'e 'cide sumpin otter be done. But 'sidderin' an' 'ciderin' don' make Sal's baby a shirt. Bum-bye de widder say, "Hullong us gotter put up wid dis dead co'pse? Hullong us gotter wait twell 'e molder? Hullong us gotter set hyuh by us own fiah, oonah, an' me, an' *him?*"

De fiddleh 'sidder; but 'e yent 'cide. Bum-bye Aaron stretch 'eseff, an', seezee: "Dis ain't berry jovy. Le's we be jovy. Le's we dance fuh limbeh us laigs."

So de fiddleh git out 'e fiddle an' 'chume 'um. De fiddle begin fuh sing. Aaron stretch 'eseff; 'e shuk 'eseff; 'e giddup; 'e tek a step or two; him begin fuh jig, wid 'e ol' bone a'crackin', an 'e yaller teet' a-snappin', an' 'e bald bonehead a-wakklin' an' 'e ahms a flip-floppin . . . roun' an' roun' an' roun'.

'E skip an' 'e prance, hidder an' yander roun' de room, 'e long shanks clockin', an' 'e knee bones a-knockin' . . . landy Lawdy! How dat dead man dance! Pooty soon a piece fly loose, an' fall on de flo'.

"My golly! Look at dat!" say de fiddleh.

"Play mo fasteh!" say de widder. De fiddleh play mo' fasteh. De co'pse 'e creak an' 'e crack. Ebry time 'e jump 'e crack. An' ebry time 'e crack a piece drap on de flo'.

"Play mo' loudeh!" say de widder.

De fiddleh play mo' loud. An' crickety-crack, down an' back, de dead man go hoppin', an' de dry bone a-droppin', disaway, data-way, dem pieces keep poppin'. Ebry hop a dry bone drap. Ebry jump 'e shuck a bone. "Oh, my Gawd!" say de fiddleh; an' 'e han' shake so's 'e cain't sca'cely fingeh de string. "Play, man, play!" say de widder.

De fiddleh fiddle fasteh; dead Aaron dance; an' all de time 'e dance de bone keep a-droppin' . . . twell all to once 'e crumble down . . . 'e rib bone roll like a barrel hoop roun' de flo' . . . an' dere dead Aaron lay, des' a heap o' dry bone on de flo' . . . an' all de time de bal' headbone dance by itseff midst er de flo', grinnin' at de fiddleh, an' crackin' it' teeth. Dat head go a-dancin' bop, bop, bop!

"Oh, my sweet Lawd! Look at dat!" say de fiddleh.

"Play mo' loudeh yet!" say de widder.

"Ho, ho!" say de bonehead. "Ain't us des' a-cuttin' de buck!" But dat fiddleh 'e ain't int'res' in head wuh do like dat head do. Sezzee: "Widder, ah gotta go git me mo' rozzum fuh ma bow!" So 'e gone fum dat house . . . an' ah reckons 'e still gittin' dat rozzum . . . cauze 'e didn't come back.

Dem gadder de bone tugedder, an' put 'em back in de grabe. But

dey ben keerful fuh lay 'em all cristy-cross an' unj'int; so's Aaron cain't 'cide wey dem bone go. An', after dat, dead Aaron didn't gie up no mo'.

But de widder stan' widder fum dat day till yet. Dat dancin' dead-head spile de match.

As told by Sarah Rutledge and Epsie Meggett

LOUIE ALEXANDER

IN THE old days when the Devil taught the fiddlers we had much better music than we have now.

Jack Calhoun was a fine fiddler; but Louie Alexander was finest of all.

Some say he was taught by Dicky Brux, the great conjure man on the Dorchester Road. Some say the Devil taught him. Old Caesar says he was taught by the Devil, not by Dicky Brux; no man could fiddle like Louie Alexander unless he had been taught by the Devil.

Louie was a Charleston man, short bodied, heavy and dark. He was a pleasant fellow, friendly with all, jovial and fond of a joke. And he could play the fiddle as if he had been born with a fiddle in his hands. There never has been another fiddler like Louie Alexander. He could play equally well the banjo, guitar or bull fiddle; he could play a lead horn fit to make a man cry. But with his fiddle he could almost conjure your heart out. When white folks heard Louie Alexander play they always said: "The Devil is in that man." They called him "The Black Pickaninny."

One who wants to learn to play from the Devil must take a yellow yam, a hen egg, and a black fowl to the crossroads in the dark of the moon, stake the fowl, break the egg, lay the yam down in the egg, and call the Devil seven times. He will come on the seventh call.

Louie did these things so; then called the Devil. There was the Devil, sitting on a burnt gum stump. "What do you want?" says he.

"To play the fiddle better than any man alive or dead," said Louie. "I will pay whatever you ask."

"That's a fair bargain," said the Devil; and taught Louie how to play the fiddle better than any man alive or dead. "Thank you," said Louie.

"Just keep your thanks," said the Devil. "I will take my own pay."

After that no man could play the fiddle like Louie Alexander. He could play a whole tune on one note; or a whole song on one string; and when he played for dancing everyone that heard him had to dance, . . . they could not keep their feet still.

When Louie played the Devil was in it. The women sang at the top of their voices; and the dancer sang tunes that could only come from the Devil. The women all pushed around him like cows, butting to be next. Louie just scratched their heads with his fiddle bow: women were about as pleasing to him as a houseful of smoke. The men whooped and hopped and jumped. They forgot their troubles, and all their cares; the girls were pretty, drink was free; and everyone might have his fill. They just whooped it up all night. Every minute the party got louder, with buckets of white mule and bottles of beer. The girls pulled their clothes off, and everything was delightful. And nobody who came into the hall ever left it from candlelighting on Saturday night to sunrise Sunday morning; they forgot how to use the door.

And never once, the whole night long, would Louie ever skip a beat or lose the time; he fiddled like the Devil himself; and the Devil never loses any time. Everybody had a pig's fill till the first dong of the old church bell put an end to the doing.

Louie gave a hot supper every Saturday night. And every Sunday morning, after Louie's hot supper, somebody got carried home, dead.

At the dong of the bell Louie laid down his fiddle; and when he laid down his fiddle the party was over. They all went home. They forgot where they had been, or what they had done, or how they had behaved themselves. All they knew was that they were too tired to go to work; so they went home and slept all day; nobody went where he was hired, or where anybody expected him to be; and nobody cared a damn. The Devil was in Louie Alexander's

music. But Louie laughed, and kept his secret.

After a while he went down to Beaufort and got him a fine string orchestra there. The people in Beaufort and Port Royal welcomed so famous a fiddler, and took the opportunity to have hot suppers and dances. And as it had been in Charleston it was in Port Royal and Beaufort; people hailed Louie Alexander as the greatest of all fiddlers, dead or alive.

But a gift from the Devil is a debt in the end.

Louie lived many years in Beaufort. His house was on the Point, behind Beaufort, a solitary place.

One day the apothecary missed Louie, who went every day by the apothecary shop. "What's become of Louie Alexander?" he asked. Nobody knew. So they went to the lonely house on the Point where Louie had lived. When they opened the door there was Louie, dead, in a heap on the bed . . . like the old song says:

> Dere lay Louie stretch' on de bed,
> Shoe on his feet, and hat on his head,
> And a stink like de Debble behine 'im!

Louie lay there on the bed, stiff, his eyes wide open, staring, and his mouth twisted. His face was gray as an alley cat at night, and there was white froth on his lips. The look on Louie Alexander's face was not that of a sweet and quiet death.

Joe Bythewood said that there had been a light in Louie's house all night. The oil in his lamp was burnt out, the wick was charred to the brass, and the brass was burnt black. The soot from the burnt wick had fallen like snow on everything; Louie's face was covered with it, and the bedding.

Some said he died of poison, from the foam on his lips. But the law couldn't prove it; nobody believed it; and nobody believes it to this day.

The Devil, who had taught him to fiddle, had come for his pay; and, willy-nilly, ready or not, he just took Louie Alexander's soul and went home. On the table by the bedside were pen, ink and paper, a regular contract paper; and across the back of the paper, in a big, sprawl hand, showing that it had been written by a big man, were the three words:

PAID IN FULL

Nobody could have written that but the Devil.

As told by Walter Mayrant

A ROOST ON THE RIM OF THE MOON

I seen a owl settin'
On de rim er de moon.
He draw in he neck
An' rumple he feather,
An' look below at de world.

He shook de horn on he head,
Wall he big eye
An' laugh at de things
Above an' below
From he roost
On de rim er de moon.

He woke de fowls
In de barnyard,
An' de dead stirred
In dey grave,
When he laugh
From he roost
On de rim er de moon.

An' de ole folks say
He were a dead man;
Dat evil did float

Wid de sound er he voice,
When he laugh
From he roost
On de rim er de moon.

An' de dead
In de graveyard
Raise up dey voice an' moan;
Dey laugh an' dey cry
At de sound er de owl,
When he laugh
From he roost
On de rim er de moon.

He stir up de fever an' chill
Wid he shadow,
When de sound er he voice
Pass over de swamp,
When he laugh
From he roost
On de rim er de moon.

Black Magic and Chance

ORIGIN OF THE VOODOO CULT

Most of the Negroes speak of conjuration as "hoodoo"—the Negro version of the familiar "voodoo" or "voudou." Some writers would derive the term from the followers of Peter Valdo, the Waldenses, or Vaudois (*vaudois,* a witch) of France—a sect later spreading into Haiti; yet the prevailing opinion today is that the term is of African origin, being derived from the *vo* (to inspire fear) of the Ewe-speaking peoples and signifying a god—one who inspires fear. *Vōdu* is not the name of an especial deity, but is applied by the natives to any god. "In the southeastern portions of the Ewe territory, however, the python deity is worshipped, and this *vōdu* cult, with its adoration of the snake god, was carried to Haiti by slaves from Ardra and Whydah, where the faith still remains today. In 1724 the Dahomies invaded Ardra and subjugated it; three years later Whydah was conquered by the same foe. This period is beyond question that in which Haiti first received the vōdu of the Africans. Thousands of Africans from these serpent-worshipping tribes were at that time sold into slavery, and were carried across the Atlantic to the western island. They bore with them their cult of the snake. At the same period, Ewe-speaking slaves were taken to Louisiana." In 1809, because of war between France and Spain, some of these Haitian planters and their slaves fled from Cuba, where they had sought refuge during the Haitian Revolution, to New Orleans and made their residence there. These Africans, too,

were faithful adorers of the serpent. Such were the principal sources
of the voodoo religion in the United States.

HOODOO

BELIEF in magic is older than writing. So nobody knows how it
started.

The way we tell it, hoodoo started way back there before everything. Six days of magic spells and mighty words and the world
with its elements above and below was made. And now, God is
leaning back taking a seventh day rest. When the eighth day comes
around, He'll start to making new again.

Man wasn't made until around half-past five on the sixth day, so
he can't know how anything was done. Kingdoms crushed and
crumbled whilst man went gazing up into the sky and down into
the hollows of the earth trying to catch God working with His
hands so he could find out His secrets and learn how to accomplish
and do. But no man yet has seen God's hand, nor yet His finger-
nails. All they could know was that God made everything to pass
and perish except stones. God made stones for memory. He builds
a mountain Himself when He wants things not forgot. Then His
voice is heard in rumbling judgement.

Moses was the first man who ever learned God's power-com-
pelling words and it took him forty years to learn ten words. So
he made ten plagues and ten commandments. But God gave him
His rod for a present, and showed him the back part of His glory.
Then too, Moses could walk out of the sight of man. But Moses
never would have stood before the Burning Bush, if he had not
married Jethro's daughter. Jethro was a great hoodoo man. Jethro
could tell Moses could carry power as soon as he saw him. In fact,
he felt him coming. Therefore, he took Moses and crowned him
and taught him. So Moses passed on beyond Jethro with his rod.
He lifted it up and tore a nation out of Pharoah's side, and Pharoah
couldn't help himself. Moses talked with the snake that lives in
a hole right under God's foot-rest. Moses had fire in his head and

a cloud in his mouth. The snake told him God's making words. The words of doing and the words of obedience. Many a man thinks he is making something when he's only changing things around. But God let Moses make. And then Moses had so much power he made the eight winged angels split open a mountain to bury him in, and shut up the hole behind them.

And ever since the days of Moses, kings have been toting rods for a sign of power. But it's mostly sham-polish because no king has ever had the power of even one of Moses' ten words. Because Moses made a nation and a book, a thousand million leaves of ordinary man's writing couldn't tell what Moses said.

Then when the moon had dragged a thousand tides behind her, Solomon was a man. So Sheba, from her country where she was, felt him carrying power and therefore she came to talk with Solomon and hear him.

The Queen of Sheba was an Ethiopian just like Jethro, with power unequal to man. She didn't have to deny herself to give gold to Solomon. She had gold-making words. But she was thirsty, and the country where she lived was dry to her mouth. So she listened to her talking ring and went to see Solomon, and the fountain in his garden quenched her thirst.

So she made Solomon wise and gave him her talking ring. And Solomon built a room with a secret door and everyday he shut himself inside and listened to his ring. So he wrote down the ring-talk in books.

That's what the old ones said in ancient times and we talk it again.

RITES

THE secret meetings of the voodoo society were held at night. Castellanos tells of the members divesting themselves of their usual raiment and putting on sandals, girding their loins with red handkerchiefs, of which the king wears a greater number and those of finer quality than the ordinary member. He also has a blue cord

about his waist and his head draped with some crimson stuff. The queen is dressed more simply, with red garments and a red sash.

The ceremony begins with adoration of the snake, placed in a barred cage upon an altar in front of the king and queen, and a renewal of the oath of secrecy. The king and queen extol future happiness and exhort their subjects always to seek their advice. Then individually the members come up to implore the voodoo god—to invoke blessings upon friends and curses upon enemies. The king patiently listens. Then the spirit moves him. He places the queen bodily upon the box containing the deity. She is seized with convulsions and the oracle talks through her inspired lips. She bestows flattery and promises of success; then lays down irrevocable laws in the name of the serpent. Questions are asked and an offering taken; new work is proposed and the oath of secrecy taken again, sometimes sealed by the warm blood of a kid.

After this the voodoo dance begins. The initiation of new candidates forms the first part of this ceremony. The voodoo king traces a large circle in the center of the room with a piece of charcoal and places within it the sable neophyte. He now thrusts into his hand a package of herbs, horse hair, rancid tallow, waxen effigies, broken bits of horn, and other substances equally nauseating. Then lightly striking him on the head with a small wooden paddle, he launches forth into the following African chant:

> *Eh! eh! Bomba, hen, hen!*
> *Canga bafio te,*
> *Canga moune de le,*
> *Canga do ki la*
> *Canga li.*

At this the candidate begins to squirm and dance—an action called *"monter voudou."* If he steps out of the ring in his frenzy, the king and queen turn their backs to neutralize the bad omen. Again the candidate enters the ring, again he becomes convulsed; drinking some stimulant, he relapses into an hysterical fit. To stop this the king sometimes hits him with a wooden paddle or with a cowhide. Then the initiate is led to the altar to take the oath, and from that moment becomes a full-fledged member of the order.

The king then places his foot upon the box containing the snake. He seems to get a sort of shock which is transmitted to his queen, and through her to everyone in the circle. Violent convulsions take place, the queen being the most violently affected. From time to time the serpent is again touched to get more magnetic power. The box is shaken, and tinkling bells on the side increase the general delirium already under way. A nervous tremor possesses everybody. No one escapes its power. They spin with incredible velocity, whilst some, in the midst of these bacchanalian orgies, tear their vestments and even lacerate their flesh with their gnashing teeth. Others, entirely deprived of reason, fall down to the ground from sheer lassitude, and are carried, still panting and gyrating into the open air.

ANATOL PIERRE

ANATOL PIERRE, of New Orleans, was a middle-aged octoroon. He is a Catholic and lays some feeble claim to kinship with Marie Leveau. He had the most elaborate temple of any of the practitioners. His altar room was off by itself and absolutely sacrosanct. He made little difficulty about taking me after I showed him that I had worked with others. Pierre was very emotional and sometimes he would be sharp with his clients, indifferent as to whether they hired him or not. But he quickly adjusted himself to my being around him and at the end of the first week began to prepare me for the crown.

The ceremony was as follows:

On Saturday I was told to have the materials for my initiation bath ready for the following Tuesday at eleven o'clock. I must have a bottle of lavender toilet water, Japanese honeysuckle perfume, and orange blossom water. I must get a full bunch of parsley and brew a pint of strong parsley water. I must have at hand sugar, salt and Vacher Balm. Two long pink candles must be provided, one to be burned at the initiation, one to be lit on the altar for me in Pierre's secret room.

He came to my house in Belville Court at a quarter to eleven to see if all was right. The tub was half-filled with warm water and Pierre put in all of the ingredients, along with a handful of salt and three tablespoons of sugar.

The candles had been dressed on Saturday and one was already burning on the sccret altar for me. The other long pink candle was rolled around the tub three times, "In nomina patria, et filia, et spiritu sanctus, Amen." Then it was marked for a four day burning and lit. The spirit was called three times. "Kind spirit, whose name is Moccasin, answer me." This I was told to repeat three times, snapping my fingers.

Then I, already prepared, stepped into the tub and was bathed by the teacher. Particular attention was paid to my head and back and chest since there the "controls" lie. While in the tub, my left little finger was cut a little and his finger was cut and the blood bond made. "Now you are of my flesh and of the spirit, and neither one of us will ever deny you."

He dried me and I put on new underwear bought for the occasion and dressed with oil of geranium, and was told to stretch upon the couch and read the third chapter of Job night and morning for nine days. I was given a little Bible that had been "visited" by the spirit and told the names of the spirits to call for any kind of work I might want to perform. I am to call on Great Moccasin for all kinds of power and also to have him stir up the particular spirit I may need for a specific task. I must call on Kangaroo to stop worrying; call on Jenipee spirit for marriages; call on Death spirit for killing, and the seventeen "quarters" of spirit to aid me if one spirit seems insufficient.

I was told to burn the marked candle every day for two hours— from eleven till one, in the northeast corner of the room. While it is burning I must go into the silence and talk to the spirit through the candle.

On the fifth day Pierre called again and I resumed my studies, but now as an advanced pupil. In the four months that followed these are some of the things I learned from him:

A man called Muttsy Ivins came running to Pierre soon after my initation was over. Pierre looked him over with some instinctive antipathy. So he wouldn't help him out by asking questions. He

just let Mr. Muttsy tell him the best way he could. So he began
by saying, "A lot of hurting things have been done to me, Pierre,
and now its done got to de place Ah'm skeered for mah life."

"That's a lie, yes," Pierre snapped.

"Naw it 'tain't!" Muttsy insisted. "Ah done found things 'round
mah door step and in mah yard and Ah knows who's doin' it too."

"Yes, you find things in your yard because you continue to sleep
with the wife of another man and you are afraid because he has
said that he will kill you if you don't leave her alone. You are crazy
to think that you lie to me. Tell me the truth and then tell me what
you want me to do."

"Ah want him out de way—kilt, cause he swear he's gointer kill
me. And since one of us got to die, Ah'd ruther it to be him than
me."

"I knew you wanted a death the minute you got in here. I don't
like to work for death."

"Please, Pierre, Ah'm skeered to walk de streets after dark,
and me and de woman done gone too far to turn back. And he
got de consumption nohow. But Ah don't wanter die before he do.
Ah'm a well man."

"That's enough about that. How much money have you got?"

"Two hundred dollars."

"Two fifty is my terms, and I ain't a bit anxious for the job at
that."

Pierre turned to me and began to give me a list of things to get
for my own use and seemed to forget the man behind him.

"Maybe Ah kin get dat other fifty dollars and maybe not. These
ain't no easy times. Money is tight."

"Well, goodbye, we're busy folks here. You don't have to do this
thing, anyway. You can leave town."

"And leave mah good trucking business? Dat'll never happen.
Ah kin git yo' money. When yo' goin' ter do de work?"

"You pay the money and go home. It is not for you to know how
and when the work is done. Go home with faith."

The next morning soon, Pierre sent me out to get a beef brain,
a beef tongue, a beef heart and a live black chicken. When I returned he had prepared a jar of bad vinegar. He wrote Muttsy's
enemy's name nine times on a slip of paper. He split open the heart,

placed the paper in it, pinned up the opening with eighteen steel needles, and dropped it into the jar of vinegar, point downward.

The main altar was draped in black and the crudely carved figure of Death was placed upon it to shield us from the power of death.

Black candles were lit on the altar. A black crown was made and placed on the head of Death. The name of the man to die was written on paper nine times and placed on the altar one degree below Death, and the jar containing the heart was set on this paper. The candles burned for twelve hours.

Then Pierre made a coffin six inches long. I was sent out to buy a small doll. It was dressed in black to represent the man and placed in the coffin with his name under the doll. The coffin was left open upon the altar. Then we went far out to a lonely spot and dug a grave which was much longer and wider than the coffin. A black cat was placed in the grave and the whole covered with a cloth that we fastened down so that the cat could not get out. The black chicken was then taken from its confinement and fed a half glass of whiskey in which a paper had been soaked that bore the name of the man who was to die. The chicken was put in with the cat, and left there for a full month.

The night after the entombment of the cat and the chicken, we began to burn the black candles. Nine candles were set to burn in a barrel and every night at twelve o'clock we would go to the barrel and call upon the spirit of Death to follow the man. The candles were dressed by biting off the bottoms, as Pierre called for vengeance. Then the bottom was lighted instead of the top.

At the end of the month, the coffin containing the doll was carried out to the grave of the cat and chicken and buried upon their remains. A white bouquet was placed at the head and foot of the grave.

The beef brain was placed on a plate with nine hot peppers around it to cause insanity and brain hemorrhages, and placed on the altar. The tongue was slit, the name of the victim inserted, the slit was closed with a pack of pins and buried in the tomb.

"The black candles must burn for ninety days," Pierre told me. "He cannot live. No one can stand that."

Every night for ninety days Pierre slept in his holy place in a black draped coffin. And the man died.

CONCERNING THE DEAD

THERE are many superstitions concerning the dead. All over the South and in the Bahamas the spirits of the dead have great power which is used chiefly to harm. It will be noted how frequently graveyard dust is required in the practice of hoodoo, goofer dust as it is often called.

It is to be noted that in nearly all of the killing ceremonies the cemetery is used.

The Ewe-speaking peoples of the west coast of Africa all make offerings of food and drink—particularly libations of palm wine and banana beer upon the graves of the ancestor. It is to be noted in America that the spirit is always given a pint of good whisky. He is frequently also paid for his labor in cash.

It is well known that church members are buried with their feet to the east so that they will arise on that last day facing the rising sun. Sinners are buried facing the opposite direction. The theory is that sunlight will do them harm rather than good, as they will no doubt wish to hide their faces from an angry God.

Ghosts cannot cross water—so that if a hoodoo doctor wishes to sic a dead spirit upon a man who lives across water, he must first hold the mirror ceremony to fetch the victim from across the water.

People who die from the sick bed may walk any night, but Friday night is the night of the people who died in the dark—who were executed. These people have never been in the light. They died with the black cap over the face. Thus, they are blind. On Friday nights they visit the folks who died from sick beds and they lead the blind ones wherever they wish to visit.

Ghosts feel hot and smell faintish. According to testimony all except those who died in the dark may visit their former homes every night at twelve o'clock. But they must be back in the cemetery at two o'clock sharp or they will be shut out by the watchman and must wander about for the rest of the night. That is why the living are frightened by seeing ghosts at times. Some spirit has lingered

too long with the living person it still loves and has been shut out from home.

Pop Drummond of Fernandina, Fla., says they are not asleep at all. They "Sings and has church and has a happy time, but some are spiteful and show themselves to scare folks." Their voices are high and thin. Some ghosts grow very fat if they get plenty to eat. They are very fond of honey. Some who have been to the holy place wear seven-starred crowns and are very "suscautious" and sensible.

Dirt from sinners' graves is supposed to be very powerful, but some hoodoo doctors will use only that from the graves of infants. They say that the sinner's grave is powerful to kill, but his spirit is likely to get unruly and kill others for the pleasure of killing. It is too dangerous to commission.

The spirit newly released from the body is likely to be destructive. This is why a cloth is thrown over the face of a clock in the death chamber and the looking glass is covered over. The clock will never run again, nor will the mirror ever cast any more reflections if they are not covered so that the spirit cannot see them.

When it rains at a funeral it is said that God wishes to wash their tracks off the face of the earth, they were so displeasing to him.

If a murder victim is buried in a sitting position, the murderer will be speedily brought to justice. The victim sitting before the throne is able to demand that justice be done. If he is lying prone he cannot do this.

A fresh egg in the hand of a murder victim will prevent the murderer's going far from the scene. The egg represents life, and so the dead victim is holding the life of the murderer in his hand.

Sometimes the dead are offended by acts of the living and slap the face of the living. When this happens, the head is slapped one-sided and the victim can never straighten his neck. Speak gently to ghosts, and do not abuse the children of the dead.

It is not good to answer the first time that your name is called.

It may be a spirit and if you answer it, you will die shortly. They never call more than once at a time, so by waiting you will miss probable death.

CONJURE DOCTORS

CONJURE doctors have to diagnose the case, tell the person whether he is conjured or not (he usually is if some of the less ethical members of the profession get hold of him) and to find out who "layed de trick." The "trick" (charm) must be found and destroyed and the patient cured. If the patient wishes we must also be able to turn the trick back upon the one who set it. Besides this, a conjurer truly up in his profession must be able to lay haunts, and to locate buried treasure or a vein of water. The treasure trove may be found by taking a divining rod (a small branch with two side limbs running off in the shape of a "V", driving a nail in the end of each branching twig and in the spot where they converge, holding these twib ends in the hands, and marching boldly over the suspected landscape. When you pass over the buried treasure the free end will be pulled suddenly toward the ground. Or, simpler still, you may put three pieces of brass in our right hand, keeping them well separated. Sniff occasionally and when you pass over the buried treasure you will find that the brass will automatically begin to smell. Water may be located by a similar rod without the nails; or if you observe a tree in the locality with the limbs longer on one side than on the other, the tree bending somewhat in that direction, you may be reasonably sure that a vein of water is located beneath the surface of the earth on that side.

HOODOO PRESCRIPTIONS
TO KILL

GET bad vinegar, beef gall, filet gumbo with red pepper, and put names written across each other in bottles. Shake the bottle for

nine mornings and talk and tell it what you want it to do. To kill the victim, turn it upside down and bury it breast deep, and he will die.

TO MAKE PEOPLE LOVE YOU

TAKE nine lumps of starch, nine of sugar, nine teaspoons of steel dust. Wet it all with Jockey Club cologne. Take nine pieces of ribbon, blue, red, or yellow. Take a dessertspoonful and put it on a piece of ribbon and tie it in a bag. As each fold is gathered together call his name. As you wrap it with yellow thread call his name till you finish. Make nine bags and place them under a rug, behind an armoire, under a step or over a door. They will love you and give you everything they can get. Distance makes no difference. Your mind is talking to his mind and nothing beats that.

BLACK MAGIC
TO FREE A CRIMINAL

SECURE a strand from the rope to be used to hang him and have 'Conjurer Doctor' say a prayer over it. Slip it to the condemned and he will go free.

TO HURT AN ENEMY

PUT his name in a dead bird's mouth and let the bird dry up. This will bring him bad luck.

A FETISH TO CAUSE DEATH

HAIR from a horse's tail, a snake's tooth, and gunpowder. Wrap in a rag and bury under your enemy's doorstep.

TO DRIVE A WOMAN CRAZY

SPRINKLE nutmeg on her left shoe every night at midnight.

TO GET REVENGE ON A WOMAN

KEEP a bit of her hair and all her hair will fall out.

TO MAKE A WOMAN DROWN HERSELF

GET a piece of her underwear, turn it inside out and bury it at midnight, and put a brick on the grave.

BLACK ART USED TO INFLUENCE PEOPLE

TO WIN LOVE

TAKE some of the desired one's hair and sleep with it under the pillow.

Rub love oil into the palm of your right hand.

Carry a piece of weed called 'John the Conqueror' in your pocket.

TO MAKE A LOVE POWDER

GUT live hummingbirds. Dry the heart and powder it. Sprinkle the powder on the person you desire.

A LOVE FETISH

PUT a live frog in an ant's nest. When the bones are clean, you will find one flat, heart-shaped, and one with a hook. Secretly hook this into the garment of your beloved, and keep the heart-shaped one. If you should lose the heart-shaped bone, he will hate you as much as he loved you before.

TO KEEP A LOVER FAITHFUL

WRITE his name on a piece of paper and put it up the chimney. Pray to it three times a day.

TO WIN BACK A HUSBAND

Put a little rain water in a clean glass. Drop in three lumps of sugar, saying, 'Father, Son, Holy Spirit.' Then three more lumps, saying, 'Jesus, Mary, Joseph.' Drop in three more lumps while making your request. Put the glass in a dark room (never before a mirror), and place a spoon on the top of the glass. Next morning stir the contents toward you, then, with back toward the street, throw the contents against the house or fence, saying, 'Father, Son, Holy Spirit, Jesus, Mary, Joseph, please grant my favor.' Water must not be spilled, for it must not be walked on.

TO GET RID OF A MAN

Pick a rooster naked, give him a spoonful of whiskey, then put in his beak a piece of paper on which is written nine times the name of the person to be gotten rid of. The rooster is then turned loose in Saint Roch's cemetery. Within three days the man dies.

TO GET RID OF PEOPLE

In New Orleans it is said that a collector or salesman will never return if you sprinkle salt after him.

Dry three pepper pods in an open oven, then place them in a bottle, fill with water, and place under your doorstep for three days. Then sprinkle the water around your house, saying, 'Delonge toi de la' (remove yourself from here), and the person will never return.

TO MAKE SOMEONE MOVE

TAKE the hair off a dead black cat, fill its mouth with lemons that have been painted with melted red wax crayon. Wrap animal in silver paper, repeat your desire over it, and place it under the house of the person.

VOODOO AND WITCHES

'I DON'T believe in no hoodoo at all,' declared Bongy Jackson. 'One time one of my nephews got into police trouble and a woman come to my house and say if I pay her she could help me with hoodoo. I give that woman some of my money and the best ham we have in the smokehouse and she give me a paper with some writing on it and some kind of powder in it and somethin' what looked like a root dried up. She told me to send 'em to that boy and tell him to chew the root in the courtroom durin' his trial and to hold the piece of paper in his hand and to spit on it now and then when the judge wasn't lookin'. I did all that and he did all that and that boy go to jail just the same. No, I don't believe in no hoodoo.'

'I never seen a witch,' admitted Rebecca Fletcher, 'but my Grandma knew lots of 'em and she done tol' me plenty times what they looks like. My Grandma told me about a witch that went into a good woman's house when that woman was in bed. That woman knowed she was a witch so she told her to go into the other roon. Ole witch went out and lef' her skin layin' on the floor and the woman jumped out of bed and sprinkled it wit' salt and pepper. Old witch come back put on her skin. She start hollerin' and jumpin' up and down like she was crazy. She yelled and yelled. She yelled, "I can't stand it! I can't stand it! Something's bitin' me!" Ole witch hollered, "Skin, don't you know me?" She

said this three times, but the salt and pepper keep bitin'. The woman took a broomstick and shooed that old witch right out and she disappeared in the air.'

WITCHES WHO RIDE

THE chief activity of the witch is riding folks, though occasionally there is that evil succubus who steals wives. One informant regards witches as identical with conjurers: "Dey's who' hoodoos, Marse Newebell, dey sho' is. Dey's done sold deir soul ter de debbil, (the old European view) an' ole Satan gi' dem de pow'r ter change ter anything dey wants. Mos' gen'ally dey rides you in de shape uv a black cat, an' rides you in de daytime too, well ez de night." You can always tell when such witches have been riding you; you feel "down and out" the next morning and the bit these evil friends put in your mouth leaves a mark in each corner. When you feel smothered and can not get up, ("jes' lak somebody holdin' you down") right then and there the old witch is taking her midnight gallop. You try to call out, but it is no use; your tongue is mute, your hair crawls out of its braids and your hands and feet tingle. My old mammy was very sick one time. Something heavy was pressing upon her chest. A good woman touched her, the load was lifted, and a dark form floated out through the window. "Hit mus' 'er been a witch." When you find your hair plaited into little stirrups in the morning or when it is all tangled up and your face scratched you may be sure that the witches have been bothering you that night. In Virginia "the hage turns the victim on his or her back. A bit (made by the witch) is then inserted in the mouth of the sleeper and he or she is turned on all-fours and ridden like a horse. Next morning the person is tired out, and finds dirt between the fingers and toes."

There is one song about an old woman who saddles, bridles, boots, and spurs a person, and rides him fox-hunting and down the hillsides, but in general, the Negroes deny that the person ridden is actually changed into a horse. But, horse or not, when a person

talks or cries out in his sleep a witch is surely after him. Horses as well as humans are ridden; you can tell when the witches have been bothering them by finding "witches' stirrups" (two strands of hair twisted together) in the horses' mane. A person who plaits a horse's mane and leaves it that way is simply inviting the witches to ride, though they will seldom bother the horses except on very dark nights, and even then have a decided preference for very dark horses.

HAGS AND HORSES

THIS connection between horses and witches is further shown by the statement that witches are synonymous with *nightmares* and may be prevented from riding you by placing a fork under your pillow. This connection with the horse is all the more strange since horseshoes hung over the doors, windows, beds and in other parts of the house, are supposed to be a sure way of keeping these unwelcome visitants away. The Maryland Negroes say, "de witch got to travel all over de road dat the horseshoe been 'fo' she can git in de house, and time she git back it would be day." A horse bridle put over the churn will free the butter from a witch's control. Without doubt the fact that the horse has been used in the past as a fetish animal for auguries has led to its present-day association with witches, and also, possibly to the fact that in New Orleans and in parts of Mississippi, at least, a hoodoo-doctor is spoken of as a "horse."

AIDS TO THE LOVELORN

LOVE charms are particularly common and seem to be mainly small bits of conjuration practice which have come into popular use. Hair from your lover's head placed under the band of your hat, worn

in your purse, or in your pocket nearest your heart, buried under your lover's doorstep, or nailed to a tree or post, will make that person love you; but, inserted in a green tree, it will run the owner crazy. The bow from your sweetheart's hat is equally effective in love affairs, worn in your shoe or in your stocking (if you lose it he will beat you to death), tied around your leg, or thrown into running water (if thrown into stagnant water he will go crazy). Else you may write a note and slip it in the hat band of the desired person, or pick up that person's track and lay it over the door. Others suggest the boy kissing his elbow in order to win a girl, or putting a letter from his lady love in a can and throwing it into running water. If a boy can contrive to have his eyes meet those of his girl and rub bluestone in his hands at the same time she is his forever. If you pass between two persons of the opposite sex you will marry both of them.

WEDDINGS

THE days of the week have the following significance as relates to weddings:

Monday—a bad day.

Tuesday—a good day. You will have a good husband and he will live long.

Wednesday—a grand day. You will have a good husband and will live happily, but will have some trouble.

Thursday—a bad day.

Friday—a bad day.

Saturday—no luck at all.

Sunday—no luck at all.

May brides will die while June brides will get rich. Colors are significant as follows:

Marry in green, your husband will be mean.

Marry in red, you wish yourself dead.

Marry in brown, you will live in town.

Marry in blue, your husband will be true.

Marry in black, you will wish yourself back.
Marry in gray, you will stray away.
Marry in pink, your love will sink.
Marry in white, you have chosen all right.

SOUTH CAROLINA SUPERSTITIONS

Don't walk over a broom or you'll spend your life in jail or you won't get married.

Don't kill a bluebird—this means bad luck—and if a spider descends on a string of his web, don't let him rise again. This means death.

If anyone is lying down, don't step over him or you'll catch all of his sickness.

If you kill a snake, be sure you don't leave it lying on its back— it'll bring rain. Also, be sure it's dead, for if it isn't its mate will come and nurse it back to health.

NAMES FOR DICE NUMBERS

2 — Snake Eyes
3 — Craps
4 — Little Joe
5 — Fever
6 — Big Six
7 — Natural
8 — Ada from Decatur
9 — Nina
10 — Big Dick
11 — Natural
12 — Boxcars

DICE SHOOTING SONG

My baby needs a new pair of shoes; come along, you seven,
She can't get 'em if I lose; come along, you seven.
Roll them bones, roll 'em on a square, roll 'em on a sidewalk,
Street and everywhere; we'll roll 'em in the mornin', Joe.

Roll them in the night,
We'll roll them bones the whole day long,
When the cops are out of sight,
We will roll them bones.

READING THE DECK

Ace means the first time that Ah met you,
Deuce means there was nobody there but us two,
Trey means the third party, Charlie was his name,
Four spot means the fourth time you tried dat same ole game,
Five spot is five years you played me for a clown,
Six spot, six feet of earth when de deal goes down.
Now, I'm holdin' de seben spot for each day in de week,
Eight spot, eight hours you sheba-ed wid yo' sheik,
Nine spot means nine hours I work hard every day,
Ten spot de tenth of every month I brought you home mah pay,
De Jack is Three Card Charlie who played me for a goat,
De Queen, dat's you, pretty mama, also tryin' tuh out mah throat,
De King, dat hot papa Nunkie, and he's gointer wear de crown,
So be keerful y'all ain't broke when de deal goes down.

LET THE DEAL GO DOWN

When your cards gits lucky, oh, partner,
You ought to be in a rolling game.
Let the deal go down, boys,
Let the deal go down.

I ain't had no money, Lawd, partner,
I ain't had no change.
Let the deal go down, boys,
Let the deal go down.

I ain't had no trouble, Lawd, partner,
Till I stop by here.
Let the deal go down, boys,
Let the deal go down.

I'm going back to 'Bama, Lawd, partner,
Won't be worried with you.
Let the deal go down, boys,
Let the deal go down.

SONG OF 4-11-44

Four, 'leven and forty-four,
Four, 'leven and forty-four.
Goin' down this mornin'
'Cause I got to go.
But if I hit this gig,
Ain't gonna bust these suds no more!
Four, 'leven and forty-four,

Four, 'leven and forty-four,
Soapy water and dirty clo'es.
I'm bustin' these suds
Up to my elbows!
Four, 'leven and forty-four,
Four, 'leven and forty-four,
My man, he's lazy.
He ain't no good,
But if I hit this gig,
He's gonna dress up like he should!
Four, 'leven and forty-four,
Four, 'leven and forty-four,
'Fore I lose my haid,
'Cause my man's in that
Yaller woman's bed!
Four, 'leven and forty-four,
Four, 'leven and forty-four,
He walked out my door.
Last night he said, Honey,
I'm comin' back
When you git your big black money!
Four, 'leven and forty-four,
Four, 'leven and forty-four,
Let me hit that gig.
I'm needin' my man so bad
I'm feelin' freakish;
It's makin' me mean, lowdown and sad!

NEW ORLEANS LOTTERY SHOPS

'Lottery shops? Yes, sir. There's three in this block. The Bag of
Gold, the Clover Bloom and the Horseshoe Blue.

'Sure, I'd rather play Lottery than gamble at a dice table. You
can't use no system with dice, but you sure can with Lottery. Like
on Monday you play a nickel gig and a nickel saddle. Then you

don't play no more until the list comes out. Then you play again. You can't lose no more than seventy cents in a week. But you gotta stick to your numbers. They bound to come out sometimes. It's just like feedin' up a little ole shoat. You gotta fatten that pig up first. Then you kills him.

'And you gotta play your hunches. You gotta play what comes to you. Dreams is a good way. Everybody plays their dreams. Sure I got me a dream book.'

There are numbers for every dream, for every hunch. Everyone has his own personal superstition about how to win at Lottery. Ideas like these prevail:

'I burns things, me. I burns candles, lamps and all kinds of powders. It sure do work too.'

'I knows a woman who mixes up black pepper and cinnamon and sprinkles it all around her house. She won lots of money that way. She lives off Lottery.'

'I always plays my numbers by what I thinks and dreams. I don't play on nothin' I can see, that's livin', or nothin' I can touch with my hand. My numbers is all from the spirit.'

'The other night I dreams a tall and handsome brown man was makin' love to me. I played sixteen for his color, seven for his height and forty-two for the age he looked about to be. All three of them numbers come out.'

'I plays Lottery like you goes to your office. It's my whole life, man. I wouldn't give it up for nothin'. If I had to choose between work and Lottery, I sure would take Lottery, 'cause I feels I can make money and still have all my time to myself.'

'Lottery ain't no sin. I feels I is justified in playin' it, 'cause then I gits what I wants without havin' to steal. So, you see, it ain't no sin.'

THE HIT

THE most popular gambling game in New York City, and especially in Harlem, is the numbers. The poorest, most miserable

creature alive can play. To try his luck, all he needs is a penny, and if his guess is right the numbers bank will pay him six dollars in return. The odds against his winning are a thousand to one, and his payoff is only six hundred to one, but this disparity is somewhat compensated for by the comparative ease with which he can play this supposedly illegal game. The fat lady upstairs who sits at home all day with her cats and dogs, the grasping little man in the candy store across the street, the furtive, overdressed loafer with glistening shoes who is standing on the corner at sunrise—each will take a bet on the numbers. The penny bet is the stock in trade of a multi-million-dollar business with its headquarters downtown in the city's financial district. This business is incorporated, after a fashion; it has its stockholders, its officers, its workers, and its payroll. Its volume of business is steady, and it is seldom in crisis, for it is based on that most solid and persistent of all American phenomena—the dream.

Noon eased itself into the Manhattan streets. The sun hung high over Harlem, and its heat was heavy as a white cloak over the flat roofs and the gray streets. Children sought the coolness of dark basements and dark hallways. The old people sat near their windows and looked with indifference out onto the shimmering streets. Behind the lunch counters brown girls and yellow girls, irritated by the heat and their own perspiration, grouchily served up frank-furters with sauerkraut, hot sausages with mustard and relish and onion, milk shakes, malteds, coffee, and orange juice; served these to impatient clerks and laborers and helpers' helpers, to shoppers, policemen, and hack drivers. Preachers napped and dreamed of churches larger than the Abyssinian. Lawyers and petty real-estate brokers planned and schemed and gamblers figured. A con man dropped a wallet with a hundred-dollar bill in it to the sidewalk in front of the Corn Exchange Bank and waited for a sucker to fall for the age-old game. A hustler sat in her apartment on Sugar Hill sipping cocktails with a white merchant from downtown who was taking a long week end, sized him up, estimated his worth. Madam Lawson shuffled her cards, Madam Fatima stared into her silver crystal ball, and turbaned Abdul Ben Said of the ebony skin mumbled an incantation to the black gods of old, and lo! all of

them saw glory in the morning if not sooner. There, near the top
of Manhattan Island, Harlem sizzled and baked and groaned and
rekindled its dream under the midday sun.

And so the great dream machine was wound tight. The nickels
were in the slots and the players waited. Only a turn of the handle
was needed to set the whole thing in motion.

Oh, Lord, please let that number be 316 today. You know my
life ain't been easy, me with three mouths to feed and that man of
mine done snuck away like a dirty little coward. I done forgive
him, Lord, the way I know You wanted me to—I never think no
evil of him no more. But it's hard trying to feed these three kids
on thirty dollars a week. Now, with a twenty-five cent hit I could
get shoes for little Johnny and Mary and Sarah Lou, and clothes to
keep them in school . . . So if you please, Lord, let that number
come 316. . . .

A girl needs nice things or men just look the other way . . .
dresses, slips, a handbag . . . Honest to goodness, I'm out of just
about everything. Just can't seem to make enough to keep up. But
if I can hit 212 today . . .

How a man can work so hard and never have any money I just
don't know. If that 530 don't come today, I just don't know what
I'm going to do. There's the television set to be paid, the refrigerator,
the furniture and the car, all of which comes due the first of the
month. Not to mention the rent that never stops and the gas and
electricity and the telephone. I could take care of these things if
530 was to jump out just the way I played it.

Let 728 come, and Harlem's gonna wake up and find out that I
am here. I'll rent myself a suite up on the top floor of the Theresa
and throw a party that will last a week. Then I'll buy myself the
prettiest Cadillac Harlem ever saw. It'll even have a television set in
it. I might even send some money to Mama down home, too. She
ain't been doing so good lately. . . .

Lord, I'm needing a new church so as I can help set these people
back on the path of righteousness. I saw a nice big store at One
hundred and thirty-sixth and Lenox, and I have made inquiries,
and I know that store can be acquired for a hundred and twenty-five
a month. Now, they want two months in advance, and You know I
don't have that kind of money. It's the perfect site for the Blessed

Lamb Holiness Church. From there, Lord, the truth of Your loving word will flow all over Harlem and bring these wayward sheep back to the fold. The number is 471, Lord, and I have played it in a six-way combination. Now, if in Your loving kindness You could see fit to make things go that way, O Lord, we would be eternally in Your debt as we are already. All these things we ask in Jesus' name.

Amen.

· IX ·

On the Levee

LEVEE LIFE

HAUNTS AND PASTIMES OF THE ROUSTABOUTS
THEIR ORIGINAL SONGS AND PECULIAR DANCES

ALONG the river-banks on either side of the levee slope, where the
brown water year after year climbs up to the ruined sidewalks, and
pours into the warehouse cellars, and paints their grimy walls with
streaks of water-weed green, may be studied a most curious and
interesting phase of life—the life of a community within a community,—a society of wanderers who have haunts but not homes,
and who are only connected with the static society surrounding
them by the common bond of State and municipal law. It is a very
primitive kind of life; its lights and shadows are alike characterized
by a half savage simplicity; its happiness or misery is almost purely
animal; its pleasures are wholly of the hour, neither enhanced nor
lessened by anticipations of the morrow. It is always pitiful rather
than shocking; and it is not without some little charm of its own—
the charm of a thoughtless existence, whose virtues are all original,
and whose vices are for the most part foreign to it. A great portion
of this levee-life haunts also the subterranean hovels and ancient
frame buildings of the district lying east of Broadway to Culvert
street, between Sixth and Seventh streets. But, on a cool spring
evening, when the levee is bathed in moonlight, and the torch-
basket lights dance redly upon the water, and the clear air vibrates

to the sonorous music of the deep-toned steam-whistle, and the sound of wild banjo-thrumming floats out through the open doors of the levee dance-houses, then it is perhaps that one can best observe the peculiarities of this grotesquely-picturesque roustabout life.

Probably less than one-third of the stevedores and 'longshoremen employed in our river traffic are white; but the calling now really belongs by right to the Negroes, who are by far the best roustabouts and are unrivaled as firemen. The white stevedores are generally tramps, willing to work only through fear of the workhouse; or, some times laborers unable to obtain other employment, and glad to earn money for the time being at any employment. On board the boats, the whites and blacks mess separately and work under different mates, there being on an average about twenty-five roustabouts to every boat which unloads at the Cincinnati levee. Cotton boats running on the lower Mississippi will often carry sixty or seventy deck-hands, who can some seasons earn from forty-five dollars to sixty dollars per month. On the Ohio boats the average wages paid to roustabouts will not exceed $30 per month. 'Longshoremen earn fifteen and twenty cents per hour, according to the season. These are frequently hired by Irish contractors, who undertake to unload a boat at so much per package; but the first-class boats generally contract with the 'longshoremen directly through the mate, and sometimes pay twenty-five cents per hour for such labor. "Before Freedom," as the colored folks say, white laborers performed most of the roustabout labor on the steamboats; the Negroes are now gradually monopolizing the calling, chiefly by reason of their peculiar fitness for it. Generally speaking, they are the best porters in the world; and in the cotton States, it is not uncommon, we are told, to see Negro levee hands for a wager, carry five-hundred-pound cotton-bales on their backs to the wharfboat. River men, to-day are recognizing the superior value of Negro labor in steamboat traffic, and the colored roustabouts are now better treated, probably, than they have been since the war. Under the present laws, too, they are better protected. It used at one time to be a common thing for some ruffianly mate to ship sixty or seventy stevedores, and, after the boat had taken in all her freight, to hand the poor fellows their money and land them at some small town, or even in the woods,

hundreds of miles from their home. This can be done no longer
with legal impunity.

Roustabout life in the truest sense is, then, the life of the colored
population of the Rows, and, partly, of Buck-town-blacks and
mulattoes from all parts of the States, but chiefly from Kentucky and
Eastern Virginia, where most of them appear to have toiled on the
plantation before Freedom; and echoes of the old plantation life
still live in their songs and their pastimes. You may hear old
Kentucky slave songs chanted nightly on the steamboats, in that
wild, half-melancholy key peculiar to the natural music of the
African race; and you may see the old slave dances nightly performed to the air of some ancient Virginia-reel in the dance-houses
of Sausage Row, or the "ball rooms" of Bucktown. There is an intense uniqueness about all this pariah existence; its boundaries are
most definitely fixed; its enjoyments are wholly sensual, and many
of them are marked by peculiarities of a strictly local character.
Many of their songs, which have never appeared in print, treat of
levee life in Cincinnati, of all the popular steamboats running on the
"Muddy Water," and of the favorite roustabout haunts on the river
bank and in Bucktown. To collect these curious songs, or even all
the most popular of them, would be a labor of months, and even
then a difficult one, for the colored roustabouts are in the highest
degree suspicious of a man who approaches them with a note-book
and pencil. Occasionally, however, one can induce an intelligent
steamboatman to sing a few river songs by an innocent bribe in the
shape of a cigar or a drink, and this we attempted to do with considerable success during a few spare evenings last week, first, in a
popular roustabout haunt on Broadway near Sixth, and afterward
in a dingy frame cottage near the corner of Sixth and Culvert
streets. Unfortunately some of the most curious of these songs are
not of a character to admit of publication in the columns of a daily
newspaper; but others which we can present to our readers may
prove interesting. Of these the following song, *Number Ninety-
Nine*, was at one time immensely popular with the steamboatmen.
The original resort referred to was situated on Sixth and Culvert
streets, where Kirk's building now stands. We present the song
with some necessary emendations:

You may talk about yer railroads,
Yer steamboats and can-*el*
If 't hadn't been for Liza Jane
There wouldn't bin no hell.
Chorus—Oh, ain't I gone, gone, gone,
Oh, ain't I gone, gone, gone,
Oh, ain't I gone, gone, gone,
Way down de ribber road.

Whar do you get yer whisky?
Whar do you get yer rum?
I got it down in Bucktown,
At Number Ninety-nine.
Chorus—Oh, ain't I gone, gone, gone, etc.

I went down to Bucktown,
Nebber was dar before,
Great big Negro knocked me down,
But Katy barred the door.
Chorus—Oh, ain't I gone, gone, gone, etc.

She hugged me, she kissed me,
She told me not to cry;
She said I wus de sweetest thing
Dat ebber libbed or died.
Chorus—Oh, ain't I gone, gone, gone, etc.

Yonder goes the Wildwood,
She's loaded to the guards,
But yonder comes the Fleetwood,
An' she's the boat for me.
Chorus—Oh, ain't I gone, gone, gone, etc.

The words, "Way down to Rockingham," are sometimes substituted in the chorus, for "way down de ribber road."

One of the most popular roustabout songs now sung on the Ohio is the following. The air is low, and melancholy, and when sung in unison by the colored crew of a vessel leaving or approaching port,

has a strange, sad sweetness about it which is very pleasing. The two-fold character of poor Molly, at once good and bad, is somewhat typical of the stevedore's sweetheart:

> Molly was a good gal and a bad gal, too.
> Oh Molly, row, gal.
> Molly was a good gal and a bad gal, too,
> Oh Molly, row, gal.
>
> I'll row dis boat and I'll row no more,
> Row, Molly, row, gal.
> I'll row dis boat, and I'll go on shore,
> Row, Molly, row, gal.
>
> Captain on the biler deck a-having of the lead,
> Oh Molly, row, gal.
> Calling to the pilot to give her, 'Turn ahead,'
> Row, Molly, row, gal.

Here is another to a slow and sweet air. The chorus, when well sung, is extremely pretty:

> Shawneetown is burning down,
> Who tole you so?
> Shawneetown is burnin' down,
> Who tole you so?
>
> Cythie, my darlin' gal,
> Who tole you so?
> Cythie, my darlin' gal,
> How do you know?
>
> CHORUS Shawneetown is burnin', etc.
>
> How the h—l d'ye 'spect me to hold her,
> Way down below?
> I've got no skin on either shoulder,
> Who tole you so?

CHORUS   Shawneetown is burnin', etc.

De houses dey is all on fire,
Way down below.
De houses dey is all on fire,
Who tole you so?

CHORUS   Shawneetown is burnin', etc.

My old missus told me so,
Way down below.
An' I b'lieve what ole missus says,
Way down below.

CHORUS   Shawneetown is burnin', etc.

The most melancholy of all these plaintive airs is that to which the song "Let her go by" is commonly sung. It is generally sung on leaving port, and sometimes with an affecting pathos inspired of the hour, while the sweethearts of the singers watch the vessel gliding down stream.

I'm going away to New Orleans!
Good-by, my lover, good-by!
I'm going away to New Orleans!
Good by, my lover, good-by!
Oh, let her go by!

She's on her way to New Orleans!
Good-by, my lover, good-by!
She bound to pass the Robert E. Lee,
Good-by, my lover, good-by!
Oh, let her go by!

I'll make dis trip and I'll make no more!
Good-by, my lover, good-by
I'll roll dese barrels, I'll roll no more!
Good-by, my lover, good-by!
Oh, let her go by!

An' if you are not true to me,
Farewell, my lover, farewell!
An' if you are not true to me,
Farewell, my lover, farewell!
Oh, let her go by!

The next we give is of a somewhat livelier description. It has, we
believe, been printed in a somewhat different form in certain song
books. We give it as it was sung to us in a Broadway saloon:

I come down the mountain,
An' she come down the lane,
An' all that I could say to her
Was, Good-by, 'Liza Jane.

CHORUS   Farewell, 'Liza Jane!
Farewell, 'Liza Jane!
Don't throw yourself away, for I
Am coming back again.

I got up on a house-top,
An give my horn a blow;
Thought I heerd Miss Dinah say,
"Yonder comes your beau."
(Chorus.)

Ef I'd a few more boards,
To build my chimney higher,
I'd keep aroun' the country gals,
Chunkin' up the fire.
(Chorus.)

The following are fragments of rather lengthy chants, the words
being almost similar in both, but the choruses and airs being very
different. The air of the first is sonorous and regularly slow, like a
sailor's chant when heaving anchor, the air of the next is quick
and lively.

Belle-a-Lee's got no time,
Oh, Belle! Oh, Belle!
Robert E. Lee's got railroad time,
Oh, Belle! Oh, Belle!

Wish I was in Mobile Bay,
Oh, Belle! oh, Belle!
Rollin' cotton by de day,
Oh, Belle! oh, Belle!

.   .   .   .   [a]   .

I wish I was in Mobile Bay,
Rollin' cotton by de day,
Stow'n' sugar in de hull below,
Below, belo-ow,
Stow'n' sugar in de hull below!

De Natchez is a new boat; she's just in her prime,
Beats any oder boat on de New Orleans line.
Stow'n' sugar in de hull below, &c.

Engineer, t'rough de trumpet, gives de firemen news,
Couldn' make steam for de fire in de flues.
Stow'n' sugar in de hull below, &c.

Cap'n on de biler deck, a scratchin' of his head,
Hollers to de deck hand to heave de larbo'rd lead.
Stow'n' sugar in de hull below, &c.

Perhaps the prettiest of all these songs is *The Wandering Steam-boatman*. Which, like many other roustabout songs, rather frankly illustrates the somewhat loose morality of the calling:

I am a wandering steamboatman,
And far away from home;
I fell in love with a pretty gal,
And she in love with me.

> She took me to her parlor
> And cooled me with her fan;
> She whispered in her mother's ear:
> "I love the steamboatman."

The mother entreats her daughter not to become engaged to the stevedore. "You know," she says, "that he is a steamboatman, and has a wife at New Orleans." But the steamboatman replies, with great nonchalance:

> If I've a wife at New Orleans
> I'm neither tied nor bound;
> And I'll forsake my New Orleans wife
> If you'll be truly mine.

Another very curious and decidedly immoral song is popular with the loose women of the "Rows." We can only give one stanza:

> I hev a roustabout for my man—
> Livin' with a white man for a sham,
> Oh, leave me alone,
> Leave me alone,
> I'd like you much better if you'd leave me alone.

But the most famous song in vogue among the roustabouts is *Limber Jim,* or *Shiloh.* Very few know it all by heart, which is not wonderful when we consider that it requires something like twenty minutes to sing Limber Jim from beginning to end, and that the whole song, if printed in full, would fill two columns of the Commercial. The only person in the city who can sing the song through, we believe, is a colored laborer living near Sixth and Culvert streets, who "run on the river" for years, and acquired so much of a reputation by singing Limber Jim, that he has been nicknamed after the mythical individual aforesaid, and is now known by no other name. He keeps a little resort in Bucktown, which is known as "Limber Jim's," and has a fair reputation for one dwelling in that locality. Jim very good-naturedly sang the song for us a few nights ago, and we took down some of the most

striking verses for the benefit of our readers. The air is wonderfully quick and lively, and the chorus is quite exciting. The leading singer sings the whole song, excepting the chorus, Shiloh, which dissyllable is generally chanted by twenty or thirty voices of abysmal depth at the same time with a sound like the roar of twenty Chinese gongs struck with tremendous force and precision. A great part of Limber Jim is very profane, and some of it not quite fit to print. We can give only about one-tenth part of it. The chorus is frequently accompanied with that wonderfully rapid slapping of thighs and hips known as "patting Juba."

Black man and a white man playing seven-up,
White man played an ace, black man feared to take it up.
White man played an ace, black man played a nine.
White man died and black man went blind.
                    Limber Jim,
              (All.) Shiloh!
              Talk it agin,
              (All.) Shiloh!
              Walk back in love,
              (All.) Shiloh!
              You turtle-dove,
              (All.) Shiloh!

Went down the ribber, couldn't get across;
Hopped on a rebel louse; thought 'twas a hoss,
Oh lor', gals, 't aint no lie,
Lice in Camp Chase big enough to cry,—
                    Limber Jim, etc.

Bridle up a rat, sir; saddle up a cat,
Please han' me down my Leghorn hat,
Went to see widow; widow warn't home;
Saw to her daughter,—she gave me honeycomb.
                    Limber Jim, etc.

Jay-bird sittin' on a swinging limb,
Winked at me an' I winked at him.

Up with a rock an' struck him on the shin,
Dog-gone yer soul, don't wink again.
                    Limber Jim, etc.

Some folks says that a rebel can't steal,
I found twenty in my corn-fiel',
Sich pullin' of shucks an' tearin' of corn!—
Nebber saw the like since I was born.
                    Limber Jim, etc.

John Morgan come to Danville and cut a mighty dash,
Las' time I saw him, he was under whip an' lash;
'Long come a rebel at a sweepin' pace,
Whar 're ye goin', Mr. Rebel? "I'm goin' to Camp Chase."
                    Limber Jim, etc.

Way beyond de sun and de moon,
White gal tole me I were too soon.
White gal tole me I come to soon,
An' black gal called me an ole fool.
                    Limber Jim, etc.

Eighteen peonies hidden in a fence,
Cynthiana gals ain't got no sence;
Every time they go from home
Comb thar heads wid an ole jaw bone.
                    Limber Jim, etc.

Had a little wife an' didn' inten' to keep her;
Showed her a flatboat an' sent her down de ribber;
Head like a fodder-shock, mouf like a shovel,
Put yerself wid yaller gal, put yourself in troubble.
                    Limber Jim, etc.

I went down to Dinah's house, Dinah was in bed,
Hoisted de window an' poked out her head;
T'rowed, an' I hit in her de eyeball,—bim;
"Walk back, Mr. Man; don't do dat again."
                    Limber Jim, etc.

Gambling man in de railroad line,
Saved my ace an' played my nine;
If you want to know my name,
My name's High-low-jack-in-the-game.
Limber Jim,
Shiloh!
Talk it again,
Shiloh!
You dancing girl,
Shiloh!
Sure's you're born,
Shiloh!

Grease my heel with butter in the fat,
I can talk to Limber Jim better'n dat.
Limber Jim,
Shiloh!
Limber Jim,
Shiloh!
Walk back in love,
Shiloh!
My turtle dove,
Shiloh!

(Patting Juba)—And you can't go yonder,
Limber Jim!
And you can't go yonder,
Limber Jim!
And you can't go-oo-o!

Lafcadio Hearn

ANNIE CHRISTMAS

OLDTIMERS say that the Negro longshoremen and all life on the riverfront are not what they used to be. It's gone soft now, say they.

In other days men were really men, yet the toughest of them all was a woman. Her name was Annie Christmas. She was six feet, eight inches tall and she weighed more than two hundred and fifty pounds. She wore a neat mustache and had a voice as loud and as deep as a foghorn on the river. The tough keelboatmen, terrors of the river in other days, stood in awe of her and there wasn't a stevedore who didn't jump when Annie snapped her fingers. She could lick a dozen of them with one arm tied behind her back and they knew it.

Most of the time Annie dressed like a man and worked as a man. Often she worked as a longshoreman, pulled a sweep or hauled a cordelle. She would carry a barrel of flour under each arm and another balanced on her head. Once she towed a keel boat from New Orleans to Natchez on a dead run and never got out of breath.

Annie could outdrink any man in the South. She would put down a barrel of beer and chase it with ten quarts of whiskey, without stopping. Men used to buy her whiskey just to see her drink. Sometimes she got mad in a barroom, beat up every man in the place and wrecked the joint. Sometimes she did it for fun. Then, every once in a while, Annie would get into a feminine mood. When this happened she was really seductive and enticing in a super sort of way.

Annie had twelve black sons, each seven feet tall, all born at the same time. She had plenty of other babies, too, but these were her favorites. Whenever she got ready to have a baby, she drank a quart of whiskey and lay down somewhere. Afterward she had another quart and went straight back to work. Finally Annie met a man who could lick her and then she fell in love for the first time in her life. But the man didn't want her, so Annie bedeckered herself in all her finery and her famous necklace and committed suicide.

Her funeral was appropriately elaborate. Her body was placed in a coal-black coffin and driven to the wharf in a coal-black hearse, drawn by six coal-black horses. Six on each side, marched her coal-black sons, dressed in coal-black suits. At the riverfront the coffin was placed on a coal-black barge and that coal-black night, with no moon shining, her dozen coal-black sons floated on it with the coal-black coffin out to sea and vanished forever.

WATERFRONT LORE

A hook on a cistern is boun' to rust,
Lot of New Orleans wimmens is hard to trust.
If we two was like we three,
We'd all git together an' then agree.

A nickel is a nickel,
And a dime is a dime,
The best work is on the riverfront
All the time.

The boys in Wisconsin they take their time,
They go to work to make eight and a dime.
The boys in Chicago they gits a draf',
They go to work to make eight and a half.
The boys in New York they oughta be rich,
They go to work to make eight, six bits.
The boys in New Orleans they oughta be dead,
They go to work for fish and bread.

They'll work for the rich and they'll work for the poor,
Will work for a man jest day long so.
They'll work for Saint Peter and they'll work for Saint Paul,
They'll be in New Orleans workin' when the roll is called.
And I ain't bluffin',
I ain't gonna work for nothin'.

Amen Corner

SERMONS
DE SUN DO MOVE

'Low me to say dat when I was a young man and a slave, I knowed nothin worth talkin bout concernin books. Dey was sealed mysteries to me, but I tell you I longed to break de seal. I thirsted for de bread of learnin. When I seen books I ached to git in to 'em for I knowed dat dey had de stuff for me and I wanted to taste dere contents, but most of de time dey was barred against me.

By de mercy of de Lord a thing happened. I got a roomfeller—he was a slave, too and he had learned to read. In de dead of de night he give me lessons outen de New York Spellin Book. It was hard pullin, I tell you; harder on him, for he know'd just a little and it made him sweat to try to beat somethin into my hard head. It was worse with me. Up de hill every step, but when I got de light of de lesson into my noodle I fairly shouted, but I know'd I was not a scholar. De consequence was I crept long mighty tedious, gittin a crumb here and dere until I could read de Bible by skippin de long words, tolerable well. Dat was de start of my education—dat is what little I got. I make mention of dat young man. De years have fled away since den but I ain't forgot my teacher and never shall. I thank my Lord for him and I carries his memory in my heart.

Bout seven months after my gittin to readin, God converted my soul and I reckon bout de first and main thing dat I begged de Lord to give me was de power to understand His Word. I ain't braggin and I hates self-praise, but I bound to speak de thankful word. I believes in my heart dat my prayer to understand de Scriptur was heard. Since dat time I ain't cared bout nothin 'cept to study and preach de Word of God.

Not, my brothren, dat I's de fool to think I knows it all. Oh, my Father, no! Far from it. I don't hardly understand myself nor half of de things round me and dere is millions of things in de Bible too deep for Jaspcr and some of 'em too deep for everybody. I don't carry de keys to de Lord's closet and He ain't tell me to peep in and if I did I'm so stupid I wouldn't know it when I see it. No, friends, I knows my place at de feet of my Master and dere I stays.

But I can read de Bible and get de things what lay on de top of de soil. Outen de Bible I know nothin extry bout de sun. I seen its course as he rides up dere so gran and mighty in de sky, but dere is heaps bout dat flamin orb dat is too much for me. I know dat de sun shines powerfully and pours down its light in floods and yet dat is nothin compared with de light dat flashes in my mind from de pages of God's book. But you knows all dat. I knows dat de sun burns—oh, how it did burn in dem July days! I tell you he cooked de skin on my back many a day when I was hoein in de corn field. But you knows all dat—and yet dat is nothing to de divine fire dat burns in de souls of God's chillun. Can't you feel it, brothren?

But bout de course of de sun, I have got dat. I have done ranged through de whole blessed Book and scoured down de last thing de Bible has to say bout de movement of de sun. I got all dat pat and safe. And lemme say dat if I don't give it to you straight, if I gits one word crooked or wrong, you just holler out, 'Hold on dere, Jasper, you ain't got dat straight and I'll beg pardon. If I don't tell de truth, march up on dese steps here and tell me I's a liar and I'll take it. I fears I do lie sometimes—I'm so sinful, I find it hard to do right; but my God don't lie and He ain't put no lie in de Book of eternal truth and if I give you what de Bible say, den I bound to tell de truth.

I got to take you all dis afternoon on an excursion to a great battlefield. Most folks like to see fights—some is mighty fond of

gittin into fights and some is mighty quick to run down de back
alley when dere is a battle goin on for de right. Dis time I'll 'scort
you to a scene where you shall witness a curious battle. It took
place soon after Israel got in de Promise Land. You 'member de
people of Gideon make friends with God's people when dey first
entered Canaan and dey was monstrous smart to do it. But, just de
same, it got 'em in to an awful fuss. De cities round bout dere
flared up at dat and dey all joined dere forces and say dey gwine to
mop de Bigyun people off de ground and dey bunched all dere
armies together and went up for to do it. When dey come up so
bold and brace de Gideonites was scared outen dere senses and dey
sent word to Joshua dat dey was in trouble and he must run up dere
and git 'em out. Joshua had de heart of a lion and he was up dere
directly. Dey had an awful fight, sharp and bitter but you might
know dat General Joshua was not dere to get whipped. He prayed
and he fought and de hours got away too fast for him and so he
asked de Lord to issue a special order dat de sun hold up awhile and
dat de moon furnish plenty of moonshine down on de lowest part of
de fightin grounds. As a fact, Joshua was so drunk with de battle, so
thirsty for de blood of de enemies of de Lord and so wild with de
victory dat he tell de sun to stand still till he could finish his job.

What did de sun do? Did he glare down in fiery wrath and say,
'What you talking bout my stoppin for, Joshua? I ain't never
started yet. Been here all de time and it would smash up everything
if I was to start.' No, he ain't say dat. But what de Bible say? Dat's
what I ask to know. It say dat it was at de voice of Joshua dat it
stopped. I don't say it stopped; tain't for Jasper to say dat, but de
Bible, *de Book of God*, say so. But I say dis; nothin can stop until
it has first started. So I knows what I'm talkin bout. De sun was
travellin long dere through de sky when de order come. He hitched
his red ponies and made quite a call on de land of Gideon. He
perch up dere in de skies just as friendly as a neighbor what comes
to borrow somethin and he stand up dere and he look like he enjoyed de way Joshua waxes dem wicked armies. And de moon, she
wait down in de low grounds dere and pours out her light and look
just as calm and happy as if she was waitin for her escort. Dey
never budged, neither of 'em long as de Lord's army needed a light
to carry on de battle.

I don't read when it was dat Joshua hitch up and drove on, but I suppose it was when de Lord told him to go. Anybody knows dat de sun didn't stay dere all de time. It stopped for business and went on when it got through. Dis is bout all dat I has to do with dis particular case. I done showed you dat dis part of de Lord's word teaches you dat de sun stopped which show dat he was movin before dat and dat he went on afterwards. I told you dat I would prove dis and I's done it and I defies anybody to say dat my point ain't made.

I told you in de first part of dis discourse dat de Lord God is a man of war. I expect by now you begin to see it is so. Don't you admit it? When de Lord come to see Joshua in de day of his fears and warfare and actually make de sun stop stone still in de heavens so de fight can rage on till all de foes is slain, you're obliged to understand dat de God of peace is also de man of war. He can use both peace and war to heap de riches and to scatter de host of de aliens. A man talked to me last week bout de laws of nature and he say dey can't possibly be upset and I had to laugh right in his face. As if de laws of anything was greater dan my God who is de lawgiver for everything. My Lord is great! He rules in de heavens, in de earth and down under de ground. He is great and greatly to be praised. Let all de people bow down and worship before Him! Dere you are! Ain't dat de movement of de sun? Bless my soul! Hezekiah's case beat Joshua. Joshua stop de sun, but here de Lord make de sun walk back ten degrees; and yet dey say dat de sun stand stone still and never move a peg. It look to me he move round mighty brisk and is ready to go any way dat de Lord orders him to go. I wonder if any of dem philosophers is round here dis afternoon? I'd like to take a square look at one of dem and ask him to explain dis matter. He can't do it, my brothren. He knows a heap bout books, maps, figgers and long distances but I defy him to take up Hezekiah's case and explain it off. He can't do it, my brothren. De Word of de Lord is my defense and bulwark and I fears not what men say nor do—my God give me my victory.

Low me, my friends, to put myself square bout dis movement of de sun. It ain't no business of mine whether de sun move or stan still, or whether it stop or go back or rise or set. All dat is out of my hand entirely and I got nothin to say. I got no the-o-ry on de sub-

ject. All I ask is dat we will take what de Lord say bout it and let His will be done bout everything. What dat will is I can't know except He whisper into my sould or write it in a book. Here's de Book. Dis is enough for me and with it to pilot me, I can't get far astray.

But I ain't done with you yet. And de song says, dere's more to follow. I invite you to hear de first verse in de seventh chapter of de Book of Revelations. What do John under de power of de Spirit say? He says he saw four angels standin on de four corners of de earth, holdin de four winds of de earth and so forth. Low me to ask if de earth is round where do it keep its corners? A flat square thing has corners, but tell me where is de corner of an apple or a marble or a cannon ball or a silver dollar. If dere is anyone of dem philosophers what's been takin so many cracks at my old head bout here, he is cordially invited to step forward and square up dis vexin business. I hear tell dat you can't square a circle but it looks like dese great scholars done learn how to circle a square. If dey can do it, let 'em step to de front and do de trick. But, my brothren, in my poor judgement, dey can't do it; tain't in 'em to do it. Dey is on de wrong side of de Bible—dat's on de outside of de Bible, and dere's where de trouble comes in with 'em. Dey done got out of de breastworks of de truth and as long as dey stay dere de light of de Lord will not shine on dere path. I ain't care so much bout de sun, though it's mighty convenient to have it but my trust is in de Word of de Lord. Long as my feet is flat on de solid rock, no man can move me. I's gettin my orders from de God of my salvation.

The other day a man with a high collar and side whiskers come to my house. He was one nice Northern gentleman what think a heap of us colored people in de South. Dey are lovely folks and I honors 'em very much. He seem from de start kinder strict and cross with me and after a while he broke out furious and fretted and he says: 'Allow me Mister Jasper to give you some plain advice. Dis nonsense bout de sun movin where you are gettin is disgracin your race all over de country and as a friend of your people I come to say it's got to stop'. . . . Ha! Ha! Ha! . . . Mars Sam Hargroven-ever hardly smash me dat way. It was equal to one of dem old overseers way back yonder. I tell him dat if he'll show me I's wrong, I give it all up. . . . My! My! . . . Ha! Ha! . . . . He sail in on

me and such a storm bout science, new discoveries and de Lord only knows what all, I hever hear before and den he tel me my race is urgin me and poor old Jasper must shut up his fool mouth.

When he got through—it look like he never would—I tell him John Jasper ain't set up to be no scholar and don't know de philosophies and ain't trying to hurt his people but is workin day and night to lift 'em up but his foot is on de rock of eternal truth. Dere he stand and dere he is going to stand till Gabriel sounds de judgement note. So I say to de gentleman what scolded me up so dat I hear him make his remarks but I ain't hear where he get his Scripture from and that between him and de Word of de Lord, I take my stand by de Word of God every time. Jasper ain't mad; he ain't fighting nobody; he ain't been appointed janitor to run de sun; he nothin but de servant of God and a lover of de Everlasting Word. What I care bout de sun? De day comes on when de sun will be called from his race track and his light squinched out forever; de moon shall turn to blood and this earth be consumed with fire. Let 'em go; dat won't scare me nor trouble God's elected people, for de word of de Lord shall endure forever and on dat Solid Rock we stand and shall not be moved!

Is I got you satisfied yet? Has I proven my point? Oh, ye whose hearts is full of unbelief! Is you still holding out? I reckon de reason you say de sun don't move is cause you are so hard to move yourself. You is a real trial to me, but, never mind, I ain't given you up yet and never will. Truth is mighty; it can break de heart of stone and I must fire another arrow of truth out of de quiver of de Lord. If you has a copy of God's Word bout your person, please turn do dat minor prophet, Malachi, what write de last book in de whole Bible and look at chapter one, verse eleven. What do it say? I better read it for I got a notion you critics don't carry any Bible in your pockets every day in de week. Here is what it says: 'For from de rising of de sun even unto de goin down of de same, My name shall be great among de Gentiles . . . My name shall be great among de heathen, says de Lord of hosts!' How do dat suit you? It looks like dat ought to fix it! Dis time it is de Lord of Hosts hisself dat is doin de talkin and He is talkin on a wonderful and glorious subject. He is telling of de spreadin of His Gospel of de comin of His last victory over de Gentiles and de world-wide

glories dat at de last He is to get. Oh, my brothren, what a time dat will be! My soul takes wing as I anticipate with joy dat millenium day! De glories as dey shine before my eyes blinds me and I forget de sun and moon and stars. I just remembers dat long bout dose last days dat de sun and moon will go out of business for dey won't be needed no more. Den will King Jesus come back to see His people and He will be de sufficient light of de world. Joshua's battles will be over. Hezekiah won't need no sun dial and de sun and moon will fade out before de glorious splendors of de New Jerusalem.

But what de matter with Jasper? I most forgot my business and most gone to shoutin over de far away glories of de second comin of my Lord. I beg pardon and will try to get back to my subject. I have to do as de sun in Hezekiah's case—fall back a few degrees. In dat part of de Word dat I'm given you from Malachi—dat de Lord hisself spoke—he declares dat His glory is gwine to spread. Spread? Where? From de rising of de sun to de goin down of de same. What? Don't say dat, does it? Dat's exactly what its says. Ain't dat clear enough for you? De Lord pity dese doubtin Thomases. Here is enough to settle it all and cure de worse cases. Wake up here, wise folks, and get your medicine. Where is dem high collared philosophers now? What dey skulkin round in de brush for? Why don't you get out in de broad afternoon light and fight for your collars? Ah, I understand it; you got no answer. De Bible is against you and in your consciences you are convicted.

But I hears you back dere. What you whisperin bout? I know! You say you sent me some papers and I never answer dem . . . Ha, ha, ha! . . . I got 'em. De difficulty bout dem papers you sent me is dat dey did not answer me. Dey never mention de Bible one time. You think so much of yourself and so little of de Lord God and thinks what you say is so smart dat you can't even speak of de Word of de Lord. When you ask me to stop believing in de Lord's Word and to pin my faith to your words, I ain't goin to do it. I take my stand by de Bible and rest my case on what it says. I take what de Lord says bout my sins, bout my Saviour, bout life, bout death, bout de world to come and I take what de Lord say bout de sun and moon and I cares little what de haters of my God chooses to say. Think dat I will forsake de Bible? It is my only

Book, my hope, de arsenal of my soul's supplies and I wants nothin else.

But I got another word for you yet. I done work over dem papers dat you sent me without date and without name. You deals in figures and thinks you are bigger dan de archangels. Lemme see what you done say. You set yourself up to tell me how far it is from here to de sun. You think you got it down to a nice point. You say it is 3,339,002 miles from de earth to de sun. Dat's what you say. Another one say dat de distance is 12,000,000; another got it to 27,000,000. I hears dat de great Isaac Newton worked it up to 28,000,000 and later on de philosophers gone another rippin rise to 50,000,000. De last one gets it bigger dan all de others, up to 90,000,000. Don't any of 'em agree and so dey runs a guess game and de last guess is always de biggest. Now, when dese guessers can have a convention in Richmond and all agree upon de same thing, I'd be glad to hear from you again and I does hope dat by dat time you won't be ashamed of your name.

Heeps of railroads has been built since I saw de first one when I was fifteen years old but I ain't hear tell of a railroad built yet to de sun. I don't see why if dey can measure de distance to de sun, dey might not get up a railroad or a telegraph and enable us to find something else bout it dan merely how far off de sun is. Dey tell me dat a cannon ball could make de trip to de sun in twelve years. Why don't dey send it? It might be rigged up with quarters for a few philosophers on de inside and fixed up for a comfortable ride. Dey would need twelve years rations and a heep of changes of raiment—mighty thick clothes when dey start and mighty thin ones when dey git dere.

Oh, my brothren, dese things make you laugh and I don't blame you for laughing except it's always sad to laugh at de follies of fools. If we could laugh 'em out of countenance we might well laugh day and night. What cuts into my soul is dat all dese men seem to me dat dey is hitting at de Bible. Dat's what stirs my soul and fills me with righteous wrath. Little cares I what dey says bout de sun, provided dey let de Word of de Lord alone. But never mind. Let de heathen rage and de people imagine a vain thing. Our King shall break 'em in pieces and dash 'em down. But blessed be de name of our God, de Word of de Lord endureth forever! Stars

may fall, moons may turn to blood and de sun set to rise no more, but Thy kingdom, oh, Lord, is from everlastin to everlastin!

But I has a word dis afternoon for my own brothren. Dey is de people for whose souls I got to watch—for dem I got to stand and report at de last—dey is my sheep and I's dere shepherd and my soul is knit to dem forever. Ain't for me to be troublin you with dese questions bout dem heavenly bodies. Our eyes goes far beyond de smaller stars. Our home is clean out of sight of dem twinklin orbs. De chariot dat will come to take us to our Father's mansion will sweep out by dem flickerin lights and never halt till it brings us in clear view of de throne of de Lamb. Don't hitch your hopes to no sun nor stars. Your home is got Jesus for its light and your hopes must travel up dat way. I preach dis sermon just for to settle the minds of my few brothren and I repeats it cause kind friends wish to hear it, and I hopes it will do honor to de Lord's Word. But nothin short of de Pearly Gates can satisfy me and I charge my people, fix your feet on de Solid Rock, your hearts on Calvary, and your eyes on de throne of de Lamb. Dese strifes and griefs will soon get over; we shall see de King in His glory and be at ease. Go on, go on, ye ransomed of de Lord! Shout His praises as you go! And I shall meet you in de city of de New Jerusalem where ye shan't need de light of de sun—for de Lamb of de Lord is de light of de saints!

John J. Jasper
(Virginia, 1812–1893)

BEHOLD THE RIB!

I TAKE my text from Genesis two and twenty-one (Gen. 2:21)

Behold de Rib!
Now, my beloved,
Behold means to look and see.
Look at dis woman God done made,
But first thing, ah hah!

Ah wants you to gaze upon God's previous works.
Almighty and arisen God, hah!
Peace giving and prayer hearing God,
High-riding and strong armded God
Walking acrost his globe creation, hah!
Wid de blue elements for a helmet
And a wall of fire round his feet
He wakes de sun every morning from his fiery bed
Wid de breath of his smile
And commands de moon wid his eyes.
And Oh—
Wid de eye of Faith
I can see him
Even de lion had a mate
So God shook his head
And a thousand million diamonds
Flew out from his glittering crown
And studded de evening sky and made de stars.
So God put Adam into a deep sleep
And took out a bone, ah hah!
And it is said that it was a rib.
Behold de rib!
A bone out of a man's side.
He put de man to sleep and made wo-man,
And men and women been sleeping together ever since.
Behold de rib!
Brothers, if God
Had taken dat bone out of man's head
He would have meant for woman to rule, hah
If he had taken a bone out of his foot,
He would have meant for us to dominize and rule.
He could have made her out of back-bone
And then she would have been behind us.
But, no, God Almighty, he took de bone out of his side
So dat places de woman beside us;
Hah! God knowed his own mind.
Behold de rib!
And now I leave dis thought wid you,

Standing out on de eaves of ether
Breathing clouds from out his nostrils,
Blowing storms from 'tween his lips
I can see!!
Him seize de mighty axe of his proving power
And smite the stubborn-standing space,
And laid it wide open in a mighty gash—
Making a place to hold de world
I can see him—
Molding de world out of thought and power
And whirling it out on its eternal track,
Ah hah, my strong armded God!
He set de blood red eye of de sun in de sky
And told it,
Wait, wait! Wait there till Shiloh come
I can see!
Him mold de mighty mountains
And melting de skies into seas.
Oh, Behold, and look and see! hah
We see in de beginning
He made de bestes every one after its kind,
De birds that fly de trackless air,
De fishes dat swim de mighty deep—
Male and fee-male, hah!
Then he took of de dust of de earth
And made man in his own image.
And man was alone,
Let us all go marchin' up to de gates of Glory.
Tramp! tramp! tramp!
In step wid de host dat John saw.
Male and female like God made us
Side by side.
Oh, behold de rib!
And less all set down in Glory together
Right round his glorified throne
And praise his name forever.
                    AMEN.

THE WOUNDS OF JESUS

Our theme this morning is the wounds of Jesus. When the father shall ast, "What are these wounds in thine hand?" He shall answer, "Those are they with which I was wounded in the house of my friends." Zach. 13:6.

We read in the 53rd Chapter of Isaiah where He was wounded for our transgressions and bruised for our iniquities, and the apostle Peter affirms that His blood was spilt from before the foundation of the world.

I have seen gamblers wounded. I have seen desperadoes wounded; thieves and robbers and every other kind of characters, law-breakers and each one had a reason for his wounds. Some of them was unthoughtful, and some for being overbearing, and some by the doctor's knife, but all wounds disfigures a person.

Jesus was not unthoughtful. He was not overbearing. He was never a bully. He was never sick. He was never a criminal before the law and yet He was wounded. Now, a man usually gets wounded in the midst of his enemies, but this man was wounded, says the text, in the house of His friends. It is not your enemies that harm you all the time. Watch that close friend. Every believer in Christ is considered His friend, and every sin we commit is a wound to Jesus. The blues we play in our homes is a club to beat up Jesus, and these social card parties.

> Jesus have always loved us from the foundation of
>   the world
> When God
> Stood out on the apex of His power
> Before the hammers of creation
> Fell upon the anvils of Time and hammered out the
>   ribs of the earth
> Before He made any ropes
> By the breath of fire
> And set the boundaries of the ocean by the gravity of
>   His power

When God said, Ha!
Let us make man
And the elders upon the altar cried, ha!
If you make man, Ha!
Father!! Ha-aa
I am the teeth of time
That comprehended de dust of de earth
And weighed de hills in scales
That painted de rainbow dat marks de end of de
      parting storm
Measured de seas in de holler of my hand
That held de elements in a unbroken chain of con-
      trollment.
Make man, ha!
If he sin I will redeem him
I'll break de chasm of hell
Where de fire's never quenched
I'll go into de grave
Where de worm never dies, Ah!
So God A'mighty, Ha!
Got His stuff together
He dipped some water out of de mighty deep
He got Him a handful of dirt
From de foundation sills of de earth
He seized a thimble full of breath
From de drums of de wind, ha!
God, my master!
Now I'm ready to make man
Aa-aah!
Who shall I make him after? Ha!
Worlds within worlds begin to wheel and roll
De Sun, Ah!
Gethered up de fiery skirts of her garments
and wheeled around de throne, Ah!
Saying, Ah, make man after me, ha!
God gazed upon the sun
And sent her back to her blood-red socket
And shook His head, ha!

De Moon, ha!
Grabbed up de reins of de tides.
And dragged a thousand seas behind her
As she walked around de throne
Ah-h, please make man after me
But God said "NO"!
I'll make man in my own image, ha!
I'll put him in de garden
And Jesus said, ha!
And if he sin,
I'll go his bond before yo' mighty throne
Ah, He was yo' friend
He made us all, ha!
Delegates to de judgment convention
Ah!
Faith hasn't got no eyes, but she' long-legged
But take de spy-glass of Faith
And look into dat upper room
When you are alone to yourself
When yo' heart is burnt with fire, ha!
When de blood is lopin' thru yo' veins
Like de iron monasters (monsters) on de rail
Look into dat upper chamber, ha!
We notice at de supper table
As we gazed upon his friends, ha!
His eyes flowin' wid tears, ha! He said
"My soul is exceedingly sorrowful unto death, ha!
For this night, ha!
One of you shall betray me, ha!
It were not a Roman officer, ha!
It were not a centurion
But one of you
Who I have chosen my bosom friend
That sops in the dish with me shall betray me."
I want to draw a parable.
I see Jesus
Leaving heben with all of His grandeur
Dis-robin' Hisself of His matchless honor

Yielding up de scepter of revolvin' worlds
Clothing Hisself in de garment of humanity
Coming into de world to rescue His friends.
Two thousand years have went by on their rusty ankles
But with the eye of Faith, I can see Him
Look down from His high towers of elevation
I can hear Him when He walks about the golden streets
I can hear 'em ring under His footsteps
Sol me-e-e, Sol do
Sol me-e-e, Sol do
I can see Him step out upon the rim bones of nothing
Crying I am de way
De truth and de light
Ah!
God A'mighty!
I see Him grab de throttle
Of de well ordered train of mercy
I see kingdoms crush and crumble
Whilst de archangels held de winds in de corner chambers
I see Him arrive on dis earth
And walk de streets thirty and three years
Oh-h-hhh!
I see Him walking beside de sea of Galilee wid His disciples
This declaration gendered on His lips
"Let us go on to the other side"
God A'mighty!
Dey entered de boat
Wid their oarus (oars) stuck in de back
Sails unfurled to de evenin' breeze
And de ship was now sailin'
As she reached de center of de lake
Jesus was sleep on a pillow in de rear of de boat
And de dynamic powers of nature became disturbed
And de mad winds broke de heads of de Western drums
And fell down on de lake of Galilee
And buried themselves behind de gallopin' waves
And de white-caps marbilized themselves like an army
And walked out like soldiers goin' to battle

And de zig-zag lightning
Licked out her fiery tongue
And de flying clouds
Threw their wings in the channels of the deep
And bedded de waters like a road-plow
And faced de current of de chargin' billows
And de terrific bolts of thunder—they bust
       in de clouds
And de ship begin to reel and rock
God A'mighty!
And one of de disciples called Jesus
"Master!! Carest Thou not that we perish?"
And He arose
And de storm was in its pitch
And de lightnin' played on His raiments as
       He stood on the prow of the boat
And placed His foot upon the neck of the storm
And spoke to the howlin' winds
And de sea fell at His feet like a marble floor
And de thunders went back in their vault
Then He set down on de rim of de ship
And took de hooks of His power
And lifted de billows in His lap
And rocked de winds to sleep on His arm
And said, "Peace, be still."
And de Bible says there was a calm.
I can see Him wid de eye of faith.
When He went from Pilate's house
Wid the crown of seventy-two wounds upon His head
I can see Him as He mounted Calvary and hung upon
       de cross for our sins.
I can see-eee-ee
De mountains fall to their rocky knees when He cried
"My God, my God! Why hast Thou forsaken me?"
The mountains fell to their rocky knees and trembled
       like a beast
From the stroke of the master's axe
One angel took the flinches of God's eternal power

And bled the veins of the earth
One angel that stood at the gate with a flaming sword
Was so well pleased with his power
Until he pierced the moon with his sword
And she ran down in blood
And de sun
Batted her fiery eyes and put on her judgment robe
And laid down in de cradle of eternity
And rocked herself into sleep and slumber
He died until the great belt in the wheel of time
And de geological strata fell aloose
And a thousand angels rushed to de canopy of heben
With flamin' swords in their hands
And placed their feet upon blue ether's bosom, and
    looked back at de dazzlin' throne
And de arc angels had veiled their faces
And de throne was draped in mornin'
And de orchestra had struck silence for the space of
    half an hour
Angels had lifted their harps to de weepin' willows
And God had looked off to-wards immensity
And blazin' worlds fell of His teeth
And about that time Jesus groaned on de cross, and
Dropped His head in the locks of His shoulder and
    said, "It is finished, it is finished."
And then de chambers of hell exploded
And de damnable spirits
Come up from de Sodomistic world and rushed into
    de smoky camps of eternal night,
And cried, "Woe! Woe! Woe!"
And then de Centurion cried out,
"Surely this is the Son of God."
And about dat time
De angel of Justice unsheathed his flamin' sword and
    ripped de veil of de temple
And de High Priest vacated his office
And then de sacrificial energy penetrated de mighty
    strata

And quickened de bones of de prophets
And they arose from their graves and walked about in
    de streets of Jerusalem
I heard de whistle of de damnation train
Dat pulled out from Garden of Eden loaded wid
    cargo goin' to hell
Ran at break-neck speed all de way thru de law
All de way thru de prophetic age
All de way thru de reign of Kings and judges—
Plowed her way thru de Jurdan
And on her way to Calvary, when she blew for de switch
Jesus stood out on her track like a rough-backed
    mountain
And she threw her cow-catcher in His side and His
    blood ditched de train
He died for our sins.
Wounded in the house of His friends.
That's where I got off de damnation train
And dat's where you must get off, ha!
For in dat mor-ornin', ha!
When we shall all be delegates, ha!
To dat Judgment Convention
When de two trains of Time shall meet on de trestle
And wreck de burning axles of de unformed ether
And de mountains shall skip like lambs
When Jesus shall place one foot on de neck of de sea,
    ha!
One foot on dry land, ah
When his chariot wheels shall be running hub-deep
    in fire
He shall take His friends thru the open bosom of an
    unclouded sky
And place in their hands de "hosanna" fan
And they shall stand 'round and 'round his beautific
    throne
And praise His name forever,
                 AMEN.

JEFF'S FUNERAL SERMON

REVEREND:

Oh, Lord, dis man was born in sin, an' he died in Christ.
He sold his lot in Egypt, an' he bought a lot in Paradise.
Watch wey you put your footsteps,
Don' put 'em in de mud.
Kiver up your tracks,
'En look out for de serpents dat's lyin' all 'bout.
Don' tell your secrets,
Don' put your trus' in mens,
But put your faith in Jesus,
He is de only fren' you got.
Keep your eye upon your footsteps,
Kiver up your tracks,
Don't walk in de mud.

OLD LUCY:

(*Walking up and down the aisles, waving her hand and hollering at the top of her voice*)
Great God, Reverend, hold your holt! I'm gwine to my Jesus!
I'll bus' heben wide open wid a trail of light leading to my
Lord. Great God, Reverend, hold your holt!

JEFF'S SON:

(*Standing by the coffin, bending up and down and hollering*)
Pa, Oh, Pa! Pa gone. I de last one talked wid Pa. Pa tell me, he say
    tear down dis shed an' buil' a better one. Pa, Oh, Pa!
Ain't you hear me? I goin' do what you say.

FEMININE VOICE:

(*in back of congregation, shrieking*)
Jesus, Jesus, gone to Jesus!

REVEREND:

Oh, Lord, dis man was born in sin an' he died in Christ.
He sold his lot in Egypt, an' he bought a lot in Paradise.
For he watch where he put he footsteps.

And he kiver up he tracks.
He place his faith in God, an' he walk aroun'
    de serpents that was lyin' all 'bout.
He put his faith in Jesus, an' he trusted in he God.
He kept his eye upon he footsteps.
He kivered up he tracks, an' he never put 'em in de mud,
For he put he faith in God.
Oh, Lord, he born in sin, an' he died in Christ,
He sold he lot in Egypt, an' he bought a lot in Paradise.

OLD LUCY:

Great God, Reverend, hold your holt! I'm goin' to bus' heben wide
    open wid a trail of light leadin' to de throne.

VOICE:

(of *sister, in middle of congregation*)
Lead us, Sister Lucy,
Lead us to de light.
Lead us from de darkness,
Lead us from de night.
Lead us toward de throne,
Where all is snowy white.

REVEREND:

Our deceased brother was born in sin, an' he died in Christ.
He sold his lot in Egypt,
An' he bought a lot in Paradise.
He has placed his footsteps on de golden stairs,
He never put 'em in de mud.
He has kivered up his tracks.
He's up in heben.
He is on his way to Jesus.
He has throwed away his crown of thorns.
He has shunned the path of serpents.
He steps beneath the silver lights,
He is walking on the golden stairs,
He is climbing to the pearley throne.
He'll set up a footstool at the feet of Jesus.
He'll tell to him the secrets
That he didn't tell to mens,

For he is walkin' up the golden stairs,
He is climbing to the pearley throne,
And he will set upon a footstool in spotless white,
Beneath the bright and shining lights of heben.
And he will tell his troubles to his God,
For he was born in sin,
An' he died in Christ.
He sold his lot in Egypt,
An' he bought a lot in Paradise.

OLD LUCY:

Great God, Reverend, hold your holt!
I'm goin' to bus heben wide open,
I'm goin' to the throne of Christ.
I'm goin' to make a trail of light.
I'm goin' out of darkness,
I'm goin' to lef' behind de night.
I'm on my way to Jesus,
I'm goin' to my Christ,
I'm goin' to shout my way thru Paradise,
Great God, Reverend, hold your holt!

SISTER LUCY

(*Fragment of a funeral sermon*)

I seen our sister in life,
An' she done her duty,
She served her God
An' done her earthly labor
As best she knowed how,
An' listened for the blowin' of the trumpet.
Death had no fears for her,
For the blowin' of the trumpet,
The Master's trumpet,

Was the music that she loved;
The blowin', the blowin' of the trumpet,
The Master's trumpet.

At the mornin' sunrise,
She was on her row,
An' when the sun had set,
Her daily task was done;
An' when the night was come
She knelt in prayer beside her bed
An' listened for the blowin' of the trumpet,
The Master's trumpet,
The music that she loved,
The blowin', the blowin' of the trumpet,
The Master's trumpet.

She had met the world
Wid strength an' grace;
Although her life was trailed by hardship,
Love was in her heart for man
An' in her soul for God.
An' she listened for the blowin' of the trumpet,
The Master's trumpet,
The music that she loved,
The blowin', the blowin' of the trumpet,
The Master's trumpet.

Wid a frosty life behind her,
Wid misery savage
As a hungry hound
Ever wid her,
She never lost her faith in God,
An' she listened for the blowin' of the trumpet.
The Master's trumpet,
The music that she loved,
The blowin', the blowin' of the trumpet,
The Master's trumpet.

SILAS

(Fragment of a funeral sermon)

De body of Silas
Stiff on de coolin'-board lies.
De battle of life is done;
His soul has passed
To his far-off home—
Passed through de pearly gates.
He passed in de night,
His soul's gone forward,
But his body is left
For de weepers and mourners,
For de singers of songs
And de prayer of prayers.
His soul's gone onward
To de golden throne.
He has no regrets,
His labors was hard
And he passed in de night,
In a heavenly flight,
By a holy light.
He's gone to his home—
His far-off home—
To de golden throne.

THE HARPS OF GOD

(Fragment of a sermon)

For de harps er God is ringin',

> VOICE IN CONGREGATION:
> For de harps er God is ringin',
> Ringin', ringin',
> For de harps er God is ringin',

Ringin' de chunes er Jesus,
Wid de angels singin'.
Come, brother, ain't you hear de harp,
De Harp wid de golden strings?

Angels' hands helt out

> VOICE OF A SISTER:
> Hands, hands, hands helt out.

For God's poor chillun,
Singin' wid de harps er Jesus,
Music ringin' through de air;
God's voice above it all.
Come, my brother, ain't you hear de harp,
De harp wid de golden strings?

> VOICE:
> Golden strings, golden strings,
> De harp, de harp wide de golden strings.

For de voice er Jesus
Is callin' you to come,

An' listen to de angels singin',
Singin' wid de harp.
For, my brother an' my sister,
Dere is peace an' rest
Wid de distant music,
For Jesus leads de far off choir,
An' God is superintendent.

ONE VOICE WITH SEVERAL JOINING:
For Jesus, Jesus leads de far off choir,
An' God is superintendent.

An' de harps is playin',
An' every sound is sayin',
"Come, my brother, father, mother, sister,
For dere's peace an' love an' kindness
Where de harps er God is playin'.

SEVERAL VOICES:
For dere's peace
Where de harps er God is playin'
De harps, de harps,
De harps wid de golden strings.

For de harps er God is playin' for His chillun
In dis sinful world below.
Come, my brother, come an' listen,
Listen to de harps of heaven;

For dey are playin' 'round de snowy throne,
For de harps er God is playin'
Is playin' for His helpless chillun here below.

WHOLE CONGREGATION:
For de harps er God is playin'.
Playin' for His helpless chillun.
De harps, de harps,
De harps wid de golden strings.

GOD

I vision God standing
On the heights of heaven,
Throwing the devil like
A burning torch
Over the gulf
Into the valleys of hell.
His eye the lightning's flash,
His voice the thunder's roll.
Wid one hand He snatched
The sun from its socket,
And the other He clapped across the moon.

I vision God wringing
A storm from the heavens;
Rocking the world
Like an earthquake;
Blazing the sea
Wid a trail er fire.
His eye the lightning's flash,
His voice the thunder's roll.
Wid one hand He snatched
The sun from its socket,
And the other He clapped across the moon.

I vision God standing
On a mountain
Of burnished gold,
Blowing His breath
Of silver clouds
Over the world.
His eye the lightning's flash,
His voice the thunder's roll.

Wid one hand He snatched
The sun from its socket,
And the other He clapped across the moon.

THE REMNANT

BROTHERS and sisters, being a duty-bound servant of God, I stand
before you to-night. I am a little hoarse from a cold. But if you will
bear with me a little while we will try to bring you a message of
"Thus sayeth the Lord." If God is willing we will preach. The hell-
hounds are so swift on our trail that we have to go sometime
whether we feel like it or not. So we are here to-night to hear what
the spirit has to say.

It always make my heart glad when I run back in my mind and
see what a powerful God this is we serve. And every child . . .
Pray with me a little while children—that has been borned of the
spirit, I mean born until he can feel it, ought to feel proud that he is
serving a captain who has never lost a battle, a God that can speak
and man live, but utter his voice and man lay down and die. A
God that controls play across the heaven. Oh, ain't He a powerful
God? He stepped out on the scope of time one morning and declared
'I am God and there's none like me. I'm God and there is none before me. In my own appointed time I will visit the iniquities of the
earth. I will cut down on the right and on the left. But a remnant
I will save.' Ain't you glad, then, children that he always spares a
remnant? Brothers (pray with me a little while), we must gird up
our loins. We who are born of the spirit should cling close to the
Master, for he has promised to be a shelter in the time of storm; a
rock in a weary land. Listen at Him when He says 'behold I lay in
Zion, a stone, a tried stone.' . . . What need have we to worry about
earthly things. They are temporal and will fade away. But we, the
born of God have laid hold on everlasting life. Every child that has
had his soul delivered from death and hell (Pray with me brothers)
stayed at hell's dark door until he got his orders is a traveler. His
home is not in this world. He is but a sojourner in a weary land.

Brothers! this being true we ought to love one another; we ought to be careful how we entertain strangers. If your neighbor mistreat you, do good for evil, for a-way by and by our God that sees all we do and hears all we say will come and woe be unto him that has offended one of these His "Little Ones." I know the way gets awful dark sometimes; and it looks like everything is against us, but listen what Job said, 'All the days of my appointed time I will wait on the Lord till my change comes! Sometimes we wake up in the dark hours of midnight, briny tears flowing down our cheeks (Ah, pray with me a little longer, Brothers). We cry and don't know what we are crying about. Brother, If you have been truly snatched from the greedy jaws of Hell, your feet taken out of the miry clay and placed on the rock, the sure foundation, you will shed tears sometime. You just feel like you want to run away somewhere. But listen at the Master when he says: 'Be still and know that I am God. I have heard your groans but I will not put on you a burden you cannot bear.' We ought to rejoice and be glad for while some day they think, we know we have been born of God because we have felt His power, tasted His love, waited at Hell's dark door for orders, got a through ticket straight through from hell to heaven; we have seen the travel of our soul; He dressed us up, told us we were His children, sent us back into this low land of sorrows to tarry until one sweet day when He shall send the angels of death to bear our soul from this old earthly tabernacle and bear it back home to glory, I say back home because we been there once and every since that day we have been making our way back." "Brothers! A-ha! Glory to God! The Captain is on board now, Brothers. Sit still and hear the word of God, a-ha; away back, away back brothers, a-ha! Before the wind ever blowed, a-ha! Before the flying clouds, a-ha! Or before ever the earth was made, a-ha! Our God had us in mind. Ha! oh, brothers, oh brothers! Ha! ain't you glad then, a-ha! that our God, Ha! looked down through time one morning, a-ha! saw me and you, a-ha! ordained from the very beginning that we should be his children, a-ha! the work of His Almighty hand, a-ha! Old John the Revelator, a-ha! a-looking over yonder, a-ha! in bright glory, a-ha! Oh, what do you see, John! Ha! I see a number, a-ha! Who are these, a-ha! I heard the angel Gabriel when he answered, a-ha! 'These are they that come up through hard trials and great tribulations, a-ha!

who washed their robes, a-ha! and made them white in the blood of the lamb, a-ha! They are now shouting around the throne of God,' a-ha! Well, oh brothers! Oh, brothers! Ain't you glad that you have already been in the dressing room, had your everlasting garments fitted on and sandals on your feet. We born of God, a-ha! are shod for traveling, a-ha! Oh, Glory to God! It won't be long before some of us here, a-ha! will bid farewell, a-ha! take the wings of the morning, a-ha! where there'll be no more sin and sorrow, a-ha! no more weeping and mourning, a-ha! We can just walk around, brother, a-ha! Go over and shake hands with old Moses, a-ha! See Father Abraham, a-ha! Talk with Peter, Matthew, Luke and John, a-ha! And, Oh yes, Glory to God! we will want to see our Saviour, the Lamb that was slain, Ha! They tell me that His face outshines the sun, a-ha! but we can look on him, a-ha! because we will be like Him; and then oh brother, Oh brother, we will just fly from Cherubim to Cherubim, There with the angels we will eat off the welcome table, a-ha! Soon! Soon! we will all be gathered together over yonder Brothers, ain't you glad you done died the sinner death and don't have to die no more? When we rise to fly that morning, we can fly with healing in our wings. . . . Now, if you don't hear my voice no more, a-ha! remember, I am a Hebrew child, a-ha! Just meet me over yonder, a-ha! on the other side of the River of Jordan, away back in the third heaven.

DRY BONES

Dry bones, dry bones,
Well, them bones, dry bones, that are
Laid in the valley.
Well, them bones, dry bones, that are
Laid in the valley,
You can hear the word of the Lord.
Or from my toe bone to my
Foot bone, or from my
Foot bone to my

Ankle bone, or from my
Ankle bone to my
Leg bone, or from my
Leg bone to my
Knee bone.
Well, them bones, dry bones, that are
Laid in the valley,
You can hear the word of the Lord.
Or from my knee bone to my
Thigh bone, or from my
Thigh bone to my
Hip bone, or from my
Hip bone to my
Rib bone, or from my
Rib bone to my
Back bone.
Well, them bones, dry bones, that are
Laid in the valley,
Well, them bones, dry bones, that are
Laid in the valley,
Well, them bones, dry bones, that are
Laid in the valley.
You can hear the word of the Lord.
Or from my back bone to my
Shoulder bone to my
Head bone, or from my
Head bone to my
Skull bone to my
Eye bone.
Well, them bones, dry bones, that are
Laid in the valley,
Well, them bones, dry bones, that are
Laid in the valley.
You can hear the word of the Lord.
Or from my eye bone to my
Nose bone, or from my
Nose bone to my
Mouth bone, or from my

Mouth bone to my—
Chin bone, or from my—
Chin bone to my
Throat bone, or from my
Throat bone to my
Well, them bones, dry bones, that are
Laid in the valley.
Well, them bones, dry bones, that are
Laid in the valley.
You can hear the word of the Lord.
Or from my throat bone to my
Breast bone, or from my
Breast bone to my
Shoulder bone, or from my
Shoulder bone to my
Muscle bone, or from my
Muscle bone to my
Elbow bone.
Well, them bones, dry bones, that are
Laid in the valley.
Well, them bones, dry bones, that are
Laid in the valley.
Or from my elbow bone to my
Arm bone to my
Wrist bone, or from my
Wrist bone to my
Hand bone, or from my
Hand bone to my
Finger bone,
Well, them bones, dry bones, that are
Laid in the valley.
Well, them bones, dry bones, that are
Laid in the valley.
You can hear the word of the Lord.

PRAYERS

PRAYER

"ALMIGHTY! and all wise God our heavenly Father! 'tis once more and again that a few of your beloved children are gathered together to call upon your holy name. We bow at your foot-stool, Master, to thank you for our spared lives. We thank you that we were able to get up this morning clothed in our right mind. For Master, since we met here, many have been snatched out of the land of living and hurled into eternity. But through your goodness and mercy we have been spared to assemble ourselves here once more to call upon a Captain who has never lost a battle. Oh, throw round us your strong arms of protection. Bind us together in love and union. Build us up where we are torn down and strengthen us where we are weak. Oh, Lord! Oh, Lord! take the lead of our minds, place them on heaven and heavenly divine things. Oh, God, our Captain and King! search our hearts and if you find anything there contrary to your divine will just move it from us Master, as far as the east is from the west. Now Lord, you know our hearts, you know our heart's desire. You know our down-setting and you know our up-rising. Lord you know all about us because you made us. Lord! Lord! One more kind favor I ask of you. Remember the man that is to stand in the gate-way and proclaim your Holy Word. Oh, stand by him. Strengthen him where he is weak and build him up where he is torn down. Oh, let him down into the deep treasures of your word.

And now, oh, Lord; when this your humble servant is done down here in this low land of sorrow: done sitting down and getting up: done being called everything but a child of God; oh, when I am done, done, done, and this old world can afford me a home no longer, right soon in the morning, Lord, right soon in the morning, meet me down at the River of Jordan, bid the waters to be still, tuck my little soul away in that snow-white chariot, and bear it away over yonder in the third heaven where every day will be a

Sunday and my sorrows of this old world will have an end, is my
prayer for Christ my Redeemer's sake and amen and thank God."

NOTE: *This prayer was offered by a deacon during a camp meeting held in South Nashville, Tennessee, in the summer of 1928.
It is reproduced here as accurately as possible from the notes
taken during the occasion.*

SAME GOD

You are de same God, Ah
Dat heard de sinner man cry.
Same God dat sent de zigzag lightning tuh
Join de mutterin' thunder.
Same God dat holds de elements
In uh unbroken chain of controllment.
Same God dat hung on Cavalry and died,
Dat we might have a right tuh de tree of life—
We thank Thee that our sleeping couch
Was not our cooling board,
Our cover was not our winding sheet . . .
Please tuh give us uh restin' place
Where we can praise Thy name forever,

AMEN.

PRAYER FOR TEACHER

Dear Lord,
Bless our dear Teacher.
Give her the brightest crown in heaven.
Give her the whitest robe that can be given.

Put golden sandals on her feet, and let her
Slip and slide up to the throne of Master Jesus.

AMEN.

TESTIMONIALS

HOOKED IN THE HEART

BEFORE God can use a man that man must be hooked in the heart.
By this I mean that he has to feel converted. And once God stirs
up a man's pure mind and makes him see the folly of his ways he
is wishing for God to take him and use him. From this time on it
is up to God and if He has ever started a work He will not stop
until it is finished and finished once and for all times. He spoke to
me once after I had prayed and prayed trying to hurry Him and get
a religion. He said, "I am a time-God. Behold, I work after the
counsel of my own will and in due time I will visit whomsoever I
will."

He showed me many things before He turned me around and
then gave me my orders. I was a great musician and at times, after
I had spent seasons at fasting and praying, I would get tired of it
and go back to the ways of the world. You see the devil knows how
to tempt a man. He always reminds him of the things he likes best
and in this way he can get his attention.

God started on me when I was a little boy. I used to grieve a lot
over my mother. She had been sold away from me and taken a long
way off. One evening I was going through the woods to get the
cows. I was walking along thinking about mama and crying. Then a
voice spoke to me and said, "Blessed art thou. An obedient child
shall live out the fullness of his days." I got scared because I did not
know who it was that spoke nor what he meant. But from this time
on I thought more about God and my soul and started to praying as
best I knew how. It went on this way until I was about grown. I
would pray a while and then stop and forget God. Finally, one day
I was plowing in a field. There was a stump at one end and as I
came to the end and turned the team around I heard a mourning

behind the stump. I turned around and sat on the plow-handle and looked but didn't see anything. Yet the voice kept on mourning. I went on about my plowing feeling sad and wondering what it all meant. The voice said nothing but just mourned. Later God revealed to me that it was my soul crying out for deliverance. The voice was within me all the time but it sounded like it was behind the stump. From this time on He began to show me things.

Once while I was sick I saw in a vision three people and one was a woman. They looked at me and said, "He is sick." The woman said, "I can cure him." So speaking she took out a little silver vial, held it before me and vanished.

At another time I saw myself travelling down a big broad road. I came to three marks across my path and it was revealed to me that those marks represented the number of times I had started to find God and turned back.

After this, one day, I was putting a top on our little log house that I was building. It was broad open day and I was as wide awake as ever I was in this world. I had just got in position to fit on the first rafters when a voice called my name three distinct times. It called, "O William! O William! O William!" I hollered and answered, "Hey!" but nobody answered. I looked all around and began to wonder about the voice. It sounded so strange. It seemed to come from afar off and still it seemed to be right at me. I never have been able to find out what it meant.

I started to praying again. That night I went to my regular praying-place. I usually prayed behind a big beech-tree, a little distance from the house, and often during the night when I would feel to pray, I would get out of bed and go to this tree. That night I said, "Lord, if I am praying right, let me hear a dove mourn three times. While I was praying I went off in a trance and I saw myself going up a broad hilly road through the woods. When I was nearly to the top I saw a big dog. I got scared and started to run back but something urged me on. The dog was chained to a big block I found out when I got closer and though she tried to get to me I passed out of her reach. I came then to a tree like a willow and there I heard a dove mourn three times.

But in spite of this it wasn't long before I was serving the devil again. I was serving him outwardly but my soul was pleading with

God. I turned back several times because the devil stayed so hot on my trail. Whenever a man tries to do right and seek God then the devil gets busy. I used to go to my praying-place and it just looked like the devil would take me whether or no. I would see him with my spiritual eye as some great monster coming down out of the tree to tear me to pieces and devour me. Or else I would recall all the good times I had had. Such temptations are the first that a man goes through before he becomes purified and fit for God's Kingdom.

You can't serve two masters. You either got to be on the one side or the other. Before any man hires another to work for him he tries to find out something about that man—what kind of a worker he is; how much interest he will take in his work and how much time he can give. If that man finds out that you cannot give his job the proper time and interest, no matter how good a worker you may be, he can't use you. The same is true with God. If we don't meet his requirements he can't use us. He calls us and gives us our orders and until a man gets orders from God he is not ready to serve Him.

When God called me I had applied in hell but my name wasn't on the roll. I saw a sharp-eyed looking man and he seemed to be walking back and forth from one end of a work-shop to the other and looking at a time-book. I went to ask him if my name was in the book and he snapped back, "No." It was from here that God delivered my soul, turned me around and gave me my orders. I saw myself on the same broad road I had seen so much of in the spirit. As I went along a voice called out, "O William! O William! O William!" When He said that He turned me around out of the big road into a little path, my face being toward the east. He spoke again and said, "Go preach my Gospel to every creature and fear not for I am with you, an everlasting prop. Amen."

MY JAWS BECAME UNLOCKED

ABOUT twelve years before I got converted I was in a crap game out on the Harding pike. I'll never forget it as long as I live. I and three or four others were gambling. I had the dice in my hands. A

voice spoke to me and it spoke three times. Every time it got nearer and nearer until it seemed right over the top of my head. It said, "Have you ever thought where you will spend eternity?" I got sorrowful and sad and slipped out of the room and prayed. It was on the fifth day of October that I made a determination to follow the Lord. I saw Him through the eye of faith and heard His voice through the spiritual ear until the heart understood.

Sometime after this—it was in June—my wife and mother-in-law were sitting in the room and I was in the bed sick. A hand came and struck me across the face three times. Then I looked and saw the very gates of heaven open and an angel come out. It flew right to my bed and said, "I am a doctor that cures all diseases." That same day I got up and dressed myself and walked for the first time in three months.

I believe in the Baptist church because before I was sure I joined the Missionary Baptist church. One day I was standing between these walnut trees—this was three weeks before I joined church—I heard the Lord and He spoke to me and I saw Him take a sun out of a sun and he said to me, "Behold, my little one. I am God Almighty. I freed your soul from death and hell. I set you in Babylon until you know that I ordained you to preach the Gospel to every creature." I didn't know what this meant. For a long time I could not spiritually call on the name of the Lord. In 1906 I prayed six months. He showed me what I was to do and my complaint to Him that I was from a poor tribe and that I had no learning and had not had the advantages of other people, he answered in a voice, "I am wisdom and possess all knowledge. I ordain you to preach."

Wisdom in the heart is unlike wisdom in the mind. I remember the first sermon I was to preach. I picked out two verses from the scripture and practised on them as my text. But when I got up to preach I started off all right but died dead right in the middle. I couldn't so much as call the name of the Lord. Then all at once I began to feel sorrowful and my jaws became unlocked and my tongue started to move so I could speak. I preached with no trouble for I just said what the spirit directed me to say. This is why I don't prepare any sermons today. I just read the word and pray. God will do the rest.

Once when I had rheumatism in my leg I was called to preach.

My wife hobbled all along the way to church with me, telling me all the time that I should have stayed home in bed but I told her that I must fill my hand. The rest is the Lord's. I felt awful bad when I first got to church and took my place on the stand waiting for the congregation to gather. And then the spirit lifted me up. I forgot all about the pain and just lost sight of the world and all the things of the world. When the spirit begins to work with one it don't have any cares for pain or anything of the world. My mind gets fixed on God and I feel a deep love, joy and a deep desire to be with God. We shout because we feel glad in the heart. At times I feel like I could just kiss the very feet of man and I had rather hear the voice on the inside cry out "Amen" when I do something than to have all the money in the world.

GOD STRUCK ME DEAD

I HAVE always been a sheep. I was never a goat. I was created and cut out and born in the world for Heaven. Even before God freed my soul and told me to go I never was hell-scared. I just never did feel that my soul was made to burn in hell.

God started on me when I wasn't but ten years old. I was sick with the fever and He called me and said, "You are ten years old." I didn't know how old I was but later on I asked my older sister and she told me that I was ten years old when I had the fever.

As I grew up I used to frolic a lot and was considered a good dancer but I never took much interest in such things. I just went many times to please my friends and, later on, my husband. What I loved more than all else was to go to church.

I used to pray then. I pray now and just tell God to take me and do His will for He knows the every secret of my heart. He knows what we stand most in need of before we ask for it and if we trust Him, He will give us what we ought to have in due season. Some people pray and call on God as if they think He is ignorant of their needs or else asleep. But God is a time-God. I know this for He told me so. I remember one morning I was on my way home with a

bundle of clothes to wash—it was after my husband had died—I felt awfully burdened down and so I commenced to talk to God. It looked like I was having such a hard time. Everybody seemed to be getting along well but poor me. I told Him so. I said, "Lord, it looks like You come to everybody's house but mine. I never bother my neighbors or cause any disturbance. I have lived as it is becoming a poor widow woman to live and yet, Lord, it looks like I have a harder time than anybody." When I said this something told me to turn around and look. I put my bundle down and looked towards the east part of the world. A voice spoke to me as plain as day but it was inward and said, "I am a time-God working after the counsel of my own will. In due time I will bring all things to you. Remember and cause your heart to sing."

When God struck me dead with His power I was living on 14th Avenue. It was the year of the Centennial. I was in my house alone and I declare unto you when His power struck me I died. I fell out on the floor flat on my back. I could neither speak nor move for my tongue stuck to the roof of my mouth; my jaws were locked and my limbs were stiff.

In my vision I saw hell and the devil. I was crawling along a high brick wall, it seems, and it looked like I would fall into a dark roaring pit. I looked away to the east and saw Jesus. He was standing in snow—the prettiest, whitest snow I have ever seen. I said, "Lord, I can't go for that snow is too deep and cold. He commanded me the third time before I would go. I stepped out in it but it didn't seem a bit cold nor did my feet sink into it. We travelled on east in a little narrow path and came to something that looked like a grape-arbor and the snow was hanging down like icicles. But it was so pretty and white that it didn't look like snow. He told me to take some of it and eat but I said, "Lord, it is too cold." He commanded me three times before I would eat any of it. I took some and tasted it and it was the best-tasting snow I ever put into my mouth.

The Father, the Son and the Holy Ghost led me on to glory. I saw God sitting in a big arm-chair. Everything seemed to be made of white stones and pearls. God didn't seem to pay me any attention. He just sat looking into space. I saw the Lamb's book of life and my name written in it. A voice spoke to me and said, "Whosoever my Son sets free is free indeed. I give you a through ticket from hell

to Heaven. Go into yonder world and be not afraid, neither be dismayed for you are an elect child and ready for the fold." But when He commanded me to go I was stubborn and didn't want to leave. He said, "My little one, I have commanded you and you shall obey."

I saw, while I was still in the spirit, myself going to my neighbors and to the church telling them what God had done for me. When I came to this world I arose shouting and went carrying the good news. I didn't do like the Lord told me though for I was still in doubt and I wanted to make sure. Because of my disobedience He threw a great affliction on me. I got awfully sick and my limbs were all swollen so that I could hardly walk. I began to have more faith then and put more trust in God. He put this affliction on me because it was hard for me to believe. But I just didn't want to be a hypocrite and go around hollering and not knowing what I was talking and shouting about. I told God this in my prayer and He answered me saying, "My little one, my grace is sufficient. Behold I have commanded you to go and you shall go."

When I was ready to be baptized I asked God to do two things. It had been raining for days and on the morning of my baptism it was still raining. I said, "Lord, if You are satisfied with me and pleased with what I have told the people, cause the sun to shine this evening when I go to the river." Bless your soul, when we went to the river, it looked like I had never seen the sun shine as bright. It stayed out about two hours and then it clouded up again and rained some more.

The other thing I asked God was that I might feel the spirit when I went down to the river. And I declare unto you, my soul caught on fire. From the minute I stepped in the carriage to go to the river. I had been hobbling around on a stick but I threw it away and forgot that I was ever a cripple.

Later the misery came back and I asked God to heal me. The spirit directed me to get some peach-tree leaves and beat them up and put them about my limbs. I did this and in a day or two that swelling left me and I haven't been bothered since. More than this, I don't remember ever paying out but $3.00 for doctor's bills in my life either for myself, my children or my grandchildren. Dr. Jesus tells me what to do.

A LOVE LETTER FROM DE LORD

"I'M GOIN', dear Jesus, yes, I'm goin' too," chanted the Negroes, rocking back and forth in their seats. "I'm goin' to Heaven to be with you. I'm goin' to Heaven to be with you."

"Take Jesus with you day by day," sang the white-robed soloist in the choir loft, and the people in the seats chanted back, "I'm goin', dear Jesus, yes, I'm goin' too."

The members of Green Valley Baptist Church were holding their annual New Year's Eve service. The night was bitterly cold. Clouds covered the sky, and a knifelike wind penetrated heavy winter clothing. Some of the members paraded down the aisle in warm, fur-trimmed coats and flashing jewelry; others hurried in, shivering in thin, shabby suits and light wraps, grateful for the warmth of the meetinghouse. Women ushers in dark blue dresses, white collars, white cuffs, white gloves, and with glittering badges pinned on their breasts, escorted the people down the aisles to their seats. On the back seat of the church sat eight Red Cross nurses in uniform with their first-aid kits beside them. The men ushers, dressed in tuxedos and also wearing badges, stood at the back of the church. After the services started, they would take over the duties of ushering and preserving order.

Brother Clark, the minister, walked to the pulpit and read the sixty-fifth Psalm. "The folds shall be full of sheep: The valleys also shall stand so thick with corn that they shall laugh and sing."

"Amen!" chanted the people. "Amen!"

The church was packed by this time, and the men ushers were sending a few more late-comers up to the gallery.

"Silence in the presence of the Lord!" sang the soloist, and the choir and congregation answered back, "Silence in the presence of the Lord!" The building rang with their voices.

Brother Clark said, "Let us pray," and all during the prayer the people kept up their chanting.

"We ask you to come an' be in the service with us, Lord—(Yes! Yes!)—You know who's right an' you know who's wrong; we can't fool you—(Amen!)—We can't tell how much farther we're goin'— (No!) for our 'magination an' our wisdom is too limited—(Yes, Yes!)—Raise up those that are bowed down—(Yes, Lord!).

"The reason I love to talk to you, Lord, is you feed the hungry— (Dat's de truf!)—You feed the fishes in the water, you feed the fowl—(Yes! Yes!)—You tol' me when I got in trouble you'd come— (Amen!)—Come to us now, Lord—(Yes! Yes!)—We don't know how much farther we're goin'—(No!)—We're in your hands— (Goin' up! Goin' up!)—Have mercy tonight—(Yes! Yes!)—We're comin' up the wrong side o' the mountain—(Goin' up!)—Guide us, O Lord—(Yes!).

"Some of us are in the hospital tonight—(Yes! Yes!)—Go out an' be with 'em—(Amen!)—We put our hand in your hand—(Goin' up! Goin' up!)—We're wrong an' you right—(Amen!)—Have mercy! (Yes, Lord!)—Make me a better servant—(Yes, Lord!).

"We don't know what the new year holds for us—(No, Lord!)— It may be dark an' we'll need you—(Yes! Yes!)—We can't get along without you—(Goin' up! Goin' up!)—Amen—(Amen!)."

The prayer was ended, and, while the choir sang, all the men and women ushers marched down the aisles, took long-handled baskets, and started collecting. First came the women, passing the baskets to each row. A few feet behind them came the men, collecting all that the women might have missed. Then the minister announced that another collection would be taken for the guest preacher who was with them that night. So again the long-handled baskets were passed through the congregation. The choir finished the song and sat down.

"I have some announcements to make," said Brother Clark. "Sister Mary Blackstone died Friday. The wake will be held at Stevens' Funeral Parlor Tuesday night. I hope a number of you will attend the wake.

"There will be the usual services in the church nex' Friday night. Nex' Sunday we will have a baptizin'. If the weather is too cold, we'll have it here in the church. Otherwise it will be at the river. I know that you much prefer for our baptizin's to be in the river than in the tub. We all follow John the Baptist, you know, an' do

like he did when he baptized our blessed Lord in the River Jordan.
But sometimes the river is so icy we have to use the tub.

"I now interduce Brother Brown, our visitor, who will talk to you
in his own way."

"De first day of dis year," began Brother Brown, "was a Sabbath
Day. De last day is a Sabbath Day. Dat means somethin'. How have
I used dis year? Brothers an' sisters, ask yourself dat question: how
have I used dis year? Have you done de Lord's will? Have you been
a part of His fam'ly? Dere's somethin' 'bout gettin' in His fam'ly
an' growin' up in it dat you can't get by comin' in late. I'm sixty
years old. I growed up in His fam'ly an' I'm still here. What is it
dat I'm here for? Others have been taken, why'm I left here?

"Lots of our people feel 'shamed of de fact dat we used to be
slaves. Dey shuns talk of de past when we wasn't a free people.
But I wants you to know dat I look upon slavery as anudder trial
or burden dat was placed upon us, an' which de Lord has helped us
to overcome. We is stronger for it. Dere is still many trials dat we
must bear, but we is strong an' able to cast dem aside, an' we can
look forward with de Lord's help to bein' a more free people as we
face each New Year.

"Ah sisters, ah brothers," he shouted, "how much of God's will
have you done dis year? Have you read your Bible—dis love letter
from de Lord? Dat's what de Bible is, a love letter from de Lord!"

The preacher paced up and down in a frenzy. The people before
him, swaying and chanting, were as so much potential dynamite,
waiting only for the spark of oratory to cause the explosion of
religious fervor.

"I've got a mother over dere waitin' for me! Is your mother over
dere waitin' for you? We're on our way to Canaan. We'll be dere
one o' dese days!"

"Goin' up! Goin' up!" shouted old Brother Smith.

One of the women in the congregation felt the power of the
Spirit. She screamed and began threshing her arms about. She
pushed out into the aisle and rushed from one usher to another.
The preacher finished his sermon with a shout and a flourish. The
congregation moaned and chanted. Then the minister of Green
Valley Baptist Church rose to his feet.

"We extend an invitation," he said, "for anyone to come into

the church by letter, baptism, or personal experience. Anyone wantin' to join with us, come forward now."

The choir began to sing:

> Oh, why not tonight,
> Why not tonight?
> We want to be saved,
> Then why not tonight?

The congregation joined in, and the song became a rolling sea of sound. Their hands clapped and their feet stamped the floor. Their bodies swayed back and forth.

> We want to be saved,
> Then why not tonight?

The monotony of sound and motion produced a state of ecstasy. A woman stood up, followed by another and then another.

"Is there a sister who wants to be saved?" asked Brother Clark. "We'll ask that sister to come forward an' let us talk to her."

One by one the applicants went forward. The first sister gave her "personal experience."

"You have heard her 'experience,'" said the preacher. "All those in favor of takin' her in, say 'Aye!'"

"Aye," said the congregation.

Another testified that she was going to a church of the same faith and order but that she wanted to join Green Valley. Again the vote was taken.

"Aye," said the congregation.

"Tomorrow's sun may not rise for you," cried Brother Clark. "Come now!"

"We want to be saved," sang the people. "Then why not tonight?"

"Now," said the preacher, "we're goin' to turn the meetin' over to anyone that wants to talk. And when the meetin' is over, if you haven't had your said, come nex' Friday or nex' Sunday an' you can have your said. It's our custom to start out with our officers, but sometimes the officers don't feel like talkin'. So now you that the

Spirit moves, you can do the talkin'."

Brother Smith stood up. "I'm eighty-six now," he said. "I been wid de Lord for sixty-one years." The congregation shouted jubilantly.

Sister Davis rose to her feet. "Somebody's touched me," she cried. "It must ha' been the hand o' the Lord."

The people were clapping and stamping to the rhythm of their chants. Each testimonial was preceded by a song or chant. The one standing sang the first line, and the entire congregation joined in on the following lines. Most of the chants were in a minor key and used the same three or four notes over and over again. The Negroes call them "meter-hymns." They have an endless number of them, and the people know the words to all of them.

"I'm on my way to Jesus. I'm a sinner, but I'm on my way."

"I rose as a witness to Jesus. I didn't rise because I was afraid I was goin' to pass out. Nobody called me to rise. I'm carryin' the blood-stained banner of Jesus."

"He's good to me. He's ever'thing to me. I been keepin' good all day. Jus' pray for me."

Several others began shrieking and jumping.

"I'm goin' to stick to Jesus. I'm goin' home. I love Jesus! I love ever'body!"

"Lord, ha' mercy, Jesus," chanted the people.

A fat sister with gold teeth and strong voice rocked back and forth as she sang: "You don't know when or where. Pray for me."

"I ain't missed a whole Sunday. I've come out ever' Sunday all dis year."

"We was born in de country. We had fam'ly prayers. You don't see dat now."

"O yes! O yes!" shouted the congregation.

"I want you all to pray for me."

"I been thirty years in this church; haven't gave no trouble. I've got religion. Ever'thing I do God is with me. Never die no more. You all will be settin' in the grandstand when I run in."

"I don't care what come or what goes."

"I've come two hundred miles to get here. I got up at six o'clock dis mornin' to get here before midnight."

"Fifty-four years I been servin' God. I was only four years old, an'

God took hold o' my hand an' led me. Tol' me to be a good boy. Didn't know I was livin' in a valley till God took hold o' my hand."

"Sisters an' brothers, I rose as a witness. Long ago as a child in Mississippi at eleven years old I was converted. I know I'm goin' over the river."

"Sometimes I feel frantic, but I know Jesus is mine. I tol' Jesus thirty-four years ago I'd live for him. I'm goin' to try to do better 'cause he's certainly been good to me."

> Jesus is mine, mine, mine,
> O Jesus is mine, mine, mine;
> Everywhere I go, everywhere I be
> Jesus is mine!

sang the people, and the building trembled with the stamping of their feet.

Down in one of the front pews a man was sitting between two women. One of the woman felt the Ecstasy coming. She began to thresh out with her arms. The man leaned over, removed his glasses, and gave them to someone else. Then he held the woman down in her seat. No sooner had she quieted than the one on his other side let out a scream. He reached over, removed his glasses, and started to hold her. Then all at once the Ecstasy come to him. He pushed through to the aisle and began to walk up and down. Faster and faster he went from one end of the aisle to the other. He shivered and jerked. Furiously he began to fight the ushers who tried to restrain him. One by one different members rushed to the aisles, screaming and running, shouting and fighting. The Red Cross nurses went into action with their first-aid kits. The choir sang:

> My soul just couldn't be content
> Until I found my Lord.

It was now three minutes before twelve. For four hours they had been testifying and singing. Brother Clark said, "Let us all kneel." And so they knelt, facing the backs of their pews. Someone started to sing "Nearer, My God to Thee." Others joined in, half-singing, half-chanting. Some, possessed by the Spirit, were still screaming

and shouting as they rushed up and down the aisles. The ushers in their tuxedos and the nurses in their white uniforms were restraining the more violent and treating the exhausted. The preacher was praying for help in the year to come.

The members of Green Valley Church lived close to God. They never fail to give credit for the blessings that come their way, and they take Jesus with them in their daily lives. Without this trust and faith they would be lost. They fervently believe what they are saying on New Year's Eve. They may go out the next day and break many of the Ten Commandments, but they will be back the following Sunday testifying, "I'm a sinner, but I'm on my way."

Outside, the whistles were blowing. A half moon hung low in the east, and stars looked down from a cloudless sky. A new year had come again.

Ruth Rogers Johnson

THE LORD SPOKE PEACE TO MY SOUL

IN 1903, October, between eleven and twelve o'clock, the Lord spoke to me and spoke peace to my soul. A person must travel before he is saved.

Twelve years before I was converted I got sick. It was something unusual. For two months and eleven days I didn't know night from day and until the eleventh of March, from the time I was taken down, I was unable to put one foot on the ground.

I believe a person must have some travel before conversion. I was ailing and I wasn't giving God a thought till I was taken sick. On Thursday morning in May, when I was lying in my bed, unable to turn my face to the north—(my face was to the south)—I had to lay wherever they putted me. I seen the heavens open up. Before this I seen a hand and it smote me across the face and then I seen the heavens open up and an angel come down. This was twelve years before I was converted. The angel sat on the head of the bed. He looked me in the face and told me he was the Doctor. What did he do to me? I am unable to tell but the moment He spoke

I came back to myself and I've been walking ever since. I've been married twice. I lay on my bed sick and the heavens opened up. The wife I had then wasn't dead but I saw the wife I have now come and sit on my bed as the angel did.

WILD GOOSE NEST

BROTHER HICKMAN: Brothers and sisters, we come before the Lord this day with prayer. Dear father, look down from the throne on high and view these children of yourn. Look into dey hearts and see if dey's pure. Jesus, if dey ain't make 'em repent and don' lu'm tell no lies dis day, Amen.

CONGREGATION: Tell us about it, Brother.

BROTHER HICKMAN: Sister Peggy, what is your experience? Has you reached a determination in your travels?

SISTER PEGGY: Brother, I is. I travel a long distance and de road been rough and mighty dark, and at a long distance and at a great height and nigh de end of de road I find a wild goose nest, and all the eggs but one is white, and it were black.

BROTHERS AND SISTERS: (*Chanting*)
> Wild goose nest,
> Wild goose nest,
> Wild goose nest.

BROTHER HICKMAN: Sister, go back in de wilderness and pray some more. Go seek again till all de eggs in de wild goose nest is white.

(*Shrill voices from Sisters in different parts of the congregation*):
> Wild goose nest,
> Wild goose nest,
> Wild goose nest.

(*Sister Peggy goes and returns*)

SISTER PEGGY: Brother Hickman, I traveled to de wild goose nest, and de road been long and de road been rough, and I come to de wild goose nest.

(*Voices in congregation*)
> Tell us, Sister.

SISTER PEGGY: Wild goose nest,
Wild goose nest,
Wild goose nest.

And de nest been soft with
Feathers, from de wild Goose' breast
Wild goose breast
Wild goose breast,
Wild goose breast.
An' all de eggs been white but one,
And it still were black.

BROTHER HICKMAN: Go back, Sister Peggy! Go back in de wilderness and seek again for a determination. There still is work to be done. Go, and pray and seek, sister, till all de eggs in de wild goose nest is white.

CONGREGATION: Wild goose nest,
Wild goose nest,
Wild goose nest.

(*Sister Peggy goes, and returns for the third time.*)

BROTHER HICKMAN: What you find Sister Peggy?

SISTER PEGGY: Brother I have been to de wild goose nest and all de eggs is white. All de eggs is white.

BROTHER HICKMAN: My Sister, you has reach a determination in your long travel and your labors is done. Rise, Sister, your journey is done.

CONGREGATION: Wild goose nest,
Wild goose nest,
Wild goose nest.

EXCERPT FROM A LETTER FROM
FATHER DIVINE TO A FOLLOWER

THE time is not far away when no man shall say to another, "Know ye the LORD:" for they shall all know ME from the least to the great-

est. I AM guiding the destiny of this nation, yea, of all humanity and I AM speaking through the officials, even as I spoke through the President, to bring this Nation home to God, where there is Peace and Security, as a sample and an example for all mankind. We shall have Peace on Earth through the Wisdom of Righteousness; and I shall not cease MY Endeavors until it shall be accomplished.

All humanity shall enjoy the Abundance of every desirable blessing, of comfort and convenience, of houses and lands, just as you have it and there shall be no division among this people from shore to shore and from land to land.

Thus, continue in faith for I am Present with you that you and all who will, may be even as this leaves Me, as I Am Well, Healthy, Joyful, Peaceful, Lively, Loving, Successful, Prosperous and Happy in Spirit, Body, and Mind and in every organ, muscle, sinew, joint, limb, vein and bone and even in every Atom, fibre and cell of My Bodily Form.

Respectfully and Sincere, I Am

Rev. M.J. Divine, Ms D., D.D.

(Better known as Father Divine)

REMARKS OF MOTHER DIVINE

REV. MJD/r
WHILST AT THE HOLY COMMUNION TABLE of the CIRCLE MISSION CHURCH HOME and TRAINING SCHOOL, INC. 764-722 BROAD STREET PHILADELPHIA, PENNSYLVANIA MONDAY AFTERNOON NOVEMBER 11, 1957 A.D.F.D. TIME—4:18 P.M.

(MOTHER speaks as follows:)
PEACE, FATHER Dear! PEACE to our Visiting Guests and Friends! PEACE, EVERYONE! FATHER, it is a glorious privilege to be here in this day and time when GOD ALMIGHTY

is here in a BODILY FORM—the hopes and dreams of all generations! We are blessed to be living in the fulfilment now. FATHER Darling, it is a wonderful blessing—more than tongue can ever tell and more than a heart can contain at times—the beauty and the mystery of GOD'S Presence on earth among HIS people. And we thank YOU, FATHER, for awakening us into this realization, because many people are living and yet they are as dead! But because YOU have awakened us, we desire to be more fully awakened into the realization of YOUR marvelous Presence here on earth, for IT IS ETERNAL LIFE TO KNOW THEE, THE ONLY TRUE GOD; and I say, THROUGH JESUS CHRIST WHOM THOU HAST SENT!

Because FATHER Dear, it's not a matter of just meeting YOU as a PERSON, but it's taking YOUR Mind and YOUR Spirit, so that we might be Spirit of YOUR Spirit and Mind of YOUR Mind and Flesh of YOUR Flesh, that we might no longer be separated from our MAKER and CREATOR, but be ONE with HIM, the only place where there is rest, the only place where there is protection, the only place where there is happiness and complete satisfaction—is being lost in the WILL of GOD!

A TRANSPARENT AIRPLANE THAT
CAN TAKE ON ANY COLOR

Proposed by FATHER DIVINE in 1941

A thought given by Father whilst in his private office 152–160 W. 126 Street, New York City, Saturday afternoon, July 5, 1941 A.D.F.D. Time—12:00 P.M.

We should invent an aeroplane that is atmospherically transparent—that could change any color of the atmosphere—just have it change any color of the atmosphere! You see, the lizard is something, if he crawls on anything blue, he will turn blue; anything brown, he turns brown; anything green; he turns green! And, you see, if you have it atmospherically transparent, so changeable as to

change any color, anything that the atmosphere may be, and also the reflection from the sky—I mean, it is to be the same color as air—no color!

Water is not any color, is it? It is just neutral. It should be atmospherically transparent, that the outside would be the reflection of whatsoever its appearance or whatsoever it is in or on; and therefore, you could not see it.

Secretary: If that were the case you could have any kind of a motor in it!

FATHER: Sure—atmospheric transparent! It does not mean you would look through it but you would not see it.

Secretary: If it were going through the clouds it would reflect the clouds.

FATHER: Yes—reflect the clouds—and then if you make it soundless in motion, it would be absolutely noiseless!

(At this point there was an interruption, and FATHER discontinued speaking on the subject.)

NO PUSHBUTTON GOD

ME, my name is Charles McCoy. I am just a good Joe. I will not call myself a good-for-nothing Joe—the song made money and I didn't. I have been to many churches and many places and I like all religions. And sometimes in life I come to myself and I draw up in a corner all by myself. Each and everybody in life, at a certain time in life, go into suspense. Suspense life is miserable. You have to pretend sometimes in life. As I said, I am not a religious man but I go to all churches, holy roller, places when they bow and where they use God to protect themselves from God. I'm just an ordinary guy but I know there is something beyond my knowledge. The day that they have pushbuttons for everything, cars and eyes and everything works automatic but people cannot use God as a pushbutton because when they are in trouble and they need and they get down on their knees and ask God or Jesus to help me, and God does not act they lose all belief but if you wait and pray He will

come whether or not He comes at the hour when you want him to act, but He will come. But you still can't push Him like you do a machine or a motor because I have called on Him in time of need and He didn't come. But later things worked out all right for me. But I give Him up, Jesus and God, because I thought when I fell on my knees and prayed, He would come just like you turn on a washing machine. But God does not act that way. He is not a push-button. Just because you are in trouble and need Him, He don't always come in that hour. He comes in His own mysterious way. I don't know who comes, Jesus or God, but They come, but not always at the time or hour that you push the button for Them to come because They do not come by pushbutton. But I am grateful to know that One of them comes. I don't know which One, but I know sombeody comes. That is the way I feel.

Statement by Charles McCoy, Harlem, January 10, 1958

Spirituals

THE SPIRITUALS

TRAVELERS through the antebellum South were struck by the singing and dancing of the slaves. Some dismissed these as uncouth barbarism, others were stirred by the vigor of the dancing and the weird sadness of the songs. Report of these reached the North in travelers' accounts, published journals, novels, and the narratives of fugitive slaves. Southern authors, in the main, did not consider the songs and dances worth mentioning, except, strangely, as proofs of the slave's contentment.

It was not until the Civil War that any of these songs were collected. In 1864, Charlotte Forten wrote down a few songs that she heard the new freedmen sing on Saint Helena Island. Thomas Wentworth Higginson, moved greatly as the black soldiers of his regiment sang in the evenings about the campfires, recorded several spirituals for an article in *The Atlantic Monthly* (1867) and included a chapter on them in his *Army Life in a Black Regiment* (1870). The first systematic collection was made by three Northerners, William F. Allen, Charles P. Ware, and Lucy McKim Garrison, in their *Slave Songs of the United States* (1867). This book, sympathetically edited, is an important landmark in American musical history.

The wider introduction of these songs to the world came a few years later in 1871, when a group of Fisk University students, under the leadership of George White, started on tour, singing the songs that they had learned from their slave parents. They had to struggle for a hearing. One tavern keeper, astounded that real Negroes and

not burnt-cork singers were advertised to sing Negro songs, drove them out of his tavern. In Brooklyn they were scoffed at as Beecher's Nigger Minstrels. But they packed churches there and in New York and went on to Europe on a truly triumphal tour. When they left Fisk, the school was in straitened circumstances; when they returned, they had enough money to construct a new building, Jubilee Hall. Their example has been followed even until the present by a large number of colleges that send out choral groups that specialize in spirituals.

Fisk University's part in establishing the spirituals is definite. The origins of the type of songs that the young college group sang is less definite. Whether they are of individual or group authorship, for instance, is one problem. An early collector heard a slave tell how the songs were made:

'I'll tell you, it's dis way. My master call me up and order me a short peck of corn and a hundred lash. My friends see it, and is sorry for me. When dey come to de praise-meeting dat night dey sing about it. Some's very good singers and know how; and dey work it in—work it in, you know, till they get it right; and dat's de way.

James Weldon Johnson, who called the makers of spirituals "black and unknown bards of long ago," believed that many spring from highly gifted individuals. Robert W. Gordon, according to his *Folk Songs of America,* discovered in the isolated Low Country of South Carolina a type of spiritual that in its primitive structure (single line of recitative alternating with simple line refrain) is probably closest to the earliest spirituals sung. For their "recitative" these spirituals demanded a highly special sort of singer:

He was not an "author" in the ordinary sense, for he did not himself create new lines. He merely put together traditional lines in new forms, adding nothing of his own . . . He gathered together and held in his memory countless scraps and fragments, and had the ability to sew or patch them together as occasion demanded.

One of the groups most productive of new spirituals, The Golden Gate Quartet, works similarly, according to report. Willie Johnson, their talented poet and leader, with an enormous stock of folk idioms

and lines, reworks these into new and original patterns. Yet the songs that this quartet sings, though obviously showing a creative gift, are not so "original" that the folk would not recognize them as theirs. "Composers" of the best of present-day blues likewise levy upon the folk storehouse, turning out products that are close to authentic folk stuff.

Something of this sort is meant by the folk origin of the spirituals. It is unlikely that any group of worshipers and singers, as a group, composed spirituals. Single individuals with poetic ingenuity, a rhyming gift, or a good memory "composed" or "remembered" lines, couplets, or even quatrains out of a common storehouse. The group would join in with the refrain or the longer chorus. When one leader's ingenuity or memory was exhausted, another might take up the "composition." About two matters of origin, however, there is more certainty than about method of composition. The first is that stories purporting to tell the circumstances and dates of individual spirituals are more fanciful than accurate. This is true of all folk song. The claims of ex-slaves that they were present at the creation of well-known spirituals are to be trusted no more than the claims of many yarn-spinners that they worked side by side with John Henry or were shot at by Stackalee. The second is that the spritiuals are genuinely folk products, regardless of the fact that gifted individuals may have played leading roles in their composition. From the folk storehouse came the ideas, the vocabulary, the idioms, the images. The folk approved the song or rejected it, as it squared with folk knowledge, memory and vision. The folk changed lines that were not easily understood, inserted new stanzas, sometimes bringing the songs up to date, and transmitted them orally to the next generation. In the long journey, stanzas were lost or imperfectly remembered; and new and often incoherent interpolations took their places. But the folk kept a very large number of the songs alive and in a rather sound condition.

A second problem of origin: whether the spirituals were derived from African music or European music, whether they were "original" with the Negro or imitations, started its controversial course at the end of the nineteenth century. In a period when the glorification of the Aryan by Gobineau and Houston Stewart Chamberlain was popular, the attribution of artistic capacity to the Negro seemed presumptuous. In 1893 Richard Wallaschek, a German musicologist,

attacked the songs of the Negro as "very much overrated," "mere imitations of European compositions," "ignorantly borrowed." Certain musical critics, irritated by the praise of the spirituals, and especially by Dvořák's use of Negro melodies in his symphony *From The New World,* gladly made use of Wallaschek's dicta. In 1915, Henry E. Krehbiel, an American musical critic of high repute, answered Wallaschek's charges. This was not difficult, since Wallaschek had included many spurious minstrel melodies in the "Negro" songs he studied. Krehbiel set out to prove, in a discriminating analysis, that the Negro songs were the only indigenous body of folk songs in America, and that these songs were the Negro's own.

John W. Work, James Weldon Johnson, R. Nathaniel Dett, N. Ballanta-Taylor, and several other Negroes allied themselves with Krehbiel. Naturally sensitive about the aspersion on the originality of their race, some of these at times overstated their argument and stressed not only the complete originality of the songs, but also their Africanism.

A cogent attack on the Africanism of the songs came from Guy B. Johnson, one of the most sympathetic and informed students of Negro folklore. In *Folk Culture on St. Helena Island* (1930) Johnson approached the Negro spiritual as a problem in anthropology: "What happened when the Negro slave, possessing a system of music admittedly different from European or Western music, came into contact with the American white man's music?" Johnson established definite points of contact between the slave and "white music," which the defenders of the originality of the spirituals had scouted. He found both musical and textual similarities in white revival hymns and Negro spirituals. Newman White in *American Negro Folk Songs* (1928) adduced proof of the slaves' participation in the camp meetings of the South, and of the similarity of white and Negro religious primitivism. He found a large number of close textual resemblances in white revival hymns and the spirituals. George Pullen Jackson in *White Spirituals of the Southern Uplands* (1934) illustrates melodic and textual similarities between white and Negro spirituals. A large school of commentators now accepts the conclusions of these scholars.

Extremists have set up the controversy as between Africanism, or complete originality, and white camp-meeting derivation, or complete unoriginality. This oversimplification does injustice to the careful

scholarship of some of the men on both sides. Certain observations, however, may be useful, since they pertain to the whole picture of the Negro in American culture. Few of the disputants know all three of the musics involved: African music (if the music of an entire continent of different peoples can be so simply categorized); Southern white music of the slavery period with which the slave might have come into contact; and the spirituals themselves. Collections of slave songs were made very late; they are at best only approximations, in a system of notation that is admittedly skeletal. Analyzing the songs collected by Allen, Ware, and Garrison is a long way from analyzing the songs as sung by folk Negroes, either then or now. That the slave had contact with white religious folk and minstrel music is no less undebatable than that whites had contact with Negro music. A give-and-take seems logical to expect. Correspondences between white and Negro melodies have been established. The complete Africanism of the spirituals was never tenable. The spirituals are obviously not in an African musical idiom, not even so much as the music of Haiti, Cuba, and Brazil. But all of this does not establish the Negro spiritual, and most certainly not hot jazz, the blues, and boogie-woogie, as imitative of white music, or as unoriginal, or as devoid of traces of the African idiom. Believing one's ears, especially where folk-music is concerned, is probably better than believing the conventional notation of that music; believing phonograph records, as recent scholars are doing, is even better. The obstinate fact of a great difference between Negro folk-songs and the white camp-meeting hymns exists. Even the strongest adherents of the view that the origin of the Negro spirituals is in white music, agree that now the spiritual is definitely the Negro's own and, regardless of birthplace, is stamped with originality. The conclusions of Milton Metfessel, derived from a use of "phonophotography" in music, are that

In bridging the gap between civilized and primitive music, the Negro sings some songs in which the analyzed elements are probably more often European than African, others in which the two are equally present, and others still in which the African element predominates. In our present group, the work songs seem to have more of the latter elements, the blues and workaday religious songs partake of both, while the formal spirituals appear to lean toward Europe.

The present state of scholarship on the subject is summarized by George Herzog:

It becomes more and more clear that Southern Negro folk music does not furnish a chapter in the rigid survival of original musical features, but an equally fascinating chapter in the recreation of musical forms. European folk song, in the hands of the Negro, achieved special forms and idiosyncrasies, one step further removed from the European proto-types and from the old European background.

To many this step is a good long one. Lovers of Negro folk songs need not fear either its detractors or the students of origins. Neither European nor African, but partaking of elements of both, the result is a new kind of music, certainly not mere imitation, but more crea-tive and original than any other American music.

The resemblance of words and ideas in white hymns and Negro spirituals is not of such great moment. The slaves, accepting Chris-tianity, naturally accepted the vocabulary and subject matter of Christianity; and, liking a good song wherever they heard it, they sang church hymns as well as spirituals. Exact correspondences be-tween lines in white hymns and spirituals have been discovered; Guy Johnson found such lines as "Ride on, Jesus"; "O, Lord, remember me"; "I am bound for the land of Canaan"; "O, could I hear some sinner pray"; "Lay this body down"; and "You will see the graves a-bursting" in a single white songbook, *The Millennial Harp* (pub-lished in 1843). Both Negro and white religious songs tell of "poor, wayfaring strangers," "a union band," on "a pilgrimage to heaven."

But, as Guy Johnson states, the line, or at most the stanza, seems to be the unit of transfer; there are not many instances (though more than generally suspected) "in which a white song was taken over in its entirety by Negroes." This fact should be considered with the fact that some of the correspondences are forced. For instance, George Pullen Jackson cites the following lines:

At his table we'll sit down,
Christ will gird himself and serve us with sweet
manna all around. (white)

as parallel with

> Gwine to sit down at the welcome table,
> Gwine to feast off milk and honey. (Negro)

and

> To hide yourself in the mountaintop
> To hide yourself from God. (white)

as parallel with

> Went down to the rocks to hide my face,
> The rocks cried out no hiding place. (Negro)

These are similar only in general idea, certainly not in the poetry. Newman White believes that white songs in "crossing over" are greatly transformed. Samuel Asbury believes "the words of the best white spirituals," cannot compare as poetry with the words of the best Negro spirituals and Carl Engel sees the spirituals as amazingly profound and beautiful verse, unlike anything in "the Bay Psalm Book or its numerous successors," though both men deny "complete originality" to the music. Louis Untermeyer writes that the slaves, having absorbed the Christianity to which they were exposed, repeated it in a highly original way:

> Only those who have heard the *cadences* can appreciate the originality of the Negro's contribution . . . The magic emanates from the unaffected nobility of the themes, the teasing-shifting rhythms, so simple on the surface, so intricately varied beneath; it rises from a deep emotional sincerity in every beat.

Where suspicions of the new scholarship were justified was in the interpretation of the spirituals, based on the verbal similarities between white hymns and Negro spirituals. Finding that white camp-meeting hymns spoke of "freedom" and of "hard trials," Newman White argued against the "abolitionist use of the spirituals as an

instrument of propaganda," as sorrow songs produced by the oppression of slavery. He bases his argument upon the paucity of songs containing "unequivocal references to the desire for freedom," and upon his assumption that the Negro "seldom contemplated his low estate in slavery." According to White, the spirituals of the slaves, when referring to freedom mean exactly what the camp-meeting hymns of slaveholders mean by their references to freedom: namely, freedom from the oppression of sin. This is ingenious but unconvincing reasoning.

There are not many spirituals that speak openly of a love for freedom and a determination to be free. The slaves were not so naïve as that; they knew, better than several of their historians, how close to hysteria the slaveholders really were, how rigid the control could be. The very fact of a group of slaves meeting and singing and praying together was cause of anxiety to many masters, even if the slaves were singing of Jordan or Jericho.

If we can believe several fugitive slave autobiographies, however, there were many not so indirect references to physical bondage and freedom. It required no stretch of imagination to see the trials of the Israelites as paralleling the trials of the slaves, Pharaoh and his army as oppressors, and Egyptland as the South. "Go Down, Moses" was a censored song, according to fugitive slaves. "O Mary don't you weep, don't you mourn; Pharaoh's army got drowned, O Mary don't you weep" is less direct, but expresses the same central idea. Douglass tells us not only of the doubletalk of the slaves' songs, but also sees the whole body of spirituals as reflecting a desire for freedom.

Nevertheless, the spirituals which without ingenious forcing are seen to have double meanings: "Didn't my Lord deliver Daniel, and why not every man?" "Rich man Dives, he lived so well—When he died he found a home in hell"; the challenging "Go Down, Moses"; the shouts of jubilee possible under the banners of a liberating army: "O Freedom, befo' I'd be a slave, I'd be buried in my grave!" are numerically in the minority. The slaves sang songs expressing Christianity, and then not as "Christian soldiers, marching on to war," but as lost sheep, all crying for a shepherd.

Yet Newman White goes too far in stating that the slave "never contemplated his low estate," and that because few outspoken abolitionist spirituals can be found, the slave's references to freedom con-

note only freedom from sin, from the bonds of the flesh and the world. Analysis of the body of white camp-meeting "spirituals" reveals fairly perfunctory references to heaven as freedom; but in Negro spirituals references to trouble here below are far more numerous, and are poignant rather than perfunctory, springing from a deep need, not from an article of faith. Such lines as

> Bye and bye, I'm gonna lay down dis heavy load.

> De blind man stood on de road, and cried
> Crying Lord, my Lord, save-a po' me.

> Keep a-inchin' along, lak a po' inchworm.

> I don't know what my mother wants to stay here fuh,
> Dis ole worl' ain't been no friend to huh.

> I'm rolling through an unfriendly worl'.

> Lord, keep me from sinking down.

surely reflect the slave's awareness of his bitter plight more than his consciousness of the oppression of sin.

The spirituals tell of hard trials, great tribulations; or wanderings in some lonesome valley, or down some unknown road, a long ways from home, with brother, sister, father, mother gone. It is only a half-truth to see the spirituals as otherworldly. "You take dis worl', and give me Jesus" is certainly one of the least of the refrains. In the spirituals the slave took a clear-eyed look at this world, and he revealed in tragic poetry what he saw:

> O I been rebuked, and I been scorned,
> Done had a hard time sho's you born.

There are spirituals, many of them well known, that spring with joy. The convert shouts when he gets out of the wilderness. The true believer sees heaven as a welcome table, a feasting place; quite as often, significantly, as a place of rest where the worn out ones can sit down, for once at their ease. The saved dilate on the activities of that great "gittin' up morning" with greater zeal and trust than that with

which Michael Wigglesworth foresaw his Day of Doom. But even
in heaven, life on earth is not forgotten:

> I'm gonna tell God all my troubles,
>   When I get home. . . .
>
> I'm gonna tell Him the road was rocky
>   When I get home. . . .
>
> I'm gonna tell Him I had hard trials
>   When I get home. . . .
>
> I'm gonna tell God how you're doing
>   When I get home.

If the spirituals that talk about heaven are often joyful, it should be
remembered that the joy is a joy at escape.

The spirituals were born of suffering. Yet Zora Neale Hurston
is right when, thinking of their rendition, she refuses the inclusive
title "Sorrow Songs." Negro folk singers, certainly today, sing spirituals with great gusto. There is much more than melancholy in their
singing; there is a robustness, vitality, a fused strength. The singing
serves as a release; the fervor of the release indicates something of
the confining pressure that folk Negroes know too well and have
known too long.

Musicologists find in the spiritual singing of today a musical relative
of the wild free improvisations of hot jazz. The resemblance is seen
especially in the singing of such groups as the Golden Gate Quartet
and the Mitchell Christian Singers. The spirituals that they sing
are often of recent origin, frequently narratives of Biblical characters,
and their arrangements of the older spirituals are probably more
dynamic and less restrained than their forefathers' singing in the
old brush arbors. With some pronounced exceptions, the new spirituals seem more evangelical in nature and less the outpourings of "a
troubled sperrit." Besides the new spirituals springing up in the rural
churches of the South, evangelists sell hymns, printed as broadsides,
as their own compositions, though many of the lines seem lifted from
hymnbooks.

Newman White states that there was a time "when most of the
literate and semi-literate members of the Negro race were desirous

of forgetting [the spiritual]." This is only a half-truth. Many Negroes in the upper strata did so, some because of what James Weldon Johnson calls "second-generation respectability," some because of the dubious uses to which spirituals were put, some because of the interpretations of them as plantation songs, reminiscent of the good ole days befo' de war, which is exactly what they are not. Some Negro college students have refused to sing them, but more colleges have stressed them in the repertoires of their choral groups, not only because of their value in gaining finances and prestige. Most of the leading race interpreters: Frederick Douglass, Booker T. Washington, Paul Laurence Dunbar, W. E. B. DuBois, Kelly Miller, Carter G. Woodson, and Alain Locke have paid honor to them. Leading musical scholars such as those mentioned earlier have praised them even extremely; leading musicians like Harry T. Burleigh, R. Nathaniel Dett, Hall Johnson, Eva Jessye, W. C. Handy, Charles Cooke, William Grant Still, and William Dawson have interpreted and arranged them; leading artists like Marian Anderson, Dorothy Maynor, Roland Hayes, and Paul Robeson sing them with utmost respect.

For nearly a century, articulate Negroes have recognized the spirituals as the Negro's first important cultural gift to America. Folk Negroes have nourished them for longer than that, and are still creating new ones, hoarding a treasure though unconscious of its value.

Sterling A. Brown

DO, LORD, REMEMBER ME

Do, Lord, remember me.
Do, Lord, remember me.
When I'm in trouble,
Do, Lord, remember me.

When I'm low down,
Do, Lord, remember me.
Oh, when I'm low down,
Do, Lord, remember me.

Don't have no cross,
Do, Lord, remember me.
Don't have no crown,
Do, Lord, remember me.

Do, Lord, remember me.
Do, Lord, remember me.

MOTHERLESS CHILD

Sometimes I feel like a motherless child,
Sometimes I feel like a motherless child,
Sometimes I feel like a motherless child,
A long ways from home,
A long ways from home.

Sometimes I feel like I'm almost gone,
Sometimes I feel like I'm almost gone,
Sometimes I feel like I'm almost gone,
A long ways from home,
A long ways from home.

Sometimes I feel like a feather in the air,
Sometimes I feel like a feather in the air,
Sometimes I feel like a feather in the air,
And I spread my wings and I fly,

I spread my wings and I fly.

CITY CALLED HEAVEN

I am a poor pilgrim of sorrow.
I'm in this wide world alone.

No hope in this world for tomorrow.
I'm tryin' to make heaven my home.

Sometimes I am tossed and driven.
Sometimes I don't know where to roam.
I've heard of a city called heaven.
I've started to make it my home.

My mother's gone on to pure glory.
My father's still walkin' in sin.
My sisters and brothers won't own me
Because I'm tryin' to get in.

Sometimes I am tossed and driven.
Sometimes I don't know where to roam,
But I've heard of a city called heaven
And I've started to make it my home.

NO MORE AUCTION BLOCK

No more auction block for me,
No more, no more,
No more auction block for me,
Many thousand gone.

No more peck of corn for me,
No more, no more,
No more peck of corn for me,
Many thousand gone.

No more pint of salt for me,
No more, no more,
No more pint of salt for me,
Many thousand gone.

No more driver's lash for me,
No more, no more,
No more driver's lash for me,
Many thousand gone.

GO DOWN, MOSES

Go down, Moses,
Way down in Egyptland
Tell old Pharaoh
To let my people go.

When Israel was in Egyptland
Let my people go
Oppressed so hard they could not stand
Let my people go.

Go down, Moses,
Way down in Egyptland
Tell old Pharaoh
"Let my people go."

"Thus saith the Lord," bold Moses said,
"Let my people go;
If not I'll smite your first-born dead
Let my people go."

Go down, Moses,
Way down in Egyptland,
Tell old Pharaoh,
"Let my people go!"

SAVIOUR, DON'T PASS ME BY

A blind man stood on the roadside,
He was blind and he could not see.
He heard that Jesus was passing by.
He felt he had need of Thee.
He called to one of the disciples,
Pray tell me, tell me when he's nigh.
He cried out, Saviour, don't you pass me by!

I'm crying, Saviour, please, my loving Saviour,
Saviour, don't you pass me by!
I'm crying, Saviour, please, my loving Saviour,
Oh, Saviour, don't you pass me by!

While Jesus was passing by
He heard a woman cry,
If I could but His garment touch,
I would go and prophesy.
She called to Peter, James and John,
Pray tell me when he's nigh.
She cried out, Saviour, don't you pass me by!

I'm crying, Saviour, Saviour,
Please, Saviour, don't you pass me by!
I'm crying out, Saviour, Saviour!
Crying out, Saviour, don't you pass me by!

NOBODY KNOWS THE TROUBLE I'VE SEEN

Oh, nobody knows the trouble I've seen,
Nobody knows but Jesus.

Nobody knows the trouble I've seen,
Glory, Hallelujah!

Sometimes I'm up, sometimes I'm down,
Oh, yes, Lord!
Sometimes I'm almost to the ground,
Oh, yes, Lord!
Although you see me going along, so,
Oh, yes, Lord!
I have my troubles here below,
Oh, yes, Lord!

Nobody knows the trouble I've seen,
Nobody knows my sorrow.
Nobody knows the trouble I've seen,
Glory, Hallelujah!

One day when I was walking along,
Oh, yes, Lord!
The elements opened and His love came down,
Oh, yes, Lord!
I never shall forget that day,
Oh, yes, Lord!
When Jesus washed my sins away,
Oh, yes, Lord!

Oh, nobody knows the trouble I've seen,
Nobody knows my sorrow.
Nobody knows the trouble I've seen,
Glory, Hallelujah!

EVERY TIME I FEEL THE SPIRIT

Every time I feel the spirit
Moving in my heart I will pray.

Every time I feel the spirit
Moving in my heart I will pray.

Upon the mountain my Lord spoke,
Out of His mouth came fire and smoke.
In the valley on my knees,
Asked my Lord, Have mercy, please.

Every time I feel the spirit
Moving in my heart I will pray . . .

Jordan River's chilly and cold,
Chills the body but not the soul.
All around me looks so fine,
Asked my Lord if all was mine.

Every time I feel the spirit
Moving in my heart I will pray.
Every time I feel the spirit
Moving in my heart I will pray.

SWING LOW, SWEET CHARIOT

Swing low, sweet chariot,
Coming for to carry me home,
Swing low, sweet chariot,
Coming for to carry me home.

I looked over Jordan and what did I see
Coming for to carry me home,
A band of angels, coming after me,
Coming for to carry me home.

If you get there before I do,
Coming for to carry me home,

Tell all my friends I'm coming too,
Coming for to carry me home.

Swing low, sweet chariot,
Coming for to carry me home,
Swing low, sweet chariot,
Coming for to carry me home.

STEAL AWAY

Steal away, steal away, steal away to Jesus,
Steal away, steal away home,
I ain't got long to stay here.

My Lord, He calls me,
He calls me by the thunder,
The trumpet sounds within-a my soul,
I ain't got long to stay here.

Steal away, steal away, steal away to Jesus,
Steal away, steal away home,
I ain't got long to stay here.

Green trees a-bending,
Po' sinner stands a-trembling
The trumpet sounds within-a my soul,
I ain't got long to stay here.

Steal away, steal away, steal away to Jesus,
Steal away, steal away home,
I ain't got long to stay here.

DEEP RIVER

Deep river, my home is over Jordan,
Deep river, Lord; I want to cross over into camp ground.

O, don't you want to go to that gospel feast,
That promised land where all is peace?

Deep river, my home is over Jordan,
Deep river, Lord; I want to cross over into camp ground.

I GOT A HOME IN DAT ROCK

I got a home in dat rock,
Don't you see?
I got a home in dat rock,
Don't you see?
Between de earth an' sky,
Thought I heard my Saviour cry,
You got a home in dat rock,
Don't you see?

Poor man Laz'rus, poor as I,
Don't you see?
Poor man Laz'rus, poor as I,
Don't you see?
Poor man Laz'rus, poor as I,
When he died he found a home on high,
He had a home in dat rock,
Don't you see?

Rich man Dives, he lived so well,
Don't you see?
Rich man Dives, he lived so well,
Don't you see?
Rich man Dives, he lived so well,
When he died he found a home in **Hell,**
He had no home in dat rock,
Don't you see?

God gave Noah de Rainbow sign,
Don't you see?
God gave Noah de Rainbow sign,
Don't you sec?
God gave Noah de Rainbow sign,
No more water but fire next time,
Better get a home in dat rock,
Don't you see?

WHERE SHALL I BE WHEN THE
FIRST TRUMPET SOUND?

Where shall I be when the first trumpet sound?
Where shall I be when it sound so loud?
Sound so loud till it wakes up the dead!
Where shall I be when it sound?

Moses died in the days of old,
Where he was buried has never been told,
Where shall I be?
Where shall I be?

God gave the people the rainbow sign
No more water, but fire next time,
Where shall I be?
Where shall I be?

GOD'S GONNA SET DIS WORLD ON FIRE

God's gonna set dis world on fire,
God's gonna set dis world on fire,
Some o' dese days. God knows it!
God's gonna set dis world on fire,
Some o' dese days.

I'm gonna drink that healin' water
I'm gonna drink that healin' water,
Some o' dese days . . . God knows it!
I'm gonna drink that healin' water
Some o' dese days.

I'm gonna drink and never git thirsty,
I'm gonna drink and never git thirsty,
Some o' dese days . . . God knows it!
I'm gonna drink and never git thirsty
Some o' dese days.

I'm gonna walk on de streets of glory,
I'm gonna walk on de streets of glory,
Some o' dese days . . . God knows it!
I'm gonna walk on de streets of glory
Some o' dese days.

OH MARY, DON'T YOU WEEP

Oh Mary, don't you weep, don't you moan,
Oh Mary, don't you weep, don't you moan,
Pharaoh's army got drownded,
Oh Mary, don't you weep.

One of dese mornings, bright and fair,
Take my wings and cleave de air,
Pharaoh's army got drownded,
Oh Mary, don't you weep.

One of dese mornings, five o'clock,
Dis ole world gonna reel and rock,
Pharaoh's army got drownded,
Oh Mary, don't you weep.

Oh Mary, don't you weep, don't you moan,
Oh Mary, don't you weep, don't you moan,
Pharaoh's army got drownded,
Oh Mary, don't you weep.

JOSHUA FIT DE BATTLE OF JERICHO

Joshua fit de battle of Jericho,
Jericho, Jericho,
Joshua fit de battle of Jericho,
And de walls come tumbling down.

You may talk about yo' king of Gideon
Talk about yo' man of Saul,
Dere's none like good old Joshua
At de battle of Jericho.

Up to de walls of Jericho,
He marched with spear in hand;
"Go blow dem ram horns," Joshua cried,
"Kase de battle am in my hand."

Den de lamb ram sheep horns begin to blow,
Trumpets begin to sound,
Joshua commanded de chillen to shout,
And de walls come tumbling down.

Dat morning,
Joshua fit de battle of Jericho,
Jericho, Jericho,
Joshua fit de battle of Jericho,
And de walls come tumbling down.

NOW LET ME FLY

Way down yonder in de middle o' de fiel',
Angel workin' at de chariot wheel,
Not so partic'lar 'bout workin' at de wheel,
But I jes' want-a see how de chariot feel.

Now let me fly,
Now let me fly,
Now let me fly
Into Mount Zion, Lord, Lord.

I got a mother in de Promise Lan',
Ain't goin' to stop till I shake her han',
Not so partic'lar 'bout workin' at de wheel,
But I jes' want-a get up in de Promise Lan'.

Meet dat Hypocrite on de street,
First thing he do is to show his teeth.
Nex' thing he do is to tell a lie,
An' de bes' thing to do is to pass him by.

Now let me fly,
Now let me fly,
Now let me fly
Into Mount Zion, Lord, Lord.

GET ON BOARD, LITTLE CHILDREN

Get on board, little children
Get on board, little children,
Get on board, little children
There's room for many a more.

The gospel train's a-comin', I hear it just at hand,
I hear the car wheels rumblin' and rollin' through the land.

I hear the train a-comin', she's comin' round the curve,
She's loosened all her steam and brakes and strainin' every nerve.

The fare is cheap and all can go, the rich and poor are there,
No second class aboard this train, no difference in the fare.

Get on board, little children
Get on board, little children,
Get on board, little children
There's room for many a more.

HAND ME DOWN MY SILVER TRUMPET

Hand me down my silver trumpet, Gabriel,
Hand me down my silver trumpet, Gabriel.
Hand it down, throw it down,
Anyway to get it down,
'Cause all my sins been taken away.

Hand me down my walking cane, Gabriel,
Yes, hand me down my walking cane, Gabriel.

Hand it down, throw it down,
Any old way to get it down,
'Cause all my sins been taken away.

Hand me down my long white robe, Gabriel,
Robe, robe, robe, my long white robe, Gabriel.
Hand it down, throw it down,
Just any old way to get it down,
'Cause all my sins been taken away.

SIT DOWN

Why don't you sit down?
Can't sit down!
Sit down, I told you!
I can't sit down.
Go 'way don't bother me,
I can't sit down
'Cause I just got to heaven
An' I can't sit down!

Who's that yonder dressed in white?
I just got to heaven
An' I can't sit down!
Looks like the children of the Israelites.
I just got to heaven
An' I can't sit down!

Who's that yonder dressed in red?
I just got to heaven
An' I can't sit down!
It looks like the children that Moses led.
I just got to heaven
An' I can't sit down.

Why don't you sit down?
I can't sit down.
Go 'way don't bother me,
I can't sit down
'Cause I just got to heaven
An' I can't sit down!

RISE AND SHINE

Oh, rise and shine, and give God the glory, glory!
Rise and shine, and give God the glory, glory!
Rise and shine, and give God the glory, glory
For the year of Jubilee.

Jesus carry the young lambs in his bosom, bosom,
Carry the young lambs in his bosom, bosom
Carry the young lambs in his bosom, bosom
For the year of Jubilee.

Oh, come on, mourners, get you ready, ready,
Come on, mourners, get you ready, ready,
Come on, mourners, get you ready, ready,
For the year of Jubilee.

You may keep your lamps trimmed and burning, burning,
Keep your lamps trimmed and burning, burning,
Keep your lamps trimmed and burning, burning,
For the year of Jubilee.

Oh, come on children, don't be weary, weary!
Come on, children, don't be weary, weary!
Come on, children, don't be weary, weary,
For the year of Jubilee.

Oh, don't you hear them bells a-ringing, ringing?
Don't you hear them bells a-ringing, ringing?

Don't you hear them bells a-ringing, ringing
For the year of Jubilee?

THERE'S A LITTLE WHEEL A-TURNIN'

There's a little wheel a-turnin' in my heart,
There's a little wheel a-turnin' in my heart,
    In my heart, in my heart,
There's a little wheel a-turnin' in my heart.

Oh, I feel so very happy in my heart,
Yes, I feel so very happy in my heart,
    In my heart, in my heart,
Oh, I feel so very happy in my heart.

Oh, I don't feel no ways tired in my heart,
No, I don't feel no ways tired in my heart,
    In my heart, in my heart,
Oh, I don't feel no ways tired in my heart.

GO TELL IT ON THE MOUNTAIN

Go tell it on the mountain,
Over the hills and everywhere;
Go tell it on the mountain,
That Jesus Christ is born.

When I was a seeker,
I sought both night and day,
I asked the Lord to help me,
And he showed me the way.

He made me a watchman
Upon a city wall,
And if I am a christian,
I am the least of all.

Go tell it on the mountain,
Over the hills and everywhere;
Go tell it on the mountain,
That Jesùs Christ is born.

RISE UP, SHEPHERD AND FOLLOW

There's a star in the East
On Christmas morn.
Rise up, shepherd, and follow!
It'll lead to the place
Where the Saviour's born.
Rise up, shepherd, and follow!
If you take good heed
To the angel's words and
Rise up, shepherd, and follow,
You'll forget your flocks,
You'll forget your herds.
Rise up, shepherd, and follow!
Leave your sheep, leave your lambs,
Rise up, shepherd, and follow!
Leave your ewes, leave your rams,
Rise up, shepherd, and follow!
Follow the Star of Bethlehem,
Rise up, shepherd, and follow!

THE VIRGIN MARY HAD A BABY BOY

The Virgin Mary had a baby boy,
The Virgin Mary had a baby boy,

The Virgin Mary had a baby boy,
And they said His name was Jesus.
He come from the glory,
He come from the glorious kingdom!
Oh, yes, believer!
He come from the glory,
He come from the glorious kingdom!

WASN'T THAT A MIGHTY DAY

Wasn't that a mighty day
When Jesus Christ was born?
Star shone in the East,
Star shone in the East,
Star shone in the East
When Jesus Christ was born'.

WHAT YOU GONNA NAME THAT
PRETTY LITTLE BABY?

Oh, Mary, what you gonna name
That pretty little baby?
Glory, glory, glory
To the new born King!
Some will call Him one thing,
But I think I'll call Him Jesus.
Glory, glory, glory
To the new born King!
Some will call Him one thing,
But I think I'll say Emanuel.
Glory, glory, glory
To the new born King!

WERE YOU THERE WHEN THEY
CRUCIFIED MY LORD?

Were you there when they crucified my Lord?
Were you there when they crucified my Lord?
Oh!—sometimes it causes me to tremble, tremble, tremble,
Were you there when they crucified my Lord?

Were you there when they nailed Him to the tree?
Were you there when they nailed Him to the tree?
Oh!—sometimes it causes me to tremble, tremble, tremble,
Were you there when they nailed Him to the tree?

Were you there when they pierced Him in the side?
Were you there when they pierced Him in the side?
Oh!—sometimes it causes me to tremble, tremble, tremble,
Were you there when they pierced Him in the side?

Were you there when He bowed His head and died?
Were you there when He bowed His head and died?
Oh!—sometimes it causes me to tremble, tremble, tremble,
Were you there when He bowed His head and died?

Were you there when the sun refused to shine?
Were you there when the sun refused to shine?
Oh!—sometimes it causes me to tremble, tremble, tremble,
Were you there when the sun refused to shine?

Were you there when they laid Him in the tomb?
Were you there when they laid Him in the tomb?
Oh!—sometimes it causes me to tremble, tremble, tremble,
Were you there when they laid Him in the tomb?

DELILAH

Delilah! Delilah! Delilah!
Read about Sampson from his birth,
Strongest man ever lived on earth.
He lived way back in ancient times,
Killed three thousand Phillistines.
He cried,
    If I had my way, Delilah,
    If I had my way, Delilah,
    If I had my way, Delilah
    I'd tear this building down.

Delilah was a woman fine and fair,
Pleasant looks and coal-black hair.
Delilah changed old Sampson's mind
When he first saw that woman of the Phillistines.
He cried,
    If I had my way, Delilah,
    If I had my way, Delilah,
    If I had my way, Delilah
    I'd tear this building down.

Delilah took Sampson's head upon her knees,
Said, Tell me where your strength lies, if you please.
He said, Shave my head as clean as your hand,
And I'll be just like a natural man.
Now Delilah was a woman mighty bold.
Delilah did as she was told,
Shaved his head as clean as his hand,
Sampson got as weak as a natural man.
He cried,
    Oh, if I had my way, Delilah,
    Oh, if I had my way, Delilah,

Oh, if I had my way, Delilah
I'd tear this building down.

Sampson called on God and started to pray.
God growed his hair back that very day.
Sampson put his hands up against the wall—
Great-God-A-Mighty, house started to fall.
Oh, Sampson had his way, Delilah!
Oh, Sampson had his way, Delilah!
Oh, Sampson had his way, Delilah!
And he tore that building down.

WHEN THE SAINTS GO MARCHING IN

When the saints go marching in
When the saints go marching in
I want to be in that number
When the saints go marching in.

I used to have some playmates
Who used to play with me.
But since I've been converted
They done turned their backs on me.

Oh, when they crown Him Lord of Lords
Oh, when they crown Him Lord of Lords
Yes, I want to be in that number
When they crown Him Lord of Lords.

When they march all around His throne
When they march all around His throne.
Oh, I want to be in that number
When they march all around His throne.

I have a dear old mother who has gone on before
And left me here below,

But I know I'm gonna meet her
When the saints go marchin in.

When the saints go marching in,
Oh, when the saints go marching in!
Oh, Lord I want to be in that number
When the saints go marching in.

Gospel Songs

ROCK, CHURCH, ROCK!

BACK in 1925, audiences at the old Monogram Theatre, 35th and State in Chicago, found themselves centering more and more attention on a lanky, foot-patting piano player called Georgia Tom. There was a boy to watch!

Georgia Tom had blues in his mind as well as in his feet and his hands. He had composed Ma Rainey's popular theme music:

> Rain on the ocean,
> Rain on the deep blue sea,

not to mention scores of other blues. The kid was a natural. If the blues idiom meant anything to you, he was your boy. The only trouble was that the more you watched Georgia Tom, the less you saw him. It was downright quaint the way he bobbed in and out of things. Presently the hard-working boogie-woogie player dropped out of sight completely, and the name of Georgia Tom was forgotten.

Five or six years later, observers of such phenomena noticed that Negro churches, particularly the storefront congregations, the Sanctified groups and the shouting Baptists, were swaying and jumping as never before. Mighty rhythms rocked the churches. A wave of fresh rapture came over the people. Nobody knew just why. True, the Depression had knocked most of the folks off their

feet and sent them hurrying back to church, but did that explain this tremendous impulse to get out of their seats and praise God in the aisles? It was also true that many new songs were being introduced from time to time—songs which were different—but what did that have to do with this new ecstasy? A few of the more inquiring members discovered that the best and most lively of the new songs were credited to Thomas A. Dorsey, composer, but there were few people anywhere who connected Dorsey with the Georgia Tom of former years. The transformation had been complete. Well—almost complete.

Dorsey—not to be confused with the white orchestra leader of the same name—was born near Atlanta, the son of a country preacher. Gawky and shy, sensitive about his looks, snubbed by the more high-toned colored boys and girls of the city, young Tom early set his mind on learning to play the piano. This involved walking four miles a day, four days a week (since there was no piano in his home), but it was worth the effort and the results were completely satisfactory.

Within two years the funny-looking country kid was able to turn a Saturday Night Stomp upside down with his playing. City youngsters started calling him Barrel House Tom. Such stomp pianists as Lark Lee, Soap Stick, Long Boy, Nome Burkes, and Charlie Spann had to move over and make room for the sad-faced newcomer, Barrel House Tom. People who gave the stomps recognized a difference, too. They were glad to pay a player like Tom a dollar and a half a night for dance music. The second-string boys counted themselves lucky to get fifty cents.

Even in those marvelous days, however, young Dorsey had more in his mind than just punishing a piano. For one thing, there was a girl—a girl with curly black hair hanging over her shoulders like the glory of a thousand queens. When she looked at Tom, he felt like a boy dazzled by the sun. Then, quite suddenly, her family picked up and moved to Birmingham, carrying the daughter with them. If they had only known what they were doing to the poor boy's heart! In this mood, as so often happens, ambition was born. Tom determined to be somebody in his chosen field.

First he tried, with such local help as he could get, to teach himself harmony, composition, instrumentation, and arranging. But

being twenty and broken-hearted, he listened to talk about the steel mills of Gary, Indiana. There was good money in those mills —money that would make the wages of a Georgia stomp musician look sick. Moreover, there were golden opportunities up North, opportunities for study, musical opportunities. Perhaps, too, there were other proud dark queens with shiny black glory hanging down over their shoulders. The lure was too great; Tom couldn't resist.

What he failed to consider was the limitation of a thin, willowy body that weighed only 128 pounds. The steel mill all but did him in, but he kept at it till he got his bearings. Which is to say, he kept at it till he could put a little five-peace orchestra together. This orchestra marked the beginning of Georgia Tom, the Barrel House and Saturday Night Stomp phase having been left in Atlanta. It gave him piano practice, and it enabled him to earn money by playing for parties in the steel mill communities of Gary and South Chicago. It provided exercises in the making of band arrangements and piano scores, and it left enough time for study at the Chicago College of Composition and Arranging. More important still, it started him to reflecting.

One of the first results of this tranquil thought was a little song entitled "Count the Days I'm Gone." The waste basket got that one, but the effort was not wasted. Song followed song; and when Dorsey joined the Pilgrim Baptist Church the following year, he took to writing church songs as some people take to drinking gin. Why Dorsey's songs should have been different from other church music can be left to the imagination.

As it turned out, 1921 was a good year in which to join Pilgrim Baptist Church, for that was the year the National Baptist Convention met in Chicago. More important still, that was the convention which was lifted out of its chairs by a song called "I Do, Don't You?" A. W. Nix did the singing, and the response by the audience was terrific. More important was the fact that a small wheel started turning in the heart of an inconspicuous young convert. The song lifted the boy like angels' wings. Nothing he had pounded out at parties or stomps had ever moved him so completely. Here was his calling. He would make such music.

The effects of that decision are still unmeasured. Dorsey con-

siders "I Do, Don't You?" the first of the so-called "gospel songs."
He credits C. A. Tindley, its composer, with originating this style
of music. All of which may be fair enough, but it should be quickly
added that the songs of this genre have come a long way since
Georgia Tom's conversion.

Tindley's productive period fell between 1901 and 1906. Most
of his compositions were gospel songs in the conventional sense:
tabernacle and revival songs. His, however, leaned heavily on Negro
spirituals. At least one widely-used song book classifies Tindley's
"Stand by Me" as a spiritual. "Nothing Between" could go in
the same group with equal reason.

Thomas A. Dorsey joined Pilgrim and commenced to write
"gospel songs" at a time when Tindley's were catching on—after
fifteen years of delayed action. It is therefore not suprising that
Dorsey's first successful songs were distinctly in the mood of his
tutor's. The earliest of these, "If I Don't Get There," published
in the popular Gospel Pearl Song Book, reveals its debt in the very
wording of its title. The second followed the same line: "We Will
Meet Him in the Sweet By and By." The Special Edition of the
National Baptist Hymnal included this one. Both have the Dorsey
touch, both have swing and bounce, both are definitely "live";
but there is little in either of the special quality that marks the more
mature Dorsey as an "influence." They are standard tabernacle
songs. Perhaps there was a reason.

Like most young fellows who join the church in their early
twenties, Dorsey had his temptations. Right off the bat, the devil
showed him a red apple: a forty-dollar a week offer to play the
blues. Georgia Tom was entranced. He fought against the allure-
ment briefly, then gave up the struggle. The blues are not thrown
off by casual resistance. Trifle with them, and they'll get you. They
got Georgia Tom. He left the church rocking and swaying to
savage rhythms.

The band he joined was called the Whispering Syncopators. It
was directed by Will Walker, and among its members were Les
Hite, Lionel Hampton, and half a dozen other boys who have since
become jazzmen of note. Georgia Tom played with the outfit
around Chicago and then accompanied them on an extended tour.
When they started a second turn through the country, he was left

behind. Instead, he organized a band for Ma Rainey, the "gold-neck mama" (thanks to a necklace of twenty-dollar gold pieces) of the early blues era. This was a step up, and he went on tour with her at an increased salary. The tricks were running his way.

One day, jittery with excitement, he found himself standing before the dog license cage in the City Hall. It was an embarrassing moment, for what he really wanted was a marriage license. When he got himself straightened out, it was just five minutes before the bureau closed. An hour later, all hitched up and everything, he was off with the band for engagements in the South. While his new wife was not the girl who provoked his sighs in Atlanta, she had her own glory, and Dorsey knew that things were breaking his way. Yet his mind wasn't right. Something told him he was straying. God had to put a stop to it.

That was the time he got sick. For eighteen months he was unable to work. The doctors couldn't do him any good. His money melted away, and his wife had to take a job in a laundry. Still he grew worse and worse. His weight went down to 117 pounds. It was then that his Godfearing sister-in-law decided to take a hand. She took him back to church. It was just what he needed; he commenced to improve immediately. As a matter of fact, it occurred to him that perhaps his sickness was less of the body than of the mind. To prove it, he sat down that very week and wrote a new song, one of his ringing successes, "Someday, Somewhere."

Even a song that has since been so widely approved by church-people of all denominations throughout the Christian world as "Someday, Somewhere" put no meal in the barrel immediately. No publisher wanted it, and when Dorsey had a thousand copies printed at his own expense, nobody would buy them. With money his wife borrowed, he bought envelopes and stamps and circular-ized people who should have been interested. Nothing happened; not a single sale. There were no choirs interested in singing this kind of number. No musical directors were impressed. The situation called to mind W. C. Handy's experiences with his blues compositions. The only thing left to Dorsey was to get out and sing his song to the people themselves.

The very next week he made a start, arranging with a preacher to introduce the number in a church service. He arrived as arranged,

took his seat on the front row, and waited for his call. The preacher preached. The people sang and prayed. The collection was raised. Finally church was dismissed. Dorsey was still sitting on the front row, waiting to be called upon for his song. The next Sunday he tried again. Then the next, and the next. On the latter occasions he got to sing his song, but the rewards were meager. He counted himself lucky when he sold a dollar and a half's worth of song sheets. Still the humiliating business went on. He wouldn't give up. Eventually the Brunswick Recording Company rescued him by giving him a job arranging music for their recording artists.

Thereafter things went better. He took his wife out of the laundry. In six months he had a thousand dollars in the bank. But he hadn't learned his lesson yet. Temptation came strolling around again. This time, oddly enough, it strummed a guitar, and its name was Tampa Red.

The young singer came to Dorsey's house one evening with some words for a song. He wanted them set to music and a musical arrangement made. Dorsey hemmed and hawed. He had had his fill of blues and stomp music and all the likes of that. Besides, this particular lyric was entitled "It's Tight Like That" and was way out of line. The guitarist pleaded; Dorsey hedged. For two hours the battle raged. In the end Georgia Tom won out over Thomas A. Dorsey. He went to the piano and knocked out the music.

The next day they took it to Vocalian Recording Company, played it. The record people jumped with glee. They promptly waxed the number and gave it to the world. Result: the first royalty statement brought $2,400.19. Tight? Well, I reckon! Dorsey rewarded his loyal wife with all the fine clothes she had dreamed about while she was working in the laundry and he was ill. The rest of the money he put in the bank. But God didn't like "Its Tight Like That," and he didn't like the money that came from it. The bank failed, and it has never yet paid off. Thomas A. Dorsey took that for a lesson.

He has behaved himself ever since. God is pleased, and the church folks are so happy you can hear them half a mile away. They are clapping their hands, patting their feet, and singing for all they are

worth. Why shouldn't they? They had as good a reason as the composer for singing

> How many times did Jesus lift me,
> How many times did my burdens bear?
> How many times has He forgiven my sins?
> And when I reach the pearly gates, He'll let me in.

Since his return to his true love, definitely and finally, Dorsey has written some songs in the tempered, conventional style of gospel music everywhere. His "Take My Hand, Precious Lord" is a good example. It seems to be almost universally approved and is sung in many churches where there is still a definite resistance to the main body of the Dorsey music. The resistance is understandable. Georgia Tom is still lurking about. The composer of "Stormy Sea Blues" and "It's Tight Like That" is entitled to come out and take a bow when a congregation sings:

Just hide me in Thy bosom till the storm of life is o'er;
Rock me in the cradle of Thy love.
Just feed me (feed me, feed me, feed me, Jesus) till I want no more;
Then take me to that blessed home above.

It is not surprising that the swing bands fell for the stuff, nor that a church singer like Sister Thorp could join Cab Calloway without changing her songs. Neither is it surprising that the church folks resented this use of their music and complained bitterly. They have their case, and it's a good one.

Meanwhile, the vogue of the ineptly described "gospel songs" continues. Dorsey's campaigns in the churches resulted in the organization of hundreds of choirs that would not blush at the strong rhythms of the new songs. Where the senior choirs wouldn't handle them, the younger elements in the churches have insisted on the organization of junior choirs to sing them. In Negro communities school children sing them on the streets. Here, indeed, is church music that can hold its own against anything on the hit parade. Taxicab drivers tune in Rev. Clarence Cobb's church on Sunday

night. His choir sings the new songs almost exclusively, and they make them jump, to say the least.

A flock of other composers have come along since Dorsey showed the way. One of the best is Rev. Cobb himself. Another is Roberta Martin. Dorsey says he discovered her when she was playing and singing in a storefront church on South State Street. Her "Didn't It Rain" is miles ahead of the old spiritual which also bears that name. Something has been added.

What these composers have evolved is perhaps a compound of elements found in the old tabernacle songs, the Negro spirituals, and the blues. Georgia Tom can probably be thanked for the latter. In any case, the seasoning is there now; and, like it or not, it may be hard to get out. Indeed, some churchgoers are now bold enough to ask, "Why shouldn't church songs be lively?"

To this Dorsey would undoubtedly answer, "Amen," but he has also stated his case in verse:

> Make my journey brighter,
> Make my burdens lighter,
> Help me to do good wherever I can.
> Let Thy presence thrill me,
> The Holy Spirit fill me,
> Keep me in the hollow of Thy han."

Clap hands, church!

Arna Bontemps

TAKE MY HAND, PRECIOUS LORD

> Precious Lord, take my hand,
> Lead me on, let me stand,
> I am tired, I am weak, I am worn.
> Through the storm, through the night
> Lead me on to the light,
> Take my hand, precious Lord,
> Lead me home.

When my way grows drear,
Precious Lord, linger near.
When my life is almost gone,
Hear my cry, hear my call,
Hold my hand lest I fall.
Take my hand, precious Lord,
Lead me home.

When the darkness appears
And the night draws near,
And the day is past and gone,
At the river I stand,
Guide my feet, hold my hand.
Take my hand, precious Lord
Lead me home.

Thomas A. Dorsey

WHAT COULD I DO?

What could I do? What could I do?
What could I do? What could I do?
What could I do if it wasn't for His word?
What could I see? What could I say?
How could I feel? How could I pray?
What could I do if it wasn't for the Lord?

He's my bread, He's my water,
He's my life, my everything.
And He helps me whatever the years may bring.
He keeps me young, keeps me strong,
Sets me right when I'm doing wrong.
What could I do if it wasn't for the Lord?

He's my mother, my father, my sister,
And he's my brother, too,

And he helps me when I don't know what to do.
When my lights go out and my clouds get dim,
Friends move out, then my Jesus moves in.
What could I do if it wasn't for the Lord?

Thomas A. Dorsey

IF I CAN JUST MAKE IT IN

If I can just make it in,
If I can just make it in,
If I can just make it in
To the heavenly gate,
I won't mind the load I'm bearing,
I won't mind the clothes I'm wearing,
I won't mind the way I'm faring
If I can just make it in.
I won't mind the work I've done,
I won't mind the race I've run.
All my trials will count as one
If I can just make it in.

I won't mind my lowly station,
I won't mind Satan's temptations,
I won't mind my tribulations
If I can just make it in.
You can have all this world's gold
And all the riches you can hold,
Just let me save my soul
So I can just make it in.
Though my pathway now is drear,
Though my heart is filled with fear,
I won't mind my every tear
If I can just make it in.

Kenneth Morris

BUILD ME A CABIN

Houses and land I may not ever own.
Oh, this world's riches I've never known.
I'll just keep on working for a home in Glory.
They tell me it was built by my God's own hand.
I am not so particular about mansions in the sky.
But all I want the Lord to do is
Just own me as his child.
Lord, build me a cabin
Somewhere in a corner up in Glory Land.
Oh, Lord, Lord, just build me a cabin,
I want a little cabin somewhere in Glory.
I'm begging, Lord! Yes, I want a cabin,
Please build me a cabin
Where I can shake my Saviour's hand.
I am not so particular about walking streets of gold.
I am not so particular about sharing riches untold.
But I want a cabin, yes, a cabin
In a corner builded in Glory Land.

Edna Gallmon Cooke

MOVE ON UP A LITTLE HIGHER

One of these mornings,
One of these mornings
I'm gonna lay down my cross
And get my crown.

One of these evenings, Oh, Lord,
Late one evening, My Lord,

Late one evening I'm going home
To live on high.

Just as soon as my feet strike Zion,
Lay down my heavy burden,
Put on my robe in glory, Lord,
Sing, Lord, and tell my story.
Up over hills and mountains, Lord,
To the Christian fountain,
All of God's sons and daughters, Lord,
Drinking that old healing water.

I'm gonna live on forever,
Yes, I'm gonna live on forever,
Yes, I'm gonna live up in glory after while.
I'm going out sightseeing in Beulah,
March all around God's altar,
Walk and never tire,
Fly, Lord, and never falter.
Move on up a little higher,
Meet old man Daniel.
Move on up a little higher,
Meet the Hebrew children.
Move on up a little higher,
Meet Paul and Silas.
Move on up a little higher,
Meet my friends and kindred.
Move on up a little higher,
Meet my loving mother.
Move on up a little higher,
Meet that Lily of the Valley,
Feast with the Rose of Sharon.

It will be always, *Howdy! Howdy!*
It will be always, *Howdy! Howdy!*
It will be always, *Howdy! Howdy!*
And never *Goodbye.*

Oh, will you be there early one morning?
Will you be there assembled 'round the altar?
Will you be there when the angels call the role?
Oh, children, I'll be waiting 'round God's altar.
Yes, I'll be watching early one of these mornings.
Yes, I'll be waiting at the beautiful Golden Gate.
Soon as my feet strike Zion,
Lay down my heavy burden, Lord,
Put on my robe, Lord, in glory,
Sing, Lord, Lord, and tell my story,
Been climbing over hills and mountains, Lord,
Up to the Christian fountain,
All of God's sons and daughters, Lord,
Drinking that old healing water.
I'm gonna live on forever,
I'm gonna live on forever,
Yes, I'm gonna live up in glory after while.

Mahalia Jackson and Theodore R. Frye

99½ WON'T DO

I'm runnin' tryin'
To make a hundred
'Cause 99½ won't do.
It's a rugged uphill journey,
But I've got to make a hundred
'Cause 99½ won't do.

John the Baptist was chosen of Christ.
They cut off his head when they took his life.
But when old Death came round with his head misplaced
John looked at him and smiled because his hundred were made!
The head was exhibited on a platter in Rome

But God took the soul from the body and carried John home.
It won't do! No, it won't do! 99, no, it won't do!
It's like this—70 won't make it.
80—God won't take it. 90 that's close.
99½ is almost—But get your 100!
99½ won't do! I said it won't do!
No, it won't do! 99½ won't do!

D. Love

WHEN I TOUCH HIS GARMENT

When I go to face my Lord,
I will face my Lord alone.
When I walk that starry street
Up to His Christian throne,
I will go all by myself,
Yes, I will go alone—
But when I touch His garment,
He'll claim me for His own.

CHORUS

When I touch His garment,
Yes, I touch His garment,
When I touch His garment,
He'll claim me for His own.
I've got to go all by myself,
Got to go all alone;
But when I touch His garment,
He'll claim me for His own.

All the troubles of this world
Such as weigh me down today,
All my heartaches, all my woes
I know He'll take away.
On the road up to His throne,

I will go all alone—
But when I touch His garment,
He'll claim me for His own.

There will be a shower of stars.
There will be a blaze of light,
All around my savior's head
A diadem so bright.
I will see it from afar,
As I stand there all alone—
For when I touch His garment,
He'll claim me for His own.

Langston Hughes and Jobe Huntley

I KNOW IT WAS THE LORD

Who found me when I was lost?
Who helped me to bear my heavy cross?
Who fixed me up, turned me 'round,
Left my feet on solid ground?
  I know it was Jesus!
  I know it was the Lord!

Who did you think it was in the Lion's den
When Daniel was put there by evil men?
Who put the lock on the lion's jaw,
And rescued Daniel from the terrible claws?
  I know it was Jesus!
  I know it was the Lord!

Tell me who do you think stopped Ezekiel's wheel
That kept on turning in the middle of the wheel?
Who fought with Joshua at Jericho?
Don't you know it was Jesus!
He'll reign for evermore.

Who do you think gave sight to the blind?
Made the lame ones to walk
And dead men rise?
Who took the fishes and the loaves of bread
And made 500 so all could be fed?
  Oh, Jesus, Oh Lord, Jesus! My Lord!
  I know it was Jesus! I know it was the Lord!

Clara Ward

HE WENT ON A MAN'S BOND

My God in creation said
If you make man he'd sin.
But if man break his Holy laws,
He'd bring him back again.

  And He went on a man's bond.
  Oh, He went on a man's bond.
  Well, He came all the way from heaven **down**
  And He went on a man's bond.

Now you read in the Book of Daniel
Somewhere about the latter clause,
Where the angel left from glory
And he locked that lion's jaws.

  He went on the man's bond.
  Well, He went on the man's bond.
  He came all the way from heaven **down**
  And He went on the man's bond.

 Now, read about Paul and Silas,
Them boys was prisoners bound,
Just before day when the trial was **made**
The jailer come easin' down.

And He went on the man's bond.
He went on the man's bond.
He came all the way from heaven down
And He went on the man's bond.

While praying in the Garden of Gethsemane,
And the sweat was rushin' down,
Just before day when the trial was made,
The jailer come easin' down.

He went on the man's bond.
He went on the man's bond.
He came all the way from heaven down
And He went on the man's bond.

As sung at the Apollo Theatre, N.Y.
by Pearl Jones (1957) Amateur Night

FATHER DIVINE'S GREETINGS TO THE UNIVERSE

It's One Eternal Merry Christmas
And One Eternal Happy New Year,
As we're conscious of God's Presence
And Know He's Everywhere.
It's One Eternal Merry Christmas
And One Eternal Happy New Year!

VERSE I.

For the Joy of Living this Christ Life
Keeps us Jubilant All the Year
And we always have an Abundance,
And are filled with this Holiday Cheer,
As we're conscious of God's Presence
And Know He's Everywhere.
It's One Eternal Merry Christmas
And One Eternal Happy New Year.

Pastime Rhymes

LOVE

Love is a funny thing
Shaped like a lizard,
Run down your heart strings
And tickle your gizzard.
You can fall from a mountain,
You can fall from above,
But the great fall is
When you fall in love.

WHEN I GO TO MARRY

W'en I goes to marry,
I wants a gal wid money.
I wants a pretty black-eyed gal
To kiss an' call me "Honey."

Well, w'en I goes to marry,
I don't wanter git no riches.
I wants a man 'bout four foot high,
So's I can w'ar de britches.

ROSES RED

Rose's red, vi'lets blue.
Sugar is sweet but not lak you.
De vi'lets fade, de roses fall;
But you gits sweeter, all in all.

As sho' as de grass grows 'round de stump,
You is my darlin' Sugar Lump.
W'en de sun don't shine de day is cold,
But my love fer you do not git old.

De ocean's deep, de sky is blue;
Sugar is sweet, an' so is you;
De ocean waves an' de sky gits pale,
But my love are true, an' it never fail.

DAY

Jackson, put dat kettle on!
Fire, steam dat coffee done!
Day's done broke and I got to run
For to meet my gal by de risin' sun.

HERE I STAND

Here I stan', raggity an' dirty;
If you don't come kiss me, I'll run lak a tucky.

Here I stan' on two liddle chips,
Pray, come kiss my sweet liddle lips.

Here I stan' crooked lak a horn;
I hain't had no kiss since I'se been born.

SHE HUGGED ME AND KISSED ME

I see'd her in de Springtime,
I see'd her in de Fall,
I see'd her in de Cotton patch,
A cameing from de Ball.

She hug me, an' she kiss me,
She wrung my han' an' cried.
She said I wus de sweetes' thing
Dat ever lived or died.

She hug me an' she kiss me.
Oh Heaben! De touch o' her han'!
She said I wus de puttiest thing
In de shape o' mortal man.

I told her dat I love her,
Dat my love wus bed-cord strong;
Den I axed her w'en she'd have me,
An' she jes say "Go long!"

VINIE

I loves coffee, an' I loves tea.
I axes you, Vinie, does you love me?

My day's study's Vinie, an' my midnight dreams,
My apples, my peaches, my tunnups, an' greens.

Oh, I wants dat good 'possum, an' I wants to be free;
But I don't need no sugar, if Vinie love me.

De river is wide, an' I cain't well step it.
I loves you dear Vinie; an' you know I cain't he'p it.

Dat sugar is sweet, an' dat butter is greasy;
But I loves you, sweet Vinie; don't be oneasy.

Some loves ten, an' some loves twenty,
But I loves you, Vinie, an' dat is a plenty.

Oh silver, it shine, an' lakwise do tin.
De way I loves Vinie, it mus' be a sin.

Well, de cedar is green, an' so is de pine.
God bless you, Vinie! I wish you was mine.

PRECIOUS THINGS

Hold my rooster, hold my hen,
Pray don't touch my Grecian Bend.

Hold my bonnet, hold my shawl,
Pray don't touch my waterfall.

Hold my hands by the finger tips,
But pray don't touch my sweet little lips.

TAKE YO' TIME, MISS LUCY

Miss Lucy she is handsome,
    Miss Lucy she is tall;
To see her dance Cachuca,
    Jes' captivates us all.

Oh, Miss Lucy's teeth is grinnin',
    Jes' like an ear of corn;
An' her eyes dey look so winnin',
    Oh! would I'd never been **born.**

Take yo' time, Miss Lucy,
    Take yo' time, Miss Lucy Long;
Oh! take yo' time, Miss Lucy,
    Take yo' time, Miss Lucy Long.

I ax'd her for to marry
    Myself de other day;
She said she'd rather tarry,
    So I let her have her way.

If she makes a scolding wife,
    As sure as she is born,
I'll tote her down to Georgia,
    An' trade her off for corn.

Take yo' time, Miss Lucy,
    Take yo' time, Miss Lucy Long;
Oh! take yo' time, Miss Lucy,
    Take yo' time, Miss Lucy Long.

SLAVE MARRIAGE CEREMONY SUPPLEMENT

Dark an' stormy may come de wedder;
I jines dis he-male an' dis she-male to gedder.

Let none, but Him dat makes de thunder,
Put dis he-male an' dis she-male asunder.
I darefore 'nounce you bofe de same.
Be good, go 'long, an' keep up yo' name.
De broomstick's jumped, de worl's not wide.
She's now yo' own. Salute yo' bride!

LOVE IS JUST A THING OF FANCY

Love is jes a thing o' fancy,
Beauty's jes a blossom;
If you wants to git yo' finger bit,
Stick it at a 'possum.

Beauty, it's jes skin deep;
Ugly, it's to de bone.
Beauty, it'll jes fade 'way;
But Ugly'll hol' 'er own.

DOES I LOVE YOU?

Does I love you wid all my heart?—
I loves you wid my liver;

Ah' if I had you in my mouf,
I'd spit you in de river.

A SHORT LETTER

She writ me a letter
As long as my eye,
And she say in dat letter:
"My Honey—goodbye!"

I'M A ROUND-TOWN GENT

I ain't no wagon, ain't no dray,
Just come to town with a load of hay.
I ain't no cornfield to go to bed
With a lot of hayseeds in my head.
I'm a round-town gent, and I don't choose
To work in the mud and do without shoes.

MISTAKE

Tell me, sister, tell me, brother,
Has you heard the latest news?
A woman down in Georgia
Got her two sweet-men confused.

One knocked on the front do',
One knocked on the back—
Now that woman down in Georgia's
Doorknob is hung with black.

A SICK WIFE

Las' Sadday night my wife tuck sick,
An' what d'you reckon ail her?
She e't a tucky gobbler's head
An' her stomach, it jes' fail her.

She squall out: "Sam, bring me some mint!
Make catnip up an' sage tea!"
I goes an' gits her all dem things,
But she throw 'em back right to me.

Says I: "Dear Honey! Mind nex' time!"
         "Don't eat from 'A to Izzard'"
         "I thinks you won' git sick at all,
         If you saves po' me de gizzard."

OLD WOMAN IN THE HILLS

Once: Dere wus an ole woman
       Dat lived in de hills,
       Put rocks in 'er stockin's
       And sent 'em to de mill.

Den: De ole miller swore
       By de pint o' his knife
       Dat he never ground up
       No rocks in his life.

So: De ole woman said
       To de miller nex' day:

"You railly must 'scuse me,
It's de onlinest way.
I heared you made meal
A-grindin' on stones.
I must 'ave heared wrong—
It must 'ave been bones.

MISS RINNER

Ol' Miss Rinner
Is a awful Sinner.
She sins all day,
She sins all night.
Won't get a man
Just for spite.

DISGRACE

Pepper and salt,
Vinegar in the face,
Woman, you so ugly
It's a disgrace!

LOUISIANA WOMEN

Jack Johnson runs the engine
And Jefferson throw the switch,
Louisiana women got no hair,
But they git them wigs that fit.

HOMELY

Her face look like a coffee-pot,
Her nose look like the spout,
Her mouth look like the fireplace
With the ashes tooken out.

ANCESTRY

I don't know your face
And I don't know your name,
But I can tell by your hair
Your papa was a bear.

I don't know your face
And I don't know your name,
But I'll talk about your mama
Just the same.

AUNT DINAH

Ole Aunt Dinah, sick in bed,
Sent for the doctor. Doctor said,
Git up, Dinah, you ain't sick,
All you need is a hickory stick.

DEACONS

Some o' dese deacons is makin' a plot,
To git dere whiskey in a coffee-pot,
They goes to church and be on time,
To pick up a collection to git a dime.

THE DEVIL

Did you ever see de devil
Wid his iron handled shovel,
A-scrapin' up de san'
In his ole tin pan?
He cuts up mighty funny,
He steals all yo' money,
He blinds you wid his san'.
He's tryin' to git you, man!

INDICATIONS

Blue gums and black eyes,
Run 'round and tell lies.
Little head, little wit,
Big long head, not a bit.

DON'T SING

Doan' sing befo' breakfast,
Doan' sing 'fore you eat,
Or you'll cry befo' midnight,
You'll cry 'fore you sleep.

UNCLE JERRY FANTS

Has you heared 'bout Uncle Jerry Fants?
He's got on some cu'ious shapes.
He's de one what w'ars dem white duck pants,
An' he sot down on a bunch o' grapes.

AUNT KATE

Ole Aunt Kate, she died so late
She couldn't get in at the Heaven Gate.
The Angels met her with a great big club,
Knocked her right back in the washin' tub.

STILL WATER

Still water it runs deep,
The shallow water prattle.

Tongue hung in a hollow head
Jus' roll around and rattle.

A TOAST

When you look at this life you'll find
It ain't nothing but a race.
If you can't be the winning horse,
At least try to place.

If they box you on the curve, boy,
Jockey your way to the rail—
And when you get on the inside track,
Sail! . . . Sail! . . . Sail!

In a race, daddy-o,
One thing you will find:
There ain't NO way to be out in front
Without showing your tail to the horse behind.

SHOO FLY, DON'T BOTHER ME

Shoo, fly, don't bother me!
Shoo, fly, don't bother me!
Shoo, fly, don't bother me,
I belong to Company G.

I feel, I feel, I feel,
I feel like a morning star,
I feel, I feel, I feel,
I feel like a morning star.

I feel, I feel, I feel,
That's what my mother said,
Like angels pouring 'lasses down,
Right down upon my head.

Shoo, fly, don't bother me!
Shoo, fly, don't bother me!
Shoo, fly, don't bother me!
I belong to Company G.

As sung by Negro troops during the Civil War.

MOTHER SAYS I'M SIX YEARS OLD

My mammy says dat I's too young
To go to church an' pray,
But she don't know how bad I is
When she's been gone away.

My mammy says I's six years old,
My daddy says I's seben.
Dat's all right how old I is,
Jes since I's gwine to Heaben.

Ballads

JOHN HENRY

Some say he's from Georgia,
Some say he's from Alabam,
But it's wrote on the rock at the Big Ben Tunnel,
John Henry's a East Virginia Man,
John Henry's a East Virginia Man.

John Henry he could hammah,
He could whistle, he could sing,
He went to the mountain early in the mornin'
To hear his hammah ring,
To hear his hammah ring.

John Henry went to the section boss,
Says the section boss what kin you do?
Says I can line a track, I kin histe a jack,
I kin pick and shovel, too,
I kin pick and shovel, too.

John Henry went to the tunnel
And they put him in lead to drive,
The rock was so tall and John Henry so small
That he laid down his hammah and he cried,
That he laid down his hammah and he cried.

The steam drill was on the right han' side,
John Henry was on the left,
Says before I let this steam drill beat me down,
I'll hammah myself to death,
I'll hammah myself to death.

Oh the cap'n said to John Henry,
I bleeve this mountain's sinkin' in.
John Henry said to the cap'n, Oh my!
Tain't nothin' but my hammah suckin' wind,
Tain't nothin' but my hammah suckin' wind.

John Henry had a pretty liddle wife,
She come all dressed in blue.
And the last words she said to him,
John Henry I been true to you,
John Henry I been true to you.

John Henry was on the mountain,
The mountain was so high,
He called to his pretty liddle wife,
Said Ah kin almos' touch the sky,
Said Ah kin almos' touch the sky.

Who gonna shoe yoh pretty liddle feet,
Who gonna glove yoh han',
Who gonna kiss yoh rosy cheeks,
An' who gonna be yoh man,
An' who gonna be yoh man?

Papa gonna shoe my pretty liddle feet,
Mama gonna glove my han',
Sistah gonna kiss my rosy cheeks,
An' I ain't gonna have no man,
An' I ain't gonna have no man.

Then John Henry he did hammah,
He did make his hammah soun',

Says now one more lick fore quittin' time,
An' I'll beat this steam drill down,
An' I'll beat this steam drill down.

The hammah that John Henry swung,
It weighed over nine poun',
He broke a rib in his left han' side,
And his intrels fell on the groun',
And his intrels fell on the groun'.

All the women in the West
That heard of John Henry's death,
Stood in the rain, flagged the east bound train,
Goin' where John Henry dropped dead,
Goin' where John Henry dropped dead.

They took John Henry to the White House,
And buried him in the san',
And every locomotive come roarin' by,
Says there lays that steel drivin' man,
Says there lays that steel drivin' man.

DUPREE AND BETTY BLUES

Dupree was settin' in a hotel,
Wasn't thinkin' 'bout a dog-gone thing,
Settin' in a hotel,
Wasn't thinkin' 'bout a dog-gone thing.
Betty said to Dupree,
I want a diamond ring.

Dupree went to town
With a forty-five in his hand.
He went to town with
A forty-five in his hand.

He went after jewelry—
But he got the jewelry man.

Dupree went to Betty cryin',
Betty, here is your diamond ring.
He went to Betty cryin',
Here is your diamond ring.
Take it and wear it, Betty,
'Cause I'm bound for cold old cold Sing Sing.

Then he called a taxi
Cryin', Drive me to Tennessee.
Taxi, taxi, taxi,
Drive me to Tennessee.
He said, Drive me, bubber,
'Cause the dicks is after me.

He went to the Post Office
To get his evenin' mail.
Went to the General Delivery
To get his evenin' mail.
They caught poor Dupree, Lordy,
Put him in Nashville Jail.

Dupree said to the judge, Lord,
I ain't been here before.
Lord, Lord, Lord, Judge,
I ain't been here before.
Judge said, I'm gonna break your neck, Dupree,
So you can't come here no more.

Betty weeped, Betty moaned
Till she broke out with sweat.
Betty weeped and she moaned
Till she broke out with sweat.
Said she moaned and she weeped
Till her clothes got soppin' wet.

Betty brought him coffee,
Betty brought him tea.
Betty brought him coffee,
Also brought him tea.
She brought him all he needed
'Cept that big old jail-house key.

Dupree said, It's whiskey I crave,
Bring me flowers to my grave.
It's whiskey I crave.
Bring flowers to my grave.
That little ole Betty's
Done made me her dog-gone slave.

It was early one mornin'
Just about the break o' day,
Early, early one mornin'
Just about break o' day,
They had him testifyin'
And this is what folks heard him say:

Give my pappy my clothes,
Oh, give poor Betty my shoes.
Give pappy my clothes,
Give poor Betty my shoes.
And if anybody asks you,
Tell 'em I died with the heart-breakin' blues.

They lead him to the scaffold
With a black cap over his face.
Lead him up to the scaffold,
Black cap over his face.
Some ole lonesome graveyard's
Poor Dupree's restin' place.

The choir followed him
Singin' *Nearer My God to Thee.*

The choir followed him,
Nearer My God to Thee.
Poor Betty, she was cryin',
Have mercy on Dupree!

Sail on! Sail on!
Sail on, Dupree, sail on!
Sail on! Sail on!
Sail on, sail on, sail on!
I don't mind you sailin'
But you'll be gone so dog-gone long!

As sung by Delaney Anderson for Langston Hughes,
Cleveland, Ohio, 1936

FRANKIE BAKER

Frankie Baker was a good gal
Everybody knows.
She paid a hundred dollars flat
For the makin' of a suit o' clothes
    For her man.
    He didn't treat her right.

Frankie went down to the corner,
She bought a bottle o' beer.
Frankie says to the bartender,
Have Albert Britton been here?
    He is my man.
    He don't treat me right.

Frankie went up Hogan's Alley,
Thought she heard a bulldog bark.
T'warn't nothin' but her good man

Tryin' to dodge her in the dark.
  He was her man.
  He didn't treat her right.

Frankie says to Albert,
Just run now if you can.
I got a razor in my pocket
And a pistol in my hand.
  You are my man.
  You don't treat me right.

She shot him in the shoulder.
He fell down on the floor.
Rooty-toot-toot and rooty-toot-toot,
She shot that man some more.
  He was her man.
  He didn't treat her right.

Frankie says to the doctor,
Help me if you can.
Here's a thousand dollars cold
For the savin' of my man.
  He is my man,
  But he didn't treat me right.

Doctor says to Frankie,
He cannot get well.
You done filled him full o' holes
And shot him plumb to hell.
  He was your man.
  He didn't treat you right.

Frankie went to Albert's mother's house,
She fell down on her knees.
Mother, I have killed your only son,
Forgive me, if you please.
  He was my man.
  He ain't done me right.

Judge Gridley says to Frankie,
Frankie, tell me, if you can,
WHY did you shoot that
Big tall yellow man?
    Judge, he was my man.
    He ain't done me right.

Judge Gridley says to Frankie,
Frankie, please tell me
WHY did you shoot that man
In the third degree?
    He was your man
    If he didn't treat you right.

Frankie said to the Judge.
Judge, it came to pass,
I didn't shoot him in no third degree—
I shot him in his yas, yas, yas!
    He was my man.
    He didn't treat me right.

Lillies of the valley,
Roses sure smell nice.
Flowers all over poor Albert,
He thought he was in Paradise.
    He was her man.
    He didn't treat her right.

Frankie's in the jail house.
Hear her weep and moan,
Cryin' for poor Albert,
And her pillow ain't nothin' but stone.
    He was her man.
    He didn't treat her right.

Listen, all you good gals,
Two things you can choose—
Livin' with a low-down man,

Or them low-down jail-house blues.
Better keep your man—
Even if he don't treat you right.

*Traditional. This version sung by Palmer Jones and
transcribed by Langston Hughes at the Grand Duc
Cabaret in Paris, 1924*

DE BALLIT OF DE BOLL WEEVIL

Oh, have you heard de lates',
De lates' of de songs?
It's about dem little Boll Weevils,
Dey's picked up bofe feet an' gone
A-lookin' for a home,
Jes a-lookin' for a home.

De Boll Weevil is a little bug
F'um Mexico, dey say,
He come to try dis Texas soil
En thought he better stay,
A-lookin' for a home.

De picker say to de Boll Weevil
"Whut makes yo' head so red?"
"I's been wanderin' de whole worl' ovah
Till it's a wonder I ain't dead,
A-lookin' for a home,
Jes a-lookin' for a home."

First time I saw Mr. Boll Weevil,
He wuz on de western plain;
Next time I saw him,
He wuz ridin' on a Memphis train,
A-lookin' for a home,
Jes a-lookin' for a home. . . . .

De fus' time I saw de Boll Weevil
He wuz settin' on de square,
De nex' time I saw de Boll Weevil
He had all his family dere—
Dey's lookin' for a home,
Jes a-lookin' for a home. . . . .

BAD MAN

Late las' night I was a-makin' my rounds,
Met my woman an' I blowed her down,
Went on home an' I went to bed,
Put my hand cannon right under my head.

Early nex' mornin' 'bout de risin' o' de sun,
I gets up-a fer to make-a my run.
I made a good run but I made it too slow,
Got overtaken in Mexico.

Standin' on de cornor, readin' of a bill,
Up step a man name o' Bad Texas Bill:
"Look here, bully, ain't yo' name Lee Brown?
B'lieve you are de rascal shot yo' woman down."

"Yes, oh, yes," says, "This is him.
If you got a warrant, jes' read it to me."
He says: "You look like a fellow that knows what's bes'.
Come 'long wid me—you're under arres'."

When I was arrested, I was dressed in black;
Dey put me on a train, an' dey brought me back.
Dey boun' me down in de county jail;
Couldn' get a human for to go my bail.

Early nex' mornin' 'bout half pas' nine,
I spied ol' jedge drappin' down de line.

I heered ol' jailer when he cleared his th'oat,
"Bad Man, git ready for de deestreec' cote."

Deestreec' cote is now begin,
Twelve big jurymen, twelve hones' man.
Five mo' minutes up step a man,
He was holdin' my verdic' in his right han'.

Verdic' read murder in de firs' degree.
I said, "O Lawd, have mercy on me."
I seed ol' jedge when he picked up his pen,
Say, "I don't think you'll ever kill a woman ag'in.

"This here killin' of women natchly got to stop,
I don't know whether to hang you er not.
Ninety-nine years on de hard, hard groun',
'Member de night you blowed de woman down."

Here I is, bowed down in shame,
I got a number instead of a name.
Here for de res' of my nachul life,
An' all I ever done is kill my wife. . . .

CAPTAIN LORD WELTON

(Tomper's Song)

She told her lover, "Come to my home,
Captain Lord Welton's on a long journey gone."
That night he come to de arms of he lover,
"Take you' time for you can hear de winding of his horn,
Captain Lord Welton is a long way from home."

Don't you hear what de sparrow say?
"Captain Lord Welton is one hundred miles from home."

Don't you hear what de footspeed say?
"Captain Lord Welton ain't but ninety-five miles from home."

"Take you' time," de ooman say,
"Ain't you hear what de sparrow say?
Captain Lord Welton is ninety miles from home."
Oh, listen to what de footspeed say,
"I can hear de soundin' of the horn,
Captain Lord Welton is only eighty-five mile from home."

"Oh stay! oh, stay!" de ooman say,
"Captain Lord Welton is a long way from home."
Ain't you hear what de sparrow say?
"Captain Lord Welton is eighty mile from home."
Oh, listen to what de footspeed say,
"Captain Lord Welton ain't but seventy-five mile from home."

"Oh, stay!" de sparrow say,
"Captain Lord Welton is seventy mile from home."
Oh, ain't you hear what de footspeed say?
"I can hear de blowin' of he horn,
Captain Lord Welton ain't but sixty-five mile from home."

"Hush you' mout'," de sparrow say,
"Captain Lord Welton is sixty mile from home."
"Listen! listen!" de footspeed say,
"I can hear de soundin' of he horn,
Captain Lord Welton ain't but fifty-five mile from home."

"Oh, listen!" de lover say,
"I must be guine,
I can hear de windin' of he horn,
Captain Lord Welton ain't but fifty mile from home."

"Take you' time; oh, take you' time,"
De sparrow say,
"Captain Lord Welton is forty-five mile from home."
Don't you hear what de footspeed say?

"I can hear de soundin' of he horn,
Captain Lord Welton ain't but forty mile from home."

Oh, listen to what de sparrow say,
"Captain Lord Welton is thirty-five mile from home."
"Oh, don't you listen to what de sparrow say,
Captain Lord Welton is ridin' hard for home.
Ain't you hear de soundin' of he horn?
He ain't but thirty mile from home."

Oh, listen to what de sparrow say,
"Captain Lord Welton is twenty-five mile from home."
"You will not listen," de footspeed say,
"I can hear de windin' of he horn,
Captain Lord Welton ain't but twenty mile from home."

"Have no fear," de sparrow say,
"Captain Lord Welton is fifteen mile from home."
"Make haste! make haste!" de footspeed say,
"I can hear de soundin' of he horn,
Captain Lord Welton ain't but ten mile from home."

"Take you' time; oh, take you' time."
De sparrow say,
"Captain Lord Welton is five mile from home."
Oh, ain't you hear what de footspeed say?
"I hear de soundin' of he horn,
Captain Lord Welton is arrive at home."

"Too late, too late," de footspeed say,
"I hear de slashin' of he sword,
Captain Lord Welton already home."

POOR LAZARUS

High sheriff tol' de deputy, "Go out an' bring me Laz'us."
High sheriff tol' de deputy, "Go out an' bring me Laz'us.
Bring him dead or alive, Lawd, Lawd, bring him dead or alive."

Oh, bad man Laz'us done broke in de commissary winder,
Oh bad man Laz'us done broke in de commissary winder,
He been paid off, Lawd, Lawd, he been paid off.

Oh, de deputy 'gin to wonder, where in de worl' he could fin' him;
Oh, de deputy 'gin to wonder, where in de worl' he could fin' him;
Well, I don' know, Lawd, Lawd, I jes' don' know.

Oh, dey found po' Laz'us way out between two mountains,
Oh, dey found po' Laz'us way out between two mountains,
An' dey blowed him down, Lawd, Lawd, an' dey blowed him down.

Ol' Laz'us tol' de deputy he had never been arrested,
Ol' Laz'us tol' de deputy he had never been arrested,
By no one man, Lawd, Lawd, by no one man.

So dey shot po' Laz'us, shot him wid a great big number,
Dey shot po' Laz'us, shot him wid a great big number,
Number 45, Lawd, Lawd, number 45.

An' dey taken po' Laz'us an' dey laid him on de commissary county,
Dey taken po' Laz'us an' dey laid him on de commissary county,
An' dey walked away, Lawd, Lawd, an' dey walked away.

Laz'us' sister run an' tol' her mother,
Laz'us' sister run an' tol' her mother,
Dat po' Laz'us dead, Lawd, Lawd, po' Laz'us dead.

Laz'us' mother, she laid down her sewin',
Laz'us' mother, she laid down her sewin',
'Bout de trouble, Lawd, Lawd, she had wid Laz'us.

Laz'us' mother she come a-screamin' an' a-cryin',
Laz'us' mother she come a-screamin' an' a-cryin',
"Dat's my only son, Lawd, Lawd, dat's my only son."

STACKALEE

It was in the year of eighteen hundred and sixty-one
In St. Louis on Market Street where Stackalee was born.
Everybody's talkin about Stackalee.
It was on one cold and frosty night
When Stackalee and Billy Lyons had one awful fight,
Stackalee got his gun. Boy, he got it fast!
He shot poor Billy through and through;
Bullet broke a lookin glass.
Lord, O Lord, O Lord!
Stackalee shot Billy once; his body fell to the floor.
He cried out, Oh, please, Stack, please don't shoot me no more.

The White Elephant Barrel House was wrecked that night;
Gutters full of beer and whiskey; it was an awful sight.
Jewelry and rings of the purest solid gold
Scattered over the dance and gamblin hall.
The can-can dancers they rushed for the door
When Billy cried, Oh, please, Stack, don't shoot me no more.
Have mercy, Billy groaned, Oh, please spare my life;

Stack says, God bless your children, damn your wife!
You stold my magic Stetson; I'm gonna steal your life.
But, says Billy, I always treated you like a man.
'Tain't nothin to that old Stetson but the greasy band.
He shot poor Billy once, he shot him twice,

And the third time Billy pleaded, please go tell my wife.
Yes, Stackalee, the gambler, everybody knowed his name;
Made his livin hollerin high, low, jack and the game.

Meantime the sergeant strapped on his big forty-five,
Says now we'll bring in this bad man, dead or alive.
And brass-buttoned policemen tall dressed in blue
Came down the sidewalk marchin two by two.
Sent for the wagon and it hurried and come
Loaded with pistols and a big gatlin gun.
At midnight on that stormy night there came an awful wail
Billy Lyons and a graveyard ghost outside the city jail.
Jailer, jailer, says Stack, I can't sleep,
For around my bedside poor Billy Lyons still creeps.
He comes in shape of a lion with a blue steel in his hand,
For he knows I'll stand and fight if he comes in shape of man.
Stackalee went to sleep that night by the city clock bell,
Dreaming the devil had come all the way up from hell.
Red devil was sayin, you better hunt your hole;
I've hurried here from hell just to get your soul.

Stackalee told him yes, maybe you're right,
But I'll give even you one hell of a fight.
When they got into the scuffle, I heard the devil shout,
Come and get this bad man before he puts my fire out.
The next time I seed the devil he was scramblin up the wall,
Yellin, come and get this bad man fore he mops up with us all.

II

Then here come Stack's woman runnin, says, daddy, I love you true;
See what beer, whiskey, and smokin hop has brought you to.
But before I'll let you lay in there, I'll put my life in pawn.
She hurried and got Stackalee out on a five thousand dollar bond.
Stackalee said, ain't but one thing that grieves my mind,
When they take me away, babe, I leave you behind.
But the woman he really loved was a voodoo queen
From Creole French market, way down in New Orleans.

He laid down at home that night, took a good night's rest,
Arrived in court at nine o'clock to hear the coroner's inquest.
Crowds jammed the sidewalk, far as you could see,
Tryin to get a good look at tough Stackalee.
Over the cold, dead body Stackalee he did bend,
Then he turned and faced those twelve jury men.
The judge says, Stackalee, I would spare your life,
But I know you're a bad man; I can see it in your red eyes.
The jury heard the witnesses, and they didn't say no more;
They crowded into the jury room, and the messenger closed the door.

The jury came to agreement, the clerk he wrote it down,
And everybody was whisperin, he's penitentiary bound.
When the jury walked out, Stackalee didn't budge,
They wrapped the verdic and passed it to the judge.
Judge looked over his glasses, says, Mr. Bad Man Stackalee,
The jury finds you guilty of murder in the first degree.
Now the trial's come to an end, how the folks gave cheers;
Bad Stackalee was sent down to Jefferson pen for seventy-five years.

Now late at night you can hear him in his cell,
Arguin with the devil to keep from goin to hell.
And the other convicts whisper, whatcha know about that?
Gonna burn in hell forever over an old Stetson hat!
Everybody's talkin bout Stackalee.
That bad man, Stackalee!

An old version, collected by Onah L. Spencer

STACKOLEE

One dark and dusty day
I was strolling down the street.
I thought I heard some old dog bark,
But it warn't nothing but Stackolee gambling in the dark.
Stackolee threw seven.

Billy said, It ain't that way.
You better go home and come back another day.
Stackolee shot Billy four times in the head
And left that fool on the floor damn near dead.
Stackolee decided he'd go up to Sister Lou's.
Said, Sister Lou! Sister Lou, guess what I done done?
I just shot and killed Billy, your big-head son.
Sister Lou said, Stackolee, that can't be true!
You and Billy been friends for a year or two.
Stackolee said, Woman, if you don't believe what I said,
Go count the bullet holes in that son-of-a-gun's head.
Sister Lou got frantic and all in a rage,
Like a tea hound dame on some frantic gage.
She got on the phone, Sheriff, Sheriff, I want you to help poor me.
I want you to catch that bad son-of-a-gun they call Stackolee.
Sheriff said, My name might begin with an *s* and end with an *f*
But if you want that bad Stackolee you got to get him yourself.
So Stackolee left, he went walking down the New Haven track.
A train come along and flattened him on his back.
He went up in the air and when he fell
Stackolee landed right down in hell.
He said, Devil, devil, put your fork up on the shelf
Cause I'm gonna run this devilish place myself.
There came a rumbling on the earth and a tumbling on the ground,
That bad son-of-a-gun, Stackolee, was turning hell around.
He ran across one of his ex-girl friends down there.
She was Chock-full-o'-nuts and had pony-tail hair.
She said, Stackolee, Stackolee, wait for me.
I'm trying to please you, can't you see?
She said, I'm going around the corner but I'll be right back.
I'm gonna see if I can't stack my sack.
Stackolee said, Susie Belle, go on and stack your sack.
But I just might not be here when you get back.
Meanwhile, Stackolee went with the devil's wife and with his
    girl friend, too.
Winked at the devil and said, I'll go with you.
The devil turned around to hit him a lick.
Stackolee knocked the devil down with a big black stick.

Now, to end this story, so I heard tell,
Stackolee, all by his self, is running hell.

A Harlem version

THE SIGNIFYING MONKEY

The Monkey and the Lion
Got to talking one day.
Monkey looked down and said, Lion,
I hear you's king in every way.
But I know somebody
Who do not think that is true—
He told me he could whip
The living daylights out of you.
Lion said, Who?
Monkey said, Lion,
He talked about your mama
And talked about your grandma, too,
And I'm too polite to tell you
What he said about you.
Lion said, Who said what? Who?
Monkey in the tree,
Lion on the ground.
Monkey kept on signifying
But he didn't come down.
Monkey said, His name is Elephant—
He stone sure is not your friend.
Lion said, He don't need to be
Because today will be his end.
Lion took off through the jungle
Lickity-split,
Meaning to grab Elephant
And tear him bit to bit. Period!
He come across Elephant copping a righteous nod

Under a fine cool shady tree.
Lion said, You big old no-good so-and-so,
It's either you or me.
Lion let out a solid roar
And bopped Elephant with his paw.
Elephant just took his trunk
And busted old Lion's jaw.
Lion let out another roar,
Reared up six feet tall.
Elephant just kicked him in the belly
And laughed to see him drop and fall.
Lion rolled over,
Copped Elephant by the throat.
Elephant just shook him loose
And butted him like a goat,
Then he tromped him and he stomped him
Till the Lion yelled, Oh, no!
And it was near-nigh sunset
When Elephant let Lion go.
The signifying Monkey
Was still setting in his tree
When he looked down and saw the Lion.
Said, Why, Lion, who can that there be?
Lion said, It's me.
Monkey rapped, Why, Lion,
You look more dead than alive!
Lion said, Monkey, I don't want
To hear your jive-end jive.
Monkey just kept on signifying,
Lion, you for sure caught hell—
Mister Elephant's done whipped you
To a fare-thee-well!
Why, Lion, you look like to me
You been in the precinct station
And had the third-degree,
Else you look like
You been high on gage
And done got caught

In a monkey cage!
You ain't no king to me.
Facts, I don't think that you
Can even as much as roar—
And if you try I'm liable
To come down out of this tree and
Whip your tail some more.
The Monkey started laughing
And jumping up and down.
But he jumped so hard the limb broke
And he landed—*bam!*—on the ground.
When he went to run, his foot slipped
And he fell flat down.
Grrr-rrr-rr-r! The Lion was on him
With his front feet and his hind.
Monkey hollered, Ow!
I didn't mean it, Mister Lion!
Lion said, You little flea-bag you!
Why, I'll eat you up alive.
I wouldn't a-been in this fix a-tall
Wasn't for your signifying jive.
Please, said Monkey, Mister Lion,
If you'll just let me go,
I got something to tell you, *please,*
I think you ought to know.
Lion let the Monkey loose
To see what his tale could be—
And Monkey jumped right back on up
Into his tree.
What I was gonna tell you, said Monkey,
Is you square old so-and-so,
If you fool with me I'll get
Elephant to whip your head some more.
Monkey, said the Lion,
Beat to his unbooted knees,
You and all your signifying children
Better stay up in them trees.
Which is why today

Monkey does his signifying
A-way-up out of the way.

Traditional. A Harlem version, Embassy Bar, 1956

SINKING OF THE TITANIC

It was 1912 when the awful news got around
That the great Titanic was sinking down.
Shine came running up on deck, told the Captain, "Please,
The water in the boiler room is up to my knees."

Captain said, "Take your black self on back down there!
I got a hundred-fifty pumps to keep the boiler room clear."
Shine went back in the hole, started shovelling coal,
Singing, "Lord, have mercy, Lord, on my soul!"

Just then half the ocean jumped across the boiler room deck.
Shine yelled to the Captain, "The water's 'round my neck!"
Captain said, "Go back! Neither fear nor doubt!
I got a hundred more pumps to keep the water out."

"Your words sound happy and your words sound true,
But this is one time, Cap, your words won't do.
I don't like chicken and I don't like ham—
And I don't believe your pumps is worth a damn!"

The old Titanic was beginning to sink.
Shine pulled off his clothes and jumped in the brink.
He said, "Little fish, big fish, and shark fishes, too,
Get out of my way because I'm coming through."

Captain on bridge hollered, "Shine, Shine, save poor me,
And I'm make you as rich as any man can be."
Shine said, "There's more gold on land than there is on sea."
And he swimmed on.

Jay Gould's millionary daughter came running up on deck
With her suitcase in her hand and her dress 'round her neck.
She cried, "Shine, Shine, save poor me!
I'll give you everything your eyes can see."
Shine said, "There's more on land than there is on sea."
And he swimmed on.

Big fat banker begging, "Shine, Shine, save poor me!
I'll give you a thousand shares of T and T."
Shine said, "More stocks on land than there is on sea."
And he swimmed on.

When all them white folks went to heaven,
Shine was in Sugar Ray's Bar drinking Seagrams Seven.

> *According to Negro belief, persons of color, even servants,*
> *were barred from the Titanic on its ill-fated maiden voyage.*
> *But folk versifiers insist that there was one Negro aboard.*
> *This is a Harlem variant of his story as heard by Langston*
> *Hughes on Eighth Avenue in 1956*

ROOSEVELT AND HITLER

You may read the Holy Bible
Where Matthew's does record
There are 'pistles (pestilences) and earthquakes
And also rumors of war
There you can see
The Bible do fulfill
There are strange things a-happenin' in the land.

CHORUS
Strange things are happenin' in this land—
Strange things are happenin' in this land.
The war is goin' on,

'Causin' many hearts to mourn,
There are strange things a-happenin' in this land.

Nations against Nations,
Are risin' in this land
Kingdoms against kingdoms,
You jus' can't understand.
But you need not to be surprise
For the time is drawin' nigh,
There are strange things a-happenin' in this land.

We have read also of famines
That shall come in this land.
But if you notice closely,
You can see and understand.
Provisions are so high,
'Til we can't hardly buy,
There are strange things a-happenin' in this land.

Roosevelt with Hitler
He tried to live in peace.
But Hitler he's destroyin'
Every vessel he could see
He's treatin' us so mean
With his dreadful sub-marines,
There are strange things a-happenin' in this land.

Hitler, he's a fightin'
And makin' every charge.
He's tryin' to win the victory,
So his land might be enlarge.
He's fightin' everywhere
On land and in the air.
There are strange things a-happenin' in this land.

Some said Roosevelt was coward,
And said he would not fight
But he was jus' only a-waitin'

'Till he got things fixed up right.
When he made it up in his mind
He got on the foughtin' line
There are strange things a-happenin' in this land.

Hitler tried to fool the Negroes,
By sayin' they ought not to fight.
They have no home or country
No flag or equal rights.
But the Negro knewed the best
They deeds did prove the rest.
There are strange things a-happenin' in this land.

When Uncle Sam called for them
They answered, "Here are we,
To perform a soldier's duty,
Where'sn-ever we may be."
They answered true and brave,
Ef the trenches makes they grave
There are strange things a-happenin' in this land.

Hitler called the Japanese
They could not help from cryin'.
They say, "Ef you go up against that race,
You comin' out behin'."
If you try to take they place,
You can't not keep from dyin'.
There are strange things a-happenin' in this land.

Hitler told his wife at the supper table
He dreamt a mighty dream.
"Ef I cut out these submarines,
I will sure save many of men.
But ef I fight and ef I win,
I will gain a many a frien'."
There are strange things a-happenin' in this land.

Now sinners, God is Power
You jes' can't understand.

The whole world will tremble
From the moving of his hand.
Hit's beyond the human sights,
But all he does is right.
There are strange things a-happenin' in this land.

*Buz Ezell's war time version of "Strange Things Are
Happening In The Land" as sung at Fort Valley, Georgia.
There are ancient roots to this ballad. John Work says
he heard an old blind guitarist in Mississippi sing a 1917
version in which Woodrow Wilson and the Kaiser were
the chief protagonists. The refrain is a theme familiar in
old mountain ballads of Civil War days; it is doubtless
even older.*

ℬlues

THE BLUES AS FOLK POETRY

I

THE Blues have deservedly come into their own, and, unfortunately for the lover of folk art, into something more than their own. They are sung on Broadway in nearly unrecognizable disguises, are produced on phonograph records by the thousands, are transmitted by radio, the T. O. B. A. circuit, carnival minstrel troupes, and the returned prodigal with his songbag full. It is becoming more and more difficult to tell which songs are truly folk and which are clever approximations.

It must be said, however, that the phonograph companies seem willing to record the crudest and most naive Blues, from most obvious folk sources. Artless cottonfield calls and levee moans are quite as likely to be found as urbanized fake folk things. Then too, the chief singers of these Blues, such as Ma Rainey, Bessie Smith, Blind Lemon Jefferson, and Cottonfield Thomas, seem to be of the folk, earthy and genuine, certainly in the main and best part of their work. Some of these singers must still sing for the jealous creators of the Blues. One likes to believe that this audience may be trusted to be severely critical of clumsy inverted rhythms, and such strained figures as this one, appearing in the "Lonesome Desert Blues," after lines speaking of the burning desert:

My mind is lak a rowboat, out on de stormy sea.
It's wid me right now, in de mawnin' where will it be?

Even with the flood of new Blues one still finds traces of the same folk imagery and attitude found in the earliest noted examples. One finds lines from the older spirituals. There has been such an assimilation that one might say: If these are not by the folk, they ought to be.

Therefore, although the word has become part of the popular music vernacular, and has been widened to cover songs that by no stretch of the imagination could be considered Blues, nevertheless, Blues of importance to students of folk life are still being produced, in considerable numbers and with a great degree of authenticity. One knows that when the river rises remorselessly above the high water mark, when a loving man takes to the road and leaves the side of his good woman, when the train blows far down the track, or the steamboat heaves in sight around the bend, some singer a long ways from happiness lifts up his voice and tells the world of his trouble.

Something of an introduction to folk life might result from the mere reading of Blues titles. This list would resemble a geographical index to the South, or to the Black Belt extensions into the North, as well as a catalogue of all the melancholy afflictions that any children of Adam have suffered. A deep knowledge would result from a close study of the songs themselves. It might perhaps be recommended that this study be done with as few preconceived notions as possible. For the Blues, unlike the early "coon" songs and East Side mammy songs, do not conform to a single pattern. It would be foolhardy to say that everything is here, any more than in more sophisticated lyric poetry. But there is a great deal. Stoicism is here as well as self-pity, for instance; rich humor as well as melancholy. There are so many Blues that any preconception might be proved about Negro folk life, as well as its opposite. As documentary proof of dogma about the Negro peasant, then, the Blues are satisfactory and unsatisfactory. As documents about humanity they are invaluable.

II

It is a popular misconception that the Blues are merely songs that ease a woman's longing for her rambling man. Of course, this pattern has been set, especially by certain priestesses of the Blues cult. Nevertheless, the Blues furnish examples of other concerns. And as the lost-lover line may be dragged into a levee moan, so may an excellent bit of farm advice be found in a song about a long-lost mamma. Blues will be found ranging from flood songs to graphic descriptions of pneumonia, from complaints about Volstead to such lines as

> I got a grave-diggin' feelin' in my heart.

The diction of most of the Blues is immediately connected, as it should be, with folk life. Cottonfield parlance is in

> Makes me feel I'm on my las' go-round.

Folk parlance in general:

> Wish I was a jaybird flyin' in de air,
> Would build my nest in some of you high browns' hair.

> I'm fresh from the country, yuh know I'm easy to rule.
> Jes hitch me to yo' cart, girls, and drive me fo' yo' mule.

> Ef I could holler lak a mountain jack,
> I'd go up on de mountain an' call my baby back.

> Sun gonna shine in my back door some day.

> Another mule kickin' in my stall.

> You been a good ole wagon, daddy, but you done broke down.

Supplementing the numerous excellent work songs we have such lines as

> Cap'n, cap'n, has my pay check come?
> Damn yo' pay check, get de cap'n's work done.

> Cap'n, cap'n, my hands is cole.
> Damn yo' hands, let de pick an' shovel roll.
>
> Pay day, cap'n, ain't got no soap.

And the native "Cottonfield Blues," as spontaneous, as unfinished on the record, as when created in the Brazos Bottom:

> I'm goin' downtown buy myself a plow,
> Goin' downtown get me a mule
> Get up in de mo'nin', fo' o'clock,
> Goin' to turn dat land in turnips.

The love for fabling, a quality of the best folklore in general and of the Negro in particular:

> What makes a rooster crow every mo'nin' fo' day?
> To let de ramblers know dat de workin' man is on his way.
>
> Tadpole in de river hatchin' underneaf of a log.
> Got too old to be a tadpole, turned to be a natchal frog.
>
> Ef a toadfrog had wings, he'd be flyin' all aroun',
> Would not have his bottom boppin' boppin' on de groun'.
>
> I wish I was a catfish, swimmin' in de sea,
> I'd have you good womens fishin' after me.
>
> Brownskin momma make a rabbit chase a hound.

Or from city animals:

> You jes lak one uh dese ole tom-cats,
> Always chasin' dese alley rats.

The superstitions of the Negro folk are frequently found. There are Blues about "Black Cat's Bones," about

> Goin' to Louisiana to git myself a Mojo hand
> 'Cause dese backbitin' womens tryin' fo' to steal my man.

You may tip out sweet poppa, while tippin' is grand,
But yo' tippin' will be over when Momma gits her Mojo hand.

When de hog makes a bed, yuh know de storm is due.
When a screech-owl holler, means bad luck to you.

Screech-owl holler dis mawnin' right beside my front door.
I know when he hollered trouble comin' back once more.

When a black cat crosses you, bad luck, I've heard it said.
One must have started cross me, got halfway an' fell dead.

Went to de gipsy to get ma fortune tole.
Gipsy done tole me: Damn yo' unhardlucky soul.

I went to see de gipsy, he opened up my hand.
He said: My friend, you're worried but I don't understand.

I heard a hound dog bayin', an' I felt so blue.
I dreamt he was in de graveyard, lookin' down at you.

True to folk literature there are shrewd proverbs:

My momma tole me, my daddy tole me too:
Everybody grins in yo' face, son, ain't no friend to you.

When I had money, had friends fo' miles aroun'.
Now ain't got no money, friends cannot be found.

When you got a dollar in New York, brother, you got lots of friends,
But when you're broke an' hungry, that's where your friendship ends.

When yo' lose yo' money, baby, don't you lose yo' mind.
You must remember all gamblers git broke sometime.

You gotta reap jus' what you sow.

When you love a man, he treats you lak a dog,
But when you don't love him, he'll hop aroun' you lak a frog.

The cloudier aspects of the sunny South get their due share of lines. There are "Chain Gang Blues," "Prison House Blues," "Ball and Chain Blues." The cell is sometimes lighted up as in the "He's in de Jailhouse Now" comic variations, but is just as often darkened.

> Waitin' fo' de evenin' mail.

> They gonna put you under de jail.

> Settin' in de jail house, face turned to de wall,
> Red-headed woman was de cause of it all.

> Two mo' months fo' to do de grind.

> Way down, way down dat lonesome road,
> De workhouse is down dat long ole lonesome road.

Or from the "Hard Luck Blues" of Ma Rainey, who might with more reasons than her own proud sayso be called the mother of the Blues:

> Mah friend committed suicide, whilst I'se away at sea.
> They wanted to lock me up fo' murder in first degree.

Or from the same Ma Rainey:

> When I went to de station, bad luck waitin' there too.
> When dey needs mo' money, dey take out a warrant fo' you.

The sorry tricks played upon these folk by Nature do not go un- sung. The St. Louis cyclone had hardly spent its rage before songs were being sung commemorating the sufferers. Happening to be in St. Louis in the immediate wake of the cyclone, the author be- lieves that he was present at the genesis of many Blues. He re- members seeing in a second-story bedroom, with its front walls torn off, an old woman sitting in an old rocker, moaning and chant- ing, weaving from the tragedy her own blues.

Soon after there were such phonograph records as the "St. Louis Cyclone Blues" and the "St. Louis Tornado Blues."

The wind was howlin', buildin's begin to fall.
I seen dat mean o' twister comin' jes lak a cannon ball.

World was as black as midnight, I never heard such a noise befo'.
The people were screamin', runnin' every which a way, Lawd, help us.

The shack where we were livin' reeled and rocked but never fell.

The floods of the Mississippi Valley bring in their wake many Blues. Especially was the 1927 disaster bemoaned and besung. For authenticity of folk utterance it would be fruitful to compare the stereotyped "Muddy Water" or the "Mississippi Flood Song," a rather wet ballad:

> On the banks of the Father of Waters
>
> . . . .
>
> I am dreaming to-night in the moonlight
> Of the friends it has taken from me.
>
> All the world seemed so happy and gay.
> The waters rose quickly above us
> And it swept my beloved ones away-ay-ay-ay.
>
> . . . .
>
> The wrath of the great river's might.

With the "Backwater Blues," or the "Mississippi Water Blues," or any of the lesser high water Blues.

> It rained fo' days an' de skies was dark as night.
> Trouble taken place in de lowlands that night.
>
> It thundered an' lightened an' de wind begin to blow.
> Thousan's of people ain't got no place to go.
>
> Dey rowed a little boat about five miles 'cross de pond.
> I packed my clothes, throwed 'em in, an' dey rowed me along.
>
> Oh, I ain't goan move no mo'.
> My house fell down; ain't got no place to go.

Water, water, mo' than I've ever seen.
The water is still risin' from Memphis down to New Orleans.

Ef it keeps on rainin', levee's bound to break,
An' de water will come an' sweep dis town away.

The gain in vividness, in feeling, in substituting the thing seen for the bookish dressing up and sentimentalizing is an obvious one and might tell us a great deal about the Blues.

The ravages of the boll weevil have produced, besides the gem that Carl Sandburg has popularized, other Blues.

Eigh, bo' weevil, don't bring them dem blues no mo'.
Bo' weevil here, bo' weevil everywhere I go.

Gonna sing dis song to ease bo' weevil's travelin' mind.

Bo' weevil got Mississippi and de women want me.

Topical allusions to other tragedies, such as the sinking of the Titanic, the death of Floyd Collins, railroad wrecks, can be found as well, although these belong more to folk ballads, or to sermons. The War, however, became a prolific source of Blues. Professor Howard W. Odum, in *Wings on My Feet,* and Lieutenant John J. Niles, in *Singing Soldiers,* tell us of this. There was the "Drafting Blues":

When Uncle Sam
Calls out yo' man . . .
Don't dress in black,
'Cause dat won't bring him back.
Jus' say I've got dose drafted blues.

III

The longing for a far country is often encountered:

I went to the deepot, an' looked upon de boa'd.
It say: dere's good times here, dey's better down de road.

I'm goin' up de country, baby, don't you want to go?

Did you ever wake up in de mo'nin', yo' mind rollin' two different ways—
One mind to leave yo' baby, and one mind to stay?

I'm got a mind to ramble, a mind fo' to leave dis town,
Got a mind my baby is goin' to turn me down.

Sometimes the long journey ends traditionally in the South; à la Jolson's mammy songs:

> Dixie Flyer, come on an' let yo' driver roll,
> Wouldn't stay up Nawth to save nobody's doggone soul.

> If it keeps on snowin', I'll be Gulf Coast bound.

> I'm goin' down South where de weather suits my clothes.

Just as often these far wanderers trek Northward.

> Michigan water it tastes lak cherry wine,
> But dis Nashville water it drinks lak turpentine.

> I'm goin' to Chicago where I been longin' to be.

> Dere's a big red headline in Chicago Defender News,
> Says my gal down South got dem Up de Country Blues.

These lovers of the open road, in their desire for the far country, turn to the train as their best friend. One young Negro author, interpreting the fascination of trains for the Negroes of the South, says: "I have often thought that the Negro farmhand would lose heart once for all, were it not for the daily encouragement he takes from the whistle of his favorite locomotives. Tied to his plow, under the red, burning sun, or aching with the loneliness of the sterile night, he can find all his desire for escape, all the courage he lacks in the face of the unknown, mingled with his inescapable hopelessness, in the deepthroated, prolonged blast of the express train, like a challenge to untravelled lands, a terrifying cry to his petty township."

This favored symbol of escape is everywhere evident in the Blues. The Blues are like a large Union Terminal. We hear of such Blues as the "Dixie Flyer," the "Santa Fe," the "Freight Train," the "Mobile Central," the "Brakeman's."

I'm gonna leave heah dis mawnin' ef I have to ride de blind.

T is fo' Texas, an' T's fo' Tennessee,
And T is fo' dat train dat took you 'way from me.

Ticket agent, ease yo' window down.

De train I ride is sixteen coaches long.

Did you evah ride on de Mobile Central Line?
It's de road to ride to ease yo' troublin' mind.

From the "Freight Train Blues," a song which, as sung on the record, expresses infectiously the naive joy in the railroad:

Jus' as sho as de Southern makes up in de Southern yard,
I'm gonna leave heah, baby, ef I have to ride de rods.

I got the Railroad Blues, freight train on my min'.
Ever' time dat train hollers, poppa gonna change his min'.

De train's at de station, I heard de whistle blow.
Done bought my ticket but I don't know where I'll go.

Ticket agent said: Lady, don't sit aroun' an' cry.
Yo' man may have been here, but he's said his las' go'-by.

I ain't gonna tell nobody what dat Santa Fe done to me.
It took my good man, come back an' got my used-to-be.

All I want's my ticket, show me in my train.
I'm gonna ride till I can't hear dem call yo' name.

Hold dat engine, let sweet momma git on boa'd,
'Cause my home ain't here, it's a long ways down de road.

Blow yo' whistle, tell 'em momma's comin' through.
Shake it up a li'l bit, 'cause I'm feelin' awful blue.

Many of these trains are northbound: the Blues throw light on the recent migrations. Though in these Northern cities the Blues become more sophisticated and more blatantly suggestive, they still serve as registers of folk life transplanted. There are "House Rent Blues," "Black Maria Blues," "Hometown Skiffles," "Market Street Blues," "Furniture Man Blues," "State Street Blues," "Chicago Gouge Blues."

In the surly but indigenous "Snitcher's Blues":

O mah babe, way down in Polock town
Where de police an' de snitchers, dey tore my playhouse down.

In the classic "St. Louis Blues":

St. Louis Woman, she wears a diamond ring,
Got her man tied around her by de apron string.

Ef it wasn't for de powder an' de store-bought hair,
De man I love wouldn't go nowhere.

Harlem comes in for its share, pseudo-folk but indicative:

Folks in New York City ain't like de folks down South.
Never say "Have dinner"; they live from hand to mouth.

The horses and the numbers keeps most of them alive,
All they buy is hot dogs when eatin' time arrive.

The Midwest:

I'm goin' to Kansas City, baby; honey, where they don't like you.

In "Kitchen Mechanic Blues" we have the transplanted idiom:

People talk about me, they lie on me; call me out of my name,
But dey men calls to see me jes de same.

I'm jes a workin' girl, po' workin'-girl, kitchen mechanic is what dey say,
But I'll have an honest dollar on dat rainy day.

IV

The Blues as expressions of the man-woman relationship have already received full treatment at the hands of authorities. As in frontier ballads, cowboy ballads, even many English and Scottish ballads, the plaint is generally of true love lost or turned treacherous. It seems to be the history of lyric poetry, however (and the Blues, unlike most folk poetry, are lyric), that it is generally the lover or lady in absentia who calls out poetry. This is true of the Blues. The stereotyping of the Blues into a woman's moaning for her departed man may be due to the dominant personality of some of the women singers of the Blues, such as Ma Rainey, Ida Cox, Victoria Spivey, Bessie Smith, Mamie Smith, Clara Smith, Laura Smith, and Trixie Smith. (The Smith Brothers aren't yet as popular as they might be.)

Love is not presented, however, in a single aspect. We have not only the "Sobbin'-Hearted Blues," the "Grievin'-Hearted Blues" ringing changes on the theme of "Careless Love," but also:

> Ef you don't want me, baby, ain't got to carry no stall.
> I can git mo' women than a passenger train can haul.

> Ef you don't love me, why don't you tell me so?
> I'm little an' low, can get a man anywhere I go.

> Ef you don't like my peaches, don't you shake my tree.

> Ef she flags my train, I'm sho gonna let her ride.

There is not only faithlessness but

> I'll love my baby till the sea runs dry
> And ever after on.

> Gonna build me a scaffold, I'm gonna hang myself.
> Cain't git the man I love, don't want nobody else.

> Have you ever loved somebody—that somebody didn't love you?
> But I love my good girl, no matter what she do.

There is the cynicism of

> There's nineteen men livin' in my neighborhood,
> Eighteen of them is dumb an' the other ain't no doggone good.

There is the fancy of

> Love is like a faucet, you can turn it off or on,
> But when you think you've got it, it's done turned off and gone.

In one vein there is the poetic imagery of

> Love, oh, love, oh, careless love,
> You fly to my head like wine.
> You brought the wrong man into this life of mine.

In another:

> A sealskin brown will make a preacher lay his Bible down.

The gamut can be found running from tenderness to cynicism, from tears to laughter. Love is a torment, or love is a humorous interlude. One takes his choice.

V

The images of the Blues are worthy of a separate study. At their best they are highly compressed, concrete, imaginative, original. Among the clichés, the inconsecutiveness, the false rhymes—one finds suddenly the startling figure:

> My gal's got teeth lak a lighthouse on de sea.
> Every time she smiles she throws a light on me.

> My man's got a heart lak a rock cast in de sea.

> I got de worl' in a jug, de stopper in my hand.

> The gal I love is choklit to de bone.

Ef blues was whisky, I'd stay drunk all de time.

Blues ain't nothin' but a po' man's heart-disease.

There is the comic hyperbole of

I creeps up to huh window jes to hear how sweet she snores . . .

A good-lookin' woman makes a bulldog gnaw his chain.

A brownskin woman makes a cow forget her calf.

Done drunk so much whisky I staggers in my sleep.

Lemme be yo' switch engine, baby, till de main line comes.
I kin do mo' switchin', momma, than yo' main line ever done.

Big fat momma wid de meat shakin' on huh bones.
Evah time she wiggles, skinny woman los' huh home.

Settin' here wond'rin' would a match box hold my clothes.

You got a handful of gimme, a mouthful of much obliged.

Want to lay my head on de railroad line,
Let de train come along and pacify my mind.

May mean good, but he do so doggone po'.

There is a terseness, an inevitability of the images dealing with suffering. Irony, stoicism, and bitterness are deeply but not lingeringly expressed. There are sardonic lines like

I'm goin' to de mountain, goin' to de deep blue sea.
I know de sharks an' de fishes gonna make a fuss over me.

I got de blues but too damned mean to cry.

Yuh can read my letters but yuh sho cain't read my mind.

The tragic sense of life:

I hear my daddy callin' some other woman's name.
I know he don't mean me; I'm gonna answer jes de same.

Standin' here lookin' one thousand miles away.

I hate to see dat evenin' sun go down.

Don't yo' room seem empty when yo' gal packs up to leave?

I never loved but three men in my life:
My father an' my brother an' de man what wrecked my life.

I'm goin' to de pawnshop to hock my weddin' ring.
My man done quit me so I don't need dat thing.

Look down, look down dat lonesome road,
De hacks all dead in line.

Been down so long, Lawd, down don't worry me.

Woke up dis mawnin' bout de break of day.
Laid my head on de piller where my momma used to lay.

I followed my momma right down to be buryin'-groun'.
You ought to a heard me cryin' when dey let her down.

Ef you ever been down, you know jes how I feel—
Lak a broken-down engine got no drivin' wheel,
Lak a po' sojer boy lef' on de battle-fiel'.

When you think I'm laughin', laughin' jes to keep from cryin'.

The poetry of the Blues deserves close attention. Crudities, in-congruities, of course, there are in abundance-annoying changes of mood from tragedy to cheap farce. There seems to be entering more recently, a sophisticated smut, not the earlier breadth of Rabelais, but the snickering of the brothel. Blues are becoming cabaret ap-petizers. Perhaps the American public, both Negro and white, pre-

fers this to the simpler, more poetic phrasing of burdened folk. But at their most genuine they are accurate, imaginative transcripts of folk experience, with flashes of excellent poetry.

They show a warm-hearted folk, filled with a naive wonder at life yet sophisticated about human relationships, imaginative here as in their fables and spirituals, living a life close to the earth. With their imagination they combine two great loves, the love of words and the love of life. Poetry results.

These Blues belong, with all their distinctive differences, to the best of folk literature. And to some lovers of poetry that is not at all a negligible best.

Sterling A. Brown

JUST BLUES

I got a sweet black gal
Lives down by the railroad track,
A sweet black gal
Down by the railroad track,
And everytime she cries
The tears run down her back.

Cryin', baby, have mercy,
Baby, have mercy on me!
Baby, baby, baby,
Have mercy, mercy on me!
If this is your mercy,
What can your pity be?

I rolled and I tumbled
And I tossed the whole night through,
Rolled and tumbled and
Tossed the whole night through.
I could not rest in peace, babe,

For worryin' about you.
I feel just like a log
Floating on the deep blue sea,
Log, log, log, log
On the deep blue sea,
A-worryin' and a-driftin'
'Cause nobody cares for me.

Can't read, can't write,
Gonna buy me a telephone.
Can't read, can't write,
Gonna buy a telephone.
Gonna talk to my baby
Till she comes back home.

White folks, white folks,
Please don't give my gal a job.
White folks, don't give my
Ugly old gal no job.
She's a married woman and I
Don't want her to work too hard.

I got something on my mind
That sure do worry me.
Something on my mind that
Sure do worry me—
Tain't my present, tain't my future,
It's just my old-time used-to-be.

*As heard and transcribed by Langston Hughes at
the Swing-Hi Club in Los Angeles, 1941*

GOOD MORNING BLUES

Good mornin', blues,
Blues, how do you do?

Good mornin', blues,
Blues, how do you do?
Good morning, how are you?

I laid down last night,
Turning from side to side;
Yes, I was turning from side to side,
I was not sick,
I was just dissatisfied.

When I got up this mornin',
Blues walking round my bed;
Yes, the blues walkin' round my bed,
I went to eat my breakfast,
The blues was all in my bread.

I sent for you yesterday baby,
Here you come a walking today;
Yes, here you come a walking today,
Got your mouth wide open,
You don't know what to say.

Good mornin', blues,
Blues, how do you do?
Yes, blues, how do you do?
I'm doing all right,
Good morning, how are you?

Traditional Blues

GOOD MORNING BLUES

Woke up this morning
Blues all around my head.
Walked in to eat my breakfast,
I had the blues all in my bread.

I got the blues so bad,
I could feel 'em, baby, with my natural hand.
Well, I'm having so much trouble,
Blues I just can't understand.

I got the blues so bad
'Til it hurts my feet to walk.
Well, I got the blues so bad,
That it hurts my tongue to talk.

I got blues in my water,
Blues all in my tea,
Blues in my water
Puts blues all in my tea.
Well, I got blues in my home, Lord,
They're between my wife and me.

Well, the blues ain't nothin'
But a workingman feelin' bad.
Well, it's one of the worst old feelin's
That any poor man's ever had.

Well, the blues got on me one morning,
Followed me to my good gal's door.
Well, the blues got on me one morning,
Followed me to my good girl's door.
Blues are just like my shadow
Follows me everywhere I go.

As sung by Brownie McGhee

SEE, SEE RIDER

See See Rider, see what you done done!
Lord, Lord, Lord!

You made me love you, now your gal done come.
You made me love you, now your gal done come.

I'm goin' away, baby, I won't be back till fall.
  Lord, Lord, Lord!
Goin' away, baby, won't be back till fall.
If I find me a good man, I won't be back at all.

I'm gonna buy me a pistol just as long as I am tall.
  Lord, Lord, Lord!
Kill my man and catch the Cannon Ball.
If he won't have me, he won't have no gal at all.

See See Rider, where did you stay last night?
  Lord, Lord, Lord!
Your shoes ain't buttoned, clothes don't fit you right.
You didn't come home till the sun was shinin' bright.

CARELESS LOVE

Love, oh love, oh careless love,
Love, oh love, oh careless love,
Love, oh love, oh careless love,
You see what careless love has done.

It's gone and broke this heart of mine,
It's gone and broke this heart of mine,
It's gone and broke this heart of mine,
It'll break that heart of yours, sometime.

I cried last night and the night before,
I cried last night and the night before,
I cried last night and the night before,
I'm gonna cry tonight, ain't gonna cry no more.

Love, oh love, oh careless love,
Love, oh love, oh careless love,
Love, oh love, oh careless love,
You see what love has done to me.

SOUTHERN BLUES

House catch on fire
And ain't no water around,
If your house catch on fire,
Ain't no water around,
Throw yourself out the window,
Let it burn on down.

I went to the gypsy
To have my fortune told,
I went to the gypsy
To have my fortune told,
She said, "Dog-gone you, girlie,
Dog-gone your hard-luck soul!"

I turned around and
Went to that gypsy next door.
I turned around and
Went to that gypsy next door.
She said, "You can get a man
Anywhere you go."

Let me be your ragdoll
Until your china comes.
Let me be your ragdoll
Until your china comes.
If he keeps me ragged,
He's got to rag it some.

JOE TURNER

They tell me that Joe Turner's come and gone,
Oh, Lord!
They tell me that Joe Turner's come and gone,
Got my man and gone.
He come with forty links of chain,
Oh, Lord!
He come with forty links of chain,
Got my man and gone.

DINK'S BLUES

Some people say dat de worry blues ain' bad.
Some people say dat de worry blues ain' bad.
It's de wors' ol' feelin' I ever had.

Git you two, three men, so one won't worry your min'.
Git you two, three men, so one won't worry your min'.
Don't,—dey'll keep you worried an' bothered all de time.

I wish to God east boun' train would wreck.
I wish to God east boun' train would wreck.
Kill de engineer, break de fireman's neck.

I'm gwine to de river, set down on de groun'.
I'm gwine to de river, set down on de groun'.
Ef de blues overtake me, I'll jump overboard an' drown.

Ef trouble was money I'd be a millionaire.
Ef trouble was money I'd be a millionaire.
Ef trouble was money I'd be a millionaire. . . .

Come de big Kate Adam wid headlight turn down de stream.
Come de big Kate Adam wid headlight turn down de stream,
An' her side-wheel knockin', "Great-God-I-Been-redeemed."

Ef I feels tomorrow like I feels today.
Ef I feels tomorrow like I feels today.
Stan' right here an' look ten-thousan' miles away.

My mother tol' me when I was a chile.
My mother tol' me when I was a chile.
Bout de mens an' whiskey would kill me after while.

Ef I gets drunk, wonder who's gwine carry me home.
Ef I gets drunk, wonder who's gwine carry me home.
Ef I gets drunk, wonder who's gwine carry me home.

I used to love you, but, oh, God damn you, now.
I used to love you, but, oh, God damn you, now.
I used to love you, but, oh, God damn you, now.

De worry blues ain' nothin' but de heart disease.
De worry blues ain' nothin' but de heart disease.
De worry blues ain' nothin' but de heart disease.

Jes as soon as de freight train make up in de yard.
Jes as soon as de freight train make up in de yard.
Some poor woman got an achin' heart.

Tol' my mother not to weep an' moan.
Tol' my mother not to weep an' moan.
I do de bes' I can, cause I's a woman grown.

I flag de train an' it keep on easin' by.
I flag de train an' it keep on easin' by.
I fold my arms; I hang my head an' cry.

When my heart struck sorrow de tears come rollin' down.
When my heart struck sorrow de tears come rollin' down.
When my heart struck sorrow de tears come rollin' down.

Worry now an' I won't be worry long.
Worry now an' I won't be worry long.
Take a married woman to sing de worry song.

Ef I leave here walkin', it's chances I might ride.
Ef I leave here walkin', it's chances I might ride.
Ef I leave here walkin', it's chances I might ride.

MAMIE DESDUME'S BLUES

De Two-Nineteen done took mah baby away.
Two-Nineteen took mah babe away.
Two-Seventeen bring her back some day.

Stood on the corner with her feets soakin' wet.
Stood on the corner with her feets soakin' wet,
Beggin' each an' every man that she met—

If you can't give me a dollar, give me a lousy dime.
Can't give a dollar, give me a lousy dime,
I wanna feed that hongry man of mine.

*Which Jelly Roll Morton said was the first blues he, no
doubt, ever heard in his life*

TRADITIONAL BLUES VERSES

Did you ever glimpse a one-eyed woman cry?
Says, did you ever see a one-eyed woman cry?
Jack, she can cry so good out of that one old eye.

My gal's got ways like a levee-camp mule before day.
Yes, my gal's got ways like a levee-camp mule 'fore day.
When she thinks I'm sleepin', she tries to steal away.

The wrong kind of mammy made the wrong kind of chile out of me.
The wrong kind of mammy made the wrong kind of chile out of me.
And a no-good daddy lemme be just what I wanted to be.

I got so many womens I cannot call they name.
So many womens, Lord, I cannot call they name.
Some is cross-eyed—but they see me just the same.

If you got a little woman, don't never hit her too hard.
If you got a little woman, don't hit her too hard.
She'll swell up like a doughnut when you throw it in the lard.

Where you goin', Mister Spider, climbin' up the wall?
Where are you goin', Spider, climbin up the wall?
Spider said, I'm goin' to get my ashes hauled.

Did you ever see peaches growin' on a watermelon vine?
Did you ever see peaches on a watermelon vine?
Did you ever see a woman I couldn't get for mine?

Lemme be your teddy until your big bear comes.
Lemme be your teddy until your big bear comes.
I can be your teddy until your big bear comes.

My gal's got legs, yes, legs like a kangaroo.
My gal's got legs, legs like a kangaroo.
If you don't watch out she'll hop all over you.

I'm goin' to the river, take my rockin' chair,
Goin' to the river, take my rockin' chair.
If the blues overcome me, I'll rock on away from here.

Sometimes you married womens
I cannot understand.
Sometimes you married womens
I cannot understand—
You serves beans to your husband,
Cooks chicken for your backdoor man.

You never miss the water
Till the well runs dry.
You never miss the water
Till the well runs dry.
You never miss a good woman
Until she up and die.

I got two women,
Can't hardly tell them apart.
I got two women,
Can't hardly tell them apart.
'Cept one woman is my money,
Other woman is my heart.

I heard my baby call me.
I said, What do you want this time?
I heard my baby call me.
Asked her, What you want this time?
She said, If you ain't got a quarter,
Can't you get up off a dime?

Used in variant forms in many blues songs, often without any
connective sequences

HOW LONG BLUES

How long, baby, how long
Has that even' train been gone?
How long? How long? I say, How long?
Standin' at the station watchin' my baby leave town,
Sure am disgusted—for where could she be gone—
For how long? How long? I say, how long?

I can hear the whistle blowin' but I cannot see no train
And deep down in my heart I got an ache and pain
For how long? How long? I say, how long?

Sometimes I feel so disgusted and I feel so blue
That I hardly know what in this world it's best to do
For how long, how long, how long?

If I could holler like I was a mountain jack
I'd go up on the mountain and call my baby back.
For how long, how long, how long?

If some day she's gonna be sorry that she done me wrong
Baby, it will be too late then—for I'll be gone
For so long, so long, so long!

My mind get's to rattling, I feel so bad
Thinkin' 'bout the bad luck that I have had
For so long, so long, so long.

How long? Baby, how long?
Baby, how long?
How long?

Work Songs

TAKE THIS HAMMER

Take this hammer—huh!
And carry it to the captain—huh!
You tell him I'm gone—huh!
Tell him I'm gone—huh!

If he asks you—huh!
Was I runnin'—huh!
You tell him I was flyin'—huh!
Tell him I was flyin'—huh!

If he asks you—huh!
Was I laughin'—huh!
You tell him I was cryin'—huh!
You tell him I was cryin'—huh!

RAILROAD MAN

Oh, French fried potatoes and a good line of beans.
I wouldn't mind eating but the cook ain't clean.

Let's move—
Big boy, we're rollin'!
Big boy, we're rollin'!

What did the hen duck tell the drake?
No more crawfish in this lake.

Let's move—
Big boy, we're rollin'!
Big boy, we're rollin'!

This is the way we line this track:
Put the rungs in the rails and snatch 'em back.

Let's move—
Big boy, we're rollin'!
Big boy, we're rollin'!

I'm a poor railroad man, ain't got no hope.
Today I'm here, tomorrow I'm gone.

Let's move—
Big boy, we're rollin'!
Big boy, we're rollin'!

CAN'T YOU LINE IT

Track Workers' Song

When I get to Illinois,
I'm gonna spread the news about the Florida boys.
  Shove it over! Hey! Hey!
  Can't you line it?
  Ah, shack-a-lack-a-lack-a-lack-a-lack-a-lack!

Can't you move it? Hey! Hey!
Can't you try?

Me and my buddy's goin' across the field.
I heard that train when it left Mobile. . . .

I heard a mighty noise around the river bend.
Must be the Southern crossin' the L & N. . . .

Tell you what the hobo told the bum—
If you get any corn bread, save me some. . . .

A nickle's worth of bacon and a dime's worth of lard,
I would buy more but the time's too hard. . . .

Wonder what's the matter with the walking boss,
It's done five-thirty and he won't knock off. . . .

I ast my Cap'n what's the time of day.
He got so mad he throwed his watch away. . . .

Cap'n got a pistol and he try to play bad,
But I'm gonna take it if he makes me mad. . . .

Cap'n got a burner I'd like to have,
A 32:20 with a shiny barrel. . . .

MULE ON DE MOUNT

Cap'n got a mule, mule on the Mount called Jerry.
Cap'n got a mule, mule on the Mount called Jerry.
I can ride, Lawd, Lawd, I can ride.

I don't want no cold corn bread and molasses,
I don't want no cold corn bread and molasses,
Gimme beans, Lawd, Lawd, gimme beans.

I don't want no coal-black woman for my regular,
I don't want no coal-black woman for my regular,
She's too low-down, Lawd, Lawd, she's too low-down.

I got a woman, she's got money 'cumulated,
I got a woman, she's got money 'cumulated,
In de bank, Lawd, Lawd, in de bank.

I got a woman she's pretty but she's too bulldozing,
I got a woman she's pretty but she's too bulldozing,
She won't live long, Lawd, Lawd, she won't live long.

Every pay day, pay day I gits a letter,
Every pay day, pay day I gits a letter,
Son come home, Lawd, Lawd, son come home.

If I can just make June, July and August,
If I can just make June, July and August,
I'm going home, Lawd, Lawd, I'm going home.

Don't you hear them coo-coo birds keep a'hollering,
Don't you hear them coo-coo birds keep a'hollering,
It's sign of rain, Lawd, Lawd, it's sign of rain.

I got a rain-bow wrapped and tied around my shoulder,
I got a rain-bow wrapped and tied around my shoulder,
It ain't goin' rain, Lawd, Lawd, it ain't goin' rain.

CHILLY WIN' DON' BLOW

The hanh! *represents the explosion of breath
at the end of a blow with an ax or a pick*

An' it's oh, Lawdy me
An' it's oh, Lawdy my
Says, I make it where de chilly win' don' blow

If I make it, *hanh!* where de chilly, *hanh!* win' don' blow, *hanh!*
Then It's oh, *hanh!* Lawdy me, *hanh!* an' it's oh, *hanh!* Lawdy my,
hanh!
Lawd, I'll make it, *hanh!* where de chilly, *hanh!* win' don' blow,
hanh!

Ol' black gal, *hanh!* you ain' no, *hanh!* mo' mine, *hanh!*
Ol' black gal, *hanh!* you ain' no, *hanh!* mo' mine, *hanh!*
An' it's oh, *hanh!* Lawdy me, *hanh!*
An' it's oh, *hanh!* Lawdy my, *hanh!*
Lawd, I'll make it, *hanh!* where de chilly, *hanh!* win' don' blow,
hanh!

Captain, Captain, *hanh!* don' be so hard, *hanh!* on long-time man,
hanh!
Captain, Captain, *hanh!* don' be so hard, *hanh!* on long-time man,
hanh!

Says, You worked me, *hanh!* in de rain, *hanh!*
An' you worked me, *hanh!* in de snow, *hanh!*
So I, Captain, *hanh!* cain' hard-, *hanh!* -ly go, *hanh!*
An' it's oh, Lawdy me
An' it's oh, Lawdy my
Says, I make it where de chilly win' don' blow.

IT MAKES A LONG TIME MAN FEEL BAD

Sung on the Cummins Farm, Twenty-five miles out of
Pine Bluff, Arkansas to the chopping of axes

Alberta, she won't write to me.
Alberta, she won't write to me.
She won't write me no letter,
She won't send me no word.
It makes a long-time man, O Lawd, feel bad.

Now Dr. John, he's got the record and gone.
Dr. John, he's got the record and gone.
Dr. John, he's got the record, he's got the record and gone.
Dr. John, he's got the record and gone.

It makes a long-time man feel bad.
It makes a long-time man feel bad.
It's the worst ol' feelin' I ever had.
It makes a long-time man feel bad.

Recorded by John A. Lomax

SOUTH CAROLINA CHAIN GANG SONG

Lawd, I'm goin' away for the summer
An' I won't be, won't he back till fall
I'm goin' to bring so much money,
That your apron strings won't hold

Don't talk about it, 'bout it, if you do I'll cry,
Don't talk about it, 'bout it, if you do I'll die

Lawd, I'm goin' down to Columbia
Goin' to fall down, fall down on my knees
I'm goin' to ax the hard-hearted governor
Will he pardon me, pardon me, if he please
"No pardon for you, partner, got to make your time
No pardon for you, partner, got to make your time"

Don't talk about it, 'bout it, if you do I'll cry,
Don't talk about it, 'bout it, if you do I'll die.

Recorded by John A. Lomax

HYAH COME DE CAP'M

Hyah come de cap'm
Stan' right steddy
Walkin' lak Samson,
Stan' right steddy.
A big Goliath
Stan' right steddy
He totin' his talker
Stan' right steddy.

Lookin' fer Jimbo
Don' say nothin'
Go 'head Jimbo
Don' say nothin'
Run in de bushes
Don' say nothin'
Cap'm ain't fin' you
Don' say nothin'.

De houn' dawgs come
Oh! hab mercy
Start to runnin'
Dey cain't fin' you
Oh, hab mercy
Good ol' Jimbo
Lawd, Lawd.

Boy you mus' be flyin'
Lawd, Lawd.
Some good day
Lawd, Lawd,
Ef ah git de drop,
Lawd, Lawd,

Ah'm goin' on
Lawd, Lawd,
Dat same good way
Lawd, Lawd,
Dat Jimbo gone
Lawd, Lawd.

Good ol' Jimbo
Lawd, Lawd,
He done gone,
Lawd, Lawd.
He done gone.

GO DOWN, OL' HANNAH

*Sung by Track Horse, Huntsville State Penitentiary, Huntsville,
Texas, April 1934. Ol' Hannah is the sun*

Well, you talk about rollin' but you don't know
You ought-a been on the river in 1904

You could find old dead man layin' cross your row
The sergeant done kilt him 'cause he couldn't go

Get up, old dead man, help me carry my row
You been here sleepin' since 1904

Cap'n, I got fever, 103,
If you believe I'm lyin' you can come and see

Little boy, did the Cap'n ever tell you why to draw your time?
Little knee high jumpin' at a steady grind

Go down, ol' Hannah, don't you rise no mo'
Go down, ol' Hannah, don't you rise no mo'

If you rise in the mornin', bring the judgment on
Oh, ain't tired of livin', but I got *so* long.

PITY A POOR BOY

Pity a poor boy? Pity a poor boy?
You ain't goin' to pity me down.
Oh, pity a poor boy! Pity a poor boy!
But you ain't goin' to pity me down.

I'm water logged, I'm fire bound,
I'm climbin' up a mountain on-a slippery groun'
My head's under water
But I ain't a-gonna drown.
And you ain't goin' to pity me,
Ain't goin' to pity me down.

Pity me down! Pity me down!
Oh, why you want to pity me down?
Oh, pity me down! Pity me down!
But you ain't goin' to pity me down.

I'm fallin' down, I'm stumblin' on,
I'm tryin' to make a livin'
But my money's all gone.
Got my toe holt broken, but I'm climbin' on
And you ain't goin' to pity me down,
Ain't goin' to pity me down.

Pity me? Don't pity me!
You ain't goin' to pity me down.

HAMMER SONG

Well she ask me—hunh—
In de parlor—hunh;
And she cooled me—hunh—
Wid her fan—hunh;
An' she whispered—hunh—
To her mother—hunh:
"Mama, I love dat—hunh—
Dark-eyed man"—hunh.

Well I ask her—hunh—
Mother for her—hunh;
And she said she—hunh
Was too young—hunh;
Lord, I wished I'd—hunh—
Never seen her—hunh;
And I wished she'd—hunh—
Never been born—hunh.

Well, I led her—hunh—
To de altar—hunh;
And de preacher—hunh—
Give his command—hunh—
And she swore by—hunh—
God that made her—hunh;
That she'd never—hunh—
Love another man—hunh.

"GOOD MORNING, CAPTAIN"

"Good morning, captain."—"Good morning, son."
"Good morning, captain."—"Good morning, son."
"Do you need another mule skinner out on your new road line?"

Well I like to work, I'm rolling all the time,
Yes, I like to work I'm rolling all the time,
I can pop my initials on a mule's behind.

Well it's "Hey little water boy bring your water 'round,"
It's "Hey little water boy bring your water 'round,
If you don't like your job set that water bucket down."

Well I'm working on that new road at a dollar and a dime a day,
Working on that new road at a dollar and a dime a day,
I got three women waiting on a Saturday night just to draw my pay.

PICK A BALE OF COTTON

Jump down, turn around to pick a bale of cotton.
Jump down, turn around, pick a bale a day.
Jump down, turn around to pick a bale of cotton.
Jump down, turn around, pick a bale a day.

Oh, Lordy, pick a bale of cotton!
Oh, Lordy, pick a bale a day!

Me and my gal can pick a bale of cotton,
Me and my gal can pick a bale a day. . . .

Me and my wife can pick a bale of cotton,
Me and my wife can pick a bale a day. . . .

Me and my friend can pick a bale of cotton,
Me and my friend can pick a bale a day. . . .

Me and my poppa can pick a bale of cotton,
Me and my poppa can pick a bale a day.
Oh, Lordy, pick a bale of cotton!
Oh, Lordy, pick a bale a day!

ALABAMA BOUND

I'm Alabama bound!
I'm Alabama bound!
If the train don't stop and turn around,
I'm Alabama bound.

Don't you leave me here!
Don't you leave me here!
If you gonna go anyhow, leave a dime for beer.
Leave a dime for beer.

Oh, the preacher preached till he turned around.
Deacon's in the corner hollerin', Sweet gal,
I'm Alabama bound.

Ella Green is gone.
Ella Green is gone.
She's way cross this country, sweet gal,
With a long tall John.

She's Alabama bound!
She's Alabama bound!
If the train don't stop and turn around
She's Alabama bound.

Street Cries

STREET CRIES OF AN OLD SOUTHERN CITY

THE streets of this quaint, old Southern City are teeming with sights and sounds of interest to those in whom Familiarity has not "bred contempt." To a stranger nothing is so amusing or unintelligible as the various cries of the hucksters as they ply their street trade, endeavoring to inform the "world and his wife" concerning their wares. To an inhabitant of this enchanted old "City by the Sea," numerous members of this "Brotherhood of the streets," become well-known friends; their several cries, familiar music.

When asked about themselves these hucksters tell you that they come "From up de road" or "Across from Jeems Island, Mam" and some from "ober de new bridge" and still others again are town Negroes who secure their wares "Down at Boyce Wharf and Tra-add Street Bre'kwater, my missis."

They congregate there to receive the boat loads of fresh "Vegetubble" and "Swimpy, raw raw." Long before even these enterprising denizens of the sleepy town are up and doing, the "Mosquito Fleet" has put to sea while the still, grey dawn is breaking and you hear them sending back in calm weather the long, faint cadence of a rowing song;

> "Rosy am a han'some gal!
> Haul away Rosy—Haul away gal!
> Fancy slippers and fancy shawl!

411

Haul away Rosy—Haul away!
Rosy gwine ter de fancy ball!
Haul away Rosy—Haul away gal."

Even in wet or windy weather when the wind is fresh and strong, sails are hoisted and silently the fishing fleet flits out like a flock of ghostly birds across the harbor, across the bar and out to the fishing banks, forty miles away. For these fishing boats are manned by intrepid sailors known far and wide for skill and daring.

All of the folk-songs have a queer minor catch in them and even the street cries have an echo of sadness in their closing cadence. Early one morning the usual shrimp "Fiend's" cry was superseded by a strange, unfamiliar, and piercing sweet cry in a boy's faint, clear soprano. Like a little lark this "Jean De Reszke" of the small, black world, gave his name and advertised his wares, in a voice that made you think of the freshness of dawn across dewy fields. He stood under the window and sang:

An' a Dawtry Daw!
An' a Swimpy Raw!
An' a Dawtry Dawtry
Dawtry Raw Swimp!

The shrimp are sold early in the morning. When the "Mosquito Fleet" puts back into port, the fish are hawked about the streets and the lusty-lunged fishermen cry then "Whit-ing" with an ominous voice, that seems to hold its queer, breaking sound, a reminder of the days and nights of danger which falls to the daily lot of these toilers of the deep who still must put out to sea in calm or storm alike, regardless of the death which threatens when "The Harbor bar be Moaning."

All is not sadness, for here and there a quaint bit of human nature or glint of humor shows. For instance, even in the Street cry parlance, "The Sex" holds its wonted superiority and you will find that "She Crabs," called through the nose of the vender, "She Craib, She Craib," bring more money than just ordinary "Raw Crabs"—by which distinguished title is meant the less desirable male crab.

"Old Joe Cole, good old soul," who did a thriving business in lower King Street under the quaint sign of "Joe Cole & Wife" was the bright, particular, tho fast-waning, star of our galaxy of street artists. He set the fashion, so to speak, in "hucksterdom." Joe had many imitators but no equals, he looked like an Indian Chief, walked with a limp that would "do a general proud," and used his walking stick as a baton, while bellowing like the "Bull of Bashan." It was a never-to-be-forgotten occasion when Joe lustily yelled:

"Old Joe Cole—Good Old Soul
Porgy in the Summer-time
An e Whiting in the Spring
8 upon a string.
Don't be late I'm watin at de gate
Don't be mad—Heres your shad
Old Joe Cole—Good Old Soul."

Porgy, it may be remarked in passing, is a much prized variety of chub, and is much esteemed among the colored brethren, "embracin of the sisterin," as one old, colored preacher said.

When asked to sing so that his remarkable cry might be correctly reproduced, Joe gravely informed the awe-struck crowd surrounding him, "Yunna Negroes gwan from here now cos little Miss done ax me to sing in de megafone so as she can write *Me* down in de white folks' book and she aint ax *none* ob yunna Negroes to do dat ting, jest *Me*." And sure enough I did.

The "Vegetubble" Maumas are wonderful, wide-chested, big-hipped specimens of womanhood that balance a fifty pound basket of vegetables on their heads and ever and anon cry their goods with as much ease and grace as a society lady wears her "Merry Widow" hat and carries on a conversation. As these splendid, black Hebes come along with a firm, swinging stride you may hear:

Red rose To-may-toes!
Green Peas! Sugar Peas!

Perhaps it will vary in season to "Strawberry." Or may be that yet again you will be informed that "Sweet Pete ate her." Which being

interpreted means that they are selling sweet potatoes to the tune of Red Rose Tomatoes, only it sounds quite cannibalistic sung thuswise.

Amongst all this babble of femininity the masculine call of "Little John," as he styles himself, comes as a relief to the ear. He sings as he wends his way: "Heres your 'Little John' Mam. I got Hoppen John Peas Mam! I got cabbage—I got yaller turnips Mam, Oh yes Mam"—and so he comes and you buy what you want and on he goes still singing what he's "got" to sell. "I got sweet Petater—I got beets; I got Spinach." And so on like the brook, forever, "Little John" sings, his approach marked by the musical sign "Crescendo" his retreat by "Diminuendo."

When I hear "Little John," I think of an old street crier, long since dead and gone, whose cry was used to advertise his load of water-melons, thusly:

> Load my Gun
> Wid Sweet Sugar Plum
> An Shoot dem nung gal
> One by one
> Barder lingo
> Water-millon.

Now—a "nung gal" is "Gullah" for young girl, as you will find out when you get a plantation Negro to tell you the ancient rhyme of the love affair of the old Oyster Opener and the Young Girl.

His tragic affair of the heart is briefly told in the dialogue which follows: The Old Oyster Opener taking the part of "Ber Rabbit." "Ber Rabbit what you de do day?" or as we would say "Ber Rabbit what are you doing there?" and "Ber Rabbit" sadly answers—"I open de oyster for nung gal. Oyster he bite off ma finger an nung gal he tek me for laugh at."

It is a curious fact that the Island Negroes make no distinction in talking, between "he and she" and when "Ber Rabbit" of the above says "Young gal He take me to laugh at," the old man gives a good illustration of that peculiar trait of their language.

There is a gentle looking old woman who gives vent to the most ferocious and nasal howl of—"come on chilluns and get yer monkey

meat." Should you hear it, do not be alarmed for it heralds nothing worse than a harmless, old body selling the children favorite cocoa-nut and molasses candy.

This performance is only equaled by the one of the mild, ante-diluvian "Daddy" who gravely thrusts his wooly head into your back-gate and emits in an eminently respectful tone of voice the following jargon:

"Enny yad aigs terday my Miss" which being interpreted means —"Do you wish any eggs which my hens have laid in my yard and which therefore are fresh eggs Q. E. D. Fresh Yard Eggs.

In Charleston, even the chimney-sweeps used to be musical. As their tiny faces appeared at the top of the chimney they were sweep-ing, you'd hear "Roo roo" sung out over the sounds of the street below. Also to this tribe the charcoal boy belongs. He drives into town a tiny donkey hitched to a tiny, two-wheeled cart. The cart and load are black, the donkey is black, the boy is black and the only other color that you can see in the whole outfit is the whites of the boy's eyes as he rolls them around and calls the eerie, long-drawn-out "Char————coal." He sounds weird, melancholy and even doomed, with his mournful cry of "char-coal." You wonder which is the saddest and blackest; the driver, the driven, cart or contents, as they wend their solitary and spooky way onward, cry-ing that ever sad minor wail of "Char - - - coal."

In closing, it may not be amiss to barely mention the little rhyme concerning "The Charleston Eagle," of the genus "Market Street," vulgarly called a buzzard.

"A gallant sight it is, to see
The buzzards in their glory
Fall out about an old beef knee
And fight 'till they are gory."

Nor may it be amiss to draw attention to the old fellow who perigrinates around selling "Honey Honey Honey—" along with his "yarb" "The Devils Shoe String." Soon he too will join the ranks of the things "gone and forgotten." I suspect he lives, as does another one of my old vendor friends, who told me he en-dured the ills of this life while living, "in the blessed hope of an

Immorality to come." So say we all of us.

All these interesting things and more too are here, jostling your elbow, passing your window, begging your custom and offering rich and picturesque effects to those who have "Eyes to see," and furnishing a queer, original but fast fading, street symphony to those who have "Ears to hear."

Harriette Kershaw Leiding

WATERMELON VENDOR'S CRY

Watermelon! Watermelon! Red to the rind,
If you don't believe me jest pull down your blind!
I sell to the rich,
I sell to the po';
I'm gonna sell the lady
Standin' in that do'.
Watermelon, Lady!
Come and git your nice red watermelon, Lady!
Red to the rind, Lady!
Come on, Lady, and get 'em!
Gotta make the picnic fo' two o'clock
No flat tires today.
Come on, Lady!
I got water with the melon, red to the rind!
If you don't believe it jest pull down your blind.
You eat the watermelon and preee—serve the rind!

WAFFLE MAN'S CRY

The Waffle Man is a fine old man.
He washes his face in a frying-pan,

He makes his waffles with his hand,
Everybody loves the Waffle Man.

CALA VENDOR'S CRY

We sell it to the rich, we sell it to the poor,
We give it to the sweet brownskin, peepin' out the door.
Tout chaud, Madame, tout chaud!
Git 'em while they're hot! Hot calas!

One cup of coffee, fifteen cents calas,
Make you smile the livelong day.
Calas, tout chauds, Madame, Tout chauds!
Git 'em while they're hot! Hot calas!

OYSTER MAN'S CRY

Oyster Man! Oyster Man!
Get your fresh oysters from the Oyster Man!
Bring out your pitcher, bring out your can,
Get your nice fresh oysters from the Oyster Man!

SIX NEGRO MARKET SONGS OF HARLEM

1. THE STREET CHEF

Ah'm a natu'al bo'n cook
Ah' dat ain't no lie,
Ah can fry po'k chops
An' bake a low-down pie

So step right up
Ah' he'p yo'se'f
Fum de vittles on
Mah kitchen she'f!

2. THE SORREL WOMAN

Sorrel! Oh, sorrel!
'e tehste lok Granny's wine,
Sorrel! Oh, sorrel!
'e sweet an' 'e too fine!
Sorrel! Oh, sorrel!
'e sure a 'trengh'nin' t'ing,
Sorrel! Oh, sorrel!
'e med to suit de king!

3. THE AH-GOT-UM MAN

Ah got pompanos!
Ah got catfish!
Ah got buffaloes!
Ah got um!
Ah got um!

Ah got stringbeans!
Ah got cabbage!
Ah got collard greens!
Ah got um!
Ah got um!

Ah got honeydews!
Ah got can'lopes!
Ah got watermelons!
Ah got um!
Ah got um!

Ah got fish,
Ah got fruits,

Ah got veg, yes 'ndeed!
Ah got any kind o' vittles,
Ah got anything yo' need!

Ah'm de Ah-Got-Um Man!

4. DE SWEET PERTATER MAN

See des gread big sweet pertaters
Right chere by dis chicken's side,
Ah'm de one what bakes dese taters
Makes dem fit to suit yo' pride

Dere is taters an' mo' taters,
But de ones ah sells is fine
Yo' kin go fum hyeah to yondah
But yo' won't get none lak mine
'Cause Ah'm de tater man!
(Ah mean!)
De sweet pertater man!

5. THE CRAB MAN

Ho! cra-ab man!
Ho! cra-ab man!
Ho! Crabs, I say!

Fresh crabs! Hyeah!
Fresh crabs! Hyeah
Fresh crabs, today!

6. THE PEPPER-SAUCE SONG
West Indian Song Poem

Make's no diff'ence what yo' eat
Whether rice or greens or meat

All de flavah sho am los'
'Less yo' got some pepper-sauce

When yo' pass by this-a-way
Keep a lis'nin' fo' mah call
Pure Jamaica pepper-sauce!
Fresh red pepper-sauce!
Dat's all!

Playsongs and Games

CHICKAMA, CHICKAMA-CRANEY CROW

Chickama, Chickama-Craney Crow
Went to the well to wash my toe
When I got back my chicken was gone.
What time old witch?

HIDE AND SEEK

I got up about half-past four,
Forty-four robbers was 'round my door.
I opened the door and let 'em in,
Hit 'em over the head with a rollin' pin.
 All hid? All hid?

COUNTING OUT RHYMES

Out goes the rat.
Out goes the cat.

Out goes the lady with the see-saw hat.
O-U-T spells out and out goes you.

One, two, three, four, five, six, seven.
All good people go to heaven.
All bad ones go down below
To keep company with old Jimbo.
O-U-T spells out and out goes you.

Eeeny, meeny, miney-mo,
Catch a boy by his toe.
If he hollers, let him go.
Eeeny, meeny, miney, mo.
Out goes you.

Eeeny, meeny, dixie, deeny.
Hit him a lick and join the queeny.
Time, time, merry go round.
Eighteen-Hundred and Ninety-nine.
O-U-T spells out and out goes you.

DID-YOU GAME

LEADER:
Did you go to the hen house?
CHORUS:
    Yes, mam!
Did you get any eggs?
    Yes, mam!
Did you put 'em in the bread?
    Yes, mam!
Did you bake it brown?
    Yes, mam!
Did you hand it over?
    Yes, mam!

Good old egg bread,
    Shake 'em, shake 'em!
Good old egg bread,
    Shake 'em, shake 'em!
Did you go to the lynchin'?
    Yes, mam!
Did they lynch that man?
    Yes, mam!
Did that man cry?
    Yes, mam!
How did he cry?
    Baa, baa!
How did he cry?
    Baa, baa!

YES MA'M

O little girl! Yes Ma'm!
Did you get any eggs? Yes Ma'm!
Did you give them to the cook? Yes Ma'm!
Did the cook make bread? Yes Ma'm!
What good egg bread! O shake, shake, shake.
What good egg bread! O shake, shake, shake.
Shoo, turkey, Shoo, Shoo. (*Shout.—Repeat over and over*)

O little girl! Yes Ma'm!
Did you go to the river? Yes Ma'm!
Did you see my turkey? Yes Ma'm!
Will you help me catch him? Yes Ma'm!
Get ready. Let's go—
O shoo, shoo, shoo,
Get ready. Let's go—
Oh, shoo, shoo, shoo.
Shoo, turkey, Shoo, Shoo. (*Shout.—Repeat over and over*)

RING FORMATION: This is a call and response game. Child in center of ring. Group makes calls. Center girl answers, Yes Ma'm. After last two lines in first verse, the answer is, "O shake, shake, shake." (*Second Verse*) Group gives calls. Child in center answers, "Yes Ma'm." After last two lines in second verse, the answer is "O Shoo, Shoo, Shoo." When second verse is ended the child in center runs and group chases her calling over and over, "Shoo, turkey, shoo, shoo."

SHOO FLY, DON'T BOTHER ME

Shoo, Shoo, Shoo, Shoo-fly don't bother me.
Shoo, Shoo, Shoo, Shoo-fly don't bother me.
Oh, Shoo-fly, don't bother me,
Shoo-fly, don't bother me,
Shoo-fly, don't bother me,
I belong to the bumble bee.

NOTE: *This game might have been taken from an old reel song of long ago. Title of original song is unknown by the collector.*

Sometimes the last line is sung "I belong to the Company D."
RING FORMATION: Children go around in circle keeping time to music. On last four lines, the group stands still and clap their hands in time to the song.

LIL LIZA JANE

Steal a partner, Lil Liza Jane,
Steal a partner, Lil Liza Jane.
That old man ain't got no wife.
Lil Liza Jane.
I wouldn't have him to save his life.
Lil Liza Jane.
Steal a partner, Lil Liza Jane.
Steal a partner, Lil Liza Jane.

RING FORMATION: Children select partners. Then form circle two by two. An odd child is in center of ring. Group sings song, clapping hands to music. The odd child crosses the ring and steals a partner. The child that is left without a partner also steals one. This movement is repeated over and over.

O, LI'L 'LIZA JANE

You've got a gal and I've got none,
Li'l' 'Liza Jane,
Come, my love and be my one,
Li'l' 'Liza Jane,

I got a house in Baltimo'
Li'l' 'Liza Jane,
Street cars runnin' by my do'
Li'l' 'Liza Jane,

Brussels carpets on my flo'
Li'l' 'Liza Jane.
Silver name plate on my do'
Li'l' 'Liza Jane.

Come my love, and marry me
Li'l' 'Liza Jane.
I will take good care of thee,
Li'l' 'Liza Jane.

MISS SUE LIZA JANE

Somebody's in your cellar, Miss Sue,
Miss Sue, Miss Sue,
Somebody's in your cellar,
Miss Sue—Liza—Jane.

Did you ever see a monkey motion,
Miss Sue, Miss Sue?
Did you ever see a monkey motion,
Miss Sue—Liza—Jane?

RING FORMATION: "Miss Sue" is in center of ring. Children march around "Miss Sue" singing first verse. When the second verse is sung, "Miss Sue" does "The Charleston"—or some other original dance step. This step usually suits the fancy of the one in the center of the ring. "Miss Sue" then selects some one to be in the center of the ring, and she takes that player's place.

GIVE THAT GAL SOME CAKE

The first day I played in the sand, the
sand got in my eye;
The second day I played in the sand, the
sand made me cry.
I went over to my Grandma's house,
and asked her for some cake.
She turned me 'round, and 'round,
and 'round, and said,
"Give that po' gal some cake!
Oh, give that gal some cake; oh, give
that gal some cake!"
She turned me 'round and 'round and
'round, and said,
"Give that po' gal some cake!"

OLD COW DIED

Ole cow died in Tennessee
Send her jawbone back to me

Jawbone walk, Jawbone talk
Jawbone eat wid uh knife and fork.
Ain't Ah right?

CHORUS: Yeah!
Ain't I right? Yeah!

If you want to see me jabber
Set me down to uh bowl uh clabber
Ain't Ah right? Yeah!
Now, ain't Ah right? Yeah!

Ole Aunt Dinah behind de pine
One eye out and de other one blind
Ain't Ah right? Yeah! Yeah!
Now, ain't Ah right? Yeah!

Wisht Ah had uh needle
Fine ex Ah could sew
Ah'd sew mah baby to my side
And down de road Ah'd go.

Double Clapping

Down de road baby
Down de road baby
It's killing mama
Oh, it's killing Mama.

Raccoon up de 'simmon tree
Possum on de ground
Raccoon shake dem 'simmons down
Possum pass 'em round.

Some love collards, some love kale
But I loves uh gal wid uh short skirt tail.

Little fishes in de brook
Willie ketch 'em wid uh hook

Mama fry 'em in de pan
Papa et 'em lak uh man.

PLAY VERSES

When you pass a mule tied to a tree,
Ring his tail and think of me.
Long as the vine grow 'round the stump,
You are my darling sugar lump.

When you pass a mule tied to a tree
Ring his tail and think of me.
Some love collards, some love kale,
But I loves a gal with a short skirt tail.

SWEET NOTASULGA

Sweet Notasulga,
Chocklit Alabama,
Date of kisses,
Month of love.
Dere John, you is my honey.
I won't never love
Nobody else but you.
I love choir practise now.
Sugar is sweet
And lard is greasy.
You love me,
Don't be uneasy.

OLD LADY SALLY

Old lady Sally want to jump-ty-jump,
Jump-ty-jump, jump-ty-jump.
Old lady Sally want to jump-ty-jump,
And old lady Sally want to bow.

Throw that hook in the middle of the pond.
Catch that girl with the red dress on.
Go on, gal, ain't you shame?

    Shame of what?

Wearing your dress in the latest style.

Many fishes in the brook.
Papa caught 'em with a hook.
Mama fried 'em in a pan.
Baby eat 'em like a man.

Preacher in the pulpit
Preaching like a man,
Trying to get to heaven on a 'lectric fan.
Do your best, papa, daddy, do your best.

AUNT DINAH'S DEAD

Aunt Dinah's dead!
    How did she die?
Oh, she died like this!
Oh, she died like this!

She lived in the country 'til she came
to town,
And she danced, danced, danced, 'til
the sun went down.

CHULA, LU!

I'm a big fat lady!
Chula, Lu!
I'm just from the country!
Chula, Lu!
Just outen' the kitchen,
Chula, Lu!
With a handful o' biscuits!
Chula, Lu!
You know I wants to marry?
Chula, Lu!
Then, Miss Fancy Chula Lu,
Fly, way over yonder!
Fly, way over yonder!
Now chose your pardner.
Chula, Lu!
And swing him around!
Chula, Lu!
I'm a bald head gen'leman,
Chula, Lu!

MARY MACK

Oh, Mary Mack, Mack, Mack,
All dressed in black, black, black,

With silver buttons, buttons, buttons,
Up and down her back, back, back.

And I love coffee, coffee, coffee,
And I love tea, tea, tea,
And the boys love me, me, me.

I went to the river, river, river,
And I couldn't get across, 'cross, 'cross,
And I paid five dollars, dollars, dollars,
For the old grey horse, horse, horse.

And the horse wouldn't pull, pull, pull,
I swapped him for a bull, bull, bull,
And the bull wouldn't holler, holler, holler,
I swapped him for a dollar, dollar, dollar.

And the dollar wouldn't spend, spend, spend,
I put it in the grass, grass, grass,
And the grass wouldn't grow, grow, grow,
I got my hoe, hoe, hoe.

And the hoe wouldn't chop, chop, chop,
I took it to the shop, shop, shop,
And the shop made money, money, money,
Like the bees made honey, honey, honey.

See that yonder, yonder, yonder,
In the jay-bird town, town, town,
Where the women gotta work, work, work,
Till the sun goes down, down, down.

Well, I eat my meat, meat, meat,
And I knaw my bone, bone, bone,
Well, goodbye, honey, honey, honey,
I'm going on home.

ROSIE, DARLING ROSIE

Rosie, darling Rosie,
Ha, ha, Rosie.
Rosie, darling Rosie,
Ha, ha, Rosie.
Grab your partner and follow me,
Ha, ha, Rosie.
Let's go down by Galilee,
Ha, ha, Rosie.
Way down yonder by Baltimore,
Ha, ha, Rosie.
Need no carpet on my floor,
Ha, ha, Rosie.
Rosie, darling Rosie,
Ha, ha, Rosie.
Rosie, darling, hurry,
Ha, ha, Rosie.
If you don't mind you gonna get left,
Ha, ha, Rosie.
Some folks say preachers won't steal,
Ha, ha, Rosie.
But I caught two in my cornfield.
Ha, ha, Rosie.
One had a bushel and one had a peck,
Ha, ha, Rosie.
The baby had a roasting ear 'round her neck.
Ha, ha, Rosie.
Rosie, darling Rosie,
Ha, ha, Rosie.
Rosie, darling hurry,
Ha, ha, Rosie.
Stop right still and study yourself,
Ha, ha, Rosie.
See that fool where she got left,
Ha, ha, Rosie.

BLUEBIRD, BLUEBIRD

Bluebird, bluebird,
Fly in the window!
Bluebird, bluebird,
Fly in the window!
Bluebird, bluebird,
Fly in the window!
Oh, Johnny, what a day!

Choose your partner,
Pat her on the shoulder.
Choose your partner,
Pat her on the shoulder.
Choose your partner,
Pat her on the shoulder.
Oh, Johnny, what a day!

Bluebird, bluebird,
Fly in the window!
Bluebird, bluebird,
Fly in the window!
Oh, Johnny, what a day!

HARLEM CHILDREN'S RHYMES AND GAGS

I

WHEN you see a guy got on brown pants you say:

Buster Brown
Went down town

With his britches
Hanging down.

Other members of the group chimed in with the following, each
voice following the other in rapid succession, giving an antiphonal
effect as varied as the colors named. While most of the jingles appear to have a set formula, there were many attempts at improvisation.

Yellow, Yellow,
Kiss a fellow.

Blue, blue,
I love you.

Black, black
Sit on a tack.

Green, green,
Eat ice cream
Stick your nose
In kerosene.

White, white,
You can fight.

The following is said by children on noticing a stranger or an
out-of-town license on a car driven by a Negro:

I'm a square from Delaware,
Jest come in town to see the Fair.
Boom da dee ah dee
Boom! boom!

The last two lines, to the tune of "Shave and a Haircut," were used
by Herbert Lambert to end each stanza he gave. Thus:

Once upon a time, goose drink wine.
Monkey chewed tobacco on the street car line.
Street car broke, monkey choke,
And that was the end of the monkey joke.
Boom da dee ah dee
Boom! boom!

You know this one, Mister? See, you meet a guy you know and he's doing something good and you say, "Gee, that's fine." And the other guy says, "Wine!" And you say,

Sho nough, that's fine as wine,
As a Georgia pine,
Two old grandmothers drinking wine.

· XIX ·

The Jazz Folk

JELLY ROLL MORTON REMEMBERS

... THOSE days I often used to like to stay with my godmother. She kept boxes of jewels in the house and I always had some kind of diamond on. Through her I came to be considered the best dresser, and this caused me to get my invitation to be an honorary member of the Broadway Swells when I was still in short pants. The members figured I was a smart kid, so, in order to beat the other clubs, they decided to display a kid as an aide.

"What do you think about it, kid?" they said, "Do you think you could get a horse—that would cost five dollars for the day? You'd have to have a streamer, too. But then you'd be an honorary member of the Broadway Swells."

I thought that was a swell idea and I personally accepted.

You see, New Orleans was very organization-minded. I have never seen such beautiful clubs as they had there—the Broadway Swells, the High Arts, the Orleans Aides, the Bulls and Bears, the Tramps, the Iroquois, the Allegroes—that was just a few of them, and those clubs would parade at least once a week. They'd have a great big band. The grand marshall would ride in front with his aides behind him, all with expensive sashes and streamers.

The members that could afford it would have a barrel of beer and plenty of sandwiches and a lot of whiskey and gin waiting at their houses. And, wherever these supplies would be, the parade would stage a grand salute. The grand marshall would lead his boys up

one side of the street and down the other while the band played on the front steps. Then the boys would go inside and get their drinks and have a hell of a time.

The day I rode with the Broadway Swells my horse wasn't exactly up to the minute. I thought I should have a small horse, since I wasn't nothing but a kid, and so the boys around that was jealous of me called my horse a goat and picked him up by his knees and hollered, "We can truck this horse on our back . . . You shouldn't be riding the horse. . . . he should be riding you." I got angry two or three times at the way my poor old pony was moving and I tried to beat him to death to show them that he could run fast. Until this day one of the things I feel most sorry for is the way I beat that poor horse.

Those parades were really tremendous things. The drums would start off, the trumpets and trombones rolling into something like Stars and Stripes or The National Anthem and everybody would strut off down the street, the bass-drum player twirling his beater in the air, the snare drummer throwing his sticks up and bouncing them off the ground, the kids jumping and hollering, the grand marshall and his aides in their expensive uniforms moving along dignified, women on top of women strutting along back of the aides and out in front of everybody—the second line, armed with sticks and bottles and baseball bats and all forms of ammunition ready to fight the foe when they reached the dividing line.

It's a funny thing that the second line marched at the head of the parade, but that's the way it had to be in New Orleans. They were our protection. You see, whenever a parade would get to another district the enemy would be waiting at the dividing line. If the parade crossed that line, it meant a fight, a terrible fight. The first day I marched a fellow was cut, must have been a hundred times. Blood was gushing out of him same as from one of the gushers in Yellowstone Park, but he never did stop fighting.

Well, if they'd have ten fights one Sunday, they didn't have many. Sometimes it would require a couple of ambulances to come around and pick up the people that was maybe cut or shot occasionally. This didn't happen all the time, but very seldom it didn't. The fact of it is, there was no parade at no time you couldn't find a knot on somebody's head where somebody got hit with a stick or something.

And always plenty to eat and drink, especially for the men in the band, and with bands like Happy Galloway's, Manuel Perez's and Buddy Bolden's we had the best ragtime music in the world. There was so many jobs for musicians in these parades that musicians didn't ever like to leave New Orleans. They used to say, "This is the best town in the world. What's the use for me to go any other place?"

Now everybody in the world has heard about the New Orleans Mardi Gras, but maybe not about the Indians, one of the biggest feats that happened in Mardi Gras. Even at the parades with floats and costumes that cost millions, why, if the folks heard the sign of the Indians

> Ungai-ah
> Ungai-ah!

—that big parade wouldn't have anybody there: the crowd would flock to see the Indians. When I was a child, I thought they really were Indians. They wore paint and blankets and, when they danced, one would get in the ring and throw his head back and downward, stooping over and bending his knees, making a rhythm with his heels and singing—T'ouwais, bas q'ouwais—and the tribe would answer—Ou tendais.

> And they'd sing on—
> T'ouwais, bas q'ouwais,
>   Ou tendais,
> T'ouwais, bas q'ouwais,
>   Ou tendais.

And then they would stop for a minute, throw back their heads and holler—

> Ala caille-yo,
>   Ala caille wais . . .
> Ouwais bas q'ouwais,
> T'ouwais bas q'ouwais,
>   Ou tendais.

They would dance and sing and go on just like regular Indians, because they had the idea they wanted to act just like the old Indians did in years gone by and so they lived true to the traditions of the Indian style. They went armed with fictitious spears and tommyhawks and so forth and their main object was to make their enemy bow. They would send their spy-boys two blocks on ahead —I happened to be a spy-boy myself once so I know how this went—and when a spy-boy would meet another spy from an enemy tribe he'd point his finger to the ground and say, "Bow-wow." And if they wouldn't bow, the spy-boy would use the Indian call, "Woo-woo-woo-woo-woo," that was calling the tribes—and, many a time, in these Indian things, there would be a killing and next day there would be somebody in the morgue.

In New Orleans we would often wonder where a dead person was located. At any time we heard somebody was dead we knew we had plenty good food that night. Those days I belonged to a quartet and we specialized in spirituals for the purpose of finding somebody that was dead, because the minute we'd walk in, we'd be right in the kitchen where the food was—plenty ham sandwiches and cheese sandwiches slabbered all over with mustard and plenty whiskey and plenty of beer. Of course, the dead man would always be laid out in the front and he'd be by himself most of the time and couldn't hear nothing we would be saying at all. He was dead and there was no reason for him to be with us living people. And very often the lady of the house would be back there with us having a good time, too, because she would be glad he was gone.

Then we would stand up and begin—

Nearer my God to thee

very slow and with beautiful harmony, thinking about that ham—

Nearer to thee

Plenty of whiskey in the flask and all kinds of crazy ideas in the harmony which made it impossible for anybody to jump in and sing. We'd be sad, too, terribly sad.

Steal away, steal away,
Steal away home to Jesus.

I tell you we had beautiful numbers to sing at those wakes.

Of course, as I told you, everybody in the City of New Orleans was always organization minded, which I guess the world knows, and a dead man always belonged to several organizations—secret orders and so forth and so on. So when anybody died, there was always a big band turned out on the day he was supposed to be buried. Never buried at night, always in the day and right in the heart of the city. You could hear the band come up the street taking the gentleman for his last ride, playing different dead marches like *Flee as the Bird to the Mountain.*

In New Orleans very seldom they would bury them in the deep in the mud. They would always bury um in a vault . . . So they would leave the graveyard . . . the band would get ready to strike up. They'd have a second line behind um, maybe a couple of blocks long with baseball bats, axe handles, knives, and all forms of ammunition to combat some of the foe when they came to the dividing lines. Then the band would get started and you could hear the drums, rolling a deep, slow rhythm. A few bars of that and then the snare drummer would make a hot roll on his drums and the boys in the band would just tear loose, while second line swung down the street, singing . . .

Didn't he ramble?
He rambled.
Rambled all around,
In and out the town.
Didn't he ramble?
He rambled.
He rambled till the butchers cut him down.

That would be the last of the dead man. He's gone and everybody came back home, singing. In New Orleans they believed truly to stick right close to the Scripture. That means rejoice at the death and cry at the birth. . . .

Those boys I used to sing with were really tough babies. They

frequented the corners at Jackson and Locust and nobody fooled
with them. The policemen was known never to cross Claiborne
Avenue and these tough guys lived five blocks past Claiborne at
Galvez, way back of town!

It was a miracle how those boys lived. They were sweet-back
men, I suppose you'd call them—always a bunch of women running
after them. I remember the Pickett boys—there was Bus, there was
Nert, there was Nonny, there was Bob. Nert had a burned hand,
which he used to wear a stocking over, and he was seemingly simple
to me. All these boys wanted to have some kind of importance.
They dressed very well and they were tremendous sports. It was
nothing like spending money that ever worried their mind. If they
didn't have it, somebody else would have it and spend it for them—
they didn't care. But they all strived to have at least one Sunday
suit, because, without that Sunday suit, you didn't have anything.

It wasn't the kind of Sunday suit you'd wear today. You was
considered way out of line if your coat and pants matched. Many
a time they would kid me, "Boy you must be from the country.
Here you got trousers on the same as your suit."

These guys wouldn't wear anything but a blue coat and some
kind of stripe in their trousers and those trousers had to be very,
very tight. They'd fit um like a sausage. I'm telling you it was very
seldom you could button the top button of a person's trousers those
days in New Orleans. They'd leave the top button open and they
wore very loud suspenders—of course they really didn't need suspenders, because the trousers was so tight and one suspender was
always hanging down. If you wanted to talk to one of those guys
he would find the nearest post, stiffen his arm out and hold himself
as far away as possible from that post he's leaning on. That was to
keep those fifteen, eighteen dollar trousers of his from losing their
press.

You should have seen one of those sports move down the street,
his shirt busted open so that you could discern his red flannel undershirt, walking along with a very mosey walk they had adopted
from the river, called shooting the agate. When you shoot the agate,
your hands is at your sides with your index fingers stuck out and
you kind of struts with it. That was considered a big thing with

some of the illiterate women—if you could shoot a good agate and had a nice highclass red undershirt with the collar turned up, I'm telling you were liable to get next to that broad. She liked that very much.

Those days, myself, I thought I would die unless I had a hat with the emblem Stetson in it and some Edwin Clapp shoes. But Nert and Nonny and many of them wouldn't wear ready-made shoes. They wore what they called the St. Louis Flats and the Chicago Flats, made with cork soles and without heels and with gambler designs on the toes. Later on, some of them made arrangements to have some kind of electric-light bulbs in the toes of their shoes with a battery in their pockets, so when they would get around some jane that was kind of simple and thought they could make her, as they call making um, why they'd press a button in their pocket and light up the little bitty bulb in the toe of their shoes and that jane was claimed. It's really the fact.

Now these boys used to all have a sweet mama that worked in white people's yards. These were colored girls I'm talking about, but it applied to the white girls, too, of the poorer class. They all practically lived out in the same section together, because there was no such thing as segregation at all in that section—in fact nowhere in New Orleans at that time.

Well, every night these sports I'm talking about would even go as far as to meet their sweet mamas—sometimes they would brave it and walk to St. Charles Avenue where their sweet mamas were working; and sometimes it would be okay for them to go in and their sweet mamas would bring a pan out to the servant's room. Some of those pans were marvelous, I'm telling you—in fact I, myself, have been in some of the homes, seeking after a pan, and I know. Take a girl working for the Godchaux or the Solaris—she would bring you gumbo, Bayou cook oysters, and maybe turkey with cranberry sauce—this wouldn't have to be on Christmas, because New Orleans is the place where no doubt the finest food in the world prevails. When sweet mama cooks and carves that fowl, sweet papa is sure to eat the choicest portions, no argument about that!

I was quite small, but I used to get in on those pans occasionally. Always hanging out with older men, anyhow. And sometimes I'd

be with um when they all get together—a whole lot of sweet mamas and their sweet papas—to have a little bit of a ball off to their self. Josky Adams would play the blues, . . .

> See, see, rider, see what you have done,
> You made me love you, now your man done come.

Josky had a beautiful sister and I always had it in my mind I wanted to marry her. Used to take her to these parties and had a wonderful time. It seemed like a family there—Josky playing and singing . . .

> I want a gal that works in the white folks' yard,
> A pretty gal that works in the white folks' yard.
> Do you see that fly crawling up the wall,
> She's going up there to get her ashes hauled.

But the one blues I never can forget out of those early days happened to be played by a woman that lived next door to my godmother's in the Garden District. The name of this musician was Mamie Desdoumes. Two middle fingers of her right hand had been cut off, so she played the blues with only three fingers on her right hand. She only knew this one tune and she played it all day long after she would first get up in the morning.

> I stood on the corner, my feet was dripping wet,
> I asked every man I met . . .
> > Can't give me a dollar, give me a lousy dime,
> > Just to feed that hungry man of mine. . . .

Although I had heard them previously I guess it was Mamie first really sold me on the blues.

Yes, "now you'll get a chance to see my red underwear!" that's what Joe used to say when he got going, with his stiff shirt bustin' on the stand, blowing for all he had, and his red undershirt showing. . . .

I have been robbed of three million dollars all told. Everyone today is playing my stuff and I don't even get credit. Kansas City style, Chicago style, New Orleans style—hell, they's all Jelly Roll style. I'm a busy man now and have to spend all my time dealing with attorneys, but I am not too busy to get around and hear jazz that I myself introduced twenty-five years ago, before most of the kids was even born. All this jazz I hear today is my own stuff, and, if I had been paid rightfully for my work, I would now have three million dollars more than I have now.

Not until 1926 did they get a faint idea of real jazz, when I decided to live in New York. In spite of the fact that there were a few great dispensers, as Sidney Bechet, clarinet, William Brand, bass, New York's idea of jazz was taken from the dictionary's definition —loud, blary, noisy, discordant tones, et cetera, which really doesn't spell jazz music. Music is music. Regardless of type, it is supposed to be soothing, not unbearable—which was a specialty with most of them. It is great to have ability from extreme to extreme, but it is terrible to have this kind of ability without the correct knowledge of how to use it. Very often you could hear the New York (supposed-to-be) jazz bands, have twelve-fifteen men; they would blaze away with all the volume they had. Sometimes customers would have to hold their ears to protect their eardrums from a forced collision with their brains. Later, in the same tune, without notification, you could hear only drums and trumpet. Piano and guitar would be going but not heard. The others would be holding their instruments leisurely, talking, smoking reefers, chatting scandals, et cetera.

Musicians of all nationalities watched the way I played; then soon I could hear my material everywhere I trod, but in an incorrect way, using figures behind a conglomeration of variations sometimes discordant, instead of hot-swing melodies.

ZUTTY SINGLETON ON JELLY ROLL

I FIRST met Jelly Roll in Chicago. He was livin' high then. You know, Jelly was a travelin' cat, sharp and good lookin' and bragging about he wrote this and that and the other thing—in fact, everything! And let me tell you this—no one ever won an argument with Jelly either!

Once I was walkin' somewhere with Louis and Lil Armstrong (they were together then), and Lil had got herself a brand new baby grand piano. We all went to Louis' place and Jelly sat down at that piano and really gave us a serenade. He played and played, and after each number he'd turn around on that stool and tell us how he wrote each number and where it came from. It was a real lecture, just for the benefit of me and Lil and Louis.

BUNK JOHNSON ON JELLY ROLL

JELLY was one of the best in 1902 and, after that, noted more so than Tony Jackson and Albert Cahill because he played the music the whores liked. Tony was dicty. But Jelly would sit there and play the barrelhouse music all night—blues and such as that. I KNOW because I played with him in Hattie Rogers' sporting house in 1903. She had a whole lot of light-colored women in there, best-looking women you ever want to see. Well, I was playing with Frankie Duson's Eagle Band on Perdido Street and sometimes after I'd knock off at four in the morning, Jelly would ask me to come and play with him—he'd play and sing the blues till way up in the day.

THE BUNK JOHNSON STORY

"Where did I learn to play cornet?
I learned to play cornet when I were 'tendin' New Orleans
    University.
I learned to play cornet under Professor Coochie Wallace's instruc-
    tion. He were our teacher at New Orleans and also our
    organist in chapel.
And he's the man that taught me cornet and learned me music.
And I taken lessons with him from the age of six years old until
    I finish New Orleans University.
I come out of New Orleans University in 1894 and I was fit for
    orchestra.

I went with Adam Olivier's band, my first band.
Played with them just a short while and I had the opportunity of
    hearing King Bolden's band at Lincoln Park.
And I got crazy to play with Bolden
And Bolden played my style of music that I liked.
I liked to read
But I rather played that head music better—
More jazz to it.
I liked to read, and I could read good—good reader—
But Bolden played mighty much by ear
And made up his own tunes.
But everything that he played I could whistle, I could play
And I jumped Olivier's band and went with Bolden.
That was in 1895.

I was crazy to play blues.
Bolden were playing blues of all kinds
So when I got with Bolden we helped make more blues.
Blues that we made a record of, too—Pallet on the Floor, Make Me
    a Pallet on the Floor—
That was played in 1894 by King Bolden.

And quadrilles—
I was crazy to play quadrilles,
This quadrille, the first eight bars of what the bands are usin' today,
    Tiger Rag,
That's King Bolden's first eight bars we would play to get your
    partner ready for quadrille.

And in later years 'twas taken and turned into Tiger Rag by musi-
    cians that could read.
Had Bolden knew music probably Bolden would have made Tiger
    Rag,
So we played the beginning of Tiger Rag before we had any Dixie-
    land Jazz Band.
The Dixieland Jazz Band is the one that taken Tiger Rag—the
    first eight bars
And turned it into the dance number what we dancin' today, we
    call Tiger Rag.
And in later years
Bolden lost his mind.
Frank Duson taken Bolden's band and he turned it into the Eagle
    Band,
And he played with Bolden just a few engagements before he lost
    his mind.
He had—Willie Cornish was his first trombone player.
Him and Cornish fell out and he got with Duson, and taken Duson,
And he lost his mind shortly after that and Duson taken the band
    in charge.
And I also played with Duson—Frankie Duson's Eagle Band.
And we played in a good many sections across Canal Street
But most of the playin' were uptown
Playin' for the High Arts Club.
We played for the San Jacinto Club,
We played for the Red Cross Club
We played at Josephine and Willow
Cole's Lawn
We played at Lincoln Park
Old Johnson Park
Also the Love and Charity Hall

Number 12 Hall
And good many halls that we played when I were workin' in bands
    across Canal Street, in the Superior Band.
And I played with Duson and I also played with the Algiers Pacific
    Brass Band."
(Say, Bunk, give us a list of the trumpet players who learned from
    you or got ideas from you.)
"A list of trumpet players?
All our good trumpet players.
Well, beginning with trumpet players,
When I were playin' the uptown section, Frank Duson's band,
Is where Louis used to follow me.
Louis was about the age of . . . Louis WAS eleven years old
And when he seed a parade
Louis tramped the street all day long, right with me.
When the band stopped playin'
He's worryin' me to carry my horn
And wanted me to learn him how to play.
And Louis done that,
Done that for a long while.
Then I seen that he were really interested in learning
I told him that I would,
I'd learn him
But he'd have to do like I would tell him.
So he told me, 'Bunk, I sure will do like you tell me.'
He say, 'All I want to do is learn.'
And I told him, I say, 'Well, all right now
You want to learn how to read music?'
He said, 'No.
I want to learn how to play Pallet on the Floor, Salty Dog, Didn't
    He Ramble and Ball the Jack.'
And a good many more numbers.
And I used to set down 'round Dago Tony's—
I was workin' at a little honky tonk, Franklin and . . .
At Franklin and Perdido—
Piano, drums and cornet.
When I'd knock off playin' at Masonic Hall,
Well, I'd go over to Dago Tony's and play.

Louis was in short pants, he couldn't go in.
But he would steal in there in the early part of the night,
Sleep behind the piano 'til I would come on.
Then after he'd git in there
Well, then I would show him and show him 'til he begin under-
    standin' me real good.
It was a short while before Louis could play the blues.
After he learn to play the blues
I learn him how to play Ball the Jack,
I learn him how to play Ball the Jack
I learn him how to play Didn't He Ramble
Then I learn him to play Didn't He Ramble
And then music become easy to him—
By head, by ear.
And Louis could play anything that he could whistle.
And then, a short while after that
Well, Louis would get arrested for goin' in the Basin Swimmin';
So when he went to Jones' Home, Louis could play.
He didn't learn at Jones' Home.
He learned with Bunk.
And he'll tell you.

And the next trumpet player was Buddy Petit.
Buddy was workin' at the glass factory.
I were livin' on Marigny between Robertson and Villere where
    Buddy used to take lessons with me.
Couldn't hold a horn.
I showed him how to hold it and he really went good.
And to execute on it.
And Chris Kelly's another one.
Me and Chris were workin' at Empire Rice Mill—
We'd knock off at the rice mill—
We'd go down on Toulouse and Burgundy to my mother's.
He'd take lessons there with me.
I learned Chris.

Then, in 1914, I were teachin' a band at Mandeville, Louisiana.
Tommy Ladnier. I taught Tommy.

First piece I learned Tommy Ladnier to play was Big Chief Battle
    Axe
And then Tommy turned out to be real good.
And Louis Dumaine, he was in the uptown section,
I taught Louis.
Also Joe Nicholas, called him Wooden Joe. I taught . . ."
(By the way, Bunk, you didn't tell us about King Oliver yet.)
"That's right.
About King Oliver, you sure is right.
I didn't mention that.
Well, Joe, I didn't start Joe.
Joe started with old man Kenchen.
Old man Kenchen started a band,
And after old man Kenchen died
George McCullons taken the band and Joe could play very little
    on cornet.
And then we begin goin'—me and Brundy, Walter Brundy—begin
    goin' to Second and Magazine where Joe was workin'
And I used to teach Joe there.
I used to help Joe.
Joe used to follow me in the street also—all parades.
Big a man as Joe was,
Joe was second line, like the rest, like Louis,
And follow me and follow me.
And we used to go to Second and Magazine and I was teachin' him.
Joe would buy music that he was unable to play
I'd make Brundy talk to Joe Oliver while I steal the music
And I'd bring it to the Superior Band and play.
And Joe asked me that in his last letter that I received from Joe
Well, that's about thirteen years ago.
I have that letter yet.
That letter's in Cleveland, Miss Mary has that.
She 'clared that she would take a copy of it and send it to me.
And I'm a few years older than Joe.
But Joe didn't really git well on cornet until he crossed Canal Street.
Joe begin playin' in the District in Manuel's place.
He played in the Superior Band in my place on engagements,
Played dance halls in my place.

When I quit Mr. Pete Lala's cabaret
Well, Joe taken that job with Sidney Bechet
And Joe begin gettin' really good then,
And he was workin' in the District every night
And playin' with Manuel Perez in the Onward Brass Band.
And Joe always did like my style of playin'
And mentioned in his letter how I played blues
How low and how wicked.
And he was crazy to learn the blues.
Joe really could play the blues in a short while.
And Joe became good 'til he went North.
And also Kid Punch.
Kid Punch was another one.
Punch used to follow me, too.
All of them was crazy behind old man Bunk's playin'.
I had a outstanding style of playin' from every man in town.
Played my own style
Just my thoughts
Used my ideas about it.
'Course I would listen at other cornet players play,
I take their ideas and put it with mine
Made me have greater ideas.
And I found out that I was 'bout toppin' all of them.
Everybody like my style of playin' and still can play now.
And I'm mighty proud to say that the men I taught made good.
Joe went North and made good,
Louis went North and made good
Tommy Ladnier went North and made good—he played with Louis
And the old man is still hittin' that horn.
I really can play yet myself.
And I think that the records I made's gon' come out real fine."

LETTERS FROM BUNK JOHNSON

To Frederic Ramsey, Jr., 1939, 1940

Dear Friend,

I am here, only making out now. For work, we have work only when rice harvest is in, and, that over, things go real dead until cane harvest. I drive a truck and trailer and that only pays me $1.75 a day and that do not last very long. So you all know for sure how much money that I make now. I made up my mind to work hard until I die as I have no one to tell my troubles to, and my children cannot help me out in this case. I have been real down for about five years. My teeth went bad in 1934, so that was my finish playing music. I am just about to give it up. Now I haven't got no other way to go but put my shoulder to the wheel and my nose to the grinding stone and put my music down.

Now for the taking of the picture of mine, you can have one or six. Now six will cost five dollars, and if you care to pay for the six, I will be glad because Armstrong wants one. I would like to give Williams one, Foster one, Bechet one, and I would like to keep one, which would be the six. Now, if you only want me to take one, I will do so. So, you can send me what you think about it, for one or six. Now, if there is some things you would want to know about music, please let me know when you answer.

Willie Bunk Johnson

My dear kind friends,

Only a few words I want to say to you about my delay in sending you these pictures and these letters. Now, I'm pretty sure that you all know just how everything is down South with the poor colored man. The service here is really poor for colored people. We have no colored studios. This is a Cajun town and, in these little country towns, you don't have a chance like the white man, so you

just have to stand back and wait until your turn come. That is just the way here. So please do not think hard of me. You think hard of the other fellow.

You all do your very best for me and try to get me on my feet once more in life. Now, here is just what I mean when I say the word, "on my feet." I mean this: I wants to become able to play trumpet once more, as I know I can really stomp trumpet yet. Now, here is what it takes to stomp trumpet, that is a real good set of teeth. And that is just what I am in deep need of. Teeth and a good trumpet and old Bunk can really go. Now, my friends, the shape that I am in at the present time I cannot help myself, so you all can judge that. Now, as I said before, that this town is very dead and it is real tough on a poor man when he do get in the shape I am in. Now, I have the very best of health and nothing but good clothes. Old Bunk is only in need for a set of teeth and a good job. Now, I truly thank you for the treat of the money. They come in need time. I did not have a penny in my house or no place else. Do tell my dear pal, Clarence Williams, to write me and to send a few late numbers of his. Now, I cannot play them but I can think them. O Boy, that will make me feel good anyway. If I have not got no teeth I can have something to look at when I get to thinking about the shape I am in and have no good way to go but work, just as I could get it, some weeks nothing at all. Now, you tell Louis to please send me a trumpet, as he told me that he would, and you all do your best for me. From a good old, kind friend, as ever, and will always be so, so answer me at once.

Willie Bunk Johnson

BUNK JOHNSON RUMINATES

When I came back to music and was out in San Francisco in 1943, Harry James was playin' at the Civics Auditorium. I knew his papa, a fine man, bandmaster in the circus.

Young Harry says to me, "Pops, I don't have to tell you. You and Louis, only men that can play this horn." That was real nice

of young Harry, but he play real good trumpet himself. I told him so. Never catch a real good musician knock a musician.

Take my boy Louis. Anybody in this world knows any more about playin' that trumpet than Louis Armstrong—show him to me. And I'll show the doubter! I'll run 'im! And if I can't run 'im —Man, I'll sure talk him down!

You should see some of those old fellows down in New Orleans I grew up with. My, they're old! Shuffling along, can't remember nothin'. Couldn't play a chorus to save their life. Whiskey got some of them. Whiskey heads are all dead! Bunk is still here!

When I look back over the objects in my life, why I can remember back to when there was no discrimination in Louisiana. When I was a boy you got on a mule car in New Orleans and walk up and put your nickle in the bandbox and sat down. Discrimination came in 1889. Too much prejudice in the South since then. And I've played music for white people all over the world and many of my best friends are white. But there's always somebody who'll come up and say to you, "Hey, nigger, play this."

POPS FOSTER ON OLIVER

YES, I remember King Oliver. He was a happy-go-lucky guy. He liked to play pool all day long, and baseball. He would eat a lot. We would order one or two hamburger sandwiches, and he would eat a dozen at a time, and a quart of milk. He got along fine with the fellows—always playing, and kidding.

JOE OLIVER

POPS, breaks come to cats in this racket only once in a while and I guess I must have been asleep when mine came. I've made lots of dough in this game but I didn't know how to take care of it. I have

been under the best management in the country but didn't know how to stay under it.

I have helped to make some of the best names in the music game, but I am too much of a man to ask those that I have helped to help me. Some of the guys that I have helped are responsible for my downfall in a way. I am the guy who took a pop bottle and a rubber plunger and made the first mute ever used in a horn, but I didn't know how to get the patent for it and some educated cat came along and made a fortune off of my idea. I have written a lot of numbers that someone else got the credit and the money for. I couldn't help it because I didn't know what to do.

I am in terrible shape now. I am getting old and my health is failing. Doctors advised me a long time ago to give up and quit but I can't. I don't have any money and I can't do anything else, so here I am.

I have been under management of both colored and white bookers in the last few years and I haven't had one yet to deal fair with me. I had one booker who collected deposits on all the dates I played for him and skipped out. I had another who bought a bus for my band and had me sign papers that put all the fellows' instruments under mortgage. I gave him money to make the payments and he kept it for personal use. The company took the bus and the instruments, but I pleaded with the manager to let me keep the instruments and told him how I had been gypped, and he opened up his heart and gave back the instruments. After this we made jobs for a week in a coal truck, as we didn't have enough money to rent cars or bus. Then my band broke up, and I had contracts for some very nice jobs so I was lucky enough to get Maurice Morrison and his band to fill the dates for me until I got another band together. Things changed a little for me after this. I got a new and better band and a bus and headed south for Florida, where I became the victim of another crooked booker and my band broke up by degrees. I played my last job under him with four men, including myself. I then went to Georgia and organized another band, the band I have now, and if you don't do something to help me I will lose them.

LETTERS FROM JOE OLIVER TO HIS SISTER

Savannah, Georgia November, 1937

Dear Sister:
  I'm still out of work. Since the road house closed I haven't hit a
note. But I've got a lot to thank God for. Because I eat and sleep.
Look like every time one door close the Good Lord open another.
I've got to do my own cooking, as my landlady and daughter both
work out. I am doing pretty fair. But I much rather work and earn
my own money. Soon as the weather can fit my clothes I know I
can do better in New York.

Joe

Dear Sister:
  I received your letter which found me well and getting along
pretty nice. I looked up another job. With little money. If hours
was money I'd be drawing more money than Babe Ruth at his best.
We are still having nice weather here. The Lord is sure good to me
here without an overcoat. I have to see by lamp here. *Smile.*

Sincerely yours, Brother

Sunday Evening

Dear Sister:
  Well I hope you don't feel like I am lying down on you. I put
in such long hours until I don't feel anything like looking at a bottle of ink or picking up my pen and you know I'm one who love
to write. But I am going to see to you hearing from me often. I
will get some cards when I go to town and will be able to drop
you a card from the place. I am feeling pretty good, but just can't
get rid of this cough. Don't like that sticking on me so long. I just

can't get rid of it. I've tried most everything. My heart don't bother me just a little at times. But my breath is still short, and I'm not at all fat . . .

I would like to live as long as I can, but nothing like making all arrangements in time. Don't think I will ever raise enough money to buy a ticket to New York.

I am not the one to give up quick. If I was I don't know where I would be today. I always feel like I've got a chance. I still feel I'm going to snap out of the rut I've been in for several years. What makes me feel optimistic at times. Looks like every time one door close on me another door open. Look how many teeth I had taken out and replaced. I got teeth waiting for me at the dentist now. I've started a little dime bank saving. Got $1.60 in it and won't touch it. I am going to try and save myself a ticket to New York.

Joe

Dear Sister:

I open the pool rooms at 9 a.m. and close at 12 midnite. If the money was only ¼ as much as the hours I'd be all set. But at that I can thank God for what I am getting. Which I do night after night. I know you will be glad when the winter say goodby.

Now Vick before I go further with my letter I'm going to tell you something but don't be alarmed. I've got high blood pressure. Was taking treatment but had to discontinue. My blood was 85 above normal. Now my blood has started again and I am unable to take treatments because it cost $3.00 per treatment and I don't make enough money to continue my treatments. Now it begins to work on my heart. I am weak in my limbs at times and my breath but I am not asking you for money or anything. A stitch in time saves nine. Should anything happen to me will you want my body? Let me know because I won't last forever and the longer I go the worst I'll get unless I take treatments.

It's not like New York or Chicago here. You've got to go through a lot of red tape to get any kind of treatment from the city here. I may never see New York again in life. . . .

Don't think I'm afraid because I wrote what I did. I am trying to

live near to the Lord than ever before. So I feel like the Good Lord will take care of me. Good night, dear . . .

Joe

EDITOR'S NOTE: *Joe Oliver died on April 10, 1938*

BUSTER BAILEY ON OLIVER

JOE King Oliver was an important figure at that time. He was an eating guy for sure. He was also a good guy, sort of sensitive in a way. He liked to joke a lot; he liked to play the "dozens" (talk about your parents and all in a joking way—it was a way of trying to get each other's goat). King Oliver was a great musician with a mute. With an ordinary tin mute, he could make the horn talk.

Joe was a jealous guy. He knew what some of the musicians who came to listen were after, and so he wouldn't play certain numbers. But they'd come in and sneak in and steal the riffs. They'd write down the solos, steal like mad, and then those ideas would come out on *their* records. When Joe would see them coming, he'd play something different, but they'd steal everything.

Some guys would come in to sit in with you and learn what you were doing. We'd call them alligators. That was our tip-off word, because they were guys who came up to swallow everything we had to learn.

RICHARD M. JONES ON OLIVER

JOE had been afraid of Keppard and Perez in New Orleans—he didn't have much confidence. He worked as a butler. Practically overnight, he woke up and started playing. He was a good reader and a good technician. Anything you'd stick up, he'd wipe it right off.

LOUIS ARMSTRONG ON OLIVER

HE WOULD have been *big,* because there wasn't nobody doing nothing except Joe Oliver in those days. Bunk hadn't even been heard of; he was down there in the cotton fields wrestling with those bales, and forgot all about trumpet. They tried to get Joe to come to New York when he got hot, but he wouldn't come. And all the time the cats were coming out from New York with those big shows and picking up on what he was playing. Joe Oliver was *the* man in Chicago. But he came to New York too late. When he got there, everybody was playing him. Even I had been here long before him. And it was all his own fault, too, because he had Chicago sewed up. The agents and everybody coming from New York had wanted to bring him in someplace, *any* night club, with his band. But Joe wouldn't leave. "I'm doing all right here, man," he'd tell them. He had good jobs with good tips. So time ran out on him. He looked around, and when he came to New York—too late.

From then on he began to get what I guess you would call a broken heart. When you wind up playing with little old Musicians down in some place like Tampa, Florida, with cats that didn't even know him . . . And if you lay off for two days, the band breaks up. And the landlady commenced to hold his trunks. I saw him at that time; it was in Savannah, when I was on some one-nighters, and as far as I'm concerned that's what killed him—a broken heart. That's what killed Joe Oliver.

I was with him until they buried him; I was at his funeral. Most of the musicians turned out. The people who really knew him didn't forget him. It would have been nice if they'd had a parade for him, but instead they took him into the chapel across from the Lafayette—that big rehearsal hall in Harlem. I didn't like the sermon the preacher gave. Just because the Guild buried him was no reason for rubbing it in. They said he made money, and he had money, and didn't keep it. The Guild isn't supposed to say that; that's what we donate our services for when they give benefits. A

lot of us didn't like that sermon, and even after all these years I still don't like to think about it.

He was a great man. I'll always remember him. But I don't care to remember him in Savannah, or the funeral. I'd rather think about a time like 1928, when I played two nights with Luis Russell's band at the Savoy, as a guest. Joe Oliver was there each night, with a new set of clothes, and that Panama hat like he usually wore. And he looked pleasant and happy. He was standing right in front of that trumpet. That was a thrill. I had run errands for his wife; he had brought me up to Chicago. And he stood there listening, with the tears coming right out of his eyes. It knocked me out.

LOUIS ARMSTRONG SPEAKS

In 1922, when King Joe Oliver, the trumpet man of those days, sent for me to leave New Orleans and join him at the Lincoln Gardens to play second trumpet to his first trumpet, I jumped sky-high with joy. The day I received the telegram from Papa Joe, that's what I called him, I was playing a funeral in New Orleans and all the members in the Tuxedo Brass Band told me not to go because Joe Oliver and his boys were having some kind of union trouble.

When the Tuxedo Brass Band boys told me that Joe Oliver and his band were scabbing, I told them the King had sent for me, it didn't matter with me what he was doing. I was going to him just the same. So I went.

I arrived in Chicago about eleven o'clock the night of July 8th, 1922, I'll never forget it, at the Illinois Central Station at Twelfth and Michigan Avenue. The King was already at work. I had no one to meet me. I took a cab and went directly to the Gardens.

When I was getting out of the cab and paying the driver, I could hear the King's band playing some kind of a real jump number. Believe me, they were really jumpin' in fine fashion. I said to myself, "My Gawd, I wonder if I'm good enough to play in that band." I hesitated about going inside right away, but finally I did.

When I got inside and near the bandstand, King Oliver spied

me. He immediately stopped the band to greet me, saying, "Boy,
where have you been? I've been waiting and waiting for you."
Well, I did miss the train that the King thought I should have been
on. They went into another hot number. In that band were King
Oliver, trumpet; Johnny Dodds, clarinet; Honore Dutrey, trombone; Baby Dodds, drums; Bill Johnson, bass; Lillian Hardin,
piano, of course she became Mrs. "Satchmo" Louis Armstrong later,
(tee hee).

When I joined the band on second trumpet I made the seventh
member. Those were some thrilling days of my life I shall never
forget. I came to work the next night. During my first night on the
job, while things were going down in order, King and I stumbled
upon a little something that no other two trumpeters together ever
thought of. While the band was just swinging, the King would lean
over to me, moving his valves on his trumpet, make notes, the notes
that he was going to make when the break in the tune came. I'd
listen, and at the same time, I'd be figuring out my second to his
lead. When the break would come, I'd have my part to blend right
along with his. The crowd would go mad over it!

King Oliver and I got so popular blending that jive together that
pretty soon all the white musicians from downtown Chicago would
all come there after their work and stay until the place closed. Sometimes they would sit in with us to get their kicks. Lillian was
doubling from the Lincoln Gardens to the Edelweiss Gardens, an
after-hours place. After our work I would go out there with her.
Doing this, she and I became regular running buddies, and we
would go to all the other places when we had the time. She knew
Chicago like a book. I'll never forget the first time Lil took me to
the Dreamland Cabaret on Thirty-fifth and State Streets to hear
Ollie Powers and Mae Alix sing. Ollie had one of those high, sweet
singing voices, and when he would sing songs like *What'll I Do?*
he would really rock the whole house. Mae Alix had one of those
fine, strong voices that everyone would also want to hear. Then she
would go into her splits, and the customers would throw paper
dollars on the floor, and she would make one of those running
splits, picking them up one at a time.

I asked Lil if it was all right to give Ollie and Mae a dollar each
to sing a song for me. She said sure, it was perfectly all right. She

called them over and introduced them to me as the new trumpet man in King Oliver's band. Gee whiz! I really thought I was somebody meeting those fine stars. I followed Ollie Powers everywhere he sang, until the day he died. At his funeral I played a trumpet solo in the church where they had his body laying out for the last time. Ump, what a sad day that was. Mae Alix is still a singing barmaid and as popular as ever.

Speaking of the Lincoln Gardens, I had been playing there about two or three months, when one night, just as we were getting ready to hit the show, we all noticed a real stout lady, with bundles in her hands, cutting across the dance floor. To my surprise it was my mother, May Ann. The funny thing about it is that King Oliver had been kidding me that he was my stepfather, for years and years. When he saw May Ann (tee hee) he didn't know her. We kind of stalled the show so I could greet my dear mother, with a great big kiss, of course. Then I said to her, "Mamma, what on earth are you doing up here in Chicago?" May Ann said, "Lawd, chile, somebody came to New Orleans and told me that you were up here in this North awfully low sick and starving to death." I told mother, "Aw, Mamma, how could I starve when I'm eating at King Oliver's house every day, and you know how Mrs. Stella Oliver (King's wonderful wife) piles up King's plate, full of red beans and rice. Well, she fills mine the same way. Now, how could I starve?" May Ann said when she asked this man who told her the false bad news, "Why in the world didn't my son come back home to New Orleans when things began to break so bad for him?" this guy told her all I could do was to hang my head and cry. Tch, tch, such lies. I was fat as a butterball.

I took my mother to the house where I was rooming and then went out and brought her a lot of fine vines, a wardrobe with nothing but the finest—from head to foot. Oh, she was sharp! . . .

Chicago was really jumping around that time (1923). The Dreamland was in full bloom. The Lincoln Gardens, of course, was still in there. The Plantation was another hot spot at that time. But the Sunset, my boss' place, was the sharpest of them all, believe that. A lot of after-hour spots were real groovy, too. There was the Apex, where Jimmie Noone and that great piano man, Hines, started all this fine stuff your 'yars listen to nowadays. They made history

right there in the Apex. The tune, *Sweet Lorraine,* used to gas everybody there nightly. I was one of the everybodies.

They had a place on State Street called the Fiume where they had a small ofay band, right in the heart of the South Side. They were really fine. All the musicians, nightlifers, and everybody plunged in there in the wee hours of the morning and had a grand time. I used to meet a lot of the boys there after we would finish at the Lincoln Gardens. That's where I first met Darnell Howard, former sax man with "Fatha" Hines. He was playing the violin at that time with Charles Elgar's orchestra over on the West Side at Harmon's Dreamland Ballroom. Darnell was weighing one hundred and sixty-five pounds then. Of course, he has accumulated a little bread-basket since then, but still sharp.

King Oliver received an offer to go on the road and make some one-night stands at real good money. Ump! That got it. The band almost busted up. Half of the boys just wouldn't go, that's all. The same situation hits bandleaders square in the face these days, the same as then. The King replaced every man that wouldn't go. As for me, anything King did was all right with me. My heart was out for him at all times—until the day he died and even now. The tour was great. We had lots of fun and made lots of money.

At the Dreamland, in 1925, we had some fine moments. Some real jumping acts. There was the team of Brown and McGraw. They did a jazz dance that just wouldn't quit. I'd blow for their act, and every step they made, I put the notes to it. They liked the idea so well they had it arranged. Benny and Harry Goodman used to come out and set in and tear up the joint when they were real young. P.S., the boys have been hep for a long time. While at the Dreamland, Professor Erskine Tate asked me (ahem) to join his Symphony Orchestra. I wouldn't take a million for that experience. The Professor's Orchestra played hot music as well as overtures.

Things were jumping so around Chicago at that time, there was more work than a cat could shake a stick at. I was doubling from the Dreamland for awhile. Then I stayed at the Vendome for only a year before I decided to double again.

Then came Carroll Dickerson, the leader who had that fine band at the Sunset Cafe, owned by my boss, Mr. Joe Glaser. He hired me to double from the Vendome Theatre. After the theater I'd go

over to the Sunset, at Thirty-fifth and Calument Streets, and swing there with them until the wee hours of the morning. 'Twas great, I'll tell you. In that band there were *the* Earl Hines, Darnell Howard, Tubby Hall, Honore Dutrey, and Boyd Atkins, who wrote the tune called Heebie Jeebies.

The Sunset had Charleston contests on Friday night, and you couldn't get in the place unless you got there early. We had a great show in those days with Buck'n' Bubbles, Rector and Cooper, Edith Spencer and Mae Alix, my favorite entertainer, and a gang of now famous stars. We had a finale that just wouldn't quit.

The Charleston was popular at that time (1926) until Percy Venable, the producer of the show, staged a finale with four of us band boys closing the show doing the Charleston. That was really something. There was Earl Hines, as tall as he is; Tubby Hall, as fat as he was; little Joe Walker, as short as he is; and myself, as fat as I was at that time. We would stretch out across that floor doing the Charleston as fast as the music would play it. Boy, oh boy, you talking about four cats picking them up and laying them down— that was us. We stayed there until old boss man got tired of looking at us. Ha, ha.

Things moved out further on the South Side of Chicago. The Metropolitan Theatre was running in full bloom with Sammy Stewart's orchestra out of Columbus, Ohio, holding sway. After Sammy, came Clarence Jones' orchestra. That's where I came in again.

On the drums in this orchestra was my boy, Zutty Singleton. We would play an overture and then run into a hot tune. Sometimes Zutty, he's funny anyway, would dress up as one of those real loud and rough gals, with a short skirt, and a pillow in back of him. I was dressed in old rags, the beak of my cap turned around like a tough guy, and he, or she (Zutty) was my gal. As he would come down the aisle, interrupting my song, the people would just scream with laughter. Zutty and I played together pretty nearly all our lives. Chicago and New Orleans. We have seen some pretty tough days right there in Chicago. Also my other boy, Earl Hines. But, we kept our heads up, believe that.

The time the Savoy opened (1927), Earl Hines, Zutty, and myself had leased the Warwick Hall on Forty-seventh Street, just around

the corner from the Savoy. They had such an opening that we never did get a chance to open our place. Ump! There we were with a years' lease on our hands and no place to get the rent. We decided to hustle. We gave a dance on the West Side of Chicago. The dance turned out to be a success. After all, the three of us were rather popular. With the three of us playing in those famous bands such as Erskine Tate, Dave Payton, and Clarence Jones in those theaters, the folks came to hear us dish that mess out.

Earl went back to the Apex and Zutty and I joined Carroll Dickerson again. This time Carroll had the job at the Savoy Ballroom which had just opened. The place was jumping, and we three paid off the lease at the Warwick Hall. The real estate people gave us a break and threw the whole thing out for a hundred and fifty dollars. Then we could breathe again . . .

All in all, the 'twenties in Chicago were some of my finest days. From 1922 to 1929, I spent my youngest and best days there. I married Lillian and Alpha there. Of course, my first wife was Daisy. We stepped off into that deep water in New Orleans, way back in 1918. Lil, my second and Alpha, my third, we did the thing (married) in Chicago. My fourth madam, Lucille, and I were married at Velma Middleton's mother's house in St. Louis, Missouri. Looks like this is it. She's still on the mound and holding things down. Oh, but she is.

Along about the latter part of 1923, I received a telegram to go to New York to join the great Fletcher Henderson's orchestra. That's how I felt about "Smack" Henderson, years before I had seen him in person, from recordings he made for years by himself, with Ethel Waters and Revela Hughes. He had the first big colored band that hit the road and tore it up. When I explained to the King that it was my one big chance to see New York, where people there really *do things,* he dug me. I knew he would and he released me so I could knock it.

When I arrived in New York I had to go straight to rehearsal. And don't you know that when I got into that rehearsal, I felt so funny. I walked up to old "Smack" and said "Er, wa, I'm that boy you sent for to blow the trumpet in your band." And "Smack," all sharp as a Norwegian with that hard-hitting steel-gray suit he had on, said, "Oh, yes, we're waiting for you. Your part's up there"

(meaning the bandstand). I said, "Yassuh," and went on up there with my eyes closed. When I opened them I looked square into the faces of Coleman Hawkins, Don Redman, Kaiser Marshall, Long Green, Escudero, Scotty, Elmer "Muffle Jaws" Chambers, and Charles Dixon.

They all casually looked out of the corner of their eyes. You know how they do when a new man joins a band, they want to be real friendly right off the bat. But they'd rather hear you play first. I said to myself these boys look like a bunch of nice fellows, but they seem a little stuckup. That was the opinion I had of them right off the reel. I guess they had theirs about me, too. Where I had come from I wasn't used to playing in bands where there were a lot of parts for everybody to read. Shucks, all one man in the band had to do was to go to some show and hear a good number. He keeps it in his head until he reaches us. He hums it a couple of times, and from then on we had a new number to throw on the bands that were advertising in the wagons on the corner the following Sunday. That's how we stayed so famous down in New Orleans. We had a new number for the customers every week. Now I was in New York getting ready to join the biggest band in New York at the time. We played the first number down. The name of the tune was *By the Waters of Minnetonka*. I had the third trumpet part, which was so pretty.

Still nobody said anything. Finally, one of the boys said something to Long Boy Charlie Green, the great trombone man. Oh yea, it was Escudero, the tuba great. Escudero was a devilish sort of fellow, and it seemed he got a great bang out of teasing Green. I didn't know all this. Anyway, Escudero leaned over and played Green's trombone part, note for note, on his tuba. Ump! You never heard such language in all your life. I commenced to relax—you know—feeling at home. The boys didn't really hear me *tear out* until one night we all were mugging on *Tiger Rag,* and believe me, it was on.

My manager and agent sent for me to come to New York alone, to join that big show which was in rehearsal at that time called GREAT DAY. Instead of my going alone, I took the whole Carroll Dickerson band with me. We were so attached, we just wouldn't part from each other. I borrowed twenty dollars apiece for every

man in the band and myself. We had about four old dilapidated cars among us. We just piled in them and went on to New York. On our way we went sightseeing, stopping in a lot of towns where they had been listening to us over the radio from the Savoy in Chicago. They treated us royally. Our money was counterfeit.

We arrived in Buffalo, New York, and went forty miles out of the way to dig Niagara Falls. Half of the cars didn't reach the "Apple" (New York). They burned out before they reached half-way there. Of course, my agent bawled me out, but I told him, "just the same, my boys are here in New York, so find something for us to do." He did. We opened at Connie's Inn and stayed there six months. All the musicians came up and gave me a very beautiful wrist watch. Every musician from downtown was there that night. What a memory of those fine days.

Our engagement at the Roseland was great. Our road tour was the same. I stayed with "Smack" Henderson until way up until 1926. Lil, my wife at the time, had the band at the Dreamland Cabaret in Chicago, and suggested that I come home because it was easier for us to starve together than be apart so long. Then I was a little homesick too. So, I cut out from those fine boys who treated me just swell. We all are just as glad to see each other right now as we were in those days.

LIL ARMSTRONG RECALLS

IN THE summer of 1918, my folks moved from Memphis to Chicago, and I made it my business to go out for a daily stroll and look this "heaven" over. Chicago meant just that to me—its beautiful brick and stone buildings, excitement, people moving swiftly, and things happening. On one of these strolls, I came to a music store on South State Street (Jones' Music Store). I stopped and gazed at all the sheet music in the window display, wishing I had every one of them, but, knowing how impossible that was, I decided to go in and buy one that I had heard so many people whistling on the street.

I hummed it over to the salesman (Frank Clemons), and he sat down and played it over for me. Well, he didn't play it well, so I asked him if I might try it over. He readily consented and was very surprised that I played at sight as well as adding something to it. When I finished, he had me try out other numbers and then asked if I'd like the job of demonstrating music. I told him I'd go home to get my mother's consent and return later to see the boss.

I didn't *stroll*, I *ran* all the way home to break the news to Mother. Oh, but was Mother indignant. "The very idea, work! And above all things, for only three dollars a week! I should say not, young lady," she said.

Well, in no time at all I sold her the idea, just to learn all the music and have something to do until time to return to school. Off I went to work the next morning, thrilled beyond words over my first job.

As soon as I got to the music store, I got busy playing all the music on the counter, and by two p.m. the place was packed with people listening to the "Jazz Wonder Child." I played on and on, all the music there, all my classics. My, what a thrill. No wonder the people called me child, I looked to be about ten years old in my middy blouse and eighty-five pounds.

Mrs. Jones ran an employment and booking agency at the store, so all the musicians and entertainers hung out there. They'd rehearse, sit around, and gossip for hours. Almost every day there was a jam session and I took charge of every piano player that dared to come in.

But one day the great Jelly Roll Morton from New Orleans came in and I was in for a little trouble. I had never heard such music before, they were all his original tunes. Jelly Roll sat down, the piano rocked, the floor shivered, the people swayed while he ferociously attacked the keyboard with his long skinny fingers, beating out a double rhythm with his feet on the loud pedal. I was thrilled, amazed, and scared. Well, he finally got up from the piano, grinned, and looked at me as if to say, "Let this be a lesson to you."

It was indeed a lesson because from then on when I played, all eighty-five pounds of me played. But do you think the people were satisfied? No, they wanted Jelly Roll to hear me play . . . Well, I'm really in for it, and, suddenly remembering that he had played

nothing classical, I sat down to the piano very confidently, played some Bach, Chopin, and the Witches' Dance, which they especially liked. The session ended with me still the winner.

The following week the New Orleans Creole Jazz Band came in town and gave an audition for Mrs. Jones. When they started out on the *Livery Stable Blues* I nearly had a fit. I had never heard a band like that; they made goose pimples break out all over me. I'm telling you they played loud and long and got the biggest kick out of the fits I was having over their music. Mrs. Jones booked them at a Chinese restaurant on the North Side immediately.

The band consisted of violin, clarinet, cornet, trombone, bass, and drums, so they had to add a piano player to accompany the girl singer. Mrs. Jones sent several men pianists but none proved satisfactory, so Frank Clemons suggested that she send me over just for one night to see what would happen. She argued that I was a minor and would not be allowed to play in a cabaret, but she took a chance anyway, and off I went thrilled again.

When I sat down to play I asked for the music and were they surprised! They politely told me they didn't have any music and furthermore never used any. I then asked what key would the first number be in. I must have been speaking another language because the leader said, "When you hear two knocks, just start playing."

It all seemed very strange to me, but I got all set, and when I heard those two knocks I hit the piano so loud and hard they all turned around to look at me. It took only a second for me to feel what they were playing and I was off. The New Orleans Creole Jazz Band hired me, and I never got back to the music store— Never got back to *Fisk University*.

Four weeks later we were playing at the De Luxe Cafe (Thirty-fifth and State) and I was making the unheard of salary of twenty-seven fifty weekly besides twenty dollars a night in tips.

The members of this band were Sugar Johnny (cornet), a long, lanky, dark man with deep little holes in his skinny face. He never had too much to say and I wondered about that, but how was I to know he was dying on his feet with T.B.? Couldn't tell by his playing. Lawrence Dewey (clarinet), he was skinny too, but much lighter in color and always smiling. Roy Palmer (trombone), was

the darkest one, but jolly and happy-go-lucky. Violinist Jimmie Palao (a decided Creole with his olive complexion and straight hair) was skinny and coughed all the time. He died with T.B. also. The bassist was Eddie Garland, who was the healthiest of the skinny ones. Tubby Hall (drums) was as fat as the others were skinny, and the youngest of the band that left New Orleans to make Jazz history.

The band was a sensation from the first night at the De Luxe Cafe, so much so that there were no available seats after nine p.m. and a line waiting outside that kept King Jones yelling to the high heavens to tell them that soon there would be seats.

Sugar Johnny played a growling cornet style, using cups and old hats to make all kinds of funny noises. Dewey's clarinet squeaked and rasped with his uneven scales and trills. Roy was sliding back and forth on the trombone, making a growling accompaniment to Sugar Johnny's breaks. Jimmie's violin sighed and wheezed while he scratched the strings with his bow. To top all this, Montudi Tubby and I beat out a background rhythm that put the Bechuana tribes of Africa to shame.

But this was New Orleans jazz, and the people ate it up. Ah, what fun! Everybody in town falling in to dig us. No dancing, just listen and be sent. De Luxe Cafe . . . deluxe business . . . deluxe jazz by the New Orleans Creole Jazz Band.

PRESTON JACKSON'S MEMORIES

I FEEL that if it wasn't for Lil, Louis would not be where he is today. She inspired him to do bigger and better things. Lil is the cause of Louis leaving Joe Oliver's band, where he was playing second trumpet, and going out for himself, and thereby gaining a little recognition. At that time, Lil and Louis were pianist and cornetist, respectively, with Joe Oliver.

Now I will tell you of my first experience with Lil. I first saw her demonstrating music at Jones Music Store in Chicago. Lil was just a young miss then but how she could swing, yes, I mean

swing, no ragtime. Lot of people think that Benny Goodman was first to play swing music, but we all know that Benny studied under Jimmie Noone, the master. Getting back to Lil, she only received three dollars a week on her first job, but I knew she wouldn't be there long, no, man, not with all that piano she was swinging. One month later she joined the New Orleans Creole Band with such men as Freddie Keppard, Ed Garland, Paul Barbarin, Jimmie Noone, and Eddie Vincent. She received fifty-five dollars per week, what a difference in salary. Man, Lil didn't know how much she could swing.

Later Lil had her own band at Dreamland Cafe, 3520 State Street, and was there five years. Joe Oliver came there from New Orleans, heard Lil play, and paid her more money than she had ever earned to join his band. That was in 1921. Joe had been there since 1918. Every band that could play anything was from New Orleans. Sidney Bechet was with the New Orleans Creole Band; Johnny Dodds was with Joe Oliver's band and mentioned Lil being responsible for Louis leaving Joe.

There were a lot of keen youngsters around Chicago in those days. Buster Bailey was a kid just beginning, while Tommy Ladnier was only just starting out. I didn't play anything then, but was thinking of taking the clarinet. I used to sit on the bandstand all night, listening.

At that time we used to hang around Joe Oliver's band on off nights. Joe was at Royal Gardens then and coaching Louis Panico, Isham Jones' cornetist. Joe's band was probably at its peak then with Johnny Dodds on clary; bother Baby Dodds drumming; Honore Dutrey, trombone; Bill Johnson, bass; little Lil Hardin on the ivory.

I used to sit behind Dutrey every night and watch him play cello parts all night long because cello parts were easier to get than trombone music. Other musicians were considered out of the ordinary if they could play just one cello part. Dutrey was wonderful about showing me fine points on the horn. I learned lots from him.

That band just went mad when they played. Usually fast stuff, the Garden was a turmoil and a tumult from the start of the evening until the last note died away. Why! I thought they'd blow

the roof off the place for dead sure, especially after Louis Armstrong joined the band.

I'll never forget the day he came into town (about 1920 or 1921). He wore a brown box-back coat, straw hat, and tan shoes. We called him Dippermouth. Satchmo was unheard of then. Well, Louis played a horn like nobody had ever heard. He and Joe were wonderful together. I had heard Louis play before in 1915 at a play-ground dedication when the Jones Waif Band featured Louis and Henry Rena. Louis was terrific even then. I was going to the school where the playground was. That's how I happened to hear him.

MEZZROW ON BESSIE SMITH

BESSIE SMITH had such a ringing vibration in that voice of hers, and her tones boomed out so clear and clanging full, you could hear her singing all the way down the street. There was a traffic jam out in front of that cafe; cats and their kittens blocked up the sidewalk, hypnotized by the walloping blues that came throbbing out of Bessie's throat. She was putting away *Young Woman Blues,* one of her greatest numbers, when we eased in.

Dave and I just melted together in the blaze of Bessie's singing; that wasn't a voice she had, it was a flame-thrower licking out across the room. Right after that Bessie launched into another one of the numbers that made her famous, *Reckless Blues.*

Bessie was a real woman, all woman, all the femaleness the world ever saw in one sweet package. She was tall and brownskinned, with great big dimples creasing her cheeks, dripping good looks— just this side of voluptuous, buxom and massive but stately too, shapely as a hour-glass, with a high-voltage magnet for a personality. When she was in a room her vitality flowed out like a cloud and stuffed the air till the walls bulged. She didn't have any mannerisms, she never needed any twirls and twitches to send those golden notes of hers on their sunshiny way. She just stood there and sang, letting the love and the laughter run out of her, and the heaving sadness

too; she felt everything and swayed just a little with the glory of being alive and feeling, and once in a while, with a grace that made you want to laugh and cry all at once, she made an eloquent little gesture with her hand. Bessie maybe never practised her scales in any conservatory of music, wrestling with arpeggios, but she was an artist right down to her fingertips—a very great artist, born with silver strings for vocal cords and a foaming, churning soul to keep them a-quiver.

Her style was so individual that nobody else every grasped it. The way she let her rich music tumble out was a perfect example of improvisation—the melody meant nothing to her, she made up her own melody to fit the poetry of her story, phrasing all around the original tune if it wasn't just right, making the vowels come out just the right length, dropping the consonants that might trip up her story, putting just enough emphasis on each syllable to make you really know what she was getting at. She *lived* every story she sang; she was just telling you how it happened to her.

When I told her how long I had been listening to her records, how wonderful I thought they were and how *Cemetery Blues* inspired me to become a musician when I was a kid, she was very modest—she just smiled, showing those great big dimples of hers, fidgeted around and said, "Yeah, you like that?" I asked her would she do *Cemetery Blues* for me and she busted out laughing, "Boy," she said, "what you studyin' 'bout a cemetery for? You ought to be out in the park with some pretty chick." That night, and every time I saw her from then on, Bessie kept kidding me about the kinky waves in my hair; she'd stroke my head once or twice and say, "You ain't had your hair fried, is you, boy? Where'd you get them pretty waves? I get seasick every time I look at them." Many's the time I almost peeled my whole goddamn scalp off, to hand to her on a silver platter.

You ever hear what happened to that fine, full-of-life female woman? You know how she died? Well, she went on for years, being robbed by stinchy managers who would murder their own mothers for a deuce of blips, having to parade around in gaudy gowns full of dime-store junk and throw away her great art while the lushes and morons made cracks about her size and shape. She drank a lot, and there must have been plenty of nights when she

got the blues she couldn't lose, but she went on singing, pouring out the richness and the beauty in her that never dried up. Then one day in 1937 she was in an automobile crash down in Mississippi, the Murder State, and her arm was almost tore out of its socket. They brought her to the hospital but it seemed like there wasn't any room for her just then—the people around there didn't care for the color of her skin. The car turned around and drove away, with Bessie's blood dripping on the floor-mat. She was finally admitted to another hospital where the officials must have been color-blind, but by that time she had lost so much blood that they couldn't operate on her, and a little later she died. *See that lonesome road, Lawd, it got to end,* she used to sing. That was how the lonesome road ended up for the greatest folk singer this country ever heard—with Jim Crow directing the traffic.

BILLIE HOLIDAY'S STORY

I USED to run errands for a madam on the corner. I wouldn't run errands for anybody, still won't carry a case across the street today, but I ran around for this woman because she'd let me listen to all Bessie's records—and Pops Armstrong's records of West End Blues.

I loved that West End Blues and always wondered why Pops didn't sing any words to it. I reckoned he must have been feeling awful bad. When I got to New York, I went to hear him at the Lafayette Theatre. He didn't play my blues and I went backstage to tell him about it.

I guess I was nine years old then. Been listening to Pops and Bessie ever since that time. Of course, my mother considered that type of music sinful; she'd whip me in a minute if she caught me listening to it. Those days, we were supposed to listen to hymns, or something like that.

This is the truth. Mother and I were starving. It was cold. Father had left us and remarried when I was ten. Mother was a housemaid and couldn't find work. I tried scrubbing floors, too, but I just couldn't do it.

We lived on 145th Street near Seventh Avenue. One day we were so hungry we could barely breathe. I started out the door. It was cold as all-hell and I walked from 145th to 133rd, down Seventh Avenue, going in every joint trying to find work. Finally, I got so desperate I stopped in the Log Cabin Club run by Jerry Preston. I told him I wanted a drink. I didn't have a dime. But I ordered gin (it was my first drink—I didn't know gin from wine) and gulped it down. I asked Preston for a job, told him I was a dancer. He said to dance. I tried it. He said I stunk. I told him I could sing. He said sing. Over in the corner was an old guy playing the piano. He struck Travelin' and I sang. The customers stopped drinking. They turned around and watched. The pianist, Dick Wilson, swung into Body and Soul. Jeez, you should have seen those people—all of them started crying. Preston came over, shook his head and said, "Kid, you win." That's how I got my start.

First thing I did was get a sandwich. I gulped it down. Believe me, the crowd gave me eighteen dollars in tips. I ran out the door. Bought a whole chicken. Ran up Seventh Avenue to my home. Mother and I ate that night—and we have been eating pretty well since.

I don't think I'm singing. I feel like I am playing a horn. I try to improvise like Les Young, like Louis Armstrong, or someone else I admire. What comes out is what I feel. I hate straight singing. I have to change a tune to my own way of doing it. That's all I know.

Harlem Jive

FIRST STEPS IN JIVE

Names of Things

SINCE Jive talk came into being because of the paucity of words and inadequacy of the vocabularies of its users, it is of primary interest that we get a good working knowledge of the Jive names for things. It is also essential to understand here that really good Jive talk is also accompanied by appropriate gestures, inflections of the voice, and other aids toward making one's meaning clear.

The simplest words in Jive are those relating to things—inanimate objects, the furniture in a room, objects which can be moved, sold, bought, exchanged, all concrete and tangible objects.

Alarm Clock—Chimer
Body—Frame
Corner—Three pointer
Door—Slammer
Elderly man—Poppa Stoppa
Feet—Groundpads
Gun—Bow-wow
Hands—Grabbers
Jail—House of Many Slammers
Liquor—Lush, juice
Moon—Pumpkin

Nose—Sniffer

Overcoat—Benny or Bear

Verbal Nouns

These are the words that move and "jump," the Jive Verbs that give the language its appeal and spontaneity, that make Jive flexible.

Here we are dealing with the words which describe bodily motion, the movement of arms, legs, hands and feet. They also denote intangible action having to do with thought, comprehension, a very important phase of Jive.

We start off by naming simple acts. In the preceding portion of this chapter we discussed the name of things, we had you going home: and, instead of saying, "I am going home," you said, "I'm going to my pile of stone." "Am going" is a perfectly legitimate expression in English denoting an intention and describing an act already taking place. In Jive you would substitute the words "cop" and "trill" in place of "am going," and your statement would be: "I'm copping my trill for my pile of stone." Simple, isn't it? Even your great-aunt Hannah could understand that, couldn't she?

There are relatively few Jive verbs, since Jive is primarily a language consisting of descriptive adjectives, rather than being replete with verbs denoting action. However, the few Jive verbs to balance the enormous number of nouns, or names of things, are thrillingly competent, graphic and commanding. Two in particular are worthy of our attention. The verbs "knock" and "lay" are the basis of Jive. "Knock" in particular is found all through the process of a Jive conversation. It is one of the key words.

"Knock a nod," says the Jiver. He means going to sleep. "Knock a scoff," he says. He means, eat a meal. "Knock a broom" is found to mean a quick walk or brisk trot away from something. "Knock me down to her" means to introduce me to a young lady; "knock off a riff," in musical parlance means for a musician to play a musical break in a certain manner. "Knock a jug" means to buy a drink.

The verb, "Lay," is another vitally important verb in the Jiver's vocabulary. It also denotes action. For example: "Lay some of that cash on me," says a Jiver. His statement means literally what it

says. But if he says, "he was really laying it," he means someone was doing something out of the ordinary, as in a stage performance or musical program, or a well-dressed entering a room and suddenly becoming the object of all eyes.

Here are some other important verbs:

Blow—To leave, move, run away

Cop—To take, receive, understand, do

Dig—To understand, take, see, conceive, perceive, think, hand over

Drag—Humiliate, upset, disillusion

Stash—To lay away, hide, put down, stand, a place

Take a powder—Leave, disappear

Jive Adjectives, or Words Signifying Quality

Before the names of things, or objects, as in standard English we need to know a special state or condition regarding them in order to get a clear mental picture in our minds. For example, a *blue* sky, a *soft* chair, the *hot* sun, etc. The language of Jive has plenty of such adjectives, more of which are constantly being added every day. The following list may prove helpful:

Anxious—Wonderful, excellent

Fine—All right, okay, excellent

Frantic—Great, wonderful

Groovy—To one's liking, sensational, outstanding, splendid

Mad—Fine, capable, able, talented

Mellow—State of delight, beautiful, great, wonderful

Righteous—Pleasing to the senses, glorious, pretty, beautiful, mighty

Solid—Very fine, okay, great, terrific

Jive Phrases, Simile and Hyperbole

As in standard English, Jive is flexible and infinitely capable of expressing phrases or rare harmonic beauty and rhythmical force. The language of the hepsters is constantly acquiring new descriptive phrases, narrative and explanatory in content, which constitute an integral and necessary part of one's equipment for gaining proficiency

in talking and writing Jive. Here are a few some of which are self-explanatory, and others of which are translated into English in italics:

Fine as wine

Mellow as a cello

Like the bear, nowhere

Playing the dozens with my uncle's cousins—doing things wrong

"I'm like the chicken, I ain't stickin' "—broke

"Dig what I'm laying down?"—understand what I'm saying?

"I'm chipper as the China Clipper and in the mood to play"— flying high and personally feeling fine

"Swimps and wice"—Shrimps and rice

"Snap a snapper"—light a match

"Like the farmer and the 'tater, plant you now and dig you later" —means, "I must go, but I'll remember you."

Jive Rhyming and Meter

The language of Jive presents an unusual opportunity for experimentation in rhymes, in fact, a lot of it is built on rhymes, which at first hearing might be considered trite and beneath the notice. However, Jive rhymes and couplets are fascinating and comparatively easy to fashion. As to meter, it is desirable that the syllables form a correct measure, but this is not essential. All that is necessary is that the end words rhyme; they do not necessarily need to make sense. Here are some examples:

"Collars a broom with a solid zoom"—left in a hurry

"No lie, frog eye"

"What's your duty, Tutti-Frutti?"

"Joe the Jiver, the Stranded Pearl-Diver"

"Had some whiskey, feel kind o' frisky"

"Swing and sweat with Charley Barnet"—means dance to Barnet's music

"Are you going to the function at Tuxedo Junction?"—Tuxedo Junctions are places, dancehalls, candy-stores, etc., where hepsters gather.

"My name is Billie, have you seen Willie?"—used as a greeting or salutation among accomplished hepcats

"Ain't it a pity, you're from Atlantic City?"—salutation
"I can't frolic, I got the colic"—I drank too much

HARLEM JIVE TALK, IDIOMS, FOLK EXPRESSIONS

ACE: Bosom friend. *He's my ace boy.*

ALLIGATOR: A jitterbug.

BABY KISSER: A politician.

BACK: Good, fine. *She's dressed back in righteous black.*

BALL: To have riotous fun. *On Saturday we ball!*

BEAT: Bad looking, depressed, tired. *I'm beat to my sox.* (Very beat).

BEAT UP YOUR CHOPS: Talking a lot. *Stop beating up your chops, gal.*

BENDERS: Knees

BLIP: Very good or very bad. *Man, this beer's a blip!*

BLINDS: Rods beneath a railway coach, or space between. *Hoboes ride the blinds.*

BLOW: To leave. *I'm gonna blow this town.*

BLOWTOP: Excitable, erratic. *Minnie's a blowtop.*

BLOW YOUR FUSE: To get angry. *That landlady made me blow my fuse.*

BLOW YOUR LID: Same. *Don't let a woman make you blow your lid.*

BLOW YOUR TOP: Same. *She went to the welfare and blew her top.*

BOON-COON: Same as ace. *Stacy's my boon-coon.*

BOOT: To explain, to describe, inform authoritatively. *That chick booted me about love.*

BREAD: Money; wages. *He makes good bread.* (Earns good money)

BRING DOWN: Depressing, unseemly, wrong, no good. *Monday is a bring down.*

BROWNIE: Cent, a penny.

BUG: To irritate. *Get away, you're bugging me.*

BUST YOUR VEST: To swell with pride. *That preacher's busting his vest.*

CAT: A male. *That little cat's sure fat.*

CHICK: A female. *She's a slick chick.*

CHINCH: A bedbug. *That rooming house is just full of chinches.*

CHINCHPAD: A hotel, a cheap rooming house.

CHIPPY: A playgirl. *Bars are full of chippies.*

CHIPPY'S PLAYGROUND: A pot belly on a man. *Money goes with a chippy's playground.*

CHIPS: Money. *He's in the chips today.*

CHOLLY: A dollar bill. *When you beg for a cholly, you're really down.*

CHOPS: Lips, mouth, jaws. *Don't you put my glass to your chops.*

C-NOTES: A hundred dollar bill. *That horse paid off in C-notes.*

CLINKER: A sour note in music. *The trumpet hit a clinker.*

COLLAR ALL JIVE: To understand everything. *Hipsters collar all jive.*

COOL: Calm, unruffled. *Be cool, man, if the whiskey gets you.*

COP: To take, receive, understand.

COP A NOD: Take a quick nap. *Between acts he cops a nod.*

COP A DEUCEWAYS: To buy two dollars worth of something. *Let's cop a deuceways of barbecue.*

COP A SLAVE: To go to work. *It's time to cop a slave.*

COP A SQUAT: To take a seat. *Cop a squat and stay awhile.*

CORN: Corn whiskey, also known as mountain dew. *Gimme some mellow corn.*

CREAKER: An aged person. *I hate to see a creaker act so chippy-fied.*

CRIB: House, home, where you can not only hang your hat, but raise hell.

CUT OUT: To depart. *I'm gonna cut out from Harlem.*

CUT SOME RUG: To dance. *Let's dig the Savoy and cut some rug.*

DEN: Apartment, room, house, home. *All couples need their own den.*

DEUCE: Two. *A deuce of chippies kept my company.*

DICTY: High hat, snooty. *The dicties live on Riverside.*

DIG: To understand, to enjoy, to go to. *I don't dig Dixieland.*

DO A HOUDINI: To disappear, to leave suddenly. *If the cops come, I'll do a Houdini.*

DOODLEY-SQUAT: Not caring. *I don't give a doodley-squat.*

DOWN WITH IT: To get acquainted with, to understand. *I'm down with your jive.*

DOZENS: Humorous but vulgar references to someone else's mother. *If you put me in the dozens, I'll hit you sure.*

DRAG: To humiliate, upset, disillusion. *You drag when you bring me down.*

DRAPE: A suit of clothes. *Man, dig my righteous drape!*

DUST: To leave.

DUST YOUR BROOM: To go away, to leave town. *She dusted her broom on a Greyhound bus.*

EARLY BLACK: Early evening. *Dig the neons in the early black.*

EARLY BLUE: Same as above.

EIGHTY-EIGHT: (88) A piano. *With Duke at the 88, the music's great.*

EYEBALL: To look at someone. *That chick's eyeballing me.*

FAULT: To blame. *If I can't make it, don't fault me.*

FAY: A white person. *Fays never could sing blues right.*

FEDS: Federal officers. *The feds are hard on junkies.*

FLIC, FLICKER: A motion picture. *Sinatra's in a frantic flic.*

FLY: Fresh, impudent, sassy, flirtacious. *She's a real fly chick.*

FLY RIGHT: To behave. *Straighten up and fly right, even if you are high.*

FOR KICKS: For fun. *I drink for kicks.*

FRACTURE YOUR WIG: Same as blow your top. *Love can make you fracture your wig.*

FRANTIC: Great, wonderful. *Dizzy's a frantic musician.*

FREEBYE: Free, without charge; a free dance, a free meal.

GAMS: Legs. *She's got gams like hams.*

GASSER: An exciting thing. *Eartha Kitt is a gasser.*

GATE: A big mouth. Used as a salutation. *What you say, gate?*

GAUGE: Marijuana. *Let's blow some gauge.*

GEECHEE: A South Carolinian, strictly speaking from the coastal areas.

GET OFF: To show off, strut your stuff, go over big. *When she rose to sing, she really got off.*

GET STRAIGHT: To clarify, speak plainly. *My husband really got me straight.*

GIG: A single engagement for a musician. *House parties ain't nothing but gigs.*

GIMME SOME SKIN: To slap hands in greeting.

GIT-BOX: A juke box, also piccolo. *Put a dime in the git-box and play a side.*

GO DOWN: The happenings. *Let's see what's going down at the dance.*

GONE: Great, fine, very good. *Rock and Roll is real gone music.*

GREAT WHITE FATHER: The president of the United States.

GREY: A white person. *Nothing but greys go to the Stork Club.*

GREASE YOUR CHOPS: To dine. *For a dime you can grease your chops at Father's.*

GROOVEY: Soothingly pleasant, also In The Groove. *King Cole sings groovey. He's in the groove.*

GUMBEAT: To talk a lot, gossip. *Women are always gumbeating.*

GUTBUCKET: Loud and low-down. *Rock and Roll is real gutbucket sometimes.*

HALF-PAST A COLORED MAN: 12:30 A. M.

HAMFAT: A phoney, a worthless character, a poser. *I hate hamfats myself.*

HAWKINS: The wind, wintertime, cold weather, ice, snow. *In February, Hawkins talks.*

HEAD KNOCK: The deity. *When the head knocks calls, you got to go.*

HEEBIES: Delerium tremens, the shakes. *Cheap wine will give you the heebies.*

HIGH: Intoxicated, also charged on marijuana. *I'm high as a Georgia pine!*

HINCTY: Same as dicty. *Muriel is a hincty hussy.*

HIP: Wise, in the know, understanding. *I'm hip to what's going down.*

HIPSTER: A sophisticate, an all-around wise guy. *Hipsters dig the jive.*

HOOKED: Addicted to narcotics. *Once hooked, Lexington is no where.*

HOT: Stolen, also under surveillance. *That watch is hot, and so is*

this bar.

HUSTLER: One who makes a living at others' expense. *Hustler's use crooked dice.*

HYPE: A pretense, a deceitful act. *Don't try to lay a hype on me.*

IF PUSH COMES TO SHOVE: When the final necessity arises. *I'll pay that bill when push comes to shove.*

IGG: To ignore, to high hat. *Miss Dicty tried to igg me.*

IN THERE: All right, fine, very good. *That dress is really in there, girl!*

JAG: A binge, a long drunk. *Never go on a wine jag, son, it's a drag.*

JAM: To make spontaneous group music, to jazz without music.

JAM-SESSION: Musicians playing spontaneously for fun.

JIVE: Kidding, double-talk, pleasant pretending. *He puts down such corny jive.*

JOHN: A dupe, a stooge, a sucker. *That chippie's got herself a john.*

JUICE: Alcoholic beverages. TO JUICE: To get drunk.

JUICED: Intoxicated. *Don't stagger in here if you get juiced.*

JUMP: To be very lively. *Let's play the juke box and make the joint jump.*

JUNKIE: A narcotics addict. *Junkie, don't bring your junkie self in here.*

KICKS: Thrills, satisfaction. *He gets his kicks from gospel singing.*

KILLER: A great thing, something or somebody wonderful. *Harlem is a killer, man!*

KITCHEN MECHANIC: A domestic servant. *Kitchen mechanic's night is Thursday.*

LANE: A simpleton, an unhip person. *Country boys are all lanes.*

LATCH ON: To become aware, to understand, to learn. *I latch on quick to anybody's jive.*

LAY, LAY IT: To strut, to preen, to show off. *Aw, lay it, girl, in your necklace of pearls!*

MAD: Fine, excellent. *That's real mad meal.*

MAP: Face. *What an ugly map!*

MELLOW: Agreeable, softly pleasant, nice. *My girl is fine and mellow.*

MOSS: Hair. *She's got some mellow moss.*

MOST: The greatest. *Smithfield ham is the most.*

NIX OUT: To freeze out, to eliminate. *Two in love nix out all others.*

NOWHERE: Of no value, uninteresting. *That old time jazz is nowhere.*

OFAY: Some as FAY, white. *Ofay food don't grease my chops.*

ONLIEST: Unique. *Belafonte's the onliest.*

PAD: Same as crib, home, house. *I'm heading for the pad to cop a nod.*

PECKS: Food. *My girl lays some pecks!*

PEEPERS: Eyes. *Dig them bedroom peepers.*

PEN: The penitentiary. *All junkies ought to be in the pen.*

PICK UP ON: Same as LATCH ON. *I don't pick up on bop.*

PINK TOES: White, usually in reference to a female. *Pink toes get all the breaks on Broadway.*

PIMP STEAK: A frankfurter, a hot dog. *All Jack eats is pimp steaks.*

PITCH A BOOGIE-WOOGIE: Raise sand; fuss, quarrel violently. *His wife pitched a boogie-woogie when he wasn't home for dinner.*

PLANT YOU NOW AND DIG YOU LATER: *I'll leave you now to see you by and by.*

POD: Marijuana. Also POT.

PUT DOWN: To leave, desert. *I'm going to put my evil woman down.*

QUIT IT: Same as above. *I'm going to quit it so far as Dollie goes.*

RAP: A prison sentence. *Old judge gave him a ten-year rap.*

REEFER: A marijuana cigarette.

RIGHTEOUS: Excellent, great, very nice indeed. *She's got a righteous smile.*

ROACH: Reefer butts, usually saved in case of a shortage. *Twenty roaches won't make a good stick.*

ROOST: Same as crib, pad.

ROPE: A marijuana cigarette.

RUG-CUTTER: A dancer, a jitterbug.

RUBBER: An automobile. *Folks like Sugar Ray always ride on rubber.*

RUMBLE: A fight, a street fight. *I cut out when the rumble*

started.

RUN IN: A quarrel, a minor fight. *Kin folks shouldn't have run-ins.*

SALTY: Disagreeable, angry, pouting, an evil mood. *When I said let's go, she jumped salty.*

SCAT: Singing in nonsense syllables. *Cab and Louis can really scat.*

SCHOOL: To teach. *That chick can really school a square.*

SCARF: To eat, also SCOFF. *We scarf good at grandma's.*

SCUFFLE: To work for a living. *After I scuffled all week, I was tired.*

SEND: To thrill, stir enthusiasm, gratify, please greatly. (Noun, SENDER)

SHARP: Well dressed. *Harlem cats are sharp.*

SIGNIFY: To cast aspersions, hint at something wrong. *Tell me plain, baby, and DON'T signify.*

SKY-PIECE: A hat. *Tip the sky-piece, man.*

SKY-PILOT: A preacher. *Get me a sky-pilot when I come to die.*

SLAMMER: A door. *Knock on the slammer before you enter.*

SLOW DRAG: A form of dancing, voluptuous and leisurely.

SNAP YOUR CAP: To become very angry. *The dozens made him snap his cap.*

SNOW: Powdered heroin sniffed up the nostrils.

SO HELP ME: That's the truth, no kidding. *So help me, I went to work.*

SOLID: Very fine, okay, great, terrific. *She's a solid sender.*

SPADE: A Negro. *Crackers don't like spades.*

SPAGINZY: Same as above. Also SPAGINZY-SPAGADE.

SPONSOR: Same as JOHN. *How'd you let that sponsor go before he paid the bill.*

SQUARE: An unsophisticated person. *Teenagers are all squares.*

SQUARE FROM DELAWARE: A very square, square, completely unhipped.

STASH: To stand arrogantly, also STASH BACK with one's legs benched. *Dressed to kill, he stashed on the corner.*

STICK: A marijuana cigarette.

STIR: A prison cell.

STOCK OF TEA: Same as STICK.

STOMPS: Footwear. *I need some new stomps.*

STONE: Very, really and sure enough whatever the word precedes. *Stone sick, stone crazy, stone ugly. Alaska is stone cold.*

STOOLIE: An informer to the police, a stool-pigeon.

STRUGGLE-BUGGY: An automobile.

STUD: A man. *He's a hip stud from St. Louis.*

TAKE POWDER: Leave, disappear. *When the law came, everybody took a powder.*

TAKE IT SLOW: To be careful, cool. *If your old lady blows her top, take it slow.*

TAKE LOW: To be humiliated. *Women love to see a man take low.*

TEA: Marijuana.

TEA PAD: A place where marijuana may be purchased or smoked.

THE LAW: The police.

THE MAN: The policeman.

THE SHORTS: Hunger, empty pockets. *I'm troubled with the shorts.*

TWISTER: Key. *My wife changed the lock so my twister's nowhere.*

TWO'S AND FEWS: Same as THE SHORTS.

UNBOOTED: Square, state of being a lane, a dull person. *Rev. is unbooted.*

UNCLE'S: Any pawn shop.

UNHIP: Same as unbooted, a square. *She's so unhipped it's a shame.*

UNCLE SAM'S ACTION: Draft call, induction.

UPPITY: Same as dicty, hincty, snobbish.

VIPER: One who smokes reefers; a marijuana addict.

WHAT'S YOUR STORY: How are things? What do you want? Why? Explain yourself. *What's your story, morning glory?*

WEED: Marijuana.

WHITE STUFF: Heroin.

WIG: Head, hair. *Mary's got a righteous wig.*

WOODEN KIMONA: Coffin. *Most gangsters end in a wooden kimona before their time.*

YARDDOG: A low, loud and boisterous person. *He ain't nothing but a yarddog.*

RHYMED JIVE

Fine as wine,
Mellow as a cello.

I dig all jive,
That's the reason I stay alive.

Let's get racy
With Count Basie.

I can't frolic,
I got the colic.

Do your duty,
Tutti-Fruitti.

I'm like the chicken,..
I ain't stickin'.

Where did you get that drape?
Your pants look like a cape.

Cut out that
Rootin' and tootin'
Then there won't be
Any shootin' and bootin'.

WILLIE COOL DIGS THE SCENE

Harlem Jive Talk with Translation

MY MAN:—The freeze has really set in on the turf, champ, and a kiddie has the toughest kind of time trying to get hold to some long bread so that he can have a ball and come on with frantic plays all up and down the line. Home, it's so bad that a lot of the cats on the stroll can't even get to their grits half the time. There used to be a few hustles that you could always fall back on for your twos and fews but nothing is happening at all. Even the soft shoe or gumshoe plays are cold. It used to be that a man could lay down a real hype by tomming to some grey but most of them plays got nixed by the hard beef laid down by some of the equal rights kids. You can still get some fast action on the single action kick because most of the pickups carry the stuff in their head and pass the scribe. This tricks the bluecoats and bulls trying to pickup on the action for a break job. It's a little tough copping any bread on the straight digit action because the boys from the ace law and order pad have been whaling like mad at the turnin' points. The heavy iron boys who didn't get snagged in the crummy play are blowing the burg if they're straight waiting for the chill to set in or they're just cooling it until somebody gets the contacts straight so that the brass will hold still for an arrangement. Con plays are out, too, cause everybody is so hip, there ain't no fools to drop a shuck on. You move in one a lane or square with the smooth tongue action and half the time he's got a riffle of his own that he drops on you behind a sob story so you wind up giving up some iron to him or her and then blow your stack when you see the action that plays behind it for the next time you eyeball the turkey, he running them around at a giggle juice joint. It is the craziest action, Jim, so it's best to go on the desperate tip and cop a slave for your ends. Later, daddy.

TRANSLATION OF *Willie Cool Digs the Scene:*

WILLIAM COOL SURVEYS THE SITUATION

MY FRIEND:—I am really sick about the way things have gotten so difficult and money so scarce a fellow can hardly hustle any easy money any more. It is so bad that many of the fellows on the street can't even make enough to cover their meals regularly. The once fertile avenues of kowtowing to the whites has been dried up by the virile campaign for equal rights. Single action on the numbers is still a possibility because the writers carry their plays in their heads instead of in writing. But the straight numbers men are either on the lams or inactive because of raids and other difficulties with the law. But things will change when the proper contacts are made with the higher ups. Confidence games are out now, too, because there are no unwary people to use as victims. In fact, you try such tricks and you may wind up falling for the other fellow's story yourself, only to be humiliated when you see the person enjoying himself with your money at a bar. Things are so difficult, Jim, that in desperation it's best to make the most drastic of all moves and go and get yourself a regular job. I'll see you later, pal.

THERE IS A SQUARE IN MY HAIR, I DO DECLARE

LET's make an oblique approach to the subject of jive chatter and take up the subject of The Square. In every age and every clime, there's always been a square around. Robin Hood could have been very good but he wasn't just a squire (British for square) in Nottinghamshire; he got under the wire because his mob wasn't for hire. On the turf if a character ain't so ain't, he's a square and maybe, beyond compare. The square population, they say, is di-

minishing as many belatedly get hip to what's on the beach for the leech or in the air for the mare and in some quarters one can observe the pert skirts operating on the plan of "Share the Square." Under such dire circumstances, the square develops ego to snare and might snare some air if the chick lamps him with a come hither stare. By that I mean, the square might swear that the chick's bold stare was directed so as to dare the square to enter her lair. That's why some glare and even blare so loud they scare even Jack the Bear. And some chicks invariably prepare to have a square to spare which is grossly unfair to those with the flair to say a prayer almost anywhere for just one of any pair if there's a square to spare. I mean, a square to share.

There's nothing difficult nor productive of disconsolation about this that can't be dug by any lug or mug however smug who likes to hug his jug, keeping same from the common thug who wipes his feet on the rug and blames it all on his pal the pug—dismiss 'em all with a drug shrug! And if your mother-in-law put some straw in the slaw which dislocated your jaw, get a crawful of tobacco chaw and head straight for Arkansas. And don't guffaw if you lamp the flaw and heehaw like your brother-in-law, who, like the mule, can be a typical fool who drooped out of school for playing it cool on the dummy's stool and tried to trick his pals with some lemon pool. So, don't worry and get in a flurry to begin to scurry to dig this jive in a hurry. You gotta get hip by taking my tip not to leave your ship unless you slip with a light flip past the cat with the cracking whip. Diggeth thou this jive?

Dan Burley

HERE I COME WITH MY HAIR BLOWING BACK

AND when the wind blows the other way, Cholly Hoss, my moss gets in my eyes! I'm in a solid groove, ole man; sorta groovey like a grade A movie, and I'm liable to blow my top doin' the Back Bay Hop. Now I know you're righteous because the cat I dug laying his spiel in the House of Many Slammers told me you'd be. On that

account, I'm gonna slay you with some fine hip-jive. I'm gonna slap some chops and come up with one of those plays you latch on to when you're roaming in the gloaming:

We're in a blue-lighted room. The rug is thick and there are soft pillows around the floor and against the walls. There's a righteous record on the juke box, and if you listen closely, you'll dig that it's the Hawk, knocking out that heavy and frantic tenor on "Body and Soul."

Says one cat, his shoes laying at his side: "Ole man, it's mellow if you get frantic, and it's fine if you're wild. I'm in the groove and I'm gonna lay a little spiel on you about a chippie I once knew.

"The chippie, stud hoss, was a bringdown, but Jackson, I'm tangled like the rope; lost in love without any hope. But, Cholly Hoss, she's gay and happy. Nope. Not much to gim, sorta beat as to her limbs, but I'm fluttering every time I dig her.

"I was a solid square. My boots were always opened and slipped off when I walked. She showed me how to lace 'em up; how to wear 'em to my hips. She was righteous, ole man. In fact, all root to the final toot. I was a homeboy; always had my umbrella like a simple fella. I'd hang my head, bow it in shame, if a pretty chick called my name. If a cat laid a spiel on me, I'd run home for my dictionary. I couldn't collar what they were laying when they'd ask me to cop a squat and slice my chops. And I couldn't dig when they'd want me to knock a scarf or loan them a brace o' chollies. I thought a skybird was a dove. A carpet, ole man, understand? I was sure a plain rug. I thought lush was water with the 'S' left off. But this chippie really hopped me. Here's part of her daily spiel:

"'You ain't a square. You're somewhere. You're in your boots to your twice-five roots. Your line can be fine; in fact, divine—but don't wade out deept: 'Cause sharks, play 'em in the light. Don't be no pearl diver when you can be mighty fine jiver. If you can't fly, don't get high.'

"Now, ole man, thanks to her, I'm hopped. When I hear you say let's trilly long down the cruncher, you mean, let's walk. When you say a deuce o' demons, I know you mean, a coupla dimes. When you say dive for pearls, I know you mean, a job washing dishes. When you mention the Squares in Their Chairs, you mean Congressmen. And when you say trotters, you mean pigs feet.

"If I hear you beefing about ruffles, I know you aren't spieling about dress, but about good old chitterlings. And ace-deuce means three, and a tray and a solo means four, and a five spot is an eggplant. And when you double an eggplant, it's breadfruit. And a goola is a piano. A lamb is a Lane, and a Lane is a Square, and a Square is a Homey, and a Homey ain't nowhere, just like the Bear's brother Jim, the pickin's are slim. And when a cat talks about his choppie, he means his chick; and chick, means broad, and broad means hen and hen means saw, and saw means fuzzy-quzzy, a solid little huzzy! Cats get their moss to lay down by taking the top of their chippie's stocking and putting a knot and a nickel in it and sleeping in it all night with a solid pound of some fine lay-me-down. And when you talk about flat sponges you mean avenue tripe. And Norwegian lard isn't at all hard. You see, Jackson, I'm flying. Dig you when I come down."

Dan Burley

John Greenleaf Whittier's
"THE BAREFOOT BOY"

A Parody in Harlem Jive

Blessings on Thee, Little Square,
Barefoot Cat with the unconked hair;
With thy righteous pegtop pants,
And thy solid hepcat's stance,
With thy chops so red and mellow,
Kissed by chicks so fine and yellow;
With the bean beaming on thy crown,
That sky of thine such a bringdown;
My own tick-tock to thee I bare,
I was once an unhipped Square,
A Lane, thou art; Poppa Stoppa
Is only a pigeon dropper;
Let the Cats with gold go trotting,

Barefoot, knock thy trill while plotting.
Thou hast more than Cat can lam—
In the reach of gin and gam;
Outward foxy, inward, mop!
Blessings on thee, Junior Hop.

Dan Burley

BOPSTER STORIES

Two bopsters who had never been in the country before saw a cow in a pasture one day. At the sight of her tits both of them cried at once, "Dig those crazy bagpipes!"

The same two bopsters were standing on a Long Island railroad trestle one day when one said to the other, "Man, this is a fine balcony but, Jack, the bannisters are too low."

After Josephine Baker had trouble at the Stork Club, two bopsters from Harlem decided they would try their luck at the joint, but they were stopped by the headwaiter who looked at them and said, "All the tables are gone."
The bopsters answered, "That's just what we want, a *gone* table."

Two other bopsters from Lenox Avenue went down to the Stork Club dressed as Argentine gauchos in wide hats, baggy trousers, boots and spurs. But they got no further than the sidewalk where the doorman informed them that only people with reservations were admitted.
The bopsters said, "No speak de Engleesh."
"Reservations *only*," shouted the doorman.
"No onderstan'," shrugged the bopsters.
"What language do you speak?" demanded the doorman.
"Spaneesh," said the bopsters.
"Then speak some," commanded the doorman.
"Adios, Bilbo's ghost," said the bopsters.

WHEN TO HIP A CHILD

You know, no longer than week before last, I was standing on the White House lawn, me and Dulles was talking. Yeh, me and Dulles was standing out there talking, you know. And Mamie she came out and admired my bangs. You understand what I mean? She liked my bangs. Nick, he came by and we sent him cross the street to get some Pepsi-Colas from the delicatessen.

Dulles said to me, said, "Mom, we called you down to Washington because we want to know what age should you hip a child?" (All that don't understand jive—*hip* means wise).

I said, "What age should you hip one, Dullie?"

He said, "Oh, when they get school age."

I said, "Oh, boy, no wonder the country is ruint with delinquency, or what you call it. I said, as soon as a child is born, the first word you say to it, that's the time to hip it. A child is born with a brain, but not a mind. It's like when you're making records. You go in a sound-proof room. Then the first noise that's made, the first word that you speak, that needle starts turning like the heart, that record starts registering. Whether a baby can answer you back or not, it's digging everything you're putting down from them first words. You get it wrong if instead of telling that baby the truth, about then you put your big hand in front of that child's face—no wonder they have all kinds of diseases—talking 'bout 'This little pig went to market. This little pig—.' That baby don't want to know nothing 'bout no dern pigs. You teaching it 'bout the dirtiest thing it is—a pig. That starts it out in life with a little piggy brain.

It gets a little older, and you want to go out and have a nice time like you're having tonight. You got to get baby sitters sitting with them children and carrying on, choking them and carrying on. Well, if you hipped it in front you wouldn't have that trouble. All you have to say is: 'Listen old man. I done straightened you. You go ahead and get some shut eye. I'm gonna cut out. I'm gonna dig you later. You're on your own!'

From the monologues of: Jackie "Moms" Mabley as per-
formed at the Apollo Theatre in Harlem and elsewhere.

RESPECT FOR WORK

I TREAT work just like I would my mother—I wouldn't hit mama a lick.

A COLD WINTER

IT GOT so cold in New York one winter about ten years ago that Abraham Lincoln, standing on that statue down in Lincoln Square, took his hand off that little colored boy's head and put it in his pocket, and everybody from Harlem was going down there to see what Lincoln had done.

The "Problem"

"HEADS, I WIN—TAILS, YOU LOSE"

In the days of "reconstruction" a white man and a Negro went hunting together, and it was agreed that whatever game might be bagged, should be divided fifty-fifty between them. Now, it so happened that at the end of the hard day's trek, they had killed only two fowl—a wild turkey and a turkey buzzard, the latter being otherwise known as a carrion crow. And when the time came to divide up, the white man put forward the following proposition as the basis for settlement:

"Now, Uncle Pete, you can take your own choice—either the turkey to me and the turkey buzzard to you, or else the turkey buzzard to you and the turkey to me."

"Say dat agin, boss," said the Negro.

The white man repeated with a slight variation:

"I say—the turkey buzzard to you and the turkey to me, or the turkey to me and the turkey buzzard to you."

The old Negro, with a pretense of straining both his ear and his mind to "get" it, said: "Gimme dem words jes' one mo' time, boss."

The white man varied again: "Just whichever you prefer, Uncle Pete—turkey to me and turkey buzzard to you, or, if you don't like that, then buzzard to you, and turkey to me."

As the Negro still looked puzzled, the white man continued. "Well, what's the trouble? It's all up to you."

"Ah's noticed, sah," said the Negro, "dat in all dem many proposi-

tions whut youse made, in nary one o' dem has you ever said tukkey to me!"

THE WAY OF A NEWSPAPER

AMONG the stories which Booker T. Washington was fond of telling out of his own experiences, was one which illustrated how the Negro may interest the American Newspapers.

Booker Washington had gone to some little border-state town to make a speech, and it seems that everybody in the town had turned out to hear him, all the whites and all the blacks. The whites sat on one side of the auditorium and the colored people on the other, as was the local custom.—Washington said that he made the best speech he was capable of, and that it was interesting to note that white and black responded exactly alike to his talk: They laughed at the same time, looked serious at the same time; clapped their hands at the same time, and—we started to say—blushed at the same time; but at any rate when the whites would turn redder, the blacks would turn darker, showing that the reaction was the same.

Now, the editor of the only town paper was there on a front seat, and he seemed to enjoy the speech more than anybody else: he clapped harder, laughed louder and blushed redder than the rest. But Washington was wise: he stayed in the little town the next day and wanted to see what this editor would be willing to say in his paper about the speech. His speech and meeting were undoubtedly the biggest thing in town the day before, and he naturally expected to find it reported on the front page. The little paper had just four pages. He found nothing on the first page, nothing on the second page, nothing on the third page—and he was just about to give it up when he discovered his name in the last column of the last page, with about two inches of space under an advertisement.

And what was said about his speech was good and sufficient. He could have wished for no more,—about his speech. But what was

said or what was not said about his speech, was not the thing that interested him; it was the contrast that interested him. On that same day in that same paper another black man had all of the front page. And this is how it happened: at the same time when Booker Washington entered that town to make a successful speech, another black man entered that town to make an unsuccessful attempt to snatch a white woman's purse,—and got the whole front page with his picture, his biography and his pedigree on it!

THE EVOLUTION OF SUSPICIONS

DURING the taking of a United States census in Alabama, a colored woman who lived in a narrow back alley and earned her living by washing, was busily plying her trade on a warm day in front of her shanty door, when she observed a young white man turning into the alley from the street, with a number of papers under his arm. She immediately showed the nature of her welcome to this intruder by seizing a broom and sweeping the dirt and dust in his direction with great vigor. And when he came within hearing, she turned her tongue loose on him: "Whut yo' doin' hyeah now? Can't cullud folkes git nowhar in de worl' dat you white folkes don't come a-meddlin' an' a-nosin'?—whut you want anyhow?"

The intruder rubbed his hands tamely and said in a conciliatory voice: "Madame, I have simply come to take your census, that's all."

"Dat's all? Well, I reckon dat is all! 'Fore de Gawd o' Jacob, whut mo' could you do nex' after dat? You done made dem radios jes' so you kin hear evahthing de Negro say, '—you done made dem airy-planes jes' so you kin watch de Negro all de time, —you done made dem 'lect'ic lights jes' so you kin see de Negro as good in de night as you kin in de daytime: an' now, 'fore de Lawd, hyeah you come to take de Negro's senses 'way from him!"

CAN'T FOOL THE EXPERTS

A TRAVELING salesman was being driven across country in Alabama by a Negro farmer. A certain winged insect circled about the horse's head and then about the head of the salesman.

"Uncle, what kind of an insect is that?"

"Jes' a hoss-fly, boss."

"Horse-fly? What is that?"

"Jes' a fly whut flies aroun' de heads uv hosses an' mules an' jackasses."

As the insect was still buzzing about the salesman's head, he saw a chance for a little banter: "Well, uncle, you don't mean to hint that I'm a horse!"

"No, no, boss, you certainly ain't no hoss!"

"Well, you don't mean to call me a mule, do you?"

The black farmer was a bit irritated: "No, sah, you ain't no mule, neither!"

Then the white man spoke emphatically: "Now, look here, uncle, do I look, like a jackass to you? You surely don't mean to call me a jackass!"

"No, sah, I ain't a-callin' you no jackass, an' you don't look like a jackass to me,—but den, you see, boss, you can't fool de hoss-fly."

PASSING THE BUCK

UNCLE ZEKE had a pig. A white man came along, fancied it, bought it, put it into his wagon and went on down the road. But the wagon gate came open, and the pig came back. Later another white man came along and bought the same pig, and again the pig came back. Finally a third white passer-by bought the pig and managed to get him to his pen.

Meanwhile the first two were looking for their pig and finally located it in the third white man's pen. A three-cornered dispute naturally arose over this pig. Finally to settle the matter they carried the pig to Uncle Zeke.

The first purchaser: "Uncle Zeke, didn't I buy this pig from you?"

"Yas-sir," said Uncle Zeke, blandly.

The second: "Look here, Uncle Zeke, I bought that pig didn't I?"

"Yas-sir," and Uncle Zeke continued to smoke his pipe.

The third: "Zeke, I bought that pig from you this morning."

"Yas-sir," was the disinterested interruption.

All three: "Well, for the sake of peace, Zeke, won't you tell us to whom the pig belongs, then?"

For the first time did Uncle Zeke show any signs of appreciation of any unusual situation, and removing his pipe from his mouth, and looking his disgust at such a foolish question, he said:

"Well, befo' de Gawd uv Jacob! Can't you three eddicated white folks gwan off an' settle a little question like dat 'mongst yo'selves?"

DEEP SOUTH

THEY say that the reason Negroes eat so many black-eyed peas in Mississippi, and in Louisiana so many red beans, is because for years after Emancipation, colored people did not dare ask a store keeper for *white* beans. Red beans or black-eyed peas, O.K. But it was not until folks began using the term *navy beans,* that Negroes had the nerve to purchase white beans, too. In a Pittsburgh hash-house one day a Negro customer said to another one at the counter, "Here you are up North ordering *white* bean soup. Man, I know you are really free, now."

THE OTHER SIDE OF THE RIVER

NEGROES in Arkansas, when you ask them what life is like in Tennessee, will tell you the white folks are so bad in Memphis that black folks can't even drink white milk. But if you ask Negroes in Tennessee what it is like in Arkansas, they will say, "Man, in that state you better not even put your black feet in no white shoes!"

RESPECT FOR LAW

IN A little southern town, a mob was fixing to lynch a man when a very dignified old judge appeared.

"Don't," he pleaded, "put a blot on this fair community by hasty action. The thing to do," he insisted, "is to give the man a fair trial and then lynch him."

DISCRETION

THEY say once there was a Negro in Atlanta who had made up his mind to commit suicide, so one day he went down to the main street and took the freight elevator up to the top of the highest building in town, in fact, the highest skyscraper in Georgia. Negroes could not ride the passenger elevators, but he was so anxious to commit suicide that he did not let Jim Crow stand in the way. He rode as freight. Once at the top of the building, he took off his coat, drew a deep breath, approached the ledge and jumped off. He went hurling through the air and was just about to hit the sidewalk when he saw a white woman come around the corner. He knew he had

better not fall on a white woman, so he curved and went right back up.

DUE RESPECT

IN TOWNS like Money, Mississippi, no quarter is given when Negroes fail to show what the local citizens regard as proper deference to white folks. Accordingly, it was regarded as a serious breach when a colored farm hand entered a grocery store and casually asked for a can of Prince Albert pipe tobacco. The store keeper turned red with anger, drew himself up stiffly. Pointing to the picture of the Prince on the can, he thundered, "What did you call him?"

The farmer trembled and stuttered as he replied, "*Mister* Prince Albert, sir."

"Well, that's more like it," the storekeeper replied, taking the money and ringing it up on the cash register.

Outside the Negro filled his pipe and continued on his way.

GOOD MORNIN' ALLIGATOR

SAM worked for a white man on the bayou down in Louisiana. He worked all day from sun up to sun down and he had only one day a week off which was Sunday. And on Sunday he liked to go fishing. One Sunday he got up very early and started down to the bayou to fish. But when he got there, the first thing he saw was a great big old alligator lying on the shore sunning himself. The alligator looked at Sam and said, "Good mornin'."

Sam dropped his fishing pole and ran right back to the big house, banged on the door and shouted for his boss. When the white man sleepily opened the door, Sam cried, "Boss, boss there's a alligator down at the bayou that talks. Come on down and see it." The white man was annoyed.

"Now Sam you know right well there ain't no alligator can talk. Why should you wake me up this time of mornin' with that foolishness?"

But Sam persisted, "Yes there is boss and if I ain't telling you the truth you can kick me right square on my backsides."

Finally Sam persuaded the white man to put on his clothes and walk down to the bayou to see this alligator. And when they got there, sure enough there was a great big alligator lying on the bank. But he did not say a living word. So Sam said, "Good mornin' alligator." The alligator didn't open his mouth. Sam said again, "Alligator, good mornin." Still the alligator said nothing.

Then the white man hauled off and kicked Sam right square on his behind and turned up the road to go back to the big house and left Sam there.

No sooner had the white man disappeared around the bend, the alligator looked at Sam and said, "Um-hum, just like a Negro! I said good mornin' to YOU. And you had to go tell a white man!"

DOWN HOME

In Harlem they say a young mother-to-be, about to bear her first child, decided to go back to her childhood home down south to be with her mother when the great event came. Her young husband tried to keep her from going, pointing out to her that aside from having better hospital facilities, New York had no Jim Crow wards, and colored physicians could attend their own patients in the hospitals. In the South upon hospitalization, one often has to have a white doctor since many hospitals there will not permit Negro physicians to practice inside their walls. Still the expectant mother insisted on going home to mama.

After she left, the father in Harlem waited and waited and waited for news of the birth of his child. No news came. The ninth month passed. The tenth month passed. Finally he phoned his wife and she said she was still awaiting the child. The husband told her something must be wrong so go to the hospital anyhow and be

examined. She went. The white physicians marvelled that her child had not yet come. Putting his earphones to his ears and baring her abdomen, he pressed his instrument against her flesh to listen for the prenatal heartbeats of the unborn. Instead, he was astonished by what he heard. Quite clearly and distinctly inside the body of the mother, was a voice singing the blues:

> I won't be born down here! No, sir!
> I won't be born down here!
> If you want to know what it's all about—
> As long as South is South, I *won't* come out!
> No, I won't be born down here!

He wasn't. She had to come back to New York to have her baby and Harlemites swear that that child had plenty of sense.

LUCKY

STERLING BROWN tells the story of the two men standing on the corner. One was a white man, the other wasn't. The first said, "I've got nothing but trouble. My house just burned down and I had no insurance. My wife just ran away with my best friend in my automobile and there are still ten payments due on it. My doctor just told me that I have to go to the hospital and have a serious operation. I sure have tough luck." The second just looked at him and said, "What you kickin' 'bout? Yuh white, ain't yuh?"

ON A STREETCAR

Two men—one Negro, the other white—stood side by side on the car. Suddenly reaching, the white man picked something from the Negro's sleeve. "Take your hands off'n me," the Negro flared.

"What you doing, touching me?"

"I didn't mean any harm," the white replied, "I was just taking a bedbug off your coat."

"Put it back," the Negro stormed. "Getting so colored folks can't have nothing but what you white folks want to take it away."

DESEGREGATION

A NEGRO of Washington, D.C. could scarcely believe his eyes when he read in the newspapers that Jim Crow had been ended in the restaurants of his city. He was overjoyed. He had never expected to live to see the day. Since the miracle had happened however, he decided to experience it for himself—at least once. But he would not act too hastily. The change-over was bound to take a little time. He decided to wait three weeks.

Then one Sunday evening he put on his best clothes, caught a taxi and directed the driver to one of the most elegant restaurants he knew.

He was greeted with a smile at the door and again inside, where the waiter gave him his choice of locations and placed a handsome menu in his hand. The Negro put on his glasses and began reading attentively. He perused the menu so long, in fact, that the waiter, still courtesy itself, came over and asked if he was ready to order.

The Negro looked perplexed. "I don't see any chitterlings here," he said.

"No, I'm afraid we don't have any chitterlings," the waiter agreed.

Once more the customer scanned the menu. "How about turnip greens and ham hock?"

"I'm sorry. No greens and ham hock."

Puzzlement turned to frustration on the face of the desegregated Negro. "I'd like to order black-eyed peas and hog jowl."

"We don't have that either," the waiter told him sadly.

The Negro put his glasses back in their case, pushed his chair back and rose slowly. "You folks," he observed thoughtfully, "you folks just ain't ready for integration."

SATURDAY NIGHT

A YANKEE once bought a plantation in Mississippi and there were many things he could not understand about the Negro plantation hands. Among these things was the importance of Saturday to them, the importance of drawing money on that day, of having the day off and the night free to go in town. So finally the Northerner asked one of the very old men who worked for him about it and the answer he got was, "Lord, sir, all I can tell you is that if you was ever a Negro one Saturday *and particularly one Saturday night,* you'd never want to be a white man in this world agin."

ON THE RAIL

AN OLD Negro was brought into a Southern court accused of insulting a white woman.

"What is the charge, madam?" asked the Judge.

"Judge, your honor," said the white woman, "I was waiting at the bus stop for a bus and this old Negra was sitting on the bench when I sat down. He didn't get up."

"I am sorry, madam," said the judge, "but in these days of integration the Supreme Court has done decreed that that is nothing to arrest a Negra for."

"But that ain't all, Judge," declared the white woman. "You know, that Negra looked at me and said, 'Baby, what's on the rail for the lizard?'"

"What!" cried the Judge. "He went too far." Whereupon the Judge glared at the prisoner and said, "Negra, *I'll* tell you what's on the rail for the lizard—a twenty-dollar fine on one end—and thirty days in jail on the other. Now you ride 'em both out."

RIGHT-OFF—RIGHT-ON

THERE's a town in Alabama called Right-Off—Right-On. Just before the train pulls into the station, the porter comes into the Jim-Crow car and says, "Next stop is Right-Off—Right-On. Everybody in this car better stay in their seats, except that old man in the corner with all the lumps all over his head. He lives in that town. There's a sheriff meets every train, and if you get off this train shame on you—because the name of this town means if a colored man gets right-off like the white folks the sheriff gets *right-on* his head with a stick."

Well, the train stopped at Right-Off—Right-On and everybody stayed in their seats except the old man in the corner who lived there. He got off, and the sheriff said, "Come here, Tom."

Tom walked over to the sheriff and took off his hat. The sheriff ran his hand over Tom's head full of lumps and bumps. There were so many knots on Old Tom's head that the sheriff couldn't find no place to put a new knot, so he didn't hit him at all. The sheriff just stood there hoping some strange Negro would get off, and looking at the Jim Crow car, swinging his stick till the train pulled away.

THE WHOLE WIDE WORLD

DURING the war even the white folks in Mississippi got worried about so much criticism from the rest of the world concerning the way they treated Negroes. So they decided to put good old Mose on an international hook-up to tell the world how happy he was in Mississippi. Mose agreed that this was a good idea and practiced his little speech which was only to take three minutes. The radio show was advertised in all the newspapers all over the world. On

the day of the broadcast the white folks sent two white policemen in full regalia to escort Uncle Mose to the radio station, and they had a big audience of white folks in the auditorium to listen to his testimony. Just before the switch was turned on the announcer told Uncle Mose that his voice was going to be heard all over the state of Mississippi, and all over the United States, and all over the world. Uncle Mose expressed surprise.

"You mean to tell me that folks are gonna hear me all over Mississippi and all over the United States and all over the world?"

"Yes indeed," the announcer assured Uncle Mose, "and when I turn this switch and announce your name I want you to speak right up."

"Now Uncle Mose you have the mike—say what you want to say," he urged.

"All I wants to say," the old man's voice boomed, "is HELP! HELP! HELP!"

NEUTRALITY

DURING the Detroit riots, the police stopped a car which was racing through the battle-area. A white pillow case was dangling from the center of the car, for all to see. "What's that for?" a policeman asked the driver—who grinned, and explained: "It's a white pillow case. That's to show I'm neutral, boss."

The policeman quickly frisked the driver, and discovered a .45 in his pocket. "Neutral, eh?" said the cop. "Then what's this gun for?"

"I'm neutral all right, boss," vowed the driver. "But that gun's in case somebody don't believe it."

FATHER TO SON

YOUNG HUMMAN TALMADGE, Senator from Georgia, who was governor of Georgia following in his father's footsteps, got so worried about integration after the Supreme Court decreed that the schools and busses and everything should be mixed, that he didn't know what to do. So he decided to try to get in touch with his father who died before the Supreme Court had come to such decisions, and who had a great reputation for knowing how to handle 'Nigras.' It took young Humman a long time to get through to the spiritual world, but he finally contacted old Gene and said, "Father, I have been trying to get in touch with you for a long time."

Gene said, "I have been trying to get in touch with you too, son, because I'm catching hell down here."

Humman said, "Pappy, we are catching hell here in Georgia and what I want to know from you is what shall I do about these 'Nigras'?"

Old Gene answered, "Son, please don't be too hard on them at home 'cause the head devil down here is a 'Nigra' and I am catching enough hell now."

BUS RIDE

A MEMBER of the Montgomery, Alabama, Bus Strike Committee spotted two drunken Negroes hovering about the bus stop one day. Worried less they got on a bus thereby weakening the fight against the abuse and segregation which the Committee was protesting, he tapped one of the men on the shoulder. He was so intoxicated that he fell against his companion. The Committee member was apologetic, "I'm sorry, fellow," he said, "but I just wanted to ask you to please not ride on a bus while our boycott is on." He was sure he

had made a mistake.

Just as he was about to walk off, one staggered closer, "Man" he said, "we dig you. Yeah, we're drunk—very drunk—but we ain't drunk enough to get on them jim crow busses."

LENOX AVENUE DIALOGUE

"WHEN I hit that white man in the mouth, he bled from his feet."

"When a white man bleeds from his feet, he hates black men to begin with."

"He does—that's one sure way to tell."

THERMOMETER: NEGRO DOMESTICS

THE colored race is the best thermometer of how things is going, because when white folks feel good we know it, and when white folks feel bad, we know it, too—even before they do—their appetites fall off.

BLACK CATS

THEY say there was once a black cat in Mobile who decided to head for Chicago because he had always heard that up North there was no color line. Hardly had that cat of color gotten to Chicago than he met a white cat. Desirous of being shown about a bit,

> The black cat said to the white cat,
> "Let's go 'round the town."

> The white cat said to the black cat,
> "You better set your black self down."

PLANTATION HELP

Mule die—
Buy another one.
Negro die—
Hire another one.

WORK

Negroes:
Last to be hired,
First to be fired.

LORD'S PRAYER

Our Father, who art in heaven,
White man owe me 'leven and pay me seven.
Thy kingdom come, Thy will be done,
But if I hadn't tuck that, I wouldn't got none.

JUST THE SAME

A yellow gal rides in a limousine,
A brownskin does the same.
A black gal rides in a old-time Ford,
But she gets there just the same.

White folks lives in a fine brick house,
Lord, the yellow gal does the same.
Poor black man lives in the big rock jail,
But it's a brick house just the same.

DIXIE MOTHER GOOSE

Mary had a little lamb,
Its fleas were white as snow—
For everywhere that Mary went
Only *white* fleas could go.

Songs in the Folk Manner

OH, DEM GOLDEN SLIPPERS

A Minstrel Song

Oh, my golden slippers am laid away,
Kase I don't 'spect to war 'em till my weddin' day,
An' my long tail'd coat, dat I love so well,
I will wear up in de chariot in de morn.
An' my long, white robe dat I bought las' June,
I'm gwinter get it changed kase it fits too soon,
An' de old gray horse dat I used to drive
I will hitch up to de chariot in de morn.

    Oh, dem golden slippers!
    Oh, dem golden slippers!
    Golden slippers I'm gwinter wear,
    Because dey look so neat;
    Oh, dem golden slippers!
    Oh, dem golden slippers!
    Golden slippers I'm gwinter wear,
    To walk de golden streets.

Oh, my old banjo hangs on de wall,
Kase it ain't been tuned since way las' fall.
But de peoples all say we will have a good time,
When we ride up in de chariot in de morn.
Dere's old Brother Ben an' Sister Luce,
Dey will telegraph de news to Uncle 'Bacco Juice,
What a great camp meetin' dere will be dat day.
When we ride up in de chariot in de morn.

    Oh, dem golden slippers!
    Oh, dem golden slippers!
    Golden slippers I'm gwinter wear,
    Because dey look so neat;
    Oh, dem golden slippers!
    Oh, dem golden slippers!
    Golden slippers I'm gwinter wear,
    To walk de golden streets.

Oh, my, good-by, children, I will have to go.
Where de rain don't fall or de wind don't blow,
An' you' ulster coats, why, you will not need,
When you ride up in de chariot in de morn.
But de golden slippers mus' be neat an' clean,
An' you' age must be jes' sweet sixteen,
An' yo' white kid gloves you will have to wear,
When you ride up in the chariot in de morn.

    Oh, dem golden slippers!
    Oh, dem golden slippers!
    Golden slippers I'm gwinter wear,
    Because dey look so neat;
    Oh, dem golden slippers!
    Oh, dem golden slippers!
    Golden slippers I'm gwinter wear,
    To walk de golden streets.

James A. Bland

THE RAIN SONG

Bro. Simmons
"Walk right in Brother Wilson—how you feelin' today?"

Bro. Wilson
"Jes mod'rate, Brother Simmons, but den I ginnerly feels dat way."

Bro. Simmons
"Here's White an' Black an' Brown an' Green; how's all you
  gent'men's been?"

Bro. White
"My health is good but my bus'ness slack."

Bro. Black
"I'se been suff'rin' lots wid pains in my back."

Bro. Brown
"My ole 'oman's sick, but I'se alright—"

Bro. Green
"Yes, I went aftuh Doctuh fuh her 'tuther night—"

Bro. Simmons
"Here's Sandy Turner, as I live!"

Bro. Turner
"Yes, I didn' 'spect to git here—but here I is!"

Bro. Simmons
"Now, gent'mens, make yo'selves to home,
Dare's nothin' to fear—my ole 'oman's gone—
My stars; da weather's pow'ful warm—
I wouldn' be s'prised ef we had a storm."

Bro. Brown

"No, Brother Simmons, we kin safely say—
'Tain't gwine to be no storm to-day
Kase here am facts dat's mighty plain
An' any time you sees 'em you kin look fuh rain:
Any time you hears da cheers an' tables crack
An' da folks wid rheumatics—dare jints is on da rack—"

All

"Lookout fuh rain, rain, rain.

"When da ducks quack loud an' da peacocks cry,
An' da far off hills seems to be right nigh,
Prepare fuh rain, rain, rain!

"When da ole cat on da hearth wid her velvet paws
'Gins to wipin' over her whiskered jaws,
Sho' sign o' rain, rain, rain!

"When da frog's done changed his yaller vest,
An' in his brown suit he is dressed,
Mo' rain, an' still mo' rain!

"When you notice da air it stan's stock still,
An' da blackbird's voice it gits so awful shrill,
Dat am da time fuh rain.

"When yo' dog quits bones an' begins to fas',
An' when you see him eatin'; he's eatin' grass:
Shoes', trues', cert'nes sign ob rain!"

REFRAIN

"No, Brother Simmons, we kin safely say,
'Tain't gwine tuh be no rain to-day,
Kase da sut ain't seen no spiders fum dare cobwebs creep;
Las' night da sun went bright to bed,
An' da moon ain't nevah once been seen to hang her head;
If you'se watched all dis, den you kin safely say,
Dat dare ain't a-gwine to be no rain to-day."

Alex Rogers

PAWNSHOP BLUES

Well, I'm walkin' down the street this mornin',
Hear someone call my name and I could not stop,
Someone called me and I could not stop,
Well, boys, you know Brownie was broke and hungry,
On my way to that old pawnshop.

Well, I went to the pawnshop, had my last suit in my hand,
Yes, I went to the pawnshop,
Had my last suit of clothes in my hand,
I said, "won't you give me a loan?
Try to help me, Mister Pawnshop Man."

Well, I went to the pawnshop,
Went down to pawn my radio,
Went down to pawn my radio,
Well, the man said, "Brownie, you ain't got a T.V.—
We don't take radios in no more."

Well, I went to the pawnshop,
'Cause the man had come and took my car.
You know I had lost my job, man, that car-man took my car.
Well, I'm goin' to the pawnshop in the mornin'
See if I can pawn my old guitar.

I asked the pawnshop man
What was those three balls doin' on the wall,
What was those three balls doin' on the wall.
"Well, I bet you two to one, buddy,
You won't get your stuff out o' here at all."

Brownie McGhee

THERE'LL BE SOME CHANGES MADE

There's a change in the ocean, a change in the sea,
And from now on there'll be a change in me.
I'm gonna change my way of living and if that ain't enough,
I'm gonna change the way I strut my stuff.
I'm gonna change my address where I'm livin' at,
Gonna change my long tall one for a little short fat.
Nobody wants you when you're old and gray,
So there's gonna be some changes made today.
There's gonna be some changes made today.

Benton Overstreet and Billy Higgins

NOBODY

When life seems full of clouds and rain
And I am filled with naught but pain,
Who soothes my thumping brain?
　　Nobody!

When winter comes with sleet and snow,
And me with hunger and cold feet,
Who says, "Here's two bits, go and eat?"
　　Nobody!

When summer comes all cool and clear,
And friends they see me drawing near,
Who says, "Come in and have a beer?"
　　Nobody!

I had a steak sometime ago.
With sauce I sprinkled it—but OH!

Who said, "That sauce is Tabasco?"
    Nobody!

When I try hard, and scheme and plan
To look as good as e'er I can,
Who says, "Look at that handsome man?"
    Nobody!

When all day long things go amiss
And I go home to find some bliss,
Who hands to me a glowing kiss?
    Nobody!

I ain't never done nothin' to
    Nobody.
I ain't never got nothin' from
    Nobody, no time—
And until I get somethin' from
    Somebody, sometime,
I don't intend to do *nothin'* for
    Nobody, no time!

                    Bert Williams and Alex Rogers

OLE MAN MOSE IS DEAD

Once there lived an old man
Had a very crooked nose.
He lived in a log hut,
They called him Old Man Mose.
Early one morning a knock came on my door.
I didn't see a single soul,
I ain't gonna do that no more!

I believe, I believe,
I believe Old Man Mose is dead.

Yes, Mose kicked the bucket!
Mose kicked the bucket!
Mose kicked the bucket!
Old Man Mose is dead!

I ran around the side of the house
And I peeped through a crack.
I saw an old man
Layin' flat on his back.
Old Man Mose is dead or sleep
I really didn't know—
But after peeping through that crack,
I ain't gonna do that no more.

I found out, I found out
I found out Old Man Mose is dead!
I found out what it's all about.
Mose kicked the bucket
Yes, Mose kicked the bucket.
Yes, Mose kicked the bucket.
Yes, Mose kicked the bucket.
Old Man Mose is dead!

Zilner Randolph

SATURDAY NIGHT FISH FRY

JACKIE: Well, as I live and breathe, look who's here!
Now, here's somebody I really didn't expect to meet.
Pearl, what you doin' down here on Rampart Street?
PEARL: Well, Jackie, I am down here to try to have me
A ball at one of these Saturday fish fries.
JACKIE: What's that?
PEARL: Ain't you ever been in New Orleans?
JACKIE: Yeah!
PEARL: Well, you can understand what I mean.

All through the week it's quiet as a mouse
But on Saturday night they go from house to house
And they're rockin'.

JACKIE: You mean they're rockin'?

PEARL: I'm tellin' you they're rockin'.

JACKIE: No kiddin'?

PEARL: You never seen such a scufflin'
And a shufflin' till the break of dawn.

JACKIE: Well, I declare!

PEARL: Oh, yes, they're rockin'.

JACKIE: Pearl, you say they're rockin'?

PEARL: These people are movin'.

JACKIE: No kiddin'?

PEARL: I'm tellin' you, you never seen such a scufflin'
And a shufflin' till the break of dawn.

JACKIE: I think I'd like that.

PEARL: Oh, you'll love it!

JACKIE: Wait a minute, listen, Pearl, what's the admission?

PEARL: Oh, nothin', just be an entertainer or a musician.
Say, look, you got anything to do?

JACKIE: No, I believe I'll go on down to the fish fry with you.

PEARL: Come on then.

JACKIE: Wait a minute, Pearl, am I seein' double?

PEARL: No, what's the matter? We just got here.
We gonna have some trouble?

JACKIE: I don't want to bring you down
But your old man's over there in the corner
Actin' like a clown.

PEARL: What is he doin'?

JACKIE: He's rockin', baby.

PEARL: Oh, no!

JACKIE: Yeah, he's rockin'.

PEARL: Is he alone?

JACKIE: You never seen such dancin' and a prancin'
Till the break of dawn.

PEARL: Well, I'm gonna undance him in a minute.

JACKIE: He's rockin'.

PEARL: Oh, you don't mean to tell me.

JACKIE: Girl, that man is rockin'.

PEARL: Oh, how can he upset my nerves?

JACKIE: You never seen such prancin' and a dancin'
           Till the break of dawn.

PEARL: Well I hate to break up the party
           But I'm gonna break it up now.

JACKIE: Now, wait a minute, Pearl. Stop.

PEARL: What's the matter?

JACKIE: Honey, here comes the cops.

PEARL: Oh, my goodness, I'm goin' under the piano and hide.

JACKIE: It's too late, sister, I think we're all goin' for a ride.

PEARL: I don't care. Did you get any of that punch that they
           serves?

JACKIE: Yes, baby, and it really upset my nerves.

PEARL: Say, look here, girl, before the cops came, oh, me, oh my!

JACKIE: We were havin' a ball at that fish fry.

PEARL: We were rockin'.

JACKIE: Baby, we were rockin'.

BOTH: Yes, we were rockin'. Aw, did you see us?
           You never seen such movin' and a groovin'
           Till the break of dawn.

PEARL: Wasn't we tearin' 'em up?

JACKIE: I mean we were rockin', we upset 'em a little.

PEARL: I thought, Jackie, we were rockin'.
           I mean we were movin'.

JACKIE: You never seen such a whoopin' and a boopin'
           Till the break of dawn.

PEARL: Yes, we were rockin'.

JACKIE: Girl, we was carryin' on, weren't we?

PEARL: Did you notice how the dress that I had on upset 'em?

JACKIE: Did you see my coat?
           Why it was disastrous.

PEARL: So much jealousy!
           But, honey, we was rockin'!
           Yes, we was rockin' . . .

Song by Ellis Walsh and Louis Jordan as sung by
Pearl Bailey and Jackie Mabley

HIT THAT JIVE

Hit that jive, Jack!
Put it in your pocket till I get back.
I'm goin' downtown to see a man
And I ain't got time to shake your hand.

Standin' on the corner
All full of jive,
When you meet old schoolboy
Ask him to give you five.

Hit that jive, Jack!
Put it in your pocket till I get back.
I'm goin' downtown to see a man.
I ain't got time to shake your hand.

Slim Gaillard

I AIN'T GONNA BE NO TOPSY

Can't you see the tint of Bergman in me,
The Cornell approach to dramatic ecstasy,
That Hepburn indecision of to be or *ain't* to **be?**
I've suffered as Ophelia,
Yes, honey, your mother has suffered!
And yet, still, regardless,
You ask me to be Topsy.
How do you sound?

I ain't gonna be no Topsy.
I've got style, I've got class,

And yet you ask me to be Topsy.
Now if I must play a part
Where I must use my heart,
I'll play Eva.
Yes, pretty golden curley-haired Eva.
Why, why should I be Topsy?
In the first place, I'd have Simon Legree
Doing favors for *me*. Could Topsy?
I've the highest ideal
Of that certain appeal called glamour,
So, why, why should I be Topsy?

Um-huh! I ain't gonna be no Topsy.
You know something? I have the feel for Camille,
And I revel in O'Neil, not Topsy.
Yes, it's a cinch in a pinch
I'd be happy or sad or simple.
But in this case, I really would be evil.
Why? Give me one good reason
Why I should be Topsy.
I can dance, I can chirp.
And she can't decently burp—not Topsy.
Yes, I could even put sex
In *Four Saints in Three Acts,* believe me.
So tell me why, why should I be Topsy?

Nay! I ain't gonna be no Topsy!
Why, every time I appear
The only thing I can hear
Is be Topsy, be Topsy, be Topsy!
The people just don't realize
I've got beautiful eyes and a dimple.
Instead, all they ever want me to be
Is just plain simple.
Oh, how simple can you get?
Tell me, why should I be Topsy?
I've no cause for alarm,
And I've got no Uncle Tom like Topsy.

That's your river, honey, not mine.
And I'm determined to tell—
Even if I catch hell or dropsy—
I ain't gonna be no Topsy.

Reginald Bean and Avon Long as sung by Mae Barnes

Poetry in the Folk Manner

LI'L GAL

Oh, de weather it is balmy an' de breeze is sighin' low,

Li'l gal,
An' de mockin' birds is singin' in de locus' by de do',

Li'l gal;
There's a hummin' an' a hummin' in de land from east to west,
I's a'sighin' for you, honey, an' I never know no rest.
For dey's lots o' trouble brewin' an' a-stewin in my breast.

Li'l gal.

What's de matter with de weather, what's de matter with de breeze,

Li'l gal?
What's de matter with de locus' that's a-singin' in de trees,

Li'l gal?
Why they knows their ladies love 'em, an' they knows they love
'em true,
An' they love 'em back, I reckon, just like I's a-lovin' you;
That's de reason they's a-weavin' an a-sighin', through and though,

Li'l gal.

Don't you let nobody fool you 'cause de clothes he wears is fine,
Li'l gal.
There's a honest heart a-beatin' underneath these rags o' mine,
Li'l gal.
Cause there ain't no use in mockin' what de birds an' weather do,
But I's sorry I can't 'spress it when I knows I loves you true,
That's de reason I's a-sighin' an' a-singin' now for you,
Li'l gal.

Paul Laurence Dunbar

THE PARTY

Dey had a gread big pahty down to Tom's de othah night;
Was I dah? You bet! I nevah in my life see sich a sight;
All de folks f'om fou' plantations was invited, an' dey come,
Dey come troopin' thick ez chillun when dey hyeahs a fife an'
drum.
Evahbody dressed deir fines'—Heish yo' mouf an' git away,
Ain't seen no sich fancy dressin' sence las' quah'tly meetin' day;
Gals all dressed in silks an' satins, not a wrinkle ner a crease,
Eyes a-battin', teeth a-shinin', haih breshed back ez slick ez grease;
Sku'ts all tucked an' puffed an' ruffled, evah blessed seam an' stitch;
Ef you'd seen 'em wif deir mistus, couldn't swahed to which was
which.
Men all dressed up in Prince Alberts, swallertails 'u'd tek you' bref!
I cain't tell you nothin' bout it, yo' ought to seen it fu' yo'se'f.
Who was dah? Now who you askin'? How you 'spect I gwine to
know?
You mus' think I stood an' counted evahbody at de do'.
Ole man Babah's house boy Isaac, brung dat gal, Malindy Jane,
Huh a-hanging to his elbow, him a struttin' wif a cane;
My, but Hahvey Jones was jealous! seemed to stick him lak a tho'n;
But he laughed with Viney Cahteh, tryin' ha'd to not let on,
But a pusson would'a noticed f'om de d'rection of his look,
Dat he was watchin' ev'ry step dat Ike an' Lindy took.

Ike he foun' a cheer an 'asked huh: "Won't you set down?" wif a
    smile,
An' she answe'd up a-bowin', "Oh, I reckon 'tain't wuth while."
Dat was jes' fu' style, I reckon, 'cause she sot down jes' de same,
An' she stayed dah 'twell he fetched huh fu' to jine some so't o'
    game;
Den I hyeahd huh sayin' propah, ez she riz to go away,
"Oh, you raly mus' excuse me, fu' I hardly keers to play."
But I seen huh in a minute wif de othahs on de flo',
An' dah wasn't any one o' dem a-playin' any mo';
Comin' down de flo' a-bowin' an' a-swayin' an' a-swingin',
Puttin' on huh high-toned mannahs all de time dat she was singin':
"Oh, swing Johnny up an' down, swing him all aroun',
Swing Johnny up an' down, swing him all aroun',
Oh, swing Johnny up an' down, swing him all aroun',
Fa' you well, my dahlin'."
Had to laff at ole man Johnson, he's a caution now you bet—
Hittin' clost onto a hunderd, but he's spry an' nimble yet;
He 'lowed how a-so't o' gigglin', "I ain't ole, I'll let you see,
D' ain't no use in gettin' feeble, now you youngstahs jes' watch me,"
An', he grabbed ole Aunt Marier—Weighs th'ee hunderd mo' er less,
An' he spun huh 'roun' de cabin swingin' Johnny lak de res'.
Evahbody laffed an' hollahed: "Go it, swing huh, Uncle Jim!"
An' he swung huh too, I reckon, lak a youngstah, who but him.
Dat was bettah'n young Scott Thomas, tryin' to be so awful smaht.
You know when dey gits to singin' an' dey comes to dat ere paht:

        "In some lady's new brick house,
      In some lady's gyahden.
          If you don't let me out, I will jump out,
      So fa' you well, my dahlin'."

Den dey's got a circle 'roun' you, an' you's got to break de line;
Well, dat dahky was so anxious, lak to bust hisse'f a-tryin';
Kep' on blund'rin' roun' an' foolin' 'twell he giv' one great big jump,
Broke de line, an' lit head-fo'most in de fiahplace right plump;
Hit 'ad fiah in it, mind you; well, I thought my soul I'd bust,
Tried my best to keep f'om laffin', but hit seemed like die I must!

Y' ought to seen dat man a-scramblin' f'om de ashes an' de grime.
Did it bu'n him! Sich a question, why he didn't give it time;
Th'ow'd dem ashes and dem cindahs evah which-a-way I guess,
An' you nevah did, I reckon, clap yo' eyes on sich a mess;
Fu' he sholy made a picter an' a funny one to boot,
Wif his clothes all full o' ashes an' his face all full o' soot.
Well, hit laked to stopped de pahty, an' I reckon lak ex not
Dat it would ef Tom's wife, Mandy, hadn't happened on de spot,
To invite us out to suppah—well, we scrambled to de table,
An' I'd lak to tell you 'bout it—what we had—but I ain't able,
Mention jes' a few things, dough I know I hadn't orter,
Fu' I know 'twill staht a hank'rin' an' yo' mouf'll 'mence to worter.
We had wheat bread white ez cotton an' a egg pone jes' like gol'
Hog jole, bilin' hot an' steamin' roasted shoat an' ham sliced cold—
Look out! What's de mattah wif you? Don't be fallin' on de flo';
Ef it's go'n to 'fect you dat way, I won't tell you nothin' mo'.
Dah now—well, we had hot chittlin's—now you's tryin' ag'in to fall,
Cain't you stan' to hyeah about it? S'pose you'd been an' seed it all;
Seed dem gread big sweet pertaters, layin' by de possum's side,
Seed dat coon in all his gravy, reckon den you'd up and died!
Mandy 'lowed "you all mus' 'scuse me, d' wa'n't much upon my
    she'ves,
But I's done my bes' to suit you, so set down an' he'p yo'se'ves."
Tom, he 'lowed: "I don't b'lieve in 'pologizin' an' perfessin',
Let 'em tek it lak dey ketch it. Eldah Thompson, ask de blessin'."
Wish you'd seed dat colo'ed preachah cleah his th'oat an' bow his
    head;
One eye shet an' one eye open,—dis is evah wud he said:
"Lawd, look down in tendah mussy on sich generous hea'ts ez dese;
Makes us truly thankful, amen. Pass dat possum, ef you please!"
Well, we eat and drunk ouah po'tion, 'twell dah wasn't nothin' lef',
An' we felt jus' like new sausage, we was mos' nigh stuffed to def!
Tom, he knowed how we'd be feelin', so he had de fiddlah 'roun',
And he made us cleah de cabin fu' to dance dat suppah down.
Jim, de fiddlah, chuned his fiddle, put some rosum on his bow,
Set a pine box on de table, mounted it an' let huh go!
He's a fiddlah, now I tell you, an' he made dat fiddle ring,
'Twell de ol'est an' de lamest had to give deir feet a fling.
Jigs, cotillions, reels an' bread-downs, codrills an' a waltz er two;

Bless yo' soul, dat music winged 'em an' dem people lak to flew.
Cripple Joe, de ole rheumatic, danced dat flo' f'om side to middle,
Th'owed away his crutch an' hopped it, what's rheumatics 'ginst a
fiddle?
Eldah Thompson got so tickled dat he lak to lo' his grace,
Had to tek bofe feet an' hol' dem so's to keep 'em in deir place.
An' de Christuns an' de sinnahs got so mixed up on dat flo'
Dat I don't see how dey'd pahted ef de trump had chanced to blow.
Well, we danced dat way an' capahed in de mos' redic'lous way,
'Twell de roostahs in de bahnyard cleahed deir th'oats an' crowed
fu' day.
Y' ought to been dah, fu' I tell you evahthing was rich an' prime,
An' dey ain't no use in talkin', we jes' had one scrumptious time!

Paul Laurence Dunbar

ITCHING HEELS

Fu' de peace o' my eachin' heels, set down;
   Don' fiddle dat chune no mo'.
Don you see how dat melody stuhs me up
   An' baigs me to tek to de flo'?
You knows I's a Christian good an' strong;
   I wusship f'om June to June;
My pra'ahs dey ah loud an' my hymns ah long:
   I baig you don' fiddle dat chune.

I's a crick in my back an' a misery hyeah
   Whaih de j'ints's gittin' ol' an' stiff,
But hit seems lak you brings me de bref o' my youf;
   W'y, I's suttain I noticed a w'iff.
Don' fiddle dat chune no mo', my chile,
   Don' fiddle dat chune no mo';
I'll git up an' taih up dis groun' fu' a mile,
   An' den I'll be chu'ched fu' it, sho'.

Oh, fiddle dat chune some mo', I say,
   An' fiddle it loud an' fas':

I's a youngstah ergin in de mi'st o' my sin;
    De p'esent's gone back to de pas'.
I'll dance to dat chune, so des fiddle erway;
    I knows how de backslidah feels;
So fiddle it on 'twell de break o' de day
    Fu' de sake o' my eachin' heels.

Paul Laurence Dunbar

WHEN MALINDY SINGS

G'way an' quit dat noise, Miss Lucy—
    Put dat music book away;
What's de use to keep on tryin'?
    Ef you practise twell you're gray,
You cain't sta't no notes a-flyin'
    Lak de ones dat rants and rings
F'om de kitchen to de big woods
    When Malindy sings.

You ain't got de nachel o'gans
    Fu' to make de soun' come right,
You ain't got de tu'ns an' twistin's
    Fu' to make it sweet an' light.
Tell you one thing now, Miss Lucy,
    An' I'm tellin' you fu' true,
When hit comes to raal right singin',
    'T ain't no easy thing to do.

Easy 'nough fu' folks to hollah,
    Lookin' at de lines an' dots,
When dey ain't no one kin sence it,
    An' de chune comes in, in spots;
But fu' real melojous music,
    Dat jes' strikes yo' hea't and clings,

Jes' you stan' an' listen wif me
   When Malindy sings.

Ain't you nevah hyeahd Malindy?
   Blessed soul, tek up de cross!
Look hyeah, ain't you jokin', honey?
   Well, you don't know whut you los'.
Y' ought to hyeah dat gal a-wa'blin',
   Robins, la'ks, an' all dem things,
Heish de moufs an' hides dey faces
   When Malindy sings.

Fiddlin' man jes' stop his fiddlin',
   Lay his fiddle on de she'f;
Mockin'-bird quit tryin' to whistle,
   'Cause he jes' so shamed hisse'f.
Folks a-playin' on de banjo
   Draps dey fingahs on de strings—
Bless yo' soul—fu'gits to move em,
   When Malindy sings.

She jes' spreads huh mouf and hollahs,
   "Come to Jesus," twell you hyeah
Sinnahs' tremblin' steps and voices,
   Timid-lak a-drawin' neah;
Den she tu'ns to "Rock of Ages,"
   Simply to de cross she clings,
An' you fin' yo' teahs a-drappin'
   When Malindy sings.

Who dat says dat humble praises
   Wif de Master nevah counts?
Heish yo' mouf, I hyeah dat music,
   Ez hit rises up an' mounts—
Floatin' by de hills an' valleys,
   Way above dis buryin' sod,
Ez hit makes its way in glory
   To de very gates of God!

Oh, hit's sweetah dan de music
    Of an edicated band;
An' hit's dearah dan de battle's
    Song o' triumph in de lan'.
It seems holier dan evenin'
    When de solemn chu'ch bell rings,
Ez I sit an' ca'mly listen
    While Malindy sings.

Towsah, stop dat ba'kin', hyeah me!
    Mandy, mek dat chile keep still;
Don't you hyeah de echoes callin'
    F'om de valley to de hill?
Let me listen, I can hyeah it,
    Th'oo de bresh of angels' wings,
Sof' an sweet, "Swing Low, Sweet Chariot,"
    Ez Malindy sings.

                           Paul Laurence Dunbar

AT CANDLE-LIGHTIN' TIME

When I come in f'om de co'n-fiel' aftah wo'kin' ha'd all day,
It's amazin' nice to fin' my suppah all erpon de way;
An' it's nice to smell de coffee bubblin' ovah in de pot,
An' it's fine to see de meat a-sizzlin' teasin'-lak an' hot.

But when suppah-time is ovah, an' de t'ings is cleahed away;
Den de happy hours dat foller are de sweetes' of de day.
When my co'ncob pipe is sta'ted, an' de smoke is drawin' prime,
My ole 'ooman says, "I reckon, Ike, it's candle-lightin' time."

Den de chillun snuggle up to me, an' all commence to call,
"Oh, say, daddy, now it's time to mek de shadders on de wall."
So I puts my han's together—evah daddy knows de way,—
An' de chillun snuggle closer 'roun' ez I begin to say:—

"Fus' thing, hyeah come Mistah Rabbit; don' you see him wo'k his
    eahs?
Huh, uh! dis mus' be a donkey,—look, how innercent he 'pears!
Dah's de ole black swan a'swimmin'—ain't she got a' awful neck?
Who's dis feller dat's a-comin'? Why, dat's ole dog Tray, I'spect'!"

Dat's de way I run on, tryin' fu' to please 'em all I can;
Den I hollahs, "Now be deerful—dis hyeah las's de buga-man!"
An' dey runs an' hides dey faces; dey ain't skeered—dey's lettin' on:
But de play ain't really ovah twell dat buga-man is gone.

So I jes' taks up my banjo, an' I plays a little chune,
An' you see dem haids come peepin' out to listen mighty soon,
Den my wife says, "Sich a pappy fu' to give you sich a fright!
Jes' you go to baid, an' leave him: say yo' prayers an' say good-
    night."

                                        Paul Laurence Dunbar

GO DOWN DEATH

A Funeral Sermon

Weep not, weep not,
She is not dead;
She's resting in the bosom of Jesus.
Heart-broken husband—weep no more;
Grief-stricken son—weep no more;
She's only just gone home.

Day before yesterday morning,
God was looking down from his great, high heaven,
Looking down on all his children,
And his eye fell on Sister Caroline,
Tossing on her bed of pain.

And God's big heart was touched with pity,
With the everlasting pity.

And God sat back on his throne,
And he commanded that tall, bright angel standing at his right
    hand:
Call me Death!
And that tall, bright angel cried in a voice
That broke like a clap of thunder:
Call Death!—Call Death!
And the echo sounded down the streets of heaven
Till it reached away back to that shadowy place,
Where Death waits with his pale, white horse.

And Death heard the summons,
And he leaped on his fastest horse,
Pale as a sheet in the moonlight.
Up the golden street Death galloped,
And the hoof of his horse struck fire from the gold,
But they didn't make no sound.
Up Death rode to the Great White Throne,
And waited for God's command.

And God said: Go down, Death, go down,
Go down to Savannah, Georgia,
Down in Yamacraw,
And find Sister Caroline.
She's borne the burden and heat of the day,
She's labored long in my vineyard,
And she's tired—
She's weary—
Go down, Death, and bring her to me.

And Death didn't say a word,
But he loosed the reins on his pale, white horse,
And he clamped the spurs to his bloodless sides,
And out and down he rode,
Through Heaven's pearly gates,

Past suns and moons and stars;
On Death rode,
And the foam from his horse was like a comet in the sky;
On Death rode,
Leaving the lightning's flash behind;
Straight on down he came.

While we were watching round her bed,
She turned her eyes and looked away,
She saw what we couldn't see;
She saw Old Death. She saw Old Death.
Coming like a falling star.
But Death didn't frighten Sister Caroline;
He looked to her like a welcome friend.
And she whispered to us: I'm going home,
And she smiled and closed her eyes.

And Death took her up like a baby,
And she lay in his icy arms,
But she didn't feel no chill.
And Death began to ride again—
Up beyond the evening star,
Out beyond the morning star
Into the glittering light of glory,
On to the Great White Throne.
And there he laid Sister Caroline
On the loving breast of Jesus.

And Jesus took his own hand and wiped away her tears,
And he smoothed the furrows from her face,
And the angels sang a little song,
And Jesus rocked her in his arms,
And kept a-saying: Take your rest,
Take your rest, take your rest.

Weep not—weep not
She is not dead;
She's resting in the bosom of Jesus.

James Weldon Johnson

WHO IS THAT A-WALKNG IN THE CORN?

Who is that a-walking in the corn?
I have looked to East and looked to West
But nowhere could I find Him who walks
    Master's cornfield in the morning.

Who is that a-walking in the corn?
Is it Joshua, the son of Nun?—
Or King David come to fight the giant
    Near the cornfield in the morning?

Who is that a-walking in the corn?
Is it Peter jangling Heaven's keys?—
Or old Gabriel come to blow his horn
    Near the cornfield in the morning?

Who is that a-walking in the corn?
I have looked to East and looked to West
But nowhere could I find Him who walks
    Master's cornfield in the morning.

Fenton Johnson

THE LONELY MOTHER

Oh, my mother's moaning by the river,
My poor mother's moaning by the river,
For her son who walks the earth in sorrow.

Long my mother's moaned beside the river,
And her tears have filled an angel's pitcher:

"Lord of Heaven, bring to me my honey,
Bring to me the darling of my bosom,
For a lonely mother by the river."

Cease, O mother, moaning by the river;
Cease, good mother, moaning by the river.
I have seen the star of Michael shining,
Michael shining at the Gates of Morning.
Row, O mighty angel, down the twilight,
Row until I find a lonely woman,
Swaying long beneath a tree of cypress,
Swaying for her son who walks in sorrow.

Fenton Johnson

AUNT JANE ALLEN

State Street is lonely today, Aunt Jane Allen has driven her chariot
to Heaven.
I remember how she hobbled along, a little woman, parched of skin,
brown as the leather of a satchel and with eyes that had scanned
eighty years of life.
Have those who bore her dust to the last resting place buried with
her the basket of aprons she went up and down State Street
trying to sell?
Have those who bore her dust to the last resting place buried with
her the gentle worn *Son* that she gave to each of the seed of
Ethiopia?

Fenton Johnson

SONG OF THE SON

Pour O pour that parting soul in song,
O pour it in the sawdust glow of night,

Into the velvet pine-smoke air to-night,
And let the valley carry it along.
And let the valley carry it along.

O land and soil, red soil and sweet-gum tree,
So scant of grass, so profligate of pines,
Now just an epoch's sun declines
Thy son, in time, I have returned to thee,
Thy son, I have in time returned to thee.

In time, for though the sun is setting on
A song-lit race of slaves, it has not set;
Though late, O soil, it is not too late yet
To catch thy plaintive soul, leaving, soon gone,
Leaving, to catch thy plaintive soul soon gone.

O Negro slaves, dark purple ripened plums,
Squeezed, and bursting in the pine-wood air,
Passing, before they stripped the old tree bare
One plum was saved for me, one seed becomes
An everlasting song, a singing tree,
Caroling softly souls of slavery,
What they were, and what they are to me,
Caroling softly souls of slavery.

Jean Toomer

NORTHBOUN'

O' de wurl' ain't flat,
An' de wurl' ain't roun',
Hits one long strip
Hangin' up an' down—
Jes' Souf an' Norf;
Jes' Norf an' Souf.

Talkin' 'bout sailin' 'round de wurl'—
Huh! I'd be so dizzy my head 'ud twurl.
If dis heah earf wuz jes' a ball
You know the people all 'ud fall.

O' de wurl' ain't flat,
An' de wurl' ain't roun',
Hits one long strip
Hangin' up an' down—
Jes' Souf an' Norf;
Jes' Norf an' Souf.

Talkin' bout the City whut Saint John saw—
Chile you oughta go to Saginaw;
A nigger's chance is "finest kind,"
An' pretty gals ain't hard to find.

Huh, de wurl' ain't flat
An' de wurl' ain't roun'
Jes' one long strip
Hangin' up an' down.
Since Norf is up,
An' Souf is down,
An' Hebben is up,
I'm upward boun'.

Ariel Williams Holloway

MOLLY MEANS

Old Molly Means was a hag and a witch;
Chile of the devil, the dark, and sitch.
Her heavy hair hung thick in ropes
And her blazing eyes was black as pitch.
Imp at three and wench at 'leben
She counted her husbands to the number seben.

O Molly, Molly, Molly Means
There goes the ghost of Molly Means.

Some say she was born with a veil on her face
So she could look through unnatchal space
Through the future and through the past
And charm a body or an evil place
And every man could well despise
The evil look in her coal black eyes.
 Old Molly, Molly, Molly Means
 Dark is the ghost of Molly Means.

And when the tale begun to spread
Of evil and of holy dread:
Her black-hand arts and her evil powers
How she cast her spells and called the dead,
The younguns was afraid at night
And the farmers feared their crops would blight.
 Old Molly, Molly, Molly Means
 Cold is the ghost of Molly Means.

Then one dark day she put a spell
On a young gal-bride just come to dwell
In the lane just down from Molly's shack
And when her husband come riding back
His wife was barking like a dog
And on all four like a common hog.
 O Molly, Molly, Molly Means
 Where is the ghost of Molly Means?

The neighbors come and they went away
And said she'd die before break of day
But her husband held her in his arms
And swore he'd break the wicked charms;
He'd search all up and down the land
And turn the spell on Molly's hand.
 O Molly, Molly, Molly Means
 Sharp is the ghost of Molly Means.

So he rode all day and he rode all night
And at the dawn he come in sight
Of a man who said he could move the spell
And cause the awful thing to dwell
On Molly Means, to bark and bleed
Till she died at the hands of her evil deed.
    Old Molly, Molly, Molly Means
    This is the ghost of Molly Means.

Sometimes at night through the shadowy trees
She rides along on a winter breeze.
You can hear her holler and whine and cry.
Her voice is thin and her moan is high,
And her cackling laugh or her barking cold
Bring terror to the young and old.
    O Molly, Molly, Molly Means
    Lean is the ghost of Molly Means.

Margaret Walker

DARK OF THE MOON

Southern Road

Swing dat hammer—hunh—
Steady, bo.
Swing dat hammer—hunh—
Steady, bo.
Ain't no rush, bebby;
Long ways to go.

Burner tore his—hunh—
Black heart away.
Burner tore his—hunh—
Black heart away.

Got me life, bebby,
An' a day.

Gal's on Fifth Street—hunh—
Son done gone.
Gal's on Fifth Street—hunh—
Son done gone.
Wife's in de ward, bebby;
Babe's not bo'n.

My ole man died—hunh—
Cussin' me.
My ole man died—hunh—
Cussin' me.
Ole lady rocks, bebby,
Huh misery.

Doubleshackled—hunh—
Guard behin'
Doubleshackled—hunh—
Guard behin'
Ball an' chain, bebby,
On my min'.

White man tells me—hunh—
Damn yo' soul.
White man tells me—hunh—
Damn yo' soul.
Got no need, bebby,
To be tole.

Chain gang nevah—hunh—
Let me go.
Chain gang nevah—hunh—
Let me go.
Po' los' boy, bebby,
Evahmo'. . . . .

Sterling A. Brown

SISTER LOU

Honey
When de man
Calls out de las' train
You're gonna ride,
Tell him howdy.

Gather up yo' basket
An' yo' knittin' an' yo' things,
An' go on up an' visit
Wid frien' Jesus fo' a spell.

Show Marfa
How to make yo' greengrape jellies,
An' give po' Lazarus
A passel of them Golden Biscuits.

Scald some meal
Fo' some rightdown good spoonbread
Fo' li'l box-plunkin' David.

An' sit aroun'
An' tell them Hebrew Chillen
All yo' stories. . . .

Honey
Don't be feared of them pearly gates,
Don't go 'round to de back,
No mo' dataway
Not evah no mo'.

Let Michael tote yo' burden
An' yo' pocketbook an' evah thing

'Cept yo' Bible,
While Gabriel blows somp'n
Solemn but loudsome
On dat horn of his'n.

Honey
Go straight on to de Big House,
An' speak to yo' God
Widout no fear an' tremblin'.

Then sit down
An' pass de time of day awhile.

Give a good talkin' to
To yo' favorite 'postle Peter,
An' rub the po' head
Of mixed-up Judas,
An' joke awhile wid Jonah.
Then, when you gits de chance,
Always rememberin' yo' raisin',
Let 'em know youse tired
Jest a mite tired.

Jesus will find yo' bed fo' you
Won't no servant evah bother wid yo' room.
Jesus will lead you
To a room wid windows
Openin' on cherry trees an' plum trees
Bloomin' everlastin'.

An' dat will be yours
Fo' keeps.

Den take yo' time . . .
Honey, take yo' blessed time.

Sterling A. Brown

MA RAINEY

1.

When Ma Rainey
Comes to town,
Folks from any place
Miles aroun',
From Cape Girardeau,
Poplar Bluff,
Flocks in to hear
Ma do her stuff;
Comes flivverin' in,
Or ridin' mules,
Or packed in trains,
Picknickin' fools. . . .
That's what it's like,
Fo' miles on down,
To New Orleans delta
An' Mobile town,
When Ma hits
Anywheres aroun'.

2.

O Ma Rainey,
Sing yo' song;
Now you's back
Whah you belong,
Git way inside us,
Keep us strong. . . .
O Ma Rainey,
Li'l an' low,
Sing us 'bout de hard luck

Roun' our do';
Sing us 'bout de lonesome road
We mus' go. . . .

3.

I talked to a fellow, and de fellow say:
She jes catch hold of us, somekindaway;
She sang "Backwater Blues" one day—

It rained fo' days an' de skies was dark as night.
Trouble taken place in de lowlands at night.

Thundered an' lightened an' de storm begin to roll.
Thousan's of people ain't got no place to go.

Den I went an' stood upon some high o' lonesome hill,
An' looked down on de place where I used to live.

An' den de folks, dey natchally bowed dey heads an' cried,
Bowed dey heavy heads, shet dey moufs up tight an' cried,
An' Ma lef' de stage, an' followed some de folks outside.

Dere wasn't much more, de fellow say:
She jes gits hold of us, dataway.

Sterling A. Brown

BLUES FOR BESSIE

Bessie Smith, the greatest of the early blues singers, died violently after an auto accident while on a theatrical tour of the South in 1937. The newspapers reported that she bled to death when the only hospital in the vicinity refused her emergency medical attention because she was a Negro woman.

Let de peoples know (unnh)
  what dey did in dat Southern Town
Let de peoples know
  what dey did in dat Southern Town
Well, dey lef' po' Bessie dyin'
  wid de blood (Lawd) astreamin' down

Bessie lef' Chicago
  in a bran' new Cadillac;
Didn' take no suitcase
  but she wore her mournin' black (unnh)
Bessie, Bessie,
  she wore her mournin' black
She went ridin' down to Dixie (Lawd)
  an' dey shipped her body back

Lawd, wasn't it a turr'ble
  when dat rain come down
Yes, wasn't it a turr'ble
  when de rain come down
An' ol' Death caught po' Bessie
  down in 'at Jim Crow town

Well, de thunder rolled
  an' de lightnin' broke de sky
Lawd, de thunder rolled
  an' de lightnin' broke de sky
An' you could hear po' Bessie moanin',
  "Gret Gawd, please doan lemme die!"

She holler, "Lawd, please hep me!",
  but He never heerd a word she say
Holler, "Please, *some*body hep me!",
  but dey never heerd a word she say
Frien', when yo' luck run out in Dixie,
  well, it doan do no good to pray.

Well, dey give po' Bessie
  to de undertaker man;

Ol' Death an' Jim Crow (Lawd)
  done de job, hand in han'
Well, Bessie, Bessie,
  she won't sing de blues no mo'
Cause dey let her go down bloody (Lawd)
  trav'lin' from door to do'

Bessie lef' Chicago
  in a bran' new Cad'lac Eight
Yes, Bessie lef' Chicago
  in a gret big Cad'lac Eight
But dey shipped po' Bessie back (Lawd)
  on dat lonesome midnight freight

Lawd, let de peoples know
  what dey did in dat Southern Town
Yes, let de peoples know
  what dey did in dat Southern Town
Well, dey lef' po' Bessie dyin'
  wid de blood (Lawd) a-streamin' down

Myron O'Higgins

HOMAGE TO THE EMPRESS OF THE BLUES:

BESSIE SMITH

Because somewhere there was a man in a candystripe silk shirt
gracile and dangerous as a jaguar and because some woman moaned
for him in sixty watt gloom and mourned him Faithless Love
Twotiming Love Oh Love Oh Careless Aggravating Love,
    She came out on the stage in yards of pearls, emerging like
    a favorite scenic view, flashed her golden teeth, and sang.

Because somewhere the lathes began to show from underneath
torn hurdygurdy lithographs of dollfaced heaven,

because there were those who feared the riotsquad of statistics,
    She came out on the stage in ostrich feathers, beaded satin,
    and shone that smile on us and didn't need the lights and sang.

Robert Hayden

YOUNG GAL'S BLUES

I'm gonna walk to de graveyard
'Hind ma friend, Miss Cora Lee.
Gonna walk to de graveyard
'Hind ma dear friend Cora Lee.
Cause when I'm dead some
Body'll have to walk behind me.

I'm going to de po' house
To see ma old Aunt Clew.
Goin' to de po' house
To see ma old Aunt Clew.
When I'm old an' ugly
I'll want to see somebody, too.

De po' house is lonely
An' de grave is cold.
O, de po' house is lonely,
De graveyard grave is cold.
But I'd rather be dead than
To be ugly an' old.

When love is gone what
Can a young gal do?
When love is gone, O,
What can a young gal do?
Keep on a-lovin' me, daddy,
Cause I don't want to be blue.

Langston Hughes

MA LAWD

Ma Lawd ain't no stuck-up man.
Ma Lawd, He ain't proud.
When He goes a-walkin'
He gives me His hand.
You ma friend, He 'lowed.

Ma Lawd knowed what it was to work.
He knowed how to pray.
Ma Lawd's life was trouble, too,
Trouble ever' day.

Ma Lawd ain't no stuck-up man.
He's a friend o' mine.
When He went to Heaben,
His soul on fire,
He tole me I was gwine.
He said, "Sho you'll come wid Me
An' be Ma friend through eternity."

Langston Hughes

BLUES AT DAWN

I don't dare start thinking in the morning.
I don't dare start thinking in the morning.
    If I thought thoughts in bed,
        Them thoughts would bust my head—
So I don't dare start thinking in the morning.

I don't dare remember in the morning,
Don't dare remember in the morning.

If I recall the day before,
I wouldn't get up no more—
So I don't dare remember in the morning.

Langston Hughes

BAD MORNING

Here I sit
With my shoes mismated.
Lawdy-mercy!
I's frustrated!

Langston Hughes

WAKE

Tell all my mourners
To mourn in red—
Cause there ain't no sense
In my bein' dead.

Langston Hughes

REQUEST FOR REQUIEMS

Play the *St. Louis Blues*
For me when I die.
I want some fine music
Up there in the sky.

Sing the *St. James Infirmary*
When you let me down—

Cause there ain't a good man
Like me left around.

Langston Hughes

MOTTO

I play it cool
And dig all jive.
That's the reason
I stay alive.

My motto,
As I live and learn,
    is:
Dig And Be Dug
In Return

Langston Hughes

DEAD IN THERE

Sometimes
A night funeral
Going by
Carries home
A re-bop daddy.

Hearse and flowers
Guarantee
He'll never hype
Another paddy.

It's hard to believe,
But dead in there,

He'll never lay a
Hype nowhere!

He's my ace-boy,
Gone away.
Wake up and live!
He used to say.

Squares
Who couldn't dig him,
Plant him now—
Out where it makes
No diff' no how.

Langston Hughes

JAM SESSION

Letting midnight
out on bail
   pop-a-da
having been
detained in jail
   oop-pop-a-da
for sprinkling salt
on a dreamer's tail
   pop-a-da
while Bebop boys
implore Mecca
to achieve
six discs
with Decca
   pop-a-da
Little cullud boys
with fears
   frantic

nudge their draftee years.
Pop-a-da!

Langston Hughes

MAE'S RENT PARTY

Say, did you go to Mae's rent party?
Let me tell you what it was all about.
They had pig's feet and potato salad.
It jumped till the man threw us out.
They had hog maws and corn pone dumplings,
White whiskey and fo' kegs of beer.
I sure hopes I get invited,
When they let her out next year.

Ernest J. Wilson, Jr.

BRINGING MOTHER HOME

The narrator of "Bringing Mother Home" is an old woman, half-Indian and half-Negro. She is literate to the extent of being able to sign her own name but for reasons of her own she has wished to sign only "Martha." Miss Rosenberg writes us that she not only set down the words exactly as they were told, but that when Martha repeated the story after a long interval the details and the wording of the retelling were almost identical with those of the version here set down. I am not sure that what follows is a poem in the most formal sense. Certainly, however, it is a rare example of a kind of folk-telling so charged and so self-formed in the telling as to suggest the very roots of poetry. We at SATURDAY REVIEW *have found Martha's story unforgettable. We think many readers will share our sense that Martha is an authentic and moving voice speaking the native matter of poetry.*

John Ciardi

I went to Louisiana to get my mother (that's where she was at)
The twenty-third of December.
(That was my borned state. I left there when I was seventeen.)
And when I got there she didn't know me.
She had to look at me a long time.
But she come to remember; she finally come to:
She said, "This is Martha.
Martha?" she says, "Is this you?"
So my brother he come from New York.
He got there on the twenty-fourth of December.
(He has two children and a wife),
And so they said, "We come after you mama,
That's what we come for."
But she didn't want to go with them,
And I didn't want her to, because
They had little children and his wife couldn't—you know—
Take care of all.
So we carried her to a doctor—Dr. King,
And he give her some examines
And he said she was a mentality case.
He told me, "Don't leave her. Stay with her."
I stayed with her 'till February,
Just me alone.

She would go out of the house and walk
In the rain and I would follow close behind—
To see would she know the way back.
A lot of times she wouldn't know where she was going.
I would come up beside her and she would look at me
And say, "Martha, *where* we going?"
"Where *you* going?" "I do' know." "Then le's go home."

Then she agreed to come back to California with me,
She agreed to. So, on the seventeenth of February,
We left in a car. But we got to the place where she wouldn't
Stay in the car no more. She would ask for the key until
We had to give it to her (Can't drive no more without the key).
Then she would get out and walk; so

I would walk too, until she was tired.
I couldn't get her to eat, not anything.
So, come to El Paso, Texas, I put her in the hospital
For five days. I asked the doctor there,
Could she take a plane or a train to California,
Or could she make it in a car. He said, "She can."

We got as far as Fresno, and rainin'!
It rained so hard the windshield wiper
Couldn't make it. Mama was laughin' and
Talkin', so I said "Mama's better. I'm glad
I had her in the hospital."
Then we went into a gas station
And all of a sudden Mama said to me,
"Martha, look at me. I'm as *white*. I'm as white as that white man
        standing over there."
So then I knew she was very sick.
We carried her to the hospital.
The lady there, she said "This is a payin' hospital."
I said, "That's all right, if you can do her some good."
The doctor, he gave her a injection, and then,
Just like that, she died.

Well, I mean
I would'uv stayed there in El Paso with her.
I asked the doctor "Can she make it?"
And he said, "She can."
I told them all, "I kin keep my mother. I kin keep her."
I wasn't thinking of no money. I didn't care.
I was thinking how to keep my mother.

Dorothy Rosenberg

OF DE WITT WILLIAMS ON HIS WAY TO
LINCOLN CEMETERY

He was born in Alabama.
He was bred in Illinois.
He was nothing but a
Plain black boy.

Swing low swing low sweet chariot.
Nothing but a plain black boy.

Drive him past the Pool Hall.
Drive him past the Show.
Blind within his casket,
But maybe he will know.

Down through Forty-seventh Street:
Underneath the L,
And—Northwest Corner, Prairie,
That he loved so well.

Don't forget the Dance Halls—
Warwick and Savoy,
Where he picked his women, where
He drank his liquid joy.

Born in Alabama.
Bred in Illinois.
He was nothing but a
Plain black boy.

Swing low swing low sweet chariot.
Nothing but a plain black boy.

Gwendolyn Brooks

LAME MAN AND THE BLIND MAN

Lame man said to the blind man,
"Hope you're doing well."
Blind man said to the lame man,
"Can't you see me catching hell?"

Blind man said to the lame man,
"How's things with you?"
Lame man leading the blind man,
"I'm catching hell, too."

Blind man playing his old guitar.
"Somebody gimme a dime—
Tired o' singing the blues
For nothing all the time!"

Lame man said to the blind man,
"Can't I sing some bass?"
Blind man said to the lame man,
"Open up your face!"

Lame man and the blind man,
Sang a too-sad song:
" 'Tain't right to be so faredown!
It's wrong! Sure is wrong!"

Blind man said to the lame man,
"Do I feel rain or snow?"
Lame man said to the blind man,
"Rain! Let's go!"

Waring Cuney

JOHN HENRY IN HARLEM

The scabby walls of tenements
Tower on either hand
Like the wind-clawed sides
Of a Dust Bowl canyon.

In the dream-dead street
The heat waves dance
Like ghosts upon a plagued river.

Stripped to the waist,
His muscles knotted like ebony cords,
Stillicho swings his mighty pick
And his lusty ballad of John Henry
Climbs the fire-trap tenements:

John Henry said: "If you give me a drink
I'll finish dis job befo' a cat kin wink.
When Gawd made me, He made a man
Who's de best pick driver in all de lan'."

The sweat rolls down Stillicho's body,
And the sweat rolls down his face,
And the blur of the street scene wavers before his eyes,
And the rag of the toiler wipes his face.

Stillicho thinks of his wife,
The big pot of cabbage and ham-hock
Waiting for him in the flat.

He sees pride shining in her eyes
When he brings home his check, Saturday nights,
And hides it where she can find it.

John Henry he had a pretty wife,
An' her name it was Polly Ann,
She loved her home an' she loved her kid
An' she loved her pickdrivin' man!

Stillicho Spikes dreams of his son
And the bright new watch he'll buy the lad
When he finishes high school in June,
The first of the Spikes to get a diploma.
Didn't the principal say
Junior was smart
And perhaps he'd be a second Booker T.?

John Henry he had a little boy,
An' he was John Henry's pride an' joy.
John Henry said, "He'll make a man
As good as any in dis wide, wide lan'."

The verve of his thoughts
Makes his pick rise and fall
Like the regal stick of a drum-major.

Stillicho looks at the slanting sun,
Spits on his horny hands,
Rubs them and grins.

John Henry worked in all kinds of weather,
'Cause a workin' man cain't do no better.
John Henry said to just keep in motion
Till you conquer de lan' an' conquer de ocean!

Melvin B. Tolson

Prose in the Folk Manner

FISH FRY

I WENT out to see Houston, Texas. The Ethiopians of the district were having their annual Fish Fry. Also, the circus was in town. I was told, of all the sights to see, don't miss the Fish Fry. They directed me down to the railroad track, where I crossed and walked a few blocks west to a vacant lot. The colored people had this lot covered with tents, cook stoves of all kinds, charcoal pots and camp-fires—all with some kind of a kettle or hot grease on them, frying fish. The customers were like a big mass of moving ants, when you step on their hill accidentally. Out on a little green spot, a man and woman were lying on the ground, eating fish offa spread-out news-paper with their hands. I stood near them and heard this conversation:

MAN: This fish sho is good.
WOMAN: Ain't they.
MAN: I wonder who first named the fish, "Fish."
(Time was past for swallowing.)
WOMAN: Christ named the fish, "Fish."
MAN: How come no one ever talked with Christ?
WOMAN: Yes, they did. The day Christ named the fish "Fish,"

He fed a whole town of people, as big as Houston, on one fish.

MAN: On *one* fish? Stop your kidding! It musta been a whopper.
. . . I've heard tell of fish as big as whales, but they don't eat 'em.

WOMAN: No, this wasn't a big fish. Christ held it in his hand: I
saw the picture of it.

MAN: A SEASONED FISH, huh?

WOMAN: I ain't never heared of a SEASONED FISH.

MAN: Hush yo mouth. You've eaten many seasoned fish. You see,
you put salt on this fish because it comes from the clear water, but
seasoned fish comes from the ocean and they don't need any salt
on them.

WOMAN: Oh, I guess you is right.

MAN: Christ sho knowed his stuff—feed all them people on one
seasoned fish. One mouthful, then they fill upon water! Ha-ha-ha-
hee!

WOMAN: Ain't it the truth.

MAN: Den Christ made the salt, too—huh?

WOMAN: Cos he did.

MAN: I forgives my elder den, an' I'se gwine back to the church
again, for dere's nothing I likes better than SALT PORK, CORN
BEEF and SEASONED FISH!

And the conversation ended in laughter. I could hear them laughing as I left the lot. There was no way for the man to stick the
woman on any questions about Christ. She had lived as intimately
with him as Esther Murphy has lived with Napoleon—Josephine
and George Washington.

Taylor Gordon

SUNDAY DINNER

AFTER my father's desertion, my mother's ardently religious disposi-
tion dominated the household and I was often taken to Sunday
school where I met God's representative in the guise of a tall, black
preacher. One Sunday my mother invited the tall, black preacher
to a dinner of fried chicken. I was happy, not because the preacher

was coming but because of the chicken. One or two neighbors also were invited. But no sooner had the preacher arrived than I began to resent him, for I learned at once that he, like my father, was used to having his own way. The hour for dinner came and I was wedged at the table between talking and laughing adults. In the center of the table was a large platter of golden-brown fried chicken. I compared the bowl of soup that sat before me with the crispy chicken and decided in favor of the chicken. The others began to eat their soup, but I could not touch mine.

"Eat your soup," my mother said.

"I don't want any," I said.

"You won't get anything else until you've eaten your soup," she said.

The preacher had finished his soup and had asked that the platter of chicken be passed to him. It galled me. He smiled, cocked his head this way and that way, picking out choice pieces. I forced a spoonful of soup down my throat and looked to see if my speed matched that of the preacher. It did not. There were already bare chicken bones on his plate, and he was reaching for more. I tried eating my soup faster, but it was no use; the other people were now serving themselves chicken and the platter was more than half empty. I gave up and sat staring in despair at the vanishing pieces of fried chicken.

"Eat your soup or you won't get anything," my mother warned.

I looked at her appealingly and could not answer. As piece after piece of chicken was eaten, I was unable to eat my soup at all. I grew hot with anger. The preacher was laughing and joking and the grownups were hanging on his words. My growing hate of the preacher finally became more important than God or religion and I could no longer contain myself. I leaped up from the table, knowing that I should be ashamed of what I was doing, but unable to stop, and screamed, running blindly from the room.

"That preacher's going to eat all the chicken!" I bawled.

The preacher tossed back his head and roared with laughter, but my mother was angry and told me that I was to have no dinner because of my bad manners.

Richard Wright

GRANDFATHER

I AM not ashamed of my grandparents for having been slaves. I am only ashamed of myself for having at one time been ashamed. About eighty-five years ago they were told that they were free, united with others of our country in everything pertaining to the common good, and, in everything social, separate like the fingers of the hand. And they believed it. They exulted in it. They stayed in their place, worked hard, and brought up my father to do the same. But my grandfather is the one. He was an old odd guy, my grandfather, and I am told I take after him. It was he who caused the trouble. On his deathbed he called my father to him and said, "Son, after I'm gone I want you to keep up the good fight. I never told you, but our life is a war and I have been a traitor all my born days, a spy in the enemy's country ever since I give up my gun back in the Reconstruction. Live with your head in the lion's mouth. I want you to over come 'em with yeses, undermine 'em with grins, agree 'em to death and destruction, let 'em swoller you till they vomit or bust wide open." They thought the old man had gone out of his mind. He had been the meekest of men. The younger children were rushed from the room, the shades drawn and the flame of the lamp turned so low that it sputtered on the wick like the old man's breathing. "Learn it to the younguns," he whispered fiercely; then he died.

But my folks were more alarmed over his last words than over his dying. It was as though he had not died at all, his words caused so much anxiety. I was warned emphatically to forget what he had said and, indeed, this is the first time it has been mentioned outside the family circle. It had a tremendous effect upon me, however. I could never be sure of what he meant. Grandfather had been a quiet old man who never made any trouble, yet on his deathbed he had called himself a traitor and a spy, and he had spoken of his meekness as a dangerous activity. It became a constant puzzle which lay unanswered in the back of my mind. And whenever

things went well for me I remembered my grandfather and felt guilty and uncomfortable. It was as though I was carrying out his advice in spite of myself. And to make it worse, everyone loved me for it. I was praised by the most lily-white men of the town. I was considered an example of desirable conduct—just as my grandfather had been. And what puzzled me was that the old man had defined it as treachery. When I was praised for my conduct I felt a guilt that in some way I was doing something that was really against the wishes of the white folks, that if they had understood they would have desired me to act just the opposite, that I should have been sulky and mean, and that really would have been what they wanted, even though they were fooled and thought they wanted me to act as I did. It made me afraid that some day they would look upon me as a traitor and I would be lost. Still I was more afraid to act any other way because they didn't like that at all. The old man's words were like a curse.

Ralph Ellison

HOSPITAL

"You're all right, boy. You're okay. You just be patient," said the voice, hollow with profound detachment.

I seemed to go away; the lights receded like a tail-light racing down a dark country road. I couldn't follow. A sharp pain stabbed my shoulder. I twisted about on my back, fighting something I couldn't see. Then after a while my vision cleared.

Now a man was sitting with his back to me, manipulating dials on a panel. I wanted to call him, but the Fifth Symphony rhythm racked me, and he seemed too serene and too far away. Bright metal bars were between us and when I strained my neck around I discovered that I was not lying on an operating table but in a kind of glass and nickel box, the lid of which was propped open. Why was I here?

"Doctor! Doctor!" I called.

No answer. Perhaps he hadn't heard, I thought, calling again and feeling the stabbing pulses of the machine again and feeling

myself going under and fighting against it and coming up to hear
voices carrying on a conversation behind my head. The static sounds
became a quiet drone. Strains of music, a Sunday air, drifted from
a distance. With closed eyes, barely breathing I warded off the pain.
The voices droned harmoniously. Was it a radio I heard—a phonograph? The vox humana of a hidden organ? If so, what organ
and where? I felt warm. Green hedges, dazzling with red wild roses
appeared behind my eyes, stretching with a gentle curving to an
infinity empty of objects, a limpid blue space. Scenes of a shaded
lawn in summer drifted past; I saw a uniformed military band
arrayed decorously in concert, each musician with well-oiled hair,
heard a sweet-voiced trumpet rendering "The Holy City" as from
an echoing distance, buoyed by a choir of muted horns; and above,
the mocking obbligato of a mocking bird. I felt giddy. The air
seemed to grow thick with fine white gnats, filling my eyes, boiling
so thickly that the dark trumpeter breathed them in and expelled
them through the bell of his golden horn, a live white cloud mixing
with the tones upon the torpid air.

I came back. The voices still droned above me and I disliked
them. Why didn't they go away? Smug ones. Oh, doctor, I thought
drowsily, did you ever wade in a brook before breakfast? Ever
chew on sugar cane? You know, doc, the same fall day I first saw
the hounds chasing black men in stripes and chains my grandmother sat with me and sang with twinkling eyes:

> "Godamighty made a monkey
> Godamighty made a whale
> And Godamighty made a 'gator
> With hickeys all over his tail. . . ."

Or you, nurse, did you know that when you strolled in pink
organdy and picture hat between the rows of cape jasmine, cooing
to your beau in a drawl as thick as sorghum, we little black boys
hidden snug in the bushes called out so loud that you daren't hear:

> "Did you ever see Miss Margaret boil water?
> Man, she hisses a wonderful stream,
> Seventeen miles and a quarter,
> Man, and you can't see her pot for the steam. . . ."

But now the music became a distinct wail of female pain. I opened my eyes. Glass and metal floated above me.

"How are you feeling, boy?" a voice said.

A pair of eyes peered down through lenses as thick as the bottom of a Coca-Cola bottle, eyes protruding, luminous and veined, like an old biology specimen preserved in alcohol.

"I don't have enough room," I said angrily.

'Oh, that's a necessary part of the treatment."

"But I need more room," I insisted. "I'm cramped."

"Don't worry about it boy. You'll get used to it after a while."

Ralph Ellison

LONESOME BOY

When Bubber first learned to play the trumpet, his old grandpa winked his eye and laughed.

"You better mind how you blow that horn, sonny boy. You better mind."

"I like to blow loud, I like to blow fast, and I like to blow high," Bubber answered. "Listen to this, Grandpa." And he went on blowing with his eyes closed.

When Bubber was a little bigger, he began carrying his trumpet around with him wherever he went, so his old grandpa scratched his whiskers, took the corn-cob pipe out of his mouth, and laughed again.

"You better mind *where* you blow that horn, boy," he warned. "I used to blow one myself, and I know."

Bubber smiled. "Where did you ever blow music, Grandpa?"

"Down in New Orleans and all up and down the river. I blowed trumpet most everywhere in my young days, and I tell you, you better mind where you go blowing."

"I like to blow my trumpet in the school band when it marches, I like to blow it on the landing when the river boats come in sight, and I like to blow it among the trees in the swamp," he said, still smiling. But when he looked at his grandpa again, he saw a worried

look on the old man's face, and he asked, "What's the matter, Grandpa, ain't that all right?"

Grandpa shook his head. "I wouldn't do it if I was you."

That sounded funny to Bubber, but he was not in the habit of disputing his grandfather. Instead he said, "I don't believe I ever heard you blow the trumpet, Grandpa. Don't you want to try blowing on mine now?"

Again the old man shook his head. "My blowing days are long gone," he said. "I still got the lip, but I ain't got the teeth. It takes good teeth to blow high notes on a horn, and these I got ain't much good. They're store teeth."

That made Bubber feel sorry for his grandfather, so he whispered softly, "I'll mind where I blow my horn, Grandpa."

He didn't really mean it though. He just said it to make his grandpa feel good. And the very next day he was half a mile out in the country blowing his horn in a cornfield. Two or three evenings later he was blowing it on a shady lane when the sun went down and not paying much attention where he went.

When he came home, his grandpa met him. "I heard you blowing your horn a long ways away," he said. "The air was still. I could hear it easy."

"How did it sound, Grandpa?"

"Oh, it sounded right pretty." He paused a moment, knocking the ashes out of his pipe, before adding, "Sounded like you mighta been lost."

That made Bubber ashamed of himself, because he knew he had not kept his word and that he was not minding where he blew his trumpet. "I know what you mean, Grandpa," he answered. "But I can't do like you say. When I'm blowing my horn, I don't always look where I'm going."

Grandpa walked to the window and looked out. While he was standing there, he hitched his overalls up a little higher. He took a red handkerchief from his pocket and wiped his forehead. "Sounded to me like you might have been past Barbin's Landing."

"I was lost," Bubber admitted.

"You can end up in some funny places when you're just blowing a horn and not paying attention. I know," Grandpa insisted. "I know."

"Well, what do you want me to do, Grandpa?"

The old man struck a kitchen match on the seat of his pants and lit a kerosene lamp, because the room was black dark by now. While the match was still burning, he lit his pipe. Then he sat down and stretched out his feet. Bubber was on a stool on the other side of the room, his trumpet under his arm. "When you go to school and play your horn in the band, that's all right," the old man said. "When you come home, you ought to put it in the case and leave it there. It ain't good to go traipsing around with a horn in your hand. You might get into devilment."

"But I feel lonesome without my trumpet, Grandpa," Bubber pleaded. "I don't like to go around without it any time. I feel lost."

Grandpa sighed. "Well, there you are—lost with it and lost without it. I don't know what's going to become of you, sonny boy."

"You don't understand, Grandpa. You don't understand."

The old man smoked his pipe quietly for a few minutes and then went off to bed, but Bubber did not move. Later on, however, when he heard his grandpa snoring in the next room, he went outdoors, down the path and around the smokehouse, and sat on a log. The night was still. He couldn't hear anything louder than a cricket. Soon he began wondering how his trumpet would sound on such a still night, back there behind the old smokehouse, so he put the mouthpiece to his lips very lightly and blew a few silvery notes. Immediately Bubber felt better. Now he knew for sure that Grandpa didn't understand how it was with a boy and a horn—a lonesome boy with a silver trumpet. Bubber lifted his horn toward the stars and let the music pour out.

Presently a big orange moon rose, and everything Bubber could see changed suddenly. The moon was so big it made the smokehouse and the trees and the fences seem small. Bubber blew his trumpet loud, he blew it fast, and he blew it high, and in just a few minutes he forgot all about Grandpa sleeping in the house.

He was afraid to talk to Grandpa after that. He was afraid Grandpa might scold him or warn him or try in some other way to persuade him to leave his trumpet in its case. Bubber was growing fast now. He knew what he liked, and he did not think he needed any advice from Grandpa.

Still, he loved his grandfather very much, and he had no intention of saying anything that would hurt him. Instead he decided to leave home. He did not tell Grandpa what he was going to do. He just waited till the old man went to sleep in his bed one night. Then he quietly blew out the lamp, put his trumpet under his arm and started walking down the road from Marksville to Barbin's Landing.

No boat was there, but Bubber did not mind. He knew one would come by before morning, and he knew that he would not be lonesome so long as he had his trumpet with him. He found a place on the little dock where he could lean back against a post and swing his feet over the edge while playing, and the time passed swiftly. And when he finally went aboard a river boat, just before morning, he found a place on the deck that suited him just as well and went right on blowing his horn.

Nobody asked him to pay any fare. The river boat men did not seem to expect it of a boy who blew a trumpet the way Bubber did. And in New Orleans the cooks in the kitchens where he ate and the people who kept the rooming houses where he slept did not seem to expect him to pay either. In fact, people seemed to think that a boy who played a trumpet where the patrons of a restaurant could hear him or for the guests of a rooming house should receive money for it. They began to throw money around Bubber's feet as he played his horn.

At first he was surprised. Later he decided it only showed how wrong Grandpa had been about horn blowing. So he picked up all the money they threw, bought himself fancy new clothes and began looking for new places to play. He ran into boys who played guitars or bullfiddles or drums or other instruments, and he played right along with them. He went out with them to play for picnics or barbecues or boat excursions or dances. He played early in the morning and he played late at night, and he bought new clothes and dressed up so fine he scarcely knew himself in a mirror. He scarcely knew day from night.

It was wonderful to play the trumpet like that, Bubber thought, and to make all that money. People telephoned to the rooming house where he lived and asked for him nearly every day. Some sent notes asking if he would play his trumpet at their parties.

Occasionally one would send an automobile to bring him to the place. Bubber liked riding through the pretty part of the city to the ballrooms in which well-dressed people waited to dance to his music. He enjoyed even more the times when he was taken to big white-columned houses in the country, houses surrounded by old trees with moss on them.

But he went to so many places to play his trumpet, he forgot where he had been and he got into the habit of not paying much attention. That was how it was the day he received a strange call on the telephone. A voice that sounded like a very proper gentleman said, "I would like to speak to the boy from Marksville, the one who plays the trumpet."

"I'm Bubber, sir. I'm the one."

"Well, Bubber, I'm having a very special party tonight—very special," the voice said. "I want you to play for us."

Bubber felt a little drowsy because he had been sleeping when the phone rang, and he still wasn't too well awake. He yawned as he answered, "Just me, sir? You want me to play by myself?"

"There will be other musicians, Bubber. You'll play in the band. We'll be looking for you."

"Where do you live, sir?" Bubber asked sleepily.

"Never mind about that, Bubber. I'll send my chauffeur with my car. He'll bring you."

The voice was growing faint by this time, and Bubber was not sure he caught the last words. "Where did you say, sir?" he asked suddenly. "When is it you want me?"

"I'll send my chauffeur," the voice repeated and then faded out completely.

Bubber put the phone down and went back to his bed to sleep some more. He had played his trumpet very late the night before, and now he just couldn't keep his eyes open.

Something was ringing when he woke up again. Was it the telephone? Bubber jumped out of bed and ran to answer, but the phone buzzed when he put it to his ear. There was nobody on the line. Then he knew it must have been the doorbell. A moment later he heard the door open, and footsteps came down the dark hall toward his room. Before Bubber could turn on the light, the footsteps were just outside his room, and a man's voice said, "I'm the chauffeur.

I've brought the car to take you to the dance."

"So soon?" Bubber asked, surprised.

The man laughed. "You must have slept all day. It's night now, and we have a long way to drive."

"I'll put on my clothes," Bubber said.

The street light was shining through the window, so he did not bother to switch on the light in his room. Bubber never liked to open his eyes with a bright light shining, and anyway he knew right where to put his hands on the clothes he needed. As he began slipping into them, the chauffeur turned away. "I'll wait for you on the curb," he said.

"All right," Bubber called. "I'll hurry."

When he finished dressing, Bubber took his trumpet off the shelf, closed the door of his room, and went out to where the tall chauffeur was standing beside a long, shiny automobile. The chauffeur saw him coming and opened the door to the back seat. When Bubber stepped in, he threw a lap robe across his knees and closed the door. Then the chauffeur went around to his place in the front seat, stepped on the starter, switched on his headlights, and sped away.

The car was finer than any Bubber had ridden in before, and the motor purred so softly, the chauffeur drove it so smoothly, Bubber soon began to feel sleepy again. One thing puzzled him, however. He had not yet seen the chauffeur's face, and he wondered what the man looked like. But now the chauffeur's cap was down so far over his eyes and his coat collar was turned up so high Bubber could not see his face at all, no matter how far he leaned forward.

After a while he decided it was no use. He would have to wait till he got out of the car to look at the man's face. In the meantime he would sleep. Bubber pulled the lap robe up over his shoulders, stretched out on the wide back seat of the car and went to sleep again.

The car came to a stop, but Bubber did not wake up till the chauffeur opened the door and touched his shoulder. When he stepped out of the car, he could see nothing but dark, twisted trees with moss hanging from them. It was a dark and lonely place, and Bubber was so surprised he did not remember to look at the chaufeur's face. Instead, he followed the tall figure up a path covered

with leaves to a white-columned house with lights shining in the windows.

Bubber felt a little better when he saw the big house with the bright windows. He had played in such houses before, and he was glad for a chance to play in another. He took his trumpet from under his arm, put the mouthpiece to his lips and blew a few bright, clear notes as he walked. The chauffeur did not turn around. He led Bubber to a side entrance, opened the door and pointed the boy to the room where the dancing had already started. Without ever showing his face, the chauffeur closed the door and returned to the car.

Nobody had to tell Bubber what to do now. He found a place next to the big fiddle that made the rhythms, waited a moment for the beat, then came in with his trumpet. With the bass fiddle, the drums, and the other stringed instruments backing him up, Bubber began to bear down on his trumpet. This was just what he liked. He played loud, he played fast, he played high, and it was all he could do to keep from laughing when he thought about Grandpa and remembered how the old man had told him to mind how he played his horn. Grandpa should see him now, Bubber thought.

Bubber looked at the dancers swirling on the ballroom floor under the high swinging chandelier, and he wished that Grandpa could somehow be at the window and see how they glided and spun around to the music of his horn. He wished the old man could get at least one glimpse of the handsome dancers, the beautiful women in bright-colored silks, the slender men in black evening clothes.

As the evening went on, more people came and began dancing. The floor became more and more crowded, and Bubber played louder and louder, faster and faster, and by midnight the gay ballroom seemed to be spinning like a pinwheel. The floor looked like glass under the dancers' feet. The draperies on the windows were like gold, and Bubber was playing his trumpet so hard and so fast his eyes looked ready to pop out of his head.

But he was not tired. He felt as if he could go on playing like this forever. He did not even need a short rest. When the other musicians called for a break and went outside to catch a breath of fresh air, he kept right on blowing his horn, running up the scale and down, hitting high C's, swelling out on the notes and then letting

them fade away. He kept the dancers entertained till the full band came back, and he blew the notes that started them to dancing again.

Bubber gave no thought to the time, and when a breeze began blowing through the tall windows, he paid no attention. He played as loud as ever, and the dancers whirled just as fast. But there was one thing that did bother him a little. The faces of the dancers began to look thin and hollow as the breeze brought streaks of morning mist into the room. What was the matter with them? Were they tired from dancing all night? Bubber wondered.

But the morning breeze grew stronger and stronger. The curtains flapped, and a gray light appeared in the windows. By this time Bubber noticed that the people who were dancing had no faces at all, and though they continued to dance wildly as he played his trumpet, they seemed dim and far away. Were they disappearing?

Soon Bubber could scarcely see them at all. Suddenly he wondered where the party had gone. The musicians too grew dim and finally disappeared. Even the room with the big chandelier and the golden draperies at the windows was fading away like a dream. Bubber was frightened when he realized that nothing was left, and he was alone. Yes, definitely, he was alone, but—but *where?* Where was he now?

He never stopped blowing his shiny trumpet. In fact, as the party began to break up in this strange way, he blew harder than ever to help himself feel brave again. He also closed his eyes. That is how he happened to notice how uncomfortable the place where he was sitting had become. It was about as unpleasant as sitting on a log. And it was while his eyes were closed that he first became aware of leaves near by, leaves rustling and blowing in the cool breeze.

But he could not keep his eyes closed for long with so much happening. Bubber just had to peep eventually, and when he did, he saw only leaves around him. Certainly leaves were nothing to be afraid of, he thought, but it was a little hard to understand how the house and room in which he had been playing for the party all night had been replaced by branches and leaves like this. Bubber opened both his eyes wide, stopped blowing his horn for a moment

and took a good, careful look at his surroundings.

Only then did he discover for sure that he was not in a house at all. There were no dancers, no musicians, nobody at all with him, and what had seemed like a rather uncomfortable chair or log was a large branch. Bubber was sitting in a pecan tree, and now he realized that this was where he had been blowing his trumpet so fast and so loud and so high all night. It was very discouraging.

But where was the chauffeur who had brought him here and what had become of the party and the graceful dancers? Bubber climbed down and began looking around. He could see no trace of the things that had seemed so real last night, so he decided he had better go home. Not home to the rooming house where he slept while in New Orleans, but home to the country where Grandpa lived.

He carried his horn under his arm, but he did not play a note on the bus that took him back to Marksville next day. And when he got off the bus and started walking down the road to Grandpa's house in the country, he still didn't feel much like playing anything on his trumpet.

Grandpa was sleeping in a hammock under a chinaberry tree when he arrived, but he slept with one eye open, so Bubber did not have to wake him up. He just stood there, and Grandpa smiled.

"I looked for you to come home before now," the old man said.

"I should have come sooner, Grandpa," Bubber answered, shamefaced.

"I expected you to be blowing on your horn when you came."

"That's what I want to talk to you about, Grandpa."

The old man sat up in the hammock and put his feet on the ground. He scratched his head and reached for his hat. "Don't tell me anything startling," he said. "I just woke up, and I don't want to be surprised so soon."

Bubber thought maybe he should not mention what had happened. "All right, Grandpa," he whispered, looking rather sad. He leaned against the chinaberry tree, holding the trumpet under his arm, and waited for Grandpa to speak again.

Suddenly the old man blinked his eyes as if remembering something he had almost forgotten. "Did you mind how you blew on

that horn down in New Orleans?" he asked.

"Sometimes I did. Sometimes I *didn't,"* Bubber confessed.

Grandpa looked hurt. "I hate to hear that, sonny boy," he said. "Have you been playing your horn at barbecues and boatrides and dances and all such as that?"

"Yes, Grandpa," Bubber said, looking at the ground.

"Keep on like that and you're apt to wind up playing for a devil's ball."

Bubber nodded sadly. "Yes, I know."

Suddenly the old man stood up and put his hand on Bubber's shoulder. "Did a educated gentleman call you on the telephone?"

"He talked so proper I could hardly make out what he was saying."

"Did the chauffeur come in a long shiny car?"

Bubber nodded again. "How did you know about all that, Grandpa?"

"Didn't I tell you I used to blow music, sonny boy?" Grandpa closed his eyes a moment. When he opened them again, he shook his head slowly. "Any time a boy with a trumpet takes off for New Orleans without telling anybody good-bye—well, sooner or later, one way or another, he's apt to hear from strange people."

"I should have hung up the telephone," Bubber mumbled, feeling ashamed of himself.

Suddenly Grandpa's voice grew stern. "You should have minded what I told you at the first. Blow your horn when you're a-mind to, but put it down when you're through. When you go traipsing through the woods, leave it on the shelf. When you feel lonesome, don't touch it. A horn can't do nothing for lonesomeness but make it hurt worse. When you're lonesome, that's the time to go out and find somebody to talk to. Come back to your trumpet when the house is full of company or when people's passing on the street. That's what I tried to tell you before."

"I'm going to mind you this time, Grandpa," Bubber promised. "I'm going to mind every word you say."

Grandpa laughed through his whiskers. "Well, take your trumpet in the house and put it on the shelf while I get you something to eat," he said. "Raising up a boy like you ain't easy. First you tell him when to pick up his horn, then you tell him when to put it

down. Some things he just has to learn for himself, I reckon."

Bubber smiled too. He was hungry, and he had not tasted any of Grandpa's cooking for a long time.

Arna Bontemps

CHURCH AND DANCE HALL

THE preacher tells of days long ago and of a people whose sufferings were like ours. He preaches of the Hebrew children and the fiery furnace, of Daniel, of Moses, of Solomon, and of Christ. What we have not dared feel in the presence of the Lords of the Land, we now feel in church. Our hearts and bodies, reciprocally acting upon each other, swing out into the meaning of the story the preacher is unfolding. Our eyes become absorbed in a vision. . . .

a place eternal filled with happiness where dwell God and His many hosts of angels singing His praises and glorifying His name and in the midst of this oneness of being there arises one whose soul is athirst to feel things for himself and break away from the holy band of joy and he organizes revolt in Heaven and preaches rebellion and aspires to take the place of God to rule Eternity and God condemns him from Heaven and decrees that he shall be banished and this Rebel this Satan this Lucifer persuades one-third of all the many hosts of angels in Heaven to follow him and build a new Heaven and down he comes with his angels whose hearts are black with pride and whose souls are hot with vengeance against God who decides to make Man and He makes Man in His own image and He forms him of clay and He breathes the breath of life into him but He warns him against the Rebel the Satan the Lucifer who had been banished from Heaven for his pride and envy and Man lives in a garden of peace where there is no Time no Sorrow and no Death and while Man lives in this happiness there comes to him the Rebel the Satan the Lucifer and he tempts Man and drags him down the same black path of rebellion and sin and God seeing this decrees that Man shall live in the Law and not Love and must endure Toil and Pain and Death and must dig for his bread in the

stony earth but while Man suffers God's compassion is moved and God Himself assumes the form of Man's corrupt and weak flesh and comes down and lives and suffers and dies upon a cross to show Man the way back up the broad highway to peace and thus Man begins to live for a time under a new dispensation of Love and not Law and the Rebel the Satan the Lucifer still works rebellion seducing persuading falsifying and God through His prophets says that He will come for a second time bringing not peace but a sword to rout the powers of darkness and build a new Jerusalem and God through His prophets says that the final fight the last battle the Armageddon will be resumed and will endure until the end of Time and of Death. . . .

and the preacher's voice is sweet to us, caressing and lashing, conveying to us a heightening of consciousness that the Lords of the Land would rather keep from us, filling us with a sense of hope that is treasonable to the rule of Queen Cotton. As the sermon progresses, the preacher's voice increases in emotional intensity, and we, in tune and sympathy with his sweeping story, sway in our seats until we have lost all notion of time and have begun to float on a tide of passion. The preacher begins to punctuate his words with sharp rhythms, and we are lifted far beyond the boundaries of our daily lives, upward and outward, until, drunk with our enchanted vision, our senses lifted to the burning skies, we do not know who we are, what we are, or where we are. . . .

We go home pleasantly tired and sleep easily, for we know that we hold somewhere within our hearts a possibility of inexhaustible happiness; we know that if we could but get our feet planted firmly upon this earth, we could laugh and live and build. We take this feeling with us each day and it drains the gall out of our years, sucks the sting from the rush of time, purges the pain from our memory of the past, and banishes the fear of loneliness and death. When the soil grows poorer, we cling to this feeling; when clanking tractors uproot and hurl us from the land, we cling to it; when our eyes behold a black body swinging from a tree in the wind, we cling to it. . . .

Some say that, because we posses this faculty of keeping alive this spark of happiness under adversity, we are children. No, it is the courage and faith in simple living that enables us to maintain this

reservoir of human feeling, for we know that there will come a day
when we shall pour out our hearts over this land.

Neither are we ashamed to go of a Saturday night to the cross-
road dancehall and slow drag, ball the jack, and Charleston to an
old guitar and piano. Dressed in starched jeans, an old silk shirt, a
big straw hat, we swing the girls over the plank floor, clapping our
hands, stomping our feet, and singing:

> Shake it to the east
> Shake it to the west
> Shake it to the one
> You love the best. . . .

It is what makes our boys and girls, when they are ten or twelve
years of age, roam the woods, bareheaded and barefoot, singing
and whistling and shouting in wild, hilarious chorus a string of
ditties that make the leaves of the trees shiver in naked and raucous
laughter.

> I love you once
> I love you twice
> I love you next to
> Jesus Christ. . . .

And it is this same capacity for joy that makes us hymn:

> I'm a stranger
> Don't drive me away
> I'm a stranger
> Don't drive me away
> If you drive me away
> You may need me some day
> I'm a stranger
> Don't drive me away. . . .

Richard Wright

BRONZEVILLE

Ezekiel saw a wheel—
Wheel in the middle of a wheel—
The big wheel run by faith,
An' the little wheel run by the grace of God—
Ezekiel saw a wheel.

—Negro spiritual

STAND in the center of the Black Belt—at Chicago's 47th Street and South Parkway. Around you swirls a continuous eddy of faces— black, brown, olive, yellow, and white. Soon you will realize that this is not "just another neighborhood" of Midwest Metropolis. Glance at the newsstand on the corner. You will see the Chicago dailies—the *Tribune,* the *Times,* the *Herald-American,* the *News,* the *Sun.* But you will also find a number of weeklies headlining the activities of Negroes—Chicago's *Defender, Bee, News-Ledger,* and *Metropolitan News,* the Pittsburgh *Courier,* and a number of others. In the nearby drugstore colored clerks are bustling about. (They are seldom seen in other neighborhoods.) In most of the other stores, too, there are colored salespeople, although a white proprietor or manager usually looms in the offing. In the offices around you, colored doctors, dentists, and lawyers go about their duties. And a brown-skinned policeman saunters along swinging his club and glaring sternly at the urchins who dodge in and out among the shoppers.

Two large theaters will catch your eye with their billboards featuring Negro orchestras and vaudeville troupes, and the Negro great and near-great of Hollywood—Lena Horne, Rochester, Hattie McDaniels.

On a spring or summer day this spot, "47th and South Park," is the urban equivalent of a village square. In fact, Black Metropolis has a saying, "If you're trying to find a certain Negro in Chicago, stand on the corner of 47th and South Park long enough and you're

bound to see him." There is continuous and colorful movement
here—shoppers streaming in and out of stores; insurance agents
turning in their collections at a funeral parlor; club reporters rushing into a newspaper office with their social notes; irate tenants
filing complaints with the Office of Price Administration; job-
seekers moving in and out of the United States Employment Office.
Today a picket line may be calling attention to the "unfair labor
practices" of a merchant. Tomorrow a girl may be selling tags on
the corner for a hospital or community house. The next day you
will find a group of boys soliciting signatures to place a Negro on
the All-Star football team. And always a beggar or two will be in
the background—a blind man, cup in hand, tapping his way along,
or a legless veteran propped up against the side of a building. This
is Bronzeville's central shopping district, where rents are highest
and Negro merchants compete fiercely with whites for the choicest
commercial spots. A few steps away from the intersection is the
"largest Negro-owned department store in America," attempting
to challenge the older and more experienced white retail establish-
ments across the street. At an exclusive "Eat Shoppe" just off the
boulevard you may find a Negro Congressman or ex-Congressman
dining at your elbow; in the private dining room there may be a
party of civic leaders, black and white, planning reforms. A few
doors away, behind the Venetian blinds of a well-appointed tavern,
the "big shots" of the sporting world crowd the bar on one side of
the house, while the respectable "élite" takes its beers and "sizzling
steaks" in the booths on the other side.

Within a half-mile radius of "47th and South Park" are clustered
the major community institutions: the Negro-staffed Provident
Hospital; the George Cleveland Hall Library (named for a colored
physician); the YWCA; the "largest colored Catholic church in the
country"; the "largest Protestant congregation in America"; the
Black Belt's Hotel Grand; Parkway Community House; and the
imposing Michigan Boulevard Garden Apartments for middle-
income families.

As important as any of these is the large four-square-mile green,
Washington Park—playground of the South Side. Here in the summer thousands of Negroes of all ages congregate to play softball
and tennis, to swim, or just lounge around. Here during the De-

pression, stormy crowds met to listen to leaders of the unemployed.

Within Black Metropolis, there are neighborhood centers of activity having their own drugstores, grocery stores, theaters, poolrooms, taverns, and churches, but "47th and South Park" overshadows all other business areas in size and importance.

If you wander about a bit in Black Metropolis you will note that one of the most striking features of the area is the prevalence of churches, numbering some 500. Many of these edifices still bear the marks of previous ownership—six-pointed Stars of David, Hebrew and Swedish inscriptions, or names chiseled on old cornerstones which do not tally with those on new bulletin boards. On many of the business streets in the more run-down areas there are scores of "storefront" churches. To the uninitiated, this plethora of churches is no less baffling than the bewildering variety and the colorful extravagance of the names. Nowhere else in Midwest Metropolis could one find, within a stone's throw of one another, a Hebrew Baptist Church, a Baptized Believers' Holiness Church, a Universal Union Independent, a Church of Love and Faith, Spiritual, a Holy Mt. Zion Methodist Episcopal Independent, and a United Pentecostal Holiness Church. Or a cluster such as St. John's Christian Spiritual, Park Mission African Methodist Episcopal, Philadelphia Baptist, Little Rock Baptist, and the Aryan Full Gospel Mission, Spiritualist.

Churches are conspicuous, but to those who have eyes to see they are rivaled in number by another community institution, the policy station, which is to the Negro community what the race-horse bookie is to white neighborhoods. In these mysterious little shops, tucked away in basements or behind stores, one may place a dime bet and hope to win $20 if the numbers "fall right." Definitely illegal, but tolerated by the law, the policy station is a ubiquitous institution, absent only from the more exclusive residential neighborhoods.

In addition to these more or less legitimate institutions, "tea pads" and "reefer dens," "buffet flats" and "call houses" also flourish, known only to the habitués of the underworld and to those respectable patrons, white and colored, without whose faithful support they could not exist. (Since 1912 when Chicago's Red-light District was abolished, prostitution has become a clandestine affair, though

open "street walking" does occur in isolated areas.) An occasional feature story or news article in the daily press or in a Negro weekly throws a sudden light on one of these spots—a police raid or some unexpected tragedy; and then, as in all communities, it is forgotten.

In its thinking, Black Metropolis draws a clear line between the "shady" and the "respectable," the "sporting world" and the world of churches, clubs, and polite society. In practice, however, as we shall see, the line is a continuously shifting one and is hard to maintain, in the Black Metropolis as in other parts of Midwest Metropolis. This is a community of stark contrasts, the facets of its life as varied as the colors of its people's skins.

St. Clair Drake and Horace R. Cayton

URBAN BURYING LEAGUES

THE burial association represents the impact of a southern culture pattern upon the northern community. The church "burying leagues" and lodges had, by 1920, been replaced in many sections of the South with associations organized by the undertaker. Each member paid weekly or monthly dues and the undertaker guaranteed an impressive burial. When a person had a policy with an insurance company and could not keep up the payments, the burial association would take over the policy in the role of beneficiary and continue to pay the premiums. The founder of the first burial association in Chicago defended the innovation thus:

"There was a need for one here in Chicago—you know they are a common thing in the South. Since the Depression, you will find more people in funeral systems than previously carried life insurance. I suppose it's because they had to cash in the policies for what they could and didn't have any protection left."

The largest burial association in Chicago was founded in 1922 by an undertaker with an eye for increased business. At this time, the masses of the migrants were unprotected except for lodge benefits. Many who had insurance policies had let them lapse or had cashed them in. White companies were charging exorbitant premiums.

Northern Negro companies had not yet attained prestige. Into the breach stepped the burial association, offering a policy which, while it had no "turn-in" or borrowing value, assured the holder of a funeral, required no medical examination, and imposed no age limit. The association buried its policy-holders from its own funeral parlors, thus seriously threatening the ordinary undertaker. The Depression made burial societies even more popular, since when a policy was turned over to the association it did not need to be listed as an asset when applying for relief. A white doctor with a large Negro clientele commented somewhat patronizingly on the funeral system as follows:

"Doug and his brother had a funeral parlor. I think he is now the owner of the Eureka Funeral Association. You pay him so much a year to get a high-class funeral—something like ten cents a week. These Negroes will do a lot to be sure of a classy funeral. You see, Doug is in the insurance end of this just as much as the funeral business. He has a $15,000 Lincoln hearse and a whole string of Lincoln limousines. He offers an 'All-Lincoln' funeral. He tells them they are getting a thousand-dollar funeral; what he really does costs him probably a hundred dollars. He uses cheap coffins with a lot of paint. The way the thing is worked, they sign over their insurance policy for maybe a thousand dollars and are promised a big funeral. So Doug gets a cut two ways because he is in the insurance company, too. You should see his funeral parlors; they are elegant."

St. Clair Drake and Horace R. Cayton

BRANDS FROM THE BURNING

LOWER-CLASS preachers have long since despaired of saving the lower class *en masse*. They content themselves, as they phrase it, with "snatching a few brands from the burning." They offer their wares from their pulpits and gratefully accept a convert here and there. For a preacher to appear on the street, Salvation Army style, is a rare event. Most churches have annual revivals, widely advertised

but poorly attended except by those already "saved." Dramatic conversion ceremonies, with prolonged praying and singing over the sinners and wild rejoicing over those who "come through" occur in a few churches, but they attract little attention and have none of the compelling fervor of such meetings in the South where many of Bronzeville's people originally "got religion."

The practical problem of recruiting and keeping members calls for numerous concessions to the secular urban world. Instead of demanding a period of praying and seeing visions, pastors of the larger churches merely require a perfunctory statement that the candidate for membership believes Jesus died to save him from his sins, whereupon he is voted into the church. (Among Baptists, the prospective member must subsequently be baptized by immersion.) Older members and most preachers speak with nostalgia of the passing of the "mourners' bench"—that conspicuous spot down in the front of the church where the sinner is supposed to sit and wait for the spirit to strike him.

The Time of the End: Realizing their impotence, lower-class ministers lean heavily upon "prophecy." They thunder away at "Sin," reminding their congregations of the destruction of Sodom and Gomorrah and of Noah's flood. Their choirs sing ominously that "God's gonna move this wicked race, and raise up a nation that will obey." Seizing upon the eschatological tradition in Christianity, they claim insight into God's "plan of the ages." They teach that we are living in the "last dispensation." After the Gospel has been preached throughout the world ("giving everybody a fair chance") "God's gonna close the books." Jesus will return "in clouds of glory," destroy the wicked and set up the millennial kingdom. Men will beat their swords into plowshares and their spears into pruning-hooks, and will study war no more. The "righteous dead" will arise to enjoy the new age, and the unsaved will be consigned to eternal torment.

We are living in "the time of the end." Men have been "growing weaker and wiser." This old world can't last much longer. Even now the Four Horsemen of the Apocalypse are riding. The impending battle of Armageddon is at hand. The persecution of the Jews, pestilences, earthquakes and famines, "wars and rumors of wars," are all signs of the end. Jesus will soon return. The sheep will be

separated from the goats. And most important of all, they see the imminent fulfillment of a much-cherished Biblical prophecy: "Princes shall come out of Egypt, and Ethiopia shall stretch forth her hands unto God."

This is the "Gospel" as it is preached in Bronzeville's lower-class churches. Some sects concentrate on this apocalyptic note, while other ministers preach occasional "special sermons" on the Second Coming and weave the myth into their regular sermons. Even when it is not hammered home continuously, this world view colors the thinking of all the faithful and is shared by large numbers of people—in combination with divers other beliefs—who do not attend church. It is a paradoxical theology of despair and hope, mirroring the realities of life in a Black Ghetto. . . .

A typical performance is Rev. Jonah Goodfriend's revival sermon on "He is Able." The Reverend, dark, and with a voice to fit his 250-pound frame, was preaching in a small Baptist church from the text, "Our God whom we serve is able to deliver us." After announcing his subject he closed his Bible and began to preach to his hearers as follows: 'You have faith in God, you know He won't let you down! . . . We need courage to run on! The Race needs courage to run on!" He ran across the rostrum, crying with rising inflection, "To run on, run on, run on!" He then began to discuss "the idols men serve"—women, whiskey bottles, policy slips, declaring that "men are mixed up about which God to serve. They got so many idols." He dropped to his knees, pantomiming obeisance to an imaginary idol while the audience responded with shouts of *"Yes"* and *"It's the truth!"* He then lauded the three Hebrew captives who refused to bow before Nebuchadnezzar's idol: "The wicked king chunked 'em in a fiery furnace, heated seven times hotter than it ought to be. But they didn't care. They knew that my God was able to deliver His children." Coming down from the rostrum, he selected three young men in the congregation to represent the Hebrew children, and led them to the pulpit, where he placed them in a corner representing the furnace. He began to mimic the wicked king, saying, "I guess now you'll bow, won't you? When those flames begin to eat you, you'll bow." The minister then roared, "But my God-a-mighty, the king jumped back, crying, 'I put three men in there—now I see four.' My Jesus

was in that furnace walking with those Hebrew children."

"Fear not, I am with thee, be not dismayed," he yelled triumphantly, while the audience shouted; "flames can't hurt you. Fire can't singe you. Bad names can't break you. Lo, I am your God. I will deliver you from *this* fiery furnace and *every* fiery furnace." Rev. Goodfriend was sweating from his exertion when he finished and the church was in an uproar. He then began to sing "Just a Little Talk With Jesus Sets It Right." A woman cried out, "That boy's really preaching." The church responded with a loud *Amen*.

St. Clair Drake and Horace R. Cayton

BAPTISM

FROM the baptismal pool Coin couldn't make out any shapes but the lighted candles in mid-air, arranged around the rostrum. When Mr. Foreman saw them earlier that evening, he declared that Reverend Brooks was introducing pagan practices into the Baptist church. Coin was too busy getting into his long white robe, in the deacons' room, to worry about his father's criticism. He was going to be washed in the blood of the lamb. Deaconess Westerfield called the water in the pool blood. Woody said it wasn't any different from bathtub water. It wasn't blood but it was different though. He was standing right in it in front of Reverend Brooks who had on his black gown and rubber boots. The water was warm for one thing and it was dark blue, blue like when his mother dipped Blue-In in washing water and it had smell of iodine . . . the holy smell. The tiny waves of real water licked against the painted fishes.

Reverend Brooks stretched up his right hand and chanted to Coin loud enough for everybody to hear, "I baptize thee in the name of the Father, and of the Son and of the Holy Ghost," and ended with a long, "amen." Amens came from the church too.

Coin was thrust into the water and came up hollering just like Deaconness Westerfield told him every Christian did when he was transformed. As he walked dripping up the ramp leading to the

deacons' room from the pool, he heard the triumphant singing of
the congregation:

> Hallelujah, it's done,
> I believe on the Son,
> I am saved by the blood
> Of the crucified One.

The song came toward him like going up steps to a door. The way
was opened for him to ask the Lord to help his mother. And so
in his flannel robe, shivering, with the music mounting in his wet
flesh, he got down on his knees . . . and began to cry.

Owen Dodson

LODGE SISTERS AT A FUNERAL

REVEREND BROOKS's hands went up, the black, birdwing sleeves
spread out, an eagle flying over the casket to carry it up to God's
nest; he stood on tiptoe to finish, ". . . and I says, farewell."

The organ swelled up: *When the Roll Is Called Up Yonder, I'll
Be There.* Sister Elba Fuller led the procession of the Dorcas Society
down the left aisle. She carried stalks of wheat in either arm. She
held her head high leading the singing. The other sisters marched
behind her three by three, rocking from side to side, tramping to
the tune. Some were crying with their heads held high and no veils
to hide their tears. Coin could feel the rocking under his feet. Most
of them were old with gray hair and white hair, many had shaking
hands. They came weeping most pitifully as if it was their own
funeral they were living through. Seeing this, all notes of the
banana tune left him and he was caught up in the solemn meaning
of age and death and the mournful celebration of them.

> When the trumpet of the Lord shall sound
> And time shall be no more,
> And the morning breaks eternal bright and fair,

> When the saved of earth shall gather
> To their home beyond the sky,
> When the roll is called up yonder, I'll be there.

Sister Fuller's voice was a trumpet piercing the church above all the singing to break the stained-glass window. All the glass would shatter down colors, letting winter sunshine in. The old sisters just rocked in their white dresses, their black badges swayed from side to side. The whole church took up the refrain.

> When the roll is called up yonder,
> When the roll is called up yonder,
> When the roll is called up yonder,
> When the roll is called up yonder, I'll be there.

The society was grouped about the casket and each sister held the stalk of wheat Sister Fuller handed them. The congregation ceased singing and clapped the rhythm out low. Softly now the Dorcas Society sang another verse.

> On that bright and cloudless morning
> When the saints of God shall rise
> And the glory of His resurrection share,
> When His chosen ones shall gather
> To their home beyond the skies,
> When the roll is called up yonder,
> I'll be there.

Again the congregation took up the refrain. Men sang the bass till the church seemed to rock from side to side and the enormous chandelier rocked with it. Then each line got softer and softer. And when the last, *"When the roll is called up yonder, I'll be there,"* was sung, it was in a scared whisper.

In silence Sister Fuller laid her stalks of wheat on the casket, paused a second with a raised hand, moved to the head, and laid one hand on the coffin.

"These sheaves of wheat is the sign that life, life keeps on growing. Life will grow from thee, our dear sister, for you have set your

days before us as a sample and as an example. You will grow in our hearts until the trumpet calls us all, and we go marching home together."

Her voice rose sharp, rose trembling, rose so high and triumphant, Coin felt a shiver up his spine.

She began the exit march up the right aisle. The others circled the casket laying their sheaves down, circling, singing.

> When the saints go marching home,
> Oh, when the saints go marching home,
> Lord, I want to be in that number,
> When the saints go march. . . .

Their faces were set, their steps firm, their tears dry. For a moment Coin was convinced that they would march right out of the church and mount a gangplank up the air and through the clouds.

Agnes put one arm around Popa's shoulder.

> Oh, Lord, I want to be in that number,
> When the saints go marching home.

Owen Dodson

HOUSE RENT PARTIES

AFTER the Stock Market crash of 1929, followed by the closing of many factories, shops and banks, large numbers of people in Harlem had no work. But they still wanted to have a little fun once in a while even during the Depression, so house-rent parties began to flourish—and not always to raise the rent either. But, as often as not, to have a get-together of one's own, where you could do the black-bottom with no stranger behind you trying to do it, too. Non-theatrical, non-intellectual Harlem was an unwilling victim of its own vogue. It didn't like to be stared at by white folks. But perhaps the down-towners never knew this—for the cabaret owners,

the entertainers, and the speakeasy proprietors treated them fine—
as long as they paid.

The Saturday night rent parties that I attended were often more
amusing than any night club, in small apartments where God
knows who lived—because the guests seldom did—but where the
piano would often be augmented by a guitar, or an old cornet, or
somebody with a pair of drums walking in off the street. And where
awful bootleg whisky and good fried fish or steaming chitterlings
were sold at very low prices. And the dancing and singing and
impromptu entertaining went on until dawn came in at the windows.

These parties, often termed whist parties or dances, were usually
announced by brightly colored cards stuck in the grills of apartment
house elevators. Some of the cards were highly entertaining in
themselves.

Almost every Saturday night when I was in Harlem I went to a
house-rent party. I wrote lots of poems about house-rent parties,
and ate thereat many a fried fish and pig's foot—with liquid refreshments on the side. I met ladies' maids and truck drivers, laundry workers and shoe shine boys, seamstresses and porters. I can
still hear their laughter in my ears, hear the soft slow music, and
feel the floor shaking as the dancers danced. Such parties still continue:

With dim lights on, and shades down tight,
We'll clown on down, 'till broad daylight.

AT A

~ PARLOR SOCIAL ~

GIVEN BY

BILL ROBERTS

—AT

498 Washington Street   Newark, N. J.

Saturday Evening, September 5th, 1931

Good Music   Refreshments

If your Sweetie ain't on the level, Come and get yourself another Cute Little Devil at

A SOCIAL WHIST PARTY.
given by

MAYBORN & BLUE
CREOLE INN, 216 W. 122nd ST.

SATURDAY EVENING
SEPT. 19

Good Music   Refreshments

200 Tickets 65c at Cor. 134th St. & Madison Ave.

Praise the Lord
and pass the Chitterlings at

CHITTERLING STRUT
celebrating? Birthday

Given by

Ida Forsyne Hubbard

225 West 121 Street   Apt. 3

THURSDAY EVENING DECEMBER 31st, 1942

Swing Music   Refreshments Served

**ONE LIGHT BLUE AND THE OTHER RED
YOU CAN STAY ALL NIGHT, BUT CAN'T
GO TO BED**

A SOCIAL PARTY
— GIVEN BY —
M A E

429 West 124 Street   Apt. 62

Saturday ~~~~~~~~~~~1946

GOOD MUSIC   **REFRESHMENTS**

Don't sit at home and stare at the wall;
Come on up and let's have a ball! at—

✾ **A SOCIAL PARTY** ✾

——Given By——

BOB and EDDIE

At 371 LENOX Avenue   Apt. 3   N. Y. C.

Saturday evening, February 7th, 1953

GOOD MUSIC!   REFRESHMENTS!

You can wake up the Devil, raise all the Hell;
No one will be there to go home and tell.

— A SOCIAL PARTY —

GIVEN BY

ROSE

— A T —

2213 Eighth Avenue   Apartment 5

Friday evening, March 18th, 1955

from 9 P. M. until ? ? ?

LATEST ON WAX   ——   REFRESHMENTS

35 Cents With Ticket   (Pay at Door)   50 Cents Without

Winding and Grinding like the old Dutch Mill,
The Boys do the work while the Girls stand still

A SOCIAL PARTY

Given By

THE ADELERETTE'S S. C.

At 170 West 136th Street   Apt. 12

SATURDAY OCTOBER 6, 1956   9 Until?

Donation 50 Cents   Free Cocktail

Hop Mr. Bunny, Skip Mr. Bear,
If you don't dig this party you ain't no where!

*   **A SOCIAL DANCE**   *
—Given By—
DELORES and GLORIA
AT 66 WEST 133rd STREET, APT. 2-N.
New York City *Until*
Saturday evening, November 24th, 1956
—— *REFRESHMENTS* ——
35c. with Ticket   45c. without Ticket

Nowadays the money collected at most of these parties is not to pay the rent, but simply to pay for the fun.

Langston Hughes

AT THE REGAL

The applause was quick. And the silence—final.

That was what Maud Martha, sixteen and very erect, believed, as she manipulated herself through a heavy outflowing crowd in the lobby of the Regal Theatre on Forty-seventh and South Park.

She thought of fame, and of that singer, that Howie Joe Jones, that tall oily brown thing with hair set in thickly pomaded waves, with cocky teeth, eyes like thin glass, With—a Voice. A Voice that Howie Joe's publicity described as "rugged honey." She had not been favorably impressed. She had not been able to thrill. Not even when he threw his head back so that his waves dropped low, shut his eyes sweetly, writhed, thrust out his arms (really *gave* them to the world) and thundered out, with passionate seriousness, with deep meaning, with high purpose—

—Sa-WEET sa-ooo
Jaust-a yooooooo—

Maud Martha's brow wrinkled. The audience had applauded. Had stamped its strange, hilarious foot. Had put its fingers in its mouth—whistled. Had sped a shininess up to its eyes. But now part of it was going home, as she was, and its face was dull again. It had not been helped. Not truly. Not well. For a hot half hour it had put that light gauze across its little miseries and monotonies, but now here they were again, ungauzed, self-assertive, cancerous as ever. The audience had gotten a fairy gold. And it was not going to spend the rest of its life, or even the rest of the night, being grateful to Howie Joe Jones. No, it would not make plans to raise a hard monument to him.

She swung out of the lobby, turned north.

The applause was quick.

But the silence was final, so what was the singer's profit?

Money.

You had to admit Howie Joe Jones was making money. Money that was raced to the track, to the De Lisa, to women, to the sellers of cars; to Capper and Capper, to Henry C. Lytton and Company for those suits in which he looked like an upright corpse. She read all about it in the columns of the Chicago *Defender's* gossip departments.

She had never understood how people could parade themselves on a stage like that, exhibit their precious private identities; shake themselves about; be very foolish for a thousand eyes.

She was going to keep herself to herself. She did not want fame. She did not want to be a "star."

To create—a role, a poem, picture, music, a rapture in stone; great. But not for her.

What she wanted was to donate to the world a good Maud Martha. That was the offering, the bit of art, that could not come from any other.

She would polish and hone that.

Gwendolyn Brooks

JAM SESSION

THAT night, at the Showboat, the Blues Singer walked over to Slim and said, "This life is killing me, I got to have myself a little fun once in a while. Let's go over to the Elkins, pick up on the jam session there after I finish here tonight." The Blues Singer finished at two. She and Slim walked across Broad Street and down toward Catherine to the Elkins Ballroom. Upstairs, over the ballroom, there was a smaller room, where the best musicians in town met to have some musical fun and talk after their chores in the night clubs around the town. "The only real music," the Blues Singer frequently said, "is extemporaneous music. And you only get that at a jam session." The Blues Singer did not think much of night clubs.

They climbed the narrow stairway to the second floor; they did not have to show membership cards, because everybody knew Slim and the Blues Singer. Inside, the Blues Singer called to some of the musicians already on the bandstand, "All right now let's play music! Let's play music!" The musicians, who had not yet started, laughed and waved greetings. "You gonna sing a couple tonight?" they asked her. "Naw, not me, I got my class on tonight. I'm gonna play lady and watch you work for a change." The initiates in the hall, some wearing goatees and horn-rimmed glasses as popularized by Dizzy Gillespie, looked at the Blues Singer, first with an air of superiority (not knowing who she was), and then with respect, as they recognized her. Some called greeting, but the Blues Singer ignored them. "Here are two seats, good ones," the Blues Singer said to Slim. "Let's take 'em." Some hundred and fifty spectators were already crowded into the room whose folding chairs were meant to accommodate slightly more than a hundred . . .

The Blues Singer took her seat beside Slim, the musicians were on a platform, the pianist struck a chord; the spectators, crowded together, warm, hot, in the smoke-filled room, leaned forward, expectantly, as the musicians began to play. First, a simple song,

rendered in the orthodox manner. Then, one after the other, the instrumentalists "took off"; using the basic melody as anchor, they each in turn took off on riffs and dives, circling the melody, dodging in and out of it, frightening it, hiding from it, creeping up on it, whirling dizzily far away from it, closing back in on it again. Trumpeter, saxophonist, trombonist, drummer, pianist, bass. "Work! Work!" cried the spectators. The musicians grinned; sweat poured down their faces, down their open necks, soaked the thin shirts they wore. "Work! Work!" The trumpeter arched backward, shook, and made his trumpet scream; the drummer prayed to the great god noise, twirling his sticks into hysteria; the pianist darted discords between the notes of the others; the bassist marched in mellow frenzy up and down the scale. "Work! Work!" The shirt-sleeved spectators laughed, looked at one another, stared leaning at the musicians, shouted, stomped their feet. "Oh, Jesus!" thought the Blues Singer, "Oh, Jesus!" The now-dimmed sidelights, and the brighter stagelights, cast arching, abstract shadows through the smoke across the crowd, against the walls. The world whirled, shrieked, stood on end, did a tribal dance. Emotions angled outward, upward. "Play music!" shouted the Blues Singer. "Play music! Play music!" echoed the crowd. "Play music!" she shouted. Echo of the slamming door. "Play music! Play music!" cried the crowd. Louder and louder the Blues Singer shouted, against the booming bass, "Music! Music!" Around her, the frantic faces, the yelling feet, the sweating laughter. "Music! Music! Music!" cried the Blues Singer, rising to her feet. "Music! Music!" cried the crowd. The music shouted on.

William Gardner Smith

THE GANG

"First we gotta decide on a name to call ourselves, and then think up someplace to meet— What about calling ourselves the 'Green Tiguhs'?"

"What about 'The Raddul Snakes'?" Henry spat with excitement.

B.J. scowled at him in disapproval. "We don want no bad name like that! Won't nobody trust us!"

Bruce had been thinking too. "Let's call ourselves somethin different," he said. "How about the 'Greeks' or maybe the 'Trojans'—?"

B.J. frowned, "Naaaaw—can't name ourselves the Greeks, cause them rookies will start calling us 'The Greasies.' What was that other name you mentioned?"

Bruce withdrew the name Trojans, himself. "We don't wanna call ourselves that neither," he said, "because the Trojans got beat."

"That's right!" B.J. agreed. "We don want no bad luck name." They all puckered in deep thought. Bruce snapped his fingers.

"I got it!"

"What?"

" 'The Warriors!' Let's call our gang 'The Warriors'!"

B.J. rolled the name over his tongue, tasting it carefully. "Wahyuhs, huh? ummm, the Wahyuhs—" He accepted it. "Kinda funny name, but it do mean bein tough and good fighters, donit?"

It was settled. They got together on a secret insignia, a double U, to be worn on the left sleeve, halfway up the forearm. And they devised a special sign to get one another's attention in a crowd—it would be three spread fingers, flashed quickly to indicate their initial letter. And if any one of them got into trouble and had to call for help, B.J. decided that such a distressed member should "holler out, 'Dubya! Dubya!' twice, and all the gang will come runnin!" Then B.J. drew them in close. "Now look, you Wahyuhs," he said. "Here's how we gonna run this gang: I'll be in charge, cause I'm the toughest and I got more sperience than the rest a yall, understand?" There was no argument. B.J. put his arm around Bruce. "And Bruce is secun in charge after me, okay?"

Henry didn't like that, but B.J. quickly silenced him. "Bruce ain as tough as me, but yall done seen that he got mo sense than all the rest a us put together. So when I ain around, yall follow Bruce, see, and do what he tell ya. He's secun in charge! Okay!" The motion carried.

"What about third in charge?" Henry demanded. "Don I git that?"

B.J. shook his head. "Ain but five of us! And a gang can't have mo rookies givin orders than it got takin um! Wait till we enroll some

mo membuhs, then we'll move somebody up to third in charge."
They glanced at one another curiously. They were organized.

Mark Kennedy

SIMPLE ON MILITARY INTEGRATION

"Now, the way I understand it," said Simple one Monday evening
when the bar was nearly empty and the juke box silent, "it's been
written down a long time ago that all men are borned equal and
everybody is entitled to life and liberty while pursuing happiness.
It's in the Constitution, also Declaration of Independence, so I do
not see why it has to be resolved all over again."

"Who is resolving it all over?" I asked.

"Some white church convention—I read in the papers where they
have resolved all that over and the Golden Rule, too, also that
Negroes should be treated right. It looks like to me white folks better stop resolving and get to *doing.* They have resolved enough.
Resolving ain't solving."

"What do you propose that they do?"

"The white race has got a double duty to us," said Simple. "They
ought to start treating us right. They also ought to make up for
how bad they have treated us in the past."

"You can't blame anybody for history," I said.

"No," said Simple, "but you can blame folks if they don't do
something about history! History was yesterday, times gone. Yes.
But now that colored folks are willing to let bygones be bygones,
this ain't no time to be Jim Crowing nobody. This is a new day."

"Maybe that is why they are resolving to do better," I said.

"I keep telling you, it has come time to stop *resolving!*" said
Simple. "They have been *resolving* for two hundred years. I do not
see how come they need to *resolve* any more. I say, they need to
solve."

"How?"

"By treating us like humans," said Simple, "that's how!"

"They don't treat each other like human beings," I said, "so how do you expect them to treat you that way?"

"White folks do not Jim Crow each other," said Simple, "neither do they have a segregated army—except for me."

"No, maybe not," I said, "but they blasted each other down with V bombs during the war."

"To be shot down is bad for the body," said Simple, "but to be Jim Crowed is worse for the spirit. Besides, speaking of war, in the next war I want to see Negroes pinning medals on white men."

"Medals? What have medals to do with anything?"

"A lot," said Simple, "because every time I saw a picture in the colored papers of colored soldiers receiving medals in the last war, a white officer was always doing the pinning. I have not yet seen a picture in no papers of a *colored* officer pinning a medal on a white soldier. Do you reckon I will ever see such a picture?"

"I don't know anything about the army's system of pinning on medals," I said.

"I'll bet there isn't a white soldier living who ever got a medal from a colored officer," said Simple.

"Maybe not, but I don't get your point. If a soldier is brave enough to get a medal, what does it matter who pins it on?"

"It may not matter to the soldiers," said Simple, "but it matters to *me*. I have never yet seen no *colored* general pinning a medal on a *white* private. That is what I want to see."

"Colored generals did not command white soldiers in the last war," I said, "which is no doubt why they didn't pin medals on them."

"I want to see colored generals commanding white soldiers, then," said Simple.

"You may want to see it, but how can you see it when it just does not take place?"

"In the next war it must and should take place," said Simple, "because if these white folks are gonna have another war, they better give us some generals. I know if I was in the army, I would like to command white troops. In fact, I would like to be in charge of a regiment from Mississippi."

"Are you sober?" I asked.

"I haven't had but one drink today."

"Then why on earth would you want to be in charge of a white regiment from Mississippi?"

"They had white officers from Mississippi in charge of Negroes—so why shouldn't I be in charge of whites? Huh? I would really make 'em toe the line! I know some of them Southerners had rather die than to *left face* for a colored man, buddy-o. But they would *left face* for me."

"What would you do if they wouldn't *left face?*"

"Court-martial them," said Simple. "After they had set in the stockade for six months, I would bring them Mississippi white boys out and I would say once more, *'Left face!'* I bet they would *left face* then! Else I'd court-martial them again."

"You have a very good imagination," I said, "also a sadistic one."

"I can see myself now in World War III," said Simple, "leading my Mississippi troops into action. I would do like all the other generals do, and stand way back on a hill somewheres and look through my spyglasses and say, 'Charge on! Mens, charge on!' Then I would watch them Dixiecrat boys go—like true sons of the old South, mowing down the enemy.

"When my young white lieutenants from Vicksburg jeeped back to Headquarters to deliver their reports in person to me, they would say, 'General Captain, sir, we have taken two more enemy positions.'

"I would say, 'Mens, return to your companies—and tell 'em to *charge on*'.

"Next day, when I caught up to 'em, I would pin medals on their chests for bravery. Then I would have my picture taken in front of all my fine white troops—*me*—the first black American general to pin medals on white soldiers from Mississippi. It would be in every paper in the world—the great news event of World War III."

"It would certainly be news," I said.

"Doggone if it wouldn't," said Simple. "It would really be news! You see what I mean by *solving*—not just resolving. I will've done solved."

Langston Hughes

SIMPLE ON BOP MUSIC

"SET down here on the stoop with me and listen to the music," said Simple.

"I've heard your landlady doesn't like tenants sitting on her stoop," I said.

"Col-ya-koo," Simple sang to an old Dizzie Gillespie record spinning like mad. "Hey Ba-Ba-Re-Bop! Be-Bop! Mop!"

"All that nonsense singing reminds me of Cab Calloway back in the old *scat* days," I said, "around 1930 when Cab was chanting, 'Hi-de-hia-de-ho! Hee-de-*hea*-de-hee!'"

"Not at all," said Simple, "absolutely not at all."

"Re-Bop certainly sounds like scat to me," I insisted.

"No," said Simple, "Daddy-o, you are wrong. Besides, it is not *Re*-Bop. It is Be-Bop."

"What's the difference?" I asked. "Between *Re* and *Be?*"

"A lot," said Simple. "Re-Bop is an imitation like most of the white boys play. Be-Bop is the real thing like the colored boys play."

"You bring race into everything," I said, "even music."

"It *is* in everything," said Simple.

"Anyway, Be-Bop is passé, gone finished—everything is cool, progressive now."

"Bop may be gone, but its riffs remain behind," said Simple. "Be-Bop music was certainly colored folks' music—which is why white folks found it so hard to imitate. But there are some few white boys that latched onto Bop right well. And no wonder, because they sat and listened to Charlie Christian, Dizzy, Thelonius, Ted Dameron, Charlie Parker, also Mary Lou, all night long every time they got a chance and bought their records by the dozen to copy their riffs. The ones that sing tried to make up new Be-Bop words, but them white folks don't know what they are singing about, even yet."

"I still say the singing sounds like pure nonsense syllables to me."

"Nonsense, nothing!" cried Simple. "Bop makes plenty of sense."

"What kind of sense?"

"You must not know where Bop comes from," said Simple, astonished at what he considered my ignorance.

"I do not know," I said, "Where?"

"From the police," said Simple.

"What do you mean, from the police?"

"From the police beating Negroes' heads," declared Simple. "Everytime a cop hits a Negro with his billy, that old stick says, 'BOP! BOP! . . . BE-BOP! . . . MOP!! . . . BOP!' And that Negro hollers, 'Ooool-ya-koo! Ou-o-o!'

"Old cop just beats on, 'MOP! MOP! . . . BE-BOP! MOP!' That's where Be-Bop came from, beaten right out of some Negro's head into them horns and saxophones and guitars and piano keys that plays it. Do you call that nonsense?"

"If it's true, I do not," I said.

"That's why so many white folks don't dig Bop," said Simple. "White folks do not get their heads beat *just for being white*. But me—a cop is liable to grab me almost any time and beat my head— *just* for being colored—from Harlem to Dixie. In some parts of the American country as soon as the polices see me outside the colored neighborhood, they say, 'Boy, what are you doing in this neighborhood?'

"I say, 'Coming from work, sir.'

"They say, 'Where do you work?'

"Then I have to go into my whole pedigree because I am a black man in a white neighborhood. And if my answers do not satisfy them BOP! MOP! . . . BE-BOP! . . . MOP! If they do not hit me, them cops have already hurt my soul. *A dark man shall see dark days.* Bop comes out of dark days. That's why real Bop music is mad, wild, frantic, crazy—and not to be dug unless you've seen dark days, too. Folks who ain't suffered much cannot play Bop, neither appreciate it. They think Bob is nonsense—like you think it is. They think it's just *crazy* crazy. They do not know Bop is also MAD crazy, SAD crazy, FRANTIC WILD crazy—beat out of my own head! That's what Bop is. Them young colored kids who started it, they know what it is."

"Your explanation depresses me," I sighed.

"Your nonsense depresses me," said Simple.

Langston Hughes

SIMPLE ON GOSPEL SINGERS

"It looks like," said Simple, "that the churches are buying up half the old movie theatres in Harlem and turning them into temples. Lenox Avenue, Seventh Avenue, Amsterdam, all up and down, it is getting so you can't tell a theatre from a church anymore. Now the ministers have got their name up in lights just like movie actors. Have you noticed?"

"I have," I said. "I guess television is driving the smaller movie houses out of business."

"Yes, and churches are taking over," said Simple. "And the church will be here when the movies are gone, that's a sure thing. But store-front churches are going out of style. From now on it looks like they are going to be movie-front churches—except that the box office has turned into a collection plate and the choir is swinging gospel songs. Money is being made."

"You are not opposed to churches taking up collections like other institutions, are you? They have to pay rent, light, heat, plus ministers' fees."

"I am not opposed," said Simple, "not when they put on a good show."

"*Show* is hardly the word to use in reference to religion," I said. "Do you think so?"

"That is the way some churches advertise gospel singers these days," said Simple. "I seed a poster outside a church last night, SISTER MAMIE LIGHTFOOT AND HER GOSPEL SHOW, and they were charging One Dollar to come in, also admission programs cost a quarter."

"Did you go in?"

"I did, and it were fine! Four large ladies in skyblue robes sung 'On My Journey Now,'—sung it and swung it, real gone—with a jazz piano behind them that sounded like a cross between Nellie Lutcher and Count Basie. Them four sisters started slow, then worked it up and worked it up and worked it up until they come

on like gang busters, led by Sister Lightfoot. Then they started walking up and down the aisle from the pulpit to the rear, making out like they was on their journey to the Promised Land—and the church fell in. They did the last part over about seventeen times. Folks leaped, jumped, hollered and shouted and started marching, too. Then they took up a collection for the benefit of Sister Lightfoot. The plates were overflowing. I put in a dollar myself."

"You mean after you had already paid a dollar at the door?"

"I were so moved," said Simple, "that I did not mind contributing again. Besides there was a young Negro there named McKissick who rocked the rafters. That boy can really sing a song! To tell the truth, gospel singers these days put more into a song than lots of night club stars hanging onto a microphone looking like they are on their last legs. Besides, you can hear a gospel singer two blocks off, singing and swinging, even without a mike. In the past, I have heard Mahalia, the Ward Singers, Sallie Martin, Princess Stewart, Elder Beck, the Dixie Humming Birds, the Davis Sisters, also the Martin Singers, and I am telling you, the music that these people put down cannot be beat. It moves the spirit—and it moves the feet. It is gone, man, solid gone! Which is why I has no objections to paying at the door, then shelling out some more when I get inside—even if they do invest most of it in automobiles.

"As good as them gospel peoples sing, why should they not ride on rubber—of any kind they want? Why, I saw a quartet come driving up to a church once, and each one of the singers in the quartet was driving a different kind of car, and each car were *fine!* Them five boys got out of them five fine cars and went into the church and started singing, 'If I Can Just Make It In,' meaning into the Kingdom. They also sung, 'I Cannot Get There By Myself,' and everybody said, 'Help 'em Jesus! Help 'em' Which the congregation did by contributing a dollar or a dollar and a half—so them boys took home a bushel of money.

"Another song I like is 'Move On Up A Little Higher,' also 'Precious Lord, Take My Hand.' Don't you? Some of them large sisters can really sing such songs. We have some *great* gospel singers in this land. They are working in the vineyards of the Lord and digging in His gold mines. Why, some gospel singers these days are making so much money that when you hear them crying, 'I Cannot

Bear My Burden Alone' what they really mean is, 'Help me get my cross to my Cadillac.' Which is O. K. by me, as long as they keep on singing like they do. Good singers derserve their rewards, both in this world and in the other one."

Langston Hughes

SIMPLE ON INDIAN BLOOD

"ANYBODY can look at me and tell I am part Indian," said Simple.

"I see you almost every day," I said, "and I did not know it until now."

"I have Indian blood but I do not show it much," said Simple. "My uncle's cousin's great-grandma were a Cherokee. I only shows mine when I lose my temper—then my Indian blood boils. I am quick-tempered just like a Indian. If somebody does something to me, I always fights back. In fact, when I get mad, I am the toughest Negro God's got. It's my Indian blood. When I were a young man, I used to play baseball and steal bases just like Jackie. If the empire would rule me out, I would get mad and hit the empire. I had to stop playing. That Indian temper. Nowadays, though, it's mostly womens that riles me up, especially landladies, waitresses, and girl friends. To tell the truth, I believe in a woman keeping her place. Womens is beside themselves these days. They want to rule the roost."

"You have old-fashioned ideas about sex," I said. "In fact, your line of thought is based on outmoded economics."

"What?"

"In the days when women were dependent upon men for a living, you could be the boss. But now women make their own living. Some of them make more money than you do."

"True," said Simple. "During the war they got into that habit. But boss I am still due to be."

"So you think. But you can't always put your authority into effect."

"I can try," said Simple. "I can say, 'Do this!' And if she does

something else, I can raise my voice, if not my hand."

"You can be sued for raising your voice," I stated, "and arrested for raising your hand."

"And she can be annihilated when I return from being arrested," said Simple. "That's my Indian blood!"

"You must believe in a woman being a squaw."

"She better not look like no squaw," said Simple. "I want a woman to look sharp when she goes out with me. No moccasins. I wants high-heel shoes and nylons, cute legs—and short dresses. But I also do not want her to talk back to me. As I said, I am the man. *Mine* is the word, and she is due to hush."

"Indians customarily expect their women to be quiet," I said.

"I do not expect mine to be *too* quiet," said Simple. "I want 'em to sweet-talk me—'Sweet baby, this,' and 'Baby, that,' and 'Baby, you's right, darling,' when they talk to me."

"In other words, you want them both old-fashioned and modern at the same time," I said. "The convolutions of your hypothesis are sometimes beyond cognizance."

"Cog hell!" said Simple. "I just do not like no old loud back-talking chick. That's the Indian in me. My grandpa on my father's side were like that, too, an Indian. He was married five times and he really ruled his roost."

"There are a mighty lot of Indians up your family tree," I said. "Did your grandad look like one?"

"Only his nose. He was dark brownskin otherwise. In fact, he were black. And the womens! Man! They was crazy about Grandpa. Every time he walked down the street, they stuck their heads out the windows and kept 'em turned South—which was where the beer parlor was."

"So your grandpa was a drinking man, too. That must be whom you take after."

"I also am named after him," said Simple. "Grandpa's name was Jess, too. So I am Jesse B. Semple."

"What the *B* stand for?"

"Nothing. I just put it there myself since they didn't give me no initial when I was born. I am really Jess Semple—which the kids changed around into a nickname when I were in school. In fact, they used to tease me when I were small, calling me 'Simple Simon.'

But I was right handy with my fists, and after I beat the 'Simon' out a few of them, they let me alone. But my friends still call me 'Simple.' "

"In reality, you are Jesse Semple," I said, "colored."

"Part Indian," insisted Simple, reaching for his beer.

"Jess is certainly not an Indian name."

"No, it ain't," said Simple, "but we did have a Hiawatha in our family. She died."

"She?" I said, "Hiawatha was no *she*."

"She was a *she* in our family. And she had long coal-black hair just like a Creole. You know, I started to marry a Creole one time when I was coach-boy on the L. & N. down to New Orleans. Them Louisiana girls are bee-oou-te-ful! Man, I mean!"

"Why didn't you marry her, fellow?"

"They are more dangerous than a Indian," said Simple, "also I do not want no pretty woman. First thing you know, you fall in love with her—then you got to kill somebody about her. She'll make you so jealous, you'll bust! A pretty woman will get a man into trouble. Me and my Indian blood, quick-tempered as I is. No! I do not crave a pretty woman."

"Joyce is certainly not bad-looking," I said. "You hang around her all the time."

"She is far from a Creole. Besides, she appreciates me," said Simple. "Joyce knows I got Indian blood which makes my temper bad. But we take each other as we is. I respect her and she respects me."

"That's the way it should be with the whole world," I said. "Therefore, you and Joyce are setting a fine example in these days of trials and tribulations. Everybody should take each other as they are, white, black, Indians, Creole. Then there would be no prejudice, nations would get along."

"Some folks do not see it like that," said Simple. "For instant, my landlady—and my wife. Isabel could never get along with me. That is why we are not together today."

"I'm not talking personally," I said, "so why bring in your wife?"

"Getting along *starts* with persons, don't it?" asked Simple. "You *must* include my wife. That woman got my Indian blood so riled up one day I thought I would explode."

"I still say, I'm not talking personally."

"Then stop talking," exploded Simple, "because with me it is personal. Facts, I cannot even talk about my wife if I don't get personal. That's how it is if you're part Indian—everything is personal. *Heap much personal.*"

Langston Hughes

SIMPLE ON HOUSE CLEANING

"Some women are fiends for house cleaning," said Simple. "They will break a husband down if he lets them, making him clean, and clean, and clean. Now, you take my wife, Joyce. Before we got married Joyce cleaned her own place. Now she expects me to work as hard as she do keeping our place not only clean, but clean-clean-cleaner-than-clean, which means that you just never stop cleaning. A house needs a rest sometime just like a human, but our place is whipped every day with a broom, a vacuum, a dust mop and a wet mop—until someday, I swear to God, that floor is going to open its mouth and holler, 'Stop!' I would not blame it because I am tired myself from just seeing how often the floor get cleaned. 'Cleanliness is next to Godliness,' so the Bible says. But if God was a married man, God would put a lot of space between Him and His wife. In my opinion, there is such a thing as being too clean. A little good healthy restful dirt never hurt anybody. Do you reckon? Two beers bartender."

"One can get immune to dirt," I said, paying for the beers. "Some people live in filth all their lives and it does not bother them."

"Too much dirt would bother me," said Simple, "but too much cleaning bothers me, too."

"What you should strike is a happy medium."

"What I have got right now is the unhappy most," said Simple. "All we got, Joyce and me, whilst we is planning to get a house, is a kitchenette apartment. But if it takes all this much cleaning to keep a little old kitchenette clean, I hate to think how much work on my part—not to speak of Joyce, it is going to take to help Joyce

keep a house clean. A whole great big old house! I am about discouraged from thinking of a house—not the renting or the buying
of it, but the cleaning."

"Maybe you were not cut out for house cleaning," I said. "Maybe
you are just not the domestic type."

"I love my home," said Simple, "as a place to set down and relax
in. But when a man comes home, the house ought to already be
clean."

"But when the woman works, too, as your wife does, you cannot
expect that. No house will just up and clean itself."

"That is what I would like to invent," said Simple, "a house that
would clean itself. As soon as a husband and wife lock the door
in the morning and go off to work, the dishes would turn on the
hot water and wash themselves, the rugs would jump up and start
shaking themselves, the dustrags would fly off their nails and start
dustin, and when I come home at night, all that would be done."

"You must have grown up on fairy tales."

"Comic books," said Simple. "More lately especially spacemen
and atoms. Maybe they will invent an atom that will annihilate
dirt, pulverize it every morning quick, and nobody will have to
bother about it the rest of the day. A man's evening hours is not
the time to worry about sweeping, mopping, dusting, and putting
things in place. When I was single, I was not bothered with no such
details. Now, for the love of Joyce, look what I have taken on!"

"Marriage has its advantages, though," I said.

"Disadvantages, too," said Simple. "Cleaning house is one."

"A home, my good man, has to be kept sanitary. Living in
crowded circumstances, as most of us do in big cities, dirt creates
a health hazard. If you do not do your part to keep your house
clean, what can you expect of your neighbor? And Negro neighborhoods are so often old and run-down that it takes a lot of cleaning to keep them up to par. You claim to be a race man. I know
you want to do your part."

"Joyce has me doing three parts," said Simple, "my part, the race's
part, and the hard part."

Langston Hughes

SIMPLE ON COUNTRY LIFE

"A MAN might only live to be seventy or eighty years old," said Simple, "and that is too short a time to waste in the country."

"What do you mean, waste it in the country?" I asked.

"I mean eighty years is too short a time to even be going to the country on vacations," said Simple. "I do not see any use wasting my life in the rurals when I can stay in New York City, Harlem, and have four times as much fun. In the country there is nothing to see but nature. In the city you can look at peoples. In the country there may be chickens, but in town there are chicks. In the country, there is moonlight, but I'll take neon signs for mine. Besides the country is dangerous."

"Dangerous?"

"A man might get snake-bit," said Simple, "else stung in the eye by a bee, or on the elbow by a wasp, maybe even on the bohunkus by a hornet. Oh, no, I do not like country! There are too many varmints there."

"In the American countryside," I said, "there are very few harmful animals."

"No, but there are mosquitoes," said Simple, "and they are vicious enough. I was setting on a porch swing with a girl out in the country down in Virginia one night when a mosquito stung me so hard I thought that chick had stuck a hatpin in my arm. Mosquitoes go for blood. They can also make a man a nervous wretch. Z-zzz-zz-z—they sound like dive bombers. Mosquitoes can make romance in the dark a nightmare. Then in the daytime in the country there are all kinds of flies, but worse of all is horseflies. Daddy-o, if you have never been stung by a horsefly, you have not been stung at all! To tell the truth, a horsefly does not even sting, it bites. And there are little old pesky sandflies and buzzflies and bottleflies and waterflies. Man, I see no need to go to the country where all them flies is when I can stay right here on Lenox Avenue and be bothered with nothing but butterflies—whose bark is worse than their bite.

"And speaking of barks, fellow, every farmer in the country has two or three big, bad, loud-barking dogs, some of which will rush at a stranger out taking a quiet walk and try to tear his leg off. There is nothing more fiercer than a country dog, be it fice or hound. And don't let the dog be one of them bristly haired mongrel kind whose fur stands up like a porcupine when he sees a Negro like me coming down the road. Sometimes I think country dogs are race prejudiced. I seed a dog down in Tidewater once, the darker a Negro was, the louder he would bark at him. Of course, that dog belonged to a very mean old white man, so I reckon it were trained to express prejudice. Well, anyhow, one reason I do not like the country is on account of loose dogs. In Harlem dogs have to be on a leash, else have a muzzle if they run loose in the parks and I have heard of nobody yet being bit by a dog in front of the Hotel Theresa. But in front of almost any farmhouse, a man just minding his own business is likely to be dogbit. I do not wish to run that risk by spending my vacation in the country. Fresh air or no fresh air, I do not want to get hydrophobia."

"You exaggerate the dangers of the country," I said. "Thousands of city folks go to the hinterlands for vacations."

"Hinter I will not go," said Simple. "Let whomsoever will go hinter, but not I. Another thing, there is no sidewalks in the country. Rain comes, you wade in the mud. There are no street lights. Dark comes, you fumble home the best way you can. There are no licker stores. Drink up what drinks you brought with you—and from there on in you get along the best way you can—just go dry, or drink spring water, of which I had enough in my youthhood. Also, it can get *so* lonesome at night in the country. And who says it is quiet? Crickets chirping, frogs croaking, mosquitoes buzzing, cows bawling, dogs howling, chickens crowing long before day. Oh, no, man, no! I can sleep much better in town with nothing but taxis going by, fire engines screeching, neighbors cursing, and folks fighting outside my windows. Them is *natural* noises. But country noises of things in the dark unseen, them kind of noises can make the hair rise on your head. I do not like no noise I cannot spy with my eye if I want to, guy—which is why, let all who wish go to the country. NOT I! Period! NOT I!"

Langston Hughes

THE BAREFOOT PROPHET

In the years gone by . . . prophets have appeared in Harlem representing the whole list of Biblical oracles, all of them with "calls" and supernatural credentials. Martin was the first to be known simply as "The Prophet." He was probably Harlem's most picturesque figure. Watching him stroll along the avenue was a pleasant thing to behold. His luxuriant mane of gray hair and flowing beard made him look as if he had just stepped from the pages of the Bible.

Prophet Martin was a beloved man and a one-man institution. He carried the word daily to stranger places than street corners. Patrons were seldom surprised to see him in gin mills, cabarets, bars or buffet flats. Usually he would quote a few passages of the Scriptures, take up a small collection, and then vanish. Small children followed him through the streets, touching his robe for "good luck." Confused parents would stop him in the streets and seek advice about their wayward offspring. Hustlers and number runners treated him with respect and unsmilingly accepted his benedictions.

Legends grew. It was rumored that he was rich; that he owned several apartment houses and that he traveled over the country in an expensive automobile. This Prophet Martin denied emphatically. He pointed out that he never accepted a church. He had no income other than the small change that he received from his listeners. He preached on the street corners for fifty years in twenty-five different states. When he died his family was on relief.

"The Prophet" was born Clayburn Martin in Henry County, Virginia, in 1851. At at early age he had a vision. "Take off your shoes, for this is holy ground. Go preach My gospel," a voice told him. He obeyed. His first audience was a group of crap shooters on a street corner. He succeeded in influencing the crap shooters so well that he continued his mission.

Mary, his wife, was over twenty years his junior. He had four daughters and one son. The latter was born when he was sixty-one years of age. Once he grew weak and listened to Mary. She

told him to cut his hair and wear shoes. Like Samson he cut his locks. Illness followed. He realized his error. He let his hair grow back and again trod his way in bare feet. His health was restored and he never cut his locks nor wore shoes again.

The vagabond preacher maintained a sanctum sanctorum at 217 West 134th Street. He received callers every evening from 6 to 8:30. Brother Russell, himself a living witness to the healing power of Prophet Martin, would assist him. Here "The Prophet" would ask whether the trouble was of the soul or of the body. If it was of the soul, confession and prayer were enough. If God's Temple—that is what he called the body—was broken down, he would administer a few drops of the ointment or drugs which he prepared himself, then console the ailing person with a few words of prayer. Once he was arrested in Newark, New Jersey, for practicing medicine without a license.

"I will make you ruler over the Nations. I will lift up my people through you," he would begin. Though he could not read nor write, God gave him his messages. "You are the temples. Every man is the dwelling place of the Almighty. He's not in the buildings we call churches." Thus he justified his nonbelief in church buildings.

The title of Elder was bestowed by "The Church of God, Pillar, Ground of Truth, House for all people, Holy and Sanctified."

Prophet Martin's short messages showed a great lyrical quality, somewhat in the style of James Weldon Johnson's "Creation." Following is one of Martin's typical sermons:

Our world is like a fox, brethern. Like a fox that catch his foot in the trap of the Devil. Fox knows, bretherns, that if he stays long enough in the Devil's trap the Devil will kill him with a long stick. So the fox gnaws off his foot and leaves the foot for the Devil and goes home on three legs and praises God he's gittin' home at all.

Now brethern, you see what I mean. We got sin and we got sinners, and better than that the sinners should lead us into the Devil's trap we must cut them off. Sin ain't no part of God, my brethern, but we righteous are part of God Himself. We got to save all we can, and let the rest go. But now, brethern, before we let 'em go, let's pray hard and long for them with His omnipresence.

Prophet Martin died in July, 1937. He was eighty-six years old. Barefooted in death as he was in life, his bushy head resting on a royal purple cushion, the aged evangelist lay in state. Hundreds heeded a last message pinned to the box, resting on his chest. The appeal written in his own shaking hand as he lay dying in Harlem Hospital read:

"Help bury the prophet."

Abram Hill

NEW YORK'S MY HOME

MARGE, sometimes out of town visitors can be a real drag if you live in New York City . . . Well, you remember the time my friend Mamie visited me for two weeks? . . . Of course I enjoyed her company, but she almost gave me a nervous breakdown! . . . Yes girl, she came here with a list as long as your arm and had every minute of her time planned right down to the second . . . No, I didn't mind that at all, but what got me was the fact that my time had to go right along with it . . . Honey! She had to see *all* the museums, the Statue of Liberty, the Empire State Building, the United Nations, Radio City, Central Park, Bronx Park, Small's Paradise, Birdland, Randolph's, the theatres, the markets, and, of course, she never got her fill of bus and boat sight-seeing trips . . . My dear, I never did so much subway ridin' and transferrin' in my natural life . . . I can tell you that I was some worn out. About two days before she left she decided to make the rounds of all the big department stores . . . Marge, we hit every floor in Macy's and then run over to Gimbel's and . . .

Girl! Are you out of your mind? Of course she didn't soak me for all the bills, in fact she made an announcement the first day she got here . . . "Mildred, I'm goin' to pay my own way everywhere I go" . . . That was great, Marge, but the fact remains that I had to pay *my* way and traipse along with her, and when she left I was two steps from the poor house and a nervous breakdown.

Wait a miunte, I haven't told it all . . . Well, she also had to

sample all the different foods in the different restaurants. We had Chinese dinners, French lunches, Italian suppers and so forth and so on, then to cap the climax she just *had* to ride one of those horse and buggy things through Central Park . . . Yes, we did that day before she left . . . There I was leaning back in this carriage, my arms full of packages and my blood pressure hittin' close to two hundred when out she comes with this remark: "New York is all right to visit but I could *never* live here. It's too much rush and hectic going all the time. The pace is too fast, the buildings are too close together, and I like peace and quiet."

My dear, you could have cut the silence with a knife because countin' to ten was not enough and I had to go past seventy-five before I dared answer her . . . But before I could open my mouth she adds, "How do you ever stand it?" I took ten more after that and mumbled something about, "Oh, I don't live this fast all the time." . . . Believe me when I say that the prettiest sight I ever saw in my life was that big train sittin' in the station waitin' to carry her away from here. That's a fact . . , and you know I'm fond of Mamie!

Today . . . listen close now . . . *today* I get a letter from her sister June sayin' that Mamie had such a good time while she was here that she . . . June . . . had decided to spend her vacation with me next summer. My ankles started to swell just sittin' there thinkin' about it, and I made up my mind then and there that I could not go through the business of bein' personal guide on a merry-go-round for another two-week stretch . . . Of course, she's welcome but no more of this jumpin' through hoops for yours truly, especially when half of the time the visitor goes back home without the least idea of what New York City is all about or why millions of people stay here and also like it . . . I know it! All these out-of-towners think we're a bunch of good-timers!

Marge, you know it is a rare thing for me to be runnin' different places . . . and even if my health could stand it, my pocketbook can't . . . That's right, there's hardly a small town in the land where you'll find people goin' less than your friend Mildred, but whenever I go away I soon find that I'm gettin' real homesick for this New York . . . because I like it!

When I'm here, I enjoy stayin' home with the thought that there

is a million places for me to go if I wanted to, but when I'm away I hate stayin' home with the thought that I *have* to because nothin's goin' on . . . Yes, ma'am, that makes a real difference.

When I'm away I miss the subway . . . No, not the rush and crowd, but the people. I like ridin' with folks of every race, color and kind . . . They make stories go round in my head, and sometimes I go past my stop because I'm so busy imaginin' their children and homes and what kind of lives they live . . . One day I was in a super-market and I saw this East Indian with a beautiful pink turban on his head . . . Oh, he was busy buyin' a box of Uneeda biscuits . . . That stayed on my mind for a long time because the turban made me think of pearls and palaces . . . but there he was big as life . . . with biscuits! . . . Yes, I miss these things when I'm away. I miss the people walkin' along with their little radios held up to their ear so's they can listen to the Dodgers, the big ships standin' still and mighty in the harbor, the tough little tug boats huffin' and puffin' up the river, the fellas pushin' carts of suits and dresses in and out of downtown traffic, people readin' all manner of foreign newspapers and such, all the big sounds of swishin' automobiles, planes overhead and children shoutin' until it all comes together and turns into one big "New York-sound."

. . . Talk about missin' things! . . . I miss the friendliness of total strangers when they gather on a corner and try to direct somebody who doesn't speak English . . . Yes Marge, I bet many a soul has ended up on the west side of nowhere tryin' to follow the advice of New Yorkers who are always gettin' lost themselves, even though they have been here ever since the flood . . . Ain't it the truth? . . . I also miss the nice way your neighbors don't bother to keep up with what time you come and go or who visits your house and how long they stayed . . . That's true, too, them same neighbors will rallyround in case of sickness or death . . . I miss seein' the line in front of the Apollo waitin' to see all those fine stars like Nat King Cole and Sammy Davis and Eartha Kitt and Count Basie and everything . . . Tell it now!

Talk about things to miss! . . . I miss the way the workmen are always diggin' at the street pipes . . . It's kind of mystifying because you never know what's bein' dug, but you can stop and watch a little while anyway and think about nothin' in particular and then

pass on . . . Oh honey! . . . I miss *life!*

But Marge, what I miss most is a feelin' in the air, a feelin' that hits you right in the railroad station . . . I can't describe it in words too well, but it seeps into you and it's real excitin'. I guess maybe you'd call it a "something's-gonna-happen-and-you-don't-know-what-it-is" kind of feelin' . . . You right . . . I get sick and tired of folks sayin' "I could never *live* here" . . . because even though I may not ever get hold of enough money to travel to far-off places, I can still say I've met some fine Puerto Ricans and Irish, and Italian, and French, and African and some of all kind of folk . . . This City is far from perfect, but it gets you to the place where you just want to try and *make it* perfect. Oh, sure, I don't mind June comin' to visit, but I'm gonna try and make her see my home the way I see it!

. . . Hold on, Marge! Now, I wouldn't go that far . . . I ain't sayin' that everything here is better than any place else and neither will I take any cracks at the South! Because home is where the heart is and everybody knows their own home the best.

All I'm sayin' is I wish people would stop tellin' us "I could *never* live here."

Alice Childress

2432

DATE DUE